The Maya Papyrus

Richard Coady

Published by Triffit-Priestley Books

First published in Great Britain in 2012 by Triffit-Priestley
Books Limited

ISBN: 978-0-9574876-0-4

Cover design by Daniel Gee

www.richardcoady.com

Dramatis Personae

Akhenaten	King of Egypt; son of Amenhotep III
Amenhotep III	King of Egypt, son of Thutmose IV
Amenhotep, son of Hapu	*See* Huya
Amenophis	*See* Akhenaten
Ahmose	King of Egypt, first king of the 18th Dynasty
Anen	Second Prophet of Amun, son of Yuya and Thuya
Ankhesenamun	Wife of Tutankhamun, daughter of Akhenaten
Ankhesenpaaten	*See* Ankhesenamun
Aper-el	Vizier to Amenhotep III
Artatama	King of Mitanni
Aye	Son of Yuya and Thuya
Bakenamun	Tiye's chef
Giludkhepa	Mitannite princess; wife of Amenhotep III
Hatshepsut	King of Egypt (a woman)
Hepu	Vizier for Thutmose IV
Heqarneheh	Tutor to Amenhotep III
Horemheb	General under Akhenaten and Tutankhamun
Huya	Vizier, sage, magician, overseer of building works under Amenhotep III
Ikheny	Nubian rebel; leader of the Nubian forces at the Battle of Napata
Iny	Theban priest; friend of Anen
Kheruef	Scribe to Amenhotep III
Kurigalzu	King of Babylon
Mahu	Akhenaten's Chief of Police
Maiherperi	Friend of Amenhotep III
Maya	Treasurer under Tutankhamun; the narrator
Meketaten	Daughter of Akhenaten
Meritaten	Daughter of Akhenaten
Merymose	Viceroy to Nubia under Amenhotep III
Meryt	Nurse to Amenhotep III
Mutemwia	Amenhotep III's mother
Nakhtmin	General, Crown Prince, son of Aye
Nebamun	Chief of police for Thutmose IV
Nefernefrure	Daughter of Akhenaten

Nefernefruaten-ta-sherit	Daughter of Akhenaten
Nefertiti	Wife of Akhenaten, daughter of Aye
Ptahmose	High Priest of Amun
Ptahotep	Vizier to Thutmose IV
Ranefer	A priest of Amun
Siese	Army scribe under Thutmose IV
Setepenre	Daughter of Akhenaten
Sitamun	Daughter of Amenhotep III
Sobekhotep	Treasurer for Thutmose IV
Šuppiluliumas	King of Hatti
Šuttarna II	King of Mitanni
Ta-miu	Thutmose's pet cat
Thutmose	Son of Amenhotep III, elder brother of Akhenaten
Thutmose IV	King of Egypt
Thuya	Wife of Yuya, mother of Tiye, Anen and Aye
Tiw	Sister of Amenhotep III
Tiye	Great Royal Wife of Amenhotep III, daughter of Yuya and Thuya
Tjenuna	Friend of Thutmose IV; advisor to Amenhotep III
Turtatama	Mitannite princess, wife of Thutmose IV
Tutankhamun	King of Egypt, son of Akhenaten
Tutankhaten	*See* Tutankhamun
Tutu	A priest of Amun
Yuya	Commander of the chariotry; husband of Thuya; father of Aye, Anen and Tiye

*"Made by the servant who is beneficial to his lord...
who does not allow anything to go wrong, whose
face is cheerful when he does it with a loving heart..."*

Inscription made by Maya on a wooden
sculpture found in Tutankhamun's tomb.

Excerpt from the British Journal of Egyptology, Vol. 19, No. 6, June 20--

First Translation of the Maya Papyrus

After last month's remarkable find in the Valley of the Kings (see *Tomb KV66: Nefertiti Revealed At Last*, BJE Vol. 19, No. 5, May 20--) the first of the papyrus scrolls found in Nefertiti's tomb have been translated from the Hieratic.

The bundle of documents appears to be the work of Maya, a royal courtier in the late 18th Dynasty.

At the time of writing, Maya's motives in composing and concealing the lengthy document remain unknown. Its hiding place would at least suggest that he hoped it would never be discovered.

The Maya Papyrus, Fragments 1-3
Egyptian Museum Acquisition Number B489356

I am Maya.

Maya, the nearly-king, the not-quite-god. The killer and the salvation. I am Maya, and there are few as damnable as I, and fewer still as virtuous.

I am Maya, and I am the last.

I have so many happy memories, but they are such fickle companions. They remind me only of that which is lost. Of course I remember perfectly the time that King Tutankhamun and his wife first celebrated the Festival of Opet. It was, after all, a time of beauty and light and colour and unconstrained rejoicing that continued unabated and unabashed for a whole month. This was shortly after we had left the city of Akhetaten for good – a source of jubilation in itself – and the royal couple were permitted to return to Thebes after their lifelong exile in the desert. Everything was organised, it goes without saying, by Aye.

I remember that at the time I held Aye in some degree of awe, as one tends to do of one's father. He was vizier, and it is impossible to exaggerate the importance of that role, especially the role as Aye filled it. I swear I never saw Aye idle for a moment. Always slightly aloof, as perfectly befits such a man, the long robes that signified his position always trailing behind him as he marched to his next duty. It is sometimes said that the office of vizier is as bitter as gall, but it has never been said of Aye.

Tutankhamun, meanwhile, was a wide-eyed child, forever clutching the hand of his wife and half-sister, Ankhesenamun. He had friends, this child, who were more staunch than he would ever have expected, and he had enemies who were closer than he would ever have desired, but for now he had us: his vizier (Aye), his treasurer (myself, Maya, your humble historian) and the general of his armies (Horemheb, my dear and true friend).

I had waited with the young king and his wife at the prow of our ship as it negotiated its way into Thebes harbour. We strained to see as the morning mists coalesced into the shape of the great Temple of Amun, the frescoes of kings and gods on its walls as big as buildings, even its doorways towering above the villas which surrounded it. After we landed it was impossible to stand in its shadow without feeling smothered and inconsequential.

Before long the entire household and its accoutrements had disembarked and the more senior members, myself included, were driven by chariot through deserted streets. Thebes has a distinct smell, quite different from every other city I have ever visited. All the usual smells are there of animals and waste and sewage, a pungent bouquet we may as well have packed in Akhetaten and brought with us. But with Thebes there is a scent underlying everything else. I believe it is the smell of worship emanating from the city's huge temples as the perfumes drift on eddies of air floating off the river. I had quite forgotten about it during my time in Akhetaten. I had missed Thebes more than I could say.

Everyone rode in silence until we reached the palace. We passed sleeping houses of white, hovering silently like vast ghosts, their high, small windows staring down at us darkly as we passed beneath. Soon enough, we saw the palaces and buildings of state, not white but gold, their majesty inspiring awe again after all these years.

As soon as Lord Aye was down from his chariot he was issuing orders and taking control. I was glad he was there, as I dare say was the king. There was little for Tutankhamun to do other than nod sagely at the appropriate junctures, merely giving his approval to instructions already being obeyed.

"We seem to be superfluous," General Horemheb observed, quietly. He did not look at me as he spoke.

"Perhaps," I said.

I barely had time to shake the dust from my sandals after our arrival at the palace before Horemheb and I were summoned to a meeting with Aye.

"The stela is up," he informed us. He had told us about the stela in Akhetaten. It was a declaration to the people of Egypt, a huge stone tablet displayed for all to see outside the palace gates. It announced a new beginning, a return to the days of glory when the gods could be worshipped freely, when the king would lead his armies in victory and when gold would be like the sand under our feet; in short, when the Two Lands could be proud and happy again. It spoke at length of the new king's plans for a country finally free of his father's stranglehold.

"Now," it read, "the gods and goddesses of this land are rejoicing in their hearts, the lords and temples are in joy, the provinces all rejoice and celebrate throughout this whole land, because good has come back into existence."

When I saw it for the first time some days later a tear rolled down my cheek at that line, leaving a skin coloured trail in my face paint. *Good has come back into existence.* It has, I thought. It really has. Looking back, my naivety astounds even me. Nothing had come back into existence. Nothing at all. Malevolence had merely changed its clothes.

Three days after our arrival in Thebes the astronomers announced the start of the inundation, the time when the Nile would flood and bring prosperity and food to us all. Aye summoned the most eminent of Amun's priests to attend the king.

"You are my priests," Tutankhamun told them, once they had risen from their knees on the floor of his throne room. "You are the priests of Amun and Mut. Today is the first day of the inundation of the Nile, and today you should be celebrating the union of your two gods. Go then and prepare the way. Prepare the barques of the gods. For today we celebrate the Festival of Opet."

Once or twice the king forgot his next line and had to be prompted by Aye, who was standing behind Tutankhamun's left shoulder. It mattered not one jot. The priests all left, unashamedly weeping tears of joy and bowing so low I thought they would scrape their noses on the floor.

I had spoken of the festival many times in Akhetaten, but always surreptitiously, and never with anyone whom I did not hold in steadfast and implicit trust. The tyrant King Akhenaten, Tutankhamun's father, had banned it many years previously, but if you have ever been fortunate enough to experience an Opet Festival you will know that it is a subject impossible to banish from fond recollection. But such talk was heresy to this heretic king, and heresy was to be feared more under Akhenaten than at any other time in our history. To be ostracised by His Majesty, Lord of the Two Lands, blessed of Aten the Sun God, King Akhenaten Neferkheprure Waenre, the ruin of Egypt, the killer of gods, meant it was then only a matter of time until the king's police came in the night to send you to the underworld before any more offence could be proffered to that most sensitive of deities, the Aten.

You could expect no more mercy than you could forgiveness, and you could expect no forgiveness at all. And there was nowhere else to go, because by following His Majesty to Akhetaten in the first place you had bolted the door by which you could hope to return to the rest of the kingdom, for the border patrols were as zealous as the king himself. Once in Akhetaten you could, like the king, expect to die there.

Before our arrival in Thebes, Aye had revealed his plans to Horemheb, Tutankhamun, Ankhesenamun and myself.

"We have to announce ourselves," he said. "The people need to know who we are and what we stand for. It will not be easy for them to forgive the privations and misery of Akhenaten's reign. The people must be made to love us."

"The people cannot be *made* to do anything of the sort," Horemheb said.

"Just so," I said. "We will not be making the people do anything. If we are to reinstate the Festival of Opet, they will love Tutankhamun of their own volition."

Tutankhamun looked at the three of us in turn.

"I will be loved?" he said.

Aye bowed. Horemheb said: "Most assuredly." I said: "Just so."

"Then it shall be done," said Tutankhamun. This time all three of us bowed.

And now all of Aye's planning had been brought to its fruition. There had been no time to alert the populace, but then there was scant need to do so. Once the events had been put into motion there was little any of us could have done to keep it secret.

Tutankhamun was to lead the procession behind the statue of Amun and Ankhesenamun was to lead the procession behind the statue of Amun's wife, Mut. Some people were already outside the palace when I left, shortly after the king. They were gathered around the stela, vociferously discussing its content. The same crowd would surround it for weeks to come, although with different membership, in the same way that the Nile is always the same river although the water is always new.

When I reached the temple of Amun at Karnak the god had already been lifted onto his shrine to be carried on the shoulders of the priests. A small crowd had gathered, pointing at Tutankhamun as he tried to look proud and regal, as he had been instructed, waiting for the procession to start. When it did, Horemheb, Aye and myself walked behind him. The four of us led the crowd down towards the harbour from whence Amun would board his barque for the river journey to the temple of his wife, Mut, where the goddess would meet him to conceive their child. Carved golden rams' heads adorned either end of the barge, while up and down its entire length it was encrusted with lapis lazuli and turquoise set in broad, deep runs of gold and silver, reflecting the approach of the procession from some distance away so pure was the metal and so highly polished was it. Set dead centre in the barge was the shrine in which Amun would make his journey. There had not been much time to prepare it. I could still make out where the name of Amenhotep III, the last king to celebrate Opet, had been crudely chiselled out by Akhenaten's fanatical soldiers. The priests had now overwritten it with the hieroglyphs for Tut, Ankh and Amun. The barge lay deep in the water, the weight of all its precious decoration almost too much for it. Amun must have been delighted when first he saw it. It was easy to forget that this was his first festival in seventeen years as well. The bearers strained down the processional route and struggled onto the barge, the weight of the statue buckling their legs and rocking the boat dangerously.

Once Amun was safely in his shrine, six tugs pulled the barge out into the current and towed it south. The procession itself followed at a respectful distance along the avenue of sphinxes.

Even if we had been trying, it is impossible to move a procession through the streets with anything less than a deafening racket, and when the military band struck up the sound of chaotic celebration was complete. People were woken as the procession spread sideways into the city itself. I could see heads sticking out of doorways ready to complain about the noise only to be silenced by the sight of a god in a shrine and a king marching alongside him. Some could not believe what they were seeing; others fell prostrate. Priests ran from the temples, distributing free food and wine, knocking on doors and running to the next house before the occupants had time to answer. Everywhere people were answering doors and believing that the king himself had knocked them out of bed.

As per his directions from Aye, Tutankhamun tried to keep his head straight and his eyes to the front. The solemnity of his role in the proceedings had been impressed upon him a number of times, although he could not help but see the multitude of people that fell weeping at his feet, crying out his name and proclaiming him to be their reason for continued life. Garlands of flowers were thrown for his feet to tread, lest his sandals be dirtied by the dusty ground. Babies were held precariously aloft for him to touch and bless. A desperate forest of arms reached out to touch the hem of his robes as he passed, and an entire garrison of burly soldiers struggled, arms linked, to push the crowd back to a safe distance. In all his nine years Tutankhamun had never been exposed to anything more uninhibited than respectful awe and he must have called on every ounce of his character to contain his excitement.

The entire city was out on the streets by the time we neared the Temple of Amun. It seemed as though happiness itself had been away for these last seventeen years but was now back, solidified and moulded into the shape of this nine-year-old boy who told the people that they could worship their gods again, that they could rely on their harvests again, that they could defeat their enemies again, that they could be free from the bonds of murderous tyranny once more.

It all seems such a long time ago.

All the walls of the great Temple of Amun itself would not provide space enough for me to expound upon the joy in my heart on that day as I strode proudly behind Tutankhamun, who strode proudly behind the statue of the god Amun as it was pulled along the Nile to meet the goddess Mut.

But lack of space is not, of course, the principle reason why I am recording these events on second hand scraps of papyrus, more mindful now of subterfuge than at any time I talked in Akhetaten about Opet.

Secrecy is all.

For this is the story of murder. There is nothing I can do about that now, although there was, perhaps, something I could have done at the time, if I had not acted too late. But by the time I had escaped the massacre, all was lost.

I am tormented with the guilt of my failure just as surely as if I myself had taken all the lives that I failed to protect. As if I myself had split open my young friend's skull, or butchered that poor girl in her bed.

Perhaps I have failed in the one good thing I was destined to do. Perhaps, come the day of my death, when Osiris judges the goodness of my life, perhaps then the gods will find me lacking and everlasting life will be denied me. But I will let history be my judge, and entreat her to be more insightful than I.

I pray to any gods still listening that I live long enough to finish my history, but of this I have no guarantee.

Aye's armies are at the gates.

Here the fragment ends. The laborious task of restoring and translating the remaining scrolls continues.

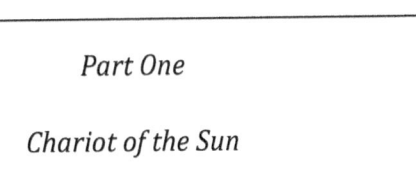

Part One

Chariot of the Sun

Chapter One

The Grandson of God

The Maya Papyrus, Fragments 5-7

SOME MEN *become gods because they are pharaohs; others become pharaohs because they are gods.*

Nebmaatre Amenhotep III, Ruler of Thebes, the Good God, Lord of the Two Lands, Son of Ra, Lord of Appearances, Beloved of Amun and grandfather of Tutankhamun was such a pharaoh, a living bridge between this world and the next, a man who could trace his lineage back to the sun god Ra himself.

Amenhotep had grown up with the story of his ancestry, always listening with a proud and silent smile, eyes bright and attentive regardless of the number of times his father, King Thutmose IV, told it. It was one of those rare tales that was never embellished in reiteration, for there could be no elaboration more compelling than the truth.

"I had become separated from the rest of the hunt," Thutmose would tell him, and Amenhotep would imagine himself alone in the desert with only tired horses for company and sand stretching unbroken to every horizon. "I had no choice but to try to find some shade. You have yet to venture far into the desert, Amenhotep, and you have no conception of the heat of the sun in that forsaken place. In the excitement of the chase I had wandered too far. I found myself before the legs of the Sphinx, and there I decided to rest."

Amenhotep could see it all. He could feel the sand shifting beneath his feet and the heat radiating from it. He could see the steam rising from the backs of the horses. He noticed how cool it was within the shadow beneath the Sphinx's great head. He could already hear the words that he knew were to come; the words of a god.

"Before long, I was asleep," Thutmose said. "But I was fated to slumber only briefly."

Amenhotep squirmed with anticipation.

"And do you know why?" Thutmose asked, knowing full well the answer.

"Ra," Amenhotep replied.

"Ra," Thutmose confirmed, with a sombre nod. "And just as I tell you that I am your father, so he told me that he is mine. He told me that he had chosen me, his son, to rule over all the lands of the living. I remember his exact words. 'To you shall belong all the land. Yours shall be a reign great in years. You are my son and my protector.' Can you imagine, Amenhotep? To be addressed in such a way by Ra himself! Can you imagine?"

Amenhotep could very well imagine. He could hear the voice and feel its reverberations in his chest. He could feel his knees sinking into the hot sand. Above all, he could understand, even at this early age, the profound implications. Every child by every wife sat upon the king's knee in order to hear the tale recounted. In fact, there was an old saying about King Thutmose, that he had children not for his love of children, but for his love of that story. But only young Amenhotep truly embraced it, for his father was the son of god, and he was his father's heir.

The door to the king's audience chamber was opened by unseen hands and in strode three men, one carrying charts and maps rolled up and tied with twine, the others with empty hands which fidgeted as though guilty through lack of employment. In one movement they sank to their knees and lay prostrate before the throne.

King Thutmose said: "May you live." Prince Amenhotep mouthed the words along with him and imagined it was his voice that commanded the men to rise.

"Gentlemen," the king said, by way of greeting, once the men in the audience chamber had regained their feet.

"Your Majesty," the men replied.

"What news from the gold routes?" the king asked.

Hepu, the southern vizier, stepped forward.

"Grave news, Majesty."

"Hepu, your news is always grave."

The group laughed politely. Hepu restricted himself to a tight lipped smile and waited for the king to continue. When he did not, Hepu said, "Your Majesty knows I report only the truth."

"Of course, of course," the king said. He was smiling. "Please, Hepu: continue."

"The Nubians are still attacking our supply caravans with impunity. Quite aside from the effect this is having on our gold supplies, news of the troubles will by now have spread throughout the Near East. The Mitannites in particular will be awaiting your response. I need not remind Your Majesty of the fragility of our current negotiations with them."

"If their king would only send me a daughter to marry this would not be a problem," Thutmose said. "How many proposals have we sent him now?"

"I think six, Majesty."

"Artatama is a very stubborn man. He must surely recognise the benefits for both our lands if we can secure a lasting peace, and yet he continues to refuse me." Thutmose sighed and rubbed his temples. "I presume, then, that we need to make war on the Nubians?"

"I see no other viable course of action, Majesty."

"How do our gold reserves stand?"

Tjenuna, the king's chief steward, stepped forward. "Majesty, the Nubians are plundering our gold, but they have neither the resources nor the information to attack every caravan. Our reserves are strong. The Nubians are nothing more than a fly that needs swatting."

"Then this presumably requires nothing more than a police action?"

Each wrongly presuming the king's question to be rhetoric, none of the men offered an answer.

The king rested his chin on his hand and tapped his lips with his fingers in thought. "Tjenuna, my friend," he said. "Yours has been the truest counsel since we were children. What do you believe?"

"Only that your decision is infallible, Majesty."

"Yes, and remind me, Tjenuna, why I ask for your advice when it is always 'think for yourself'?" Tjenuna knew the king well enough to recognise when his comments were in jest, and the two were firm enough friends for Tjenuna to answer in the same vein.

"Because you only ever ask me when you have already made up your mind."

"Quite," Thutmose said. "Here is my decision, gentlemen. I believe that Nebamun's police would be more than equal to the task of destroying these bandits, but I shall not send the police; I shall send the army, and I shall do so for two reasons. Firstly, we need to assure our neighbours that any disobedience to the crown will not be tolerated. We must take these common criminals and leave them as nothing more than a red smear in the sand. Secondly, my father, King Amenhotep, was a fearsome warrior. So much so that I inherited from him enemies that had already submitted. I have little enough chance to fight for my country, and so I cannot pass up the opportunity when it arises. This shall be a military campaign, if only a small one. It can be an outing, and I would like to bring along a guest. He will be pharaoh after me, and it is about time that he learned what it entails."

He looked over at Prince Amenhotep. "How would you like to smite some Nubians?"

"Me?" Amenhotep said.

Thutmose made a show of looking behind the boy for anyone else to whom he may have been referring. "Yes," he said, with mock solemnity. "You."

Amenhotep could scarcely stay seated in his excitement.

"If you were to smile any more the top of your head would topple off," said the king, but Amenhotep's grin grew all the broader.

The king turned back to his audience. "Yuya, I believe this will be a job for your chariotry. The bandits will be mobile, hard to find, and perhaps harder to catch. We need the speed of horses. We shall meet again en route to discuss our tactics."

Yuya bowed. "Your Majesty," he said. Yuya's prominent hooked nose loomed over the lower half of his face, forming a permanent shadow over his fleshy lips, and when he bowed it suddenly brought to Amenhotep's mind the countenance of a wading bird bobbing for fish. The prince put his hand to his mouth to stifle a giggle.

"For now, you may all take your leave," said Thutmose. "We leave the day after tomorrow. I trust that is enough time for preparations to be made."

The men nodded and bowed like puppets on the same string and then backed away, bowing all the while, until the doors closed and cut them from view.

As soon as the latches clicked Amenhotep was on his feet and bouncing up and down before Thutmose's throne.

"Can I ride in your chariot?" he was saying. "Can I shoot a bow? Will it be like hunting lions?"

"Amenhotep, you will be going nowhere if you behave like that. Remember who you are." Thutmose was suddenly stern. "Sit here," he said, patting his knee, "and listen to me very carefully. Yes, you may ride in my chariot. No, you may not fire a bow. You are young and do not have the strength to bend the bow back. And no, it is not like hunting lions. Lions do not shoot back. Tomorrow I will pray for you in the temple of Ra. We shall see if you have such an appetite for war when we return."

"Oh, I will, father, I will. The Nubians will tremble before us."

"Shush now," Thutmose said, holding his finger to the child's lips. "I said we shall see. For now, I must retire. I want you to go and find my physician and bring him to my quarters. Tell him my stomach ails me again. If I knew no better I would swear his spells were making me worse."

He took Amenhotep by the hand once more and led him back towards the door through which they had entered a short while earlier. As the doors swung open to admit them, Amenhotep turned his gaze upwards to Thutmose's face and said, "Father? What are Nubians?"

The next morning Heqarneheh, Amenhotep's tutor, sought to keep him occupied with his studies, expecting and getting no real work from him. He sat with the prince long enough to present him with his ivory palette, a new reed brush, and instructions to copy out classical texts on the wars of independence against the Hyksos.

"Can I study with Maiherperi today?" Amenhotep asked.

Heqarneheh shook his head. "You are to study alone."

"But I always study with Maiherperi. Send for him."

"Not today."

"I want to study with Maiherperi," Amenhotep said. "I order you to send for him."

Heqarneheh sighed. "Amenhotep, do not make this difficult for me. You will study alone. It will aid your concentration."

"I hate you," Amenhotep pouted. "You never do what I say. When I am pharaoh..."

Heqarneheh lost his patience. "Amenhotep, pick up your brush. I have no time for this. I must prepare for the trip. I will come back in a little while to check on you."

He left the room, closing the door firmly behind him.

"When I am pharaoh..." muttered Amenhotep to himself, but he knew that further dispute was useless. He picked up the brush. He got as far as dipping the newly chewed brush into the water, but it remained hovering over the block of ink as his finger traced the words of the text he had been given to copy, his lips moving in sympathy. Over the next hour he repeated a profitless cycle of daydreams and half-hearted pretences at work. Only a few lines into the text he had forgotten about Heqarneheh's insolence. He would see himself as his ancestor King Ahmose standing at the head of his army, watching the Hyksos flee in terror before him. After a few moments his finger and his lips would falter and fall still in his reverie, until the hurried slapping of sandals on the tiles outside his door would break the spell and he would remember where he was.

He decided that he would go to see Maiherperi after all. Heqarneheh had no hold over the future king of Egypt. Amenhotep put down his brush and went in search of his friend.

Amenhotep and Maiherperi had been inseparable since either of them could remember. Maiherperi was a Child of the Inner Palace. These children were the offspring of court officials, tutors, nurses and foreigners who had been installed at the palace for any number of reasons. Maiherperi's parents had been brought over as high profile hostages years before, guarantees of their homeland's subservience in its dealings with Egypt, and had simply never returned, until it became unclear to everyone but themselves whether they were here under duress or preference. Maiherperi had been brought up as an Egyptian, an equal alongside others with far better pedigree, until any distinction blurred into unimportance.

Between Amenhotep's quarters and those of Maiherperi and his family lay the throne room, the nucleus of activity before any campaign. It lay up ahead, on the left hand side of the corridor along which Amenhotep was walking, behind one of a series of doors. He knew it would be occupied today. He briefly considered turning back, but it was never a truly serious consideration. He was unsure how his father would react to the dereliction of his studies.

And then the door opened. For a second, Amenhotep froze. Shadows fell out of the throne room, elongated across the floor of the corridor as though they had been leaning against an obstacle that had been suddenly removed.

He heard his father say "... of being outnumbered. Defeat would be the undoing of twenty five years of..."

Amenhotep leapt backwards and pressed himself against the side wall of the doorway nearest to him. His heart was beating so hard he was sure the sound of it would betray him. Thutmose and two men walked past, deep in conversation and intent on nothing but each other. When he was sure his movement would not be seen from the corners of their eyes Amenhotep stepped across to the other side of the doorway and tried to press his back into the stonework. The voices began to recede. After a moment he risked a glance out into the corridor to see his father's back disappearing around the corner he himself had tiptoed past only moments before.

Just as he was preparing to step out once more into the corridor, the door next to him swung open. The commander of the chariotry took a step forward before seeing Amenhotep cowering against the wall. Both were as surprised as each other, and both exclaimed out loud.

After he had taken a moment to regain his composure, Yuya said: "I was not expecting to see you today, Your Highness."

"I..." Amenhotep said. "I was just..."

"Are you looking for the king? He is somewhere hereabouts. Would you like me to take you to him?"

"No!" Amenhotep blurted out, too loudly. "No thank you, Yuya. I was just going to see my friend."

"Really? Is this not a time for your studies?"

"Yes, it is. I... I needed some help with my work. Everyone appears so busy today that I did not want to disturb them. I thought my friend could help."

"Your friend being...?"

"Maiherperi."

Up until then Yuya had been indulging the child. Now his face grew stern. "I am surprised you would want to see him," he said.

"Why?"

"Perhaps the king should hear of this, after all."

"Please, Yuya. Please do not tell my father. He is very busy. Why do you think I should not see Maiherperi?"

Yuya seemed to think for a moment before he next spoke. "You know, Your Highness, that I have children?"

Amenhotep shook his head.

"Well, I do," Yuya said. "Three. Two boys and a girl. This Maiherperi, he is the son of a hostage, is he not?"

"Yes, but..."

"I think you would enjoy more the company of my children, Your Highness. They are Egyptian, and more refined than these foreigners."

"Yes, but..."

"They are your age, and intelligent. You would like them. My daughter's name is Tiye. It is a pretty name – Tiye – do you not think?"

Amenhotep had not the slightest idea of what could possibly constitute a pretty name. "Yes, Yuya," he said.

"Good boy. Now, you think about what I have said. I do not think there will be any need to speak to the king about this. You stay out of trouble, and I shall see you tomorrow."

"Thank you," Amenhotep said. "I will."

Yuya stepped past him and strode away. Amenhotep turned and ran towards Maiherperi's quarters.

Maiherperi's mother answered the door and seemed surprised to see him. She let him in and directed him towards her son's room. Maiherperi was studying when Amenhotep entered. He looked up from his palette and said: "Oh. It's you."

"I cannot stay for long," Amenhotep said. "I need to return to my room before Heqarneheh comes to find me."

"Good," said Maiherperi.

Amenhotep sat down next to him. "Have you heard?" he asked.

"That the king is to wage war on the Nubians? Yes, I have heard."

"Have you heard that I am to be there with him? That I am to ride in his chariot?"

"This I have heard also."

"That I am to fight alongside him and slay the vile enemy?"

"That I did not know. I hope he is comfortable with you hiding in his skirts."

"What are you saying?" Amenhotep said. "Put down your palette. Are you not pleased for me? I thought you were my friend."

Maiherperi's gaze remained fixed on his hands, which refused to relinquish their grip on the palette and brush. "And I thought you were mine," he said. "Yet you do not even know me."

Amenhotep stood up again. "Why are you being like this?" he asked. I am Crown Prince Amenhotep, he told himself. I will not cry.

"Why are you fighting the Nubians?"

"Because they are stealing our gold," Amenhotep said. "I think," he added.

"But you do not know?"

"Of course I know. It is as I said."

"Do you remember my arrival here at the palace?" Maiherperi asked.

"You know I do not. I remember us being friends. I know of nothing before that."

"Then when you are in battle tomorrow and the Nubians lie dead around your father's chariot, and you toast yourselves on their blood, remember this: that I am one of them."

Amenhotep looked down at the top of his friend's head. Maiherperi's hands were kneading the sides of the palette.

"Heqarneheh will be looking for me," Amenhotep said, finally. He turned on his heel and walked out of the room.

The next morning Amenhotep was awoken from a deep sleep by Meryt, his nurse. He had lain awake for hours the previous night, staring into the darkness until his eyes invented dancing shapes of pale colour in the air over his head. In turns he brooded over the revelation of Maiherperi's ancestry and fantasised about the battle to come. In his waking dream his father lay injured by the side of his upturned chariot while Amenhotep protected him from hordes of rampaging Nubians (none of which he could prevent having Maiherperi's features) swinging his father's sickle shaped *kepesh* sword around his head in shining arcs that left trails in the air. After the battle, Thutmose clambered out from under the pile of men that Amenhotep had rendered into corpses and hailed his son as a military genius and hero of the realm.

Meryt dressed him in a linen loincloth and kilt ("This will be ruined," she sighed) and braided his hair down the side of his head. Amenhotep scowled and fidgeted throughout the entire procedure.

"I have given Heqarneheh some tunics," Meryt said. "Stop squirming. I have sewn the sleeves onto them. It gets cold in the desert at night. Remember to ask him for them if he forgets to offer."

Finally, he was ready. Meryt made a grab for him as he tried to make a run for the door. "Remember who you are," she said. "All eyes will be on you."

As they walked together from the room Amenhotep struck a regal pose.

When they reached the docks they found them to be a scene of recently abated pandemonium. Men stood in small conspiratorial cabals or leant against walls, the rivulets of sweat on their torsos betraying their spent labours. Other teams hoisted and pulled at wide ramps that linked the ships to the dockside, their cargo of horses and chariots already loaded. Soldiers waited in ranks on the decks of the ships as though they were statues of themselves, the only sign of life the ruffling of their heavy black wigs in the breeze. Sailors mingled among them making final preparations for the voyage or settling themselves into the seats from which they would row.

Meryt and Amenhotep were halfway across the dock towards the lead ship when the murmuring of the workmen stopped and those recumbent or crouched struggled to their feet to stand in solemn silence, as though mocking the soldiers that stared back at them from the ships. For a fleeting instance Amenhotep's heart lurched and he looked quickly around him. He was just about to raise his hands, the words of blessing teetering on his lips, when he noticed that the gaze of the men fell back towards the entrance to the dockside. Meryt had also noticed the change in the men's demeanour. The pair stopped and turned to look back the way they had walked in time to see Thutmose step onto the dock. In one well practised motion, the men lowered themselves first to their knees, then all fours, and finally lay prostrate on the ground. Those still struggling with the ramps dropped what they were doing and followed suit. With a startling clatter and a splash one of the ramps fell into the water and Amenhotep thought he heard a quiet curse over his left shoulder. Within a matter of seconds, only Amenhotep and his father remained standing on the dock, Thutmose comfortably ignoring the crowd as he strode towards his ship, Amenhotep feeling strangely vertiginous at this illusion of altitude. Even Amenhotep was awed by the sight of the king. The tall blue Crown of Upper and Lower Egypt was sitting atop his head, two cobra heads standing proud from it. He wore a long kilt, around the waist of which hung a heavy pendant depicting his father, the disc of the sun, which shone as though of its own volition rather than merely reflecting the proud, paternal rays that Ra beamed down from the vault of the heavens. Wrapped around his neck and upper arms were thick bands of gold that threw darting patches of pale light around the dock as he moved. As he passed Amenhotep he said, "You may embark with me," although he did not slow his pace to allow the boy a moment's decision. Amenhotep turned and, stepping over Meryt, who still lay at his feet, he ran after his father.

The men Amenhotep had seen in his father's throne room two days previously, along with the captain of the fleet, were standing at the bow of the ship waiting to welcome their king. As he boarded, they bowed low.

"May you live," said the king. "Are we prepared?"

Tjenuna spoke. "The men, chariots and horses are all loaded. The members of the household chosen to accompany the expedition are all aboard. We await your command."

"Consider it given."

Tjenuna nodded at a man who must have been standing behind Amenhotep and the king. The dockside sprang back into life. Ropes were untied and thrown onto the ships and men pushed and heaved the boats away from the moorings. A hundred splashes marked the entry of the oars into the water and the ships laboriously turned towards the narrow passage that led out into the Nile.

"Tjenuna and Yuya may join me," Thutmose said. "Someone find Heqarneheh. Take the boy."

As Yuya followed the king towards his cabin he caught Amenhotep's eye. He smiled broadly and nodded his head in a private bow.

The fleet made good progress, and it only took a week and a half to reach their destination. Even so, it was a time of unrelenting boredom for Amenhotep. There was no room to run or play, even if either activity had been an option in such close proximity to his father. He would wave frantically at fishing and trade boats as they passed on their way back to Memphis. Occasionally someone would wave back and Amenhotep would settle down and wait for the next one.

Once docked and unloaded, the charioteers, with Yuya and the king at their head, made their way across the verdant land bordering the river into the desert, towards a gap in the range of cliffs that were waiting before them. The breach was the Wadi Mia, through which the Egyptian caravans would pass to and from the gold mines beyond. It was the only navigable point for miles to the north or the south, and somewhere within it was the bandits' lair.

It was not until the fourth morning since leaving the ship that the troops passed through the gateway of the cliffs to the Wadi Mia. Amenhotep, riding in his father's chariot, sensed a change in the ranks that followed behind. The men no longer rode confident and proud in their chariots. Without cowering, they nevertheless gave the impression of men who perhaps should be. Their heads swivelled this way and that to stare into the fissures and shadows that lined the sides of the wadi. Occasionally a man would point and all eyes would follow the line of his arm into the overhangs and crevices that towered above them. Chariots, in twos and threes, raced ahead and disappeared quickly from view. A phalanx of chariots moved up the line and surrounded Amenhotep and the king.

"Is this a bad place, father?"

"It could be. Here is a lesson of war for you to learn. What would happen if within these walls were hidden a host of Nubians with bows?"

Amenhotep considered it for a moment. "Then we would have found them and we could fight."

"No, Amenhotep. They would have found us, and they could fight. Try not to give me the answer you think I want."

"They could shoot us," Amenhotep said, vacantly, as though it was a thought unrelated to the conversation. Now he too was staring at the wadi walls as they passed.

"When you command an army of your own," Thutmose said, "Never, never bring them through an unsprung trap such as this unless it is absolutely necessary. Are you listening?"

Amenhotep's head turned back to his father. "Yes, father."

"Then what did I say?"

"Never bring an army through a trap."

"Good boy."

Yuya trotted up and the guards parted to grant him access to the king. As he drew level he said, "Amenhotep," by way of greeting, and bowed with a smile. His familiarity was beginning to make Amenhotep uncomfortable. He could not decide whether or not it was disrespectful.

"Majesty," Yuya said. "May I make a humble suggestion? Do you think it would be wiser for your son to travel with the household?"

Thutmose did not turn to Yuya when he spoke. "Are you trying to tell me my business, Yuya?"

"Your Majesty knows I would never presume. I wish no sleight. It is my duty as a loyal servant to risk your displeasure in order to safeguard Your Majesty and Your Majesty's family."

"If you displeasured me, Yuya, you would know about it. Amenhotep is happy where he is, aren't you, boy?"

"Yes," said Amenhotep, without conviction. He was still staring nervously at the wadi walls.

"The future pharaoh will not cringe at the rear with incompetents and nursemaids. See you remember that," Thutmose said to Yuya.

Yuya bowed as low as he could within the constraints of his chariot. "Your Majesty," he said.

Reports began to come back from the advanced guard that the Nubian camp had been located. It was strategically well placed, situated in a narrow defile which arced out from the wadi and rejoined it perhaps a mile further on. From there they could strike any commercial travellers with impunity, using the defile to divide their forces to form a pincer attack. It also gave them an escape route should they come under attack themselves, and was narrow enough to prevent a large force from attacking more than a few ranks at a time. The scouts estimated that the camp could hold a thousand men.

"Split the men into two sections," Thutmose told Yuya. "You will lead the second section through the main route of the wadi. Find the second turning to the defile. Split your section into two further groups. One group is to wait this side of the turning, the other on the far side. I will take the remaining men and lead the charge on the camp. You will await us there. We will be preceded by any number of enemy soldiers."

"As you wish, Majesty," Yuya said. "Perhaps Your Majesty would prefer me to take charge of the child. He may be of hindrance to you."

Thutmose retained his temper, but said: "Yuya, were we not on the threshold of battle you would answer for your impertinence. We have discussed this already."

Paling slightly, Yuya bowed and went to organise the men.

Once strapped in beside his father, Amenhotep tried to persuade himself that he felt safe. He eyed the outriders surrounding Thutmose's chariot and tried to count the troops following behind. Once Yuya's contingent had split from the column, their number appeared feeble. *What can happen to me?* he thought. *I am Crown Prince Amenhotep, and I ride in the chariot of the pharaoh. The gods of the empire ride with us and protect us. I am in the safest place in the world.* He was having difficulty convincing himself that he was convinced.

They passed through the entrance to the defile without incident. Thutmose held up his hand and the column slowed to a walk.

I am Crown Prince Amenhotep...

The sheer walls towered over them, making Amenhotep appear puny to himself regardless of whose chariot he rode in.

...and I ride in the chariot of the pharaoh...

From an unseen fissure in the rock an arrow hissed by, almost too fast for the eye. It missed the king's chariot close enough for an outreached arm to have been its target and buried itself with a solid thud in the side of the chariot immediately to Amenhotep's left. From the walls of the defile came the warning shouts of the Nubian sentries. The king's hand chopped through the air, and the Egyptian horses sprang into a charge.

...The gods of the empire ride with us and protect us...

In quick succession, another arrow, and another, flew from nowhere. One clattered along the ground. The other found its target behind Amenhotep. A man screamed.

Thegodsoftheempireridewithusandprotectus

Thutmose turned his face to the sky and cried out *Amun!* The men roared in echo. *Amuuuuuuun! Amuuuuuuuuun!*

The chariot flew so quickly around the corner of the defile that Amenhotep feared it would topple over. Before him lay the enemy camp, a jumble of tents and rudimentary huts from which men were already emerging, many armed with swords or bows. Others ran this way and that in search of weapons. Amenhotep could tell they had been taken unawares, but some of the Nubians were already advancing to meet the attack. Thutmose raised his bow.

Thegodsoftheempire...

The king's first arrow struck an approaching Nubian full in the face, puncturing his left cheek and travelling far enough through his skull for the arrowhead to poke out of the back like a flower sprouting from seed. The man perished before he hit the ground and fell into a heap so grotesquely arranged it looked to Amenhotep to be painful even to the dead. The king's horses widened their eyes and plunged headlong into the chaos of the camp while Amenhotep hid in his father's shadow and tried to suppress his rising panic. Thutmose reached for a new arrow and fired, reached and fired, in a well practised fluidity of motion.

...ridewithusandprotectus

The full force of the Egyptians fell onto the Nubian camp in a rolling thunderclap of hoof and wheel on stone, careering heedlessly through men and tents alike. Bows were less help than hindrance at these close quarters and the men discarded them in favour of their *kepesh* swords, which flashed in the afternoon sun as they rose and sliced through the air.

Amenhotep had never heard noise like it and had his hands not been gripping the sides of the chariot tightly enough to burn he would have clamped them to his ears and prayed for silence.

The horses did not falter but surged ahead, mindless of the enemy that rose and fell around them. The chariot bucked over rocks and holes in the unyielding stone ground and threw Amenhotep this way and that as though it was angry at having to carry him. His hips and waist would be bruised black for days to come where they had banged against the chariot sides.

By now the Egyptians had reached the centre of the Nubian camp. The battle raged on whichever way Amenhotep turned. His head darted from side to side, but all he could see were the faces of black men falling under chariot wheels and swords. Any one of them could have been Maiherperi's brother or father.

The royal guards had managed to retain their shape around Thutmose's chariot, shielding him from attack, although this in itself was enough to label him a worthy target in the eyes of an enemy who knew their only hope of salvation lay in the slaying of the king. Those Nubians who had been at the far end of the camp when the battle started had time to arrange themselves into some semblance of organisation and as the king ploughed on a determined group of them threw themselves towards him, their battle cries lost in the clamour. The royal guards prevented all but two reaching their goal. One fell under the king's horses. Amenhotep lost the last of them and crouched lower, suddenly aware of the vulnerability of his fingers.

Without warning, a face loomed over the left side of the chariot, its teeth bared. High above his head the Nubian held a long sword, its edge already tarnished brown and red. The chariot's momentum meant that the Nubian's blow would miss the king but fall directly where Amenhotep crouched. He cried out involuntarily and cowered back, his hands at last relinquishing their grip and hovering over his head in a pose akin to that of prayer. The king's *kepesh* arced through the air. It sliced easily through the Nubian's left arm and embedded itself deep in his chest with a crack as ribs splintered beneath it. Blood sprayed into the chariot. Squirming, Amenhotep failed to avoid it. For a moment the sword stayed fast in its victim and dragged him along as the king cursed and tugged it free. Behind, Amenhotep saw the body trampled to mulch by the horses that followed.

The backbone of the Nubian defence had been broken. Those who still could turned and fled, brave groups of them fighting a determined but ultimately suicidal rearguard action to slow the king's pursuit. As they rounded their final corner the leading Nubians fell under a storm of arrows as Yuya's waiting troops launched themselves into the fray. Such was the devastation wrought by the initial attack that the Egyptian second wave was able to swamp them within moments and advance with ease back towards where the last of the Nubians held their ground against the king. Finding themselves under attack from the rear, they fell like harvested corn.

Amenhotep saw nothing of the last stages of the battle. Even had he wanted to stand again, his legs would have been unable to hold him. He crouched, his eyes level with the backs of his father's knees, sobbing uncontrollably. Only when silence fell was he aware of any change in his circumstances. He realised that the last shouts he had heard were ones of victory. When he finally wiped his eyes and looked up, his gaze was met by the stern faces of his father and Yuya. They were sallow with whipped up sand and piebald with blood, their eyes the only evidence of their identity.

For now, there was little for them to say and little time in which to say it. The soldiers' job was not yet done. The piles of Nubian corpses had yet to be searched and prodded and probed for survivors. Those who were too badly wounded to be of use were dispatched to their place of rest forthwith. The remainder were bound at the elbow and wrist with their arms behind their backs and left to wait in sullen, bloody groups until transport could be arranged for their delivery back to Memphis, where they would be sold as slaves. The bands of men selected as trophy gatherers roamed the battle site with serrated knives and ashen faces, sawing the genitalia off fallen Nubians and depositing them in linen sacks. The veterans found some small comfort in forced humour and comments on size and shape.

Amenhotep remained foetal in the chariot, thankfully forgotten. After a time he saw Thutmose and Yuya approaching. They looked down at him silently. Amenhotep was expecting a punishment for his cowardice, but he saw no reproach in their gaze. Yuya was smiling, but it was a smile laced with pity.

"Perhaps he was too young for this after all," Thutmose said, as though this was the last sentence in a conversation to which Amenhotep had not been privy.

"Perhaps now you are not so keen to smite," Thutmose said to him. "We may need to toughen you up."

Amenhotep's eyes remained downcast. He gave no sign that he had heard anything that Thutmose had said.

"Do you no longer feel the need to answer your father?" Thutmose asked.

Amenhotep made no reply.

"I think we may be seeing the influence of Maiherperi in this upset," said Yuya.

"Maiperi?"

"He is a Child of the Inner Palace. The son of a hostage. A Nubian, Your Majesty."

"And is this Maiperi a friend of yours, boy?"

"Maiherperi," Amenhotep said. "Yes."

"A king cannot afford sentimentality, Amenhotep. A king only knows friends of Egypt, or her enemies. No friends of yours died this day. It is of no consequence if Maiperi has Nubian blood."

"Maiherperi," Amenhotep said.

Thutmose sighed and stepped onto the chariot. Amenhotep shuffled out of the way, but did not stand. Yuya looked as though he was about to say something, but as he opened his mouth the king said, "We are departing for the ship. I leave you in charge, Yuya. We shall travel leisurely, with a small guard." He picked up the reins.

"Perhaps," Yuya managed to stutter, "if young Amenhotep were to be placed in the company of other Egyptian children of good and trusted birth..." but the king's horses were already turning.

"See that you overtake us before sunset," Thutmose said.

"...Very good, Majesty." Yuya bowed, blushing slightly. He watched as the king signalled for a handful of men to follow. As the dust of the king's departure settled, Yuya turned to shout perfunctory orders to the men around him.

The return journey passed with as little incident as the first, although Amenhotep now found himself grateful for the monotony. The king did not venture from his cabin for the entire trip and there were rumours among his attendants that he was once again stricken with unbearable stomach pains. Amenhotep somehow found it impossible to care, stricken as he was himself by dreams of the battle. He felt himself to be angry, although he had no clue at whom or why.

The ships must have been seen on the approach to Memphis because a welcoming party awaited them on the dock. They waved and cheered once the lead ship reached hailing distance, and continued to do so throughout the rigmarole of docking. Amenhotep watched them from his vantage point and sneered. He caught sight of Meryt in the crowd and hoped that she saw him turn his back.

Thutmose did not appear for a long time after the rest of the men and materials had disembarked. When he did, he was being helped by Tjenuna. The king was stooped, one arm hugging his stomach, the other around Tjenuna's shoulder. He shuffled painfully across the deck. Before the crowd was able to catch a glimpse of him over the rail he pushed Tjenuna to one side and tried to stand under his own strength.

"Majesty, allow me to..." said Tjenuna, but Thutmose shook his head.

"They need to see a conquering hero," he said. "Not an invalid." He took a step forward and leant against the parapet, waiting for the renewed shouts of the onlookers to die down.

"We return as victors!" he shouted. It was not much of a shout and the news had to be relayed in murmurs from the front of the crowd to the back. "The Nubians lie in their own blood!" He paused to get his breath. "Our gold is safe from the bandits!"

He turned and hobbled towards the gangplank. "Hardly my most inspiring piece of oratory," he said to Tjenuna as he passed. "But it will have to do for now."

Tjenuna followed him pace for pace, his hands held away from his body in readiness to catch the king should he stumble. Now a new murmur ran round he crowd. The king was hurt. Thutmose smiled and waved.

Yuya appeared next to Amenhotep and said, "Perhaps I could accompany you from the ship?"

"What is wrong with my father?"

"He is a little unwell, that is all. He has a stomach ache."

"Is he going to die?"

Yuya laughed. "No, he is not going to die."

The pair met each other's gaze for a silent moment.

"He is *not* going to die," Yuya said again. "Now, the quicker we start, the quicker you can be back at the palace." He held out his hand. Amenhotep walked away without taking it.

Meryt was waiting for him at the bottom of the gangplank.

"What happened to the king?" she said. "People are saying he has been wounded. Are you all right?"

"He is dying," Amenhotep said. He had believed Yuya when he had said that Thutmose was merely unwell but a malicious part of him inexplicably wanted to hurt Meryt. When he saw her stricken expression he relented immediately. "He only has a stomach ache," he said, quickly, and then worried that he sounded too repentant. "You cannot die from a stomach ache," he added, as though explaining the situation to a child half his age, and then: "I want to go home."

Meryt led him through the crowd, who annoyed him by standing up once the king had passed.

"Well?" said Thuya, once the drama and excitement of Yuya's homecoming had abated somewhat and the children had been settled in their beds.

"He is a fine and determined warrior," he replied. "We had but few losses, and no men of name."

"That is not what I meant," she said. "You know what I meant."

"He is as intractable as he is fierce. His mind was turned only to the fight."

"Did you ask him?"

"My dear, he is not a man to be asked. I may as well ask the rocks in the field."

The couple sat in silence as the sun dipped low enough in the sky to shine in broad bands of gold through the window. Motes of dust floated like grains of sand caught in amber.

"Your hair has a glowing aura in this light," Yuya said, but his wife was not so easily distracted.

"So you said nothing? Yuya, we may never have another opportunity like this. Have your family travelled all the way from Akhmim for nothing other than sore behinds?"

"It does not become a woman of your beauty to be so coarse."

"Well," she said, as though an explanation of a temper driven momentarily beyond the bounds of decency and a defiant apology could all be couched in one word.

"I have had a long and tiring trip," Yuya said. "I am ready for my bed." He yawned voluminously and stretched until he felt bones crack deep in his back.

"There has to be something we can do," she said.

"Thuya, if I were to leave the room, would you carry on this conversation on your own? I have said all I can to the king. Too much, in all probability. Another word and my head would have joined a thousand others, face down in the sand."

"I do not wish to return to Akhmim with nothing."

"You have nothing? You are the wife of the commander of the king's chariotry, and you have nothing?"

"Do you think you could arrange an audience?"

"Are you serious? On what pretext?"

"That you are leaving for Akhmim and you wish to pay your respects to the king before you go. He will be touched."

"*I* will be touched. By the edge of his sword. I want this every bit as much as you do. I would thank you to remember that. But I see no profit in angering the only person who could help us. Anyway, he is not well. He had to be helped from the ship today. His doctor has told him he is beset by demons in his stomach. He looks to me as though he has started to lose weight, so they may even be digesting his food for him."

"He will not be unwell forever. Demons are no match for the son of Ra. Stop looking for excuses. We can start making preparations to leave as soon as he begins his recovery. Everything must look as though we really mean to go. And if our entreaties are to no avail, then I will happily leave Memphis anyway. It would only serve as a constant reminder to what I almost had."

Yuya knew better than to resist his wife when she was in such a determined mood. He sat back in his chair and stared at the ceiling as though inspiration for the fight might be found lurking there. Perhaps if he was not so tired he would find resistance easier to ensnare. "I shall visit the palace in the morning," he said finally, when revelation eluded him.

"You are a good man, Yuya," Thuya said, and leant over to brush his cheek with her fingers. "You shall thank me for this when you are God's Father."

"And you God's Mother."

"Of course," Thuya smiled. "They may remember us in history yet, my darling."

"They may, God's Mother, they may."

They retired, but despite Yuya's fatigue he managed little sleep that night.

Yuya could have afforded to postpone his nervousness, at least for the immediate future. Neither King Thutmose nor Prince Amenhotep were to be seen around the palace for the next few days. Rumour absconded with the truth and paraded with brazen familiarity on the tongues of courtiers and palace staff. The king was deathly ill, some said. Others claimed such doom mongering was out of date and that the king was already dead; and with each retelling the poor man's demise grew increasingly legendary. He clutched his unlucky and ineffectual physician to his chest and, in his death throes, squeezed the life from them both. Or at his last exhalation a cloud of black demons swarmed from his throat, gloating and infesting all in the room with the king's affliction. Or his father, Amenhotep II, appeared, resplendent in immortal glory, and led his son by the hand down to the vaults of the underworld.

For his part, Prince Amenhotep was in fine health and poor spirits. He had not been seen outside his own apartment since his return from the campaign. As soon as Meryt had led him through the palace doors he had released her hand with a contemptuous shake and had disappeared into the maze of corridors. Only Heqarneheh had seen him since, to provide progress reports on the king that were never requested and that were mostly received with a disinterested raise of the eyebrows. Heqarneheh had tried talking, cajoling and finally shouting at the prince to provoke any sort of reaction, with no discernable result. After the first couple of days he gave up, in the hope that boredom or loneliness would succeed where entreaties and threats had failed. But still Amenhotep did not step over the threshold.

Tjenuna found him sitting on his bed, writing on his palette with a worn brush. It was four days since Amenhotep's return.

"Do I find you well, prince?" Tjenuna asked, after a moment's awkward silence during which Tjenuna was unsure as to whether

Amenhotep even knew he was there. Amenhotep raised his head, but did not reply. Tjenuna tried again.

"Do I find you studying? What are you writing?"

Amenhotep made a show of unburdening himself of a weary sigh and putting his writing materials to one side. "Nothing," he said.

"I have good news for you. Your father is on the road to recovery. He is asking after you."

"He is still alive then?"

Tjenuna stared at the floor and rocked backwards and forward on the balls of his feet until a brief flash of temper abated. Saying nothing, he strode across the room and sat next to Amenhotep on the bed. The boy edged away from him slightly; not so far as to seem afraid, but far enough to make his point.

"Amenhotep, you are a still a child, but in a very brief time indeed you will be a man. No, it is true. You will be surprised how quickly the time passes. But while you are a child you need to act like you are a man already, or when the time comes you will not know how to do it and you will stay a child forever. Everybody in the palace is worried about you, even while your father lies grievously ill. Only yesterday Yuya was at the gates. It is the third time he has visited since your return from Nubia, and each time he has come he has asked after your wellbeing before that of the king. And that, my boy, is an honour you would do well not to ignore. I am your father's oldest friend, and I have known you since you were born. I flatter myself that I am as close to an uncle to you as I could be without a blood tie. Now, tell me what troubles you, and perhaps I can help."

"You cannot help me."

"I can try. Egypt needs you to be strong. Your father is not a well man. I am aggrieved to say it, but there it is. What would happen if anything untoward befell your father? You would be king. Is Egypt to have a pharaoh that never ventures beyond the four walls of his apartment?"

"I don't want to be king!" Amenhotep said.

"You will be king one day, whatever happens. Who would not want that?"

In a move so sudden that Tjenuna flinched, Amenhotep threw himself across the bed, flattened his face against Tjenuna's chest, wrapped his arms around his neck, and began to sob.

"I don't want to be king!" he was shouting. "I don't want to be king!"

Momentarily stunned, Tjenuna could do nothing more than stroke the boy's hair and whisper useless nonsense. "Come now," he said. "There, there. Try not to cry."

Gradually, Amenhotep's energy ebbed and he brought his weeping under control. He pulled his head far enough away from Tjenuna's chest to look him in the face. "I don't want my father to die," he said.

"Your father has asked to see you," Tjenuna said. "He may be ill, but you can see for yourself how strong he is."

When Tjenuna and Amenhotep arrived at the king's quarters, they found the court physician already there.

"No more excuses," Thutmose was saying to him. "I want no more stale beer and dates. I fail to see how your medications are helping at all. In one week's time I will be married to a daughter of the king of Mitanni, and I expect to be able to do so on my feet. Now go away and consult who you need to consult and read what you need to read, and be back here in one hour. We have come to a sorry pass if the son of Ra and the greatest doctors and spell-casters in the land cannot deal with a simple infestation of lowly demons. And *don't*," he said, holding up his hand, "tell me to rest. Go."

Amenhotep and Tjenuna stood to one side to allow the doctor's hurried egress. Thutmose beckoned Amenhotep into the room, and then patted the bed where he wanted Amenhotep to sit. Tjenuna remained outside and closed the door between them.

"Is there anything you would like to discuss with me?" Thutmose asked.

Amenhotep stared resolutely at a spot on the floor just in front of where his feet dangled. "No, father," he said.

"Certain reports have been made to me concerning your behaviour. Would you care to explain them?"

"No, father."

"Is all this because of Nubia?"

There was a pause. "No, father."

"Remember, Amenhotep, I do not want you to give me the answer that you think I want to hear. I just want the answer. Now, is all this because of what happened in Nubia?"

"Yes."

"There is nothing I can say to cushion the blow, Amenhotep. These things come into the life of every king. A king needs to be just but strong. Even merciless when the occasion demands. If he is not prepared to be so, Egypt will be quickly swallowed up by her enemies, who know full well how to be merciless. You do not want that, do you?"

"Of course not."

"Then what do you want?"

"Father," Amenhotep said, taking a deep breath as though air were courage. "Father, I do not want to be king."

"I think you underestimate the importance of what you are saying, my boy. Do you have no respect for the concept of duty?"

"No," Amenhotep muttered.

"I beg your pardon?"

"Duty has no respect for me. It makes me sad and afraid. Why should I hold duty in such high regard?"

"Because," Thutmose said, "it is demanded of you by your country and your gods. Do you think I want to endure a marriage ceremony in the condition that I find myself? I am in pain, and I wish to do nothing but sleep, but I have my duty and I shall stand by it. This marriage will safeguard our kingdom and make a friend of our enemy, and so I shall honour it, however onerous I find it."

Silence fell over the room. Finally, the king said: "Do you know the story of Hatshepsut?"

Amenhotep was not in the mood for one of his father's stories. He briefly considered lying and telling the king that he knew all about it in the hope that this would forestall him from launching into it. But what if Thutmose were to ask questions? Reluctantly, Amenhotep shook his head.

"Hatshepsut was pharaoh before my grandfather. You will not have seen any pictures or statues of Hatshepsut, because my grandfather had them all smashed." Thutmose shook his head ruefully. "Now it seems a shame," he said. "Although at the time I am sure it was the right thing to do. You know the mortuary temple at Deir el-Bahri? Hatshepsut built that. It is my favourite building in all of Thebes. Anyway, Hatshepsut ruled for twenty years, and was a very successful pharaoh, bringing prosperity and riches from Punt, but also, when it was necessary, leading the army, as you and I have done, in fierce battles in Nubia. But here's the thing, Amenhotep. Hatshepsut should never have been pharaoh, for Hatshepsut was not heir to the throne. And more than that, she was a woman. She took to having herself depicted as a man, and even showing herself with a beard in order to safeguard her position. She stood up to the might of the clergy of Amun. She went through all that in order to take up the duty and the challenge that the gods had handed to her. Are you, a young man, really telling me that you balk at a role that even a woman can fulfil?"

Thutmose leaned back on his pillows and let out a long and weary sigh. The exertions of the conversation were beginning to exhaust him. Amenhotep did not look up, although it seemed that the lecture was over. He made no effort at rejoinder.

"Sometimes," Thutmose said, and then subsided into a weak coughing fit. "Sometimes," he said again, once he had caught his breath, "I wonder about the quality of the youth of today. If I did not know you better I would think you an ingrate. I know that I will recover from this illness, because Ra himself, that day when I fell asleep between the front legs of the sphinx, personally promised me a reign long in years, and six years does not a long reign make. You are lucky, if only you could see it. You have your father at your side to teach you, and years of learning and growing ahead of you before you have to take up my mantle. All of this, and yes, Nubia as well, will seem distant and trivial before you wear my crown. You will be king, Amenhotep. Of that there is no question. Now I want you to go back to your quarters. I will send for Maiperi. You can study and play together."

For the first time, Amenhotep's gaze shifted. "I do not wish to see Maiherperi," he said.

"Why?"

"I do not know."

"Yes you do. Why?"

"Because," Amenhotep said, "because I am ashamed."

"Of what?"

"Before the battle I gloated about killing Nubians."

"And so you should, my boy. They were enemies of Egypt. A prince should never be ashamed. Should you be ashamed of protecting your homeland?"

"I will not see him."

"Amenhotep, there are two things in life that you obey without question. One is your father and the other is your king. As I happen to be both, you will do as I command. There is an old saying that my father taught me, on many an occasion. 'A child's ears are on his back: he listens when you beat him.' Do not make me illustrate it."

Thutmose may have been weak from illness, but Amenhotep thought he probably still had strength enough to hurt. He did not need telling again.

Back in his quarters, he sat and waited for Maiherperi's arrival, trying to plan the conversation in advance. His father had told him not to be ashamed, so presumably he should not apologise. But then his father wanted him to be friends with Maiherperi, so perhaps he should apologise after all. Or at least explain. A prince of Egypt should have to do neither, he told himself. Especially when he has done nothing wrong. He gave up his planning and simply stared. Over in the far corner was a table, upon which rested a half finished game of Senet he had been playing against Maiherperi before the departure for Nubia. Heqarneheh had made them stop playing until they had finished the study assignment he had set them, but events had overtaken them and the game had remained as it was, with

Amenhotep a few turns away from defeat. Amenhotep wondered if it would ever be finished.

Although he was expecting it the knock at his door startled him. Maiherperi stepped into the room, looking every bit as nervous and awkward as Amenhotep felt. He closed the door gently behind him, but approached no further.

"Hello," he said.

"Hello."

"Are you well?"

"No."

"How was the campaign?"

"Horrible."

"Good."

"I was not fighting you," Amenhotep said. "I was fighting enemies of Egypt."

"I have heard that you were not fighting at all. I have heard that your contribution to the victory was the contents of your stomach."

"From whom?"

"My father has a friend whose cousin rode a chariot in the campaign."

"Well that just goes to show how much you know. I fought alongside my father."

"How many Nubians did you kill?"

"Lots."

"How many?"

"Shut up, Maiherperi. I do not know. Lots. When you are in a battle it is difficult to keep track. You should remember whom you are addressing. Are you here just to insult me?"

"I was sent here."

"And if I were to send you away again?"

Maiherperi shrugged. "I presume I would be sent back."

"Then you may as well make yourself comfortable."

Maiherperi walked across the room and sat down in the far corner.

"I had to go, Maiherperi. I had no choice."

"You wanted to go. You were looking forward to it."

"Only because I had no idea what it was going to be like. Now I wish I was never there. I cannot even begin to describe... I am never going to fight again, Maiherperi."

"You will have to fight when you are king."

"I do not want to be king."

Maiherperi sat forward and raised his eyebrows. "What?" he said. "Does your father know?"

"He just told me about Hatshepsut."

"Who?"

Amenhotep sighed as though Hatshepsut's story was one with which he had been familiar all his life. "She was a woman who became king. You know the mortuary temple at Deir el-Bahri? Hatshepsut built that. My father says I shall be king whether I want it or not."

"He is probably right."

Amenhotep shrugged and said nothing. Maiherperi followed his gaze. "Anyway," he said. "You are just annoyed because I am beating you at Senet."

"You are not."

"I am so. In…" Maiherperi made a small calculation. "In three turns."

Amenhotep went and looked over the board. He cast his throwing sticks and moved one of his counters. "And what if I were to do that?"

"It is not your turn."

"It is so my turn."

"When Heqarneheh came in and made us stop, I was thinking about my next move. I remember it distinctly."

"Maiherperi, I know for a fact it was my turn." Amenhotep pulled a chair over and sat at the table. Maiherperi shuffled his chair over to sit opposite him and examined the board.

"I can still beat you in three turns."

"Nonsense."

When the game was over, Amenhotep said: "I let you win."

"I *did* try," said Yuya. "I could not get past the gate."

Yuya and Thuya were in the sparse but spacious Memphite residence provided to them by the crown. Although they were already packed and ready to leave there was little evidence to suggest so. Here and there boxes awaited removal to the docks, as though abandoned by owners long gone. The couple sat in the central hall of the villa, well away from the punishing midday heat. Empty doorways allowed cool air to circulate around Yuya's legs. The low roof was supported by four sturdy pillars, against one of which Yuya was now leaning, having pushed the front two legs of his chair off the ground. On the table at which Yuya and Thuya sat were the remains of a meal of goat's meat, bread and fruit. Thuya's food had hardly been touched.

"Did you think of telling them who you are?" Thuya said.

"They know exactly who I am. They are acting under orders from a higher authority."

"Well, have you told them that you wish to see the king?"

"Thuya, please. Do not treat me like a child. Do you think I just stand there silently? Nobody gets to see the king at the moment. By all accounts he is at death's door. Anyway, now it is all immaterial. Today we will get to see the king anyway."

"Us and half of Memphis. It is hardly a private audience. Anyway, we may be too late."

"We are not too late. How can we be too late?"

"Should we be worried about this marriage, Yuya?"

Yuya took a sip of his barley beer and picked a seed from where it had got lodged between his teeth. "It is a marriage of alliance," he said. "Thutmose is trying to secure our lands to the north, which he can only do if the Mitannite threat is removed."

"And?"

"And if, Amun forbid, Thutmose was to die from this sickness that afflicts him so, the need for an alliance would not die with him. In fact, with a new and untried king on the throne it would become a great deal more important than it already is."

Thuya started to speak, but cut herself short when a servant entered to clear away the plates. The couple sat in silence until the ritual was completed. As the heavily laden servant left the room, Thuya whispered: "They would not make her his principal wife, would they?"

Yuya shrugged.

"Not a foreigner," Thuya said. "They wouldn't. She would be a minor wife. Even..."

The servant reappeared with a cloth. "Leave it!" Thuya shouted across the room. It was an outburst so sudden that Yuya, who had his glass halfway to his lips, spilt some beer down his chest. The servant quickly retreated.

"Even the needs of an alliance would not force them to make her his Great Royal Wife," Thuya said.

Yuya, using the hem of his skirt to wipe the drips of beer from his stomach, could only shrug again. "We can only wait and see," he said, without looking up.

"You need to see the king, Yuya. I do not care what it takes."

"Yes," he said. "Absolutely. This afternoon at the wedding I shall disguise myself as the High Priest of Amun, and instead of conducting the ceremony I shall whisper your instructions to His Majesty, and then you can bring the children to the front..."

"Oh, shut up," Thuya said. "This is too important for flippant remarks."

"Fine," Yuya said. He could think of nothing more constructive to add that he had not already said. "Fine," he said again. He stood up from the table. "I shall try to find a way. Again."

"Think of the rewards, my love," Thuya said. But Yuya no longer found pleasure in the promise of rewards. He knew that the king, under the influence of certain priests, could be persuaded that Yuya's actions were ones not wholly borne from patriotic motives.

"Now," he said. "If we are to stand any chance at all, we must get ready for this wedding. Where are the children?"

"I have the servants preparing them. They should be ready before we are."

They changed into their finest clothes. Servants platted Yuya's hair, and helped Thuya into her favourite wig. They applied each other's eye paint and jewellery. Thuya wrapped herself in layers of pleated, semitransparent linen while Yuya was happy to wear his best kilt, freshly starched, the glare of its whiteness almost painful to look at under the shine of the afternoon sun.

Finally, they were ready. The children were assembled before them for inspection, which they passed, and the family set off for the palace. Yuya was preoccupied and left the management of the children to Thuya and her practised string of commands. He was still thinking about the priests and what their reaction would be should Thutmose consult them about Yuya's proposal. Yuya would have to couch his words in such clever camouflage that everything could be creditably deniable.

The priests were always going to be a problem. The power of the priesthood of Amun reached out from its Theban temples and encircled Egypt in arms of gold that could, should it have so wished, throttle the very life from the country and all those within. Even the king, on occasion, had been known to be answerable to Amun's priests. At the best of times the monarch had at the very least to be circumspect in his dealings with them. The priesthood owned almost as much land as the crown itself, and therefore the loyalty of the people who lived upon it. The mention of Amun's name was enough to sway the few tenants who continued to profess fealty to crown above god. Should the High Priest so wish it, he would be able to manufacture a sizeable and popular opposition to the throne.

Yuya and his family passed from the residential district into the square of the marketplace. Thuya told the children to hold hands and stay close. Suddenly, they were surrounded by a swarm of people, all seemingly in everyone else's way at the same time. Yuya was buffeted and pushed, jarred and elbowed by traders and shoppers alike. Stalls were like boulders in a flood, the competing shouts of their keepers a babbling cacophony. He hated the marketplace and was forever grateful that he had servants to do his dealings here for him. He pushed past stalls selling meat and fish and fruit, and incense and statuettes of Ra for the tourists and pilgrims. He elbowed his way through crowds vociferously disputing the prices offered to them by the hawkers, and pushed past servants and slaves bowed low with the teetering loads they carried back for their masters. The stench was unnameable, as ugly and distasteful as the dirty brown achieved when mixing together every colour on the palette in equal measure.

He finally pushed his way through to the far side of the square and took deep cleansing breaths as he checked that all his family had weathered the storm. Free from concentrating on simple navigation, Yuya's thoughts turned back to the priesthood. They could be an obstacle that Thuya did not fully appreciate. A persuasive word from them in the king's ear could be all that was needed to finish Yuya and his wife's dreams, and the priesthood would most certainly be hostile to the notion of a king's wife of low birth, over whom they would have little or no control.

When Yuya, Thuya and the children reached the palace courtyard they found most of the seats already taken. They made their way to the back row, from where they awaited the arrival of the king and his latest bride.

When Thutmose and his bride finally appeared from a palace doorway and climbed the steps to the wedding thrones a murmur ran through the crowd like a breeze. Thutmose ignored it, but he knew that his ceremonial garb could not hide the rampaging desecration the illness was perpetrating on him. His refusal of his bride's offer to help him up the steps only accentuated the fact that such help was obviously needed. When he sat heavily onto his throne the crowd seemed to collectively exhale, as though they had not been expecting him to get that far.

"Hmm," Thuya said, without much thought for discretion, and without taking her eyes from Thutmose's bride. "She could hardly be described as a beauty, could she?"

"Hush, woman!" Yuya hissed. One or two heads turned in his direction.

"I merely mean to say that Artatama could have sent a daughter with... less about her. I hope Thutmose has his chefs on standby."

One or two disapproving tuts were heard in the crowd around them.

"Keep your voice down!" Yuya said, leaning close to his wife. "An ample daughter is a traditional foreign bride. It shows us that Artatama is rich enough to feed his family."

"Hmm," Thuya said again, unconvinced. "I would be surprised if he could afford to feed anyone at the same time as feeding her."

Ptahmose, the High Priest of Amun, appeared on the stage and began to recite the rites of marriage. Yuya thanked the mercy of the gods that this was enough to capture Thuya's attention. It was an unusually brief ceremony, at the end of which the congregation got to its feet and crowded around the stage to proffer its congratulations to the newlyweds before heading into the palace for a feast in their honour. Thuya ushered her children ahead of her and dragged Yuya through the crowd, unceremoniously barging her way through knots of people. Yuya was reminded of the marketplace, and was content to move in the relative calm of her wake. They reached the front of the crowd just as the king and his new wife were leaving the platform. They were retiring to their marriage bed, although most of the onlookers believed the king would be lucky to muster the strength to complete his obligations once the couple reached that sanctuary. Thuya pushed Yuya forward, almost into the king's path.

Yuya did not have to walk very fast to keep up with the king but even so, bowing low enough to show the necessary respect whilst on the move was quite awkward and Yuya had to make one or two false starts before managing to successfully complete the procedure. Walking behind, Amenhotep was unable to suppress a smile that this commander of men could be reduced to such a bumbling fool under the gaze of the king. Yuya saw his smile and, misinterpreting, returned it.

"How fares Your Majesty?" he said to the king.

"All goes well as long as I have my lovely new wife by my side." The king turned and shared a smile with his bride, patting her ample hand. She smiled the uncertain smile of one whose translator was not within earshot to explain the compliment.

"I crave an audience with Your Majesty. My family leaves for Akhmim soon and we wish to pay our respects before we depart."

"Yuya, I have never rewarded you for your role in the Nubian campaign. I seem to have been indisposed since our return. I shall be glad to receive your respects. Be at my audience chamber in one hour."

"In one hour, Majesty?" Yuya glanced at the bride and, forgetting himself, added, "Aren't you... I mean..."

"In one hour, Yuya," Thutmose said, sternly.

Yuya bowed again. "As Your Majesty wishes."

Yuya gathered his family together and herded them off to a quieter part of the courtyard.

"Well?" Thuya asked.

"We are to see him in one hour, in the audience chamber."

"Finally," Thuya said. "Was that really so difficult?"

After the dignitaries had entered the palace the crowd pushed its way in like sand running through the neck of an hourglass until only isolated pockets of well-wishers remained in the courtyard. An official appeared from the palace doorway and beckoned for Yuya to follow.

"Let me do the talking," Yuya said, as they were led through the labyrinthine corridors to the audience chamber. "This has to be handled very delicately."

"Just as long as you see to it that what needs to be said is said."

Outside the audience chamber they waited impassively for the doors to open, Yuya holding a child firmly by each hand as though his grip could control their mouths as well as their bodies. Thuya fussed around the three children, straightening their hair and spitting on her finger to wipe imagined dirt from their faces. The children scowled and flinched but were too nervous to complain any more vociferously than that.

The throne room doors opened to reveal the king's herald, who stood to one side and said, "His Majesty will see you now." Yuya nodded at him, took a deep breath, and stepped forward.

Thutmose and Amenhotep awaited them. Amenhotep seemed bored and distracted.

"So you are to be leaving Memphis for a while, Yuya?" Thutmose said.

"Yes, if it please Your Majesty. Before setting off I wished to pay my respects one more time before your throne and pass on my heartiest congratulations at your marriage. Although I will of course remain forever at Your Majesty's command in Akhmim."

"Thank you, Yuya. I have also heard that you have been attending the palace on a daily basis to ask after myself and the boy. Your loyalty, and your role in the fighting at Nubia have not gone unnoticed. I would like to confer upon you this."

Thutmose made a signal and a courtier stepped from the shadows holding a gold upper arm bracelet.

"It is a small token," Thutmose said.

Yuya took the bracelet with trembling hands and was surprised at its weight. "I am indeed honoured high among men," he said

"Nothing more than you deserve," Thutmose said.

"Perhaps Your Majesty would do me one final honour. I would deem it a blessing upon my family if I were to be allowed to introduce them to you."

"By all means."

"This is my wife, Thuya. She is chief singer in the harem of the god Min in Akhmim."

Thutmose waved his hand vaguely in Thuya's direction. "May you live," he said. Thuya bowed.

"Furthermore," Yuya continued, "I would also like to introduce my children to Your Majesty. My daughter –" here, Yuya touched his daughter's shoulder and she nervously stepped forward, "– is named Tiye."

Another wave. "May you live." Another bow. Amenhotep glanced briefly at this girl with the supposedly pretty name but found nothing there to interest him.

Thuya stepped forward and said: "It may interest you to know that Tiye is a direct descendent of Ahmose, the founder of your glorious dynasty."

"Thank you, Thuya," Thutmose said. "I am aware whom Ahmose was."

Yuya scowled at his wife but recognised that to reproach her any further in the king's presence would be undignified. Instead, he touched his younger son on the shoulder and said: "This is my son Anen."

Anen stepped forward and bowed low.

"You have taught your children manners, I see," Thutmose said. He turned to Amenhotep. "You could learn something here other than kingly duties, boy. My son is distracted, Yuya. Tell me, at what age were you when you first saw battle?"

"I believe I was a young man of sixteen or seventeen."

"And how did it affect you?"

"I was pleased only to be able to serve my country, Your Majesty."

"There," Thutmose said. "Exactly. Since our return from Nubia Amenhotep has been nothing but obnoxious and reticent. He refuses to take any interest, he refuses to see his friends, he tells me, if you can believe this, that he does not want to be king."

Yuya saw what would perhaps be his only chance.

"Perhaps, if I may be so bold, Your Majesty, you may be seeing the influence of his friends in his behaviour. I believe one of them is a Nubian himself. Perhaps if Amenhotep were to have the opportunity of mixing with Egyptian children he would see the error of his ways. I would deem it a huge honour if my children were allowed such an opportunity."

"But you are leaving for Akhmim, are you not?"

"There is nothing in Akhmim that could ever outweigh such an honour. It can wait."

"What do you say, boy? Would you like some new friends?"

Amenhotep looked around the group and took a moment before replying. "I have friends," he said.

"Well then, that settles it. You will spend some time with these children and perhaps learn some manners from them. And should you fail to do so, you will regret it, that much I promise you."

"Who's he?" Amenhotep said, pointing at the boy Yuya was yet to introduce.

Before Yuya could say a word the boy stepped forward.

"Your Majesty," he said. "I am and will remain forever your most humble servant, and I shall strive to the very limits of my ability to prove myself worthy of the honour that you have bestowed upon me." He bowed, and then turned to Amenhotep.

"My name," he said, "is Aye."

Chapter Two

Remember Hatshepsut

TJENUNA MADE his way to Amenhotep's apartments in the palace. He had no clue what his visit could possibly achieve other than his own peace of mind, but that seemed reason enough. Amenhotep's entire demeanour had changed since the king's insistence that he associate with Yuya and Thuya's children. At first, as Tjenuna had expected, he had been even more antagonistic and irascible than he had been immediately after his return from Nubia. He was a strong minded boy and he had not readily accepted that his father, and indeed Yuya, had been right all along. But it seemed that his new companions had slowly won him around. His studies were coming on apace, and although for a long while he had remained more reserved than he had been before Nubia, the intervening time had made him at least approachable.

But as Amenhotep had grown so had his father withered away, as though one was feeding off the other. There had been a time, quite recently, where it seemed as though the king's illness was finally in abeyance, although this lasted long enough only for optimism to take a hold before the demons returned, seemingly well rested by their absence. It was obvious to all except the king himself, who still clung to Ra's promise of a reign long in years, that the demons would soon vanquish their host. Indeed, the king's physicians privately professed amazement to Tjenuna that Thutmose was not already dead. Tjenuna prayed otherwise, but it appeared as though the king's latest attack would be his last, and this inevitably led Tjenuna to questions concerning the safe future of the realm.

Tjenuna found Amenhotep at study with Anen, Tiye and Aye.

"I wonder if I may have a few words alone, Amenhotep? You other children may finish your studying for today. Run along home."

"We have yet to finish today's assignment for Heqarneheh," Aye said.

"I will explain to Heqarneheh," Tjenuna said.

"May I ask after the good king's health today? I trust he is improving?" Aye said.

"The good king will, I am sure, outlive us all. Now be off with you. You may return in the morning."

Aye led his siblings from the room.

Once they were alone, Tjenuna said: "He is very grown up for his age, is he not?"

"Aye?" Amenhotep said. "He is very stern. He never laughs. Anen is nice though. I can beat him at Senet."

"And Tiye?"

Amenhotep wrinkled his nose. "I don't like girls," he said.

Tjenuna laughed. "You will," he said. "In a year or two girls will be your favourite thing."

"Heqarneheh says the same thing."

Tjenuna sat down. "Amenhotep, do you remember how you felt after our return from Nubia?"

"Yes, I do. I was sad."

"Do you still feel sad?"

"A little, but I am not as bad as I was. I still miss Maiherperi. He was my best friend."

"And are you ready to be king?" Tjenuna asked, before realising the implicit meaning in his question. "Eventually?" he added.

"Does every king have to go to war?"

"That would depend on the circumstances of his reign. No king should go to war simply because a king should fight wars. But if the occasion demands, then yes, a king should fight."

"Who was the last king not to wage war?"

Tjenuna thought for a moment. "I admit, none readily spring to mind," he said.

"I have no choice but to be king," Amenhotep said. "But I do not want to fight wars."

"You will have to wait to see what prevails during your time on the throne. But always remember that you will have the wisdom of the pantheon of the gods behind you. You will know what to do when the time comes."

"And how is my father? Am I still not allowed to see him?"

"He will recover soon enough. But it is perhaps better if you do not see him at the moment. He is still unwell. You will be able to see him when he is stronger."

"He is improving then?"

Tjenuna considered lying, but thought better of it. "You would need to ask that of his physician. I am no expert."

"Then send his physician to me."

"He is very busy caring for your father. I am sure you would prefer him spending his time tending the king rather than answering questions about it."

"Does he work every hour of the day? Or is there something you would prefer me not to know? If I am to be king I need people around me I can trust to be honest."

Aye is not the only one old for his age, thought Tjenuna. Perhaps this association with Yuya's children is having more of an effect than anybody anticipated.

"I shall endeavour to have him sent to you at the earliest opportunity."

"Thank you, Tjenuna. See that no opportunity is missed."

Tjenuna bowed and took his leave, his fears for the future somewhat assuaged. If Ra saw fit to take Thutmose back into his bosom Egypt had a strong king in waiting. Tjenuna went to find the physician to explain what he needed to say in reply to Amenhotep's questions. He would have a narrow path to walk.

As Tjenuna rounded the corner towards the physician's quarters the doctor himself careered around the turn, his arms full of papyrus sheaves, his wig thrown onto his head at a precarious angle, his kilt half tied and trailing. The two men collided and papyrus flew into the air and scattered around the floor of the corridor. The physician scrambled around gathering up the manuscripts, his breathing short, quick and clearly audible. Tjenuna tried to help him. The physician made one brief check that nothing vital had been missed and stood up. His wig lay discarded in the corner like a sulking pet.

"I know!" he shouted in Tjenuna's face. "I know! The message has already arrived! For the love of Amun, do not hinder me!"

And with that he was off, one hand holding the crumpled papyrus pages to his chest, the other grasping at the precariously tied waistband of his kilt.

"Wait!" Tjenuna shouted, but the physician had already disappeared around the next corner. Tjenuna took off in pursuit, but he reached every corner only in time to see the physician disappearing around the next. He needed to overtake the physician before he reached Amenhotep's quarters in order to prime him with the delicacies of the situation. In his alarm it did not occur to him to ask how the physician had heard of Amenhotep's summons so quickly, and only when he saw that he had sprinted past the prince's quarters without breaking stride did he realise that something far more alarming than Amenhotep's distress was afoot. Tjenuna stepped up his pace.

Apart from the servants, Yuya and Thuya ware alone at home when the children arrived back early from the palace. Aye explained that Tjenuna had sent them away. Thuya sat them down.

"Your father and I hardly see you any more," she said. "Tell me, how are you finding life at the palace?"

"We are working very hard," Aye said. "But it is interesting work."

"And you, Tiye? How do you find the prince?"

Tiye shrugged. "He talks mainly to Anen and Aye."

"Are you being nice to him? You should always be nice to him."

"I try."

"Good. Do more than try. Always remember: one day he will be your king. And perhaps more. Do you think you would be happy living at the palace?"

"Living there? Why would..."

"Thuya!" Yuya interjected. "You should not say such things. Leave the child be."

"I am only asking her if she would like to live at the palace. It is an innocent enough question. Who would not like to live in a palace?"

"And what if this conversation were to be repeated within earshot of..." Yuya glanced at the children. "...of certain people?"

"Stop fussing. There is nothing to fear."

"Nothing to fear?" Yuya repeated, hardly able to believe his wife's nonchalance. "*Nothing to fear?*" He stopped and took a deep breath. "Children, go to your rooms."

"But we have done nothing wrong," Anen said.

"Why would I want to live at the palace?" Tiye said. "I live here, with you."

"Do you see?" Yuya said to Thuya, pointing at the girl.

Aye stood up and, taking the hand of each sibling, led them from the room.

"We have *everything* to fear," Yuya hissed. "We are walking in the shadow of high treason, and you must remember to be circumspect in your dealings with the children. Children talk freely without considering the wisdom of their utterances. Not unlike you yourself, it seems."

"You are overreacting, Yuya. How can this possibly be high treason?"

"Amenhotep's mother was Mutemwia, whom Thutmose did not even recognise as a wife, which makes Amenhotep only half royal. If he needed to cement his claim to the throne, he would need to marry someone with royal blood in their veins. Someone from his own family. Without that, the legitimacy of his accession to the throne could be challenged."

"Amenhotep's claim is strong enough, whoever he marries. He has been named as heir. Who would challenge him?"

"We shall see. You may be right. But for now, I beg you to show some discretion in your conversations with the children."

"I shall try. Call the children down. We shall see if we can take their mind off my question to Tiye."

Amenhotep desperately wanted to see the royal physician. His failure to glean anything more detailed than the most rudimentary information regarding the king's health was a matter of intense frustration to him. He thought about summoning Tjenuna back to the apartment to insist, as Aye had told him he was well within his rights to do, that the physician be sent forthwith.

He took to pacing his apartment. He was near the door when it burst open and had he not instinctively jumped backwards it would have cracked him on the head.

The messenger was falling to his knees even as he came into the room.

"I humbly beg your forgiveness for such an intrusion, Your Majesty, but I have been given instruction to ask you to attend the throne room on a matter of the utmost urgency."

Amenhotep looked around for his sandals, decided they were not needed, took a step towards the door, and then stopped.

"Wait," he said. "What did you call me?"

When Tjenuna and the physician had entered the king's bedchamber the physician had dropped his paperwork on a nearby table and immediately started chanting invocations to the gods, but Tjenuna had known instinctively that the physician's skills were no longer needed here. He knelt at the side of the bed and took the king's hand in his own. Thutmose's breath rattled in his chest. His eyes, protruding from within their sunken sockets, were more closed than open, and his gaze fell unfocused into the middle distance.

"What befalls me, Tjenuna?" he managed to say. Tjenuna had to hold his head next to the king's mouth to hear him.

"Nothing at all, Majesty. You seem to have had a slight relapse, nothing more."

"The pain."

"The physician is here now. He is taking care of everything."

"The pain is so great, and yet I cannot move."

"Just a few moments longer, my old friend, and the pain will go away."

The physician was issuing instructions to assistants to fetch herbs and flowers from the apothecary.

"Ask my father to stop bellowing," Thutmose said. "It hurts my head. I cannot tell him yet."

Tjenuna and the physician exchanged glances. The physician shook his head slowly.

"Has the messenger from the Mitanni arrived yet? I shall see him now."

"Thutmose, you are confused. No messenger awaits you."

Suddenly, Thutmose gripped Tjenuna's hand with a strength that no arm so frail should have possessed. He turned his head and his eyes focused on his friend.

"Tell Amenhotep," he said, "to remember Hatshepsut. You must promise me that you will tell him. Remember Hatshepsut. I leave the boy in your charge."

"My friend, I promise..."

But the king's grip had loosened and his eyes had lost their momentary focus. His rattling breath faltered in his throat, and stopped. The room fell silent.

Tjenuna placed Thutmose's hand on his chest and slowly stood up. "Menkheperure Thutmose, King of Upper and Lower Egypt, son of Ra, has joined his ancestors," he said, quietly. "Send for the king."

The physician looked quickly between Tjenuna and Thutmose.

"Amenhotep," Tjenuna said. "Send for Amenhotep."

Once in the throne room, Tjenuna and the viziers awaited Amenhotep's arrival in silence. Tjenuna eyed the empty throne and somehow found it more upsetting a sight than that of the dead king himself. The thought that Thutmose would never again sit there and joke with him was one that he could hardly bear. He cleared his throat and looked at the floor, trying to think of other things. For him to weep now would not be the most helpful way of starting a meeting with the new king.

The doors opened and Amenhotep entered, ashen faced.

"Has something happened?" Amenhotep said. "Is it my father?"

"Amenhotep, I have grave news. Please sit down."

Amenhotep sat on the dais to the left of the throne. Out of the corner of his eye Tjenuna saw the two viziers, Hepu and Ptahotep, exchange a glance and he knew the thought they shared.

"Amenhotep, you may sit here." Tjenuna gestured towards the throne.

The prince looked at it as though it had come to life and bitten him.

"That is my father's chair," he said.

"It was. And now it is yours."

"My father is dead."

"He has become immortal. His soul will pass into the underworld, where he will live forever. He will travel the sky every day in Ra's chariot. He can fear illness and pain no longer. You will grieve, as will I. The whole of Egypt will grieve, when in truth we should rejoice for him."

Tjenuna sat next to the boy and held him while he wept. When his sobs had calmed somewhat, Hepu stepped forward.

"Your Majesty, there are matters that need to be discussed. Arrangements need to be made."

"I think these things may wait, Hepu," Tjenuna said.

"It is not your place..." Hepu began.

"Nevertheless. Summon the embalmers. We will meet again when His Majesty has had a little time to adjust."

"Do not call me that," Amenhotep whispered. "My father is His Majesty."

"Tjenuna, you are not authorised to make..."

Ptahotep touched his colleagues elbow. "Tjenuna is right," he said. "Let us go and make whatever arrangements we can. His Majesty needs time."

"Do not call me that!"

Amenhotep and Tjenuna watched the two viziers leave the room.

"I am not His Majesty," Amenhotep said. "I am Amenhotep. The Crown Prince. The boy."

"You are no longer a boy. You are now a man. Your father's last words were a message to you that I am afraid I did not understand. He was a little confused towards the end, and I am not sure that they will mean any more to you than they did to me. But knowing your father as I do... as I did... they may be words of comfort to you."

Amenhotep wiped his red eyes. "What did he say?"

"He said that you should remember Hatshepsut. I know the name, but not the significance."

"He meant that I should honour the kingship as much as she did."

"He was right."

"I know, Tjenuna. I shall try my best."

Amenhotep was allowed the luxury of an undisturbed evening to come to terms with his father's death. It was an evening that profited him little. The next morning in the throne room he apprehensively crossed the floor, climbed the steps of the dais, and stopped in front of the throne. Although he recognised the fact that it was now his, to use it still felt close to sacrilege. He took a deep breath and sat down. He felt ridiculous.

"It is time to admit your dignitaries," Tjenuna said. Amenhotep hesitantly nodded to the doormen.

In strode the viziers. In their choreographed move, they stopped before the throne and prostrated themselves. Amenhotep stared down at them. Tjenuna caught his eye and gave him a meaningful look. They all seemed to be waiting for something.

"Oh," Amenhotep said. "May you live. Get up. Arise."

Hepu stepped forward.

"May I first of all pass on our sincere and deep regrets at the passing of your father."

"Thank you."

"May I ask how Your Majesty is coping with his bereavement?"

"I feel like an impostor."

"That is perhaps understandable. Your father cast a long shadow. However, although we hate to impose on your grief at a time like this, and despite the wishes of Tjenuna, who seems to have appointed himself royal guardian, there are matters which cannot wait for your attention any longer."

Tjenuna stood impassively and let the barb slip by as though unnoticed.

"What do you want me to do?" Amenhotep said.

"I assure Your Majesty that it is not a question of what anyone wants you to do. You are pharaoh now. It is for you to command us. All we can do is offer advice."

"And what advice do you offer?"

"That all depends, Majesty, on what you command us to do."

"But how can I command without your advice?"

"Such is the lot of a king, Majesty."

"I fear that Hepu is being deliberately obtuse," Tjenuna said.

"Very well, then," Amenhotep said. "I command that Maiherperi be reinstated as my friend."

Hepu smiled in a way that reminded Amenhotep of Yuya. "That is really not a matter for court, Majesty. If you wish to see Maiherperi there is nothing stopping you from just going to see him."

"Then I have no more commands."

"We need to discuss Your Majesty's taking of a wife."

"A wife? I have no wish for a wife."

"A king needs a wife, Majesty."

"Why?"

"Because it is proper."

"Why?"

"Because, Majesty, throughout Egypt's long and illustrious history, the king has always had a wife."

"But I am pharaoh. Can I not do as I like? Surely I, of anyone, am in a position to break whatever traditions I see fit?"

The delegation looked momentarily horrified as though Amenhotep had uttered some damnable heresy. Hepu seemed to take a moment to reign in his temper.

"Majesty," Ptahotep said, before Hepu had chance to say something that he would later regret. "Although you are pharaoh and can, as you say, do as you like, you are also the guardian of Egypt, and you have a number of duties and traditions that you must observe. Without it Egypt cannot survive. You must lead the daily worship. You must enact the secret rites and rituals in the temples' sacred places. And you must take a wife. Without such observances the harmony of the gods and the universe will be compromised and chaos will reign, as it did in the primordial ocean before the world was created."

"I have taken the liberty of conducting some research," Hepu said, calmer now. "And if I may be so bold, I would like to suggest the name of your sister Tiw for Your Majesty to consider. Obviously, she has the advantage of royal blood, and, as your eldest sister, she has been coached in the matters of court during her upbringing in the harem."

"I do not know her."

"Nevertheless, Majesty, it would seem that she is the most apt candidate for your hand."

"If I am to marry, I would prefer not to marry a stranger."

"As long as you acknowledge, Majesty, that marriage is unavoidable."

"I shall think about it."

"I must implore Your Majesty..."

"I meant, Hepu, that I shall think about which wife I will take. Now do please shut up."

Hepu turned crimson. Tjenuna examined his feet in an effort to hide a smile.

"Is there any other business?" asked Amenhotep.

"No, Majesty."

"Then we shall meet again tomorrow."

The viziers bowed and backed out of the room.

"It seems that Hepu may well have met his match," Tjenuna said, smiling broadly. "Congratulations, Amenhotep. I am immensely proud of you. I only wish your dear father could have seen the way you dealt with him. He would have laughed and laughed."

"I think my father was helping me."

"I think he may have been, Majesty, I think he may have been."

"Aye said I should be strong with my subjects."

"True; but strength without wisdom is like a mother without a father. Both are needed to make a king. As, indeed, is a wife."

"I know. But who is Tiw?"

"I do not believe I have ever had the pleasure of her company."

"Then how do you know it would be a pleasure?"

Tjenuna had to concede the point.

"I will not marry Tiw. Not unless I have to," Amenhotep said. He pushed himself off the throne and yawned.

"Your Majesty, there is more to do here, unfortunately. Ptahmose, the High Priest of Amun, is waiting to see you."

"Really? What does he want?"

"He needs to discuss the funeral and your coronation. We need to begin training for both as soon as possible. They are both very complicated rituals."

Amenhotep sighed and sat back down again. When Ptahmose entered and prostrated himself, Amenhotep said: "May you live, Ptahmose. Please stand." It already seemed to be an accomplished salutation.

It was seventy days, as tradition dictated, before Thutmose was ready for his tomb. Amenhotep officiated at the funeral in Thebes, reciting the spells of life and ritually opening his father's eyes and mouth with a ceremonial adze. After the necessary observances had been made, the funeral party snaked through the crags and valleys wherein Thutmose's tomb lay, back to the Theban palace where further guests awaited.

"I trust everything went according to plan?" Aye said, before Maiherperi could ask, when Amenhotep was back in the palace courtyard.

The reinstatement of Maiherperi into the inner court was King Amenhotep's first act after that first official audience with the viziers and the High Priest of Amun. It had not been entirely welcomed. While Tjenuna took great comfort in the support that Maiherperi could offer the king, Aye for one became sullen and monosyllabic at the mere mention of Maiherperi's name. For his part Maiherperi made a determined show of how little he felt threatened by Aye's continued presence. He was so convincing that nobody quite believed it.

"Everything was perfect," Amenhotep said. "I would like to thank you for all your help. It will not be forgotten."

Maiherperi looked downcast.

"And you too, Maiherperi."

Maiherperi bowed. "Thank you, Majesty."

"Maiherperi, we have been friends as long as I can remember. There is no need for you to be so formal. Please call me Amenhotep."

Maiherperi beamed and bowed again. "As you wish, Amenhotep," he said, no doubt savouring the words for Aye's benefit, who said nothing.

Amenhotep disguised a smile by turning away as though interested in the crowd surrounding them.

Over towards the entrance to the courtyard he saw Tjenuna. Here was someone else whom Amenhotep should thank for all his help. Tjenuna had taken something of a risk by defying convention and unilaterally declaring himself as Amenhotep's advisor after Thutmose's death. It was not an action that would go unrewarded. A few yards away from Tjenuna,

Amenhotep caught sight of Yuya, deep in animated conversation with his wife. They seemed to be arguing in whispers and controlled gesticulations. If Yuya was trying to quieten his wife down he was failing abjectly. Suddenly, in the middle of a tirade from Thuya, Yuya turned away and headed through the throng. His face was red with anger, his fists clenching and unclenching as he walked. Amenhotep lost sight of him for a second or two in the eddies of the crowd. When he reappeared he was a few steps away from Tjenuna, his hands relaxed, his face a calmer shade. He was smiling. He approached Tjenuna and started talking. Thuya watched them both as intently as was Amenhotep himself.

"Interesting," Amenhotep muttered.

Yuya had no choice but to go to talk to Tjenuna, although he thought it tasteless to discuss such matters at the king's funeral. More importantly, he thought Tjenuna would see it as tasteless as well. To raise the subject now would do more harm than good but there was no other way to stop Thuya from discussing Yuya's reluctance at an indiscreet volume, and Yuya was more worried about who would overhear her than he was about Tjenuna's reaction.

"If not now, then when?" she had said.

"We will discuss it later," Yuya replied, without much hope.

"Should we wait until Amenhotep is already married to someone else before we broach the subject at court?"

"Keep your voice down, woman!"

Already, one or two heads were turning in their direction.

"Go and speak to Tjenuna. He is but a few steps away from you. You know him. Just ask him if there are any plans for Amenhotep to take a wife."

"I will if you promise me you will shut up. You will be the death of both of us."

"Ask him if anyone has been named."

Yuya turned on his heel and walked away.

"May I offer my condolences," he said to Tjenuna. "I know the late king was a friend of yours."

"He was, Yuya. Thank you."

"I suppose that life at the palace has been very unpleasant of late?"

"There have been better times."

"You must have been very busy."

"It has understandably not been easy for the new king. I have been doing my best to smooth the transition for him."

"There must have been a lot to organise."

"Indeed," said Tjenuna.

"For instance," said Yuya, trying to sound nonchalant, "have any plans been made for the king to take a wife?"

"It is still a matter for some debate."

"Really? Are there no sisters for His Majesty to marry? Presumably he will be looking to reinforce his claim to the throne."

"That is really a matter for the court and the priesthood to discuss. It would be unseemly to do so here. I am sure you understand."

"Of course," Yuya said. "Of course."

"Only," said Thuya, who had crept up behind Yuya, "it may be that we are able to help you with your decision."

"Thuya!" Yuya blurted out.

"And you are?" asked Tjenuna.

"My name is Thuya. I am Yuya's wife."

"I see. And how exactly do you think you may be able to help?"

"Well, as you know, Amenhotep is already acquainted with my daughter, Tiye..."

"*His Majesty*," interrupted Tjenuna, emphasising the title, "will be looking for a wife with royal descent. But thank you for your interest."

"I should think so, too," Thuya said. "It is only right and just that Amen... that His Majesty should not lower himself to marry someone of common birth. But Tiye is a direct descendent of King Ahmose. He was..."

"I am aware of the name, thank you, Thuya. I shall mention your daughter the next time the matter is discussed."

"And when will that be?" Thuya asked.

"Thuya," Yuya said. "Enough. Tjenuna is a very busy man."

"I was just asking..."

"Enough. Please."

Yuya led his wife away through the crowd. They were arguing as they walked, her voice much louder than his. Tjenuna heard her say "...if I left everything up to you..." before he lost sight of them. She was a very strong woman. He raised his cup to their backs. "My sympathies, Yuya," he said to himself. But still, she may have had a point. There was indeed nobody at court who had the necessary attributes to be a Great Royal Wife other than Tiw. Tjenuna, with no little skill, had so far managed to avoid this gaping hole in his case against her at the meetings with the viziers and priests, where Amenhotep's reluctance, and his own loyalty to the new king, were his only bargaining tools. He stretched his neck to try to catch a glimpse of the girl Tiye across the courtyard. She was growing into a pretty young woman, and seemed to carry herself with the deportment necessary of a royal wife. Perhaps this was the answer. Her mother may be a nuisance though, Tjenuna thought. A woman so headstrong could cause a lot of problems at court. Tjenuna made a note to consult the scribes on his return to Memphis. They at least could tell him if Thuya's claim to royal ancestry was justified. But for now Tjenuna decided not to concern himself with it. This was still his friend's funeral, after all.

Back in Memphis with the worries of the funeral behind him, Amenhotep quickly settled into his new role. When he was not leading the daily worship he spent most of his time in meetings with his officials, discussing his coronation and marriage. He had come to accept that he needed a wife. He was finding it difficult to worship alone. Certain roles needed to be taken by a Great Royal Wife to reflect the wives of the gods that Amenhotep himself imitated during the daily rituals. To worship alongside stand-ins and understudies was demeaning both to him and the gods that he worshipped. It could be overlooked for the moment because as yet he was still not crowned, but once he was a king in name as well as deed it would simply not be good enough. The gods were responsible for the safety of Creation, for the protection of Egypt and the dependability of the inundation. It would not do to fail in their appeasement.

Tjenuna had put forward the name of Tiye. Amenhotep thought it an interesting suggestion, and one with which he was not wholly at odds. If he was going to have to associate with girls it may as well be one with whom he was already familiar and bore no particular ill will. It would, of course, mean a closer association with her family. Aye and Anen were already good friends, but Yuya would perhaps have to be spoken to. His unwanted familiarity had been barely pardonable when Amenhotep had been a prince and Yuya could hide behind his loyalty and usefulness to Thutmose, but it could be tolerated no longer.

Nevertheless, as the days leading to the coronation slipped by, Amenhotep increasingly saw Tiye as his future bride. For her part, she behaved flawlessly, always supportive without sycophancy, always demure without weakness. And it was indeed a pretty name.

The day before the coronation there was one last meeting. The viziers Hepu and Ptahotep were there, as was Ptahmose, the High Priest of Amun. Tjenuna positioned himself, as always, next to the king's throne.

"Gentlemen, the time has arrived for decision making. We can procrastinate no longer," Tjenuna said. "The coronation is tomorrow. The king needs to be betrothed by the time we leave this room. The consequences, should we fail to reach a decision, do not bear thinking about."

"I have heard rumours," Hepu said, "that a decision has already been reached, Tjenuna. Surely this cannot be the case without consultation with the king's ministers?"

"I do have a name to put forward."

"Please enlighten us."

"Tiye. She is the daughter of Yuya, the Commander of the Chariotry."

"Are you serious? May I remind you that this is a king's bride we are discussing? Are you really ready to grant that honour to a commoner? On what grounds?"

"She is already acquainted with the king..."

"I am not sure that I see the relevance."

"...and she is no mere commoner. I have documents from the scribes that confirm her royal blood line."

Tjenuna passed a sheaf of papyrus rolls to Hepu, who quickly scanned through them and passed them to Ptahmose.

"The connection seems tenuous, to say the least," the priest said, without looking up.

"It is there, nevertheless," said Tjenuna.

Ptahmose passed the papers on. "I am not sure that I am happy with this at all," he said. "Are we to entrust our daily worship and the very existence of our great land to the daughter of a mere soldier?"

"I believe that my opinion may be of some bearing here," Amenhotep said.

The room stopped to listen. He already has an authority to his voice, Tjenuna thought. He has a gravitas that comes not from the mere influence of his position. He will not need me much longer. It was a thought that did not dismay him. Rather he felt pride in his role in the creation of a new monarch. He knew that Thutmose would be pleased.

"And what is your opinion, Majesty?"

"That Tiye shall be my wife."

"Your Majesty," said Ptahmose. "May I offer you my advice?"

"You may. But it will not change my decision."

"But is it your decision, Majesty?" Hepu gave Tjenuna a meaningful look. "Or someone else's?"

"Do not patronise me, Hepu. I am your king. I make my own decisions."

Hepu bowed. "Yes, Majesty."

"It seems, then, that our services are no longer needed here," said Ptahmose. "If Your Majesty has made the decisions already, then so be it. I shall arrange for a message to be sent for Yuya to attend you forthwith. Congratulations, Majesty."

After the ministers and priest had left, Amenhotep turned to Tjenuna. "Are we doing the right thing, do you think?" he said.

"I believe so, Majesty. Tiye will make a good wife. Although there may yet be a price to pay. Take care not to alienate the priesthood. They are powerful friends and dangerous enemies. It would perhaps be prudent to at least appear to listen to their advice in the future."

"I will not tread lightly around anyone, Tjenuna. I am king. And anyway, the priesthood of Amun do not represent my grandfather. The god Ra is my grandfather, and it is to him that I answer."

"Be careful, Your Majesty. We answer to all the gods in the end."

Tjenuna and Amenhotep were still in the audience chamber discussing the final arrangements for the marriage and coronation when Yuya and Thuya were announced.

"I doubt that Ptahmose included the woman in the invite for an audience," Tjenuna muttered as the doors opened and the couple bowed into the room and prostrated themselves before the throne.

"May you live."

Yuya and Thuya stood. Yuya looked nervous, his eyes darting from Amenhotep to Tjenuna and back again.

"I have brought you here to tell you that, as part of my coronation ceremony tomorrow I am to marry your daughter, Tiye."

Yuya fell abruptly to his knees. "Oh, thank you, Your Majesty!" he spluttered. "This is a unique honour!"

"Hardly unique," Amenhotep said. "Kings have been married before."

"What my husband is trying to say," said Thuya, bowing slightly, "is that it is unique for us."

"I know," said Amenhotep, dryly.

"Your Majesty," said Thuya, "may I ask what titles will be bestowed upon us after the happy event?"

Yuya looked momentarily as though his heart had given out at the audacity of his wife's question.

"You are a very forthright woman," said Amenhotep. Thuya bowed, obviously mistaking the comment for a compliment. "I can only hope that your daughter has more awareness of manners and protocol." Thuya stopped mid-bow and straightened up awkwardly. "However," continued Amenhotep, "I can tell you that Yuya will become God's Father and you God's Mother. Although," he added, "I am sure that you already knew that. Now you may take your leave to tell Tiye the news."

After they had left the room, Amenhotep said to Tjenuna: "I find her vexing."

"I would consider it a miracle if you did not, Majesty."

Yuya and Thuya allowed themselves to sleep late on the morning following their daughter's wedding. Their private celebration had lasted long into the night and they had drunk far more wine than was customary for either of them. When Yuya finally opened his eyes to squint at the sunlight streaming through the window, he saw that Thuya was already awake.

"Good morning, God's Mother," he said.

"And good morning to you, God's Father."

They both smiled. Thuya reached out and held her husband's hand. They lay for a moment in silence, staring at the ceiling, both allowing the resonance of their titles to absorb into them as though it was an unguent soaking into healing flesh. After all Thuya's machinations, the fact that Yuya still had flesh was an unexpected joy that made even Memphis air taste sweet.

"Darling," Thuya said, at last. "Do you think it would be possible for us to see Tiye at the palace today?"

"Today? I would much rather stay in the shade today. My head is unhappy with me about last night's excesses."

"Nonsense. The walk will clear it."

"Why do we need to see her today? What is so urgent that it will not wait until morning?"

"I wish to talk with her, that is all."

"Then talk with her tomorrow."

Thuya turned to face him and rested her arm across his chest. "Are you hungry?" she said.

The thought of food provoked a brief stab of nausea, and Yuya groaned. "I could not eat a thing," he said.

"Then we can have a pleasant walk, and when we return you will be ravenous, and the servants can prepare us a repast befitting our new positions."

"Thuya, we do not have new positions. We have new titles. There is a difference."

"Perhaps," she said, in a singsong tone of voice.

It was almost gratifying that Thuya had been wrong and the walk to the palace did nothing to clear Yuya's head. In the bracing cool of the early morning, when he could still see his breath before his face, the exercise would have been the perfect cure, but now the sun was too high in the sky and Ra was not so much shining as throwing his heat down from his chariot with such ferocity that the very light itself seemed to weigh on Yuya's shoulders. Yuya briefly wondered whether the god was angry with him. By the time they reached the palace Yuya was feeling even worse than he had when he had woken up. The tapestry of smells in the marketplace had done nothing to appease his stomach.

At the gates Thuya announced herself and Yuya as God's Parents, making Yuya feel faintly ridiculous. They awaited Tiye in an audience chamber smaller than the king's, but grand for all that, with wall decorations bright and gaudy enough to make Yuya's tender head swim. When Tiye finally appeared she was wearing a full length diaphanous dress of many layers, heavily laced with gold and silver and studded with turquoise. She was wearing a large wig of a thousand braids that cascaded across her head like a black waterfall which danced when she moved. Yuya had never been in the company of a Great Royal Wife before and the richness of her apparel made him realise, almost for the first time, exactly what he and Thuya had achieved. His eyes followed her as she flowed across the room.

"You look beautiful," he managed to say as she reached her throne.

She sat down carefully. "It is all very heavy," she said, with a coy smile.

"And how are you finding your first day as the king's wife?" Thuya asked.

"For now I am just learning how much there is to learn. It is such a lot."

"Of course it is, my dear," Thuya said. "And there are some things to learn that no king or minister can teach you."

"Such as?"

Thuya smiled. "You will know them when their time arrives. But always remember, I am still your mother. I am always here to help you, whatever it is you require."

"Thank you, mother."

"No thanks are necessary. It is my duty. Just as it is your duty to offer the same support to your husband. Always remember, Tiye, that he may be king, but he will sometimes benefit from help like any other man. As I can advise you, you can advise him."

"He has ministers to perform that duty."

"Ministers." Thuya made a dismissive noise. "They are all men. They do not have the insight that our gender bestows upon us. You will have your place."

"Thuya," Yuya said. "I am not sure that it is wise to meddle in..."

"Oh, hush. I am not meddling. I am merely helping. Can a mother not help her daughter?"

"Well, yes, of course, but..."

"There is one thing that causes me some concern, though."

"Concern?" said Tiye. "Mother, I am the king's Great Royal Wife now. Everything I am I owe to you. There should be nothing that causes you concern. Name it, and I shall resolve it."

"It is just that the world now owes you respect. It is every Egyptian's duty to love you as a child loves its mother, and every foreign king's obligation to honour you with praise and gifts."

"And this causes you concern how, exactly?" Yuya interjected.

"Well, it is only that all this is impossible if they do not know who she is."

"They know that there is a Great Royal Wife," Tiye said. "The king always has a Great Royal Wife."

"Yes," said Thuya. "But they love the Great Royal Wife, when they should love Tiye."

Yuya held a hand to his head and rubbed at his throbbing temples. "Are you never happy?" he said.

"If only," Thuya said, "there was some way of informing them of your existence."

She paused for the briefest of moments before continuing.

"I have been thinking," Tiye said to Amenhotep when they were finally alone later in the day. The sun had sunk low enough for the influence of the underworld to almost extinguish its glow, which remained only as a dull orange smudge across the palace ceilings.

"It seems to me," she continued, "that the world deserves to know more of you. You are the king of the most powerful land under the heavens. Your authority should reach over the whole world."

"And so it does."

"Until you have proclaimed yourself, it does not."

"What are you saying?"

"Only that the world should hear of your exploits. Your fame and glory can only grow."

"And how would I achieve this fame and glory? Even I cannot magic my likeness around the world."

"I have no idea. Perhaps you could send out bulletins."

"Bulletins? You mean scrolls? To everywhere? It is impossible."

"Not scrolls. Papyrus is not hardy enough to survive long enough to be seen by enough people."

"I see you have given this much thought."

"No, not really," Tiye said. "It has just occurred to me."

"And has a convenient solution just occurred to you as well?"

"You have craftsmen who could produce such a proclamation in stone."

"To be carried by my envoys around the whole world? I still say it is impossible."

"No," Tiye said. "A message in stone need only be carried to key locations. It would complete any further journey by itself, being passed from hand to hand. Send it to the mayors of your cities and the kings of our neighbours. They will do the rest."

The couple sat in silence for a few moments. Servants came into the room and began lighting lamps.

"Think of the fame," Tiye said. "Think of the glory. A king deserves of such things, if nothing else. The whole world would know your name."

"If such a thing were to be successful, it would be a famous exploit in itself, would it not?"

Tiye reached over and held his hand. "An exploit telling of exploits. Summon a scribe. We can compose the message now."

"To say what?"

"We can report your coronation." Tiye said. "And your marriage. This bulletin could be the first of many. More could be sent with news of the events of your reign as they happen."

When the scribe, Kheruef, arrived, Amenhotep said: "We wish to dictate a letter."

Kheruef bowed and prepared his writing materials. "To whom should it be addressed, Your Majesty?"

"To the whole world, Kheruef."

"Majesty?"

"Nothing. I shall explain after the message has been composed. Now then, my dear," Amenhotep said, turning to Tiye. "Are there words that you can pluck out of the air?"

"Some," Tiye said. "The letter should start with your name and titles."

Kheruef knew the details and wrote quickly.

"Put 'son of Ra' also," Amenhotep said. Kheruef's head bent over the papyrus again. Amenhotep turned back to his wife. "And now, my dear?"

"And now perhaps your marriage."

Amenhotep thought for a moment, composing the words in his mind. "Put 'The Great Royal Wife is Tiye, may she live'," he said.

"'May she live long', perhaps?" said Tiye. "And what about my father and mother?"

"What about them?"

Tiye thought back to the meeting with her parents earlier in the day, and for a moment could not remember the explanation her mother had provided for the inclusion of their names.

"People should know their names. It is who I am." She worried for a moment that it sounded too rehearsed, but Amenhotep seemed not to notice anything untoward. As her mother had explained to her, although the king may need the occasional help of his new family he would be far from happy knowing that they even thought help was a necessity. *All things must come from the crown*, Thuya had said. *Even if the crown knows nothing about it.*

"Very well," Amenhotep said. "Kheruef, add 'The name of her father is Yuya and the name of her mother is Thuya.'"

"'She is the wife of a mighty king'," Tiye said.

The royal couple looked at each other and shared a smile. "Indeed she is," Amenhotep said. "Indeed she is."

Chapter Three

Ikheny, the Braggart

"I HOPE you will forgive the intrusion," Tjenuna said after the servant had led him through to the living quarters.

"Not at all, not at all. Please sit down," Thuya said. Tjenuna could not help noticing that Yuya watched him walk across the room a little like a mouse might watch the progress of a snake. *He knows why I am here,* Tjenuna thought. *Thank you, Yuya. I could leave now and know the truth without uttering a single word.*

"It is not often that you are seen beyond the confines of the palace. To what do we owe this pleasure?" Thuya asked.

"Even now I am here only on palace business, I fear."

"And what may that be?"

"It has come to my attention that you have been visiting Tiye at the palace."

"Yes? What of it? She is still my daughter."

Not *our* daughter, Tjenuna noted. Yuya had still not opened his mouth.

"Absolutely," Tjenuna said. "Equally, it cannot fail to have come to your attention that your names have been included in the news scarab that His Majesty has distributed throughout Egypt and abroad."

"Yes, it was a lovely gesture. We are both very honoured."

"Indeed. Do you believe there to be a connection to such an inclusion and your palace visits?"

"I am not sure where this is leading, Tjenuna. Are we being accused of something?"

Thuya was very calm. Her polite indignation would have been persuasive enough to force Tjenuna into embarrassment had she not been betrayed by her husband's nervousness. Tjenuna almost wished that Yuya and Thuya had been more blatant in their interference in the king's dealings. This was nothing more than an act of vanity and Tjenuna would have felt petty in confronting them were it not for his fear that this was the first raindrop in a deluge. Amenhotep was still a vulnerable boy, for all his affectations of mighty kingship. Until his reign was well established in experience and knowledge, the slightest impediment could bring it toppling to the ground. There was something in Thuya's manner that made

Tjenuna uncomfortable, although he would have been hard pushed to name it had someone asked him. Interference in the king's decisions by those who had no business there was always worrying; with Thuya it was somehow terrifying.

"This is not an investigation, Thuya. I merely wish to establish a chain of events. Did you visit Tiye before the news scarabs were produced?"

"I say again, what of it?"

"To be blunt, I wish to know whether the idea for the news scarabs came from you, or from Tiye, or, as I have been led to believe, from the king."

"It seems to me that your suggestion is straying dangerously close to treason, Tjenuna."

"Your logic eludes me," Tjenuna said.

"Well, it seems that you are not only suggesting that the king is a liar in his claim to be the originator of the scarabs, but that he is weak enough to be influenced by the likes of myself and my husband. Although we are good people, Tjenuna, we do not have the wherewithal to dictate policy to the pharaoh. To underestimate His Majesty is a very dangerous thing to do. He was very generous in his acknowledgement of his wife's parents in the scarab. Perhaps your accusations stem more from the exclusion of your own name than the inclusion of ours."

Perhaps the king was not the only person who Tjenuna could be accused of underestimating. Thuya was obviously at her most dangerous when cornered, and in taking the offensive she had left Tjenuna no avenue of rejoinder that would not sound as though he were making excuses for his behaviour. Instead of replying, he turned to Yuya.

"And what say you, Yuya? Are you of the same mind as your wife?"

"My husband is always of the same mind as his wife," said Thuya, and Yuya flushed with belittlement.

"Then you have answered my questions and I bid you good day," Tjenuna said. He stood up to leave.

"Please feel free to drop in whenever you are in the neighbourhood," Thuya said, with a smile of victory.

Tjenuna left the house feeling embarrassed and defeated. It was small consolation that he now knew what he was dealing with.

"We shall have to watch that one," said Thuya, once the door had slammed shut after him. "Come, we must go to see Tiye."

"I warned you this would happen," Yuya said, as they walked. "You cannot, you just *cannot* dispense with protocol entirely without provoking some evil consequence. That is why protocol is there."

"Stop whining, Yuya. I thought you were a soldier. Are you this cowardly on the battlefield?"

Yuya stopped as though he had walked into a wall, his mouth gaping in astonishment that his wife could bandy about these insults with such nonchalance. When she did not break her stride, or so much as turn her head, he was forced to run to catch up to her.

Yuya could not bring himself to pass a civil word with his wife for some time after her intimation of cowardice on the walk to the palace. He did not speak throughout the interview with Tiye, where Thuya once again warned her daughter to be circumspect in deciding which conversations should be allowed to reach the king's ear.

"He has an entire kingdom to rule," Thuya had said. "It is of the utmost importance that he is not troubled with every meaningless piece of news. To distract him could be disastrous for Egypt. The future of the nation may rest upon your discretion. Do you understand me? You do understand me, do you not? If you are ever in doubt, you must come to me."

Tiye had assured her with such gravity that she had no cause for alarm that even Yuya was partly satisfied. It was only when they were readying themselves to leave that Tiye said, "I have a surprise for you." She reached under her throne and produced a scroll of papyrus. Yuya eyed it with suspicion and wished that Tiye would continue unrolling it forever so that he would never have to hear the words it contained.

Trying to control a smile that threatened to destroy the majesty of the occasion, Tiye cleared her throat and began to read. The scroll was the template for another news scarab, this time dealing with the details of a bull hunt in the Fayum. As the story in the scroll was revealed, Yuya began to breathe more easily. This seemed innocuous enough.

As she came to the end of the tale, Tiye read: "'The total which His Majesty took on the hunt on this day – fifty-six wild bulls.'" Then she paused and looked at her parents in turn. Perhaps this is just a wife's pride in her husband, Yuya thought. But Tiye continued to read.

"'Under the Majesty of Nebmaatre Amenhotep, Ruler of Thebes. His Great Royal Wife is Tiye, may she live.'"

Another pause. A broader smile.

"'Her father's name is Yuya,'" she said, and her voice broke into an excited laugh as she continued, "'and her mother's name is Thuya!'"

"Oh, Tiye, that is marvellous!" Thuya exclaimed. "Yuya, is that not marvellous?"

Yuya did not look up as he spoke. "It is a death sentence," he said. "It is the first cut on the tree trunks upon which we will be impaled. What do you think Tjenuna will make of this?"

"Ignore your father, dear," Thuya said. "He is sulking because we have had words."

Amenhotep was tightly clutching a papyrus scroll as he walked into the throne room where his most senior officials had already gathered before him.

"Do not bow," he said, as he crossed the floor. "Speak to me. What is the meaning of this?"

"The meaning of what, Your Majesty?" Hepu said. "We have not been informed of the reason for this summons."

"This." Amenhotep brandished the scroll at them. "Has Ptahmose not spoken?"

"I thought it better to come from you," the High Priest of Amun said.

"Very well," Amenhotep said. He sighed as though about to embark on a long story for which he did not have time. "Ptahmose has travelled up from Thebes to deliver this message to me. It has come via Merymose, our viceroy in Nubia. I shall read it to you. 'To Nebmaatre Amenhotep, King of Egypt. From Ikheny, King of Nubia, the land of gold. The four lands of Kush, Irem, Tarek and Weresh that constitute Nubia all lie under my control. We reject you, Nebmaatre Amenhotep. The gold of this land is not Egypt's, but ours. Your weakling armies are useless before my mighty word. Read this and tremble, Nebmaatre Amenhotep. Nubia is mine forever.'"

Amenhotep looked at the shocked faces around the room and allowed them a few moments to digest the information.

"Who is this Ikheny?" he asked.

"The name is not familiar to me," Hepu said. "I would guess that he is nothing more than a tribal leader."

"Merymose informs me that this tribal leader has ten thousand men behind him."

"If I may speak, Majesty," Ptahmose said. "The viceroy's messenger informed me that Merymose has retreated some distance, as far as Tabo, near the third cataract of the Nile. He may be exaggerating numbers to explain his rather, shall we say, *enthusiastic* withdrawal."

"And then he may not."

Ptahmose bowed and opened his arms as if to graciously concede a point. "As you say."

"Then we must act decisively and immediately, gentlemen," Amenhotep said. A murmur of agreement flitted around the room. "Do you have any suggestions?"

Ptahotep stepped forward. "There is only one sane alternative, Majesty. We must mobilise immediately and crush this wretch before he can do any further damage. Nubian gold is the life-blood of this nation. We cannot allow its supply to cease."

"What are your thoughts, Tjenuna?"

"Only those which I used to share with your father. That whatever decision you make is the will of the gods."

"I have already successfully appeased more than one hostile power by sending them plentiful amounts of gold. Can I not apply the same logic here?"

"What can we send him that he does not already have, Your Majesty?" Hepu said. "It would be like sending sand to appease the desert. There is no alternative but to fight."

"There are always alternatives, Hepu. I wish to correspond with this upstart."

"You wish to *correspond* with him? But..."

"I have spoken, Hepu. I may be able to talk him out of this madness. Fetch me a scribe."

While they were waiting for the scribe's arrival, Amenhotep whispered, "What are your thoughts, Tjenuna? I need advice now, not platitudes about the will of the gods."

"I think that to avoid war now will be a miracle, however repugnant it is to you. Have you spoken to Maiherperi about this?"

"Maiherperi has nothing to do with this. Is that what you think?"

"Not if you say otherwise."

The scribe arrived and Amenhotep began to dictate.

"To the false king Ikheny, the braggart. From Nebmaatre Amenhotep, king of Egypt. Your threats are but a trifle to me. Already my army sets out with its mighty king at its head. My charioteers and archers are too many to count, my infantry like the grains of sand in the desert. If we meet in battle you will be destroyed as my forefathers destroyed yours. Nubia will be laid waste to its furthest extremes, its women and children sold into bondage. Your descendants will spit upon your name for all eternity. Flee now, before you and all who follow your banner perish in the heat of my wrath."

The scribe wrote it all down and then read it back.

"Good," Amenhotep said. "Send one copy to the Nubian. Send another to Merymose with instructions to tell me what effect it has. Perhaps if he believes he has an army behind him he will venture close enough to find out."

The scribe scurried away.

"And now we must wait, gentlemen," Amenhotep said. "If we are fortunate, Ikheny will take me at my word and simply disappear."

"And if we are not?" Hepu said.

"Then we will have some more thinking to do."

"Majesty, we may not have the time..."

"I have spoken, Hepu."

The ministers trooped out of the room. In the corridor, Ptahmose took Tjenuna by the arm.

"This is a strange turn of events, do you not think?" he said.

"There has always been trouble in Nubia," Tjenuna said.

"Not that. The king's response to it. If he were his father the army would be halfway to Nubia by now, with the smell of blood in their nostrils."

"He acts under the will of the gods. As High Priest of Amun surely you would concur?"

"Yes, yes, I know all that. But if this rebellion is not crushed our gold routes will be compromised, and what would Amun's temples be without gold? Gold is Amun's blood. It is his food and his pillow. I must confess to a certain degree of concern over His Majesty's decision making."

"It is not his decision making that concerns me," Tjenuna said, quietly.

"You have other concerns?"

Tjenuna was reluctant to continue. Ptahmose had advised against Amenhotep taking Tiye for a wife all along. It was Tjenuna's influence that had given the king the confidence to insist on it. Indeed, Amenhotep would never even have considered it if it was not for Tjenuna's suggestion in the first place. But Ptahmose was a wise man, a man of religion and duty. Tjenuna had no other place to turn for advice than the priesthood or the two viziers, and he could already hear Hepu's gloating and sarcastic remarks. He was not about to subject himself to that humiliation so soon after the one he had received at the hands of Thuya. And so he quashed his doubts, and spoke.

"I think Tiye is going to make a Great Royal Wife of whom all Egypt can be proud," he said.

"But?"

"But there may be a problem with her family. Her father seems to be a weak man when he is not in command of his chariot and his men. Thuya is the head of that household. And I think Thuya may have ideas above her station. I believe that she may be manipulating the king, through Tiye, to enhance her status somewhat."

"Have you any evidence?"

"Only the inclusion of Yuya and Thuya's names on the news scarabs. They went to see Tiye before the first one was produced."

"But even if your suspicions were correct, that would surely amount to vanity, not treason."

"I agree, but I have spoken to Thuya and she is a very clever woman. An ambitious woman, I fear, but no more ambitious than she is headstrong. If she has succeeded thus far, I doubt she will be content to let the matter rest where it does. If I am correct, we have not heard the last of Thuya."

"And of Yuya?"

"Yuya does what he is told. If you had seen his face when I broached the subject to them both you would have seen that he was terrified of the truth being discovered. But not as terrified as he is of his wife. He does not have the spine to oppose her. Sometimes I pity poor Yuya."

"Of course," Ptahmose said, "if His Majesty had married his sister..."

"...then the problem could have been a hundred times worse. What if they had hated the sight of each other? Anyway, it is not Tiye that is the problem."

The corridor had emptied now, leaving the two men face to face in silence. After a moment, Tjenuna spoke again.

"I am asking for advice, Ptahmose," he said. "I have only conjecture, not proof."

"Then there is little you can do but stay close to the king until you have the proof you need. I will pray on the matter. Amun will guide me, and I will relay his instructions to you."

"Thank you, Ptahmose. And I need not impress upon you the necessity of keeping this conversation between ourselves."

"Of course," Ptahmose said. "There is something you could do for me, though. Perhaps you could speak to His Majesty on his own and persuade him of the importance of military action against Ikheny? Amun would look very favourably upon it."

"It would be my pleasure."

"Excellent. But for now I must retire to my quarters. I only hope the servants have been notified of my arrival and made preparation for me. It has been an arduous journey all told, and I am in need of some rest."

Tjenuna watched the High Priest as he disappeared around the corner. He had no intention of persuading the king to take a course of action to which he was opposed. That would make him no better than Thuya.

But then neither did Ptahmose have any intention of retiring to his quarters. As soon as he was out of Tjenuna's sight he stepped up the pace and went in search of Hepu.

He found him in the palace gardens, lost so deeply in thought that he did not hear Ptahmose's approach and flinched when the priest coughed politely to announce his presence.

"Ah, it's you," he said.

"Do I perhaps find you considering your options?" Ptahmose asked.

"I have no options. I have done everything I can to persuade His Majesty of his folly. There is nothing more to do but hope he comes to his senses."

"Perhaps," Ptahmose said. "Perhaps not."

"What do you mean?"

"It is obvious to all but the king that there is only one solution to this crisis, and it is only a matter of time before His Majesty realises the error of his ways and orders military retribution. The problem is that it may take too long to persuade him to act."

"And yet I fear we can do nothing but wait."

"Are you aware, Hepu, of what will happen to this country if the temples' coffers are allowed to run dry? Without a steady supply of gold from Nubia such a thing will be impossible to avoid. It is up to us to protect Egypt from such an eventuality. You must speak to the king again. We can only hope that you will be able to spur him on before disaster strikes."

"Even if I were to do so in a matter of days or a week, we may be too late," Hepu said. "The army will need to be mobilised. Have you seen the extent of the building works that His Majesty has commissioned around the country? Temples and monuments are springing up everywhere. And who is quarrying the stone, and transporting it from the quarries to the building sites? The army, that's who. We will have to gather men from the four quarters of Egypt. It will take time, and we have no time to spare. Ikheny will be in control of Nubia before we have chance to act, and then what? Do you think he will be content with Nubia alone? These people never are."

"And what if we were to mobilise the army now?"

"Without the king's orders? Impossible."

"Perhaps not. If I were to find a man willing to do it while you were persuading the king we could save days, or weeks. Enough time to make a difference, anyway."

"But who would be willing to do such a thing? If you approach the generals then we never had this conversation. I want nothing to do with you. They are loyal to His Majesty and would deliver your head to him without a second thought."

"Not the generals. I know just the person. Some valuable information has come into my possession. He will not be able to refuse."

"And when the king discovers what has been transpiring behind his back?"

"We can safely deny all knowledge of it. My man will make an excellent scapegoat and an awful witness. Our hands will be clean. And by then the army will already have been readied for the fight."

"And who is this man who is to sacrifice himself for the good of his country?" said Hepu.

"It is perhaps better that you do not know. It will probably become evident in time anyway. Suffice to say he is influential enough to get the job done, but at the same time completely expendable."

"I don't know," Hepu said, rubbing his chin.

"I cannot do this alone, Hepu. Without your say so I will do nothing. But I need a decision now. There will be ramifications for our actions, but they will be nothing as to the ramifications of indolence."

Hepu thought Ptahmose a trustworthy man with dependable judgement, but he was still not sure. He stared into the flowerbeds for a few moments, unable to fully comprehend the enormity of such a course of action. To defy a king's wishes to this magnitude was not something to be taken lightly.

"Do it," he said, finally.

Ptahmose gave him a reassuring clap on the shoulder and went to find a trustworthy acolyte to summon Yuya to the palace.

Thuya pretended not to notice Yuya's sullenness for days. She was not prepared to give him the satisfaction of knowing that she cared enough to acknowledge his displeasure and so the silence continued, punctuated only by civil but brief exchanges when such things were unavoidable. Such a stalemate would have continued indefinitely had it not been for a hammering on the door one early evening, perhaps a week after Tjenuna's visit. Yuya had learned to be wary of the sound and eyed the entrance to the living quarters nervously as he waited for the servant to show the visitor through. It was an envoy from the palace who informed Yuya that he had been summoned to attend the High Priest of Amun. Suddenly Yuya wanted to talk to Thuya, but their impasse had reached the level where staying in the same room for any length of time weakened both their resolves to remain silent. Thuya was in the bedroom, sewing.

"He is in Memphis?" Yuya said.

"He arrived this morning from Thebes, sir," the messenger said.

"Why does he wish to see me?"

"I know only that he does, and that it is a matter of some urgency. I was given no further information to relate."

"Very well," said Yuya. "I shall set off momentarily."

"Very good, sir," the messenger said, but did not move.

"Yes?" said Yuya.

"The High Priest has asked me to wait for you and accompany you to the palace."

Yuya's racing pulse stepped up another notch. He felt slightly nauseous.

"I shall inform my wife of my whereabouts," he said, and went to find her.

"I am to go to the palace," he told her. "Something urgent has come up."

"Fine," she said.

"Is that all you can say? Fine?"

Thuya did not look up from her needlework. "I imagine that you are panicking," she said, pretending to be enthralled by the movement of her fingers. "It will be something and nothing, but there is nothing I can say to persuade you of that until you find out for yourself."

Without another word Yuya turned on his heel, went back into the living quarters and then followed the messenger out into the front courtyard, where he was pleasantly surprised to discover that there was no armed guard waiting for him. As Yuya and the messenger set off for the palace he tried to persuade himself that Thuya was right. Surely they would both have been summoned if this concerned the news scarabs?

When they reached the palace the messenger led him not to the front gates but around the side of the walls, through alleyways that Yuya had not known existed.

"Where are we going?" he said, hesitantly. He was not sure he wanted to know.

"The High Priest has asked that your entrance be discreet," the messenger said. He led Yuya around to the rear of the palace. There was no courtyard here, so a small door set into the wall led directly into the building. A constant stream of servants and tradesmen flowed in and out. The messenger pushed his way through and Yuya followed. Inside he found himself in a series of dimly lit corridors and intersections which the messenger seemed to know well enough to stride through without hesitation. Yuya was acutely aware of the fact that this was the sort of place that you could leave only when you were expressly permitted to do so.

They stopped at an unmarked door. The messenger opened it and Yuya had to squint in the brightness of the room beyond. A skylight channelled sunlight into the room with such efficiency that the floating motes of dust in the air seemed to shine with a luminescence all of their own. The room was sparsely furnished, with only two chairs and a table to break the lines of the floor. A pitcher and two cups sat on the table next to some papyrus scrolls. In the chair opposite Yuya sat Ptahmose. He motioned to the chair and Yuya sat down. Behind him he heard the door close, but there was no sound of footsteps retreating down the corridor. He is standing guard by the door, Yuya thought. Is that good or bad?

"Thank you for coming so quickly," Ptahmose said.

"My pleasure," Yuya croaked, and cleared his throat.

"Tell me, Yuya: have you yet been informed of the situation in Nubia?"

"What situation?"

"I shall take that as a no. Excellent. May I offer you some wine?"

"I... yes. Please. Thank you." Just as a precaution, Yuya waited for Ptahmose to drink out of his own cup before Yuya sipped from his.

"Before we go any further," Ptahmose said, "I wish to make something clear. What passes between us within these walls is for us alone to know. You are a senior member of His Majesty's armed forces, and I know I can rely on you to keep this meeting secret, can I not?"

"Of course," said Yuya. "But my wife knows I am here."

"Then you must think of a reason for this meeting that you can share with her. For you must not tell her the truth. You must tell *no-one* the truth. Do we understand each other implicitly?"

"We do," said Yuya. "I will tell her... I will think of something."

"Excellent." Ptahmose said again. He pushed the scroll across the table. "This is a copy of a letter delivered to His Majesty this morning. I take it you can read?"

Yuya nodded and unrolled the papyrus.

"Ikheny?" Yuya said, after he had read the message.

Ptahmose shrugged. "Nobody seems to have heard of him."

"I did not know the Nubians even had a king," said Yuya.

"Exactly," Ptahmose said. "They do not. We do not know from whence this one has sprung."

"And why are you telling me this?"

"Ah, Yuya. Now we get to the nub. More wine?"

Yuya shook his head.

"Firstly, I would remind you that Amun himself is witness to your oath of secrecy regarding the matter."

"Of course."

"Excellent. I have brought you here to ask you to begin arrangements for mobilising the army. Rebellions of this nature have a tendency to grow apace if they are not dealt with decisively and without mercy. Nubia must see us cleave this Ikheny in two."

"You would like me to do that? I am commander only of the chariotry, not of the entire army. I cannot. Under whose authority would I act?"

"What other authority is there greater than Amun himself?"

"With the authority of all the gods in the firmament such a task would still be beyond me. I have no knowledge of the troops' whereabouts. Even if I did, I would have no means of contacting them."

Ptahmose pushed another scroll across the table. "This will tell you everything you need to know about where you can find the troops. And I understand that, as Commander of the Chariotry, you have charioteers at your disposal?"

"Of course," said Yuya.

"Then use them as messengers. We need the troops ready to embark onto ships for transportation to Nubia at a moment's notice."

"Should these orders not come directly from His Majesty?" Yuya asked.

Ptahmose took a draught of his wine, his eyes drilling into those of Yuya as though he were trying to see through him to the wall behind his head. "The king is momentarily engaged in other business. There is no need to trouble him with every detail of the goings on in his realm. But you ask too many questions, Yuya. I was led to believe that would not be the case. I was led to believe that you are a man of discretion who loves his country and his king and his gods more than he loves life itself."

"I am," Yuya said. "I do."

"And will you defy them?"

Yuya swallowed hard. He could not meet the priest's eyes any longer and he allowed his gaze to fall to the scrolls on the table, realising too late that to do so immediately after a declaration of religious and patriotic fervour may look like he had a guilty secret to hide. Instead, Ptahmose obviously took it as a sign of some sort of victory and sat back in his chair as though he had just finished a hearty meal.

"It will be impossible to do this without it coming to the attention of His Majesty," Yuya said.

"That is of no matter. By the time the king comes to know of it, he will be grateful that it has been done. You will merely be carrying out his orders before he has given them."

"I do not know about this," Yuya said.

When Ptahmose spoke he did so slowly and clearly, enunciating each word with such precision that they seemed to contain a threat independent of the words themselves.

"I see that your name has been included once again in the king's latest news scarab. Very curious."

"I..." started Yuya.

"Your station does not really justify such an honour, does it?" Ptahmose continued. "I wonder, then, how such a thing came to be? If I did not know better I would assume that someone had been putting words in His Majesty's mouth. That would be a very dangerous thing to do, would it not? It would imply that the king would be vulnerable to, shall we say, *unauthorised* influences. Such influences cannot be allowed. Tjenuna has asked for my advice on the matter. I am currently undecided as to whether the situation merits an investigation."

Yuya paled, but said nothing.

"Excellent," Ptahmose said. "Then you will do as I bid you."

Yuya noticed that it was not a question, but he nodded his agreement anyway.

"My messenger is waiting outside," Ptahmose said. "He will lead you back out the way you came in."

Yuya left the room without a word. On the way home a belated fury at the way he had been treated increased with every step. Ptahmose had spoken to him as though he were nothing more than a servant, or worse, a child. The patronising buffoon. Yuya had left the room with his head bowed as though he had been scolded. By the time he reached his door he was ready to explode, as much at his own behaviour as anything else. He marched into the house and found Thuya in the living quarters, still sewing.

"Are you happy now?" he shouted. "Do you see where your constant meddling has got me?"

"You are speaking to me again, then?" Thuya said, calmly.

Yuya was quickly pacing back and to across the floor. "What am I to do?" he was saying, more to himself than to Thuya. "What am I to do?"

"Husband," Thuya said. "Calm down. Sit here, next to me. Tell me what has happened."

"I cannot."

"Why ever not?"

"I have sworn an oath of secrecy before Amun himself."

"Surely that does not include me?"

"Of course it includes you. Secrecy is secrecy."

"Then I cannot help you."

"No, you cannot."

"And from the look of you, you cannot help yourself either."

"I fear not."

"And whatever has happened is so grave as to make you fear for your life?"

"For my life and my soul."

"Then you are doomed." She picked up her needle and continued sewing where she had left off. Yuya stopped dead.

"What?" he said.

"If you are in fear of your life and soul and you cannot help yourself, and you will not allow me to help you," she explained, "then you are doomed."

Yuya started pacing again.

"If, on the other hand," Thuya continued, as though merely thinking out loud, "your life and soul are doomed anyway, then you have nothing further to fear by breaking your oath and telling me your secret. What could possibly happen that would be any worse? Perhaps I am your only hope."

Yuya's marching gradually slowed until he lost his momentum completely and slumped into a chair.

"You must promise me one thing," he said. "You must swear by all the gods in the pantheon that you will not reveal a word of this conversation to any living soul. Especially Tiye. For the sake of your husband's life, you must not tell Tiye."

Thuya carefully placed her sewing to one side. "Go on," she said.

"Swear to me first."

"I swear, I swear. Now tell me."

Yuya related the details of his meeting with Ptahmose. He explained how the order to mobilise obviously came from none other than Ptahmose himself. He explained how the king clearly knew nothing of the move. Perhaps there was no Ikheny. Perhaps Yuya was being implicated in a plot. But to disobey Ptahmose would be to disobey the king of the gods directly. And yet to obey him could be a betrayal of the king of men. Yuya had two choices. He could either march directly to the palace and explain everything to the king, in which case Ptahmose would undoubtedly have him killed and Amun would damn his soul forever, or he could carry out Ptahmose's orders, in which the king would find out, have him killed and damn his soul forever. Worst of all, to even speak about the matter to anyone who may be able to help would be tantamount to cutting his own throat.

At the story's end Yuya sat with his head in his hands, a breath away from sobbing.

Thuya picked up her sewing.

"Is that all?" she said. "I will speak to Tiye about it. Do try not to get so agitated, dear."

It was early on the morning following Yuya's meeting with Ptahmose. Thuya and Yuya were once again in Tiye's throne room, waiting for the Great Royal Wife to appear.

"I suppose you have a better idea, do you?" Thuya said.

"You know I do not."

"Then stop scowling."

When Tiye arrived it amazed Yuya that his wife could be composed enough to find the time for small talk before broaching the subject of Ptahmose's demands. It was a full ten minutes before she even alluded to the fact that there was a reason for their visit.

"There is something worrying me which I hope you can help with," she said. "We have heard that there is trouble brewing in Nubia."

"How did you know?" Tiye asked.

"Oh, there is very little that goes on in this palace without my becoming aware of it one way or another."

"You should be careful with whom you share such information."

"Only with you, my dear, only with you. I am very discreet."

In any other situation Yuya would have laughed out loud. He contented himself with looking at the ceiling and saying nothing.

"This is a matter for my husband and his ministers," Tiye said. "How could I help? What worries you so?"

"Look around you, Tiye. Look at your beautiful clothes, at the palace, at the temples in which you worship alongside the king. How is all this possible?"

Tiye did not understand the question and she looked to her father for help. Yuya was too intrigued by what Thuya would say next to offer her any.

"It is possible," Thuya continued, "because of Nubian gold. Nubian gold is the foundation of everything we hold dear. It would be a shame, would it not, if everything you have taken possession of through your illustrious marriage was to be taken away from you before you have had chance to enjoy it?"

"Who will take it away?"

"Ikheny will take it away. If he continues to hold Nubia, no more gold will come. If no more gold comes, Egypt will sink into disarray. For one so young, Amenhotep is a singular diplomat. He has turned Egypt's enemies into her friends with presents of gold. When those presents are forgotten and no more are sent, Egypt's friends will become her enemies once more and all your husband's work will be undone. He will be remembered not as a mighty king, but as a failure. And you will be the wife of a man ridiculed in history."

Tiye's eyes grew wide as her mother spoke. She looked to Yuya for confirmation, who nodded sadly.

"But what am I to do?" she said.

"Amenhotep must go to war. He must mobilise the army and take it to Nubia. If he does not he will be destroyed, one way or another."

"I cannot influence Amenhotep's decisions."

Thuya laughed. "My sweet child," she said. "My sweet, innocent child. But of course you can!"

After Thuya had coached her thoroughly, Tiye left the throne room.

"There," Thuya said, clapping her hands together as if to shake dirt from them. "Now Amenhotep will mobilise the army. Your problems are solved."

"You are putting a lot of faith in the hands of a little girl," Yuya said.

"She is not a little girl. She is my daughter. It will come naturally to her."

Tiye flawlessly remembered the script her mother had drilled into her. Amenhotep sat opposite her, listening without interrupting. Only when she had finished did he speak.

"You seem very keen to risk the lives of others," he said, calmly.

"And you seem keen to risk the land of your fathers. When will you be prepared to fight? When Ikheny secures Nubia and Egypt has to learn to live without gold? When Ikheny decides that Nubia is not enough and pushes over our southern border? Perhaps when the Hittites see your reluctance to defend yourself and pressure us from the north? You forget that I have studied history with you, Amenhotep. We both know what life was like when Egyptians had to live under the rule of the Hyksos."

"You have seen history," Amenhotep said, "but you have never seen war."

"I have not," she said. "But your forefathers have seen war in all its horror. Are their deaths fighting the Hyksos to stand for nothing? Did they go through all that just to have you endanger the land all over again?"

Amenhotep was making a supreme effort to stay calm, to avoid the indignity of shouting. "You perhaps forget to whom you are speaking," he said.

"I am speaking to my husband."

"And your king."

"The protector of the land," she said.

"Leave me be," Amenhotep muttered, standing up and stalking from the room. He walked the palace corridors aimlessly. If he heard approaching footsteps he would duck down a side passage and continue until he heard footsteps again. He did not want to be bowed to. He did not deserve it, whichever decision he made. If he chose not to fight it seemed he was endangering the nation, and people who endanger the nation did not deserve bows. If he led his army into Nubia a large proportion of palace personnel would accompany him, and he did not want to be bowed to by people whose deaths he was about to arrange.

After a time he found himself outside Maiherperi's quarters. He stood there silently, staring at the door, remembering his furtive trip to see his friend on the eve of his last expedition to Nubia with his father. He knocked on the door and Maiherperi's mother was just as startled to see him as she had been the last time.

"Please do not bow," he said, before she had chance to lower herself to her knees. She led him through to Maiherperi's room.

Amenhotep told him about Ikheny's letter. "I am not your king tonight," he said. "I am just your friend. What would you say if I told you that I am to lead an army to Nubia and engage Ikheny in battle?"

"I would ask to come with you."

It was not the answer that Amenhotep was expecting. "Are you not the same Maiherperi who turned against me for fighting the Nubians with my father?"

"Firstly, I did not turn against you. I was merely annoyed with you. Secondly, no, I am not the same Maiherperi. That was Maiherperi the boy, while I am Maiherperi the man. And thirdly, you have already admitted to me that you fought nobody when you went to Nubia with your father. You said as much as soon as the bravado had worn off."

"Ah, but my heroic screaming served to distract the enemy long enough to ensure victory."

They both laughed and the tension in the room began to lift somewhat.

"But you would come to fight against your own countrymen?" Amenhotep asked, serious once more.

"They are not my countrymen," Maiherperi said. "You are my countryman. I may have the skin of a Nubian, but I am still an Egyptian. Everything I have I owe to Egypt, and to you. Egypt is all I know. That is what I did not appreciate as a child. And anyway, I would not trust you to go anywhere without being there myself to look after you."

"Very well then," Amenhotep said, failing to muster any real enthusiasm. "If we fight, we fight side by side, and we can look after each other."

Hepu and Ptahmose begged Amenhotep for another audience the day after the king had dictated his letter to Ikheny. Ptahmose had reported to the vizier that the interview with Yuya had succeeded flawlessly. The army would be made ready to go to war. Now all they needed was a war to go to. Amenhotep seemed distracted as he listened to Hepu's appeal for an armed response. His eyes, Hepu noted, were encircled by red patches, as though he had been crying, or had not slept, or both. When Hepu stopped talking it seemed as though Amenhotep did not realise that Hepu's oration had come to a close. Amenhotep remained silent for a few moments. Hepu caught Ptahmose's eye. Ptahmose shrugged.

"Your Majesty?" Hepu said.

"It seems I am surrounded," Amenhotep said. "My ministers, my priests, my family, my friends: they all want me to fight."

"Even Tjenuna," Ptahmose said.

"He does?"

"Has he not spoken to you?"

"No, he has not."

The room lapsed once again into silence.

"Very well then," Amenhotep said suddenly, as though abruptly coming to a decision he had not spent all night wrestling with. "Mobilise the army. Inform me when arrangements are complete. We march on Nubia."

As they left the throne room, Ptahmose said: "He mentioned that his family wanted him to fight this war."

"What of it?" said Hepu.

"Nothing. But I think Tjenuna may be interested to hear it."

Tjenuna did not see Yuya again until they were aboard the king's ship, *Rising in Truth*, sailing south for Nubia. He managed to engineer some time alone with him late in the voyage. They were standing at the stern. Ships had joined them at every port, and now the fleet stretched into the distance further than either of them could see.

"I have been speaking to Ptahmose," Tjenuna said, and saw immediately that not only did he have Yuya's undivided attention but that Yuya was at pains to hide the fact from him. Yuya's hands immediately began to squirm, brushing imaginary specks off the handrail against which they were leaning.

"Really?" said Yuya, his voice labouring with unconvincing nonchalance.

"He told me a curious thing," Tjenuna continued. "It appears that His Majesty felt pressured by his family to undertake this expedition."

Tjenuna watched the following ships as they cut silently through the water, as though counting them. He wanted Yuya to feel every iota of tension. Tjenuna believed Yuya would betray himself, or his wife, under pressure.

"You wouldn't know anything about it?" Tjenuna said, finally turning to look directly at his companion. Yuya pretended he had not noticed, and continued watching the river.

"Perhaps his sisters...?" Yuya said.

"He has no contact with his sisters."

"Then I do not know."

"Could it have been Tiye?" Tjenuna asked. "What other family is there to speak of?"

Yuya thought desperately of another name to be the hook upon which he could hang the accusation. None came to him.

"Yuya?" Tjenuna prompted.

"It could have been Tiye," Yuya conceded. "But I do not know for sure. She has not spoken to me of it."

"You surprise me," Tjenuna said. "I would not have expected Tiye to take such an active interest in matters of state. I wonder why she felt the need to intervene."

"She is the Great Royal Wife. There is no crime in her speaking with her husband."

"Yes, but even so. Perhaps," Tjenuna said, as though the thought had only just occurred to him, "she was prompted. Do you think that possible, Yuya?"

"I do not know."

"You do not know whether it is possible?"

"It is not impossible," Yuya said.

"Who would prompt her to try to steer matters in such a way? Who would gain from His Majesty taking up arms? This is no small matter. A battle is not a safe place, even for a king surrounded by his bodyguard. Imagine if something untoward befalls His Majesty. Imagine if the battle goes badly. It is a risky venture, this strategy of Tiye's, is it not? Amenhotep was prepared to win this fight with diplomacy, with no risk to himself or his army. Think of the questions that will be asked should Egypt not see the end of this battle unscathed."

"We will be docking soon," Yuya said, pushing himself off the rail to stand upright. "I need to prepare my horses."

"Yuya," Tjenuna said. He finally succeeded in catching Yuya's gaze in his own.

"Yes?"

"I know everything."

"I... I need to..." Yuya said, and gestured broadly towards the foredecks of the ship. He scurried away before completing the sentence. What did Tjenuna mean? Surely Ptahmose could not have told him about the plan to mobilise the army. That would endanger Ptahmose's life as much as it would Yuya's. Unless Tjenuna had wrestled the information from him just as he was trying to do with Yuya, and the High Priest was at that moment languishing in some cell in Memphis. *Unless*, thought Yuya, with a shock that lurched his heart into a briefly faster rhythm, unless Tjenuna himself had been the originator of the plot. But why go through Ptahmose? And why confront Yuya with it now? He is covering his tracks, thought Yuya. Out of sight of the stern of the ship, Yuya sat down heavily and put his head in his hands. Perhaps the king has heard of this and I am to be the scapegoat, he thought. The foundations of his life had turned to mud, and Tjenuna was the water that lapped against them.

Tjenuna, who in fact knew nothing, turned back to watch the ship's progress with a smile.

Merymose, Egypt's viceroy in Nubia, had withdrawn as far as Tabo, just below the Nile's third cataract. This was the last stop of the fleet's southerly journey, about a day's march from where Merymose informed the king the Nubians had made their camp. The king, Tjenuna and Yuya were sitting at the king's table in his quarters on *Rising in Truth*. Throughout the journey from Memphis, Amenhotep had grown increasingly irritable and withdrawn. Now he was sitting in silence, staring at the table as though engrossed by the grain of the wood.

"Is there something that troubles you, Majesty?" Tjenuna asked.

Had Yuya not been there Amenhotep would have considered telling the truth; that the thought of the imminent battle distressed him to such a degree that he felt close to panic. That men were to have their lives ripped and shredded from their bodies at his command. And that, in his torment and despair, his father was frowning down at him and thinking, *coward!*

Instead, he said: "Why are our archers Nubian?"

"Nubians are the best archers in the world, Majesty."

"Can they be trusted? Will they fire on their own countrymen?"

"Nubians have fought faithfully for Egypt for generations," Yuya said.

"Against Nubians?"

"Sometimes, yes."

"I want the spearmen to keep watch on them. I do not wish to be brought low by treachery."

"So shall it be, Your Majesty," Yuya said.

Merymose entered the cabin, bowed and nervously sat down opposite them.

"Appraise us of the situation, Merymose," Amenhotep said.

"They are billeted in the town of Napata, Majesty. It lies on the east bank of the river, about a day's march south east from here. There are too many of them to all fit into the town itself. They are also camped outside it, on the side furthest from the river."

"What fortifications will we find there?" asked Yuya.

"Around the camp itself there are none. The town is surrounded by mud brick walls, about three times the height of a man."

"On all sides?"

"On all sides but the river. Napata has a harbour where the rebel fleet is at anchor."

"Has my message reached Ikheny?" asked Amenhotep.

"I believe so, Majesty."

"And what effect did it have?"

"None discernable."

"None discernable from here, perhaps," said the king.

Merymose dropped his gaze. "Some rebels may have fled," he said, in a quiet voice.

"Leaving how many remaining?"

"Too many to count."

"Your Majesty," said Yuya. "Do you remember the exact wording of your letter?"

"Only that he would be destroyed if he opposed me."

Merymose fished in the waistband of his kilt and drew out the copy that the king had sent him. He offered it to Yuya, who read it aloud.

"'My charioteers and archers are too many to count, my infantry like the grains of sand in the desert.' There is no mention here of a navy."

"Should there be?" asked Amenhotep.

"Indeed not, Majesty. Ikheny is holed up in a town with no riverside wall. From your letter he may be expecting a land based attack. I suggest that we attack him from the river."

"It is only a small harbour," Merymose said. "You will not be able to fit more than five ships in there at any one time. You will not be able to unload your men fast enough. That is why there is no need of fortifications."

"Then with Your Majesty's leave, I have a suggestion," said Yuya.

Amenhotep, Yuya, Tjenuna and Maiherperi could see nothing of the land before them. Only an absence of stars in the blackness in front of them denoted where the sky became the ground. The only sounds were the horses and men behind them. The Nile lay far to their right where it took on a broad loop that would bring it back into their path by morning. They were marching south east towards Napata, and marching hard. Eight ships had set off from Tabo shortly before the march commenced, heading for the enemy's harbour. It was imperative that the troops were in position before the ships began their attack. They were taking no great effort at concealment, which would have been impossible anyway with a force of this size. They will have lookouts, Yuya had said. Let them see us. It will only add to their confusion and fear once the attack begins.

As Amenhotep rode his chariot he thought about the day ahead of him. He still prayed that the Egyptians would crest the last hill to see a deserted town before them, the rebels having evaporated upon news of the king's arrival. But what if they have not? he thought. What if I am to lead my men into battle this day? There was only one option left to him, and it was the option he most feared. If there was to be a battle, the Egyptians had to be the victors. The alternative was death and disgrace, not only for him but for the thousands that followed him as well. In order to save lives, he and his men had to kill.

By the time the eastern sky had segued from black to navy blue and the stars had begun to fade the men were tired, but in position. Directly in front of them an indistinct and irregular patch of black marked the position of the town. The encampment in front of it was delineated by an untidy cluster of lights. The chill night breeze occasionally wafted the shouts of men up to the high ground that the Egyptian forces had occupied.

"They know we are here," said Yuya. "They are preparing a welcome for us."

Amenhotep tried to remain impassive.

As Tjenuna disappeared into the night to gather the unit commanders together one last time, Amenhotep turned to Yuya. He had been meaning to speak to him for some time, ever since their departure from Memphis in fact, but had managed to postpone the moment under various pretexts that even he had recognised as poor excuses. But while he was indisposed to call Yuya a friend he could not question the man's prowess on the battlefield. All Amenhotep had seen of war had been from the bottom of his father's chariot, and that did not qualify him to make military decisions that would shape Egypt's future.

"I am king," he said, "but I readily confess my inexperience in these matters. I am depending on you, Yuya."

By the time the unit commanders had arrived, Yuya had coached the king in what he was to say.

"I trust you are all aware of the plan of battle," Amenhotep said to the officers. "If any of you are not, you may speak freely now." The officers glanced at each other, but remained silent.

"Good," Amenhotep said. "Pass this news to your men. When we charge, we do not stop until we are at the gates of the town itself. I want no man stopping to loot the enemy camp. There will be plenty of time for that after the victory. Too many battles have been lost for the love of plunder. Is that clear?"

The officers nodded.

"Is that *clear*?" Amenhotep said.

"Yes, Your Majesty."

"Good. And keep close watch on our archers. They are fighting their countrymen. Cut down any man that falters."

The officers bowed away into shadow.

"It is perhaps time for you to address the men," Tjenuna said.

"Now?" Amenhotep said. "But what should I say?"

"The usual, Your Majesty," Yuya said. "That the Nubians will murder our children, that the gods are on our side. Blood, honour, victory. It is a standard formula."

Maiherperi and Tjenuna helped the king into his armour, a tunic crafted from overlapping scales of gold, and his blue battle crown. The outfit was a heavy burden that would take some getting used to.

"Where should I stand?"

"Anywhere you see fit, Majesty. Your words will be relayed to those who cannot hear you."

Amenhotep walked over to his chariot. It was a highly ornate affair, its wood finely decorated with gold foil and glass. As Amenhotep approached he ran his hand down the flank of the stallion nearest to him. It nodded as though in greeting, the plumes atop its head shimmering as it did so. His driver held the horses steady as Amenhotep stepped onto the back of the chariot and took a moment to draw strength from the foreign foes trampled under his feet on the golden frieze that ran around the interior. He raised his arms to the sky and tried not to think about the target that such an imposing vehicle would make him.

The front ranks of the army were standing on the grass just a few feet in front of him. The sky had by now lightened enough to silhouette him against the predawn glow. The men nearest to him fell silent, and that silence seemed to radiate from them in a great arc until nothing could be heard apart from the calls of birds and insects.

"You are a mighty sight, sons of Egypt!" Amenhotep shouted. "The pitiful Nubians will scatter before you like seeds thrown to the soil. You are to write history here this day. For make no mistake – if you fall, so does your homeland. But if you stand, the whole of Egypt will stand with you and sing your names in grateful praise for years innumerable! All the glories of the heavens will be yours for the plucking!

"The Nubians are an evil and cowardly foe who would defile our temples and our women, and murder our children in their beds were it not for the valiant defenders of life arranged before them now. Victory is already ours, my brothers! For Ra is behind us and before us and within us! His light shall be our shield, and our eyes and swords will shine in the heat of his power and glory!

"Let the Nubians pray to whom they will. For no force of heaven or earth can prevent us from wreaking our havoc over these men who try to take the land from under our feet!

"Let the earth itself recoil at our battlecry! For it is *VENGEANCE!*"

"*Vengeance!*" the men shouted. The cry spread to those who had not heard the speech, until the whole army took up the shout. Amenhotep stood before his men, valiant and noble and wishing he could suck in the noise of the men's cries and use it to fuel his own bravery. And then the cheers stepped up to fever pitch and Amenhotep saw rapture spreading over the angry faces of the men closest to him. They were pointing, but not at him. He followed the line of their fingers over his right shoulder and there, at the rim of the world, he saw the mighty Ra breach the horizon. Amenhotep prostrated himself. Behind him, his army did the same.

"Was that all right?" Amenhotep asked when he had descended from his chariot and rejoined Tjenuna, Yuya and Maiherperi.

"It was... *perfect*," Yuya said. He had tears in his eyes. "Your dear father could not have done better."

Amenhotep turned towards the town. The enemy camp was now clearly visible in the dawn light. In the harbour behind the town he could see ships manoeuvring. He watched them intently. After a few moments a single fire arrow shot into the sky and burned for a few moments before it fell onto the town.

"The signal," Amenhotep said. "We march."

Orders were relayed and the huge body of men started forward. They held a steady pace but did not break into a run. If Yuya's calculations were correct they would not reach the encampment until news of the attack from the rear had reached the enemy and thrown them into turmoil.

As they drew closer, Amenhotep began to make out knots of men running back from the camp into the town to defend the harbour. He tried to count them, knowing that each one was a man less for his soldiers to have to contend with, but there were too many. There were more already arranged into ranks directly in the path of the oncoming Egyptians.

Before reaching arrow range the spearmen formed a wall with their shields which the archers crouched behind, and continued to advance until the enemy was within range of their bows. Volley after volley of arrows fell onto the camp. The Nubians' replies fizzed through the air and buried themselves with a thud deep into the roof of Egyptian shields. Only a few met their mark.

The screaming began.

Yuya was watching the scene intently, his gaze flicking between the Egyptian and Nubian front lines and the enemy running for the rear.

"When do we charge?" Amenhotep shouted over the noise of the arrows and the wounded, hoping that Yuya would say 'never'.

Instead, Yuya said: "We wait. Chariots will fail against men who have the bravery to stand firm against them. Only when the enemy is ready to run do we unleash them."

The Egyptian archers continued their advance under the spearmen's shields, firing as they walked. Only when they were twenty yards away from the Nubian lines did they stop. More Egyptians were falling now, the enemy archers able to aim for the gaps in the sheet of shields. Suddenly, responding to orders that Amenhotep could not hear, the shield wall fell and with screams of *Vengeance! Vengeance!* the spearmen threw themselves into a charge. From all over the camp Nubian spearmen stepped from where they had been taking cover behind tents to repel the attack.

Yuya signalled for the charioteers to edge closer. The royal guard, including Tjenuna and Maiherperi, closed in around Amenhotep. Yuya's skilled eyes saw signs of the faltering in the Nubian defence that he had been waiting for.

"*Charge!*" he yelled, and suddenly Amenhotep's horses were careering forward, his driver furiously whipping their flanks with the reins. Gaps appeared in the Egyptian ranks to allow the chariots to pass. They crashed through the Nubian front line and a scream of panic welled up in Amenhotep's chest as he saw black faces – those same black faces he had seen from the back of his father's chariot – disappear below the feet of his horses and the wheels of his chariot, throwing him violently from one side to the other. He slashed blindly with his sword, his eyes closed for fear of making contact and seeing its results, and managed to turn his cries of repugnance to those of defiance as they met his lips.

A block of Nubian spearmen forced his charge to the left, through a gap in the enemy that opened up and then closed just as quickly behind him, cutting him off from the majority of his guard. He looked to the right and left and saw Tjenuna and Maiherperi matching his pace, their swords hacking through the air again and again, their mouths wide in screams that he could not hear. Tjenuna's entire face was already streaming with blood. Maiherperi's driver was hurt and was listing awkwardly to one side.

Amenhotep's momentum carried him deep into the camp. Pockets of chariots had done the same at intervals along the front but they were too few to do anything other than cause confusion in the massed Nubian ranks and too far apart to be able to reach one another. They were heavily outnumbered and Nubians were suddenly able to get within thrusting range with their spears. Amenhotep again and again put all his weight into his blows, and again and again his sword bit deep into the heads and shoulders of the men that assailed him. Blood and brains sprayed from the blade at the top of each arc. All fear was gone now, leaving only his screams of fury and the metallic taste of blood at the back of his throat. Amenhotep measured his life in moments between one blade fall and the next, and was grateful for each one.

And then suddenly there were no more tents. He had ridden the entire length of the enemy camp. Only Tjenuna, Maiherperi and two guards had remained with him this far. The five wheeled round defensively. Nubians were streaming past them, desperate to plug the gaps in their harbour defence and prevent an encirclement. Few stopped to trade blows. Amenhotep had time to notice that one of his horses, the one that seemed to greet him before his speech, was limping badly from a deep cut on a foreleg. Maiherperi's driver was clutching his stomach and gasping for breath as blood trickled between his fingers.

"Are you badly hurt?" Amenhotep shouted across to Tjenuna, who was trying to wipe the blood from his face. Tjenuna shook his head.

"Your Majesty," Amenhotep's driver said, signalling the wounded horse. "I fear this injury may hinder our return."

Amenhotep turned to Maiherperi. "Will you drive me?" he shouted.

"Of course!"

Tjenuna and the two guards placed themselves between the king and the Nubians while Maiherperi and Amenhotep helped the wounded driver into the king's chariot.

"Bear this load back safely," Amenhotep said to his own driver. "And take care of my horses."

Amenhotep jumped aboard Maiherperi's chariot and prepared himself for the fight back to the Egyptian lines. As the group began to accelerate back towards the fight he saw that the battle's tone seemed to have changed. The Nubians were now in full retreat, but in full retreat towards him. And the Egyptian soldiers were no longer in pursuit. No doubt unaware of their king's precarious position, they had stopped to loot the abandoned Nubian tents. Their officers raged about them, shouting and punching, knowing that they would be ultimately held responsible for a failed attack if the Nubians were given enough space to regroup.

Maiherperi frantically spurred his horses forwards but it seemed as though the entire Nubian army lay between them and safety. The horses could do no more than canter through this terrain of fallen bodies, and even those Nubians in full flight had enough of their senses remaining to recognise Amenhotep's crown and armour and know the value of bringing him down. They clamoured at the chariot. Amenhotep wildly lunged and slashed at any face that came within his reach but there were too many of them. He could kill and kill until he dropped from exhaustion, and yet still more would surge forward. He gulped down lungfuls of air that never seemed to be quite enough and cries escaped his lips at every exhalation. Try as he might, despite every scene of carnage that assaulted him, despite the fear and the noise and the smell, despite the jolting of his chariot and the pain in his arms and legs, Amenhotep could not help thinking of home, and what it would be like without him.

King Nebmaatre Amenhotep knew he was about to die.

Yuya was lost. His place was at the head of his chariots or at the side of the king, and he could find neither. The Nubian defenders had proved hardier than he had expected and their line had broken only in half a dozen unconnected places. The chariots that had failed to get through and had managed to survive were now scattered around the battlefield, vulnerable and leaderless. The foot soldiers were pushing relentlessly forward though a quagmire of blood and flesh, but at a great cost.

Yuya wheeled his horses around and shouted orders to the men fighting in front of him. Praying that they had heard and understood, he went to find help.

He found charioteers where he could and pulled them from the fight, keeping some with him and sending others off to find more. Within a few minutes he had a force of about a dozen men, none without wounds. He doubted that half of them were able to continue fighting, but they could ride, and he hoped that was all he would need. He had not the time to gather more. He took them in a wide sweep behind the Egyptian lines to gather their pace and led them straight into the heart of the battle. As they neared the fight the ground became treacherous with corpses. Three or four of the more badly wounded charioteers did not have the strength to keep their balance and their charge faltered as they disappeared from sight behind the sides of their chariots.

Just before they reached the line, those spearmen who had heard Yuya's orders and who could extricate themselves from the enemy flung themselves to the side. The chariots crashed though, trampling enemy and friend alike but opening up a gaping hole in the Nubian line which the Egyptian spearmen rushed to fill. The Nubian defences were split into two, each half now under attack from both the front and the side. More Egyptians leapt into the breach to take the places of the comrades that fell before them.

The Nubian defences could cope for no more than a few minutes before they were overwhelmed. They turned and fled, the Egyptian foot soldiers snapping at their heels, and the battle was decided.

When the blow finally came it was not what Amenhotep had been expecting and he cried out as much from astonishment as anything else. He had been successfully defending Maiherperi's chariot for so long that each swing of his sword arm sent shooting agony across his shoulder and down the right side of his back and made the next swing seem impossible. But then the next swing would come and the pain would flare anew. He was fighting for his life with a fury of which he had not thought himself capable.

Ahead and to his right, a Nubian stepped forward, his spear held high over his head. Amenhotep timed his swing to take off the Nubian's head as the chariot carried him past but the Nubian thrust the spear forwards early and drove the point deep into the belly of Maiherperi's right hand horse. It screamed in pain and toppled over, its weight and momentum pulling its companion down to its knees and flipping the chariot over as though it was a toy. Amenhotep and Maiherperi went with it and crashed to the ground, the chariot tumbling on top of them. Something connected with the back of Amenhotep's head and colour exploded behind his eyes. He remembered no more.

Tjenuna saw them fall. Together with the guard he reined his horses in, untied himself, and jumped to the ground. A chariot at rest was a liability, and he needed to be mobile at close quarters to protect the king. His horses immediately bolted. Maiherperi's chariot lay upside down on top of the king, hiding him from ally and enemy alike. Maiherperi had managed to untangle himself from the reins. He climbed to his feet, picking up a fallen Nubian's spear on the way. He did not have the time to see whether Amenhotep was alive or dead before the enemy was upon him. Tjenuna, Maiherperi and the remaining guard stood with their backs to the upturned chariot, and they screamed their rage and swung at anything that came within their range.

Tjenuna took a glancing spear thrust to his arm that ripped flesh and left white fat and red muscle hanging from the wound. He fought on with one arm dangling uselessly by his side, no longer aiming at a specific foe, just thrashing, thrashing desperately through a gauze of sweat and blood that stung his eyes.

The Nubian attacks were increasingly hampered by the pile of corpses that surrounded the king's defenders and increasing numbers of the enemy chose to hare past rather than stop and fight, and yet slowly, step by reluctant step, the three were beaten into retreat until their backs rested on the chariot they fought so valiantly to protect.

Even when they were routed, pockets of Nubian resistance fought on, but those Egyptians not immediately engaged quickly became distracted at the contents of the tents that had been strewn around the battlefield. Yuya and the chariots he had mustered spurred their horses on in pursuit, scanning the battlefield for places where they could be of most use.

Ahead and to his left Yuya saw three men on foot, desperately fighting to keep a horde of Nubians at bay. Near them were two chariots, one of which was overturned. Yuya turned his chariots to face them and as he drew closer he could make out their faces.

Tjenuna saw him and began shouting.

Yuya knew it was within his power to save him. He also knew that Tjenuna had the same power to save Yuya, but Yuya doubted whether he would use it. *I know everything*, Tjenuna had said on the ship. He was a man devoted to his king beyond all else. He would have no compunction in betraying the man that saved his life, if he thought that betrayal was in the interests of the crown.

"Help us!" Tjenuna screamed. "*We need help!*"

We all need help, one way or another, Yuya thought. He turned his chariots away to the right and went in search of the king.

Tjenuna was the first to fall.

When he had seen the chariots approaching he had felt a brief surge of euphoria and known that he need only survive a few moments longer before the remaining Nubians would have no choice but to scatter. But the charioteers must have somehow failed to see him because they took his hope and turned their backs. As he turned to shout again he momentarily dropped his guard, allowing a Nubian to duck under the swing of his sword and thrust a spear into his back. His legs gave way in an instant and he fell, wrenching the spear from the Nubian's grasp, able neither to breathe nor scream. He looked down and saw the skin of his belly unbroken but stretched to a point. Forgive me Thutmose, he thought, for I have failed your son.

The last sounds he heard were Maiherperi's screams.

"*You shall not have him!*" Maiherperi was shouting. "*You shall not have him!*"

And then, silence.

When Amenhotep swam back into consciousness he was unsure where he was, only that his mouth was dry and tasted of soil and his head thudded with pain at every beat of his heart. He was dizzy and nauseous and it was a few moments before reality soaked back into him. Only then did he realise that the sounds of battle had receded to nothing. From somewhere nearby he could hear voices of the wounded crying out in pain.

"Help," he croaked. And then, louder: "Help!"

He heard footsteps approaching. The chariot was lifted from over him and he squinted at the sunshine that seemed to pierce his eyes to the very back of his skull.

A silhouetted face looked down and said: "It's the king!"

Two more faces appeared and soon the shout was being relayed across the battlefield.

"It's the king! It's the king! We found him! Fetch Yuya! The king's alive!"

Hands reached in and pulled him free of the chariot and then helped him to his feet, only to be withdrawn as their owners fell to their knees.

"We thought you were dead, begging your pardon, Your Majesty," someone said. "The whole army has been scouring the battlefield for you. Thanks be to Amun for your safe return to us."

Someone else echoed: "Thanks be to Amun."

"What has happened here?" Amenhotep said. He turned and saw that there were three Egyptians lying where his chariot had fallen, surrounded by a ring of Nubian corpses.

"The enemy has surrendered, Your Majesty."

He took a step towards the bodies. He vaguely recognised the first as one of his guards.

"The town has fallen, Your Majesty."

Tjenuna lay in a black pool of blood, the broken shaft of a spear still protruding from his back, one arm lacerated almost beyond recognition.

"Victory, Your Majesty!"

Maiherperi lay on his back a little further off, one hand still clutching a Nubian spear. A deep wound ran across the width of his abdomen, exposing the organs within.

"Victory?" Amenhotep said, quietly. "What victory is this?"

What little strength there was in his legs left him and he staggered sideways for a couple of steps before falling to his knees, too dazed to put his hands out to break his fall. He looked up at the sun, at the chariot of Ra which his father rode through the heavens, and shouted through his tears.

"*What victory is this?*"

There came no reply.

End Of Part One

Part Two

The Amun Conspiracy

Chapter Four

The King's Appetite

The Maya Papyrus, Fragments 17-24

THAT I, Maya, treasurer to Nebkheprure Tutankhamun, the Good
God who was lord of these Two Lands; that I should be reduced to
this. I, who have seen such riches, such happy times, who can now
be found skulking in the subterranean gloom of a Theban
outhouse by candlelight, recording this loathsome history. For
today I must bring myself to write of two portentous births.

The first was Akhenaten, born to Amenhotep and Tiye,
although he was not born with that name. That came later, when
it became a byword for terror and hardship and unjust death.
Akhenaten was born with the name Amenophis, after Amenhotep
his father, which means 'Amun is Satisfied'. If ever a name was
given in error, this was it. He was Amenhotep's second born son.

The other birth was your good scribe, Maya: Maya the
Damned, Maya the Late, Maya the Betrayed. I was born to Aye
and his wife Tey, and I have at times cursed my birth as much as
any other. I too had an elder brother, who was to become the
Crown Prince, General Nakhtmin.

But to be a similar age as Amenophis and to be somewhat
outshone, like he, by an elder brother would be the only
similarities between myself and the tyrant king, and for that I
thank the gods. Amenhotep's first born was poor, doomed
Thutmose, named in honour of Amenhotep's father, doted on like
no other by the king, despised by jealous Amenophis and groomed
from the outset as the heir apparent. Thutmose was born shortly
after the costly victory of the battle at Napata. It was said that
Amenhotep never fully recovered from the loss of his friends in
that fight. When I was growing up around the palace Amenhotep
frightened me, although I am sure that he never intended me
harm and I am told that his frequent bad tempers could be
equally well explained with reference to his bad teeth as to
youthful traumas. Even so, Tjenuna and Maiherperi were not just

friends but also advisors, and after that battle Amenhotep suddenly found that he had to face Egypt, and her ministers, alone.

Or not quite alone, for he had Tiye by his side. And Tiye had Thuya by hers.

In the years following the battle Amenhotep replaced the viziers and many of the officials that had served under his father with his own men, upon whom he could rely, and who would not see him forever as some interloper in his father's demesne. One such replacement was named Amenhotep, son of Hapu, although everyone knew him as Huya for reasons that never became entirely clear to me. Huya was widely recognised as the wisest man in the kingdom, a magician and sage who, despite his lowly birth, rose through the ranks of society with such speed and aplomb that he was elevated to the status of a demigod on his passing and was said to relay prayers directed to him without delay to the appropriate deity. He was handsome too, with heavy brow ridges that seemed to accentuate the thoughtfulness of the man and dark eyes that some said could pierce the heavy veil of the future itself.

Egypt was a peaceful land under Amenhotep, and the king expended much of his effort in keeping it that way. Gifts were sent in an almost constant stream from Egypt to her neighbours and vassals and Amenhotep regarded the cost as light indeed when set against the price he had paid in war. But war, like any predator, was ever vigilant, always awaiting a moment of weakness in which to strike. It had come to Amenhotep's attention that the Hittites, that ancient enemy, were rousing from the slumber of peace and looking to Egypt and her dominions in their thirst for riches and land. Knowing the fatality of indolence, Amenhotep summoned his advisors to him.

Huya and Aye were already in the throne room when Amenhotep arrived.

"May you live," Amenhotep said, as he lowered himself onto the throne. "I have been hearing rumours about the Hittites, and they concern me. Their power is waxing, and no powerful king of Hatti has ever been content to sit on his throne without a sword in his hand. I look to your advice, gentlemen. I need a full appraisal of the situation. Is my concern justified?"

Huya bowed and said, "Majesty, it is justified indeed. The Hittites eye the empire of Egypt with envy. As you say, their power grows. They are not yet powerful enough to challenge the Two Lands directly, but they can wait, and while they wait they will be happy to topple our allies one by one, until nothing stands between us but sand."

"Are our allies to be trusted?"

"I believe so, Majesty, but only in so far as they will defend themselves against the Hittites to the best of their ability. It is the quality of that ability which is doubtful. Hatti's immediate neighbour is Mitanni, who will fight courageously but fail. To the south of Mitanni is Amurru, who will be able to hold Hittite warriors at bay for no longer than it takes for the Hittites to arrive. And then it is us."

"Is that an estimation or a prophecy?"

"A little of both, Majesty."

"Then what is to be done?"

"We could strike first," Aye said.

"That would not be a good idea," Huya said. "Our troops would have to march through Amurru, and then Mitanni. It would leave us with tired soldiers having to fight in unfamiliar terrain."

"I hope, Huya, that you are not suggesting that we should wait for the Hittites to arrive at our border?" Aye said.

"Must you always be thinking of war?" Amenhotep said. "Ra does not create men simply for them to fall under the sword. Need I remind you of the good men Egypt has lost in battle? Need I tell you of the good counsel your king has lost through the deaths of Tjenuna and Maiherperi? Can the Hittites not be placated? An alliance, perhaps?"

"I fear not, Majesty," Huya said. "We could offer them nothing that they do not already think they are capable of taking for themselves."

"I am pleased in a way," Amenhotep said. "The thought of an alliance with the Hittites would not sit comfortably with me."

"Then perhaps our present alliances need to be reinforced, Majesty," Huya said.

"Go on."

"We must make the Hittites afraid to test the friendship between ourselves and Mitanni. Your father married a Mitannite princess. Perhaps it would be prudent for you to do the same. The Hittites have only the strength to take one country at a time. They could not survive a war against two."

"It would be a risk, Your Majesty," Aye said. "Should the Hittites ignore the warning and attack Mitanni anyway, we would have no choice but to be drawn into the fight."

"But if we do nothing we will have to fight anyway, will we not?"

"But on our terms and in defence of our own land, not another," Aye said.

Aye did not have to meet with his mother to know what her reaction would be to this news. He knew that she saw herself at the head of a new line of kings through Tiye and her sons and she would see this as a threat to her position. If Amenhotep were to take another bride there would be nothing stopping him making her Great Royal Wife in preference over Tiye. And then the foreigner's offspring could take precedence over Tiye's when it came to choosing Amenhotep's successor. But there was little Aye could do. He had heard Huya's arguments against the pursuit of war, and they were good ones. He had no answer for them.

Instead, he just said: "I would beg you to reconsider."

Amenhotep let out a weary sigh. Every decision he made seemed to be a battle with those who claimed to serve him. "Why?" he said.

"May I remind you that your father had to ask seven times before Artatama sent his daughter to be married? You should not permit such an indignity for yourself."

"And yet I would consider such an indignity meaningless under the alternative threat of the subjugation of my kingdom. I thank you for your concern, Aye, but I have decided."

Aye would have to take time to reconsider his options. For now, he had no choice but to let the king make any choices he saw fit.

"Huya, fetch me a scribe," Amenhotep said. "I believe I am to take a new wife."

"A *what?*" Tiye said to Amenhotep. They were walking the palace gardens together, where Amenhotep had brought her in the hope that the colours and fragrances around them might soothe her temper. Prince Thutmose walked between them.

"My dear, it is in the interests of diplomacy alone. Anyway, I have a harem so full of wives I do not even know how many there are. One more will make no difference."

"This is not the same," Tiye said. "She will be a Mitannite princess."

"Which means what?" Amenhotep said. He was pointing out a hoopoe bird to his son, bending down to allow Thutmose to follow the line of his arm.

"She will expect things."

"Tiye, she will be no threat to you. You are my Great Royal Wife. That will not change."

"My mother will not be happy with this," said Tiye, and then realised immediately that her mother would be even less happy to know that her name had been brought into the conversation.

"Your mother?" Amenhotep said. "What concern is this of hers?"

"Just that she wishes to see me happy," Tiye said, quickly.

"And are you not happy, oh Great Royal Wife of Egypt, whose name I send to the four corners of the earth for the betterment of her glory? Mistress of these Two Lands, who is worshipped even as a goddess in the Sudan? Are you unhappy with your life?"

"Of course not," she said, somewhat abashed.

"Then talk to me not of your mother. I am to be married for the good of Egypt. The king commands it."

Ta-miu, Thutmose's pet cat, crept out of the undergrowth, its head low and its shoulder blades poking up from its back like two pyramids. Its tail swept through the air as it watched the hoopoe bird and edged forwards. The bird sensed the danger and darted away, its wings a blur of black and white. Thutmose and Amenhotep waved it goodbye and Ta-miu immediately forgot it had ever been there and started to wash.

"I am worried about Amenophis," Tiye said, and Amenhotep and herself were both glad of a change of subject. "He is so unlike his brother."

Amenhotep looked down at Thutmose, who was trailing a long stemmed flower along the ground for Ta-miu to hunt in the absence of any wildlife. Thutmose had been born to Amenhotep and Tiye less than a year after the battle at Napata and had grown, both mentally and physically, with such speed that he seemed to have changed each time Amenhotep saw him. Amenhotep had briefly flirted with the idea of naming him after Tjenuna, but Thuya had spoken firmly to Tiye and Tiye had spoken firmly to Amenhotep and the idea had been quickly laid to rest in favour of following the fashion of the time for naming the firstborn son after the king's father.

The king had been transformed by the birth of his son. Since the battle he had relapsed back into the uncommunicative and sullen mood that followed his first Nubian campaign. Courtiers and ministers alike were afraid to approach him for fear of his unguarded tongue, and only Tiye remained unbowed before his temper. He seemed content to listen to her advice and rule accordingly. But when Thutmose came along the light of his father rekindled in Amenhotep's eyes and he was rarely to be seen without the child in his arms or at his feet. He now understood his father's love of stories, for he used to sit with Thutmose on his knee and tell him the same tales. To merely have the child's attention, to see the reflection of his own face staring up at him, was enough to entertain Amenhotep for hours at a stretch.

Although it was not quite a reflection. All who saw little Thutmose saw in his face the likeness of another king, his namesake and grandfather. Only Amenhotep claimed not to see it, but few doubted that his attitude to

Thutmose would have been different had the boy inherited the looks of his maternal grandfather, Yuya.

A daughter, Sitamun, who looked like Tiye, had followed on Thutmose's heels. And then Amenophis, who looked like nobody who had come before him and nobody since.

"He seems so unhappy," said Tiye.

"That boy has been unhappy since the moment he was born. I would not trouble yourself over it."

"You are very cold towards him, you know. He is still your son."

"I can be a good father or a good king, but not both," Amenhotep said. "I have not the time. Amenophis is well provided for with tutors and guardians. It is they who should worry, if worry is justified."

Amenhotep did not think Amenophis an easy child to love. He was a solitary boy, happiest when in no company but his own. He undertook his studies in the royal harem alongside a growing troop of sisters and the children of courtiers, ministers and hostages, working meticulously and undoubtedly intelligent but somehow never excelling.

"He deserves more of your attention," Tiye said. "He thinks you do not care about him."

"Well, that is just ridiculous," Amenhotep said. "It is just that I am so busy. Egypt cannot govern herself, you know. Amenophis wants for nothing. He should appreciate that. But I have other concerns that I can neither ignore nor delegate. These damned priests, for one."

Amenhotep had just come from a meeting with Ptahmose, the High Priest of Amun.

"Your Majesty," Ptahmose had said. "This simply cannot continue."

"Do I hear you right?" Amenhotep asked. "Are you seriously telling me what I can and cannot do?"

"Please do not misunderstand me. I am merely pointing out what is possible and what is not."

"I have done it since the first days of my reign. I see no reason why I should not continue to do so."

"It is a matter of economics."

"You dare speak to me of economics?"

Ptahmose bowed, but did not do so nervously. Engineering the mobilisation of the army before the battle of Napata had not been the last time that Ptahmose had seen fit to guide the policy of the pharaoh. He had continued, and would continue, to do so whenever the needs of Amun conflicted with the wishes of the crown. Anyway, Amenhotep was too much like his father to disconcert the priest, and Ptahmose had too many years' experience of dealing with indignant monarchs to be thrown off balance by one more fit of royal temper. Pharaohs always seemed to interpret any input by the priesthood as a threat to their authority. It was almost as though Amenhotep and Ptahmose were actors in a play whose lines had been written centuries before and would endure for centuries to come. The High Priest would point out the reality of the situation and the king would bluster and blow before the priest's spirited show of humility, but Amun would always have his way.

"May I remind you," Ptahmose said, reciting his lines, "that I speak only the words that the Great God Amun himself desires me to say. Please try not to be angry with me. I am nothing more than his humble messenger."

"Is Amun not pleased that he is the god of the greatest nation under the heavens? Have I wronged him by my actions?"

"Indeed you have not, Your Majesty."

"Have I not brought glory upon his name by building him the greatest temple in the world?"

"Indeed you have, Your Majesty."

"Then perhaps you would deign to tell me where I am going wrong?"

"I am merely telling you that to continue shipping gold to our allies in such quantities as you have made customary will be to do so at the expense of gold that Amun expects to be given to his temples in return for his patronage."

"I see. And that would be why, I presume, my gold shipments travelling through Thebes have been diverted without my permission?"

This was a deviation from the script that Ptahmose had not been expecting.

"Your Majesty?" he said, his face eyebrows raised in a look of purest innocence.

"You know very well what I mean, Ptahmose, and it will not bode well for you to deny it."

"I do not deny it, Majesty. I am merely surprised that you ask. There are more workmen than inhabitants in Thebes nowadays. Everywhere I look I see stonemasons raising temples to the sky in your honour. Amun's temple is the greatest building work in the whole of Egypt. I requisitioned some gold, I admit, but it has to come from somewhere. I did not deem it necessary to trouble Your Majesty with the details."

"It can come from somewhere other than my envoys to our allies abroad. If I make promises to our allies, I expect them to be kept. Do not mistake me, Ptahmose. If this happens again, you will personally answer to me for it. Now get you back to Thebes."

"These damned priests," Amenhotep said to Tiye again, as they walked in the palace gardens with Thutmose.

"Damned priests!" Thutmose exclaimed. "Damned *priests!*"

"Enough!" Tiye said, and shot Amenhotep a withering glance.

"These damned priests," Tiye said to Thuya.

They were in Tiye's throne room at the palace, their customary meeting place. Aye and Yuya were standing a few paces off, talking quietly between themselves. After Maiherperi's death, Aye was one of Amenhotep's few remaining confidantes. Anen counted himself blessed to be among the king's friends, but Amenhotep never troubled him with matters of state. Only Aye seemed capable of dispensing advice that proved flawless time after time. Even Thuya occasionally allowed her judgement to be swayed by Aye's word.

Thuya turned to him now.

"It seems His Majesty is having trouble controlling the priesthood," she said.

"I know," Aye said, crossing the room with Yuya in tow. "He has told me. They are becoming troublesome indeed, but what is the king to do? He cannot fight the word of Amun."

"Ptahmose is a very disagreeable man," Yuya said, but nobody replied. Since his return from Napata, Yuya had sworn to himself that he would have no more part in his wife's meddling in the affairs of state. He had withdrawn and allowed Thuya to do as she would. He could no longer bear the guilt and found it easier to simply step back rather than continually fight something he knew he could not win. During the return voyage from Napata Yuya had been as despondent as the king himself. Everyone assumed this to be a sign of his grief at the deaths of Tjenuna and Maiherperi, but nobody recognised the remorse that coloured his sadness. I am not an evil man, Yuya repeatedly told himself on the trip back to Memphis. I did what I did purely as an act of self-preservation, as viable and justified as any act in battle. But he was not convinced. He had risked a glance back towards Tjenuna even as his chariot had turned away and had seen Tjenuna slump forward as the spear pierced his back. There had been a momentary rush of elation that a great danger had been removed, but this quickly paled under the weight of a deeper shame at such a treacherous misdeed. This shame turned quickly to terror when the soldiers brought Yuya to where Amenhotep knelt weeping on the battlefield, his dead friends to either side, and Yuya realised that Tjenuna had been crying for help not for himself but for the king who lay unconscious under the protection of his overturned chariot. A shock of intense cold flushed through his body, making him shiver.

He resolved to tell Thuya nothing of the battle other than that Tjenuna and Maiherperi were dead, but upon his return he told her everything, as though a god of remorse was in control of his mouth. Thuya's reaction surprised him, in so much as the fact that she did not react at all.

"Do you have nothing to say for once?" he had asked her.

Thuya merely shrugged. "What is done is done," she said. "I am sure that Tjenuna was less of a threat than you imagine. But now he is removed and nothing stands in the way. Are you sure you were not observed? Could the king blame you for Tjenuna's death?"

Yuya shook his head. "In the confusion of battle nobody is watching anything other than where the next sword blow is coming from. And what people do see they cannot be sure of. What do you mean, nothing stands in the way?"

"Do you trust Amenhotep?"

"Of course I trust him. He is the king. Nothing stands in the way of what?"

"Even though he seems a little reluctant to fight for his country?"

"You are answering questions with questions again."

"Nothing stands in the way of the throne," Thuya said.

"Except the king, of course."

"No, Yuya. The king *is* the throne. And Tiye has his ear, and we have hers, and Amenhotep now has no advisors to interfere with our counsel. The king will make whatever decisions we like, and if we are clever he will never suspect that they did not come from his heart, but from ours."

"What are you saying?" Yuya said.

"Do not look so frightened, husband. You have no need of fear. I have made you a pharaoh."

"You are being ridiculous!" Yuya said, standing up. "You will never repeat those words!"

"Your grandchildren will be pharaohs, coached in the ways of the world by us. Their children will succeed them. Do you not see what we have done? The descendents of Thuya and Yuya will rule the world. Are you not proud?"

He was proud indeed, but not of his wife, not of the dynasty she claimed to have created. He was proud enough not to fight her, proud enough not to lose any more arguments, proud enough not to be trampled any more by her public admonitions. Although he continued to attend these meetings between Thuya and her children, he did so only because it was expected of him and to do otherwise would provoke his wife's temper. He had no more stomach for lost arguments. And so he was here today, watching his wife and children slowly bleed the power from the king, his objections unspoken for fear that they would be not be heard. Or worse, that they would.

"What does Anen do around the palace all day?" Thuya asked Aye suddenly, as though on a completely different tack.

"These damned priests," Aye said to Amenhotep.

"I know. They have dogged me since my first day on the throne. Everything is subordinate to their gold. I sometimes think that Ptahmose forgets that he is duty bound to serve me, and not the other way around."

"Well, strictly speaking," Aye said, "he is duty bound to serve Amun."

"Does he think that I do not notice that whenever he wants something it coincidentally appears to be Amun's will?"

"But what can you do?" Aye said. "Amun is your god."

"Ra is my god," Amenhotep said. "He is my grandfather, and I revere him above all others, even Amun."

"But still you must obey Amun."

"Of course. That is the problem. But I really think Ptahmose has gone too far this time. He has taken gold I had intended for King Kurigalzu in Babylon. How will this look? Can I not remove Ptahmose?"

Aye shook his head. "Not safely. He is appointed by Amun himself, remember."

"I told him today that I will no longer tolerate such actions, but I do not know what effect it will have. Thutmose has had harsher scoldings for dirtying his clothes."

"What you need," Aye said, "is an ally in the temple. Someone who can let you know what is happening there. He could be your eyes and ears, and your mouth also."

"But who? Everyone in the temple is loyal to Amun, and therefore to Ptahmose. I could never trust a spy to not be spying on me at the same time."

"Who indeed?" Aye said, and tapped his front teeth with his fingernail in thought.

"Anen was asking after your health today," Tiye said to Amenhotep. "He has not seen you in such a long time."

"I trust you passed on my good wishes in return?"

"Of course," Tiye said. "He has always been a very loyal friend to you, you know."

"I know."

"Very loyal," said Tiye.

Amenhotep sighed heavily. "I know," he said again.

From the earliest days of his reign, Amenhotep had privately acknowledged Tiye's importance in the running of the kingdom. Himself excepted, she was the one truly indispensable person at the palace, without whom Amenhotep would have quickly foundered. Unlike the Great Royal Wives of Amenhotep's predecessors, Tiye was not only keen to share the burden of power, but trustworthy to do so. He had once joked to her that under different circumstances she could have been a modern Hatshepsut. Demure to the last, she had laughed and said that she was hardly worthy to take the crown from a head as great as his. But there was no question in Amenhotep's mind that she would remain as Great Royal Wife as long as he drew breath.

"In fact," she said, "I would say that there are none more loyal."

"Tiye, please. I know."

And yet she was not without her faults. She was the only person who truly spoke unguardedly to him, and for that he loved her. But, he thought, she had a voice like beer, refreshing at first, even intoxicating, but if you have enough it soon palls. You lose the ability to see things as they really are. You get headaches. Soon, the thought of more beer is enough to make you nauseous.

Amenhotep sat back heavily in his chair. Before him on the table were arrayed a whole range of bowls and baskets, each proffering the remains of a different dish. Here were the bones of fish and birds, ragged with shards of flesh, here a plate of fruit, each piece with one or two bites taken from it. The crumbs of sweet and savoury loaves, baked with eggs, nuts, spices or milk, were scattered on the table as though sown there. Amenhotep rubbed his hands over his belly, took a deep breath and then blew it out through distended cheeks, as though this would relieve his bloated feeling.

"A truly excellent meal," he said. "My compliments to Bakenamun. And that Syrian wine is delicious. Are you sure you will not try some?"

"You are getting fat," Tiye said. "Your belly is starting to hang over your kilt. Another meal or two like that and you will need help getting out of your chair."

Amenhotep burped, his mouth closed and cheeks ballooning in an effort to disguise the sound.

"And I am still worried about Amenophis," Tiye continued, as though this was the logical next step in the conversation. Amenhotep resisted the temptation to put his hands over his ears and flee the room. He suspected that if Ra himself appeared in a tower of flame and commanded her to be quiet she would simply tell him about her day.

"Have you seen him recently?" Tiye asked. "There is something strange about the boy that eludes me. He never asks after you. Do you not think that odd?"

"I never ask after him, either."

"You should see him. Summon him to you tomorrow. I would like your opinion about something."

"Tiye, if it will stop you talking about it I shall carry him to my quarters myself."

"You will forget."

"I will not."

"I shall remind you anyway," Tiye said.

"I have every confidence that you will."

"You should see Anen as well. You are always so busy. He has not seen you for such a long time. He has always been a good friend to you, you know."

When Amenhotep appointed Anen – who was Tiye and Aye's brother, and Thuya's son – to be Second Prophet of Amun at the temple at Thebes in order to keep a check on the comings and goings of Ptahmose, he fully believed it to be an inspired idea of his own making, a spark of genius of which only a pharaoh was capable. As Tiye said, Amenhotep could be more sure of Anen's loyalty than he could of almost any man in the kingdom. Second Prophet was a role exalted enough to ensure that Anen would be close enough to Ptahmose and the other senior clerics for them to be forever in his earshot, and yet not exalted enough to be a blunt snub. It was a warning without being a threat, and it left the priesthood nothing to reasonably protest about.

Abutted to the southern side of the Memphis palace was a temple to Amun. It was small in comparison to the temple at Thebes – as all temples were in comparison to that great mansion – but it contained rooms set aside for the purification of the priests. Images and statues of the great god lined the walls and watched the goings on within with stern approbation. It was here that Anen was being prepared for his new role. He needed cleansing, and was standing naked with his legs apart and his arms held out horizontally either side of him whilst servants busied themselves shaving his head and body. They were working meticulously in silence and Anen was worried that the presence of the king, who was sitting on the other side of the room, would make the servants nervous enough to make their hands shake. He looked down at the servant who knelt before him and swallowed nervously.

"And so everything is clear?" Amenhotep asked.

"Yes, Majesty. It grieves me to leave your side, but I shall start my journey to Thebes at dawn."

"Very good," Amenhotep said. "Although it grieves me also. But I am sure we shall be seeing plenty of each other."

"I shall return to report to you as soon..." Anen said, and then stopped. Amenhotep had raised his hand to his lips to signal for silence and was glancing with trepidation at the statues of Amun that stared back at him.

"Not here," he said. "I shall take it that your understanding of the situation is complete."

"As you wish."

Amenhotep stood up. "I can come no closer for fear of contaminating you. I would hate for them to have to start cleansing you all over again."

Anen smiled. "Me also, Majesty."

"But I send you on your way with my blessing," he quickly looked around the room again, "and with the blessing of whichever gods you feel most appropriate."

"Why is uncle Anen going away?" Thutmose asked Amenhotep when the king had returned to his quarters. "Has he upset you? Have you banished him?"

Amenhotep sat down and tore a hunk of bread off the loaf that sat on the table. He talked between mouthfuls.

"No, I have not banished him. He is going away to do a job for me."

"Good. I like uncle Anen."

"I like your uncle Anen as well. He is a good man, and I shall miss him until I see him again."

"What job?" Thutmose asked.

"Come here," Amenhotep said, and hoisted the boy onto his knee. "I have a lesson for you, and you need to pay attention because it is an important one. You know that one day you will be pharaoh?"

Thutmose nodded.

"Well, years ago, I did not want to take the throne."

"Why?"

"It is a long story that one day I shall tell you about, but not today. But suffice it to say that I was wrong. I should have been proud to be pharaoh and today I can see that I was being a foolish child. But before your grandfather died, he left me a message. He told me to remember Hatshepsut."

Amenhotep told the boy the story of the woman who was king. "It was a long time before I fully appreciated that advice," he said, "for there were two meanings hidden within it. The first was that Hatshepsut had gone through a great ordeal to claim and retain her crown. The other was how she had managed to hold on to it for so long. It was because of one thing, and one thing only: the priesthood of Amun. Their support was all she needed to stay in office and to keep your great-great-grandfather off the throne. And here is today's lesson. Are you listening?"

Thutmose nodded again.

"Never, ever underestimate a priest," Amenhotep said. "They are powerful men. When you are king, you will need to watch them like a lion watches its prey. And vice versa."

"Why?" asked Thutmose.

"Because they will try to run the country behind your back."

"Why?" asked Thutmose.

"Because they are the tools of Amun, and they believe that he is the true power in Egypt."

"Why?" asked Thutmose.

"Because he is the king of the gods."

"Why?" asked Thutmose.

"If you ask why again you will be sorry."

"Why?" asked Thutmose, starting to smile.

"Because," Amenhotep said, placing the remaining bread back on the table, "I am your father and if you so wilfully disobey me, you will suffer... *this!*"

Suddenly, Amenhotep's hands were around the boy's waist and his fingers were quickly kneading the soft flesh below his ribs. Thutmose shrieked with laughter and struggled to get free but Amenhotep's grip was too strong for him.

"Don't laugh! Sit still!" Amenhotep was shouting, which just made Thutmose laugh and struggle all the more.

"Why!" Thutmose was shouting, in between gulps of air and whoops of hilarity. "Why why why why why!"

"Don't laugh and I'll let you go!"

Thutmose managed to struggle off his father's lap and Amenhotep slid off the chair to pursue the boy on his hands and knees, growling and pawing at the air. Thutmose crouched behind a chair and peeked out, still laughing, his body tensed to evade Amenhotep's lunge.

Then the door opened and Amenhotep stopped mid-growl and looked around, suddenly intensely aware of how ridiculous he must look. In the doorway stood Tiye, holding Amenophis by the hand.

"You said you would see your other son today," she said. "I knew you would forget."

"I did not forget," Amenhotep said, standing up and straightening his kilt. "I was just passing the time until his arrival."

"Profitably, I hope?" she said, looking down at Thutmose, who was now standing uneasily by the chair he had been hiding behind as though he feared he was about to fail an inspection.

"Come in, Amenophis," Amenhotep said, ignoring her. "I have been wanting to see you for some time. I always regret being so busy that I sometimes have trouble finding the time for my sons."

Now Amenophis too glanced at Thutmose, just long enough to catch Amenhotep in his lie.

"Sit here with me," Amenhotep said. "Thutmose, you may accompany your mother."

Thutmose looked momentarily stricken but walked to the door without a word. Tiye took his hand.

"We shall go and find Ta-miu," she said, "and see if he has brought us any presents today."

"So," Amenhotep said, once he and Amenophis were seated, and then realised that he could not think of a word to say. He did not know enough about the boy to start a conversation. "How are your studies progressing?" he said, by default.

"I am finding them difficult," Amenophis began. "Nobody helps me."

As Amenophis talked, Amenhotep suddenly remembered the reasons for Tiye's concern over the child. There was something odd about him, she had said. Something that she could not place.

"The other children laugh at me behind my back," Amenophis said. "They should not be allowed to do that. I am a prince."

"Of course you are, my boy. Of course you are," Amenhotep said, vaguely. Tiye had spoken the truth. There *was* something odd about Amenophis but it was a few moments before Amenhotep realised what it was. It seemed a ridiculous thought but the boy seemed out of proportion, as though some parts of him were growing faster than the rest. His fingers had started to take on an arachnid quality, each knuckle jutting outwards like knots in rope. Amenhotep glanced down and saw that Amenophis' toes poked over the front edge of his sandals. It was not that his sandals were too small, but that the toes looked as though they belonged to bigger feet. It was not an obvious effect and if Tiye had not mentioned it, Amenhotep doubted he would have noticed. But now that it had been brought to his attention he found it impossible to ignore, like a face in a cloud that remains even if you try to imagine the cloud as something else.

Amenhotep realised that the boy had stopped talking and he had no idea of what he had just said. "And what of your friends?" he said, to fill the silence.

"I do not have friends," Amenophis said.

"Oh," said Amenhotep, somewhat taken aback. "Why?" he said, in the absence of anything more intelligent, and thought of Thutmose. Perhaps he should try to tickle Amenophis. That would be the loving, fatherly thing to do. But somehow it did not seem appropriate. The boy's melancholic demeanour begged pity, not levity. It seemed to soak through him, wrapping itself about the very pith of him, and Amenhotep feared that no amount of joviality would loosen its grip.

"I do not know," Amenophis said. "Perhaps they are too busy making fun of me."

"What do they say?"

"I do not know. I just see them laughing when they think I am not looking."

"Well," the king said. "The next time you see them laughing you just remind them of who you are. You are my son. The king's son. Your great-grandfather is Ra. Your grandfather is a god, riding in Ra's chariot across the sky every day. Every time they laugh, you tell them that your grandfather is looking down from his chariot and he will not take kindly to people making fun of his family. Stand up for yourself. You are a prince, with divine blood in your veins."

"Very well," Amenophis said, but he did not seem convinced.

Amenhotep was standing with Tiye and Thutmose in the courtyard, surrounded by his ministers and courtiers, awaiting the arrival of Princess Giludkhepa, the daughter of King Šuttarna II of Mitanni. Giludkhepa's retinue was later counted to be three hundred and seventeen persons in total, and even the princess did not know who they all were or what they were all for. They surged through the gates like flood waters bursting through a Nile cataract and almost swept Amenhotep and his delegation away, Thutmose looking momentarily frightened at the size of the crowd and the strange animals locked unhappily in their cages.

And then Giludkhepa stepped forward and she was an island of sunlight in the mass of people that suddenly filled the courtyard. Her long straight hair shone black, framing a countenance as pleasing as any Amenhotep had beheld. She was slim, with shapely breasts and hips and long legs that peeked from within her robe with every step. She sank to her knees and bowed before the king. Tiye saw the smile on his face that he made no effort to hide and took a step closer to him as though to protect him should Giludkhepa try to snatch him away from her there and then. He did not take his eyes off his new bride, but he could feel Tiye's scowl burning at the side of his face.

"May you live, Giludkhepa," he said, and he meant it.

The marriage was celebrated without delay. Tiye and Aye, together with their parents, sat on the dais on either side of the king and Giludkhepa, each face set immovable. Only Yuya seemed unable to decide on a suitable expression, caught as he was between offence to the king and disloyalty to his wife.

Thuya was unhappy with the marriage and made no secret of her opposition to it, although even she recognised that to voice her censure beyond the confines of her family would be more dangerous than allowing the marriage to go ahead unchallenged. The king's mind was set, and neither Tiye nor Aye, encouraged though they were by Thuya, had succeeded in dissuading him.

"What harm is there in a new wife?" Yuya had asked her.

"It threatens our dynasty," Thuya had said.

"Dynasty? What dynasty? Anyway, he will just pack her off to the harem at Gurob."

"Not necessarily," Aye had said. "She will be given a high profile. The alliance demands it."

Yuya had known as much and he cursed Aye for speaking the truth.

The king did not emerge from the conjugal bedchamber for a day and a half and when he did he looked positively ill. Now that Tiye could see that her prayers for a fat, ugly bride had been far from answered she could hold her silence no longer.

"Your son has been wondering where you are," she said.

"Thutmose?"

"Of course Thutmose. Who else? You see precious little of Amenophis as it is. He would hardly notice his father's absence for an extra day or two."

"My dear, I have not the energy for this now. I need to rest."

"You have certainly had the energy for something," she said. "You are not as fit as you once were, Amenhotep, and it would do you good to remember it. It is not as if you hunt any more. You do nothing but sit around the palace and eat. I will perhaps have to speak to this Giludkhepa and warn her that you are not as sprightly as you would like to think. You are easily old enough to be her father. She needs to treat you gently."

"I am not an old man yet. You will probably find that she is just as exhausted as I."

"All I mean to say is that she should not feel obliged to pleasure you as enthusiastically as she seems to think. She will welcome the news. I am sure that she does not find it overly enjoyable having someone such as yourself pinning her to the bed."

Amenhotep smiled mischievously. "She was not the one who was pinned," he said.

That Amenhotep had fallen in love with Giludkhepa the moment he saw her – or at least at some point during the following thirty six hours – was obvious to all the palace, despite Amenhotep's casual dismissal of such talk.

"Nonsense," he would say. "It is a marriage of alliance only."

"She needs to be treated with respect," he would say. "Without it our friendship with Mitanni would be worth nothing."

"Really," he would say. "I see more of Amenophis than I do of her. And I see barely anything of him."

But still, Giludkhepa was not hidden away in Gurob where Amenhotep would have to travel to see her. In fact, she hardly left the palace at all and when she did it was only to accompany the king on one of his increasingly infrequent forays out into public life to tour this town or that, or inspect one garrison or another.

She was always pleased to see him, always endeavouring to ensure his happiness, always smiling, always eager to slip off to bed, always enthusiastically submitting to acts that Amenhotep would never dream of suggesting to Tiye. Her voice never snagged on his nerves. She never complained. She never commented on his weight.

"She will," Tiye told him. "She is an attractive young woman. She sees your belly just as I do. Just wait until she has learned enough Egyptian to tell you about it."

"She sees nothing but a mighty king," Amenhotep replied. "She sees me as you once did."

"She sees only that you love her. The whole palace sees it. You are acting like a fawning child."

"Ridiculous," Amenhotep said. "What if her father was to send messengers asking after her? I need her to be able to tell him that she is being treated the way he would expect."

Tiye made noncommittal noises.

"Which reminds me," Amenhotep said, as though the thought had just occurred to him and he was adding an unimportant footnote to the conversation. "I wish to compose a news scarab to announce my new marriage."

"Are you not making me feel bad enough without telling the world? I feel as though I have lost my husband."

Amenhotep suddenly and unexpectedly felt sorry for her. He had not loved her when they were first married – he had not had time – but the feeling had grown with familiarity and he could no longer imagine what his life would be without her. Giludkhepa was never going to be a replacement for her and he believed he spoke the truth when he told people that he was not in love with the Mitannite princess, but Giludkhepa had stirred a fresh love in him, a different love. A love of the new, of the untried, a love of novelty that his old wife by very definition was unable to provide. He was not yet growing tired of Giludkhepa but he nevertheless believed that one day he would. Tiye had never been a novelty wife and so his feelings for her, never having peaked in quite the same way, could never trough either.

"You are losing nothing," he said. "You are still my Great Royal Wife. This marriage is pointless unless the Hittites hear of it. Where is the deterrent otherwise?"

"Very well," she said. "If you are intent on humiliating me in public I can do nothing to stop you."

"I will make sure that your name as Great Royal Wife, and the names of your parents, are included on the scarab also. I can do no more."

But I am king, he thought, after Tiye had silently left the room. I *can* do more. After he had spoken to the scribe he summoned Huya, who, as well as vizier, took on the role of overseer of all Amenhotep's building works.

"I wish to honour my wife," he told Huya.

"Which one?" Huya said.

Huya had drawn up the plans for the digging of a lake for Tiye. Amenhotep thought it a good present to persuade her of his continued loyalty.

"In any case," Amenhotep said, "I believe that I have news for her that she may find unpalatable. This may help to take away the taste somewhat."

"May I ask what this news is, Majesty?"

"You may, but I would ask you to keep it to yourself for the moment."

"Of course."

"I am to marry again."

"Again, Majesty? To whom?"

"That, my dear Huya, is a detail with which I am yet to concern myself."

"A princess? Are we to be allied again? With Amurru perhaps?"

"Perhaps. But probably not."

Giludkhepa had awoken something that Amenhotep had never felt before their marriage. He had been a boy and then he had been married, with no interlude during which he could have explored what were to become euphemistically known as his recreations. One day he was sexless, with no idea of what sex would entail, and the next he was procreating. But he was never making love. Not until Giludkhepa. She was an artist. She was a scribe of love and he was her papyrus. And he found that he liked it more than he could ever have imagined.

"Where is good for women?" he asked Huya.

Huya was taken unawares by the question, and had to think for a moment before he spoke. "I have heard reports that the women of Gezer are very agreeable, Majesty. It is just to the south of a town named Jerusalem, in Canaan."

Amenhotep summoned a scribe.

"I wish to dictate a letter to whomever is in charge at Gezer," he told the scribe. "Tell him this. 'I am sending you the Chief of the Army together with goods, in order to fetch beautiful women. The total of women should be...' let me see."

He thought about it for a moment, the scribe sitting cross legged on the floor, his brush poised.

"'Total women forty,'" Amenhotep said, "'amounting to...' Huya? What would be a fair price?"

"Forty debens, Majesty?" said Huya, who in reality had no idea.

"Yes," Amenhotep said. "'Amounting to forty debens of silver for each woman.'"

He stopped again, and thought of Tiye. He could imagine what her reaction to this would be. I am a king, he would tell her. They will be concubines, not wives. They will populate the harem, where I will see to it that they will be comfortable, happy and fulfilled. They can work as seamstresses when not... otherwise occupied. But he did not doubt that Tiye would have something to say on the matter, and at great length.

"Add this," he said to the scribe. "'Send none with harsh voices.'"

The Maya Papyrus, Fragments 28-31

Amenophis had not been lying to his father when he told him that his classmates laughed at him, but he was perhaps unwittingly exaggerating the situation somewhat. His classmates in the harem – myself among them – were more wary of Amenophis than spiteful towards him. But it was hardly our fault. He would choose to sit apart from us and would only reluctantly and monosyllabically enter into conversation or class discussions. For the most part we did not laugh at him, although some classmates, my brother Nakhtmin for example, did not consider themselves above the occasional barbed remark and barely disguised snigger. But then this was not directed towards Amenophis alone. Perhaps he heard the laughter and assumed the worst, that we were all involved, that he was the only member of the harem to be the butt of my brother's jokes.

For my part I always tried to be sympathetic, without stepping outside the bounds of respect, and my sister, Nefertiti, was of the same mind. Nefertiti was the only school friend that Amenophis even made a pretence at liking. He would stop and talk to her. He would never do so with anyone else. This, in fact, was the main source of Nakhtmin's occasional teasing.

"Do you like my sister?" he would rhetorically ask Amenophis, and the prince would blush and hurry away.

"He likes you," Nakhtmin would say to Nefertiti, couching more meaning in the word 'like' than anyone could reasonably expect it to hold.

I would watch and say nothing. It was not my place to scold an elder brother, but I felt sorry for Nefertiti. Even then she was a pretty child and everyone acknowledged that one day she would grow into beauty and, being Amenhotep's niece, would make an excellent choice for Thutmose to take as his Great Royal Wife when he acceded the throne. It would not be becoming for her to be placed in the position of having to reject Amenophis' advances. Luckily, Amenophis never progressed further than asking after her health.

Amenophis sat alone now, at the back of the classroom, chewing on his reed brush and tapping on the palette upon which his tutor had written out, in hieroglyphic form, the family triads of the gods. The prince was squinting with such concentration that he looked to be in some pain. I was watching him surreptitiously, having long finished my own work, and I saw him glance around the room at his fellow students. Nobody else seemed to be having any trouble with this. The problem was, I was to discover later, that the hieroglyphs were blurred. Everything, in fact, was becoming blurred. He was losing the detail in life. He picked up his palette and moved it backwards and forwards in front of his face, his eyes betraying the shame of his failure at such a basic task.

Amun of Thebes, *I wanted to shout at him.* His wife, Mut. Their son, Khonsu. *The next line read* Ptah of Memphis. His wife, Sekhmet. Their son, Nefertem. *It took him three or four minutes to read it. He could see that many of the other students had finished the task and were sitting upright in their seats, awaiting further instructions.* Osiris of Abydos. His wife, Isis. Their son, Horus. *He had learned to read and write hieroglyphs within a matter of months and was fluent well before even I, usually so keen to display my mastery of any form of academic endeavour, had grasped the basics. But that was when the writing had been clear, before his eyes had started to betray him.*

He had one more line to copy. The tutor was by now watching him as keenly as was I. One or two of our classmates had begun whispered conversations. Amenophis' eyes followed the sounds to their source, anger brewing in his face.

He put his hands over his ears, his elbows resting on the table, and stared at the palette.

"Amenophis," the tutor said. "We cannot wait all day."

And here came the laughter. Muted and hidden behind turned backs, but apparent all the same.

I was unlucky enough to be seated next to Amenophis that day. He turned to me and spluttered, "How dare you laugh at me, Maya! Do you know who I am? My grandfather is Ra, and he will be very angry when he sees how you mock me."

I was dumbstruck, and automatically looked to the tutor for support. I, too, had heard the laughter, but it came not from me but from Nakhtmin, seated to my right. I was so surprised at Amenophis' uncharacteristic outburst that I thought it wise not to correct his family history. Thutmose was your grandfather, I wanted to say. Ra was your great-grandfather. I looked over to Nakhtmin in the hope that he would confess to the sniggering but he was pretending to be enthralled with the work that I knew he had already finished.

Amenophis stood up from his chair so suddenly that his palette skittered off the table and clattered onto the floor. He strode from the room with as much dignity as the situation would allow. The tutor rushed out after him and Nefertiti immediately twisted herself around in her chair to address Nakhtmin.

"You are very cruel," she said. "He does not deserve ridicule."

The class sat in silence until the tutor led Amenophis back into the room, his head downcast to such an extent that his chin rubbed on the top of his chest. Nefertiti managed to catch his eye with a sympathetic smile as he passed. I could not tell whether or not it was returned.

The matter was soon forgotten, at least by everyone but Amenophis. I feared no retribution even though he believed that it had been I who had laughed at him. Nakhtmin certainly did not. To this day I am unsure whether Nakhtmin had the intelligence to be frightened of anything. But then, none of us were truly scared of Amenophis. Not then. Not until he became a monster.

Not until he began to change shape.

Chapter Five

The Taming of Šuppiluliumas

NOBODY WAS surprised when Giludkhepa fell pregnant, least of all Tiye, who took the news with stoic ambivalence. Her anger had been already largely spent on the attention that Amenhotep had been showering on his new wife, her worry consumed by the physical changes that seemed to be taking place in her second born son. When she broke the news of the pregnancy to Thuya she did so with a downcast face that reflected not despondence but resignation, and Thuya's response seemed all the more vehement in the light of her daughter's prosaic manner.

Tiye had taken Amenophis along with her to the throne room. She was aware of his troubles at school and his apparent unpopularity with the other children, and the sickly pallor of his skin brought out a mother's sympathy in her. She blamed Amenhotep for it all. Perhaps if he had shown Amenophis some real affection the boy would have grown up as cheerful and healthy as his brother Thutmose. Tiye had taken to ensuring that Amenophis was in her company as much as possible, as if to balance out her husband's disproportionate love.

"How did we come to this?" Thuya stormed at the news of Giludkhepa's pregnancy, pacing the throne room floor like the animals brought in cages by Giludkhepa from the king of Mitanni. Aware of the rarity of such displays of emotion her husband and daughter watched open-mouthed as she strode to the opposite wall and back again. Usually, Thuya's temper ebbed as quickly as it rose. Aye watched her also, but with a look of guarded amusement playing around his lips.

"To have everything threatened by his lascivious libido!" Thuya said. "It simply does not bear thinking about. I should have stopped it. I knew I should have stopped it. Did I not tell you I should have stopped it?"

"Stopped what?" Yuya said.

"The marriage, you imbecile. Do you think I mean the sex? Would you have me stand over their bed and slap his backside every time he goes near her?"

Yuya cringed. "My dear, *please...*"

"*Mother!*" Tiye said, tempted to laugh.

"I told you I should have stopped it."

"Getting upset about it now serves no purpose," Yuya began, but was cut short.

"What would you like me to do?" Thuya said. "Congratulate him? At least I am doing something. You just stand there as though it was of no matter at all."

"Well," Yuya began, unsure of how to word the question without angering his wife further. "Why exactly are you so upset? I do not see how this changes matters."

"Imbecile I said, and imbecile you are. What if this baby is a boy? What is to stop Amenhotep naming it as his heir? Then everything I have done will come to naught. There will be no dynasty, no royal grandchildren. History will forget us, as surely as it will forget little Amenophis here."

"Why Amenophis?" Tiye asked. She pulled the boy close to her, her arms around his shoulders as though to protect him should Thuya launch a physical attack.

"Because, my dear, he is a *nearly*. He is an *almost*. He will not be king, and history does not trouble herself with second sons. Especially not dim-witted ones."

Tiye put one hand over Amenophis' ear and pulled his head to her breast, pressing the other ear deep into her bosom.

"Are there any statues of Amenophis?" Thuya continued. "Are there any paintings? No, there are not. And why? Because that rutting bull of a father of his has not been out of bed long enough to commission any. History is forgetting him already, as she will us. And history no more cares about almost dynasties than she does about almost kings."

Amenophis peered out from his soft haven, silent, eyes wide, able to hear every word, but like Yuya too intimidated to reply.

"But the baby may be a girl," Tiye said, eager to steer the conversation back to the problem in hand.

"Yes," Thuya said. "The baby may be a girl. It may not, but it may. And what if it is? Who would make a better wife for the future king Thutmose than his own sister? It would be ideal for Amenhotep. Both the king and the Great Royal Wife would be his children."

"Yes?" Yuya said. "Well?"

Aye spoke for the first time. "My daughter Nefertiti is to be Thutmose's Great Royal Wife," he said.

"She is?" said Yuya. "Who decided this?"

"I did," said Thuya in a menacing tone, and gave Yuya a look that defied him to question her. Yuya fell silent and stared at his sandals.

"And so something must be done," Thuya said, once she was sure that there were no dissenters in the room.

"Should we be talking this way in front of the boy?" Yuya said.

"Him?" Thuya said. "He understands little, and speaks less. Do you, my lad?"

Amenophis did not take his eyes off her. He shook his head hesitantly.

"But what would you suggest?" Yuya asked, without particularly wanting to hear the reply.

"I would suggest that you take that wide-eyed look off your face. Have I ever done anything to place you in danger?"

Yes, thought Yuya. Every time you open your mouth I take a step towards death.

"Do you need to do anything at all?" he said, instead. "Amenhotep still dotes on his son." He glanced at Amenophis. "His other son," he said. "I see no reason why he would change his allegiance."

"I too would advise forbearance," Aye said. "Perhaps action now would harm the dynasty more than aid it."

"It is forbearance that has been the only threat to the dynasty so far," Thuya countered.

"Would everyone please stop talking about a dynasty?" Yuya said. "The only dynasty is that of the king's."

"Could we undermine the marriage?" Thuya asked Aye.

"No easy method readily springs to mind," Aye said. "At least, none of which Tiye would approve."

"Then there is a way?"

"Perhaps if the king were to marry again. Another high profile marriage. Another princess, perhaps? Or perhaps more than one. A whole crowd of them. It could serve to distract him from the Mitannite. It will make it easier to push her into the background and surround her with her peers until she is lost in the pack."

"No," Tiye said. "I have only half a husband as it is. Would you divide his affections further? Would you have *me* lost in the pack?"

"We have higher matters to consider, my dear," Thuya said. "We must all make sacrifices to history on occasion."

"And what do you know of sacrifice?" Tiye asked, abruptly overwhelmed with anger. "What have you forfeited, other than life in a provincial backwater?"

"I have endured much for you, and I would not have you do me the disservice of forgetting it!" Thuya's voice was raised again, and Amenophis sank even deeper into the safety of his mother. "I have seen danger and death, and risked everything I have to make you the king's wife and give you everything from the crown on your head to the child who cowers in your arms. I have made you a ruler of Egypt, and yet you begrudge me the security in my old age of knowing that all my work has not been for nothing. Ingrate!"

"Tyrant!" Tiye spat back. "What use is there in giving me the king only to take him away again?"

Tiye fled the room, pulling the bewildered young Amenophis behind her. She knew she would never be favourite to win an argument with her mother, especially over something as important to Thuya as this, and there was no reason to stay and allow Thuya the comfort of a victory. Tiye had registered her displeasure, and that was as much as she could hope for.

Behind her the room was silent for a few moments, partly in embarrassment at witnessing such a scene but also in quiet wonder that Tiye had been daring enough to shout insults into her mother's face.

Yuya awaited a backlash, but Thuya only said: "She has spirit, that girl."

News scarabs commemorating the marriage of Amenhotep and Giludkhepa had been distributed widely around the kingdom and abroad and had found their way, in time, to the court of the Hittite monarch, King Šuppiluliumas I. He knew full well that he could not take up arms against Mitanni now that an alliance with Egypt would commit Amenhotep to acting in the Mitannites' defence. The Hittite king was ambitious but not suicidal. He addressed a letter of conciliation to Amenhotep and sent it with an envoy through the hostile lands of Mitanni, Canaan and Amurru, a passport tied around his neck in the hope that it would be enough to provide him safe passage.

Aye was the first to hear of the envoy's arrival at the palace. He had anticipated such an event and had informed the officer in charge of the gate guards that the appearance of any Hittite ambassadors should be brought directly to his attention. It would not be fitting for the king to address someone still filthy from the journey. And so when Aye walked into the gate commander's hut and exchanged formal bows and greetings with the envoy, he did so confident in the knowledge that the king knew nothing about it.

He led the envoy through the corridors of court and into a set of sumptuous apartments put aside for the comfort of visiting foreign dignitaries.

"Please," he told him. "Relax. Shake the dust from your shoes. I shall inform His Majesty of your arrival. What shall I tell him it concerns?"

"I have a letter from King Šuppiluliumas," the envoy said.

"Ah," Aye said. "Then you had better read it to me."

"It is for the king."

"Yes, of course. But His Majesty likes to be appraised of the situation before he meets with ambassadors such as yourself. He does not like to be caught unawares."

"I am sure. But I am under instruction from my own king, you understand, and…"

"Yes," Aye said, with a friendly smile that was betrayed by the firmness of his tone. "But you are in Egypt now, and I am sure that you would do us the courtesy of respecting our custom."

Reluctantly the envoy dug into his bag and produced a role of papyrus.

"You may skip the preliminaries and just give me the meat of it," Aye said.

"'My brother, I am desirous of peace between our nations,'" the envoy read, "'so let us establish only the most friendly relations between us. Let us be helpful to each other. There is no need for war between us. Whatsoever you request of me I will indeed do absolutely everything, and in doing so I know that whatever I request of you Your Majesty will do likewise. Send my messenger back with friendly greetings and I will rejoice.'"

"Excellent," Aye said. "That is good news indeed. I shall request an audience with His Majesty forthwith and then I shall send for you. His Majesty will exult in this report. In the meantime, please make yourself at home."

Aye followed the corridors back towards his own quarters. Once there he enjoyed a cool draught of beer to take the edge of the afternoon heat from his throat and, remembering that he had not eaten since breakfast, broke off a hunk of bread and chewed it pensively. Then he summoned a guard unit and led them back to the guest quarters.

"His Majesty will see you now," he said to the envoy, who quickly became lost when, escorted by the guards, he followed Aye through seemingly endless corridors. He noticed as he walked that the decoration on the walls was becoming increasingly sparse and drab.

Every now and again Aye would turn and, with a smile, say, "Not much further now."

They finally arrived at a long, featureless corridor lit at extended intervals by small skylights that were scarcely capable of the job asked of them and seemed to create more shadow than illumination. Heavy wooden doors lined either wall, only one of which, at the far end, was open.

"Just through here," Aye said. The envoy followed him haltingly. This did not look like an area of the palace where the king would meet honoured guests. As he drew level with the doorway he saw that it led not to a throne room, but a small, brick lined cell, bereft not only of a throne but of furniture of any description. Too late, the envoy stopped dead in his tracks and tried to turn. He immediately came against the resistance of the guards, who had closed in around him while he had been intent on his foreboding surroundings. They bundled him forward and he fell into the cell, turning just in time to see Aye's impassive face as the door closed between them. Bolts clanged into place.

In the corridor, Aye turned and strolled away without a word.

The royal physician was standing in the centre of the room, a confused look on his face that he hoped he was disguising as thoughtfulness. Amenophis was sitting before him, naked but for a loincloth, his mother sitting to his left, holding his hand in hers.

"Hmm," the physician said, and took a step to the left as though to gain a better perspective on the patient. "I have seen nothing like it."

Amenophis was not happy. He was feeling exposed and vulnerable and did not care what the physician said as long as he could get dressed again as quickly as possible. He had been prodded and poked. The physician had measured his arms and legs, his fingers and toes, his hips and chest and head. He had asked him about his diet and his bowels. He had tested his reactions and his eyesight and measured his pulse. And now Amenophis was hunched in a chair, his muscles held tense enough for him to tremble, watching as the physician stared down at his misshapen body with unconcealed curiosity.

"Nothing at all like it," the physician said.

Those who saw Amenophis every day were slow to notice the distortions, so gradual and subtle were they. After his fingers started to grow beyond their normal bounds and his toes began to peek out from the front of his sandals, his limbs began to follow suit. He began to look as though he had been tied between two chariots and then someone had driven the horses off in opposite directions. His face, everyone now noticed, was longer than would normally have been expected. Had it always been this way? Nobody could remember, and his father had commissioned no paintings or sculptures of Amenophis to which they could refer.

"Do this," the physician said to the boy. He held his hand up in a fist, but with the thumb on the inside. Amenophis did likewise.

"Extraordinary," the physician said. The tip of Amenophis' thumb was poking out past his little finger.

"Do you have no treatment for him?" Tiye asked.

The doctor shook his head. "I cannot contend with this," he said. "I do not even know whether there is anything with which I should have to contend. I can find no physical faults with him, other than his poor eyesight, and I can imagine no link that would explain how his physique could be causing that. Although it looks strange it does not seem to be hurting him."

"It is hurting me," Amenophis said.

"But you said..."

"The other children in the harem laugh at me."

"We have been through this already," Tiye said to him. "I have spoken to your uncle Aye and he assures me that his children are not laughing at you. They would not dare."

"But they do. I hear them. I hear them all the time."

"Can you hear them now?" the physician asked, tentatively. He had heard of cases of possession where the demons spoke and laughed in the ear of the afflicted in voices that nobody else could hear. That would perhaps account for a lot.

"Of course not," Amenophis said, and then paused for a moment in thought. "Why? Can you?"

The physician shook his head again.

"Well then," Amenophis said.

"Does he have any enemies?" the physician asked Tiye. "Anybody who may wish him harm?"

"Of course not. He is a child. Why?"

"Just a thought. Magic could perhaps explain this."

"You mean he is cursed?"

"Just a thought," the physician said again.

"Ridiculous. Is there nothing you can do?"

"I shall have to consult the medical texts. In the meantime I would prescribe a vigorous regimen of prayer. Perhaps his father could say a few words during daily worship?"

"Very well," Tiye said. "But I want you to contact me when you have conducted some research into the problem. This is no way for a prince to look."

The physician bowed his way out of the room. To admit as much to Tiye would have appeared defeatist and neglectful but he knew that there was little point in reading any of the medical texts in connection with this case. He had studied them at length during his years as a healer and he knew for a fact that they contained no information on people who gradually change shape. He decided to leave it for a day or two before telling her that nothing further could be done.

Tiye waited for Amenophis to get dressed and then walked with him back to the harem, despite his protestations.

"When your brother leaves for Heliopolis you will be the senior prince at court," she told him. "Nobody will dare laugh at you then."

It had been decided that Thutmose needed to see more of the world as part of his pharaonic education. Amenhotep had quickly decided against sending the boy to Thebes, stronghold as it was of the Amun clergy. Amenhotep would be much happier knowing that the likes of Ptahmose were not poisoning the boy's mind against him, for the king was sure that the priesthood would not miss such an opportunity for furthering their own ends. How much easier their lives would be with one of their own acolytes occupying the throne! Even the dutiful Anen would not be able to protect the boy. No, Heliopolis seemed a much better prospect, for Heliopolis was the home of Ra and his priesthood, and Egypt's centre of learning. The wise men of Heliopolis were renowned around the world.

"Send a messenger to us as soon as you arrive," Tiye said to Thutmose as a chariot was brought to the palace doors for him. Amenhotep, Tiye and Amenophis had gathered at the palace doors to see him off. Amenophis was unsure how he should feel, despite his parents' glum expressions. He was annoyed to have been summoned here, knowing as he did that any corresponding farewell on his part would scarcely have been noticed at all, but was simultaneously delighted to have Thutmose out of the palace for a while. He was as hopeful as his mother that his fortunes may change once out of his elder brother's shadow.

Thutmose's driver held the chariot steady as he stepped on board.

"I fail to see why I cannot go by road," Thutmose said. "If you say I should see the country I should travel through it, not simply see it from a distance."

"You will see enough of the country from the boat," Tiye said. "The roads are not safe. There are bandits."

"I could take an escort. I could stop in towns and villages on the way."

"Thutmose," Amenhotep said. "Do as your mother says."

The driver stepped up and took the reins. Thutmose had expected to lose the argument and his excitement was not dampened having done so.

"You can write to us as often as you wish," Tiye said.

"Mother, please. I will be fine."

Amenophis watched with glee as Thutmose's chariot pulled away from the courtyard, leaving a cloud of dust as his goodbye.

A small group of shaved heads awaited Anen on the dockside at Thebes harbour but they seemed to be in no hurry to greet him as he walked down the gangplank, his servants burdened with his luggage behind him. One of the priests wandered over in a desultory fashion as though wanting to make it absolutely clear that he was not here of his own choice.

"You are Anen?" he said.

"I am."

"Then follow us. Quarters have been allocated to you."

As they walked the priests closed around him as though to guard him from passers-by, or passers-by from him. Anen looked at each of his escort in turn. They all looked remarkably similar, their lack of hair making them as alike as the statue armies of servants that were buried with dead kings. Anen realised that he must look exactly the same. It was a depressing thought. Each of the priests kept their heads turned firmly towards the front and their countenances emotionless, except one. He walked to the right of Anen and was so tall that the crown of Anen's head barely reached his shoulders. When Anen glanced at him he returned the look with a smile and a shrug of the shoulders that seemed to apologise for the sternness of his companions. Anen smiled back, and it felt as though the two men had shared an illicit secret.

It was a short walk. He had been housed in a modest villa next to Amun's towering temple. The priests left him at the door. None had spoken so much as a word to him since leaving the dock, although Anen and the tall priest traded nods as the clerics turned to leave. He let himself in and, for want of anything more profitable, wandered from room to sparse room while he waited for his luggage to arrive. The house was in the shadow of the temple and he doubted if it ever received any more sunlight than the frugal ration it was currently being allowed.

Over his first few days in Thebes he learned that the gloom of his home was a blessing. His rooms were permanently infused with the scent of incense that dallied over on the breeze from each day's worship and his walls rang incessantly with the clanging echoes of hammer falls as the craftsmen worked on the temple extensions and adornments ordered by the king. The noise and the smell combined to give him a permanent headache which the lack of sunlight helped to ease.

He confined himself over the first few weeks to his house and the grounds and interior of the temple. He attended worship as was his duty as the Second Prophet of Amun. He attended those meetings to which he was invited: in other words those meetings which were to discuss matters of little import or significance to his cause. He quickly found that he had few friends in Thebes. Ptahmose had announced Anen's arrival in advance and made it clear to all that they could be either Ptahmose's friend or Anen's, but not both. The priests and prophets and servants knew their choice had been made for them, for the High Priest had spent many years cultivating a network of alliances that criss-crossed the rooms of the temple and tripped anyone in opposition to it. Ptahmose, Anen knew, would make a fearsome foe.

The only exception was the tall priest who had escorted Anen from the docks on the day of his arrival. Anen learned that his name was Iny, and that he was no more scared of Ptahmose than Ptahmose was of him. Amun and his priesthood held no particular fascination for Iny. He came from a family whose principle living came from farming the fertile land around the Nile delta. They had their own gods of the sea and river and sand and soil. They had no need for the god of Thebes. But for generations, like hundreds of other families, they had sent their men into the priesthood for a short time. It was a position of status and it gave their men a break from the rigours of the land and it did no harm to encourage the patronage of any god, however removed he may be from the realities of life. Iny was left in no doubt as to how he was regarded by the temple establishment. The tasks entrusted to him, like those given to Anen, were ones that could have been equally well executed by the more capable of the servants. And so their shared alienation was catalyst to the tentative beginnings of a friendship which blossomed from silent nods as they passed each other in the corridors of Amun's temple, where Anen often came to clear the noise and stench of his house from his head.

The temple complex was a vast sprawl of rooms choked with decorated pillars that had seemingly been placed at random with no line of sight running between them. Thick doors and walls shielded the inner temple from the sounds of building from without, and instead there reigned a comforting silence that caressed the senses like a cool breeze on a hot day. Only echoing footsteps and hints of conversation could be heard as unseen people hurried by behind the forest of pillars. There were no windows in the inner temple, and light was provided by flaming braziers hanging from columns and walls. Viscous shadows pooled in corners. Smoke hung in the air and stung the eyes. Everywhere, the reflections of flames danced on gold.

It was here, in perhaps his third week in Thebes, that Anen finally met Ptahmose. Neither had known the other would be there and both were surprised into momentary silence when they almost walked into each other around a pillar. Anen was mortified. All his resolve evaporated under the gaze of the High Priest. He was an imposing man, a man prepared to risk the anger of a king, and Anen had to fight the urge to be ingratiating towards him.

"Ah," Ptahmose said, finally. "Anen. I have been meaning to see you."

"And I you."

"I trust you have been able to make yourself at home in the temple?" Ptahmose continued, as though Anen had not spoken. "Have your duties been explained to you?"

"They have," Anen said.

"Excellent," Ptahmose said, and the pair lapsed back into an uncomfortable silence.

"How fares His Majesty?" Ptahmose eventually asked, as much to fill the silence as to elicit a response. "Does he send us his greetings?"

"He does indeed," Anen said. "The priesthood of Amun is never far from His Majesty's thoughts."

Ptahmose raised his eyebrows. "Evidently," he said. "And I would hope he understands that whatever he desires shall be delivered to him upon his every command."

"I shall ensure that he does," Anen said. "Especially now that I am here."

Ptahmose was unable to maintain his pleasant demeanour, and his expression settled into a scowl. "Then I hope that His Majesty enjoys conversing in veils and riddles," he said. "I know very well why you are here, Anen. You should know that Amun does not take kindly to being spied upon."

"I have no intention of spying on Amun, High Priest."

"Just remember where you are, Anen. Your every action is being judged by one greater than I."

With that, Ptahmose walked away. Anen took a deep breath. Every sentence had been a battle for will over circumspection. He needed no prompting to remember where he was. But even here, in the stronghold of Amun's keep, the god was not the one of whom Anen was afraid.

"And there is still no word from King Šuppiluliumas?" Amenhotep asked.

"None, Majesty," Aye said.

"Perhaps I should write to him."

"I would advise against it. It would be seen as a sign of weakness. We should not allow him the luxury of knowing that we are even thinking about him. He is inconsequential to us, his actions and threats too puny to register. If you write, he will know you are worried."

Aye had not been down to the cells to see the Hittite envoy since his incarceration. Although he held no malice towards the man, it would be impossible for him to ever be released. His imprisonment was an act of necessity, nothing more.

He knew he was taking a gamble. Should the king discover what had happened it would more than likely mean Aye's head. But Aye had spent many a sleepless night considering the risks involved and had decided at length that they were outweighed by the risks to his family's prominence should Amenhotep be allowed to grow as fond of Giludkhepa as he was of Tiye, or as loving towards her unborn child as he was towards the present and future sons of the Great Royal Wife. There was no reason why anything other than extraordinary coincidence could lead to his discovery. The king never ventured into the bowels of the palace, and none of the guards there would ever take it upon themselves to speak to him directly. As long as Aye kept vigilant in his watch for further ambassadors, there was no need for concern.

Thuya had hinted to him that she was better inclined towards more drastic measures but Aye had persuaded her that his plan would be enough to secure her family's future. He found her thoughts on the matter disquieting, but recognised that necessity was a cold master. Should this scheme fail there was no reason why Thuya's ideas could not be put into practice. But Aye would have to find a willing and trusted intermediary. He had no taste for the blood of innocents.

"Perhaps," Aye said to Amenhotep, "Šuppiluliumas intends to ignore the warning. Perhaps he intends to attack Mitanni anyway."

"Such a course of action would be extreme folly," Huya said.

Aye shrugged his shoulders. "Nobody ever accused a Hittite king of intelligence."

Amenhotep smiled. "Diplomacy is all very well as long as the opposition notices it."

"Of course," Aye said, "we may have miscalculated."

"How so?"

"Perhaps the Hittites do not plan such a quick route to reach Egypt. There are other kingdoms under just as strong a threat as us. Babylonia, Arzawa, Assyria. All may fall before the Hittites turn their eyes to us. It will take them longer to come, but come they will."

"Then we must continue to conspire against them," Amenhotep said. "We need a network of alliances such as the world has never seen. Send our ambassadors to Arzawa, and to Babylonia and Assyria. Send them wherever the shadow of Hatti may fall. Tell their kings to send princesses, not just to me but to each other. Šuppiluliumas needs to know that if he attacks one of us, he attacks us all."

"Inspired, Majesty," Aye said, trying to keep the relief from his voice. "I shall attend to it immediately."

Bringing the plan to fruition had been much easier than Aye had expected, but then he should have realised that Amenhotep's loathing of war would have led him eagerly towards such a solution. Three, four or more princesses would soon be on their way to Memphis. Knowing the king as Aye did, he was confident that their arrival would be the cue for Amenhotep to redouble his visits to the harem at Gurob. Giludkhepa may be forgotten altogether, her offspring consigned to obscurity along with all the other minor children in the harem. At the very least her influence over the king would be diluted to more manageable proportions. Thutmose's succession would be secure, as would his marriage to Aye's daughter, Nefertiti. The future was looking bright once again.

Aye went to make the necessary arrangements for the diplomatic missions abroad, looking forward to sharing the good news with his mother.

The princesses duly arrived. None possessed Giludkhepa's beauty, but then none were unsightly enough to dissuade the advances of one such as Amenhotep. They were all the object of his recreations before long. The treaties established with Egypt's neighbours could not fail to hold Hatti in check, at least for the foreseeable future. Huya, that infallible prophet, had even had a dream in which the sun fell to earth before him, crushing into oblivion a red haired man. What surer sign could there be for Ra's grandson that his nation was protected against evil?

A second ambassador arrived from Hatti, enquiring after the first and carrying with him a copy of Šuppiluliumas' letter. Aye led him to the same plush quarters where his predecessor had briefly rested, asking after the contents of the letter as though he had no idea of what it might contain. Of the first messenger he claimed ignorance.

"The lands between Egypt and Hatti are dangerous ones," he said. "Many a good man has fallen prey to the bandits of those regions. You have perhaps been luckier in your travels than the man who came before you. I wish you the same luck upon your return."

That the last statement had seemed almost to be a threat the messenger put down to paranoia brought on through exhaustion. Aye left him and went to find the king. Now that the foreign princesses had arrived and were firmly ensconced at court there was no harm in allowing Šuppiluliumas to communicate his good wishes to Amenhotep.

Aye could not help but smile as he walked the corridors. He even found himself humming a tune as he neared Amenhotep's quarters.

The messenger's audience with the king went without a hitch. Aye had informed Amenhotep of the contents of the letter before the messenger was shown into the throne room and so the king could afford to be magnanimous in his reception. The envoy unfurled the scroll with a great show of pomp, cleared his throat at length, and then read.

"So says Šuppiluliumas, king of Hatti," he began. "My brother, I am desirous of peace between our nations..."

Amenhotep hardly heard the rest of his speech. War was, at least for now, avoided. He would lose no more friends to the swords of marauding foreigners. He would not feel the bolt of pain across his back as he cleaved fierce heads from shoulders. He would not have to see the sun rise across a distant black swarm of men whose sole aim was to bring his life to an end. He had saved lives.

"Congratulations, gentlemen," Amenhotep said, once the door had closed behind the messenger. "It seems we have succeeded flawlessly."

"If Šuppiluliumas is as good as his word," Huya cautioned.

"Now, now. We must continue to be vigilant, but this is not the time for talk of treachery. We must celebrate. Tonight we will feast. I shall set Bakenamun to work like never before."

Back in his quarters he found Tiye and Amenophis and greeted them both enthusiastically, his arms wide in welcome.

"Good day to you both, wife and son," he said. "Tiye, you must make yourself ready for a celebratory feast the like of which you have never seen. Amenophis, would you care to attend the festivities with us?"

Tiye and Amenophis both looked surprised at the offer and then broke into smiles. "Amenophis would love to attend," Tiye said. "Wouldn't you?"

Amenophis started to nod, but then a thought occurred to him. He had heard laughter and whispered comments all day at school. He was increasingly becoming the centre of the class's attention as his misshapen body continued to grow in unexpected ways. His limbs were now longer than they had been, his fingers and toes thinner and increasingly nodular. Further changes seemed to be occurring in his face and head. His lips were fleshing out, his skull elongating so that his chin jutted forward and his cheekbones sat proud and highly defined on either side of his face. They were changes that would have driven him to the extremes of despair were it not for one lone voice that held him by his fingertips over a black chasm. The voice of Nefertiti.

"You should ignore them," she had said to him one day after class, nodding her head back to indicate the children that followed them from the classroom.

"How can I?" he had replied. "Look at me."

Nefertiti stopped in the corridor, allowing the crowd to pass. Amenophis stopped too. She turned to look him squarely in the eye.

"Your face is changing," she said. "That much is true. But it is not necessarily a bad thing." She turned her head to look at him first from one side and then the other. "I think it makes you look handsome. You are beginning to take on a noble beauty all of your own."

He felt his face flush with embarrassment and joy.

"I," he stammered. "Well. I mean."

Every time he looked up from the floor he found her staring at him, an innocent smile on her lips, and his gaze would slide away to less emotive subjects.

"Thank you," he said, finally. "I have to go." And with that he hurried away before he could say anything even more inane.

And so when Amenhotep invited him to attend the feast, he was only half way through nodding his acceptance when a question jumped to his lips.

"Will there be any other children there?" he asked.

"Possibly," Amenhotep said. "But I do not want to hear you complaining any more about people talking behind your back, do you understand? You will enjoy yourself. The king commands it."

But that was not what Amenophis had meant at all.

Bakenamun had worked like a slave to prepare the food and drink in time, and all agreed that he had done a magnificent job. The table could hardly be seen beneath the cornucopia of dishes that covered its surface. There were gazelle and pigeons, ducks and geese, beef and lamb cooked in coriander. There were olives, watermelons, figs, pomegranates and dates. There were breads baked into the shapes of animals and the royal family. There was even a new dish that Bakenamun had been saving for an occasion such as this. It looked a little like duck, or a small goose. Amenhotep tried a small piece before declaring it delicious and laughingly advising the guests to help themselves before he devoured every morsel. He summoned Bakenamun from the kitchens.

"What is this?" he asked him, through a mouthful of the new fowl. "Why have I never had it before?"

"It is a flightless bird, Majesty. It is called 'chicken'. I have just had it imported from Syria."

"Good man," Amenhotep said, spraying one or two lumps onto the table.

"Interestingly, Majesty, chickens lay eggs every day. I have kept some birds to one side to assure us a steady supply."

"Really?" Amenhotep said. "Every day, you say? Extraordinary. And are these chicken eggs good to eat?"

"I have taken the liberty of baking some into the bread, Majesty."

"First class, Bakenamun. As always. Absolutely first class."

Amenhotep heard snatches of a conversation from further down the table that drew him away from the chef. Bakenamun left with the compliments of his king lightening his step.

There was an inexhaustible supply of wine and beer that flowed in a never ending torrent from large jars in the shape of Bes, the god of festivity and drunkenness. Musicians played loud and long into the night. All in all, it was a ribald evening that few would soon forget. Amenhotep was in an ebullient mood, entertaining the whole table with stories and anecdotes. Even Amenophis enjoyed himself, despite Nefertiti's absence.

But even as the palace reverberated with the laughter and shouts of the revellers, events were unfolding elsewhere that, in the fullness of time, would bring the jaws of chaos clamping down on the throat of all Egypt.

The following morning a messenger clattered into Amenhotep's throne room unannounced, sweat dappling his face and forehead like dew, and fell to his knees, breathless before the throne. Amenhotep knew that good news is rarely relayed with a preamble such as this, but even so, he was unprepared for the blow that was to come.

It was the start of it all. It was the first of the murders.

Chapter Six

A Downward Glance

IT WAS the afternoon after the feast to celebrate the taming of Šuppiluliumas. A messenger from Kadašman-Enlil, King of Babylonia, was standing before the throne. Neither Amenhotep nor his ministers were well-disposed to the business of court today. It had been a late night and they were all still suffering the effects of the beer and wine they had consumed in such careless quantities. The king himself was in a particularly foul mood. Not only was his head pounding but a persistent throbbing ache in one of his teeth had awoken him in the night. Despite the application of herbs, carob and honey by a bleary eyed dentist the pain had grown steadily worse until it seemed to consume the whole of his head. All he wanted to do now was sleep.

The Babylonian envoy had brought the latest missive from Kadašman-Enlil in a long running dispute. The disagreement was a simple one, and one over which Amenhotep was not going to be swayed. It was a matter of pride. When Kadašman-Enlil had sent his daughter to marry Amenhotep, she had brought with her a letter.

"My brother," it said. "So that our alliance may be hewn out of the very rock of our two lands, send a daughter, that I may marry her and mix my blood with yours."

Amenhotep had been surprised that Kadašman-Enlil had even asked. He had sent a perfunctory letter back.

"From of old," part of it had said, "no daughter of an Egyptian king is given to anyone."

It had never been done, and with good reason. Although Amenhotep was enthusiastic in his dealing with Egypt's allies, it was less in a spirit of friendship than patronage, and while his associates abroad called him 'brother' it was only ever a term of servile hope rather than true fraternity. It would not be wise for a pharaoh to afford a foreign king the misguided impression that the two really were equals. Amenhotep appreciated the stubbornness and courage with which his forebears had harboured the crown. He was not about to dilute his blood with the likes of Kadašman-Enlil and allow him to put his shoulder against the door of Egypt's throne room. And so the bridal traffic flowed only one way, into Egypt where it could be watched and contained.

Amenhotep knew this. Kadašman-Enlil knew this. And yet here stood this envoy, almost shredding the papyrus scroll he held between two fists, such was his trepidation at the affront he knew he must recite.

"Have a care," Amenhotep muttered, massaging his temples. "This had better not be about my daughters marrying foreigners."

The envoy swallowed heavily.

Although he knew it would hurt to do so, Amenhotep could not help but tentatively touch his fingertips to his cheek where his tooth roared. Out of the corner of his eye he saw Huya cough gently and then grimace at the pounding that ran laps around his skull.

"Your Majesty," the envoy said. "I have word from my king." He emphasised the last two words, as though keen to distance himself from the correspondence he must relay.

"Go on, if you must," Amenhotep said.

"'Say to Nebmaatre Amenhotep, the king of Egypt, my brother,'" the envoy read. "Thus speaks Kadašman-Enlil, the King of Babylon. You say that no Egyptian king's daughter may be given in marriage even to loyal friends such as myself, and yet you demand this same tribute to be afforded you with no recompense. If that is the way it must be, then so be it. But someone's grown up daughters, beautiful women, must be available. So send me a beautiful woman as if she were your daughter and who will say 'She is not the king's daughter'? Thus I will have my wife and you will have your pride.'"

Amenhotep raised his head to look at the envoy. "Is he serious?" he said.

The envoy stayed uncomfortably silent, unsure as to whether the question had been rhetorical, deciding that unwanted silence was safer than an unwanted reply.

"Are the women in Babylon so unsavoury that your king must beg for Egyptian leftovers?" Amenhotep said, conveniently forgetting for the moment his own trade in foreign brides. "Tell Kadašman-Enlil that I have eaten heartily, and there are no scraps on my table."

Knowing the king may well regret such harsh words once his toothache and the effects of the previous night had worn off, Huya said: "Majesty, I shall compose a fitting reply and send it with this messenger to the court of Babylon."

"Yes," Amenhotep said. "Do so. And stress that I wish to hear no more on this subject."

The envoy and ministers bowed low, and were preparing to take their leave when the doors flew open with such force that they crashed against the walls on either side, where the handles left small discoloured indentations in the plaster. Amenhotep jumped in his seat, unused to anyone coming into his presence without being preceded by polite introductions. Huya and Aye instinctively jumped forward to shield their king from the man who had thrown himself through the doorway. His body was held almost horizontal, his legs pinwheeling behind him, and such was his precarious gait that he had fallen to his knees in front of the throne before he could stop himself. He skidded to the base of the dais. His eyes were wild, but Aye and Yuya could see that they held no threat. They were stained red from a long, sleepless journey, his hair matted and clogged with dust. He tried to speak between the laboured gulps of air that whistled down his throat.

"Your..." he said. "Your..."

"Spit it out, man!" Amenhotep said. He was on his feet now, staring down over the shoulders of Aye and Huya. "What warrants this intrusion?"

"Your Maj..." the man said. "Your..."

He seemed to make a supreme effort to bring himself under control.

"Your Majesty, forgive me," he said, finally. "But I bring heinous news that I must impart with all urgency."

At the back of the room, forgotten, the Babylonian envoy looked from one man to the next and took a hesitant step backwards, torn between making a quiet exit and waiting to hear something which Kadašman-Enlil could use.

Amenhotep's first thought had been that the Hittites had attacked and that Egypt was at war. When he heard the messenger's news, he wished he had been right.

Tiye's chief steward knocked at the door of her apartments and waited for the command to enter. He found the Great Royal Wife reading by the light from the window.

"Your Highness," he said, bowing. "I have been charged to ask you to attend His Majesty in his quarters."

"Thank you, Kheruef. Please inform the king that I shall be along shortly."

"Forgive me, Highness, but I have been instructed to inform you that it is a matter of some urgency and gravity."

Tiye put down the manuscript and looked up for the first time. "Concerning what?" she said.

"I have not been told, Highness."

"Nobody tells anybody anything in this palace," she muttered as she made her way into the corridor.

She found the king in his quarters, sitting loose and motionless in a chair. A blanket hung over the window and threw long shadows across the room. Here and there chinks of light escaped the blanket's clutches and fell onto the floor, as though they had dripped from the sun.

"You had better sit down," Amenhotep said, his voice in a monotone of shock.

"Whatever is the matter?"

"Sit down," he said again. "You must prepare yourself, my dear."

Her eyes never leaving his, she gently lowered herself into a chair, taking the weight with her arms. Only when she was settled did Amenhotep speak again.

"I have received some news," he said. "Some bad news."

"From whom?"

"From Heliopolis," he said.

Tiye's breath caught in her throat. "Thutmose?" she said.

"There has been an incident."

"What sort of incident? Is he safe?"

Amenhotep shook his head. "No," he said. "He is not safe."

"Is he hurt?"

Amenhotep took a deep breath and embarked on the story that the distraught messenger had relayed to him.

After the messenger had gathered himself enough to speak coherent sentences, he had told Amenhotep that Thutmose had been planning a return trip to Memphis during a lull in his studies. He had spent hours visiting the artisans and tradesmen of Heliopolis, picking presents to bring back to the palace. When he had finally set off there was barely enough room in the chariot for himself and the driver between the packages that piled up around their legs. He had begun his journey in good spirits, excited to be seeing his home and family again

One or two of his tutors had voiced their concern that he had chosen to travel back to Memphis by road, following the route of the Nile.

"You sound like my mother," he had told them. "Who would dare attack the Crown Prince?"

"How will bandits know you are the Crown Prince?" they had asked, but he was not to be dissuaded.

"I was sent here not just to learn from books and priests. I was sent to embrace the country I am to rule. I cannot embrace it over a stretch of water. I will travel through it, not past it."

And so the journey was planned. Thutmose and his driver would immerse themselves in the country. It was an adventure. They would rest where they could, taking rooms in the villages they travelled through, or simply sleeping out under the stars.

His friends had waved him off as the chariot pulled away.

It was still somewhat unclear what had happened next. Thutmose's driver had staggered into the outskirts of Gebel Ahmar, which lay beside the Nile between Heliopolis and Cairo. He had been viciously beaten and dried blood formed a cracked shell around his head and upper body. Here and there his skin lay off him in shredded strips. The sun had blistered what remained of it and reduced his speech to a babbling incoherency. He was given to the care of a physician, but it was some time before he was lucid enough to explain whom he had been driving. On hearing the news the local authorities, in something of a panic that they may be blamed for this disaster, sent a contingent of soldiers to retrace the driver's steps. An hour or so along the road they found the remains of the chariot, one of its wheels smashed. Later, the commander of the unit said that there was nothing along the road that could have done such damage. The wheel had presumably been smashed to prevent the occupants fleeing or seeking help. A short distance from the chariot, partly obscured by undergrowth, a black smear of blood led the soldiers to Thutmose. His body had been dragged from the road in a half-hearted attempt at concealment. The stab wounds were so numerous as to be impossible to count. Of the presents that had been piled into the chariot there was no sign.

Amenhotep spared his wife the most distressing of the details that the messenger had given him. Not only was there no reason for her to be burdened with the images that would haunt Amenhotep for the rest of his life, but Amenhotep did not think he could bring himself to say the words even if he had wanted to. It was almost a blessing that the messenger had told him that the driver was not expected to live, and so further details were unlikely to be forthcoming. Amenhotep did not want to know them in any case.

The king and his wife sat in silence for a long time. They mourned the death of their son as the puddles of sunlight crept furtively across the floor and the sun sank into the underworld.

When Giludkhepa went into labour some three weeks later, nobody had the courage to inform Amenhotep. Few outside his family and immediate friends were bold enough to approach him over any matter since the loss of his son had driven his disposition to unpredictable extremes. In the weeks since Thutmose's death he had received good news with scorn and bad with an uncharacteristic acceptance of defeat, but all news with anger and contempt. Courtiers came to dread any assignment that took them into the company of their king. Added to this was the fact that Ptahmose was currently in residence at the palace. At the best of times Amenhotep's good humour would take a sharp dip in the proximity of the High Priest of Amun.

Giludkhepa's screams could be clearly heard throughout the corridors that surrounded her apartments in the palace. Women would wince in empathy as they passed and men would grimace and hurry on, talking loudly of other things.

In the room Giludkhepa crouched on a birthing stool, held steady by two maids. Around her a host of nurses mopped her brow and told her to push. The baby's emergence was expected at any minute, although it had been expected at any minute for a number of hours and Giludkhepa's strength was beginning to desert her. Her screams were becoming quieter and taking on an air of resignation. Various remedies had been prepared and administered. She had been fed a mixture of fresh salt, honey and wine. After one sip she had refused to take any more until the pain grew so strong that she eagerly slurped down anything that was offered to her in the hope that it would bring an end to her discomfort. White emmer, pine oil, beer, beetles and parts of a tortoise had been applied to her abdomen and then held secure with bandages. A range of concoctions had been pushed into her vagina, including shredded onions, beer, salt, juniper berries, the resin of fir trees and the excrement of flies. All the while priests chanted incantations. Nothing seemed to help.

The doctors began to fear the worst.

As Giludkhepa's screams of pain subsided into moans of exhaustion, Amenhotep and his ministers, unaware of her agonies, were sitting around a banquet table with Ptahmose, discussing the succession. Now that the Crown Prince was dead another had to be found to take his place. Amenhotep found the discussion distasteful. Thutmose was not yet in his tomb and yet they spoke of him as though they had never mourned at all. The king could find no enthusiasm for the debate and spent most of the time eating in silence. His toothache had ebbed and flowed since the night of the banquet to celebrate the diplomatic defeat of Šuppiluliumas. It was currently manageable, but he had learned from experience to only eat on one side of his mouth.

"I am pleased to see that your appetite has not suffered from your grievous loss," Ptahmose said.

"What business is it of yours? Should I starve to death and join my son?"

"Not at all, Majesty. I was merely afraid that I would arrive to find you wasting away in grief."

Amenhotep did not reply, but picked up a roasted chicken, pulled off a leg and bit deeply into the breast. The juices ran down his chin and he wiped them off with the palm of his hand. While he chewed he eyed

Ptahmose suspiciously over the top of the carcass. He found him repellent. He wore enough jewellery to adorn every man at the table, and even the slightest movement would result in a musical jangling as his trinkets would dance against each other. He had ear rings, circlets around his arms, a broad chest plate, a belt and three identical necklaces long enough for their pendants to rest on his knees when he sat down. And all were fashioned from gold. Amenhotep was surprised he had the strength to stand up under all that weight.

"A, shall we say, *smooth* succession is of the utmost importance," Ptahmose said. "We must appoint a crown prince. He will need to begin his training in the ways of kingship as soon as possible. He will have a lot of ground to make up."

"We?" Amenhotep said. "This is a matter for your deliberation, is it, Ptahmose?"

Yes, Ptahmose thought to himself, for me and my god both. Ptahmose had lost count of the hours he had sat in contemplative silence in the innermost sanctum of Amun's temple, the incense stinging his eyes to tears as he wrestled with the ramifications of a succession such as this. Amun brought pictures to his mind, images of a king with Amenhotep's weakness for peaceful solutions but without Amenhotep's strength for diplomacy and negotiation, a king whose very appearance was enough to provoke ridicule from the kings of Egypt's neighbours, whose physique would be taken as a manifestation of incompetence. Who, in short, would be incapable of guaranteeing the safety of the quarries and goldmines outside Egypt's borders. And then Amun vouchsafed him more images: of a temple without the funds or stone to complete Amenhotep's ambitious construction projects, of a priesthood bereft of the wherewithal to worship their god as he intended. Of a god impoverished and a priesthood sold into destitution. And then Amun had given him a gift of this child that Giludkhepa had carried around in her belly, a son of Amun if ever there was one. Here was the escape that Ptahmose had craved. Amenhotep was already visibly aging. He would perhaps not be far from taking up his place in Ra's chariot, and so the time he had available to influence a newborn in his peculiar ways of kingship was limited. There was a finite amount of damage he could do to the throne before the child took up his mantle. Giludkhepa's baby was the way forward. It was the way of Amun.

All of these thoughts ran through Ptahmose's head at the king's question, but he deemed it prudent to voice none of them. Instead, he said, "Majesty, whoever is to be king after you needs the blessing of his church."

"Why?"

"*Why*, Your Majesty?"

"Yes, Ptahmose. Why? How did it profit Thutmose to have Amun's blessing? Did he protect him? Was Amun watching over him when he was waylaid by bandits?"

"Was Ra?" Ptahmose said, calmly.

Ptahmose was right. Amenhotep had no answer. He looked down at the food arrayed before him on the table and struggled to hold his temper in check. He felt the blood rise to his cheeks. It would be undignified to allow the rage within him to explode, but it was an explosion he feared he would be unable to suppress for much longer. He had been finding it much harder to censor shows of emotion since Thutmose's death, and such shows often became rising spirals of anger as he became further enraged at his own loss of control. Ptahmose was stretching the already taut bonds with which Amenhotep kept himself in check. It was one thing making his unwelcome views known about the succession, but to call into question the magnanimity and protection of Amenhotep's ancestral god was quite another matter. To do so in such a way as to leave Amenhotep no opportunity for recourse was even worse. His attitude had implications. It was disloyal to Ra, and to be disloyal to Ra was but one step away from being disloyal to the king. A disloyal man so highly placed in society was a dangerous thing. The man would have to be taught a lesson, Amenhotep decided. Now it was not appropriate, but the time would come soon. Ptahmose must have a weakness, he thought. There must be a way past the bravado and conceit of Amun's patronage to the man beneath. Amenhotep decided to contact Anen. It was time he became useful.

"As I was saying," Ptahmose said, once it became evident that Amenhotep had nothing to add, "a smooth succession is essential if the gods of chaos are to be prevented from gaining a foothold in this world."

"There is surely only one candidate," Aye said. "The only sensible option is to proclaim Amenophis as heir."

"If that is a sensible option I would be interested to hear your foolish ones," Ptahmose said. "I have heard that Amenophis would not be the, shall we say, *ideal* candidate."

"He is the king's son," Aye said.

"He is slow," Ptahmose said. "He is deformed. He would not make an able king. When is Giludkhepa due to bestow upon His Majesty another child?"

"Imminently," Aye said. "But would you hand our throne to the Mitannites? Giludkhepa's child cannot be made heir. It is unthinkable. Anyway, the child may be a daughter."

"If it is we will have to rethink our options. But I would like to wait and see," Ptahmose said, and leaned forwards in his seat. "Better a Mitannite than an imbecile. Majesty, it would be a disastrous folly to miss the point of my argument."

"I will be pressured by no man, Ptahmose," Amenhotep said. "Do not test my patience."

"Your Majesty, it is not I who pressures you. Amun may make demands of his pharaoh, but I will not. Your subjects hear his demands, even if their king is deaf to them. Do you think the common man will allow you to buck Amun's word? Do you think the people will accept a dunce like Amenophis on the throne? I tell you, sir, they will not."

"And I tell you, sir, that I am not a man to be trifled with. Do you really presume to issue me with orders?"

"Not in the least, Majesty. Like all loyal subjects, I simply mean to safeguard your throne."

"By which you mean that my throne is in jeopardy? Am I being threatened, Ptahmose? I suggest you choose your words carefully."

While Amenhotep's demeanour was calm and measured his heart hammered in his chest. He was calling on every ounce of his deportment to prevent himself leaping from his chair and taking the priest by the throat. Even the most harmless of conversations with the most well meaning of friends had served to put the heat of wrath in his heart since Thutmose's death. To hear such calumny from this upstart was almost more than he could bear.

Every word that Ptahmose spoke fuelled Amenhotep's anger. The fact that he may be correct about Amenophis did not give him the right to speak about members of the royal family with such disrespect. The man obviously thought himself above the common constraints of society. He even dressed as though he were in competition with the king, as though his golden adornments could elevate him above the crown itself. The king's mounting anger consumed him, until Ptahmose's words faded into silence behind it.

"Where did you get all that gold?" Amenhotep suddenly said, cutting him off. Ptahmose stumbled into silence.

"Your Majesty?" he said.

"Are you deaf? I said, where did you get all that gold?"

"Your Majesty, I can assure you..."

"I do not ask for your assurances. That gold is no present from this court. How came you by it?"

"Perhaps, Your Majesty, it may be more profitable for us to stick to the matter at..."

"You come here bedecked like a king and you sit there and insult my family? How dare you, Ptahmose? How dare you, you... *priest!*" Amenhotep spat the last word as though it was the worst insult he could think of.

For once, Ptahmose seemed genuinely shocked. Aye was staring at the table

There came a knock at the door.

Amenhotep span round to face it. *"What?"* he shouted.

A courtier appeared. He had been standing in the corridor outside the room for some time, his hand poised to knock, listening to the shouting from within. It had taken him more than a few moments to gather the courage to bring his knuckles against the wood. When he spoke it was all in one nervous sentence.

"Your Majesty I apologise for the intrusion but I beg to report that Her Highness Princess Giludkhepa has given birth to a son Your Majesty and both mother and child are doing well although it was a long and troublesome labour."

The courtier bowed, exited, closed the door and ran.

Ptahmose was immediately calmed, and smiled.

"Ah," he said. "Excellent. Congratulations, Majesty. May I ask if you have considered a name for the child?"

"I care not what they call him," Amenhotep muttered.

"Yes, well," Ptahmose said. "It is of no matter. Perhaps now we could return to discussing making him your heir?"

After the meeting was over Amenhotep paced the floor of his quarters like a man awaiting the reprieve of a death sentence. He occasionally made small detours to bring pieces of furniture into his path so he could throw them violently to one side. After a few minutes the room looked as though it had been the scene of a very localised storm.

On one circuit of the room he did not stop at the door but opened it and took a step into the room beyond. It was an anteroom where nervous servants awaited the king's errands.

"You," Amenhotep barked, pointing at the room in general. "Fetch me Kheruef the scribe."

There was a brief hiatus in conversation as everyone looked at everyone else, hoping they would not have to be the one to volunteer.

"Now!" Amenhotep shouted, and four servants jumped up at once and collided with each other as they ran for the door. Amenhotep went back to his pacing.

Kheruef arrived shortly. He was out of breath, having undoubtedly been told of the king's poor humour.

"I wish to dictate a letter," Amenhotep said. "I want you to send your best man with it to Thebes. It is for the eyes of Anen only, and any man who allows it to be seen by any other than him will have me to deal with. Is that absolutely clear?"

Kheruef assured him that it was abundantly clear. Amenhotep dictated quickly. It was a short note.

After Kheruef had bowed his way out of the room Amenhotep righted a chair and sat down heavily.

"Now we shall see who may call himself king," he muttered.

Giludkhepa was carried to her bed, almost unconscious with exhaustion. Honey, carob water and milk were mixed together and placed in her vagina to aid the expulsion of the placenta, and oil was allowed to soak in between her legs to aid the healing of injuries she had sustained during the labour. The child was declared healthy by the physicians, but the priests watched carefully as it was carried to its crib and as one man they moaned in despair and called upon Bes, the god of childbirth, when they saw the child look down to the ground from the arms of the nurse.

"What?" a physician asked. "What have you seen?"

"The child has turned his face to the floor. It is a sign."

"A sign of what?"

One of the priests touched the physician's shoulder and guided him to the far corner of the room where there was no risk of Giludkhepa overhearing their conversation.

"If a child says '*ny*' when it is born, it is a good sign. It means the child will live. If it says '*mebi*' it will certainly die. Also, if it turns its face to the floor, it will die."

"It will die? Are you sure?"

The priest shrugged. "So it is written," he said. "We will pray for him."

Aye's plan had failed, and it was small comfort that its failure was no fault of his own but the product of events over which he had no control. He explained the situation to Thuya, but she just made noncommittal noises that made it clear that she held him ultimately responsible for his failure to remove Giludkhepa's offspring as a threat to her dynasty.

"Perhaps now we can stop pussyfooting around the real issue," she said.

For once, Aye remained silent. In the luxury of believing that his plan would suffice he had been stoical about Thuya's suggestion. But now that it seemed as though he would have to act on it after all, his enthusiasm deserted him.

"Is there really no other way?" he said.

"We have tried other ways and they have failed us."

Aye and Thuya were walking alone along a deserted road that ran parallel to the Nile. To their left the villas of the blessed and powerful were indistinct shapes in the darkness. The only evidence of the river's proximity was the sound of water gently lapping against the stone bulwarks that protected the town from flooding during the time of the inundation. The river itself was empty of boats at this time of night and in the silence Aye could almost believe himself to be lost in some remote place in the desert. He understood the loneliness that Prince Thutmose must have felt as the life seeped from him.

Aye wished that Yuya was here. He would have made a good ally in this discussion. Although, Aye reflected, his effectiveness at opposing Thuya's wishes did not have a very promising record. Thuya had specified that they should meet here, and that they should meet in secret. Even Yuya and Tiye would know nothing of their discussion.

"It seems so drastic," Aye said. They were walking slowly, in no hurry to arrive anywhere. Aye absently kicked at stones that lay in his path.

"Of course it is drastic. That is the whole point. Are you telling me that you do not have the stomach for it?"

Aye did not speak for a few moments.

"Yes," he whispered, finally, as though ashamed.

"Need I remind you what is at stake here?"

"No," he said. "You need not. Need I remind you of the same thing?"

"This is not a time for squeamishness, Aye. We need to be strong if our line is to prevail. The eye of history is not sharp enough to see one or two lives. Who will speak of them in ten years, or a hundred, or a thousand? And if they will not be remembered then consequently they cannot matter. It is the grand picture with which we must concern ourselves."

"I will need someone to act on our behalf."

"No," Thuya said. "That is out of the question. Who could we trust?"

"I cannot do this."

Thuya rounded on him. "Then you would have your own mother do it?" she shouted. "What kind of a son are you?"

"Please, mother, show some restraint," Aye said, his gaze flitting between the windows of the villas that lined the road. "Would you have the whole city know our dealings?"

"You sound like your father," she said. "Be a man, Aye. It is your duty to protect your family. They should be your first concern, not some foreigner."

"Perhaps if I spoke to the king. If I could persuade him to make Amenophis his heir over Giludkhepa's child there would be no need for this."

"And what if you were to fail and that priest were to have his way? Then there would be no avoiding the necessity to act. How would that look? You try to prevent Giludkhepa's child from being named as heir, and when he is named anyway he mysteriously dies. No, it would be too suspicious."

"And so how would you have me do it?"

"However it is done, it must be done soon and it must be done subtly. If there is even a hint of murder there will be an investigation, and we cannot afford that. I believe I am correct in saying that both mother and baby are still weak from the birth?"

"It was a protracted affair. The doctors say it will be some time before she is back on her feet."

"Good. Then she can have a relapse and succumb to the pressures of the labour. It will be easy enough. She can be smothered. She can be poisoned. She is often alone in her apartments, so access will not be a problem. The problem lies with the child. He will be surrounded by nursemaids."

"Perhaps it is too hazardous, after all," Aye said, hopefully.

"Where will the child sleep?"

"With his mother, I presume."

"Alone? I mean, without a wet-nurse in attendance?"

"The wet-nurses will come and go as the feeding schedule dictates."

"Then our plan is clear."

"Mother, you talk as though this were of no more import than ridding your home of vermin."

"My dear boy, that is exactly what I *am* doing."

They had reached a junction at the end of the road. To their right they could hear the creak of timbers as ships rolled in the Nile current, their hulls rubbing against the dockside where they had been tied. A cold southerly breeze blew off the river, ruffling Thuya's plaited wig and waking little vortices of dust on the path.

"Do not underestimate what you are about to do," she said. "The future of Egypt rests in your hands. Do not condemn her to be ruled by the son of a foreigner."

"We should return separately," Aye said. "We should not be seen together this night."

"Who will see? The streets are deserted."

"Mother, you must learn caution. What if we were to meet a police patrol?"

"Very well," Thuya said, with a sigh. "Return the way we came. I shall stroll through the city. Meet me again after the deed is done."

Without a word, Aye turned and retraced his steps. Thuya watched him for a few moments before heading off to her left, her footsteps soon lost in the soporific sounds of the night.

The palace was deserted and dark, and as silent as an empty cell. It was as though the entire building was nothing more than a reflection of the king's mood. There were no banquets, no parties. There were no late night revellers returning to their apartments. There were no chinks of light escaping beneath doors. A palace mourned the death of a prince.

The sound of Aye's footsteps seemed to follow him as though they belonged to someone else, as though, if he halted suddenly they would continue for one or two steps more. He would occasionally stop and search the corridor behind him but would find only a wall of darkness staring back. He had decided not to bring a lamp with him and he was regretting it already. He had thought it would be safer to be able to step into an alcove and cloak himself in shadows should he come across anyone else along the way, but he now realised that a lack of light gave him as little notice of someone else as it gave them of him. As he neared his destination his pace began to slow. Now he walked timorously, placing the toes of each foot against the floor before allowing the heel to gently fall. His calves were already beginning to ache. But he had only one more junction to traverse before he would find himself outside Giludkhepa's quarters. Beyond that landmark he would not allow himself to think.

Giludkhepa lived in a series of rooms along the southernmost corridor of the palace. Three doors punctuated the wall on Aye's left. The first led into the princess' day room. The next door along opened into the bedroom where Giludkhepa and her baby would be sleeping. The third door was the entrance to the room currently occupied by the infant's wet-nurse. All three rooms were linked by connecting doors inside the apartment.

He reached the second doorway without incident and waited for long moments with his ear to the rough wood, listening for sounds from within. There were none. He looked to his right and left, straining to listen for footsteps above the beating of his heart. Again, there were none. Holding his breath, he pushed the door open.

Inside, the bedchamber was barely better illuminated than the corridor. The small, high windows afforded an inadequate ration of moonlight into the room, enough only to differentiate the shapes therein against the deeper darkness behind them. Now Aye could hear sounds, both coming from ahead and to his left: the measured, sonorous breathing of one in a deep sleep, and the gurgling, mewling sounds of a baby. Aye felt his way across the room, his outstretched arms blindly waving in front of him. On his way he picked up a pillow from a couch. It was square and well padded, and he could feel the raised intricacies of the pattern embroidered into one side. He held it to his chest with one arm as a child might hold a comforting toy, and edged forwards once more.

He thought it prudent to deal with the baby first. In the exhaustion of her labour it was unlikely that Giludkhepa would wake until she felt the cushion on her face. The baby, though, could wake of its own volition at any time and unwittingly sound an alarm. And the princess was only a secondary target. Her death would ensure only that this situation would not arise again. The baby had to die first because only it was an immediate threat to the succession of the throne, and Aye had no idea when its wet-nurse would arrive to discharge her duties.

Aye looked down over the crib and found that he could not move.

I cannot harm a baby, he thought.

But you have to harm the baby. Anyway, it is not as if you will be harming it. It will feel no pain. A few moments of discomfort, nothing more.

It is an innocent, he thought.

Only for now can you call it innocent. Let it live and ask yourself again in twenty years, when it has stolen the crown of Egypt from those who are owed it. When your mother is wasted by age and unfulfilled destiny, or dead and forgotten by all save those who loved her. When Amenophis has suffered the ravages of a disused life, too blind to be a scribe, too slow to be a priest. When Amenhotep marries this innocent to one of his own daughters to cement the succession and Nefertiti is shackled to some simpering bureaucrat, forever blaming her father for not securing her future. When Egypt is ruled by a Mitannite king's grandson. Ask yourself then whether this child is innocent.

The discussion went around and around in his head, bringing him always to the same conclusion. The child must die. For the sake of everyone, for the sake of Egypt. The child must die.

He took a step forward placed the cushion over the child's face. The baby was tightly swaddled and unable to struggle. It was the work of moments, and when it was done, feeling the chill of tears on his cheek, Aye turned to face Giludkhepa's bed.

She lay under one or two light sheets. She was on her side, which did not help. Afterwards, Aye would not be able to estimate the time that he spent standing over her, simply staring, hoping that she would awake so that he could flee, unrecognised in the dark. But she did not.

He leaned towards her. He wanted to practise the movement he would have to make so that he could be sure it would be smooth and effective, but he dare not risk disturbing her while his face was so close to hers. Instead, he held his breath and sprang. He clamped one hand on the back of her head, just above the nape of the neck, and with the other pushed the decorated pillow into her face. She woke immediately, her cry of surprise muffled by the cushion. Her right arm thrashed, her left caught under her body. Her legs feebly kicked out, quickly becoming entangled in the sheets.

Aye's grip remained firm but Giludkhepa's struggling did not abate. Swearing to himself under his breath, taking short breaths between clenched teeth that sprayed small flecks of spittle over the bed with every exhalation, Aye realised that the pillow could not be forming a tight seal over Giludkhepa's nose and mouth. Somehow, she was getting air.

He took his hand from the back of her head to push her onto her back, but as he released the pressure she snapped her head backwards, took in a huge whoop of air and managed to let fly half a terrified scream before she was on her back and Aye was pressing down on the cushion on her face with all his weight. It was not much of a shout, but it was enough to terrify Aye. In the still air of the palace night it would perhaps have been enough to be heard from the wet-nurse's quarters next door.

But worse; in that moment before he had managed to push the cushion back over her face, their eyes had met. Hers had been wide and uncomprehending, but fully focused in the flow of panic that ran through her veins. She had seen him, and she had recognised him, their faces close enough to momentarily feel each other's breath. Her eyes had not asked *What is happening to me?*, but *Why is Aye doing this?*

Aye wanted to stop. He wanted to lift the cushion and explain himself. He wanted to apologise. But of course he could not. He could not allow her to raise the alarm, for his sake, and he could not allow her to see her dead child, for hers. Instead, he climbed onto the bed, his legs astride her body, and threw all of his weight into his shoulders, waiting for her struggling to subside.

She was thumping him but her efforts were growing weaker. Aye was amazed at the amount of time she continued to fight. Three minutes passed, then four. Still Giludkhepa kept up her assault on his arms and shoulders. A hand found his face and pushed against it with surprising strength for one so weary, but his arms were longer than hers and he was able to keep up the pressure by simply tilting his head backwards.

Finally, her assault petered out and her arms grew weak and fell back onto the bed by her sides. Her fingers still twitched spasmodically and still Aye dared not lift his weight from the cushion. And then, just as he was about to lean backwards and remove the pressure, her arm shot out to the side in one last bid for escape and struck a vase containing flowers that was standing on a table by her bedside. Aye watched in horror as the vase rocked and tried to right itself before finally toppling, rolling across the tabletop and falling with a startling crash to the floor. Aye redoubled his efforts, cursing the woman he had pitied only moments before.

He heard a noise from behind the door that led to the wet-nurse's quarters. His head swivelled between the door and Giludkhepa's fingers, which were still occasionally spasming. He could not risk being caught here. He launched himself off the bed and ran for the door that led into Giludkhepa's day room, throwing the cushion back onto the couch where he had found it. As he moved the darkness of the room lifted slightly. He risked a glance behind him to see the dim yellow light of a lamp seeping from under the door to the wet-nurse's room.

Once into the day room he forced himself to close the door as slowly and quietly as he could. As it slid into place he heard the wet-nurse's door open.

"Your Highness?" the wet-nurse said, around a yawn. "Is everything all right? I heard a noise."

Aye walked through the dark day room towards the door that led back out into the corridor. He got as far as the junction before he heard the wet-nurse's scream, and then he could no longer prevent himself from breaking into a run.

Once back in his quarters, Aye waited for a long while, his hands resting on his knees, gasping for breath with fearful sobs, waiting for a knock at the door.

He was certain that the wet-nurse had not seen him. There had always been at least one door between them. But he was just as confident that Giludkhepa had glimpsed his face and known exactly who he was.

But was she alive or was she dead? Aye could not remember whether or not her fingers had still been twitching when he had heard the wet-nurse rousing and he had to jump from the bed. There was no question of going back to check. The room would already be full of physicians and maids and Aye could think of no creditable reason he could have for accidentally stumbling across her room at this time of night.

He tried to comfort himself with the thought that if she was still alive she would have identified him as her attacker and the guards would already have been hammering at his door. Unless, of course, he had left her unconscious and the physicians were merely waiting for her to regain her sensibilities. Aye had no doubt that his name would be the first word across her lips should she do so.

He briefly considered flight before dismissing the idea. There was nowhere to run, other than into some interminable exile where he would be reduced to scratching in the soil for a living. He preferred to take his chances here at the palace than sentence himself to such a fate. And what if Giludkhepa was dead? Other than the vase that she had knocked from the bedside table there was no sign of a violent end. Would the doctors not assume that her death was brought about by the extreme exhaustion and physical distress of her labour? Every third pregnancy seemed to result in the death of the mother or the child, so it could not be unfeasible to expect fatalities in both participants once in a while.

No, if Aye were to run it would seal his fate more than if he were to stay. There may yet be no case to answer, and if there is he may not even be a suspect. If he took to his heels every eye in the palace would follow him.

And so, when Ra freed himself from the grip of the underworld and vaulted through the barrier of the horizon he found Aye still awake, sitting in his apartment, tapping his feet nervously and watching the door as he awaited his fate.

Every footstep in the corridor outside the door thrilled him with fear, and as the room grew brighter those footsteps became increasingly frequent. He fully expected each one to terminate at his door and be followed by the rapping of a sword handle on the wood. But even so, when such an eventuality did indeed take place the insistent hammering startled him out of his wits. It was still too early for his servants to be in attendance, still too early for his wife and children to be out of bed, and so Aye answered the door himself, feeling a loneliness and trepidation almost beyond measure.

Chapter Seven

Veils and Riddles

AYE WAS surprised to see not an armed guard but a lone messenger at the door. The messenger had the look of one who has just recovered from a severe fright and Aye guessed it was the after effects of a summons to the king that had bled the colour from his complexion.

"My Lord," the messenger said, "His Majesty the king demands your urgent attendance in the throne room."

What little comfort Aye had gained from the sight of a messenger rather than a group of burly soldiers dissipated. The king did not request his attendance, he demanded it. And it was not in his quarters but in the throne room. Aye followed the messenger on weak legs, inwardly rehearsing his look of surprised horror at the unexpected news of Giludkhepa's death. If she was still alive and he was to be accused of her assault the expression would serve him just as well.

The pair stopped outside the throne room doors, which Aye watched intently as they opened, hoping to catch an early glimpse of the king in order to gauge his disposition. He inhaled deeply, as though to imbue himself with the room's ambience, and by that the humour of those within, but all he smelled was his own sweat. He stepped forwards.

Only now did he see that there was another man in the room. He was the overseer responsible for the palace's painting and decoration. Amenhotep was issuing orders, and the man was bowing almost at every word.

"Your artists will begin work immediately in my bedchamber," Amenhotep was saying. "I expect the work to be finished within the hour to allow the paint to dry. You will hear from me should I have to go to sleep with the stench of it."

"As you command, Your Majesty," the overseer said, bowing again.

Aye walked into the room and prostrated himself before the throne. The king did not look at him, but continued addressing the overseer.

"I wish the walls of my bedchamber to be covered with the hieroglyphs *ankh* and *sa*," Amenhotep said. "My priests will accompany you and chant the invocations as you work."

"As you command, Your Majesty."

Aye's nose was still pressed to the ground, but his ears were attentive to every word, wringing the hidden meanings from each one, probing each syllable for a clue as to his fate. If the king wanted those hieroglyphs on his wall, the first symbol meaning 'life' and the second 'protection' it meant he was in fear of his safety. If he was afraid it meant that there was a threat against him, which meant that he perhaps thought there was a killer loose in the palace. Aye felt despair and hope in equal measure. Despair that Amenhotep knew Giludkhepa and the child had been murdered, hope that the king would only feel the need for magical protection if he did not know who had perpetrated such an act.

"Aye," Amenhotep said. "Get up."

Aye stood.

"Giludkhepa and her child are dead," Amenhotep said.

For the briefest of moments Aye felt himself relax. He prayed that a look of relief had not been discernible on his face. He immediately employed the expression of shock and dismay that he had practised on the way, and then worried that it looked rehearsed and that in trying to look innocent he looked all the more guilty.

"Your Majesty, this is..." Aye began, but the king held up his hand for silence.

He turned to the overseer, who was still contorted in an awkward half-bow, unable to decide whether leaving without being explicitly commanded to do so would be impertinent.

"Why are you still here?" Amenhotep asked him. The overseer took this as the only command he required and backed hastily from the room, bowing all the while. Aye watched him leave before continuing.

"This is devastating news," he said. "How did they die?"

"It seems they were overcome with the protracted labour they had both endured."

Aye did not want to put ideas into the king's head, but he could not prevent himself from asking his next question when its answer could determine the length of his life.

"Are you sure that no foul play was involved?" he said.

"It seems not. There was not a mark on either of them. It was a difficult labour. It lasted twenty eight hours and I am informed that the child turned his head to the floor shortly after the birth. The priests tell me it is a sign of impending death."

Aye had not known that and did not know what to make of it. Did it mean the child was going to die anyway? That he need not have stained his soul with murder? Or was that stain now washed clean if he had only done so much as bring forward the child's death by a matter of days, or even hours? It made him feel better until he realised that the death the child foretold may have been the very one that was visited upon it. The thought terrified him. It somehow signified the involvement of the unseen, of the divine, and Aye did not want any of the gods even remotely involved in this sorry affair.

"Then," he said, "the fates were stacked against them, and they had no chance."

"Why must everyone I love be doomed to perish?" Amenhotep asked, suddenly. "Maiherperi, Tjenuna, Thutmose, Giludkhepa, Rahotep. Did you know, Aye? That I was going to name him Rahotep? It means *Ra is Satisfied*. I thought it would be apt."

Aye said nothing, for there was nothing he could say.

Amenhotep laughed mirthlessly, a derisive snort. "Perhaps *Ra is Angry* would have been better. Or *Ra Deserts His Friends*."

"You cannot blame Ra," Aye said. "I cannot imagine that this is his doing."

"Then who shall I blame? Amun? He wanted Rahotep to be named as my heir. You heard Ptahmose. He was most adamant on the subject. Why would Amun harm the child he had marked for the throne?"

"Sometimes babies just die, Majesty. And sometimes mothers too. You know how often it happens. It is the way of the world."

"It is the will of the gods," Amenhotep said. "Perhaps I have offended them. You should distance yourself from me. They may not have finished punishing me yet. It would perhaps be safer for everyone if I loved no more."

"I can do nothing but stay by your side, whatever the cost," Aye said. "I would die happy if I did so as your friend. Anyway, if the gods were punishing you they would take you, not those you loved."

"That would not hurt me enough."

"But you have done nothing to offend them. No king in the history of these lands has done as much for Amun as you have. The temples you have built to him cover half of Thebes or more. His church is more affluent now than it has ever been. He could not possibly be angry with you."

Amenhotep looked up, and Aye saw that his eyes were empty. They looked like the eyes painted on the lid of a sarcophagus, looking but not seeing.

"Perhaps that is the problem," he said.

"What?"

"That I have favoured Amun too highly. Perhaps Ra is jealous."

"Really, Majesty, I fail to see..."

"Think about it," Amenhotep said. "Nobody close to me died before I came to the throne, save my father, and he was old and sick. As soon as I wore the crown I began building to Amun, and my friends have been dying ever since."

"Your father rides with Ra through the heavens. Do you really think he is responsible for any harm that befalls you?"

"No," Amenhotep admitted. "Perhaps not. But who, then? Do I lay the blame for all that has befallen me at the feet of Amun? After all that I have done for him?"

"I think it more likely that there is nobody to blame, Majesty."

"Oh no, Aye. Someone is to blame. There have been too many deaths for mere coincidence. I shall have to give it some thought. Either Amun is punishing me for something I cannot understand, or he is unable to protect me against evil, despite all the offerings I have made him. Either way, his patronage does not seem to be of any use to me. His priest certainly does not seem to be my friend. Perhaps that is all the sign that I need."

Aye did not consider this to be a healthy topic for discussion. He felt touched by the divine through the child's prophecy of death and feared that one could not accuse the gods of such petty jealousies without paying a price.

"So who is to be king after you now that Rahotep is..." he did not want to use the word 'dead', and left the sentence unfinished.

"It must be Amenophis," Amenhotep said. "I am not overjoyed with the arrangement, but there is nobody else."

Aye bowed, and as he did so he took a long, deep breath. But that night his dreams took him back to that dark bedchamber, to the moment when he placed the cushion over the baby's face. Except that in his dream the baby's face was turned to the floor, and Aye felt his gaze drawn to shadows that ran like water into the corner of the room. He watched as those shadows coalesced into a solid form: that of a man with the swaying head of a cobra that flicked its tongue and hissed in Aye's direction. The form of Amun, watching, alert, and ready to strike.

A new change came over Amenhotep after the deaths of Giludkhepa and her child. It was as though he was beyond mourning. His very character had been ingrained with a grief that seemed immune to the consolations of time.

His dealings with Amenophis were brusque at best, although he recognised that the child had been thrust into this situation as much as he had himself and it was unfair to blame the boy. The two of them adopted the habit of taking long walks in the palace gardens under the glare of the sun. Amenophis was by now almost blind under the effects of even the slightest gloom and he found that he could concentrate more when the sun's rays helped to permeate his abiding fog, and the heavy scent of the flowers seemed to clear his head.

The prince was eager to learn but could not help but think that he was a constant source of displeasure to his father, who seemed short tempered whatever response Amenophis gave to his questions. For his part, Amenhotep fretted that he was not a good teacher. He could recognise the intelligence of his son and somehow sense the inspired thinking that lay dormant beneath that look of trepidation, but however the king coaxed him the prince would flounder and the correct answer would elude him. And the harder he grasped at it, the more elusive it became. The lessons took the form of Amenhotep describing at length some fictitious scenario at court which Amenophis, playing the king, would have to solve.

"A messenger arrives from Amurru," Amenhotep said. He was walking slowly with Amenophis at his side. "He tells you that the gifts you have sent his king have been deemed insufficient and demands a further one hundred talents of gold, or he will make war upon you. What do you do?"

"Send the gold?" Amenophis said.

"No."

"I declare war and march on Amurru."

"No, no, no," Amenhotep said, rubbing his index fingers against his temples and failing to keep the resignation from his voice. "Amenophis, please think before you answer. This is not a contest of speed. It is one of thought and deliberation and cunning. You cannot sprint with cunning. You can creep and you can stalk, but you cannot sprint."

"Yes, father," Amenophis said.

"The messenger has arrived from Amurru. He will have been travelling for a month or more. You will profit nothing by answering him so swiftly. If you feel you need more time you simply tell him so. But, and this is important, you do not allow him to know why you need more time. Mislead him. Confuse him. It will not harm you to allow him to think you are stalling while the army mobilises against his king."

Amenhotep paused to ensure that Amenophis was following the logic. The boy was attentive and bright eyed, but somewhat nervous.

"You realise," said the king, "that you are not mobilising the army. That you are only saying as much to gain the political advantage."

Amenophis nodded eagerly.

"Good boy. If you are to remember anything of our talks it is to be this: never rush towards war, for there are almost always alternatives that will achieve your ends easier, swifter, and with no loss of blood. Blood, my boy, outweighs even glory on the scales of history."

Amenophis nodded again, frowning too much in an effort to accentuate his concentration and the gravity of the subject.

"You have a lot to consider," Amenhotep said. "Is the king of Amurru bluffing? Does he have the strength of arms to attack? More importantly, does he believe he has such strength? What will be the consequences of paying him a tribute under duress? How will it affect your relationship with him?"

Amenhotep looked at his son again. "Are you following all this?" he asked. "It is important that you tell me if you are not."

"I think so," Amenophis said.

"So," Amenhotep said. "I am the ambassador from Amurru. Your Majesty, these gifts you make to my king are paltry. He has instructed me to inform you that should you not send him a further one hundred talents of gold forthwith his armies will march against your borders. What say you, Your Majesty?"

"I say wait outside while I have a think."

"Well... yes," Amenhotep said, hesitantly. "But you see, there are ways of wording these things. 'You bring grave matters indeed before my court, ambassador. Matters upon which I would be remiss not to deliberate. Please step outside a moment.' And then you make sure he is within earshot and the doors are still open when you command your vizier to fetch your generals. Do you see?"

The boy nodded again with the same eagerness he displayed to all Amenhotep's questions. The pair walked on in silence.

The messenger from Amenhotep found Anen at home with Iny.

Anen was rarely to be seen anywhere else. He tried not to venture into the temple whenever he could possibly avoid it. Since his unexpected meeting with Ptahmose it ceased to be a refuge and became instead a trap where the High Priest lurked behind every corner and every pillar. The rest of Amun's priests were hardly more welcoming. A bad air awaited him in the temple, an oppressive atmosphere grown fat and heavy on harsh glances and turned backs.

Only in Iny did Anen find any respite from loneliness. Iny had no career to pursue other than the one that awaited him in his home village. Iny made no secret to Anen of his disdain for the temple simply because he could see no disadvantage to himself in doing so when the alternative was a friendship with a friend of the king. As the weeks drew on, Anen and Iny became closer as the temple pushed them further away. They developed a private joke where they would greet each other, both in the company of others in the temple and on their own, with a silent, conspiratorial nod, as though they were the only members of a secret society. They spent much of their time in one or another of their houses.

When the message arrived Anen thought it was to recall him to Memphis and, Iny's companionship notwithstanding, he ushered the messenger in excitedly. When he read the letter he visibly sagged.

"What is it?" Iny asked.

"Tell the king his will shall be done," Anen said to the messenger, looking not at him but at the floor.

After the messenger had departed, Anen put his head in his hands. This was an unwelcome turn of events, and one that could not be further from a recall to Memphis. To make matters worse Anen could read Amenhotep's temper in the written word. He knew there was to be no questioning this, no requests for clarification.

"What is it?" Iny asked again.

"It is a message from the king."

Iny sighed in a way that he usually reserved as a response to instructions from the temple. "Do you know, I had guessed as much. I meant, what does it say? From the look on your face I can only surmise that it is an announcement of death. Possibly yours."

"I cannot tell you. But, yes, it is bad news." Anen unravelled the papyrus scroll again. It was creased from where it had been crushed within his fist.

"Ptahmose has outgrown himself," the note read. "He thinks himself my equal. From whence come his riches? You are my only ally in Thebes. Make some investigations. I need weapons against him."

"But how?" Anen whispered. "How?"

"How *what?*" Iny said in an exasperated tone.

After a sleepless night, Anen let himself out of the house. There was no need for Amenhotep to write of the urgency of Anen's mission. Urgency was couched in every word. There was nothing in its tone that would have allowed Anen the luxury of prevarication. He walked south, past the immense columns that guarded the temple's entrance. The smell of incense was thicker here, sickly sweet and catching the back of his throat. Head down, he pushed on. Chariots raced by him in both directions, their occupants shouting the occasional greeting to each other as they passed. There were no priests on the road. It was morning and they would all be occupied with the frenzy of cultic activity that took place at this time each day, all bowing or chanting or offering or sacrificing until even Amun himself must despair at the cacophony directed towards him. Anen doubted his absence would be noted, either by the god or his minions.

He was on the straight road that led to the temple of Luxor, which was still at a stage in its construction that made it difficult to tell whether it was half completed or a ruin. Workmen were hammering and shouting to each other high in the scaffold. It seemed that the entire city was enveloped within the sound of tool on stone. Off to his left lay the marketplace. The breeze brought him the occasional cries of its vendors.

He looked around. The residences hereabouts would be badly served by such a mundane description as 'house'. They were set far apart in their own grounds, shaded by trees, provided for by armies of servants. Here, somewhere, lay Ptahmose's home.

He continued further into the suburbs. Before long the roads grew broader and the houses larger, although they remained uniform enough to make it impossible to discern who lived where with any degree of certainty.

And then he saw it. He had turned a corner that opened up not onto another road, but a square. And within this square stood a mansion within its own walled garden. The walls of the grounds were so white they took the sunlight and bleached it before throwing it back out into the city. Anen squinted and shaded his eyes with his hand.

"Here we are," he muttered.

He walked across the square feeling peculiarly exposed. Over the walls to the grounds he could see, set well back, the roofs of buildings clustered around a centre with bushes and shrubs growing around their perimeters. He did not want to go to the gate for fear of meeting someone who would question his presence there. One or two chariots passed and Anen did his best to look inconspicuous. Once at the wall he surreptitiously glanced once more around the square and, seeing nobody there, threw himself upwards and pulled himself up so that his head poked over the parapet. The rough stone dug into his fingers and his arms began to tremble under the strain almost immediately and so he was able to afford himself only a few seconds grace in which to take in the view. Gardens separated him from the cluster of buildings in the centre of the grounds. A rectangular lake, in which lilies seemed to have been allowed to grow only at specific points which would be pleasing to the eye, ran most of the length of the gardens.

Anen let himself fall to the floor and rubbed his fingers. Here are riches, he thought. Perhaps riches more than even the High Priest of Amun had legitimate claim to. And yet he had nothing more than a scant glimpse upon which to base this accusation. He could not report this to the king, for the king would only ask for further details.

Anen could be confident in not meeting Ptahmose, who at this time would undoubtedly be at the temple with his acolytes, should he choose to take a closer look. There would be the matter of servants to take into consideration, and Anen prayed he would be able to formulate some fabrication to explain his presence should he be discovered.

He stood for long minutes, reluctant to make his first move into a powerful foe's lair, his mind a blank for fear of coming to a decision. Perhaps it would be safer to retreat. After all, this was already a significant step towards the completion of his mission. Amenhotep would surely not begrudge him some time to catch his breath before plunging headlong into danger? And yet, despite his own protestations, Anen knew that there would never be a better time. If he had already been seen by a servant there was no doubt that his presence here would be reported to Ptahmose and Anen would not be able to bring himself to try something this foolhardy knowing that the High Priest may have been forewarned.

He turned back to the wall and hoisted himself up once more, this time with the aim not just of peaking over it but of scaling it and dropping to the other side. For a few seconds his sandals could not find purchase in the stone and he found himself running on the spot, but just as he feared his grip was about to betray him he managed to launch himself upwards and over, but only after he scraped his knees on the top of the wall.

He dropped onto the grass, wincing and rubbing his knees as he searched the area for residents. He was almost disappointed to see none and so have no real excuse for withdrawing. He set off towards the back of the house before his fear could catch him and drag him, secretly joyful, back over the wall and into the street.

As he drew closer he realised that Ptahmose's home would be better described as a small village than a house. Outbuildings huddled around a central palace as though jealously guarding it from visitors such as Anen. He crouched beneath one or two windows, listening for occupants before risking a glimpse of the rooms beyond. They were mainly store rooms, piled high with linen or discarded furniture, or packed with huge pots whose contents Anen could not guess.

He moved closer to the main building via a narrow paved path lined with flowering plants, resisting the urge to break into a run. Before him was the main residence. The roof, which was all Anen could see over another wall which barred his way, was on two levels, both of which were flat, and both of which served as the stage for more decorative gardens. Anen once more felt the bite of rough stonework on his fingers as he hoisted himself over the wall. He could see that there were only one or two windows along the walls of the lower level but these were, at least, low enough for him to stand on tiptoes and peer through. There was a heavy wooden door to his left. It had about it an air of impregnability.

Anen crept forwards, aware of the scrape and crunch of every pebble beneath his feet on the flagstones. As he approached the windows he could see already that they would give him no worthwhile view. The shapes within revealed nothing but more store rooms. The evidence he sought lay on the other side of the rooms' internal doors.

He was unsure as to the advisability of continuing. Ptahmose was a powerful and quick tempered man who would not take kindly to an imposition of this sort. It was not beyond the bounds of possibility that he would react to Anen's investigations in an uncompromising manner. Especially if, as Anen suspected, he had hidden in this house such riches as would make Amun himself blush. Such monies could come only from the temple itself, and could only do so via a road of subterfuge and dishonesty that robbed gold directly from the hand of the king. Ptahmose would undoubtedly be at pains to prevent the discovery of such a diversion and Anen could, should Ptahmose so wish it, simply disappear. There were plenty of hidden places in the desert hills around Thebes where a body could lay undiscovered forever.

And yet Anen had his duty to consider. This was a task handed down to him by the king himself, and it was one that could not be shirked, whatever risks it may entail. And would Ptahmose really be so bold as to end the life of a man appointed to the temple by the king? Quite possibly, Anen thought, should he believe he is able to do so without fear of discovery.

Grasping his courage as one would a wayward child, he turned, reached up to the window ledge and pulled himself up. To open the internal door the merest crack and to peer through to the living quarters beyond would be the work of moments. He could be in and out in the time it took a weaker man to pluck up the resolve to continue. He was halfway there, resting his belly against the parapet, his body inside and his legs scrabbling for purchase outside, when he heard a voice from behind. It was an authoritative voice, but one cracking under a weight of years.

"You know," said the voice, "entrance via the door would be the more, shall we say, *customary* route."

"Try another one," the king said to Amenophis. "Despite your best efforts, the king of Amurru continues to talk of war. You are attempting to diffuse the situation. This time I am the High Priest of Amun. I have just arrived from Thebes and marched into your throne room."

Before continuing, Amenhotep reached forward and pulled a leg from the half eaten chicken carcass on the table at which they sat. Amenophis could not take his eyes from Amenhotep's chin, which was shiny with grease. He had been eating constantly since the boy had arrived in his quarters an hour and a half earlier. Before taking a bite he offered it to his son, who shook his head.

"Are you sure?" Amenhotep said. "They really are very good, you know."

Amenophis took the proffered leg, not because he was hungry but because he felt that it would somehow be an act of solidarity. Amenhotep ripped the remaining leg from the bird.

"Now," Amenhotep said, through a mouthful of food, "I believe Your Majesty is about to go to war."

Amenophis looked up from his food, momentarily surprised until he remembered that this was all part of the lesson.

"I might be," he said.

"You might be? But surely there is no other option. Would you allow this upstart dictate your policy without retribution? Not only is Egypt's freedom at stake, but her honour also."

"Well..." Amenophis said.

"Well, Your Majesty? Well? Will you allow the land of Amun to fall under the influence of her neighbours? I must inform Your Majesty that Amun will not look kindly on the subjugation of his people."

"I am king..." Amenophis began.

Amenhotep decided to see just how much insubordination and impertinence Amenophis would be prepared to allow.

"If you are king, then act like one," he said. "I serve Amun, a higher power than all the thrones of Egypt. And Amun demands war, not cowardice. What say you, Your Majesty?"

Amenophis took a deep breath. He did not enjoy these lessons. He had no idea what the correct answer would be. He had learned so far that there were usually two routes the king could take. He could appease or he could crush. Amenophis consistently seemed to choose the wrong one.

"I would remind you that I am your pharaoh," he said.

"...yes..." Amenhotep said, the word drawn out to encourage the boy to continue.

"And that the responsibility for decisions such as this rests solely with me, not the temple of Amun."

"...good..."

"I do not appreciate your efforts to control my decisions, but if, as you say, Amun commands me to protect his people then I am not at liberty to disobey such an order, and..."

"No!" Amenhotep said, and threw the bones of the chicken leg back onto the table in frustration. "No, no, no. Amenophis, what have I told you about the temple of Amun? It is a manipulative institution. Why is the High Priest so adamant that you go to war?"

"To protect the people?"

"Not a bit of it," Amenhotep said. "For one reason, and one reason only. War brings booty. Booty that the High Priest will attempt to commandeer the very moment it crosses our border. Amun craves gold for his temples, when the foundations of those temples already creak with the weight of the stuff that is piled within them. You must never give in to the High Priest in his demands for war, or for that matter in his demands for anything else. He is motivated by one thing. Do you understand?"

Amenophis nodded.

"I confess I am worried, Amenophis, by your lack of backbone. I am sorry, but there is no easier way of phrasing it. Remember that you will be king. Remember this above all else. You will have been appointed by the gods themselves. Nobody, not even the High Priest of the king of the gods, may talk to you without the proper respect and deference. If he spoke to you as I have just done, you should destroy him. He should leave your company a broken man. You must have authority. You must prove to me that you have the strength for this."

"Yes, father."

"Do you have the strength?"

Amenophis said nothing and stared at the floor. Amenhotep relented. Amenophis seemed so despondent that the king could not stay angry with him. He could not deny that the boy was attentive and eager. It was not his fault that he was not yet equal to the task with which he had been charged.

"Listen," Amenhotep said. "You are doing very well. Every day is an improvement. For a moment there I really thought you had it. Do not be downcast. We will make a king of you yet."

Smiling, he reached forward and with a finger lifted the boy's chin from his chest.

"I did not mean to be angry with you," he said.

Amenophis smiled back and wiped his eyes with the back of his hand.

"Now run along," Amenhotep said. "Return in the morning and we will continue."

"Yes, father."

Despite the setbacks that the relationship with his father took, Amenophis was a happier child than he had been at any time during his schooling. Although he was aware of his father's disappointment in him he was also aware that success seemed to be imminently within his grasp, and while it evaded him he always had the consolation of the king's sympathy.

Free from the tyranny of the classroom he was able to relax, and in so doing grow more confident with every passing day. He would still occasionally see his classmates but he no longer dreaded such meetings. He would even go so far as to actively seek out Nefertiti whenever he could do so without fostering rumours of romance. It helped him immeasurably to know that Nakhtmin had joined the army and was now rarely to be seen within the confines of the palace, and when he was he was usually in the company of a fellow new recruit, a wide-eyed young man who went by the name of Horemheb. Horemheb was somewhat overawed by the experience of being in the palace, where he may turn a corner at any moment to find himself face to face with the king himself.

Nakhtmin obviously enjoyed having a protégé around. Walking the corridors with Horemheb, he would casually point out rooms and statues of interest, and he would greet with easy familiarity those he hardly knew, who would reply out of politeness and then continue on their way. Horemheb thought him exceptionally popular.

Amenophis was leaving his father's quarters, inwardly berating himself for his lack of strength and his unerring ability to choose the wrong answer, and yet clinging to his father's simple act of kindness, when Nakhtmin and Horemheb rounded the corner. They were there specifically so Nakhtmin could nonchalantly wave his hand towards Amenhotep's door and say "oh, and this is where the king lives" as though it was a matter of little import for one so well placed in the society of court.

The three stopped dead facing each other at arm's length and for a moment nobody spoke. His poor eyesight had prevented Amenophis from recognising Nakhtmin until the last possible moment when it was too late to find an excuse to turn tail and disappear in the opposite direction. Horemheb looked from Nakhtmin to Amenophis and back again, wondering if he was to be introduced. Nakhtmin and Amenophis, meanwhile, eyed each other with mutual nervousness. Nakhtmin would never have treated the prince as he had in school had he known the stratum that Amenophis was to occupy. One did not mock the heir to the throne. Nakhtmin was still unsure as to the eventual ramifications of his actions and whether there was any attitude he could adopt that would undo what had been said.

For his part, Amenophis was still stinging from the lashes of Nakhtmin's laughter. He feared not what Nakhtmin may say, but that Amenophis may not find a reply disdainful and bellicose enough to do justice to the words of a future king. He was still aware of his shortcomings, and was repeatedly made more so by the exasperated tone that Amenhotep tried to disguise as he explained yet again why Amenophis' latest answer was wrong. Amenophis yearned for the opportunity to display the qualities that his father was desperately trying to instil in him. And now perhaps here was such an opportunity. His father was not here to see it but he would hear of it. It would make him proud at last.

He tried to recall all the advice given to him by his father, all the phrases handed down to him that must make up a king's vocabulary. The knowledge that he was descended from the sun god himself, that these people were his subjects in waiting. He pictured himself not standing in a corridor looking up to a young man taller than himself, but sitting upon his throne, looking down with the strength of a thousand kings in his stare.

Nakhtmin was the first to gather his wits. He could perhaps salvage something from this meeting. Horemheb would at least witness him in conversation with the heir to the throne.

"Ah, Amenophis," he said. "It is good to see you again."

The old Amenophis would have demurely responded in the positive. The new Amenophis, with the wisdom of his father reverberating around his head and with a tremor in his voice that he hoped would be interpreted as barely contained rage rather than fear, said: "You may refer to me as Your Royal Highness. And do you not bow to your future king?"

Nakhtmin was visibly surprised. He eventually bowed as though he had calculated exactly how much he had to move in order to convey the minimum amount of respect that decorum dictated. Amenophis did not wait for him to rise before walking away. He was shaking, his breathing shallow and quick, his knees hardly holding the strength to keep him on his feet. He needed to escape before Nakhtmin could reply, and before he himself could say something to betray his fear. He had amazed himself. But he felt good. He felt very, very good.

"Tiye tells me that Amenhotep is worried about Amenophis," Thuya said. "He feels the boy may not be up to the role he has been allotted."

"Really?" Aye said. "And what would you have me do about it? Perhaps you would like me to kill again?"

"Kill? Who would you kill?"

Aye shrugged. "Anyone you like, mother. Amenhotep himself, perhaps? Is he becoming troublesome for you? Would you like him removing?"

"I am your mother, Aye. Do not take that tone with me. We have discussed this before. You did what you had to do."

Aye knew she was right, but it did not make the feeling any easier to bear. He thought that if he had murdered Giludkhepa alone he could have dealt with the emotional aftermath. It was the child who haunted his dreams. The child and Amun, the snake headed god, coalesced from shadows made flesh, always to be seen out of the corner of the dream's eye. But ultimately, Egypt had to come first. The needs of the Two Lands would always outweigh those of the individual and Aye would expect harder sacrifices from anyone else. It was hypocritical to resent it in himself.

He looked out over the choppy waters of the Nile. Mother and son had met again on the road running parallel to the river where they had decided that Giludkhepa had to die. It was early morning and the sun was struggling to wring the chill from the air. Already, one or two boats could be seen leaving the harbour, buoyant enough to seem excited at the shedding of their cargoes. Only the rumours of sounds from the docks reached Thuya and Aye at this distance.

"I apologise," Aye said. "I am not myself."

"So it would seem."

"What does it matter if the king is worried about Amenophis? He is heir to the throne now. Our work is done, is it not?"

"Our work is not done until the crown sits atop his head. If we have learned anything it is that plans may go awry when least expected."

"And so what are we to do?"

"Amenophis must be crowned king."

"Amenhotep is the king."

"True," Thuya said. "But there is a precedent, is there not, for the heir to the throne to be crowned as coregent while the king is still on the throne?"

"There is, but never in a case such as this. Amenophis is simply not ready to assume a position of such heavy responsibility. He would be a liability."

"Precisely. That is exactly why he must be given the opportunity."

"I do not follow."

"He must be made coregent before his deficiencies are fully appreciated by those who would oppose him. And now is the perfect opportunity to persuade the king of the merit of this appointment. What better way would there be for Amenophis to learn the ways of government? It will be trial by fire, but the boy can only come out of it the stronger."

"If he is to be coregent he will need to be found a wife," Aye said. "Have you any thoughts on this?"

"He has plenty of sisters. I am sure that will not pose a problem."

Aye looked crestfallen and Thuya laughed.

"Oh, my dear, do not look so glum. I am teasing you. Amenophis will marry Nefertiti. Although I am sure that she will be less than overjoyed to hear the news."

"That is no concern of mine. If she marries the king she will grow to be overjoyed, and she will thank me in the end."

"Possibly," Thuya said. "Although marriage to that dunce will not be easy for her."

"Have you spoken to Tiye and my father with regards to this?"

"They are both in agreement."

"Then why have you brought me here? Not merely for the fresh air, I presume."

"I wanted to speak to you privately. It seems to me that the Giludkhepa affair has affected you more strongly than you admit."

"I killed..." Aye said, and then stopped to check that nobody had wandered into earshot. "I killed a baby. Would you have me forget that it ever happened?"

"On the contrary. I would have you remember it forever, for then you would not forget why it was an unavoidable consequence of the situation. I would have you remember exactly what you have done in service of your country, and I would have you remember what your country may ask you to do, without question and without comment. For if you do not accept what is required of you there is no sense in you even trying to help me, for your lack of commitment will be nothing but a hindrance."

Aye said nothing. On the dockside workmen were struggling under the weight of the loads they carried from the ships. Thuya nodded towards them.

"They do not care who has been killed and who allowed to live. All they care about is the food in their stomachs and the safety and happiness of their families. It is within your power to grant them peace of mind. Would you begrudge them that? They are relying on you, whether they know as much or not. Will you forsake that power?"

Aye shook his head. "No," he whispered.

"Would you?" Thuya said.

"No," he said again, louder this time. "I understand."

"See that you do," Thuya said. "And see that the picture of that child never leaves your mind. That child's face encompasses everything that you hold to be dear and true."

Aye kicked at a stone and watched it skitter into the grass at the side of the road.

"Now," Thuya said. "Do you think it is safe for you to accompany me back to my house? We should talk of other things. We never just talk any more."

"Of course, mother," Aye said.

Amenophis was looking in the mirror, lamenting the fact that he would never see his own features again. The mirror was the work of some of the greatest craftsmen in the Two Lands and offered an unrivalled clarity of image, but all Amenophis saw was an anonymous figure outlined against the white walls behind him. Today it was his shape that concerned him.

His features, he knew, were normal, or at least as normal as they could be expected to be in a head the shape of this one. But as for the rest of him…

"I look like a woman," he muttered to himself, turning this way and that in order to gain a more rounded perspective. His hips had swollen out to become a shape that could only be described as curvaceous. It was a word that did not sit well in the description of a young man. His torso was so thin as to show his ribs and the hollow directly beneath them but then jutted out into a belly the shape of an upturned bowl. He tugged his kilt up to try to hide it but it became uncomfortably tight and only accentuated the convexity of his shape.

"A pregnant one at that," he said.

He pulled the hem of the kilt up to look at his legs. Like the rest of him, they defied proportion. His thighs were fat enough to chafe when he walked any distance in hot weather and forced his thin calves apart to such a distance they looked as though they were barely on speaking terms. His elongated toes made his feet look like those of a bird.

He let the hem of the kilt fall back into place and leant forwards until his forehead was resting against the mirror.

This was why he could not command the respect of those who owed it to him. This was why his classmates had ridiculed him and why, he felt sure, they ridiculed him still. How could any air of authority be expected to force its way through the image of a man in a woman's body? It had felt too good when he had forced Nakhtmin to bow to him for him to allow the opportunity of further bows to pass ungrasped. He was owed not only the respect but the happiness.

"They must bow to me," he said to himself. "And if they will not bow to my body then they must bow to my mind. If they laugh at my weakness then I must be strong, and if they laugh at my strength I must be stronger still. Until they dare not laugh at me. Until they can do naught but bow."

He pushed himself off the mirror and again stared at the muddy reflection of himself staring back. He took a deep breath and tried to imbue his chest with some semblance of solidity.

"They will bow," he said. "They will."

A knock came at the door and shattered his reverie. He opened it to find a messenger waiting in the corridor.

"His Majesty requests Your Royal Highness' presence in his quarters," the messenger said.

"But why? My lessons are over for today."

"I know not, sir."

Amenophis tried not to notice how the messenger stared at his feet as he struggled to slip his wayward toes into his sandals.

"Thank you," Amenophis said to him. "That will be all."

The messenger bowed and retreated.

As Amenophis walked the familiar corridors to the royal chambers he tried to imagine why his father had asked to see him at this relatively late hour. His father never asked to see him unless it was with regard to his lessons.

When he arrived he found both his parents awaiting him.

"Ah, Amenophis," his father said. "Come in. Sit down."

He did so nervously. Tiye smiled at him but it did little to ease his mind. It was a smile that could have been designed to put him at his ease before giving him bad news.

"Have I done something wrong?" Amenophis asked.

"I have been talking with your mother," Amenhotep said. "Well, actually, I have only been listening to your mother, but I have been doing so at great length."

Tiye gave Amenhotep a stern look, but the comment had been made only half-seriously and Amenhotep patted her knee and smiled before continuing.

"She feels that it is time you took a great step. I have to confess that I am not convinced, but she has assured me that it will be the making of you. I am fervently hoping that you will prove me wrong."

Tiye looked at her husband and coughed pointedly. Amenhotep glanced at her.

"In fact," he said. "I am sure you will. I am sure you are a very capable young man. I have been told that you will relish the challenge."

Amenophis looked from his father to his mother and back again. He had no idea what Amenhotep was talking about, but whatever it was sounded worrying. He was sure that he was not going to like this at all.

"Amenophis," Tiye said. "What your father is trying to say is that you are to be made coregent alongside him. It is time you tasted the ways of kingship first hand."

"You will still be subservient to me," Amenhotep said.

"Of course," Tiye said.

"You will still attend your lessons as you have been doing. You still have a lot to learn. I do not want this news going to your head. It is little more than a title. Up to now you have been the king in waiting. Now you will be the king. That is all the difference."

"Husband," Tiye said. "Do not destroy the moment for him. I am sure he understands the limits of his appointment, and I am equally sure that he possesses the wisdom to curtail the power that you have granted to him. But for now, let him have his moment. He has had so little in life. He has just been made king."

Amenophis simply stared.

"Look at his face," Tiye said, smiling. "He barely knows what to do with himself."

He hardly heard her. He had been made coregent. He was a king. This was infinitely worse news than he could possibly have imagined. How could he, a boy who squinted into the mirror and fretted over his woman's hips, possibly be made king? People would not respect him yet. He needed time to build his character, to earn the fealty of his subjects. He needed to plan. He felt as though he had been thrown into the Nile in order to learn how to swim.

"I cannot do this," he said, quietly. "I am not ready."

Amenhotep began to speak, but Tiye interjected. "Nonsense. That is what your father thought when he came to the throne, and look at him now. He was ready because he had to be, and it will be no different with you."

Amenhotep closed his mouth again.

"Mother, I..."

"Now," Tiye continued. "We need to make some arrangements. You will look back on this as the happiest day of your life. We cannot let it pass without commemoration. It is about time we had something to celebrate again. I shall command Huya to make the necessary preparations. Come along."

Tiye stood up and took Amenophis by the hand, almost dragging him to his feet, before marching him to the door. Before he crossed the threshold, the coregent had time to glance back at his father, who was watching his egress with a look approaching that of sadness on his face.

Their eyes met momentarily, and Amenhotep nodded slowly to his son.

"I know," he whispered, loud enough for just Amenophis to hear. And then the boy was gone, tugged through the doorway by his mother.

In years to come Amenophis would look back on that moment with a peculiar fondness, for in his father's sadness there was a moment of unprecedented empathy. It would never happen again.

Chapter Eight

A Beautiful Woman Has Come

"Do you think me a fool, Anen?" Ptahmose said.

Anen shook his head, too afraid of betrayal by a quivering voice to speak out loud. The pair were sitting on sumptuous chairs in Ptahmose's living quarters. Servants bustled around them with bowls laden with a dozen different dishes. After every sip of his wine an acolyte would refill Ptahmose's cup.

"But you obviously do," Ptahmose continued, "for if you did not, you would not think me foolish enough to leave whatever it is you are looking for unguarded in my home."

"I do not think you a fool," Anen said, quietly.

"Well, my dear chap, one of us must be," Ptahmose said. He turned to the servants who were ladling various dishes into the empty bowls arranged on the table. "Thank you," he said. "You may leave everything here. We will take our pick. I am sure Anen is ravenous after his exertions."

The servants glided from the room and left the two men alone.

"Please," Ptahmose said, indicating the food. "Help yourself."

Anen had no appetite, but he felt compelled to nibble on one or two morsels.

"So," Ptahmose said, waving a goose drumstick around to indicate the room in which they sat. "Have you found what you were looking for?"

Anen looked around him. The room was richly decorated. Expensively made and finely woven drapes covered almost every available surface, their verdant colours giving the place a healthy glow of its own. The plaster on the walls was painted with religious scenes. Over by the door through which they had entered stood a large delicately painted bust showing Ptahmose in his priestly headgear. It was a room of exquisite taste and luxury that few outside the royal household could have envisioned.

"Possibly," Anen said.

"So you do not deny you were looking for something?"

"I would not insult your intelligence."

"Very wise," Ptahmose said. "And you do not deny that you are here under the king's bidding?"

While there was little point in pretending that he was here for any other than the real reason, Anen had to be careful not to divulge too much information. Having been so clumsy and ineffectual in pursuing the mission that Amenhotep had given him, he could at least limit the damage he had done.

"My motives are my own," he said.

"I see," Ptahmose said. "I hope you will forgive me if I do not believe you. It is just that I presumed you would be keen to bring the king's name into this. You are an intruder in the house of the High Priest of Amun. Some people would assume that you are only here to perpetrate some crime against my person."

Anen started to protest, but Ptahmose signalled for him to be quiet.

"I did not say that I believed such a thing," he said. "But most people would disagree with me. Think about it, Anen. You do know what I could have done to you, do you not? You do realise how, shall we say, *unpleasant* it would be?"

Anen did not doubt for a second that Ptahmose was capable of the worst type of cruelty. The type of cruelty that issues orders to others and then turns its back to save itself the gruesome details.

"Now," Ptahmose said. "Are you here under the king's orders?"

"No," Anen said, without giving himself the time to consider the consequences of his reply.

"Some would think you brave for your stubbornness," Ptahmose said. "I think you foolhardy. You see, I know why you are here. Or, rather, I know why you are not. I know you are not here of your own volition. What possible motive could you have? There is nothing here that will profit you. And, of course, there is the question of why you are in Thebes in the first place. You are not a religious man, Anen. I know. I have checked. The first time you have been known to show any interest in the priesthood was the day you arrived off the boat. You are not here for yourself. So for whom?"

Ptahmose paused and awaited an answer. When none was forthcoming, he continued irrespectively, as though he was prompting a child at school.

"You are here for the king," he said.

Anen remained silent.

"The king would like to know how much of a threat I am towards him," Ptahmose continued. "He does not think that he needs to be loyal towards the god of Thebes, and he thinks that I, the god's High Priest, take exception to that. And he is right."

Anen was trying his best to remain inscrutable but Ptahmose must have registered some look of surprise.

"Oh yes," he said. "He is right. I take great exception to it. Should I stand by and allow anyone – even the pharaoh – to bring Egypt to ruin? How could I possibly not oppose the naming of Amenophis as heir? The boy is obviously a simpleton. You only need to take one look at the shape of his head to know it. The gods are slowly transforming him into an ass to prove the point. It is the clearest of signs, Anen, and one which I cannot ignore, even if the rest of Egypt can. If the boy is weak minded, which he surely is, then he will not have the strength of purpose to rule these Two Lands in the manner they deserve and demand. He will have been moulded to the shape of his father, who, we should not forget, is a man already reluctant to defend our borders against those who would threaten them. It will be weakness upon weakness. I have thought long and hard on the matter and I cannot foresee any other outcome than disaster, the impoverishment of the temples, and the end of everything we hold dear. My conclusions do not please me, Anen, and the actions I must take to prevent such calamity please me even less, although I dare say you would think otherwise. But I take comfort in the thought that I am guided by Amun himself, and he has made his views quite clear on the subject. He does not wish to be a pauper's god."

Anen knew that he should speak in Amenophis' defence, but he could not force himself to form the words. He should warn the priest that the king would hear of such treachery but the beating of his heart compelled him to silence. Ptahmose had already indicated the fate that could befall Anen should Ptahmose so command it. It would be unwise to risk angering him further.

As if he was reading Anen's thoughts, Ptahmose said: "Say you nothing on the matter? Will you not be on the next boat to Memphis to repeat my words to the king?"

"No," Anen said, hating himself for his cowardice. "My place is in Thebes, at the temple. I have no call to return to Memphis."

"I find that as unbelievable as all your other denials. However, before you leave and head straight for the river I would like to make you a proposition. I would like you to help me. Upon your return to Memphis I would like you to be my eyes and ears at court. I would like you to tell me if there are any, shall we say, *developments.*"

Anen was flabbergasted.

"You expect me to betray the king?" he said.

"It is not a betrayal, Anen. To do nothing would be a betrayal of Egypt."

Anen needed time to think. What would Ptahmose do to him if he refused? To stand by his king would be the honourable thing to do, but

Anen doubted his honour would be as valuable to him once he was in the hands of the priest's enthusiastic policemen. It would perhaps be more prudent to accept now, and once safely out of Ptahmose's clutches, tell the king all.

"It seems I have no choice," he said. "I will do it."

Ptahmose laughed. "I doubt you are really so eager to please," he said. "Yes, you will do it, but not because you want to. Did you know, Anen, that I have had dealings with your family before? I recall a conversation I had with your father, just before the battle of Napata. It was before your time, but this was the battle that saw the end of two of the king's closest friends."

"I have heard of it," Anen said.

"Have you really?" Ptahmose said. "Excellent. Then perhaps your father has spoken of his role in bringing it about? The king was most opposed to it at the time. I am sure he would be fascinated to hear of Yuya's involvement. Quite fascinated. I remember your father being quite enthusiastic in his secret dealings to force the king into a war he did not want."

"I do not believe you."

Ptahmose shrugged. "Ask him," he said. "It was probably not exactly how I describe it, but it will be a simple matter to persuade the king of the verity of whatever scenario I choose."

"Then I really do have no choice?" Anen said.

"None whatsoever. Not if you care for your father's, shall we say, *well-being.*"

Anen stood up. He was visibly shaking, and close to tears. How had such a thing come to pass? He was to betray the king or he was to betray his father. Neither choice seemed possible.

"I need to think," he stammered, moving towards the door.

"Shall I take it that you will be in touch?" Ptahmose asked.

Anen nodded and Ptahmose broke into a broad smile.

"*Excellent,*" he said.

Amenophis was more nervous now than he had ever been running the gauntlet of mockery from his classmates. He paced the floor from doorway to window, from shade to sunlight and back again, continuously wringing his hands as though to wash the sweat of fear from them. He estimated that the messenger had been gone for eight or ten minutes, which meant that Nefertiti's arrival was imminent. His mind was awash with contradictory feelings. He had asked his father to be able to break the news to her himself but his father had shaken his head and told him that there were certain procedures that needed to be followed in these circumstances. So Nefertiti already knew that she was to be married to him upon his coronation.

This was good and bad. He would liked to have told her himself. He felt it was somehow the honourable thing to do. But then, of course, there would be the matter of how to broach the subject, and how to make his proposal sound less like an order. And what if she were to say no? At least he was spared that fear.

But now there was no small talk to hide behind. As soon as the door opened he would be face to face with his betrothed, and he found that thought the most terrifying of all. He expected that they would face each other in an embarrassing silence, neither knowing the correct words to breach their awkwardness. His face flushed at the prospect and he tried to remember his father's words of encouragement.

"She will be honoured," Amenhotep had said. "How else could any woman be when told she is to be the king's Great Royal Wife? She will throw herself into your arms and weep tears of gratitude and joy."

Amenophis winced at the idea. He doubted he had the strength to hold himself on his feet if she took it into her head to do such a thing.

"Anyway," Amenhotep had said. "I hear from your mother that Nefertiti is in love with you. Perhaps she has been lying awake for long nights, just dreaming of this news."

Amenophis doubted it. It was true that Nefertiti had shown him kindness, but he found it far easier to imagine that she would walk into his quarters with a look of disgust on her face and take a nervous pace away from him should he try to approach her.

His pacing took him by the mirror and he caught a glance of his shape as he walked past. He shuddered and briefly thought about hiding behind the bed. She would see the room was empty and leave and then he could go and see his father and explain just what a terrible idea this betrothal was.

Before he could give the idea any serious consideration the door opened. The messenger took a step into the room and bowed.

"Your Royal Highness," he said. "Nefertiti, daughter of Aye, has answered your summons."

"Thank you," Amenophis said. "That will be all."

The messenger stepped out of the room and there, nervously playing with the hem of her robe, was Nefertiti. She was not smiling, but there was no malice in her gaze, only wonderment.

"It was not a summons," Amenophis said to her. "It was an invitation."

Nefertiti smiled but said nothing. There was a moment of silence during which Amenophis trawled his mind for suitable subjects for conversation before he remembered that she was still standing on the threshold.

"Please," he said, too loudly. "Please come in."

"Thank you." She took a step forwards.

"Sit down," Amenophis said, and then worried that it sounded like a command. "If you like," he added, indicating a chair. Nefertiti sat and Amenophis realised that the nearest chair, a heavily ornate affair, was pushed against the opposite wall. He dragged it across the floor, its feet juddering and squealing against the tiles, and then, sweating with the exertion, took his seat opposite her.

"So," he said, as his breathing slowed.

Nefertiti raised her eyebrows. "So," she said.

"I take it you have heard the news," he said, after a moment.

"That we are to be married? Yes, my father told me."

"And what..." Amenophis said. "I mean, do you have..." He stopped and rubbed his temples. "How do you view the matter?" he said, finally.

Nefertiti laughed. "How do I view the matter? I am happy, of course."

"Are you really?"

"Of course," she said again. "I like you. You will be king."

"You like me because I will be king?"

"No, Amenophis. I like you *and* you will be king."

Amenophis nodded slowly. "Well, I like you as well," he said, and not only because he felt he ought to. He suddenly became aware that he was staring and he tried to focus on a point over her shoulder.

"That..." he said, and stopped. He seemed unable to martial his thoughts into any sort of coherent order. "Nefertiti," he said. "That is a pretty name."

"Thank you."

"What does it mean?"

It was Nefertiti's turn to feel embarrassed. "It means 'A Beautiful Woman has Come'," she said, hugging her knees and demurely looking away. "It flatters me."

"Not at all, not at all. I think it is a very apt name."

"Thank you," she said again, giggling.

"Really," he said. "I do. I think you are beautiful. Too beautiful for me, at any rate."

"You are very handsome," Nefertiti said. "I have told you so before. Those who disagree with me cannot see it. It is a failing of theirs, not of yours."

"So you have heard them discussing me, then?"

Nefertiti shrugged. "They mention you occasionally, although I am sure it is not as rife as you believe."

"Did your brother mention that we saw each other?"

"He mentioned that you humbled him. I think he was quite surprised. His young friend Horemheb was shaking with fear by the time they returned to my parents' apartments."

"With fear?"

"Of course with fear. Horemheb is nothing more than a recruit in the army. He had never even seen the palace before he met Nakhtmin."

"I was not shouting at Horemheb."

"Nevertheless," Nefertiti said.

Shortly after being told by her father of the plans to marry her to Amenophis, Thuya had taken Nefertiti to one side during one of the old lady's rare visits to Aye's apartments.

"We never see enough of each other as it is," she had said. "Now you are to be the Great Royal Wife, I imagine there will be even less time for me to enjoy your company. Visit me tomorrow morning. Come alone. This may be the last chance we get to have a good old heart to heart."

Thuya had not waited for Nefertiti to accept and so had not seen the look of surprise in her granddaughter's face. Thuya had never before so much as acknowledged her existence with anything more enthusiastic than a stern nod as they passed in a corridor. The following morning, Nefertiti, almost as nervous as she would be when meeting Amenophis for the first time as his fiancée, was welcomed effusively into Thuya's private quarters.

"So," Thuya said, cupping Nefertiti's chin in her hand. "My favourite granddaughter is all grown up and is to be married to the king. Who would have thought it? Come. Sit down and tell me all about it."

Nefertiti explained how it had come about: that Amenhotep himself had requested the marriage.

"Splendid!" Thuya said. "This is a great honour for you and your family, you know. It is a singular opportunity for you to serve your country."

"And my king," Nefertiti reminded her.

"Of course," Thuya said. "But surely your king and your country are the same thing?"

Nefertiti nodded.

"What do you think of Amenophis?" Thuya asked.

"I like him," Nefertiti said, and Thuya looked momentarily surprised.

"Really?" she said. "Well, that is a bonus. Do you not find him a little peculiar?"

"In what respect?"

"In his appearance. And in his manner also. Do you not think him a little weak?"

Nefertiti tried to understand what her grandmother was driving at. "Weak?" she said.

"Weak," Thuya said again. "Ineffectual. Uninspiring."

"It has not occurred to me," Nefertiti said.

"It has to me," Thuya replied. "He strikes me as a man who would need the help of a strong woman. Are you a strong woman, Nefertiti?"

"I am not sure," Nefertiti said.

"But of course you are. And that is why you have the opportunity to do so much good. Let me take an example. Did your father tell you about Amenophis trying to assert his authority over Nakhtmin?"

"Nakhtmin told me."

"Then I assume he told you how comical he found the whole experience?"

"He said he was embarrassed because Horemheb was there, but that it was like being shouted at by a mouse."

"And yet a king needs his authority. How do you think Amenophis would feel should he discover that Nakhtmin found his attempts at authority laughable?"

Nefertiti shrugged.

"He would be understandably mortified," Thuya said. "There are already those who would oppose Amenophis' accession to the throne. Should he lose his confidence at this early stage it will make their opposition all the easier. And so here you are, not even married, and yet you are being asked to perform your first duty to the king."

"What are you asking me to do?"

"My dear," Thuya said. "*I* am not asking you to do anything. History is asking you. Your country is asking you. A mere exaggeration. Not even a lie. All you need to do is let Amenophis believe that his confrontation with Nakhtmin had the desired effect. Nakhtmin was humbled by it. Amenophis taught him a lesson in respect and authority. Imagine what it will do to his confidence, to his ability to rule these Two Lands with the skill and judgement that they require. Imagine the service you will be doing him and your country."

Nefertiti left Thuya's house that day believing that she had learned an important lesson. She did desire to serve her king and her country, and it seemed that to serve one was to serve the other, that to strengthen one against its foes was to deliver the other, that to nurture one was to cherish the other.

And so, when she told Amenophis that Nakhtmin had been humbled by his encounter with the prince she knew that it was a lie, but that it was a lie born in patriotism and love which, after all, it appeared were the same thing.

It seemed to have the desired effect. Amenophis sat back in his seat and held his head straight, his hands resting on his knees, just as he had seen his father sit.

"Then perhaps Nakhtmin will think twice before tangling with me again," he said.

Nefertiti replied, but Amenophis did not hear her. He had been speaking not to her but to the reflection he had confronted in the mirror, the insecure boy with the feminine hips and elongated limbs. It had been a small victory against Nakhtmin but it had been one that enabled him to address the boy in the mirror as a man. When he stood and reached out to take Nefertiti's hand, he did so with a confidence that had never until now been at his command. He stood over her like his father would stand over one of his wives, not like a boy reaching out for the unattainable object of his desires. He suddenly believed that she could love him after all.

"When I am king men will marvel and envy me for your beauty," he said to her, wondering where such elegant words had come from.

"My beauty will be nothing against your power over the living and the whole world that they inhabit," she said, and for a fleeting moment, he believed her.

The Maya Papyrus, Fragments 33-36

Apart from the servants, I was alone when Uncle Anen arrived. My grandmother was at the palace visiting Tiye and had allowed my grandfather to run some meaningless errand in the city rather than join her. I often came to my grandparents' house when I knew they would be absent. The quiet of the garden where I was now sitting was a balm in which I could immerse myself until they returned and bickered me back to reality.

Anen was shown in without my knowledge and may have been standing behind me in the garden for some time before something told me I was no longer alone. I looked up from the papyrus scroll in which I had been engrossed and nearly cried out in surprise, so silent had been his approach. I hardly recognised him.

We had not had the opportunity of bidding him farewell since the temple barbers had worked their transformation on him, and his complete lack of hair – even his eyebrows had been excised – made him seem much thinner and older than he had been before he left for Thebes. He looked naked, although in his priestly garb he was wearing more than I.

But when I took a second to look closer I realised that it was not just a matter of his lack of hair that had so transformed his appearance. He looked older not just because of this but also because of the lines that had etched themselves into his face around the eyes. His demeanour told me that they were not the result of excessive laughter. There was a deadened sadness in his gaze that had not been there before his departure. If he had returned home looking like this after a number of years I would have remembered him in a second, but he had been away for only a matter of months and such changes, which seemed impossible in so short a time, initially rendered him a stranger to me.

Regardless, I could do nothing but jump from my seat, scattering papyrus sheaves hither and thither, and throw myself into his arms. That the strength of the hug he returned was minimal I put down to tiredness after his long journey.

"What are you doing here?" he said, not unkindly.

"I could ask you the same question."

"Myself and the High Priest have been summoned to attend the king. He has not told us why. I do not suppose that you would know what it concerns, would you?"

I shook my head. I was not yet of an age where I would be admitted into the secrets of life at the palace until they were revealed to the populace at large. I was, however, old enough to recognise the etchings of unhappiness on a careworn face.

"Does something trouble you, uncle?" I asked.

"Yes," he said, simply, and although I silently awaited further details, none were forthcoming.

"Is it anything I may help with?" I asked, eventually.

"If only that were so," he said. "I am in a quandary that, while it is not of my making, I fear that only I may solve."

And with that he turned and walked inside. He passed into the shade where I could not make out his features before he turned and spoke again.

"Do you have any idea when your grandfather will be home?"

I shrugged. "At any moment, I expect," I said. "He generally waits long enough to ensure that grandmother has left for the palace and then returns with instructions for the staff to tell her that he was out for hours."

"I expect nobody will have any objections should I wait for him?" said the faceless figure.

I shrugged again. "May I wait with you?" I said.

"Dear Maya, please take no offence, but I would prefer to wait alone."

"Just so," I said, and returned to my garden seat. I gathered the scattered papyri around me and sorted them back into order, but I was only able to make a pretence at reading any further. The entirety of my concentration was bent to the sounds of my grandfather returning from his retreat, and to the silence that seemed to lay in wait for him.

I almost dropped the papyri again when I finally heard the door from the front courtyard slam shut. My heart was almost a match for it in volume, although I was careful to keep my head bowed as though I had not even noticed. I dared not move from my seat, for to do so would betray my eavesdropping, but from where I sat it was impossible to glean anything more than the briefest snatches of conversation, the participants' voices raised though they were.

They seemed to be discussing a battle that had occurred at a town of which I had never heard in Nubia when my grandfather had been a young man.

"I had no choice!" I heard my grandfather shout at one point. "Do you condemn me for that?"

I decided to risk a move inside where I would be able to more clearly hear what was being said. If I was confronted I could just explain that the sun had grown too hot for me. I made a pretence of mopping my brow and fanning myself with a papyrus in case I was being watched before gathering my belongings and stepping into the relative cool of the anteroom.

"Anyway," my grandfather was saying, "it all came to naught. The king chose to go to war before I had time to intervene."

"But you were asked to intervene, and you agreed," uncle Anen said. "Were it not for circumstances out of your control, you would have committed treason."

"Yes," Grandfather said. "I was lucky to have your mother then. It was she who engineered the battle, not I. It was she who, through Tiye, persuaded the king to act so that I did not have to."

"This is a pretty mess," Anen said.

"Why? It was so long ago that nobody remembers it."

"I am sure the king remembers it. Did he not lose friends in the fight?"

The room fell silent for so long that I began to think they had somehow managed to leave without my knowing it. I edged around towards the doorway in an attempt to catch a glimpse of the room beyond. The two men were still there. Yuya was staring at the floor, his back to me, his head bent so low he looked as though he had been decapitated. Anen was watching him closely.

"Yes," Grandfather said, so quietly that only the sibilance of the word had the strength to cross the room to my ears. "Perhaps it is for that that you should condemn me."

"What do you mean?"

"Poor Tjenuna. And Maiherperi. He was just a boy. I have never forgotten them, you know. They have stalked me every day of my life since Napata."

"Father?"

Yuya seemed suddenly to remember where he was. He looked up with a start. "Nothing," he said, and gave a humourless laugh. "It is nothing. You cannot reach my age without the attendance of one or two ghosts. You are lucky to be a priest and not a soldier."

"You have no idea," Anen said. "Thank you for your time, father, but unfortunately I am expected at the palace."

"Say goodbye to Maya before you go," grandfather said. "He often asks about you."

I skittered away from the door and quickly arranged myself into a nonchalant pose, noticing after a few moments that the papyrus I was holding was upside down. It quickly became evident, though, that Anen was not coming to see me. I heard doors close before venturing into the main hall.

"Has uncle Anen left?" I said to my grandfather's back. He span around as though I had disturbed him from deep thoughts.

"He has," he said. "He was needed at the palace. He asked me to pass on his best wishes."

The walk to the palace was a long one but it passed too quickly for Anen. He had managed to speak with his father about Napata without the old man becoming too suspicious about the motives for his interest, but what he had learned had dismayed him. Ptahmose had been lying when he told Anen that Yuya had been instrumental in the king's persuasion into war, but it had been a lie close enough to the truth to at least be believed by the king, and that was all that mattered.

He has me, Anen thought. I betray my king or my father's life will be surely forfeit. By all accounts Amenhotep had loved Tjenuna and Maiherperi more dearly than he had loved anyone. He would undoubtedly wreak a terrible vengeance on any man he held responsible for their deaths, even if that man happened to be the father of his wife.

The palace walls loomed. The windows in the building beyond seemed to stare at him as though his heart were transparent and his thoughts were on display for them to see.

Amenhotep's audience chamber had filled up quickly. Anen was standing with Ptahmose in the centre of the room, craning his neck to see over the heads of those who crowded around him. Everybody of any influence in the kingdom was here, all silently facing the empty thrones, all motionless save for the occasional nod at a remade acquaintance. Anen could see the back of Aye's head as he stood at the centre front of the audience.

Finally, the king arrived. With him were Tiye, Nefertiti and Amenophis, who looked nervous and out of sorts. The king and his wife took their seats at the thrones on the dais, Amenophis and Nefertiti standing on either side of them. Anen noted that his niece was becoming a young woman of remarkable poise and beauty.

Amenhotep took a moment to look over his subjects before speaking.

"I have gathered you all here today that you may rejoice with me," he said. "For today I wish to make an announcement of immeasurable import. Amenophis, take a step forward."

Amenophis did so, looking abashed and nervous. All eyes were on him and he felt uncomfortable under their gaze. He stared at a point on the floor between himself and the feet of those who looked on, his hands held firmly behind his back.

Perhaps sensing his discomfort, Amenhotep stood and rested his hand on his son's shoulder. He gave it a gentle squeeze as he spoke.

"Today I proclaim that I sit alone on the throne no more. As from today, my son Amenophis will reign alongside me as coregent. I present to you all your new pharaoh."

A quiet murmur of indeterminable meaning drifted over the crowd. There was so little movement in the room it seemed as though nobody was so much as breathing. Amenhotep looked over the crowd, his expression darkening.

"You may bow," he said, pointedly.

The audience shuffled to its knees, but the significance of the fact that Amenhotep had been forced to order them to do so was not lost on Amenophis. He looked over the heads of those who did not accept him.

From his prostrate position, Anen glanced sideways at Ptahmose. The priest's eyes were fixed firmly on the dais, his lips set tight in indignant disapproval.

After his initial surprise, Anen had difficulty in disguising his elation. Perhaps now that matters had been taken out of his hands Ptahmose would no longer desire to have a hold over him. Perhaps he could escape this situation with his honour and his father's head intact.

Amenhotep nudged his son and motioned towards the crowd. Amenophis knew he had to speak just three words, but he had rehearsed endlessly before the mirror in his quarters, trying different inflexions on each syllable. He took a deep breath.

"May you..." he said, and his voice cracked. He cleared his throat. "...live," he said. The crowd rose in silence.

Amenhotep announced the betrothal of Amenophis and Nefertiti.

"Step forward," he said to her. She too was self-conscious under the stare of the people gathered before her, and adopted a pose similar to Amenophis'.

Misunderstanding her awkwardness, Amenhotep leant forward and whispered, not too harshly: "At least look as though you are pleased with the situation, young lady." He gave her a gentle nudge on the arm and she sidled across the dais to stand at Amenophis' side.

The announcements over, the onlookers began to filter through the doorway. Anen took a step to follow them but was stopped by a firm grip on his upper arm. He looked around to see Ptahmose, a determined look on his face, nodding in the direction of the dais where the royal foursome were now sitting. Aye had joined them. As the crowd thinned Ptahmose started edging towards them, his grip on Anen's arm still firm enough to hint at pain.

"Remember your father," Ptahmose whispered to Anen as they crossed the room.

Anen saw that Amenhotep was pretending not to notice Ptahmose's approach, as though this would deter the priest from speaking. Anen realised that nothing short of the personal intervention of Amun himself would prevent the priest from having his say. Ptahmose did not wait for an invitation to address the throne.

"Your Majesty," he said. "This is nothing short of an outrage. I must protest in the strongest possible terms."

Amenhotep made a noticeable effort to control his anger at the impertinence of the man.

"An outrage, Ptahmose? You will not be celebrating with the rest of us then? You, the champion of a smooth succession?"

"A smooth succession is one thing, Majesty, but the flouting of the wishes – nay, the commands – of the king of the gods is entirely another. I have made his position very clear to you on more than one occasion, and yet you dare not only to disobey him but have the temerity to present this fait accompli as a matter of celebration. No good will come of this, Your Majesty, you mark my words before these witnesses."

"A very interesting speech, Ptahmose. Should I take it as a threat?"

"Your Majesty knows I would never presume. I am merely taking this opportunity to state Amun's case."

"And Amun opposes Amenophis becoming king?"

"He does, Majesty. Anen here can vouch for that."

"Can he indeed? Anen? Do you wish to add your voice to this argument?"

Amenhotep, Ptahmose and the rest all turned to stare at him, and Anen looked from one to the other, stricken for words. What could he possibly say? His friend the king met his gaze and held it implacably. He could feel the stares of his brother and sister burning into the side of his head.

"Anen?" Ptahmose said. "You do remember our conversation, do you not?"

"I remember," Anen muttered. "Your Majesty, I have to report that Ptahmose speaks the truth. I am sorry."

"I see," Amenhotep said. "Interesting. Anen, we will speak at length later. But for now perhaps you could enlighten me as to the source of Amun's displeasure?"

"He is unsuitable for the throne," Anen said quietly, staring at the floor. "He is simple minded."

"Should we perhaps discuss this in private, Majesty?" Ptahmose added, glancing at Amenophis.

"Do you not think this matter concerns him?" Amenhotep said. "I am sure he will be interested in hearing what you both have to say. Is that not so, Amenophis?"

Amenophis nodded hesitantly. In truth he wanted to hear nothing. He wanted to flee to his quarters and hide himself away. The day had been trying enough as it was without hearing about the anger of the king of the gods directed personally at him.

Ptahmose cleared his throat. Amenophis tried to level his gaze on Ptahmose and will him to desist.

"One only has to look at him to see his unsuitability," Ptahmose said. "Under his rule Egypt will be ruined, either through his own incompetence or Amun's wrath at your disobedience."

Despite his unease Amenophis felt an anger rising within him. He knew that every day his body betrayed him further with its continuing distortions and he knew that his eyesight grew weaker seemingly with every blink, but he resented the implication that this was some reflection on the strength of his mind. His mind was sharp. He almost spoke in his own defence before his courage failed him. Instead, he surreptitiously reached out to his side until his hand found Nefertiti's

Amenophis concentrated on the warmth of her hand within his and the defeat of Nakhtmin by the power of his words. He drew strength from both and took a deep, faltering breath while he gathered his thoughts and bundled his courage as though he could clutch it to his chest like a linen sack.

"I would advise you to choose your words carefully, Ptahmose," he said. The room fell abruptly silent and all within turned to face him with varying degrees of surprise.

The sack of courage he had been gripping so tightly began to slip from his grasp under the weight of the room's gaze and he stammered to a halt as he fumbled for it.

"Yes," he said, looking from one to another. They were waiting for him to continue. His father seemed to have the rumour of a smile gestating in his eyes.

"You should consider the possibility that Amun may be mistaken about me," he said.

"But..." Ptahmose said, and without thinking what he was doing Amenophis held up his free hand for silence. To his amazement, Ptahmose's mouth snapped shut.

"And you should also consider that I am to be your king one day," Amenophis continued, acutely aware that he would only have a short time in which to press his advantage before Ptahmose gathered himself. "Should you live that long," he added, realising as he said it that it could be interpreted – wrongly – as a threat. He allowed it to linger in the air. Nefertiti squeezed his hand. He hoped it was in encouragement and not a warning that he had overstepped the mark.

Amenhotep's smile had spread from his eyes to his lips. Amenophis remembered the interminable lessons where they had walked in the gardens together, Amenophis desperately trying to say the right thing, his father growing increasingly exasperated as his efforts failed him.

Until now, Amenophis thought. Perhaps now I am saying the right thing. He did not see me deal with Nakhtmin. Now he can witness my worthiness for the throne.

"It would not be wise for you to antagonise me," continued Amenophis. "You do not know me. You can have no estimation of my true character. You do not know what I will do."

Amenhotep could contain his glee no longer, and he broke into a laugh.

"There, Ptahmose," he said. "I believe you have your answer. The coregent has spoken, and spoken with a skill and eloquence that I wager you did not expect. And now I believe this conversation is at a close. You may take your leave."

"But..." Ptahmose said again.

"I said, you may take your leave."

Ptahmose turned without another word and shuffled towards the door.

"Anen," Amenhotep said. "Where are you going? I still have not had that word with you."

Anen stopped short and turned back to the throne. Amenhotep waited until the doors had closed behind Ptahmose before speaking.

"There goes a defeated man," he said. "Was it wise for you to take the losing side, do you think?"

Anen had to think quickly. Without the benefit of Aye's advice on the matter he felt lost and adrift in crocodile infested waters.

"That is not what happened," he stammered. "I would never do such a thing."

"Really?" Amenhotep asked. "It certainly sounded as though he had your support. Did it not, Amenophis?"

But Amenophis' courage had deserted him as though it was physical strength after a sudden and intense exertion. He could only nod and look away. Amenhotep frowned and turned back to Anen.

"Well?" he said.

"I merely confirmed that Amun had made his thoughts plain on the situation."

"Nonsense!" Amenhotep shouted. "Either you are very gullible or you believe me to be so. Do you think I have never noticed that Amun always coincidentally wants what Ptahmose wants?"

"And yet it could be the reverse," Anen said. "Ptahmose believes that the gods have distorted Amenophis' body as a sign of their displeasure."

"Enough," Amenhotep said, malice lacing his voice. "You have disappointed me immeasurably, Anen. I sent you to Thebes as my ally. I did not consider the possibility that you would return as the friend of my enemies. Since the first days of my reign I have had two true friends, Maiherperi and Tjenuna. I have always known that their deaths were a grievous loss to this nation, but only now do I see how truly alone I have been since the battle at Napata, for it seems that I cannot trust even the brother of my wife. I see that I am unaided and friendless."

Tiye leant across and touched his forearm. "My husband..." she said, quietly.

"Yes, yes, I know," he said. "I have you. But my point remains. Anen, you had better run to your priest."

Anen hesitated, resisting the urge to flee while he had the chance. He wanted to explain himself. He wanted to blurt out the reasons for his betrayal of Amenhotep's friendship and wash the guilt clean, but he knew it was impossible for that would entail explaining the manner of the blackmail and allowing the threat that hovered over his father's head to descend in a fury.

There was nothing to say. He turned without another word and tramped from the room. Only then did Amenhotep allow his face to collapse into sadness.

"He may as well have stuck a knife in my heart," he said. "Have I no real friends?"

"Your Majesty..." Aye started, but Amenhotep waved him down.

"I know," he said. He turned to Amenophis. "I think today has been more valuable than any lesson we could have undertaken in the palace gardens. I hope you have learned something."

"Yes, father," Amenophis answered, automatically.

"And what would that be?"

Amenophis swallowed heavily and looked around the room as though the answer could be found in the tiles that had been trodden under Anen's feet. Now more than ever Amenophis prayed that the answer he would give would be the one that his father desired. To have come so far – to have even coaxed a proud smile from his father's lips – and then fail now would be a fall further than that to which even he was accustomed.

"I have learned," he said, tentatively, as though he could judge the quality of the answer by watching his father's reaction to the preliminaries, "that the church of Amun is an enemy of the throne."

Amenhotep smiled, although it was a smile without humour. "Good," he said. "And particularly, it seems an enemy of you yourself. What else?"

Amenophis' joy at the acceptance of his answer sputtered out. How many questions would he be asked here? Was his life from now on to be nothing more than an extended lesson where he could not relax for a second for fear of failing to glean every grain of information from a situation? What else had he learned?

"That," he said. "That I should trust nobody." Encouraged by a nod, he added: "That the king has no friends."

"Precisely," Amenhotep said, slapping his knee with the palm of his hand. "It seems that the grasp of Amun can reach even those I considered to be incorruptible. You should trust nobody, Amenophis, least of all the minions of Amun, for they are evidently capable of perverting even those you hold most dear."

"No, Amenhotep," Tiye said. "Do not tell the boy that. That is such a cynical outlook."

"But it is also sensible," he replied. "The truth cannot be cynical any more than it can be sentimental. The truth is just the truth. The sooner he learns to watch every blink of those he considers to be his friends the sooner he will learn what it is to be king."

"What about Maiherperi and Tjenuna?" Tiye said. "They were as loyal as any man in the kingdom."

"That much I admit," he said. "But you remember what happened to them. It would perhaps have been better for them if they had not regarded themselves as my friends in the first place. I would gladly have died for them just as they died for me, and then two lives would have been saved instead of one."

"There is no talking to you when you are in this frame of mind," Tiye said, rising from her throne. "You are determined to pity yourself. You are talking nonsense. Two lives over one, indeed! Do you forget that you are the king? You are worth any number of your countrymen, and you know as much. Come, Amenophis. Your father is upset. He will make better company when he has calmed down somewhat."

She stepped down from the dais. Amenophis followed her, and Nefertiti followed him. Aye and Amenhotep watched them leave.

"You have friends, Your Majesty," Aye said, once they were alone.

"Perhaps," Amenhotep said. "I would not pretend to know. I shall undoubtedly find out when I join my father. There must be an unequalled view of the truth from Ra's chariot."

Aye said nothing. He was thinking of Giludkhepa and her child, and was silenced by the sudden thought that his was a secret he would not only have to take to the grave but beyond, and forever.

A crown had been made for Amenophis, and now he regarded himself in the mirror that had already told him too many truths. The royal sculpture, Men, was due at any minute to take preliminary sketches for Amenophis' inaugural statue.

The crown fitted Amenophis' misshaped skull as though it was reluctant to do so. It was wider at the top than the bottom and it felt as though it would topple to the floor at the slightest movement of his head. It accentuated his strange angles and distortions. It made him look ridiculous. He adjusted it one more time and, turning his head this way and that, regarded himself through the corner of his eyes.

Nefertiti's reflection appeared behind his own.

"You look regal," she said.

"I look like a joke."

"I love the way you look."

"You do?" he said.

"Of course," she said, straightening the crown. "There. Perfect. You should be proud of your appearance. It is who you are."

"How can I possibly be proud? I am judged by the way I look. You heard Ptahmose."

"But if you cannot change it you should use it to your advantage. It can be a weapon."

"How?" he said, turning from the mirror to face her.

"Wear it like a badge. Remember the advantage it gives you. If you are deemed to be a failure before you act, think how much glory your actions will bring you when they succeed."

"Ptahmose thinks I look this way as a judgement of the gods, as a warning to all that see me that I am not worthy of the throne."

Nefertiti took a step back and viewed him from crown to sandal.

"Perhaps the gods do have a hand in it," she said.

"Do you really think so?"

"I think it is a possibility. How many people do you know who look like you?"

"None."

"And how many people do you know who are touched by divinity as you are?"

"Only my father. I fail to see..."

"So perhaps this is a sign of that."

"That I am divine?"

"That you are closer to divinity than the people who accuse you of incompetence."

Amenophis walked to a chair as though he was balancing a bowl on his head, still aware of the uncertain grip the crown had on his head. He sat down carefully.

"You think I am marked by the gods to be king rather than the contrary?"

"It makes better sense that Ptahmose's rantings. If the gods did not want you to become king they would have better ways at their disposal to display their feelings than this. It would have been you found dead under a bush in the desert, not your brother."

"The thought has never crossed my mind," he said.

There was a knock at the door.

"This will be Men," Amenhotep said. "Do I look presentable to be sketched?"

"You look perfect."

After Men had entered and prostrated himself, Amenophis said: "I know the tricks of you sculptors, you know."

"Your Majesty?"

"You will sculpt me not how I look, but how you think I would like to look. You will square off my chin and my torso. You will shorten and widen my arms, and add muscles where muscles have been forever absent. You will make me look handsome and regal and proud."

"But, Your Majesty, you *are*..."

"Enough." Amenophis said, and although he turned his eyes towards Nefertiti, he continued to address Men. "I am as the gods have made me, and from this day I shall be proud of their handiwork. Sculpt me as I am, Men, for I am a child of the gods."

The coregent and his Great Royal Wife shared an indulgent and private smile.

Chapter Nine

The Sed Festival (1)

The Maya Papyrus, Fragments 44-47

KING AMENHOTEP *was growing old. His girth had expanded to such an extent that even Tiye no longer felt the need to comment on it. It hurt him to sit or stand for long periods of time. His teeth were growing increasingly troublesome. The periods of intense pain in his jaw were beginning to outnumber the times of relief, and his periods of good humour were shortening correspondingly. He began to grow contemplative about the years he had spent on the throne and took to discussing them in melancholic tones to anyone who would listen. All gave him the same reply: that, in respect to his reign, melancholy was an entirely inappropriate emotion.*

That he had lost friends and people he had loved could not be denied. That, in his dotage, his mourning for them and loneliness in their absence increased was also not a moot point. But as for Egypt, the Two Lands could hardly have prospered more. He was a glorious monarch, respected by his friends and feared by all others. After Napata he had avoided war with a skill that could only be attributed to diplomatic genius. Under his guidance and his personal communing with the gods during daily worship the annual inundations of the Nile had not missed a beat and the harvests grew more bountiful with each passing year. The store houses were full of grain and hardly a hungry belly was to be found from the northern coast to the southern border with Nubia. I, and all the young men and women of my generation, had never experienced anything even approaching a time of hardship, much less a famine.

Although expensive gifts were still sent abroad to sweeten his relationship with his neighbours, the king could well afford it, overflowing as his coffers were. If, as he still remarked during his blacker moods, Amun was indeed punishing him through the deaths of those close to him, the god evidently did not bear a grudge against the rest of his kingdom.

It was around this time that I was judged to be of sufficient age to assume my first official appointment at court. After leaving the school I had earnestly undertaken the studies to become a royal scribe. It was a position much less glorious than that of either of my siblings but I would have made as poor a soldier as I would a Great Royal Wife, so I was happy to leave such roles to my brother Nakhtmin and sister Nefertiti. But while less exciting, my position as a scribe was no less important. The scribes were the overlooked cement that held the palace together. A king could not survive without those who have devoted themselves to his administrative service, and I was proud of my achievements, less conspicuous though they were than those of my siblings and the rest of my illustrious family.

I had always been studious, even after my studies finished, and when many young men of my age busied themselves with excessive drinking and the pursuit of women, I could often be found, perhaps in the garden of my grandparents' house, my head buried in reams of ancient manuscripts, alone and quiet, but never happier.

I like to think that it was this unassuming devotion to knowledge rather than my connections to the king via my father that elevated me to the position in which I now found myself. Of course, of this I have no proof.

Those few kings who live long enough to enjoy thirty years of power are entitled to celebrate a jubilee, or sed festival. It is a moment of rejuvenation, when the old king is visited by the gods and granted a second youth, when although the body may remain outwardly old, the soul is reborn. It is a celebration of great solemnity and gravitas, but also one of great rejoicing.

Thirty years was such a long reign that a sed festival had not been held for ten generations or more, and should the gods grant him the longevity to meet it, Amenhotep wanted it to be right. The last king to celebrate a jubilee was Niuserre, and it was still said of him that the festivities were so grand they were enough to make the gods themselves jealous. I was tasked with discovering exactly how it had been done.

My duties would take me to the very borders of Egypt, far from my family and, although I was not to know it at the time, just as far from the machinations at court that were to rob so many of so much, and from the decline of a king and his rebirth as something entirely new.

By the time Amenhotep's *sed* festival came around, in the thirtieth year of his reign, the king was in poor health. The decline had been so gradual as to have almost gone unnoticed, but gradual though it was, the deterioration was deep.

Rare was the night that Amenhotep did not awake from troubled dreams with a start, his toothache having crept up on him in his sleep and erupted in his head. There would be an evil taste in his mouth and an offensive odour that would seem to permeate the whole room. The pain now enveloped not just one or two teeth but the whole right hand side of his face from the temple to the shoulder. He would spit into a bowl by the side of his bed, and his spittle would be yellow and viscous.

On these occasions Amenhotep had learned from bitter experience that to shout for his dentist would unleash an explosion of pain. He would creep, treading carefully to prevent the jolting that would send shards of agony through his head, into an anteroom where he knew a servant would be on duty to attend to the king should there be anything he need during the night. Amenhotep would whisper his command and then gingerly return to his bed, where he would lie in voluntary paralysis.

Invariably, by the time the dentist arrived the pain would have levelled off somewhat, as would the amount of pus in Amenhotep's saliva. The dentist would bring with him honey, carob and ground malachite, which he would concoct together and pack into the side of the king's mouth before retiring to the antechamber to await further developments. Both the king and the dentist knew that these treatments were having a negligible effect and it made them both nervous. Amenhotep was always aware that however little relief the medication brought, there was no telling how bad the pain could be if nothing was done at all.

After a while the court physicians would take it in turns to sleep in the antechamber to be on hand at a moment's notice.

To add to his troubles, the king's weight had now grown to an extent that made it difficult for him to rise in the morning even when the pain in his teeth had abated to a more manageable level. But still (he would tell people with a wry smile) a hearty meal was one of the few pleasures he had left.

Certainly gone was any pleasure he had once garnered from his place on Egypt's throne. Everything was an unequal effort. The diplomatic jousting with foreign kings and potentates became interminable rather than stimulating. The thrill of command became a chore, and visits to other towns and cities, or in fact to anywhere outside the palace walls, became impossible for fear of his toothache striking and staying with him through a jolting chariot ride. His news scarabs were still sent out at intervals but now contained more fiction than fact. There was no point in worrying the population unnecessarily, or indeed of alerting Egypt's watchful neighbours to his state of health. The names of Thuya and Yuya were still regularly included in the scarabs. To do so had become customary.

Increasingly he began to rely on those around him for assistance in his royal duties, and especially on Tiye and Amenophis, although his reliance on the latter came more through necessity than choice for it quickly became obvious to all at court that Amenophis was not destined to be the same calibre of king as his father.

Of this Amenhotep was painfully aware, delegating tasks to his son only when Tiye was unavailable. Even Amenophis began to hear the rumours about his abilities, although none were ever voiced to his face. He would glean small snatches of conversation on entering a room, or see the look that passed between two of his servants as he issued them with instructions for this task or that, expressions that were tantamount to knowing smiles, evidence of shared, if unspoken, satires.

It had quickly become evident around the palace that Amenophis' tempers were nothing more than cosmetic and that, while they were unpleasant to bear they were transitory and for the most part there only to show that such passions were possible. He would shout when talking was appropriate, and rage when shouting would suffice. He would storm when his meals arrived too early or too late, or when they arrived on time but he was not ready for them. He would bellow when his chariot was driven too slowly or too fast, or when he arrived too early or too late for an appointment, although he never confided in his driver exactly when the appointment was due, for fear of losing an opportunity to show his mettle. Only with Nefertiti did he moderate his moods, and only to his parents did he deign to show respect. He professed to fearing no man, and in reality feared only one: Ptahmose. The priest seemed to carry with him an impermeable authority, a constant expression of disdain against which Amenophis felt powerless. The memory of his defiance in the face of Ptahmose's insults in Amenhotep's audience chamber had grown into a source of horror rather than strength. He was a man awaiting revenge. The thought of an accidental meeting with the priest would always confine him to his quarters on a series of dubious pretexts, and even Amenhotep would be unable to induce him to venture forth. When Ptahmose was in residence at the palace Amenophis' mood would become darker still, and he would unleash his frustration on those around him with a renewed vehemence. But always, no matter how much he blustered and roared, he would see those looks on the faces of those he berated that said *See how he tries to bully us, this pathetic monster.*

"They are laughing at me, you know," he said one day to Nefertiti.

The couple, along with members of the highest echelons of court, were aboard *Rising In Truth*, sailing south towards Thebes. In Thebes now stood Malkarta, the House of Rejoicing, which had been commissioned and built to house the court during the celebration of Amenhotep's *sed* festival. Amenophis was nervous about the trip, taking him as it did into the heart of Amun's, and therefore Ptahmose's, powerbase. They were sitting under an awning that kept off the worst of the afternoon sun. The canopy would occasionally flutter in the breeze and areas of shade and light would dance on the deck like landed fish.

"Who are?" Nefertiti asked, looking around her.

"Everyone," Amenophis said.

"Everyone here?" Nefertiti asked.

"At court. Everyone at court."

"Nonsense, my dear," she said, taking his hand in her own.

"But they are. I have seen the looks on their faces. I have heard comments."

"Comments? What comments?"

"I know they call me The Old Woman," Amenophis said. "They see my shape and they laugh. How dare they? Do they not know who I am?"

"Nobody calls you that. Nobody calls you anything other than His Majesty. You are being paranoid. You thought people were laughing at you when you were at school."

"Yes I did," he said, "but they were."

Nefertiti had no answer. She too had heard her husband referred to as The Old Woman, although the servant she overheard would not dare ever repeat the phrase again. She had begun to sense the slipping of Amenophis' power, which only quickened the more he fought to prevent it.

And yet how could it be so? How could it be that commoners and courtiers could find the courage to mock the divine? It was a matter that had never been discussed beyond the privacy of the royal apartments but there were certain facts that could not be disputed, and they all seemed to point towards the same conclusion. There was the matter of Amenophis' unique appearance. No physician, or indeed anyone else, had ever encountered another man with even remotely similar physical characteristics. If men were created by gods, it was safe to assume that pharaohs were created with more care than anybody else. There must have been a reason for Amenophis' appearance. Nothing else made any sense.

Another issue, if Ptahmose could be trusted to be telling the truth, was the attitude of Amun towards Amenophis. It was nothing short of open hostility. Nefertiti and Amenophis talked of Montu, the old god of Thebes. Where was he now? Supplanted by Amun during Amun's own rise to supremacy, Montu had disappeared from the firmament as though he had never existed. Surely a god with such a history as Amun's would be careless if he did not take care to protect his position. Perhaps his opposition to Amenophis stemmed from a fear of sharing Montu's fate? Only another god, and a powerful one at that, would cause Amun so much concern.

And what of poor Thutmose? Why had he met such an ignominious end? Had he not, as heir to the throne, been under the powerful protection of the gods? Perhaps so, Amenophis reasoned. But perhaps his attackers had been under the protection of a god more powerful still, for only in Thutmose's passing would Amenophis ever have come to the throne. And the fact that Giludkhepa's child had turned his face to the floor shortly before his death, and the death of Giludkhepa herself, was the clearest indication yet of the involvement of the unseen.

Alone, these events would have seemed nothing more than coincidental. Taken together they seemed portentous. Nefertiti had urged her husband to keep his suspicions to himself, at least for a little while. She recognised that, given his current standing at court, they would not be welcomed as good news and she feared that he would be openly mocked. She knew there would come a time when Amenophis would have to announce himself for who he really was, and when he did she would be standing proudly by his side, but that time was not now. For now the two of them needed to be patient.

The Maya Papyrus, Fragments 51-53

> *Amenhotep was as unwell as I had ever seen him. This was only my third or fourth meeting with him since my return from the fact finding mission, and it seemed as though each time I saw him he had taken a step further towards death. He did not rise from his bed throughout the entire journey to Thebes and this may have perhaps made him appear worse than he actually was, but even I, in the brief time I spent with him, could see that the slightest movement of the ship caused him pain. His face was red and*

swollen along its entire right hand side and he could only move his jaw a miniscule amount, making his words difficult to decipher. Aye and Tiye sat with him, Tiye's hand never leaving his during the entire interview, and one or the other would interject at intervals to explain what the king was trying to say.

"I want you to work with Amenophis," he told me, and then added something I did not hear well enough to understand. I looked questioningly at my father.

"He said that you must explain to Amenophis what needs to be done," Aye said.

I saw that the indignity of his need for a translator caused Amenhotep as much pain as did his teeth and I took a step closer to the bed and turned my head slightly to one side, as though this would make his words clearer. I felt overwhelming sorrow and pity for the man, although it was hardly my place to feel such things for so mighty a king. But there, in his bed, he did not look the king. It was strange, and I thought the idea may have been blasphemous, but he looked just like any other man in the kingdom who suffers. Prince or peasant, all men fall to the same level in the face of pain. Why, I thought, do the gods not intervene? Do they not take heed of the fate of their intermediary on earth?

"You carry with you the procedures for the celebration of the sed festivals of old," Amenhotep said. "You have served me well, Maya, and I shall not forget it, but I am too ill to use the information you have imparted to me. Meet with my son. Teach him what he needs to know."

Gathering the necessary information had been no easy task. I had travelled the length of Egypt in my quest, visiting every temple and tomb accessible to me and, through the hieroglyphics engraved on their walls, I had consulted the minds of kings past. I read the words of King Den, who ruled when the world was young, and King Niuserre, who has been dead these past five hundred years. I spent hot days and cold nights examining King Djoser's step pyramid at Sakkara almost stone by stone.

A sed festival is a time of rejuvenation for a king, a celebration that enables his soul to become young again to give him the strength, after thirty long years on the throne, to continue with vitality and verve.

If ever a king needed a sed festival, it was this one.

And yet I did not welcome the prospect of renewing my acquaintance with Amenophis. His reputation preceded him. His bullish temper and unreasonable demands were legendary *enough for me to have heard of them even on my travels. And now here I was, with orders to issue him with instructions regarding his role at the festival. It was not a happy thought, and even balanced the joy I felt at the opportunity to spend some time with my sister after this long separation. I had seen the pair of them on board the ship, but as yet had neither the opportunity nor the courage to approach them. I had been hoping to find her alone but the couple were never to be seen one without the other. I hoped she was happy but, from what I had heard of Amenophis, I feared my hopes were in vain.*

I decided to wait until our arrival at Thebes before I requested an audience. It would give me time to brace myself. Had I known that bracing myself would be an entirely ineffectual act, and that my audience with Amenophis would lead where it did, I believe I would have jumped overboard and taken my chances in the Nile. At least when a crocodile smiles you have a fair estimation of his plans for you.

On the day that the ship was to dock in Thebes harbour any attempts that Nefertiti made to engage Amenophis in conversation were met with a blank silence. He seemed ill at ease and fretful, pacing the floor of his cabin, his hands grasped firmly behind his back, his eyes never leaving the floor. Even the servants found that they could carry out their duties unmolested.

After his untouched midday meal had been removed he suddenly turned to Nefertiti and said: "Am I the only one who can feel that?"

"Feel what?" she said.

"You can feel nothing? It is sort of a... a tugging... a pressure..." He placed the flat of his other hand against his stomach. "Here," he said.

Nefertiti shook her head.

"I know what it is," Amenophis said. "Don't think I don't, because I do. I know exactly what it is."

He lapsed into silence and continued pacing. Eventually, Nefertiti said: "What is it?"

"It is him."

"Him?"

"Amun," Amenophis said.

Nefertiti glanced around the room nervously. "He is here?" she asked.

"No, I think not. But he knows I am here. Oh, he knows. He is waiting for me."

"Are you sure? Perhaps all this travelling is having an effect on your constitution."

"Do you not think I can tell the difference between the gaze of a god and indigestion?"

In one swift movement Amenophis strode across the cabin, sat down next to Nefertiti and took her hands in his.

"Do you not see?" he said. "I can feel him! You cannot. Does that not tell you something? We are attuned, Amun and I. We are communicating. Directly. As equals."

"Is it unpleasant?"

"It is making me nauseous. Amun is very unhappy with me. He sees me as a threat. Oh, Nefertiti, what am I to do? I am not ready to face him yet. I must prepare for that. The divine in me must grow. I must not go to Thebes, Nefertiti. I must *not*."

"And show him you are afraid?"

"I *am* afraid. I feel as though I am walking into a trap."

Nefertiti felt as though the conversation was being conducted by her mouth alone, while her mind was stammering through a host of thoughts that assaulted it. Could it be true? Could Amun be somehow attacking Amenophis? It seemed incredible, but then it also seemed to make sense. After all, why would Amun not attack him? If all their other conjecture about Amenophis' divinity was true then this was surely the only sensible outcome.

A shudder ran through her body. She had always wanted it to be true, and now she no longer believed there was merely a possibility that Amenophis was in some way divine. Now she knew it to be so. She leant over and hugged him.

"Listen to me, my husband," she whispered in his ear. "If Amun is taking these steps against you it means he must be afraid of you. For why else would he care? You cannot turn your tail now. You must confront him. You must come to Thebes and show him you are not afraid of him as he is of you. In any other direction lies defeat. I am proud of you. I am by your side. Let us march against him together."

Amenophis returned her hug, but made no reply. He was suddenly beset by doubts. Surely venturing unprepared into the heart of Amun's lair must be a mistake, even for a god? How could he hope to resist Amun, the king of the gods, in a direct confrontation? Amenophis had been recently troubled by his own lack of reference. With whom did he compare? Surely, if he was as powerful as Amun there would be no keeping his divinity a secret, even should he so wish. He would not have to announce it because people would see it. They would sense him just as he had sensed Amun. And yet nobody had. Nobody had fallen at his feet in awe and proclaimed him worthy of worship; nobody had brought him offerings of appeasement; nobody, as far as he knew, had offered prayers up to him.

Amenophis could not meet Amun eye to eye until he knew he had the power necessary to combat the other god's nefarious attacks, and he could not know that until he knew the extent of his own divinity. Amenophis decided he needed to consult someone whose judgement and discretion he could trust.

When *Rising in Truth* docked in the harbour at the palace of Malkarta, at the other end of Thebes from the temple of Amun and on the opposite bank, Amenhotep needed to be carried from the ship in a palanquin held on the shoulders of four servants. He was a heavy burden and their steps were unsteady. Towards the bottom of the gangplank one of them stumbled and, although he managed to regain his footing before Amenhotep was spilled to the ground, it was enough of a jolt to tease a small cry of pain from the king.

"Be careful, you dolts!" Aye shouted from the deck of the ship.

A welcoming committee had been prepared. A troop of musicians lined the dockside and played regal and uplifting music as the king's palanquin was lowered precariously to the floor. An array of priests lowered themselves to their knees. Watching from the safety of the deck, Amenophis noted that Ptahmose was not among them. He felt himself relax slightly, although part of him felt paradoxically slighted that the high priest had not felt it necessary to welcome the royal household to the city.

Scripted pleasantries were exchanged between king and priests and then, as the ship's passengers disembarked, the priests and musicians formed up into two columns flanking the royal party. They set off, at the necessarily slow pace set by Amenhotep's palanquin bearers, towards the palace.

It was a huge construction, more than simply a palace, that had been the employment of a whole army of men – so many, in fact, that they had to be housed in specially constructed villages to the north and south of the palace complex itself. Amenhotep, Tiye and Amenophis had separate adjoining palaces. To the north lay a newly constructed temple to Amun where Amenhotep felt he would be able to worship away from the prying eyes and quick tongue of Ptahmose. To the west lay a village of villas where those outside the immediate royal family, together with foreign kings and their representatives, were to be housed. The level of opulence was staggering for those who were visiting the site for the first time. Each and every apartment had its own bathroom and toilet facilities. Hardly an inch of wall space had remained undecorated and everywhere one turned were complex designs in pastel shades of papyrus groves, river scenes, and flora and fauna of every description.

Amenhotep only wanted to retire to his bedchamber, but formalities needed to be observed first. He was carried through his palace, followed by his family and courtiers and surrounded by gyrating dancers and singers and musicians playing harps, lyres and lutes. Under any other circumstances it would have been a pleasing scene, but his mouth was too swollen to smile and, after such a long and exhausting journey, he was too tired to care.

Once in the large audience chamber to the north of his palace Amenhotep was set down and helped to his feet. He sat down on his throne and watched wearily as the rest of the household trooped in and prostrated themselves before him.

"May you live," he said to the first few, but it hurt him too much to speak. When Amenophis arrived he motioned for him to stand next to him on the dais. From then on Amenophis conferred the blessing. Once the audience had assembled Amenhotep leant heavily on one arm of his throne and motioned for Amenophis to approach. Amenophis bent down to hear the king's words, and was hardly able to prevent himself from wincing at the smell of decay that wafted up from his father's mouth.

"Say a few words," Amenhotep said.

Amenophis was momentarily panic stricken.

"What?" he said. "What should I say?"

"Anything, Amenophis. Anything brief will suffice."

Amenophis straightened up and looked at the crowd before him, although from the distance of the dais he could see nothing more than indistinct shapes. He had no idea what to say. He turned to where he imagined Nefertiti to be and tried to draw strength from a skin coloured oval which may or may not have been her face. *Remember who you are*, he imagined her saying. *A god cannot be afraid to address his people.*

Amenophis took a deep breath.

"Welcome," he said. "Welcome to the House of Rejoicing."

This was greeted with silence. He cleared his throat.

"We are here to celebrate the rebirth of our king. It is a much deserved honour."

There were one or two murmurings of assent and Amenophis realised that the silence was attentive rather than uninterested. They were listening to him. His voice grew stronger.

"His Majesty's entire life has been led in dedication to his country," he said. "He was, and is, and shall remain forever, a mighty king of Egypt."

"Hear, hear," someone in the crowd said.

"Thank..." Amenophis began.

"In his *sed* festival His Majesty's soul shall return to youthfulness so that he may continue to rule over us, as he has these past thirty years, in beneficence, wisdom and courage."

"Yes, thank..." Amenhotep began.

"He has brought these Two Lands peace, wealth and happiness, and I am sure that you will join me in the conviction that no king more deserves this honour than does His Majesty, King Nebmaatre Amenhotep."

The room broke into spontaneous applause.

"Yes, thank you, Amenophis," Amenhotep said.

Amenophis was clearly enjoying himself. In a few short sentences he felt himself transformed from a nervous impostor, a stand-in for the king, into a skilled orator. The audience was his. His imagination was so empowered by enthusiasm that he decided he could actually see smiles on the faces of the front row. The rest of the audience was hidden behind the gauze of his vision, but he had no reason to believe that they were any less enthralled by his address.

"And furthermore," he said.

"Amenophis, that will be *enough*," Amenhotep said, with as much strength as he could muster. With enough strength, at least, for his words not to be carried to Amenophis alone but to the rest of the room as well.

Amenophis stumbled into silence.

Amenhotep signalled to his palanquin bearers. Amenophis helped him to his feet and then watched the complicated rigmarole of his father climbing into the palanquin, being lifted aloft, and then carried from the room. The crowd silently followed him while Amenophis stood immobile and squinted as he scanned the faces that passed before him. He still saw smiles but now attributed an entirely different motive to them. Now they were superior smiles, the barely concealed precursors to laughter. They may as well have been his classmates, laughing at the harsh words of his tutor. Before long only Nefertiti and himself were left in the room. It seemed suddenly barren, as though it had never been used.

"Well done," Nefertiti said. "A rousing speech."

"Well done? He belittled me. In front of all these people, he belittled me."

"Nobody noticed," Nefertiti said. "They were too in awe of your words."

"Nonsense. They saw. They heard. They were laughing as they left. I could see them."

"They were doing no such thing. How could you see them from there? You are too far away."

"I see well enough," Amenophis said, although they both knew it to be a lie. He stepped down from the dais.

"Come," he said. "I wish to retire to our quarters."

As they walked the corridors, hand in hand, servants and courtiers prostrated themselves. Amenophis bid none of them rise and they remained on their knees until the royal couple had passed out of sight.

Nefertiti was walking through the palace gardens with Nakhtmin, who had arrived at Malkarta the previous evening, military manoeuvres having kept him occupied elsewhere for almost two weeks after the royal party had disembarked from *Rising in Truth*. It was dawn, and the air was cool enough to envelop their faces in mist with every breath. A haze clung to the floor, where it would remain until the sun rose high enough to burn it off.

"At least you have no more scars," Nefertiti said.

Nakhtmin looked down at his body. It was indeed scarred, but none of the marks were fresh and all had healed to a series of pale lines that reminded him of a map of an irrigation system.

"I am no longer a lowly recruit," he said. "I no longer receive beatings. Since my last promotion I am too important even to administer them. I have someone do that for me. Now I am Host Commander I have five hundred men at my disposal."

"I hope you are not as harsh on your new recruits as your officers were on you. I remember you and Horemheb visiting mother and father when you could both hardly be seen beneath your welts and wounds."

"It does a man good to receive a beating occasionally. Look at me, and at Horemheb also. In a few years we can expect to be generals in charge of five thousand troops or more. I doubt either of us would have had the strength to achieve so much had it not been beaten into us. We are a hardy breed, us soldiers."

"Horemheb has done well. Is he here?"

"He is due to arrive tomorrow. Anyway, we have both done well," Nakhtmin said, pointedly.

"Of course you have. I merely meant that Horemheb has not had your advantages of birth."

"And how is your husband?" Nakhtmin asked.

"I am worried about him."

"I am hardly surprised. I would worry if I was married to him."

"Nakhtmin!" Nefertiti said, shocked. "You are speaking of your pharaoh."

"I know," he said. "But I cannot help it. I cannot see him as a pharaoh. I see him only as a little boy in class who was slower than everybody else."

"That is the problem," Nefertiti said. "I think that is the way that most people see him."

"Then perhaps there is some truth in it."

"If only you knew how wrong you were, you would repent such remarks on your knees."

"And if you were not my sister I would take that as a threat."

"I am merely saying that you should not underestimate him."

"I doubt I ever will," Nakhtmin said. "I have heard it said that the High Priest of Amun was opposed to Amenophis taking to the throne."

"You have heard correctly, although we have heard precious little from him since."

"Have you ever considered that he may have been correct in his opposition?"

"No," Nefertiti said.

"That Amenophis may in fact be unsuitable for such an appointment?"

"Nakhtmin, listen to me," Nefertiti said. She turned to face him and grasped him by the shoulders. "You should not say such things. I implore you to guard your tongue. There is much that you do not know."

Over Nakhtmin's shoulder, unbeknownst to him, the sun began to glide over the rim of the world, as though it was a cat stalking its prey, as though it was an all-seeing eye glaring malevolently down from the heavens. Nefertiti watched it move.

"What?" Nakhtmin said. "What is it that I do not know?"

Nefertiti took a deep breath. "Nothing," she said.

"There is much that I do not know, but it is nothing? You are not making sense. I suspect that there is something you wish to tell me."

Nakhtmin was correct in his supposition. Nefertiti had been carrying her husband's secret like a burden ever since their arrival at Malkarta. Her better instincts told her to remain tight lipped on the subject, but it was an impossible command to obey. She could think of no advantage to be gained from sharing the truth with anyone, and yet share it she must, in the same way that she knew she could not suffocate herself by simply deciding to hold her breath. And now here, at last, was a reason to which she could cling, for how could she not share the news with her brother when her silence would do nothing but endanger him? Under any other king Nakhtmin would be acting treasonously by making such remarks: under this one he was compounding the crime with blasphemy. And so when she spoke, she did so having persuaded herself that her motives were justified.

"Amenophis is a god," she said at last.

Nakhtmin laughed. "He is a *what*?" he said. "Now you are teasing me."

The sun continued to rise, now almost completely free from the horizon, casting long shadows that seemed to reach for Nakhtmin's back.

"No," Nefertiti said. "I would not joke about such a thing."

"And you actually believe this?" Nakhtmin asked.

Nefertiti had told him almost despite herself, without a thought to how she would break it to her husband that his news was out, and that his secret had been shared not by an official announcement to his father or the priesthood, but as gossip to Nakhtmin, the bully, the bane of his childhood. But Nakhtmin was still Nefertiti's brother and she could not help but try to protect him. He could not be allowed to ridicule Amenophis so vociferously when such opposition was bound to reach Amenophis' ear before long.

Now she had spoken so freely there was no option but to continue. Nakhtmin was acutely aware of the absurdity of Amenophis' claim without the evidence to support it, so she told him everything. She told him of the real reason for Ptahmose's opposition, of the convenience of the deaths which led to Amenophis' accession to the throne, of his sensing of Amun's presence, of the divine reasons for his outlandish physique.

She could tell as she spoke that Nakhtmin was unconvinced. It only served to make her more determined to persuade him of the veracity of her claims.

"How else can you explain his appearance? It does not make sense that the gods made him like that as a punishment, or a warning to keep him from the throne. It would have been so much easier for the gods to arrange to have him in Thutmose's place, or in Giludkhepa's. They could have taken him from us at birth and we would have been none the wiser. But look at him. Apart from his eyesight he is in perfect health, and yet he has the hips and belly of a woman. What does that tell you? Does his androgyny not remind you of anything? Of the Creator, perhaps?"

Nakhtmin was suddenly stern. "Now it is you whose words are straying dangerously close to blasphemy."

"Blasphemy?" Nefertiti said. "Blasphemy? How do I blaspheme? I am defending the name of a god."

"Nefertiti, listen to me. Amenophis is not a god. He is a pharaoh, and as such he is an intermediary between the world of men and the heavens. It is an exalted enough position, and he is very honoured. He should be happy with that. You are walking a road of folly. Turn back now, before the way behind you is obscured by the ego of your husband."

Nefertiti was dumbstruck. She had expected to be doubted at first, but she had not thought it would be possible for the evidence to leave any doubt in the minds of those who heard it. And Nakhtmin's disbelief made her next request all the more difficult to ask.

"You must not breathe a word of this to anyone," she said.

"Does Amenophis intend to keep his divinity secret? If he is a god, does he not expect people to notice?"

"Do not mock me, Nakhtmin. Promise me you will repeat this conversation to nobody. When the king is ready he will announce it."

Nakhtmin bowed his head slightly in agreement. "I promise," he said.

The Maya Papyrus, Fragments 58-59

As I was ushered into Amenophis' audience room at Malkarta for the first time my limbs were shaking as though all the strength had been drained from them in my sleep. I had spent the previous fortnight revisiting my notes and consulting the clergy over every aspect of Amenophis' role at the festival. I was not about to risk the erroneous repetition of facts and then spend the rest of the festival chasing him with amendments and errata. Everything had to be just so.

And so I am not ashamed to admit that I was nervous, especially now that I had more than Amenophis' famous temper to frighten me. I had encountered Nakhtmin the previous evening, as I had been tramping the palace corridors, a sheaf of papyrus in my hands as I read and re-read my own notes, reciting them as I went.

Nakhtmin was never the most trustworthy of confidantes and I had often cursed the fact as a child when he had gleefully revealed some misdemeanour to my parents. As an adult, since his discovery of the pleasures of beer and wine, his dependability was even more in question. His opening words were as indiscrete as they were slurred.

"Amenophis believes himself to be a god," he said.

I stopped dead.

"I beg your pardon?" I asked.

"Amenophis thinks he is a god," Nakhtmin repeated. There was a smirk on his lips, a superior smile he habitually adopted when imparting the most succulent of scandal. He then proceeded to relay his conversation with Nefertiti in minute detail.

"I am to see Amenophis tomorrow," I said, thoughtfully.

"I know. That is why I came to find you. If I were you, I would be careful how I handled him," Nakhtmin said, the smirk growing broader by the second. I swear he saw my discomfort and was entertained by it. There was a malicious side to Nakhtmin that was accentuated when he was in his cups. "There is no telling how a god will react to the most trivial of slights. And if Amenophis'

imagination is keen enough to think himself divine, there is no telling what else it will conjure up."

"Yes, thank you, Nakhtmin," I said. "That is a great comfort to me."

"Enjoy," he said, simply, and was off along the corridor in purposeful steps, his priggishness spreading before him like a bow wave.

"Ah, Maya," Amenophis said as I walked towards his throne, wondering if there was enough strength left in my legs to return me to my feet once I had prostrated myself.

"Your Majesty," I said, and bowed until my nose touched the floor.

"May you live."

"Your Majesty," I said again once I was upright, "His Majesty, your father, has asked me to appraise you of the situation with regards to the sed festival. He is anxious for you to take a major role in the proceedings."

"Of course he is," Amenophis said. "I am his son."

"Just so, Majesty."

It took a number of hours to describe the proceedings and his role in them. Foolishly, I had prepared a number of papyri for Amenophis to peruse at his leisure, realising only when I handed the first one to him that his eyesight made it impossible for him to read any of them. He took a disdainful glance at the first one and handed it back without a word. I did not offer him any of the others. Despite this, few points needed repeating more than once. I was impressed by his faculties. There was a great deal of information to be absorbed, and to do so without the aid of written materials in so short a time was a striking indication of his intelligence.

"You are a very knowledgeable man, Maya," he said as I tidied up the scrolls I had unrolled on the floor before the throne. "You are too young to be called wise, but you are very knowledgeable. It takes a man of no mean intelligence to gather all this information."

"Your Majesty is very gracious," I said.

"In fact, now I come to think of it," he said. "I remember you being one of the cleverest students in our class."

"Your Majesty excepted, of course," I said.

"Of course," Amenophis said, absently. He was only half attending the conversation. "I never remember you laughing at me, either."

I decided it would be unwise to remind him of the time he accused me of being the source of Nakhtmin's giggles.

"Maya," he said suddenly, as though his mind had returned from a long journey. "I have a question for you."

He turned and signalled to the servants and courtiers that decorated the audience chamber like statues. As one they left the room.

"Majesty?" I said, and swallowed heavily.

Amenophis leaned forward on his throne.

"Why do you think I look as I do?" he asked me.

I was trapped. What could I possibly say? Because you are diseased? Because you are cursed? Because the gods have a sense of humour? I said none of these, but is it any wonder I have blamed myself all these years? Perhaps, if I had the courage of a warrior, or the stupidity of a Nakhtmin, I would have answered differently. Perhaps that one sentence could have changed the whole of history. I would undoubtedly have been punished for my insolence, but think who I would have saved! My sister, my brother, my father, my nephew, my niece. My country. I would have saved the gods themselves.

But Amenophis only needed confirmation. He only needed to be told by someone else what he already believed to be the truth. And so, when I spoke, when my cowardice came bubbling up through my throat to be spewed forth like bile, he took me at my word, and it was all he needed. How I thanked Nakhtmin at the time, and how I have cursed him since for the information he gave me in the corridor that day.

"I have always assumed, Your Majesty," I said, "that there must be some trace of a god's blood running through your veins. Forgive me for speaking so bluntly, but I have always considered you to be in some way divine."

Amenophis smiled, and I was condemned.

Nakhtmin promised himself that every person he told about Amenophis would be the last. He swore each to secrecy, and each swore everyone they told to secrecy as well. Before the day was out half of Malkarta knew the young king's suspicions. News reached Aye and Tiye, and Yuya and Thuya, and would have travelled as far as Amenhotep had anyone possessed the courage to wake him from an afternoon sleep. By the following day the news had spread as far as the temple of Amun in Thebes, where Ptahmose received it with a mixture of joy and incredulity.

"Now I have him," he said to the young priest who brought him the news.

He issued instructions for the senior members of the priesthood to gather in the anteroom of the temple's inner sanctum. Ptahmose's heart was racing as he strode purposefully through the maze of corridors that ran through the temple like veins, his robes fluttering behind him as though struggling to keep up. He was smiling without realising it.

Ptahmose had little to say to the priests who crowded into the antechamber. Most of them left after a few minutes none the wiser as to the reason for their attendance, and had they suspected why they were there a good many of them would have slipped from the room a good deal sooner. Ptahmose surveyed the faces before him as they filed in. He was looking for someone specifically, although he had no idea who they may be until they arrived. And then, just as the stragglers were arriving, he saw them. There were two, and they arrived together.

They were ideal.

The day of the *sed* festival dawned at last, and although all those with a part in its preparation and execution had waited long for its arrival, none felt truly ready now that it was finally here. Everyone would have preferred perhaps just one more rehearsal, just one more opportunity to scan their instructions for that one small but crucial step they had forgotten that would make the difference between success and an ignominious and calamitous end for the festival and themselves.

The crowds began forming long before daybreak. These were the less celebrated of the attendees, those who had not been housed at the palace during the previous days and weeks, who would not be escorted to the *sed* festival site by an honour guard, and who would not be shaded from the heat of the desert sun by brightly coloured canopies. Groups huddled together for warmth and, shivering, prayed for the sun to rise. A constant stream were soon arriving at the site, endlessly ferried from Thebes by river craft of every size and shape. Few remained in the city, and those who did remarked to each other on the eerie silence of the place. The shouts of traders echoed off the walls of the buildings surrounding the market place and came back as parodies of themselves. The few stalls that had opened were closed again by mid morning.

As the sun rose the guests at Malkarta began making their way along the causeway that linked the palace to the festival site at Kom el-Samak, where a gaudily painted mud brick platform had been built on the desert sand. Soldiers lined the road along its entire length, their spears held before them. Behind the soldiers were standing row upon row of chariots, their horses as well-trained and still as the charioteers who held the reins. The show of strength was not lost on those foreign potentates that walked the causeway.

In his dressing room King Amenhotep was preparing himself, with the help of his family and a host of servants, to appear before his public. Only Amenophis and Nefertiti were not present. They were already at the festival site, leading the ceremony and complicated rituals designed to prepare the ground for the coming day's events. The dressing room was small and the number of people present prevented any activity appearing anything other than chaotic. When one person moved, everybody else had to move to accommodate them. Only the king was allowed the luxury of staying stationary. The impression was one of storm battered branches swaying around a steady trunk.

One woman was delicately threading ear rings through the piercings in Amenhotep's ears. Another was applying the heavy ceremonial face paint. A third was attaching a rearing cobra fashioned from gold and lapis lazuli to the front of Amenhotep's kilt. Another was struggling to fix sedge-plant blossoms to a sash that hung around the king's huge belt. His arms were fed through armbands, his wig adjusted and readjusted, wide *shebyu* collars and sun-disk pendants placed around his neck and delicately arranged to be as pleasing as possible to the eye.

"What are we to do?" Tiye said.

"Please try to stay calm, my dear," Amenhotep replied. "There is nothing to be done until after the festival anyway. I will speak to him then."

Every time he spoke the woman kneeling before his seat had to stop applying make-up to his face. She rubbed at a line of red ochre that had smeared from his lips onto the white face paint of his cheek, and prayed the king did not notice her involuntary show of annoyance at the disruption.

Aye noticed the frustration in the king's voice. This was undoubtedly not the first time Tiye had raised the matter of Amenophis since Nakhtmin had spread the news around the palace. Aye thought it prudent to change the subject.

"How are your teeth?" he asked.

"Bearable."

"And your strength? Will it serve to carry out your physical duties today?"

"I am sure I shall be fine."

Privately, Amenhotep had been worrying about his tasks at the festival for some time. A large part of the day would be spent with him sitting on his throne on the stage, simply watching the celebrations take place before him, and that in itself was going to be a strain, craving as he would be for food and his bed. But the rest of the time Amenhotep would be expected to take part. He would be expected to symbolically claim the land by running – *running!* – between boundary markers that represented Egypt's borders. He would be expected to erect the huge *Djed* pillar, symbol of stability and the backbone of Osiris, by the force of his hands alone. He would be expected to drive cattle around the walls of Thebes four times.

Amenhotep felt suffused with exhaustion merely at the thought of it all. As he stood up he said a silent prayer to Ra to not beat down too enthusiastically on the proceedings. His jubilee cloak was wrapped around him and the crown of Upper and Lower Egypt placed atop his head.

"Come," he said, and started for the door.

Outside, a fleet of chariots awaited the royal party. Amenhotep had ordered that there should be one chariot more than was needed to accommodate them all.

"It is for Tjenuna and Maiherperi," he had explained. "I am only able to celebrate my jubilee because of their sacrifice. It is only fitting that they should be invited to attend."

It was a grand procession. Aye and his wife Tey, Yuya and Thuya, Huya and the one chariot empty save for its driver all followed the chariots of the king and queen along the colonnade. The sentries on either side, as custom dictated, prostrated themselves as the king approached, glad of the opportunity to change position.

The crowd around the festival stage had by now swelled into the thousands. A huge roar of approval went up as the king mounted the steps to his throne. The royal party fanned out behind him, each sitting in the chair that had been allocated to them.

The festivities could now begin in earnest. In front of the stage was a large square area of desert that had been cordoned off and around which rows of tables had been placed, creaking under the weight of the food and drink that had been piled upon them. The wine began to flow from jugs fashioned into the shape of Hathor, the goddess of love and joy. At each table were sitting the lesser royal wives and courtiers and dignitaries from every level of Egyptian life. Nearer the stage, served by an army of waitresses, were the tables of the guests of honour, the kings from abroad. They had already made significant inroads on the generous repast. Most had travelled for weeks to attend, and now they were here they were going to make the best of it.

On the far side of the tables, and behind another line of soldiers, was the crowd. Its members pressed forward at the first sight of the king and it was all the guards could do to keep them back and prevent them from spilling onto the tables and into the laps of the guests of honour. The roar that greeted the king was unimaginable. He could remember nothing that rivalled it in volume since the cries of the Nubians at the battle of Napata. He raised his hand in a wave and the cheers grew even louder. Amenophis was already sitting to his father's right, and his expression of forced bonhomie told Amenhotep that the young king's reception had hardly approached this.

In the square were the boundary markers that Amenhotep would have to run between, and the Djed pillar which he would have to erect. They were currently difficult to make out behind the troops of singers, dancers and musicians who surrounded them. Wishing to waste as little time as possible, Amenhotep nodded towards Kheruef the scribe, who had been especially honoured today by being given the role of master of ceremonies. Kheruef signalled the performers, who immediately launched into a complicated and cacophonous interpretation of the forming of order from chaos at the beginning of time. Amenhotep felt a short pang of pain in his mouth. Wondering how long it would be before the pain became excruciating, he held the side of his face and attempted to appear enthusiastic.

Ptahmose did not expect his absence from the jubilee celebrations to be noticed by any other than those few of his enclave who knew he would not be attending, and who were only there themselves to occupy those seats which would otherwise have looked conspicuous for lack of employment. Ptahmose had more important things with which to occupy himself than sunning himself in the desert. Besides, the High Priest of Ptah had been asked to officiate at the festival, and Ptahmose had felt the snub as keenly as he was sure Amenhotep had intended him to.

Ptahmose had been making himself busy while the fops and the gentry fawned over their idol and his son, the false god. He had been granted the shortest of times in which to make his preparations and he applied himself to them to the exclusion of all else, foregoing even food and sleep in his determination to ensure Amun's success in this undertaking.

After the antechamber had been filled with his priests Ptahmose had made a short and meaningless speech before allowing his confused audience to disperse. The priests had only been there in order to allow Ptahmose to select two from their number, and now he had done so he had no further use for them. He asked the chosen two to wait behind as their colleagues filed from the room.

Anen had been amongst them, unnoticed by Ptahmose, and he left the room as nonplussed as any of the other priests. Ptahmose was not known as a motivational speaker and rarely went to the trouble of calling the priesthood together without having a pressing reason for doing so. Anen was one of the last to leave the room and, presuming that he was being addressed, turned to face Ptahmose when he heard him say, "You and you. Wait. Close the door."

Ptahmose was pointing to two young priests whom Anen vaguely knew from his walks around the temple. He had shared ceremonial duties with them once or twice, but knew nothing of them beyond that. His interest was piqued. What reason could Ptahmose have to speak to two lowly characters such as these? Once outside the door he made a pretence of picking a stone from the inside of his sandal and allowed the press of priests to move off without him. Once alone in the corridor he backed up and, feeling a surge of fear in his chest, stood with his ear against the door that had been closed behind him.

What he heard filled him with dismay.

"I have a very special duty for you both," Ptahmose told the two priests who had remained behind. "You alone have each been singled out by Amun himself, so highly does he value each of you. He spoke your names to me himself. He has a task for you which will earn you eternal life at his right hand and glory and blessings beyond counting."

In reality, Ptahmose had no idea what their names were. He had picked them because he did not recognise their faces in the crowd and logic told him that any priest who had never before come to his attention must be dispensable.

They appeared as enthusiastic to do the god's bidding as he had known they would be, but he also knew that their resolve would have to be strengthened further before he could fully trust them with their assignment.

He held up his arms as though he was about to embrace them both.

"Follow me," he said, and turned towards the god's inner sanctum. They did not move, as he had known they would not, and halfway to the door he stopped and turned to face them.

"Come," he said with a smile, and gestured to them to follow.

"High Priest," the taller of the two men said, a look of nervous confusion on his face. "Do you mean for us to enter Amun's room?"

"I do."

"But, High Priest, it is forbidden. It is the holy of holies."

"Amun would like to see you. He specifically gave me instructions to that effect. You have been given, shall we say, *special dispensation.*"

The two priests took one or two hesitant steps forward, as though they feared that Ptahmose's invite was a trap.

"Really," he said. "Come."

He walked forwards and opened the large double doors that led to the god's inner sanctuary. This time the two priests followed.

Outside the audience chamber Anen was taking brief, shallow breaths because, although the voices that melted through the door were muffled and difficult to decipher he was afraid that the persons within would be able to hear the air passing in and out of his throat. He had understood the majority of what had passed between Ptahmose and the priests, and knew that they had been picked for some momentous mission. Ptahmose was yet to explain to them the exact nature of their duties, but Anen was troubled by the conversation he had heard. What could be so important and yet could not be shared with the rest of the temple? He heard Ptahmose leading the two priests into Amun's inner sanctum and knew that he would gain nothing by remaining where he was any longer. A sensible course of action now would be to alert the authorities. But who? He could certainly not approach another priest, and even if he were lucky enough to find a soldier who did not sympathise with the priesthood and who would not turn him over to the temple, what could he say? That two priests had been given extra duties but that he had no idea what those duties were? He would be laughed at and dismissed.

It would be so easy for Anen to decide that this was none of his business. To turn away, follow the other priests back out into the main corridors and courtyards of the temple and forget that anything out of the ordinary had occurred. He could already feel the release of tension that such a course of action would grant him. He would be fully justified in telling himself that, whatever happened, there truly was nothing he could have done about it without placing himself in mortal danger. It was beyond his power to intervene in any meaningful sense. And yet Anen also knew that here lay an opportunity. He entertained a brief fantasy of being welcomed back to court in Memphis, showered with honours and embraced by the king, having proved his worth and his loyalty in an act of selfless courage that prevented... what? Could it really be that Ptahmose was involved in some plot? The circumstances could be called nothing more than suspicious, and perhaps the proximity of the *sed* festival was merely coincidental.

The voices from within had faded into silence and Anen knew the three men had passed from the audience chamber into the inner sanctum. Slowly, pushing with one hand and pulling with the other to make the movement as smooth and silent as possible, Anen edged the door ajar. The room beyond was indeed empty. Convinced in equal measure that he would hear nothing but Ptahmose commanding the priests to undertake some meaningless cleaning work and that he would be discovered at any second, Anen stepped into the audience chamber and made his best attempt at gliding silently across the floor towards the other doorway. Each scrape of a sandal stopped him as though he had encountered an invisible wall and he waited in agonising silence, not daring to breathe, until he was sure that his subterfuge had not been detected.

Past the doorway was a small room, smaller than either of the two priests had been expecting, with only a few paces separating the four walls. It was oppressively dark, lit only by the light that fell through the doorway and half a dozen lamps that dotted the walls. Ptahmose closed the door behind them and suddenly the areas of illumination in the room seemed to become nothing more than places where even the shadows feared to lay themselves. The priests could see, in those areas nearest the lamps, that the walls were painted the purest white and decorated with scenes of Amun appearing before the people at the festival of Opet. He stood tall in these scenes, caught in mid-stride as the populace cowered around his feet and his wife and child awaited him.

Before Ptahmose and the two priests, beyond a hazy veil of lamp smoke and the sweet odour it carried, was the shrine, and upon the shrine stood Amun's ceremonial barque, and upon the barque stood Amun himself, the king of the gods, the Hidden One. He was crafted from gold and his torso glimmered with reflected points of lamplight that still flickered in the draught from the closing door. He was not tall, perhaps the height of a young child. The priests were afforded only the briefest of glances before they instinctively fell to their knees in prostration and, perhaps confused by the lamplight and the wall painting, it seemed to them that Amun was small and close but at the same time much larger and further away, and their eyes had to fight to find their focus.

This place was neither earth nor heaven. It was a borderland, ill-defined, somehow here and yet somewhere else at the same time. The priests were under the gaze of god in a very palpable sense, in the entrance hall to his kingdom, the ephemeral in the presence of the eternal.

"You may rise," a voice said, and the priests did so, realising almost with a sense of disappointment that it had been Ptahmose who had spoken and not Amun.

"Amun is very pleased with you," Ptahmose said. He could see, even in this dim light, that the two priests were trembling, their gaze captured by that of Amun. He knew now that they would not fail him, that their courage would be buoyed aloft by this audience and that the memory of it would compel them to complete whatever task was asked of them.

"Out of all the peoples of the world," Ptahmose said, "you alone are chosen. Amun asks if you are willing to carry out that which is in his heart."

"Yes, High Priest," the priests said together.

"Excellent," Ptahmose said. Despite their awe, and still staring at Amun, the priests were smiling now, too afraid to show any more emotion than that but so clearly elated that Ptahmose thought he would sense it even if the lamps in the room were extinguished.

As he explained the duty for which they had been chosen, their smiles began to fade.

Ptahmose did not speak of cleaning duties. What he said made it impossible for Anen, who was once again pressing his ear to the door, to retreat to any place of safety, despite the fact that the peril of his situation increased with every word that Ptahmose spoke.

For the moment all he could do was wait and listen. There were no circumstances under which he could enter Amun's inner chamber and, even if he were to flout such laws, once inside he would be quickly overpowered and would have served no cause other than Ptahmose's. He needed every advantage that could be bled from the situation, and that meant hearing everything that Ptahmose had to say.

Fighting every instinct that told him to flee, that he could have no warning before the door would reopen and leave him to tumble into the room beyond, Anen remained where he was. This was a heavier door than the one which had been Anen's previous resting place, and the voices that leaked through it were more muffled and difficult to understand, but Anen managed to gather that Ptahmose was taking his acolytes through every step of his plan from start to fruition, reiterating the salient points and then asking the priests to repeat them once again. Anen was missing one piece of information, and that was where the act was to take place. He had obviously still been traversing the floor when Ptahmose had furnished the priests with the information.

Once or twice he fancied that the voices from within grew suddenly clearer and closer and he would take one or two instinctive steps towards the corridor before getting a grip on himself and skulking back to the door, cursing himself for what he could have missed.

He continued listening, waiting for the door to open and his life to be over. When the latch did finally click open and the door swung on its hinges it did so with no warning ample enough for Anen to make even an instinctive bid for escape.

Had it opened more quickly and given Anen less chance to react it would have given his claims of innocence more credence, but as it was it gave him time to adopt the guilty posture of a man about to devote all his energies to flight. He was caught in indecision by the time he had taken his first step, and he stopped. Had he continued running he may have been able to make good his escape. Had he made no attempt to run at all he may have brazened it out.

But Anen was not a man for whom acts of bravery and adventure were instinctive, and as it was he did both, and neither, and he was lost.

Ptahmose and Anen faced each other in silence, shock apportioned equally between them.

Chapter Ten

The Sed Festival (2)

PTAHMOSE WAS the first to recover.

"Anen?" he said, surprise pitching his voice in a tone higher than he would have liked.

"High Priest," Anen said. "I was... I was looking for you."

"For what reason?"

For what reason? Anen thought. *For what possible reason?*

"I wished to ask if you were ready to come to the festival."

"Despite the fact that, were I going to the festival, I would have already been there hours ago?"

"Erm," said Anen.

"And I presume that there is a good reason for you, having found me, to turn tail and lose me all over again?"

"The door frightened me," Anen said. "I was close to it when it opened and it took me by surprise."

"I see," Ptahmose said. "You were close to it when it opened, were you?"

"Yes, High Priest."

"And was there any particular reason for that?"

"I was looking for you, High Priest."

"And you could not see from the outer doorway that I was not in the room? You had to examine the area fully before you could be sure, did you? Do you have the eyes of an Amenophis, that you need to be within arms' reach of every wall before you can tell whether anything stands between you and it?"

"No, High Priest."

"What about these gentlemen over here?" Ptahmose said, waving his arm to indicate the two priests, who were standing nervously in the doorway to the inner sanctum. "Can you see them?"

"Of course, High Priest," Anen said.

"Really? You can? From there? Well done. *Excellent.* Perhaps, then, you could tell me why you were so close to the door that it startled you when it opened."

"I was looking for you, High Priest."

"We have already established, Anen, that you could tell the room was empty from the corridor, a full fifteen paces away. What I am trying to ascertain now is why you took it upon yourself to walk over here." The arm waved again to indicate exactly where 'here' was. "Were you perhaps going to open that door to look for me within? The door which, under the sacred law of Amun, you are strictly forbidden from opening? You would risk that just to find out whether I was going to the festival?"

"Of course not, High Priest."

"*Of course not, High Priest*," Ptahmose repeated, and paused. "Well?" he said, finally.

Anen knew he was caught. It smarted to be outwitted a second time by Ptahmose, and it was twice the humiliation to know how little effort the High Priest needed to put into his argument in order to defeat him. He looked at the ground in front of his sandals.

"I was listening at the door," he said, for he could think of nothing else that he *could* say. This was the answer that Ptahmose wanted, and Anen did not think he had the wit to avoid speaking it. "I was listening to see if you were in there," he said. "If you were I thought I might wait outside for you."

"Ah," Ptahmose said. "Now perhaps we approach the environs of the truth. To sum up: you saw the room was empty, came in, and listened at this door."

"I was about to listen when the door opened, High Priest."

"Of course you were, Anen. Of course you were. What exactly did you hear?"

"Nothing at all, High Priest. As I said, I was about to press my ear to the door when it opened."

"You have tangled with me once before, have you not, Anen?"

Anen wanted to defuse the situation. He wanted to agree with Ptahmose, but he did not want to admit to something as confrontational as having tangled with him. He wanted a less abrasive word, but the word would not come and finally he said, simply, "Yes."

"And do you feel that you did so well the last time that you would try to oppose me once more?"

"No, High Priest."

"Then do not try to outwit me again. You have neither the stomach nor the intelligence. What did you hear at the door?"

"Nothing, High Priest."

"Who are these men?"

"I know not, High Priest."

"What are they to do this day?"

"I know not, High Priest."

"You have always been an awful liar, Anen. I cannot say that this performance is any more remarkable than all the other times you have lied to me. But now you have a problem, for now you are no longer any use to me. You have no value alive and free that is not outweighed by the value of you dead, and silent."

"Ptahmose, I swear..."

"Enough," Ptahmose said. "You." He indicated one of the priests. "Fetch me a couple of guards."

The priest began to walk from the room.

"Look sharp, man!" Ptahmose shouted. The priest broke into a run.

When he returned, he was accompanied by two burly looking guards.

"Take this man to a secure place and hold him there," Ptahmose told him. "I shall be along shortly to deal with him."

"High Priest..." Anen began, but was cut short by a firm hand on each shoulder that twisted him around and pushed him towards the door. "High Priest, please," he said as he was propelled from the room.

With a guard before and behind him, he was marched along temple corridors he rarely frequented. Here his way was lit not by the sun but only by lamps that cast menacing shadows. Before long the leading guard stopped by an open doorway. Although he offered no resistance and turned into the doorway of his own volition, the guards gave Anen one last shove which sent him headlong across the room beyond. The door slammed shut behind him and he heard the latch click into place.

He stared at the door for a long while without a thought in his head, as though everything he knew was locked away on the other side where he could not put it to use. The only sounds were the occasional cough or shuffle of feet from beyond the threshold to indicate that the guards were still present.

I am doomed, he thought. There will be no deals. Not this time. I have nothing to offer that could profit the High Priest one iota. All he requires of me now is that I remain silent, for I am the only man under the heavens with knowledge of the events he is about to set in motion, and of his culpability in them. And there is only one truly flawless way to ensure I keep that silence.

He looked around him. The room was lit by a small window set high into the wall above his head that cast a misshapen rectangle of light at his feet. The room was empty of furniture and adornments save for a worn mat of rushes that lay in one corner to serve as a bed.

Anen lay on it and wondered how long he would have to wait, and how long it would be before the king's fate was sealed.

The two priests, whose names Ptahmose had since discovered to be Tutu and Ranefer, quickly changed out of their priestly garb. They laboriously removed their face paint and replaced it with make up more fitting a layman. They donned plaited wigs in an attempt to divert the eye from their ritual hairlessness. By the time they were finished even Ptahmose himself would not have recognised them as priests. He was delighted with the results.

"Excellent," he said, as he walked around them to examine them from every conceivable angle, and then again: "*Excellent.* You are to be congratulated."

Unfortunately the priests were no longer receptive to congratulations. They were beginning to balk at the full enormity of their task, and even the promise of an eternity spent at Amun's right hand paled somewhat against the backdrop of what they were about to face.

Even Ptahmose, who had sat and silently watched them transform themselves, had surprised himself with a momentary weakening of his resolve. He reminded himself that he was doing nothing but defending the prosperity of his god, that anything that befell Amenophis was a consequence not of Ptahmose's actions, but of Amenophis' desire for divinity. If the coregent's conceit had raised him, in his own mind, to the level of a god, was it not possible that such conceit was boundless? Was it not possible – nay, likely – that his arrogance would bear yet more poisonous fruit, and that the prominence of Amun in the firmament would one day itself be put under threat?

Ptahmose and Amun had no choice but to defend their position.

By the time the priests had prepared themselves, Ptahmose's steadfastness had reasserted itself. Anyway, Ptahmose himself had nothing to fear. The young priests would be dead or disappeared before long, and would have no opportunity to point an accusatory finger back towards the temple of Amun. With the priests disguised as laypeople, Ptahmose was confident of being able to successfully deny any involvement in the day's events.

"You are clear on your instructions?" Ptahmose asked of the two priests. Tutu and Ranefer nodded.

"Then away to your business," Ptahmose said. "And remember that you are under the protective gaze of your god. There is nothing to fear. Seek guidance through prayer, but do not for one second comfort yourselves with the mistaken belief that either Amun or myself will consent to failure. Carry with you in your mind the image of Amun himself. To you alone has it been granted, and there is no power in this world or the next to which you should have greater loyalty, or greater fear. Amun has seen you and he watches your every deed. And so I ask you again: are you clear on your instructions?"

The priests nodded again, and Ptahmose rested a hand on each of their heads in blessing.

"Godspeed," he said.

The exertions of his run between the boundary markers to symbolise his claim over the Two Lands had been enough to reduce Amenhotep to weak-kneed wreck, and the erection of the *Djed* pillar had been no easier, although it had at least given him something to lean against while he awaited the death that he thought surely imminent. Still, the crowd had roared its approval and he had the relative ease of the giving of gifts to look forward to.

But now the gifts were expended, the honoured guests had returned, laden, to their tables, and Amenhotep was still exhausted. It had taken nearly three hours to distribute all the presents and it had not been the rest-cure that he had been expecting. Throughout, the pain in his jaw had magnified, matched only by the ache in the small of his back from sitting immobile for such a length of time. It was impossible for him to call a halt to the proceedings, although the yearning to simply pace the length of the stage with his hand upon his back, as he had seen Giludkhepa do when she was heavily pregnant, had become so desirable as to be almost a fantasy. But the eyes of Egypt and beyond were upon him and this was no time for displays of infirmity. And so there he sat, without an audible word of complaint, and assayed to transform grimaces to smiles.

And now it was over, but only discomfort beyond his measure awaited him, and he was a man who had measured discomfort like an astronomer would measure the travels of the stars and the passing of the seasons.

The guards parted the crowd as Amenhotep approached. He walked through a forest of outstretched arms with Tiye and Amenophis at his side. Following closely behind were other honoured guests who would participate in the parade around the city walls, Nakhtmin and Horemheb among them. A ship waited to ferry them to the opposite bank of the Nile, where a number of chariots waited.

As Amenhotep mounted the chariot on the far side of the river he could see, a little way off, a herd of cattle, somnolent in the afternoon heat, surrounded by more guards who prevented them from moving beyond the limited confines of the space in which they found themselves. Amenhotep, with the help of his wife and son, and with a troop of family and courtiers in tow, was tasked with driving the cattle four times around the walls of the city. The knowledge that most of the work would in fact be carried out by the guards and that his presence there was nothing more than symbolic did little to raise Amenhotep's spirits. He took the opportunity of a moment's rest, leaning against the side of the chariot. His face pained him so acutely that his head was involuntarily twitching to one side with every beat of his heart.

"Have a care," he said to his driver. "I need this to be the smoothest ride of my life."

The three chariots containing Amenhotep, Amenophis and Tiye fanned out behind the herd, with Amenhotep in the middle and Amenophis behind and to his left. Behind them the other riders formed an untidy phalanx. Even here Amenhotep was required to remain the strong and unbowed king, for those residents of Thebes who had not been able to join their neighbours for the proceedings on the far bank took up position to cheer him along his route, some even standing atop the walls themselves.

Amenhotep raised his hand, hoping that its trembling could not be perceived from where the crowd stood, and an apprehensive silence fell. Amenhotep allowed his arm to drop and, with the aid of whips and cries of encouragement, the guards began the laborious process of persuading the lackadaisical cattle to embrace the exertion of a slow walk.

Amenhotep's chariot followed behind, the king wincing with every pebble and pothole negotiated.

The day was a hot one, and Tutu and Ranefer had to shade their eyes from the glare of the midday sun on the white buildings that surrounded them. The streets were empty and silent, and the whole of Thebes had the air of a town that had recently been abandoned to the desert. At intervals they would hear distant shouts. The occasional cat and, at one point, a small child ran across their path, but apart from these diversions they were alone in the city. Despite its lack of impediment their pace was a slow and reluctant one. Neither relished the prospect of what awaited them beyond the city gates. In the main, they walked in silence. As they drew closer to the city walls a change seemed to come over the atmosphere. A noise which, at first, had sounded like a breeze blowing through the deserted streets, increased in volume until it became the aimless chatter of a thousand voices. Expectation and excitement hung in the air like heat. Tutu and Ranefer turned a final corner and saw the city walls stretching out before them, disappearing in the maze of streets and houses to the priests' right and left. It was from beyond this wall that the noise of the crowd came, close enough now for the priests to be able to discern individual voices which would be raised now and then above the hubbub. Judging by the cornucopia of accents and dialects, the gathering was a cosmopolitan affair. Tutu and Ranefer turned to their right to search for a gate that would lead them out into the throng.

The cell was growing hotter by the minute. There was nowhere for the air to circulate and the cell faced west where it took the full brunt of the afternoon sun. The very stones of the walls seemed to radiate warmth. Anen was lying on the reed mat again, breathless and sweating. The thin veneer of his initial calm had dissolved within a few minutes to leave him at the mercy of the panic within. The full enormity of his situation had ricocheted around the cell, bouncing at him from every wall and consuming him with anguish. He had no doubt that he was about to die, and suddenly he was unwilling to accept that fate with equanimity. He was happy to forego his dignity and pride as a small ransom for his life.

He spent some time hammering against the door and pleading with the guards that he knew were still there, without eliciting any noticeable response. He wept and he begged, he promised them everything within his power to grant, and a number of things that were not, in return for mercy, but was accorded only silence. Realising the futility of this course of action, Anen turned his attention to escape without the aid of the guards. He grazed the skin from his knees and elbows and tore off one of his toenails in attempting to jump up the wall to reach the window, although he knew it to be too small to accommodate him. It stayed resolutely out of his reach. Favouring desperation over logic, he rolled up the reed mat and leant it on one end against the wall under the window. He tried half a dozen times to climb onto it to give him a vantage point from where he was sure he could reach the window. It collapsed each time before he had put even a fraction of his weight onto it.

Finally, he had despaired. He had thrown the mat back into the corner of the room and himself on top of it, comforting himself with the thought that escape would perhaps be more likely when the guards opened the door in order to dispatch him. He decided to rest and gather his strength.

When he heard voices outside the door he leapt immediately to his feet, not hearing or caring what they were saying. The very presence of voices was enough to convince him that his fate was at hand. He began to curse himself for accepting defeat with the rolled up mat so easily. Perhaps if he had continued in his efforts he would have eventually met with success. Now there was no time, and he had to think quickly and without panic. He moved across the room to hide behind the door, planning to pounce and run as soon as it opened before him.

The door remained closed. It was a moment before he realised that the voices without were continuing in conversation. He strained to hear them through the thick wood of the door, but caught only the occasional

word. *Anen*, he heard. *Ptahmose*, he heard. *Imperative*, he heard. *Urgency.*
Utmost.

There was the sound of footsteps retreating, and then the door
opened. Crying out, Anen threw himself forward.

It appeared that every gate to the city had been thrown open and,
uncharacteristically, left unsecured. As they approached, it became
obvious why there was so little need for security. Thebes had been
granted the most effective guard it had seen in its entire history. The
population itself was guarding the gates and, as the two priests began to
push their way forward through the almost impenetrable forest of torsos
that pressed against each other on the outside, they could see that hardly
a stone of the walls had been allowed to remain visible to the eye of any
with hostile intent.

The crowd was the largest gathering of people that Tutu or Ranefer
had ever seen. It was perhaps twenty or thirty deep, and stretched away
to either side, following the line of the wall, as far as the priests could see.
For all they knew, it enveloped the entire city.

Every neck was craned, every leg ached with the effort of stretching
onto tiptoes, every head turned towards where the royal party would
eventually emerge, preceded by the cattle. Despite the effort this involved,
every mouth chattered or sang or laughed or shouted, but hardly an ear
was tuned to anything other than each person's internal voice and the
knowledge that history was about to be made.

Only Tutu and Ranefer remained silent as they pushed their way
towards the front of the crowd, each of them wondering if any actually
realised the true history that was to come to pass, and how unique and
dreadful it would be.

Anen clattered to the floor with one of the guards beneath him. He had not
allowed himself, as he crouched in readiness, to admit the futility of his
struggle, to acknowledge that he was one against two, and that the two
were trained in the ways of combat and were armed. He would not allow
the thought to take hold that he was merely exacerbating his situation and
quickening his death. He fought not because it was brave or noble to do so,
but because he was to die in any event. If he fought he had a negligible
chance of success: if he did not, he had none. Still, he fully expected his bid
for freedom to last as long as it took for the remaining guard to bring his
sword down on Anen's head.

He had so convinced himself that the second guard would slay him in
a heartbeat that he quite forgot to implement the second phase of his plan,
and instead of maximising the advantage gained from the surprise of his

attack and darting for the door, he simply lay there, pinning the first guard to the ground and waiting for the deadly blow, his eyes tightly closed.

For a moment, nothing happened.

And then a voice, a voice that Anen recognised, spoke.

"Are you finished?" it said.

Anen opened his eyes and saw that the man he had bundled to the ground was not a guard at all. It was Iny.

"What?" Anen managed to ask.

"I suggest we make our way out of the temple rather quickly," Iny said.

Anen looked around. There were no guards.

"What?" he said again.

"If we are to make good our escape," Iny said. He gave Anen a nudge and the pair got to their feet.

"The guards believe they have been summoned to attend Ptahmose on a matter of some urgency," Iny said. "It would be advisable for us not to be here when they return."

Anen was immobile. Iny shoved him towards the door.

"I saw you being escorted here," he said. "I could hardly leave you to your fate, could I? You can thank me later. For now, we need to devote all our energies to flight."

Anen seemed to come to himself, as though he were waking from a sleep.

"I need to get to the city walls," he said. "The king! Has the cattle drive started?"

"I think so," Iny said.

The pair ran through the convoluted corridors of the temple, expecting to meet the guards at every turn. The temple had never seemed as large as it did now. Anen prayed to see sunlight at every junction, and every new corridor was a frustration. On they ran, surprised priests pressing themselves against the wall to avoid collisions, until, finally, just as Anen was beginning to believe that the temple would never be rid of him, the pair turned into a corridor that was suffused with sunlight. They hared out into a courtyard and turned left to go through a series of gateways and more courtyards, each larger and more exhausting than the last. By the time they had passed through the final gateway that led out onto the road that ran to the temple of Mut, Anen was beginning to flag. Iny overtook him, urging him onwards, but Iny was a man accustomed to physical effort, whereas Anen had grown up in a palace. Gradually, his pace began to slow. The soles of his sandals began to slap against the floor where previously they had barely touched it. Eventually, he stopped and leant with his hands resting on his knees.

"We need a chariot," he said, between whooping gulps of air. "I cannot... Get me a chariot."

Iny cast him an exasperated look before turning and running back towards the temple. With an uneven gait, Anen followed behind.

Tutu and Ranefer had managed to secure themselves a position at the front of the crowd, from where they had an unequalled vantage point to watch the approach of the cattle drive. As yet they could only see the heads of the foremost animals, the rest being obscured behind a choking cloud of dust that rose from around their hooves. Spectators stood on either side of the royal route, the gap between both sides narrowing as each person took a step further forward than the person to the side from which the king approached in order to gain as long and as clear a view as possible. This was a sight with which each spectator would be able to regale their grandchildren and each one of them wished to be able to commit as many details as possible to memory. The two priests' fidgeting and nervous glances passed unnoticed. Many people, even those who had spent some time sharing the same modest patch of ground with them, would later struggle to remember their faces, or even their presence.

The rumble of the cattle's hooves and a shaking of the ground preceded the herd as they drew closer. Tutu rested his hand on the waistband of his kilt, under which lay an unobtrusive bulge. Ranefer swallowed heavily. Had anyone been watching them, they would have seen a general readiness overcome them, a tensing of the muscles, a quickening of the breath, as though they were preparing themselves to fight or fly, or both.

The herd had by now been coaxed into quickening its step into an uninterested trot. The royal chariots became visible as silhouettes through the dust cloud and the priests were forced to step backwards as the crowd parted to allow the herd's passage.

Both Tutu and Ranefer had been secretly hoping that they would find that Amenophis' chariot, when it approached, would be on the far side of those of Tiye and Amenhotep. Should this have been the case it would not have enabled them to resign their mission, but they would have been forced to allow the party to pass before redeploying themselves in a more advantageous position for the second lap. Such was their fear that even this small reprieve would have seemed to them to be the sweet breath of Amun himself. As it was, Amenophis' chariot was closest to them, and they were already perfectly placed. The herd was level with them now. They shared a glance, each hoping the other would speak first with a creditable reason why they could not complete their assignment. Both remained silent and the moment was lost.

The herd passed, and then the soldiers who ran behind it, their whips still occasionally cracking the air. An unimportant number of paces behind them trundled the royal chariots, their drivers and passengers as oblivious as the crowd as to the intentions of the two priests who simultaneously stepped out from the throng as the chariots drew level.

Amenophis was bored and irritated. A breeze blew in exactly the wrong direction, wafting the distasteful stench of the herd directly into his face. To either side his vision rendered the crowd into a featureless mass of brown and white as though he was travelling between two dirty tributaries decorated with the white crests of waves. It was a claustrophobic feeling made all the worse by the knowledge that everyone here, every shout and every wave of the arm, was for the benefit of his father. As coregent, Amenophis privately seethed at the fact that he had not been invited to ride in his rightful place alongside his father. Instead, here he was, relegated to the ranks, lumped together with the boorish Nakhtmin and his clan. Glancing around, Amenophis saw Horemheb's chariot directly behind his own. The very idea! Who was Horemheb, other than a common soldier? He was not yet even a general. What right did he have to be here, almost alongside one of his kings, other than a remote association with court via Nakhtmin? None, so far as Amenophis could determine. Amenophis decided to discover who had been responsible for the organisation of this part of the festival and have a few harsh words with him. Perhaps, he thought, he could even take the opportunity to tear a strip or two from Horemheb himself. It was always important to stress the relative positions of those around him. It would do Horemheb good to fully understand that a friendship with the king's brother-in-law would benefit him nothing, especially when that brother-in-law was as distasteful as Nakhtmin. The thought of some new targets at which he could vent his spleen momentarily cheered him, and he even ventured a wave in the direction of the crowd to his left.

He did not see the two young men that lunged forward until it was far too late to react to save himself.

Tutu and Ranefer had discussed their strategy in as much detail as time and circumstances would allow. But come the moment for action any intricacies of a plan, such as they were, were lost as though in the cloud of dust that rose around the two priests. The crowd had become euphorically unruly at the proximity of the king, and the priests were able to use the confusion as cover when removing bronze daggers from the waistbands of their kilts. They both stepped forward. Amenophis' chariot was perhaps a dozen paces from them, and moving slowly.

Tutu was in front, torn between a sprint and a more relaxed pace that would take longer but draw less attention. He settled for something between the two, which had the advantages of neither.

The roads of Thebes were not designed for chariots travelling at speed. Anen and Iny could hardly hear themselves shout over the noise of the wheels rumbling against the uneven path. Occasionally they would hit stones and potholes large enough to lift them from their feet. As they neared the area where they knew the cattle drive had started, they could see that it was almost deserted, the crowd having dispersed itself along the royal route. Anen and Iny raced past and followed the route that the cattle drive had taken. Within moments they were charging through the crowd, which had closed up behind the royal party. Fearing that they may already be too late, Anen barely slowed down, but instead shouted and cracked his whip over the heads of the throng in the hope that they would part before his chariot.

Up ahead he could now make out the chariots of Amenophis, Amenhotep and Tiye. He saw two men step out from the crowd and advance towards Amenophis' chariot. Although they were no longer dressed in priestly garb, and although their heads were now decorated with wigs, Anen recognised them immediately. They were a few paces from Amenophis' chariot, one in front of the other. Anen handed the reins to Iny. The chariot sped onwards.

Horemheb, in the chariot behind Amenophis, saw the two men emerge from the crowd. Even before he had seen the daggers clutched in their hands, some soldier's instinct told him that their intentions were nefarious. He had no idea what those intentions may be, only that the two men were heading towards the Amenophis' chariot. He jumped from the back of his own chariot and broke into a sprint towards the two interlopers. It was only when he had closed half the distance between them that he noticed the knives. He stepped up his pace.

"Amenophis!" he shouted as he ran. "*Amenophis!*"

Amenophis was still oblivious as Tutu reached the side of his chariot. Even if his eyesight had not been flawed, the priests were approaching from behind his left shoulder. The only clue to his predicament came when he heard Horemheb's shout of warning. As he was turning, he saw an indistinct shape fill his vision to his left and felt the chariot buck under the sudden application of another man's weight.

An arm snaked its way around his neck, the bony forearm pushing painfully against his prominent larynx, restricting his breathing so that his cry of alarm emerged as an ineffectual wheeze.

"I act for Amun," a voice whispered in his ear. "He declares you a false god."

Horemheb had known he would be too late. He was intent only on the man who had clambered aboard Amenophis' chariot. The assailant's colleague was only three or four steps behind him but it was enough for Horemheb to discount him from being an immediate danger to the king. Horemheb knew he would beat him to the chariot and so could safely relegate him to a secondary threat, but he saw equally well that he would arrive too late to prevent the first attacker's knife thrust. He ran on regardless, hardly registering the chariot that raced past him.

Anen saw the priest step onto the back of Amenophis' chariot. He saw the priest's arm draw back in preparation for a blow. He saw the glint of the knife in the sunlight.

Too late, he thought. *After everything, we are too late.* He grabbed Iny's arm and pointed towards the second priest. Iny nodded his understanding and subtly adjusted the chariot's angle of approach until it targeted the second priest head on. Anen turned his attention back to the priest who was standing on Amenophis' chariot. He seemed to be whispering something in the king's ear. It was enough of a delay to the final blow to give Anen the opportunity to strike. The chariot passed Horemheb as though he was standing still.

As the chariot closed in, Anen launched himself forwards at full stretch.

Unaware of Anen's desperate leap, Tutu drew his free arm back even further and plunged the knife forwards towards Amenophis' ribcage. Anen landed on Tutu just as the knife struck home. Amenophis tried to cry out again as he felt a line of fire trace itself across his back and side. His strength fled from him and he collapsed sideways.

The entire drama was played out before any of the audience could react. There was a moment of quiet before everyone began to shout and scream and run in aimless panic from one place to the next with no regard as to what they would do when they got there.

Anen's momentum had thrown him clear of Amenophis' chariot, and he lay a few paces away from it, dazed and bruised. Ranefer lay in the road with his own crowd of spectators forming around him. The hooves of Iny's horses and the wheels of his chariot had crushed the breath from his body.

Meanwhile, on Amenophis' chariot there lay three men. The topmost was Horemheb, who was wrestling Tutu away from the fallen king with one arm wrenched painfully up his back in a grip which Horemheb seemed in no hurry to loosen. Nakhtmin stepped in to help him while Tiye, Amenhotep, Nefertiti and Aye crowded around the chariot, their faces speaking more of their horror than could a month of words. Amenophis lay face down, a trickle of blood meandering out from underneath him to drip off the edge of the chariot. Nefertiti was the first to reach down to him, whispering his name over and over, as though she was afraid to wake him.

She gently turned him onto his back and searched his face for signs of life.

End of Part Two

Part Three

King Sun

Chapter Eleven

The Tiller Unmanned

The Maya Papyrus, Fragments 54-55

I HAD been angry at the time, when I was told that I would not be honoured with an invitation to accompany the royal party around the walls of Thebes. I could almost reconcile myself with the fact that Nakhtmin had been included; after all, he was by now a senior military figure and brother to Nefertiti, while I was only a scribe and brother to Nefertiti, which is a wholly different thing. But that Horemheb had been invited, purely at the insistence of his friend Nakhtmin, I found completely mystifying.

I remained at the festival site, kicking at pebbles as I watched the crowd dissipate until I picked a stone that, unhappy at my assault, broke my toenail. I swore under my breath and tried to hide my limp as I walked away lest anybody had witnessed my childish tantrum.

Of course, when I heard what had happened I was more than grateful for my absence, and as my toenail blackened its significance paled. The news spread around Thebes and to Malkarta with the speed that only an eagerly relayed story can attain, and arrived long before the ships docked at Malkarta harbour and unloaded their frantic cargo of passengers. I had plenty of time to make my way to the dockside to await their arrival.

The rumours, as is a rumour's wont, only seemed to specify details enough to feed one's appetite for more, and omitted everything but the fact that Amenophis had been attacked. Not even the application of a hand to a throat, had I the courage or desire to attempt such a tactic, could have wrung any further details from those who ran from one person to the next, proclaiming the news. And so my first thought was that Amenophis had been killed, and I discovered that it was a prospect that did not displease me. I was ashamed of myself at the *time, and I asked the gods to forgive the thought that life may become much easier if he did not survive. I thought it was a reflection that would weigh against me come the day of the judgement of my soul. Of course, now I think my prescience a positive boon, and I often remind the gods of it in my prayers.*

It had been quickly ascertained that Tutu's attack had not been a fatal one. Amenophis was not only breathing, but, as panic had already set in, was doing so at an alarming rate. Blood was flowing freely from his back and side in a long wound. Nefertiti arranged him into what looked a more comfortable posture and ran alongside his chariot, together with what seemed to be half of Thebes, as he was transported back towards the river.

Despite being efficiently pinned to the ground by all of Horemheb's weight Tutu refused to stop struggling. A host of hands reached down to restrain him and Horemheb quickly had to turn from assailant to defender when it became evident that those hands were intent on restraining him limb from limb. Horemheb had been in the army too long not to know the worthlessness of a dead prisoner. Tutu's fate would come soon enough. He was finally manhandled to his feet and then marched, with soldiers guarding him from the mob at his back, in the wake of Amenophis' chariot.

Having satisfied himself that his son was alive, it seemed that only Amenhotep had the presence of mind to resist the descent into panic. As pandemonium flowed around him he walked, untouched by it all, to where Anen still lay in the dust. He held out his hand for Anen to grasp and pulled him to his feet. The pair regarded each other for a few silent moments, Anen too scared to speak, Amenhotep too contemplative. It was a personal silence that encompassed only these two in the tumult that surrounded them, and it was all the more powerful for it. It was Amenhotep who broke it.

"You are my friend," he said. He held his arms wide and Anen gratefully stepped forward into his embrace.

Tutu was held in the bowels of the ship while Amenophis was carried to the dockside. Once in the palace, Amenophis was laid on his bed. He was quickly lost from view behind the heads of the physicians who crowded him so thoroughly it seemed as though the greatest threat to his life was from smothering rather than loss of blood.

The royal party who had accompanied him thus far withdrew to allow the doctors to practise their trade. Within a matter of minutes one of the physicians appeared from the room. He immediately prostrated himself before Amenhotep.

"Please, enough of that," Amenhotep said. "How fares my son?"

"Your Majesty," the doctor said. "His Majesty has suffered only a minor wound. It is long but shallow. The bleeding has been brought under control with the application of bandages."

The occupants of the room let out a collective sigh.

"Thanks be to Ra," Amenhotep said. "We were under his protection today."

"And not only his," Nefertiti said.

Amenhotep turned to Horemheb.

"Indeed," he said. "Horemheb, your country owes you a debt of thanks. Your part in preventing calamity will not soon be forgotten. You shall not go unrewarded for this."

Horemheb bowed deeply.

"My reward has already been granted me, Your Majesty," he said. "His Majesty lives. Any other boon would be meaningless in comparison to this."

Amenhotep was pleased with the answer, and was about to speak again when the doctor coughed politely. The occupants of the room turned back to face him.

"Only..." he said, uncertainly.

"Well?" Tiye said. "Spit it out. Have you bad news?"

"It is just, Your Highness, that, well, His Majesty seems to be convinced that he is about to die."

Tiye held her hand up to her throat as though the breath had been robbed from her. The doctor waved his hands in front of him to quickly belay any anxiety.

"No, no," he said. "There is no need for alarm. He is mistaken. A minor wound such as this is very rarely fatal. It is just that we cannot persuade him of that fact."

"I shall persuade him," Tiye said. "I am his mother. He will listen to me."

She took a step towards the bedchamber.

"Er..." the doctor said.

"There is more? Are we to drag each piece of news from you one drop at a time?"

"Well, His Majesty is not just convinced that his life is over. He is..." The doctor took a deep breath, "Your Highness, he is raving."

"Raving?" Tiye said. "Explain yourself."

"He seems to be labouring under the misapprehension that he was attacked today not by a man, but by a god. Specifically, by Amun."

"He is in shock. He is confused."

"He is quite adamant on the subject."

Nefertiti had been listening to the conversation with a growing disquiet. She could not meet the significant glances that Nakhtmin was throwing across the room at her. She had no idea of the indiscretions he had courted with the secret she had confided in him and would never have expected that the rest of the room knew as well as she did the image Amenophis had of his own divinity.

"This has gone on long enough," Tiye said. And then, to Amenhotep, she added: "Time and time again I told you that you should have spoken to him, but there was always something else more important. It has always been the same, ever since he was a boy. Perhaps these are the fruits of your disinterest."

"My dear," Amenhotep said, surprised at the harshness of her words, "it *was* a sed festival."

Ignoring him, Tiye turned back to the doctor. "I shall come in and see him."

Nefertiti betrayed her nervousness by answering in a tone that was nearly a shout almost before Tiye had finished speaking.

"No!" she said, and then, in a more measured tone, added, "I am his wife. It is my duty to attend my husband. I shall see him."

Before Tiye could protest, Nefertiti let herself into her husband's bedchamber.

"Leave us," she commanded the doctors within.

Amenophis was lying face down on his bed. He tried to rise when he saw Nefertiti come into the room but fell immediately back into a prone position with a grimace. As she drew closer, Nefertiti saw a sheen of sweat on his face and back. The edges of the bandages were stained with it.

"My dear," Amenophis said. "Come closer, come closer. Sit with me. Hold my hand. I do not wish to be alone."

She did so, and said, "You are not dying."

"Dying?" Amenophis said, a stratum of panic breaking in his voice. "Who told you I am dying?"

"Nobody did, my dear."

"Then why tell me? Why come in here and tell me I am not dying unless it is to console me in my last hours?"

"Hush," she said. "Calm yourself. The doctors told me you thought you were breathing your last. I am here to tell you that you are going to be fine. It is a flesh wound. You could no more die of a shaving cut."

"Nefertiti, he is *here*." He shivered and looked around as much of the room as he could take in without reawakening the pain in his back.

"Here?" she said. "In the room? Now?"

"Now. He is with me wherever I go in this damned city. The palace reeks of him."

"Are you sure? Perhaps you are being too sensitive. You have been put under tremendous stress."

"Nefertiti, who do you think it was who attacked me today?"

"I have no idea," she said. "But we will know soon enough. He is held captive. He will be persuaded to talk."

"Did you see him? Did you get a good look at him?"

"Yes, husband, I did." Amenophis was becoming increasingly agitated and Nefertiti reached out to smooth his brow with her hand. "I was standing an arm's length away from him and Horemheb."

"Nefertiti," Amenophis said, and lifted his head from the pillow as though about to impart some great secret. Nefertiti leaned in close, and he whispered: "Did he have the head of a cobra?"

"Did he…? No, of course not. He was a man."

"Are you sure?"

"Of course I am sure. He was just a man. Amenophis, your assailant was not Amun."

"Do you know what he said to me? Just before he tried to kill me, he called me a false god. How do you explain that? Nobody apart from ourselves knows of my divinity. Why would he say that?"

Nefertiti had the presence of mind to remain silent, although one word was writ large in her mind. Nakhtmin. To tell Amenophis that she had shared his secret without his knowledge would be to face his not inconsiderable wrath which, while it had never been directed at her, would undoubtedly break the leash of constraint that Amenophis had placed around it. She feared for herself should Amenophis discover the truth, and not only for herself. Nakhtmin too would bear the brunt of Amenophis' anger should it be discovered that he had used Amenophis' secret as a delicacy with which to titillate half of Thebes.

Nefertiti was relieved when Amenophis broke the silence.

"I must leave this place," he said. "Amun has weakened me. I am not safe here."

"You are too unwell to move," Nefertiti said. "You said yourself that you are weak. You must rest. When you have recovered we will return to Memphis. You will be safe there."

Amenophis held his finger to his lips. When he spoke it was in a hoarse whisper. "We cannot discuss it here. He is listening. I cannot return to Memphis. He will expect that and search for me there. Ptahmose will be on the next ship downriver after we leave. I have always suspected that he was a spy. No, I want to go on a tour. We will go where Amun could never hope to find us and while we are away I will gather my strength around me like a cloak. The people can see me. Their worship will give me all the fortitude I need. I see now where my destiny lies, and there can be no destiny until my rival is removed. I want you to make preparations for us to depart as soon as possible. There must be nobody aboard the ship apart from ourselves and the crew. Do you understand?"

Nefertiti nodded.

"Then go," Amenophis said. "Tell everyone that I am much calmer now and that I am resting and do not wish to be disturbed."

Nefertiti turned to leave. As she reached the door, Amenophis spoke once more.

"And an armed guard," he said. "We will take an armed guard."

Tutu was shivering, although he was far from cold. Neither was he in a prison, although he was far from free. In fact, had he been of a mind to appreciate it, he would have seen that the room in which he found himself was luxurious beyond anything he had ever encountered. It was light and aired well, and the furniture was plush and inviting. There was nothing in the room to give the casual observer the impression that it was a place of confinement, save perhaps the frequent passing of shadows across the floor, cast by the guards that passed to and fro along the path outside the window.

Tutu was not shivering because of the imminence of his death, although this was his second day in the room and he had thought of little else. He comforted himself with the image of Amun he had been granted before he had been sent forth to do the god's bidding. He tried to draw strength from the thought of his rewards in the afterlife and the knowledge that, however unpleasant may be the following hours or days, the eternity he was to be granted was one he would spend basking in the glow of the blessings of his god. He was to die, and he was to die soon, but he was not frightened of death. It was but a doorway through which lay greater happiness than the mortal frame can accommodate.

Tutu was not even shivering because of the manner in which he expected to die. The traditional end for those who attempted regicide was to be hoisted aloft and then impaled through the belly on a sharpened wooden stake that had been driven into the ground.

No, the cause of the tremors that ran through his body was the thought of what would come before the impaling. There would be questions. For whom had he been acting? Who had given him the orders, and why? He expected no quarter in the interrogation. There were no depths to which the human spirit would not stoop in pursuit of the truth. Tutu was shivering because, when the time came for him to be pushed slowly onto the top of a stake, he might welcome it as a blessed release.

Tutu knew that when he died he would come face to face with Osiris, the god who judged all the souls who came before him. Tutu's heart would be held in Osiris' hand, and then it would be placed upon scales to be measured against the weight of a feather. His heart, being the centre of all thought, memory and experience, would be weighed down by deeds of evil or cowardice, and should his heart weigh more than the feather, Tutu would be denied entry into the afterlife. All this would have been for nothing.

To admit the truth to his captors would be contrary to Ptahmose's very explicit instructions on the matter. It would be a betrayal, and any betrayal of Ptahmose, Tutu knew, would be a betrayal of Amun also. It would not be looked on favourably by Osiris.

The question Tutu was asking himself, and had been ever since he had been unceremoniously thrown into this room, was whether the weight of his heart would be affected by torture. Would it be lightened if he was compelled under duress to name Amun as the originator of the plan, or would it be weighed down as efficiently as if he had volunteered the information willingly? And if Osiris would not forgive him his transgression whether he was tortured or not then why submit himself to it?

All these matters and more were still unresolved in Tutu's mind when he heard the latch click on the door to his improvised cell. The door opened, and when Tutu saw who stood before him he fell backwards and huddled into the corner, his arms and legs drawn about him defensively, unable to prevent himself from whimpering.

"I see that you recognise me," Amenophis said, from between the heads of the two guards who were standing in front of him.

Tutu said nothing. A quiet sob escaped him.

"It is just as well," Amenophis said. "For I recognise you, too."

This was much easier than he had been expecting. He had imagined that he was to come face to face with a defiant foe, a god in a man's skin, and yet here was this wretch, cowering in the corner. And unless Amenophis was very much mistaken, the prisoner had soiled himself.

"Although I doubt," Amenophis continued, a look of distaste painted across his features, "that you recognise this man. His name is Mahu, and he is a man especially well known for his cruelty."

A man wearing the robes of a policeman stepped from within Amenophis' shadow. He smiled and affected a little bow as though he had been complimented.

"I have assigned Mahu with the task of finding out who you are. He will, I assure you, take great pleasure in his work. There is nobody here to help you. You are all alone, and I have it on the best authority that Mahu here will not offer you any mercy, however much you plead and beg. In fact, I am told he will rather enjoy it if you do. I have offered Mahu the role of my chief of police if he extracts the information I require, and so you can assume that he is going to be especially dedicated to his task."

Mahu produced a rag and some cord from behind his back and leant down to gag the prisoner.

"Open," he said. Tutu dutifully opened his mouth and Mahu stuffed the rag within, tying it tightly in place with the cord.

"Nothing can save you now," Amenophis said, and left the room. He had no desire to see what was to ensue.

Apart from a rather stilted walk and a bandaged torso, there were no longer any signs that Amenophis had been attacked. Despite what the doctors had told him, he was sure that he had suffered what would have been in any other man a mortal wound. He wondered how his divinity was not yet visible to all.

Wishing to rid his nostrils of Tutu's stench, he wandered outside and strolled down to the harbour. Four ships were docked there, and the foremost was the scene of frenetic activity. It was being prepared to sail and men were running to and fro with armfuls of supplies and ropes, tools and weapons. Each seemed to be in competition with the next with regards to how much he could carry or how fast he could run. It was a scene which both pleased and annoyed Amenophis. He thought it likely that he had been seen, and this display of dedicated employment was nothing more than a show for his benefit. He imagined that moments before his arrival the men had been leaning against whichever walls were available, their loads lying in untidy piles along the dock. Amenophis was equally sure that once his back was turned the workmen's burdens would be abandoned and forgotten in favour of lethargy and sloth.

He had rather enjoyed his encounter with Tutu and his appetite for authority had been whetted by it. There had been precious few opportunities to flex his tongue since his arrival at Malkarta and he only now realised how much he had missed it. Smiling, he walked down to the dockside. He imagined the eyes of the men following him with sidelong glances, as though they were paintings on a temple wall. He picked one man who was approaching him from a distance and timed his walk so that the two would meet before the man reached the ship. As the pair drew closer, Amenophis was pleased to see the man's heavy burden coming slowly into focus.

The workman's pace faltered, slowed, and then finally increased, as though he was uncertain how to act in the presence of his king and had finally decided that increased toil was the safest recourse. Amenophis stopped in the man's path and allowed him to approach.

"Do you not bow to your king?" Amenophis said, when the man was close enough for the king to make out the nervousness in his face.

The man faltered as though he had tripped on something lying in his path and then, as quickly as he could manage, he placed the teetering load of supplies on the dockside. One or two of the topmost trinkets clattered to the floor. He stuttered his apologies as he prostrated himself.

"Do you perhaps think yourself indispensable to your king?" Amenophis asked the man's upturned back.

"No, Your Majesty," came the muffled reply.

"Then perhaps your load is too important to be placed to one side even for a moment?"

"No, Your Majesty."

"It isn't? Are you sure?" Amenophis asked. "You carry the king's possessions, do you not? Do you not rank them valuable?"

The man hesitated, unsure as to what the correct answer may be. Amenophis smiled to himself. This was sport. There was no answer the man could give that would not give Amenophis the opportunity to humiliate him.

"Your Majesty's ownership transforms them into objects beyond worth, Your Majesty," he said, weighing the wisdom of each word on his tongue before allowing it to escape. "And yet even their value pales into nothing in your presence, Your Majesty. I was wrong not to bow before you, and for that I humbly beg your forgiveness, but I was momentarily confused by the value of these objects and the joy at seeing you alive and unharmed after the treacherous attack on your person."

Amenophis pursed his lips. He tapped his foot and clenched and unclenched his fists. He sighed dramatically.

"Get up," he hissed at last. "On your way, and care not to cross me again."

Quickly and gratefully, the man gathered up his load and scampered off across the dock. Amenophis looked around him for a victim less likely to provide a clever answer.

He spent a happy hour on the dockside, stopping men who did not prostrate themselves voluntarily, and berating those who did for neglecting their labours. He quickly realised that these men were different from the servants at the palace in Memphis. Here at Malkarta, only part of his reputation had preceded him; the part that declared him a formidable king whom every lesser man should fear to cross. When they addressed him there was genuine fear in their voices, untarnished by the indulgence he heard from the servants in Memphis. Here he would not be called an old woman, and he could no more imagine the servants glancing at each other with barely concealed smiles than he could conceive of them sprouting wings and flying away. Here, even under the shadow of Amun himself, he felt more power than he ever had in his life. It was as though he had been crowned anew and that Memphis was not just a river journey but an entire country away, as though these men were his true subjects and that those in Memphis were merely actors. Here, in these insignificant moments, Amenophis tasted real kingship for the first time, and he could not remember a finer meal.

He hardly wished to admit it to himself, but there was another reason, beyond the enjoyable diversion of flexing his regal muscles, that kept Amenophis on the dockside for so long. He would at intervals be reminded of the unpleasant business that was taking place within the palace walls. He had never regarded squeamishness as one of his defining traits, so the thoughts of what horrors Tutu may be facing did nothing to dampen his spirits. Rather, it was an image that rose unbidden, time and again, into his mind. It was a picture that he simultaneously regarded as being laughably ridiculous and terrifyingly possible. He saw himself striding purposefully back into the palace and crashing through the door that led to Tutu's improvised cell. He would stand on the threshold, feet apart, head high, clenched fists resting on his hips. But before him he would not see Tutu mewling in a pool of his own blood and filth, and he would not receive Mahu's report with justified glee, for Mahu would be beyond making a report of any kind. Tutu, no longer disguising himself in mortal form, would be standing over Mahu's wrecked body, laughing, and when he spoke it would be with a voice that shook the plaster from the walls.

Amenophis never heard what Tutu had to say because he would always manage to force himself back to the present before the words could form. But it worried him that the thought had the strength of a vision, and that the foresight of a god such as he was not a faculty to be questioned. When he could bear it no longer, and when the heat of the afternoon sun had started to make his head ache, Amenophis left the dockside. He felt his power and resolve bleeding from him with every step that drew him closer to Tutu's cell. Inside, the palace was refreshingly cool and Amenophis could feel the beads of sweat on his brow and back in sharp relief.

He stopped outside the door that led to Tutu's cell. He had decided during the short walk that striding through the doorway with no knowledge of what lay beyond would be an act of folly. There should be no doorway in the kingdom, he told himself, at which a pharaoh should have to knock, and no room's threshold should be a barrier of fear, and so he made a short examination of the immediate area to ensure that nobody would see as he rapped his knuckles on the wood and politely waited for an invitation to enter.

When Mahu opened the door, Amenophis' first instinct was to turn and flee before he noticed that none of the blood that decorated Mahu's body and clothes had originated where it lay. Amenophis enquired as to the success of the proceedings within.

"Your Majesty," Mahu said, "I believe I am in possession of the information which you seek."

Realising there was nothing to fear, Amenophis took a bold step past Mahu and into the room. Inside, the stench was unnameable. Amenophis instinctively held his hand up to his nose.

What was left of Tutu was sitting on the floor in a corner of the room, trembling violently, his hands held up in front of his face in supplication, his knees drawn up in a useless attempt to protect his body. Although the gag had been removed from his mouth, Tutu was no longer capable of screaming. Weakened though Tutu was, Amenophis stopped before he was within arm's reach of him; but despite his revulsion he could not prevent himself from leaning forward to make out as best he could the injuries that the priest had sustained. Such was the mutilation that he felt unexpected pangs of pity until his hand strayed to the bandages around his waist as though to remind himself what this man had done to him.

One of Tutu's eyes was missing, and in its place was a ragged hole from which strips of flesh hung like miniature banners. Most of his fingernails were gone and those that remained had sharpened pieces of wood protruding from beneath them. Everywhere there was blood.

"He claims to have been acting on orders from Ptahmose," Mahu said, from over Amenophis' shoulder.

It took a few moments for Amenophis to respond. "What?" he said, finally, not taking his eyes from the scene before him, and having heard nothing other than Tutu's pathetic whining. Mahu repeated himself.

"The other one, the dead one, was named Ranefer," Mahu added.

Amenophis had heard and seen enough. He backed from the room. As he crossed the threshold he pointed in Tutu's general direction.

"Have him executed with all haste," he said to Mahu. "The sight of him offends my eyes."

Mahu bowed. "As you wish, Majesty," he said.

Amenophis walked away along the corridor in a stupefaction. His worst nightmares had not been realised, but if these events were dreams they were ones from which he would awake in a cold sweat. The orders had come from Ptahmose. As a prince, Amenophis had been raised with his father's doctrine of never trusting a priest, and of trusting a priest of Amun even less. He had been brought up to respect the enmity of the high priest of Amun as a sailor respects the sea, but even after all his father's warnings, after all that had happened, he had never truly believed that any man, even Ptahmose, would conspire to have him murdered.

The power he had felt only minutes before had been whipped away from him. People may have been sniggering at him behind their hands in Memphis, but at least while they were sniggering they were not plotting his death. It was evident from the work he had seen on the dockside that his ship would be ready to sail by the following day. Amenophis determined to spend not a second longer at Malkarta than he positively had to. He went to find Nefertiti. She would undoubtedly require a number of hours to prepare herself for the trip, for they would not be heading homewards, from the luxury of one palace to the comforts of another. They would be heading south, out into the country that Amenophis purported to co-rule. They would meet his people, a populace not tainted with the proximity of Amun or the preconceptions of Memphis, a multitude who would be happy to bow at his feet. Amenophis quickened his pace.

The Maya Papyrus, Fragments 57-60

> *I saw Tutu's execution. It was a sight that will remain with me forever, even after all the deaths of Akhenaten's reign. Even after all the people I lost, Tutu's death is one that continues to wake me in the silence of the night. There was little ceremony about the affair and I would have known nothing about it had I not been in that particular courtyard at that particular time. I had been crying, and had been ashamed enough of my emotion to mutter something that nobody heard about fresh air before stumbling clumsily through the door. I found myself in the courtyard having had no design to make that place the object of my flight.*
>
> *I had assumed that everybody would feel as I did, that their sorrow at this latest piece of news, although perhaps disguised with more efficacy than mine, would still have been welling in their throats, so I was surprised to find that I was not alone. On the opposite side of the courtyard stood Amenophis, and the closing of the door behind him informed me that his arrival there had preceded mine by a matter of seconds. He did not see me, or if he did he did not recognise me, for I was not standing within touching distance of him. I was too afraid of the emotion in my voice to call out a greeting, and so I simply watched him and remained still. The door behind him opened once again and*

Amenophis jumped to one side as though his thoughts had been far away and the noise had startled him.

Behind him emerged a heavy set, surly looking policeman I recognised but did not know, and shortly after him appeared two more men, obviously soldiers, who carried between them what looked at first sight to be a corpse. They each held one of the corpse's arms around their shoulder and they dragged him, with his legs trailing behind, into the centre of the courtyard, where I noticed for the first time a wooden post that had been driven into the ground. It's pinnacle had been sharpened into a fine point. Next to it was a small set of steps. It was towards these that the soldiers were dragging the corpse while Amenophis and the heavy set man looked to be exchanging polite conversation as though they were acquaintances that had met by chance in the marketplace.

I gasped when I saw the corpse suddenly raise his head. I recognised him as Amenophis' would-be assassin. He saw, with what I now noticed was his one remaining eye, the post towards which he was being dragged, and he let out such a howl that it chills me to even write of it. It was the cry of a man who knew his fate and knew equally well that all earthly help was beyond him. I have heard that cry many times since that day, on the lips of others as well as in the ears of my memory, and I have often contemplated how it must feel to anticipate the onset of such horrific pain and know as well as you have ever known anything that there is nothing you can do to prevent it, and that there is nobody under the heavens who will help or hear you. Such was the torment conveyed to me that day by Tutu's screams.

The soldiers by now were at the top of the steps next to the stake. They hoisted Tutu up between them until they were holding him aloft with their hands under his shoulders and buttocks. Tutu was begging them to let him go, loudly enough for me to make out each sorry word, although he must have known as well as I did, as well as Amenophis and the heavy set man knew, that his pleading was nothing more than an irritant to the soldiers, who must have only wished to expedite his removal from this earth all the more quickly because of it.

With one final push the soldiers had him over the tip of the stake. They let go, but Tutu did not have far to fall. The spike bit into him halfway between his shoulders and his hips. Rather than them being redoubled, as I had expected, his screams abruptly ceased, although the frantic flailing of his limbs alerted all of his onlookers to that fact that he was alive still.

Amenophis' conversation with the heavy set man stopped, both having become fascinated with the proceedings in the middle of the courtyard. The heavy set man took one or two paces forward and, with a stern expression, mimed something to the soldiers that involved him holding his arms out horizontally before him and sweeping them towards the ground. Confused as to his meaning, the soldiers looked to each other and Tutu and finally back to the heavy set man, but took no further action.

"Pull him down!" the heavy set man shouted. "He will wriggle his way off it!"

Finally comprehending, but none the more enthusiastic for it, the soldiers turned back to Tutu. One grabbed his arms while the other took hold of his legs and, after counting to a prearranged number, they applied all their weight to them in short bursts. In this manner was Tutu's torso dragged in spasms further onto the stake until at last the point of it rent the skin of his stomach and emerged, gleaming red, into the morning air.

"Not too far!" the heavy set man shouted, undoubtedly concerned that Tutu should quit this world too quickly. Their job completed to everyone's satisfaction except Tutu's, the soldiers retreated back to their audience, whereupon they were dismissed and lost no time in vacating the area.

His conversation still muted, Amenophis walked slowly towards the stake, the heavy set man following behind with no visible sign of reluctance. They came to rest directly in front of Tutu's upturned face, stopping at a distance that would have enabled Amenophis to reach out and touch him without straightening his arm. Amenophis remained there, impassive but curious, and watched as Tutu's silent struggling gradually abated until, finally, it was quelled altogether. Only then did Amenophis turn away. Once again, the heavy set man followed him, a respectful number of paces behind.

Although throughout these proceedings I had made no great effort at concealment I had remained undetected. Amenophis and his companion disappeared through the door by which they had entered the courtyard, and it seemed as though a spell was broken. With the taste of bile in my mouth, I staggered back towards the doorway through which I myself had passed, wanting to cry out as though on Tutu's behalf. All thoughts of the reason why I had entered the courtyard in the first place, and the sorrow that had driven me there, and all the mornings events up until that time, were driven from my mind, which had space only to accommodate the sight of Tutu's face as he hung from the stake, and Amenophis' look of detached interest as the man's life dripped down the wood and soaked into the dust of the ground.

I ran for my quarters and, once I was there, locked the door and threw myself onto the bed. For hours I could not rid my mind of the images that paraded before it and it was difficult to marshal them into any sensible order. It was as though my horror could not be limited by thought alone. My mind would show me Tutu's fate and then skitter away from the subject, as though it was a stone skimming along the surface of the Nile, but then it would return refreshed and show me not Tutu's fate but the fate of another, and a fate a million times more horrible. It would show me the fate of Egypt, with a king at her head who would have the presence of mind to remain calm and curious while those around him tumbled into the deepest pits of agony and torment.

It occurred to me that the distance between curiosity and enjoyment was not a large one.

It had been an eventful day, a far from displeasing one, and one over which Amenophis enjoyed ruminating as he watched the river waters disappearing beneath the hull of his ship, a cup of wine in his hand and the sun setting picturesquely to his left as though eager to enhance his mood. Thebes was behind him now, and the dangers that lurked in its shadows were nothing more than shadows themselves. A significant threat had been removed with Tutu's execution. Even as the priest's last moments had passed, Amenophis had felt an instinct, an apprehension, that Tutu was toying with him and that, imbued with the spirit of Amun, he was about to leap, laughing, from the tip of the stake. Amenophis had to watch him expire with his own eyes before he trusted him to remain where he had been put.

He had not been as disgusted with the procedure as he had been expecting. He had told himself, and Nefertiti when she would hear such thoughts, that it would not be proper for him to have excessive feelings for the people under his rule. He had a higher vantage point from which he could see their lives. He knew that their time on this earth was but a transitory one and that their main concern should be not for this life but for the next. It was different for Amenophis. He was a god and as such had the prospect of forever to contemplate. And on the scale of eternity, the span of a man's life may as well be a sneeze. No, it was the manner of one's life, not the length or the quality of it, that was important. It was not the manner of death or degrees of pain that mattered, but the method by which one came to that death. Tutu, Amenophis imagined, had led an impious life, and his attempt on the king's life had most likely only been the culmination of a lifetime of evil, and so Amenophis knew that Tutu had already ceased to exist, that Osiris had snuffed out his soul as though it had never been. Amenophis was confident that everlasting life would not be granted to one such as Tutu.

And there, Amenophis mused as he leant against the rail of the ship carrying him south from Thebes, there is the essential difference between all men. Death holds only terror for men such as Tutu, for they know that they have failed the test of life. The only way to confront death is to do so without fear, and the only way to do that is to have lived without sin.

A sudden gust of wind off the river brought Amenophis back to himself. He drained his cup and, sighing heavily, turned to head back to his cabin. Nefertiti was within. He could hear her sobbing even before he had opened the door.

The Maya Papyrus, Fragment 61

> *It was dark when I finally lifted my head from my pillow. I could only estimate the time I had lain there by the strength of my hunger, which told me that I had not moved from my bed in a matter of hours. It had been a harrowing day and I was glad to see the setting of the sun bringing it to a close.*
>
> *The morning had started with so much promise it would have been impossible to imagine it tumbling into so much dread and horror so quickly. It should be decreed by the gods that days like this should not start with sunlight and stolen hours in the peace of one's quarters with a soothing cup of wine, but with gloom and storms and the wailing of disembodied voices. It would give people time to prepare, for bad news can only be made worse in contrast to the happy ignorance that precedes it.*
>
> *I swore when the messenger had arrived that morning and I answered the door reluctantly. Good news is rarely heralded by such urgent knocking.*
>
> *"Your attendance is required immediately in the apartments of your grandmother, Thuya," he told me. "She has been taken ill. Her family is required to make all haste to her bedside."*

I had never been particularly close with my grandmother but the news was still unwelcome. While Thuya had never been a loving grandmother, she was a woman whose presence could be felt from several rooms away. She was old now, and everybody knew that she could not live forever, but the frailty of her body had never deleteriously affected her voice and so it sometimes seemed that the sound of her would remain behind long after her. Loving or not, close or not, the prospect of life without her influence seemed strange and alien.

The family gathered in an anteroom outside her bedroom. Only Yuya and Amenophis failed to join us. Yuya was already inside, at his wife's bedside. Nefertiti was forced into the position of making excuses for her husband's absence.

The physician briefed us on what had happened, and what to expect. Thuya had been eating a frugal breakfast when a sickness had gripped her with such ferocity that Yuya had assumed that she was choking on a morsel of food. She fell from her chair and Yuya rushed to her side, helpless to administer any other balm but love and worry. When the attack continued, Yuya knew she could not be choking. People who choke either die or expel the foreign body, but Thuya was doing neither. Physicians were summoned and Thuya was taken to her bed.

"She complains that her chest hurts, and that the pain has spread to her left arm and her jaw," the physician told us.

"What does that mean?" Tiye asked.

"She has what we call the wedj-*disease," the physician said. "I am sorry, Your Majesty, but I cannot contend with this. Death is approaching."*

One or two sobs escaped from their owners.

"And that is all you have to say on the subject?" Tiye said. "She will die? You will do nothing?"

"Majesty, modern medicine can do many things, but the wedj-*disease is beyond even us. We have given her a heart shaped amulet to hold next to her breast. There is little else we can do. She is old. Her pulse is almost non-existent. It is only due to the strength of her soul and the will of the gods that she has remained with us this long. You may see her, but I would ask you not to excite her. She is very weak."*

We filed into Thuya's bedchamber in silence. Yuya looked up at us as we entered. He was kneeling next to Thuya's bed, his hands enveloping hers. Thuya herself seemed to be sleeping. We gathered at the foot of the bed and still nobody spoke. For what could we say? The matriarch, the woman who held the tiller of the entire family, was dying. What possible words of comfort could we conjure up that would not taste of lies?

Thuya opened her eyes.

"Ah, you have all come to see me off, have you?" she said. There was a weakness in her voice, a distance that I had never heard before. It did not seem to fit. It was as though a crocodile had opened its mouth and miaowed like a kitten.

There was a chorus of 'nonsense' and 'don't be ridiculous' and 'you'll outlast all of us'. Thuya smiled.

"Thank you," she said, "but we all know the situation. There is no sense in denying it."

She looked at each of us in turn, although none could meet her gaze for long.

"I see someone is missing," she said.

"We were unable to find Amenophis," Nefertiti said. "He would be here if he knew."

"It is probably just as well," Thuya said. "For I wish to speak on the subject of our absent friend. Now may be my final chance."

One or two of Thuya's audience exchanged glances. Nefertiti looked at me enquiringly as though I would know what Thuya was about to say. I made a face that made it clear that I knew as much as she did.

Yuya leant in close to his wife and said: "You should not exert yourself. You will only slow your recovery."

"There will be no recovery, my dear husband. Do not look so stricken. We have had a good life, have we not, you and I? Have the gods not smiled upon us, and granted us everything we ever wished for? Have I not mothered a Great Royal Wife, and has she not mothered a pharaoh? Think of it, Yuya! When you first saw me singing in the temple in Akhmim, could you have ever conceived that this is where life's road would bring us? No, I shall not recover from this. My heart is weary and longs for rest. But I leave in happiness and I go to Osiris with a smile on my face, knowing the services I have performed for my country."

I looked at the floor throughout Thuya's speech, unable to shake the feeling that it was something that should be heard only by the ears of a husband. Although Thuya herself was speaking – and although only someone of her stature and self-assurance would consider giving a eulogy to herself – it seemed to be an essentially private moment upon which we were all intruding. But then, nothing was ever haphazard in Thuya's life, and if we were there to hear her words it was only because she planned it so.

"But," Thuya said, and the timbre of her voice told me that she was now addressing the room, "I have one wish left, and I have gathered you all here not only to bid me farewell, but to hear me one final time. I have been blessed to have mothered a dynasty of kings, and my grandson is on the throne and will soon take over from his father as this realm's sole regent. I was overjoyed when he came to the throne, as you all know, but only as a substitute for his brother Thutmose, whom I still miss and look forward to meeting again in the next world. Now it has come to my attention that Amenophis has begun to get some strange ideas in his head. That he is a god, and so forth. You must not allow him to jeopardise everything for which I have striven for all these years. I exhort you – all of you – to watch him, and to do so closely. You are all pharaohs now, all guardians of Egypt. I bestow the title upon you. Let Amenophis believe what he shall, for his beliefs do not matter in any place that falls outside of his own heart, as long as you are with him to guide his hand in the rule of this land. Learn from Tiye. My heart bursts when I think of what she has become, and through her this son of hers may sire generations of men who will lead these Two Lands to greatness unsurpassed."

Thuya's voice, which had been struggling to make itself heard through the frailty of her chest and throat, finally gave out to a fit of quiet coughing. Yuya took the opportunity to speak.

"Thuya, you should not say these things..." he started.

"Oh, hush, Yuya," Thuya said, in a loving and indulgent tone. "If I cannot be indiscrete now, when can I be?"

Yuya looked at us all for help. When he looked back at his wife, her eyes were closed, and she was gone.

I could contain my tears no longer, and I fled from the room to the courtyard. Tutu's execution was not the only memory that would endure from that day. The other was something that Thuya had said.

"Let Amenophis believe what he shall," she had said, "for his beliefs do not matter in any place that falls outside of his own heart."

It was the only mistake of Thuya's life, and she had waited for her dying breath before uttering it.

Chapter Twelve

Exodus

LATER, AMENOPHIS would feel himself foolish for having worried about his tour. *What if I am wrong?* he had asked himself, on the nights when the blind dark of his cabin threatened to suffocate him and he had to reach out to Nefertiti to anchor himself and stave off the panic. *What if they do not worship me? What if they laugh? They have never seen me before, or any representation of me. What if I am ridiculed?*

Nefertiti, of course, was always there to quash any fears that he did not feel too ridiculous to voice, and while he willed himself to believe her he could never quite shake the suspicion that her support and encouragement were more the product of duty than belief.

It was not until after the first stop of the tour, at the quarry of Gebel el-Silsila just north of the border with Nubia, that Amenophis began to relax. His reception there had been rapturous. Nefertiti's brief mourning for her grandmother had passed and she too was able to bask in the adoration of the crowd. It did not escape her attention that she was viewed by many of the men in that remote outpost with something approaching lust, and the power of her beauty was not lost on her. There was a short tour and a long speech and before either of them knew it the royal couple were back on the ship, heading north for their next stop.

The rest of the tour continued in a similar fashion. The stops were brief and, for the most part, identical: enthusiastic crowds would listen with rapt attention to Amenophis' speech, which varied very little from place to place, and then, at the conclusion of a short inspection, Amenophis and Nefertiti would rejoin the ship and set off for the next stop. Nefertiti would notice the eyes of the men following her and, on one or two occasions, would listen demurely to respectful declarations of her beauty. Amenophis would leave each port of call more buoyant than the last. Only when the ship passed once again through Thebes did Amenophis' good humour threaten to desert him, but it was a brief dip from which he easily recovered once the temple of Amun began to recede behind them.

They were on board the ship for a number of weeks, meandering northwards with the Nile and stopping at nearly every settlement that came their way. They stopped for an entire day and night at Cusae, north of Thebes, and Amenophis treated himself and his wife to every delight that the town could offer them, although it was neither Thebes nor Memphis so the delights were not so easy to come by. The inhabitants possessed an accent that Amenophis found amusing, and such was his good humour that he attempted to copy it for days afterwards.

The night they left Cusae, Nefertiti and Amenhotep were standing together at the stern of the ship. The town's lights were glimmering behind them in an otherwise empty ocean of night. They shimmered in the air's rising heat, and as they receded they slowly merged together and dimmed like the dying flame of a candle. Above them the stars were vivid enough to look as though the gods were holding a host of mirrors in the sky above the town. It was a scene of such beauty that Nefertiti could not bring herself to look at her husband, who faced towards the lights purely as a coincidence. When the bow of the ship turned, Amenophis' head turned with it and he gazed with equal enrapture at blackness. Nefertiti thought the gods nothing short of cruel to steal such a view from him. She shivered in the breeze and leant against him, resting her head on his shoulder. He put his arm around her.

They remained silent for a moment or two, listening to the insects that seemed to line the riverbanks to provide them with a chorus as they passed, and feeling the earth exhale after the rigours of the day.

"In the desert," Amenophis said, "every night is spring."

Nefertiti smiled but said nothing for fear of breaking the moment's spell..

"Do you know," Amenophis said, "I do not believe I have ever been this happy. From the moment my mother bore me I was ignored and then bullied. When my brother died I was pressured into becoming him in his place and I had to endure those interminable lessons with my father. By the time I was old enough to comprehend my role, it changed and I became co-regent. Now even gods turn against me to engineer my despair. But here, with you, feeling the breeze on my face and sharing in the earth's nightly rebirth, it is as though nothing untoward has ever befallen me, as though I have been standing here for my entire life, and will continue to do so for its remainder, removed from court and adversaries and free to simply be content. I love you, Nefertiti. You are the strength that my body denies me."

"I love you too," Nefertiti said. She slipped one arm around his waist and hugged him tighter.

They were still on deck hours later when the dim light of dawn began to bleed into the sky. They had spent the entire night talking while they held each other and drank wine to keep the chill from their bones. When the uppermost rim of the sun finally struggled free of the underworld's grip, Amenhotep turned to face it.

"Ra greets us," he said, shielding his eyes with his hand. "He brings me my vision. I can see so much clearer during the day."

In direct contrast to the western bank of the Nile here, which was verdant and fecund, the eastern bank, beyond a thin strip of alluvium, was desolate despite the proximity of the river. Further inland a semicircle of cliffs enclosed the area, split almost exactly in the centre by the deep cleft of a wadi. It was beyond this notch that the sun was rising, framed on either side by the cliffs.

"Nefertiti," Amenophis whispered. And then again, louder: "*Nefertiti.*"

When she turned to face him she found Amenophis on his knees. He was pointing at the sun with a trembling hand.

"Look!"

Nefertiti followed the line of his finger but could see nothing that could be responsible for such a reaction.

"What?" she asked.

"The sun! Look at the sun! Can you not see the sign that it gives me?"

She could still see nothing out of the ordinary. Amenophis turned to face her.

"Nefertiti," he said. "I know who I am."

By the time Amenophis and Nefertiti returned to the palace in Memphis, Amenhotep's condition had deteriorated. He spent most of each day in his bed and, despite the ministrations of the goddess Ishtar of Nineveh, sent by King Tušratta of Mitanni to help the ailing king, the pain was unbearable and constant. Even the extraction of his bad teeth by trembling physicians had not helped. If anything it had made the pain and the flow of pus even worse.

When Amenophis entered his father's bedchamber for the first time since his return he could barely remain in one place, such was the compelling nature of his excitement. He paced from the door to the window and back again, gesticulating as he spoke like a man infested with demons. He was so transported that he utterly failed to notice his father's wan complexion.

"I know who I am, father!" were his first words, before even the pair had greeted each other.

Amenhotep did not have the energy even to watch Amenophis' performance. He had not slept since the previous morning, borne as he was on a tide of pain, and he found Amenophis' pacing and gestures irritating.

"Well done," he said, carefully. "As do I. I am Amenhotep and you are Amenophis. Is it for this that you have disturbed my rest?"

"But!" Amenophis said, spinning to face his father and jabbing his finger in the air. "But!" he said again.

Amenhotep waited for the rest of the sentence. It seemed as though Amenophis was mentally composing it before commending it to the air.

"But I may not be Amenophis," he said at last.

"Really?" Amenhotep said. "That *is* important news. Thank you for bringing it to my attention. Make sure to inform the guards of your news on the way out, that they may arrest you as an impostor."

"Father, you are being deliberately obtuse," Amenophis said.

"Yes," Amenhotep said. "Yes, I am. You said you had important news, and instead I get fairy tales."

"Father, I have had a sign. A sign from the gods themselves."

"Telling you who you are?"

"Telling me who I have always been."

"And what was the nature of this sign?"

"A hieroglyph. A hieroglyph written in the sky. An omen that the gods fashioned from the very earth and the heavens."

"Tell me."

Amenophis told him. He explained how, as his ship had drawn alongside the notch in the cliffs formed by a wadi, the sun had chosen that exact moment to breach the horizon. As Amenophis had watched, the sun had climbed the sky until it had been perfectly framed by the sheer cliffs that rose on either side of it. Just for a few moments, until the sun's continuing journey took it out of reach of the cliffs, the scene had been the flawless rendering of a hieroglyph. The hieroglyph had been a god's name.

The god had been the Aten, the deity of the sun's disk.

As Amenophis spoke he grew increasingly agitated. His pace increased and he seemed to have less and less control over the shapes that his arms formed in the air.

"You are telling me that the Aten appeared to you?"

"Is that so incredible? I did not have a conversation with him, as my grandfather did with the Sphinx."

"Then how do you know what he was saying?"

"What else could he have been telling me other than that I am chosen?"

"Chosen?" Amenhotep asked. He was becoming tired of the company and wished to be alone to enjoy the relative absence of pain. "I thought you were a god."

"Yes!" Amenophis exclaimed. He clapped his hands together. "Yes!" he shouted again. "That is exactly my point! Father, do you not see? I am he. I am the Aten. The Aten is me. I am the god in human form. My whole life I have been waiting for some meaning, for some purpose to my appearance, for some knowledge that everything I am and everything I have suffered has been due to the plans of the gods. And here it is. Do you not think me blessed?"

"I think you are mad, not blessed. As will the rest of court."

Amenophis' enthusiasm and excitement disappeared as quickly as it had arrived, as though it was a piece of jewellery that Amenhotep had snatched from him.

"I fear you are right," he said. "They will not understand."

"If you are lucky they will not understand. If you are not, they will see the truth."

Amenophis momentarily brightened.

"You think so?" he asked.

"The truth as *I* see it, Amenophis."

"Oh," Amenophis said. "I see."

"If you truly believe yourself to have some connection with this god of which you speak, there is little I can do to dissuade you of the fact. But I would give you one piece of advice. Perhaps one last piece of advice. Take care to whom you reveal yourself. I am sorry to say this to you, but you have put me in a position where I cannot afford the luxury of sentiment. You have precious little personal authority around court as it is, Amenophis. Announcing your divinity will do nothing but erode what little there is. You will be mocked. Perhaps not to your face, but mockery in secret is the worst form of deceit. It gives you no opportunity to belie it. Think, Amenophis. That is all I ask."

Amenophis turned and marched from the room, his dignity trailing torn and dismembered at his feet. He had quite forgotten to deliver his other piece of news.

Amenophis slept fitfully that night until, waking to darkness, he could not stay in his bed another moment. He rose and shuffled across his bedchamber with short, tentative steps, his arms held out in front of him in anticipation of an obstacle, scowling at the indignity of it all.

Once in his living quarters he summoned a servant to light some candles. To his eyes they shone like estranged stars, unwilling to light the space between themselves. The effect was a discomforting one. Amenophis remained silent and stationary until sunlight began to bleed into the room and compensate for the deficiencies of the candles. It had been a long night, but worthwhile. Amenophis stretched and yawned.

He had come to a decision. It was something that had occurred to him when he first saw the Aten in the sky, but it was something as daunting as it was inspirational and it was only now that he was able to truly commit to it. His father had been right: there were very few at this court who would understand any proclamation of his, and without understanding there could be no empathy.

"It is a strong man who resists the temptation to mock that which he does not understand," Amenophis thought to himself. "And this palace is overflowing with weaklings."

He heard a noise behind him and turned to see Nefertiti in the doorway, frowning in the way of those who have just woken.

"Amenophis?" she said. "Is everything... why are you not in bed?"

"Even weaklings, in sufficient numbers, can foil the ambitions of a single man, though he may be many times stronger," he said.

"Amenophis?"

"Come. Sit with me."

She sat, and he explained the tortuous meanderings of his thoughts and the conclusion to which they had eventually and unavoidably led.

"Are you sure?" she said, when he had finished.

He shrugged, but it was a gesture of resignation rather than indecision. "What else can I do?" he said. "The Aten has spoken to me. It is the only meaning I can put into the sign that makes any sense."

"It seems so... drastic," Nefertiti said. "So final."

"It is both," Amenophis said, and gently patted her stomach. "This is a time of new beginnings."

He called for his messengers, who were sent to visit everyone of note at the palace to deliver a summons to some and an invite to others, depending on the recipients' rank at court.

Amenophis began to prepare himself to deliver his news.

Aye and Tiye had known the substance of Amenophis' announcement before they heard it officially in the audience chamber, for Amenophis had been unable to keep it entirely to himself until the allotted hour of the audience later that afternoon. Yuya had heard nothing, because Tiye had only ever visited her mother for advice, never her father, and she doubted that Yuya would have cared enough to listen to her anyway. He had not yet recovered enough from Thuya's death to take an interest in anything that was not the memory of his late wife and Tiye doubted that he ever would.

Thuya's death had hit Tiye almost as hard. Tiye now found herself thrust into the role that her mother had always occupied; that of the family matriarch. It was now she who was expected to dispense advice rather than seek it. No announcement had been made, no invitations issued, but still it was to her that they came and Tiye had nobody left to ask. When Amenophis told her and Aye of his decision her instinctive first thought had been *we shall see what my mother has to say about...* before remembering that her mother would have nothing to say about it at all, and a fresh wave of sadness broke over her at the recognition of yet another aspect of her life that her mother had taken with her into the underworld.

"You cannot," she had told Amenophis, in a tone that did not accept the possibility of disagreement.

"I must," he had replied, and she had been taken aback.

"Amenophis, I am your mother. I say you cannot. It is impractical. It is... wilful. You may not. I do not grant you my permission."

"You are my mother, but I am your king. I was not asking for your permission."

Tiye was aghast.

"The audacity!" she exclaimed. "Do you forget who put you where you are today? If your grandmother could hear such things...!"

Aye stepped forward and made soothing noises.

"Please," he said. "We will solve nothing if we attack the problem as adversaries. Amenophis, you have presented us with an announcement that we will have to digest. You should leave us now and allow us to discuss it. We will need to consult with your father also."

Amenophis looked as though he was going to say something else but thought better of it. For the second time in as many days he found himself storming from a room, his anger and humiliation unexpressed.

"Discuss?" Tiye said, once the door had closed on his back. "What is there to discuss? The whole idea is preposterous. Amenhotep will never agree to it."

"Well..." Aye said. He rubbed his bottom lip between his thumb and forefinger in thought. "What harm could it do? I mean, if someone was to watch over him. It would certainly prevent him from doing himself any more injury at court."

"But..." Tiye said.

"Think about it. It is a major project. He could be away for years just supervising the work. And in the meantime Egypt will be free to be ruled by those who deserve to rule over her."

"*Those?*" Tiye said. "He. By *he* who deserves to rule over her."

"Yes," Aye said, absently. "Yes, of course."

But Tiye and Aye were both thinking the same thing.

"You realise," Aye said, "that Amenophis will be sole ruler of this kingdom after Amenhotep joins his ancestors?"

"Of course I do. Why?"

"Oh, no reason," Aye said. "Except..."

"Except?"

"Well, it seems that we are on the threshold of the future, and we can make a choice whether or not to follow it, or whether to stay with the past."

"Are you asking me to choose between my husband and my son?" Tiye asked.

"I am asking you to make a decision for Egypt and your family. Imagine our mother was here. What would she say?"

Tiye smiled, but it was an expression without humour.

"She would undoubtedly say that you are your mother's son," she said. "I cannot turn my back on my husband."

"Nobody is asking you to. I am merely saying that it would be good for everyone for you to stay close to your son. It will be good for Egypt because you can offer him advice and the advantage of your experience and wisdom. It will be good for your family because we will have a friend in the pharaoh, and it will be good for you because, well, you will be with your son. It will even be good for Amenophis. He will see that he has your love and support. It is not as though it will be forever. It is not as though this insanity will ever come to fruition."

And so once again the decision was made before Amenhotep even realised he had made it. Tiye and Aye chose the opportune moment, when he was still groggy with sleep and toothache, and spoke to him in hushed, reverential tones, planting the seeds of decision and allowing them to germinate.

"Anyway," Amenhotep told them. "I do not suppose there is much we can do about it. He is co-regent, after all."

"Exactly," Aye said.

"And it is not as if anything will ever actually come of it. He does not have the brains."

"Exactly," Tiye said.

"Or the organisational abilities," Aye added.

"Exactly," Amenhotep said.

Of course, all three did not need to be told how unprecedented this all was, and each thought that perhaps they should be protesting a little more, but the thought of court without the embarrassment of Amenophis was too tempting to be dismissed.

Amenophis was granted his wish, and although he had neither sought nor needed permission he was grateful for it.

The Maya Papyrus, Fragments 64-68

After the audience, news spread around the palace hardly pausing at one gossipmonger before being passed onto the next. It was news too unexpected, too bewildering, too unprecedented to be comfortably held in the breast without sharing its burden with whomever happened to be within earshot. It was the sort of news that would reveal itself in the faces of those who were party to it, and I could tell simply by seeing someone's expression whether or not they knew. Before the afternoon aged into evening there were very few ignorant faces left.

I had been one of the lucky few, one of the chosen. Amenophis undoubtedly saw all of us who crowded into his audience chamber that afternoon as being among the blessed. I thought he was about to announce his divinity at last, but even that would have been too predictable for this unlikeliest of men. I had kept the secret of it for so long that it no longer seemed shocking to me, or at least it was not shocking that Amenophis believed it to be true. To have discovered that he was correct would have knocked me from my sandals.

And so to have Amenophis gather us all together to announce what I already knew would have left me singularly unmoved, but when he explained his latest departure from sanity and reason I actually felt momentarily dizzy.

Impossible! I thought, beginning to understand that nothing was beyond the whims and follies of this king.

Presumably his eyesight was not able to relay to him the faces of those who looked up from the foot of his dais, for he continued to smile proudly back at our bemused expressions as though he believed our silence to be the product of awe at his majesty. It reminded me of the look I had seen on his face once before, at the foot of a stake in a courtyard at Malkarta.

Every major figure at court – barring Amenhotep, who was still recovering from the extraction of his teeth – shared the space of that room, and many of them were not of the type to be awestruck by anything that Amenophis could say. Tiye was there, and my father Aye, both inscrutable and surprisingly calm. Yuya was there, looking as though he had shared his wife's breath for his entire married life and could no longer fill his lungs without her contribution. Anen was there, too delighted at his reinstatement at court to be anything other than radiating happiness, whatever the news. Nefertiti was there, of course, sharing the dais with her husband, looking as though she would never stray further from his side again..

I knew, of course, that this news was monumental, and that it would change everything. It would change Egypt, without doubt, although it was not immediately apparent how much of an understatement this was. This news would change history itself. There are few places where history and life touch. History flows around one's life like water around a stone, always there, but one having no real bearing on the other.

Not so with the news I heard that morning. History was to have the profoundest effect on my life, directly and irretrievably.

There were few preliminaries to Amenophis' speech. He was too excited and nervous to delay the news any longer than absolutely necessary.

"I have two announcements," he said. "The first is a matter of great joy to me. Nefertiti, my wife, is with child."

A brief murmur disturbed the silence of the audience, as though in mild surprise that Amenophis should be able to distinguish himself in that department. He waved them once more into silence.

"You may offer me your congratulations shortly," he said. He took a deep breath. The announcement that he was to be a father was only the preamble to the real business of the day, and now the moment was upon him. Upon them all. He felt history gird herself around him.

"I am to leave court," he told the room. "In all probability, I shall do so permanently."

Before he had spoken there had been in the room the subliminal hum of a crowd neither pleased to be where it was nor particularly interested in the unravelling of events. After Amenophis' introductory remarks a deep silence fell with the abruptness of the unexpected. He savoured the moment and allowed himself the luxury of a long and indulgent pause.

"I have given instructions," he said, finally, "to the architects of this court. They are to build me a city."

Amenophis lowered his voice. It was a device employed by his father on many an occasion, an orator's art that Amenophis had until now never braved. He could sense its efficacy. There was an added gravitas to his voice and every ear in the room was strained to sense each nuance.

"My city shall be named Akhetaten, which means The Horizon of the Aten, for it will be situated in a place where the Aten himself appeared to me in the guise of the rising sun and commanded me to build a new centre for Egypt, just as Ra commanded my grandfather to clear the sand from the legs of the Sphinx."

Amenophis paused again, this time partly for dramatic effect and partly because he had forgotten what he had decided to say next. The room, he noticed, was so hushed it was as though it was empty. Faces were turned towards him, but he was not close enough to discern their expressions. His ears told him all he needed to know. He could not help but smile, and his words came back to him in a rush.

"Akhetaten is to be situated on virgin land in the desert. It will be on the east bank of the Nile, north of Cusae. It is land which has not belonged to any god or man since the creation of the world. Now it is to be dedicated to my god, to the god that is within me and around me, to the Aten. I shall be taking my own court with me, and those chosen will be notified forthwith. They will need to make immediate preparations, because I have ordered that the city be completed within a year. Upon the death of my father, which with the blessing of Ra is a long way away yet, the rest of the court will join me there."

The silence was usurped by a hum, a cumulative whisper that revealed nothing to Amenophis' ears. In a sudden moment Amenophis the orator was vanquished and quite forgotten, and his place was taken by Amenophis the schoolboy struggling to read the information on his palette, and his classmates were muttering, undoubtedly about him, and any second now he would hear laughter and feel the blood rush to his face, which would only add to his humiliation.

The hum grew into a murmur.

"Memphis..." Amenophis began, with the tone of a man who knows his words are not heard.

He spoke again, louder this time, almost having to shout to make himself heard, speaking quickly as though afraid the audience would leave before the end of his sentence.

"Memphis will cease to be Egypt's capital!" he said. "Instead, Akhetaten will enjoy that particular honour!"

The mutterings of the crowd did not dissipate. Rather, upon reception of Amenophis' closing sentence, they redoubled. Amenophis rose from his throne, knowing as he did so that it was a mistake, a sign of weakness, an acknowledgement of the supremacy of the crowd. It still sounded to him like the mumblings of the classroom, and Amenophis' eyes were not well attuned enough to betray the impression of his ears as a lie.

"Get out!" he said, all pretension of regality long fled. "All of you! Leave me! How dare you mock me so? How *dare* you?"

The audience turned their backs – they did not even bow! – and took their mutterings with them. How glorious it would be to be rid of this city!

How light his steps would feel being a week's sail away from a childhood that followed him to this day. A fresh start, surrounded by people he could trust the most; his wife and the children she would bear him, and those of his family he wished to accompany him. Free too from the burden of his secret self, where he could announce his true identity to this city he was to create from nothing where the occupants would see his power and worship at his feet!

Amenophis returned to his seat visibly shaking, although whether from rage or fear few in the room could have said. The announcement could hardly have been any more of a disaster. There was little salvageable, and yet Amenophis knew that he must salvage what he could. Against a multitude of weaklings he may have been ineffectual, but he could at least flaunt his authority over one of them. There was someone to whom he had intended to speak anyway.

The Maya Papyrus, Fragment 69

> *"Maya," he said.*
>
> *"Your Majesty?"*
>
> *"You will accompany me to this new city of mine."*
>
> *Not "I request that..." or even "I have decreed that..." but simply "You will accompany me to this new city of mine" in the same tone that he would have said "the sun will rise tomorrow morning."*
>
> *"Majesty?" I said. "Are you sure? I mean, I am hardly worthy to be chosen..."*
>
> *"Nonsense. You are too modest."*
>
> *There are very few men who could say such a thing and make it sound like a threat. By now the room had emptied of everyone save myself, the king and Nefertiti, all the others having fled before his pitiful wrath, no doubt delighted that their name was not called in place of mine.*
>
> *"I have not forgotten that time in Thebes before my father's festival," he continued. "You saw me for who I am, and apart from my wife, you are the only person so far to have done so."*
>
> *"But of course, Your Majesty," I said, thinking quickly, "and it is a matter of amazement to me that everyone does not see what I see, but I do not think it would be wise for me to accompany you."*

"Wise?" Amenophis said. He had actually been smiling at my disingenuous reply until I unwisely mentioned wisdom. Then his face fell back into a scowl.

"Not that I am calling your wisdom into question," I added, quickly. "I just do not feel that I would be up to the task."

"Task? What task? I have not yet given you a task. Maya, if I did not know you better I would think you ungrateful and disloyal to show such reluctance to do your king's bidding."

His tone told me that although he did indeed know me better, he still thought me ungrateful and disloyal. I feigned shock and horror. It was not a difficult part to grasp.

"Your Majesty," I said, with all the gravitas at my disposal. "I would rather die in a pit of scorpions than lead you to think me disloyal."

His smile did not readily return.

"How could I show disloyalty to a god such as yourself?" I added for good measure. It seemed to pacify him.

"Then you will accompany me."

It was not a question.

"I would be honoured beyond my worth," I said. What else could I do?

"Of course, I shall have to go with him when he goes," Tiye said to Amenhotep, who heard not a word that she said. He was sitting at his dining table, an array of food and drink laid out before him in a semicircle, so that no one thing was any further to reach for than any other. Grease ran in rivulets down his chin. It ran down his chest and belly, from where it dripped onto his kilt. It was even, although Tiye had no clue how it had got there, glistening on the rim of one of his ears.

"Do you know," Amenhotep began, and then paused to finish chewing and swallowing his current mouthful. "Do you know," he began again, "I have not felt this well in years. Why did I not think to have those teeth removed sooner?"

"Are you listening?" Tiye said. "I said that I shall have to go with him. To this new city he has been talking about. Akhe... whatever it was."

Amenhotep stopped chewing and looked up.

"Go with him?" he said. "Why? When? For how long?"

"Why? Because we cannot trust him on his own. He is talking about making the place the capital of Egypt. Can you imagine? Anyway, he will need someone you can trust to watch over him, and someone to whom he will listen. I am the only person to fit that description. I may take Aye with me for support, and to remind me of home."

"But you will not be leaving for a while. Not until the city is built."

"My darling, the city is never going to be built. It is an undertaking larger and more complicated than all the pyramids put together. Amenophis does not have it in him to organise it. He is taking a party to the site he has chosen within the next few days. I shall accompany them. I do not know how long I will be away. It may be for some time."

Amenhotep had stopped eating and was staring with his mouth open. Tiye grimaced and held up her hand to block the view of his half chewed food.

"Amenhotep, please," she said.

The chewing resumed, but with a fraction of the enthusiasm.

Chapter Thirteen

The Gods of Akhetaten

"It is an inspired choice, Majesty," Mahu said, once he had been bidden rise.

"It was not mine," Amenophis said. "It was the Aten who led me here."

Mahu shrugged. "Still..." he said. He looked around him at the panorama that was to become Amenophis' city. He pointed at the cliffs that ringed them on three sides. "With these," he said, "there is almost no need of city walls. We could defend this site for a thousand years against all the hordes of Hatti and Mitanni combined."

Amenophis smiled. "I hope it will never come to that," he said. "If I have learned one thing from my father it is the folly of war. In any case, I have other concerns. Now you are my chief of police, Mahu, you have only one concern, and it is not Akhetaten, or Egypt, or her enemies. Your duty now is towards me, and me alone. Do I make myself clear?"

"Abundantly, Your Majesty."

"Good, then you will understand that I will take very personally indeed any failure on your part to protect me."

Mahu bowed deeply. "Majesty, your life and wellbeing are more dear to me than my own. You have no need to worry. And anyway, I am sure that your people love you as I do. You are in no danger from them."

Amenophis turned to face him. The king towered head and shoulders over Mahu, who looked as though he had put all his energy into growing wider rather than taller. Amenophis glared at him.

"I was not safe in Thebes," he said. "You did not protect me there."

"Your Majesty," Mahu protested. "I was not your chief of police in Thebes. That would never have happened under my command."

"That is as may be. But there are people who would do me harm. You will never be off duty, Mahu. You will never relax. You will treat every situation with the utmost suspicion, every man, woman or child in my vicinity as a conspirator. You will personally organise an armed guard of the highest calibre of troops to accompany me everywhere. I never wish to be alone, Mahu, and if I am, if I ever suspect that I am in danger, I will personally see to it that you provide a reason why."

Even at that moment, Amenophis felt exposed. He knew it would not be a popular move, this jettisoning of tradition, and that by extension he would not be a popular king.

At least, not at first. Not until his reforms had been digested by the populace and meshed themselves into the weave of Egyptian life. And mesh they would, although the building of Akhetaten was only the first of the revolutions gestating in Amenophis' heart. After it would come a reformation that would eclipse it entirely. Amenophis allowed himself a private smile as he watched the workers below him struggle through their toil. They had been transported from every outpost of Egypt and brought here to fulfil the king's vision of a new city. Amenophis tried to think himself into their place but it made his head swim. Each one knew only this section of wall or that foundation pit. Their world was encompassed by the bricks and mortar that they carried upon their backs or dragged in teams along the floor. Only Amenophis himself could see the entire city as it would appear. It was as though his mind was the summation of all of theirs. He supposed that if his knowledge was to be stuffed and squeezed into a mortal frame it would explode like a ripe fruit thrown against a wall.

There was only one shadow. Nowhere in Egypt did he feel truly sheltered from the machinations of Amun. Still, Amenophis thought, it was only a matter of time. It was only until the revolution was complete. Amun and his priesthood would learn to regret making an enemy of a god as powerful as Amenophis. Amun was about to learn that gods could be as susceptible to the oblivion of death as the mortals they purported to rule.

Oh yes, thought Amenophis as he watched his workers tramp to and fro before him. There are going to be changes indeed.

A warm gust of wind whipped up the sand around his legs as though the desert was feebly angry with him. Amenophis turned his back to it.

The Maya Papyrus, Fragments 81-83

> *I profess myself astonished to this day at the thought of the building of Amenophis' great new city. That it was built at all was nothing short of a miracle. Each day that passed during its construction was one of wonder piled upon the awe of the day before. He did not grow bored of this project. He did not wander back to Memphis with vague orders to continue in his absence that he knew but did not care would be ignored. He stayed. He watched, as did the Aten, who shed his light there as he slid across his heavens, and looked down, undoubtedly as astonished as the*

rest of us, as this city that was dedicated to him sprang from the ground.

Akhetaten rose like a desert flower, only faster. A flower grows in secret, invisibly and surreptitiously. Akhetaten grew with a defiant pride it inherited from its father, brick upon brick, roof upon wall.

It was an entire city, and it was built from foundations to flagpoles in a little over one year. Its vast palace complexes, its confusing temples that were open to the sky, its trade district, its workers' suburb, its irrigation, its police and army barracks, its storehouses and offices, inns and harems, all of this veritably leapt from the desert sand as though thrust upwards from below by some subterranean god.

To walk its embryonic streets during these days of construction was to descend into a maelstrom. One was constantly buffeted by men hurrying about their business, by teams of slaves sweating and struggling to pull a sled loaded high with bricks along the uneven ground, by donkeys and by skittish horses and their chariots. Every footstep was a trap evaded. Foundation pits and discarded piles of rubble threatened to engulf or trip the imprudent pedestrian and innumerable potholes lay in wait for the unwary ankle. Wide ramps led up to the tops of walls and summits of buildings, up which stones and mud bricks would be dragged in stuttering lurches.

The air was so full of dust and sand that everyone was constantly thirsty, and merchants would ply their trade along the busier streets, selling beer covered in a layer of scum and adding to the general atmosphere of melee.

I must admit that Akhetaten frightened me even this early in its history. Everything was set at such a feverish pace that it seemed nobody had the time to avoid standing on my feet or elbowing me out of their way or barking my shin with the sled they dragged behind them. Nobody shared so much as a glance and the visitor would soon learn to keep his gaze set on objects that could not return it. Of course, the atmosphere was not helped by the presence of Mahu's men. They had perfected the difficult art of not being conspicuous as such, but of merely not making much of their attempt to remain unobtrusive. It was a very powerful effect.

Amenophis later claimed, at great length and at every available opportunity, that the planning, organising and overseeing of the construction of Akhetaten was his responsibility alone, and that no other man had a hand in it. Incredible though that may be – and I have heard many a repudiation by those who were not there – it was the truth. Paranoid Amenophis would not allow anyone take a decision from him. There was no delegation, no committee to decide where this palace should be placed or that temple. The construction of Akhetaten took an army of men, and these men had to be organised and housed. Stone had to be quarried, and mud bricks made in their millions. Tiles had to be fired and bread baked and beer brewed. All were set in motion by orders from the king, and the king alone. Many of us in his entourage were forced to reconsider our assessment of him, for his decisions were flawless. It was as though Memphis had been a gag that prevented his ideas from spilling forth. Here, without the stifling personalities of those who would mock and question him, without the sidelong glances and the silent judgements of his servants and slaves, Amenophis' confidence bloomed. Here, where he was surrounded by those he trusted most – or, more accurately, distrusted least – he could voice the thoughts that had previously remained smothered for fear of being the wrong answer to one of his father's interminable questions.

He was able, at last, to take risks with his decision making, and this freedom unearthed a genius previously unimagined by even those closest to him. They who had been so eager to judge found Amenophis' appearance to be an unreliable reference point. Ptahmose the priest may have believed that the gods were slowly transforming Amenophis into an ass, but even Ptahmose would have raised his eyebrows in wonder at Amenophis' skill in the construction of Akhetaten. The size of the project was unprecedented in history. A whole town sprang up simply to house the innumerable soldiers, workmen and slaves that worked on Akhetaten in every capacity. I grant that I have never seen a battle, but I would wager that there were enough men there to fight an entire campaign, and the king seemed to know the whereabouts of every team of workmen, and at what stage of their labours they should be. He knew exactly what needed to be done, and when. He knew what needed to be finished so that whatever was next could be started. He knew what it was that was next. Under his watchful gaze, Akhetaten was born.

And it was a thing of beauty. Whatever my thoughts and beliefs about Amenophis, in whatever disdain I hold his memory, I cannot deny him this. It was white and gold and dazzling in a way that even Memphis and Thebes could not be, for Memphis and

Thebes are cities built by generations of men, where anything new and dazzling tends to be crowded on all sides by neighbours who are old and flaking and decrepit. Here in Akhetaten, nothing was older than anything else, and the buildings competed to outshine one another, lying in wait for unwary travellers who approached along the Nile at dawn.

But as beautiful as Akhetaten was, as stunning was its rise to glory, I cannot pretend to look back on the time of its construction with anything approaching fondness. I was tormented there, and not just by the austerity of my surroundings while I waited for the city to take shape, but by the company of those who surrounded me and the absence of those who did not. Nefertiti was my only friend during those days, and I ask the gods to bless her memory for that.

Amenophis himself became even more insufferable. One would hear his approach from some distance away in the tramp of the men who surrounded him. He was never to be seen without his guard, but for that matter he was never to be seen with them either, so effectively did they surround him. To be spoken to by Amenophis was akin to being eaten alive, for any discourse was prefaced by the advance ranks of his guards opening up and enveloping his prey with an unnerving pincer movement that left the target feeling helpless and suffocated, as, I am sure, Amenophis fully intended.

Meanwhile, Akhetaten grew apace. The palaces and temples were erected first, followed by the public buildings and homes of the honoured members of court, which by now included your humble historian. We all chose sites as far away from Amenophis' palace as we could whilst still appearing keen to be in his company. It became almost a competition between us, each nervous on behalf of the next while we awaited a disingenuous question: 'Is there a reason for your home to be so far away from my palace?' But Amenophis never asked.

The lesser nobles and friends of court were provided for next, and so it continued through the strata of society, until the hovels and slums of the workmen and destitute were allowed to huddle along the banks of a river of sewage that flowed from the suburbs. But whatever the home, however grandiose or humble, however sprawling and orderly or cramped and unkempt, each had one thing in common. Each had a shrine. Of course, the extravagance of the shrine changed from one home to the next, but not a single building in the city would not have one placed carefully before the threshold. They were shrines to the new god, the Aten. But the Aten was not alone, for he was joined by two other gods, previously unknown in the firmament; gods who were his children and his siblings and his parents and even him, all at once. He was flanked on one side by depictions of a tall god who appeared rather distorted, with women's hips and breasts and a head too long and large for his body. On the other side of the Aten would be standing a rather striking looking woman whose captivating face seemed to radiate sternness and love in equal measure. And we were all expected, however lowly or esteemed, however close we were already to the people that these statues represented, we were all expected to prostrate ourselves before them on entering and leaving the building. We were expected to leave them offerings and tend to their needs. My sister the goddess.

Amenophis himself had explained it to me. He summoned me especially to hear the explanation, although it was one I had never sought.

"You are a wise man," he told me, after I had risen from the ground at his feet. "You will understand."

I had no doubt that I would understand at least enough to look interested and nod in the right places. These audiences with Amenophis always made me nervous, even, as was the case this time, when Nefertiti was in attendance. I always sensed that he was the sort of man who would snap with very little provocation and Nefertiti's slight frame in the throne next to him was scant protection indeed.

"Look at the other gods," he said. "They all have families. There are always three of them; the father, the mother and the child. Amun the father, Mut the mother and Khonsu the child. Osiris the father, Isis the mother and Horus the child. It did not make sense that the Aten should be alone. It was a detail that caused me not a little concern."

I nodded and looked interested.

"And then it struck me," he said, and beamed a smile.

I nodded and looked interested. There was a moment of silence. Amenophis stared at me, still smiling. I nodded again, uncertainly. Amenophis nodded back, in a manner which said 'Yes...? well...?' It suddenly occurred to me that he was waiting for me to speak.

"Oh," I said. "The Aten is part of a triad?"

"Ye-es..." Amenophis said, prompting me.

And then, in a revelation undoubtedly less profound than had been Amenophis', but just as welcome, it came to me. I looked from Amenophis to Nefertiti and back again.

"You are the triad?" I said, unable to keep the incredulity from my voice. I coughed and said it again, with more conviction.

"You are the triad," I said.

Amenophis laughed and clapped and fairly bounced in his seat with glee and excitement.

"Yes!" he said, and then, to Nefertiti: "Do you see? I told you he would understand. Your brother has the eyes for our divinity."

I could hardly believe that Nefertiti was a willing participant in this madness, but she did not protest.

"It came to me on the journey from Memphis," Amenophis said. "And once it had, it seemed inconceivable that it could be any other way. What say you on this matter, Maya? Can you see the reflection of divinity in your sister?"

I prostrated myself before her and proclaimed her to be my goddess, feeling ridiculous and humiliated as I did so.

She said not a word. Not 'stop being silly, Maya' nor 'stand, please, you are embarrassing me' nor 'really, this is not necessary'. Not a word, except, "May you live."

The words of a king.

I rose to my feet and took a moment to knock the dust from my kilt and knees. It seemed faintly defiant at the time, but I doubt if either of the gods before me even noticed it. Their minds were on higher things, as my own would be before long.

For Amenophis had one more surprise for the people of his new city. He chose to deliver it at the city's official inauguration.

Construction work would continue at Akhetaten for most of the remainder of Amenophis' reign, but before two years had elapsed from the laying of its first foundation stone the city was fit to be occupied by a king. A day's holiday was declared for all the inhabitants save the slaves, and Amenophis and Nefertiti toured the streets in a chariot of gold and silver.

Through the centre of Akhetaten, running roughly north to south, was the arterial road around which the city had been constructed. Amenophis had been thinking of his processions when he issued the instructions for building it, and his overseers shared a worried glance when they received them. Like everything else in Akhetaten, it was imposing and august, and it was said that twenty five chariots could have ridden it abreast, with space between them for a man of Amenhotep's ample girth to comfortably walk. Known as the King's Way, it was an avenue lined with fragrant bushes and trees, and it was along this that the crowds began to gather early on the morning of the king's procession. Amenophis and Nefertiti were to travel along the length of the road from the south, followed by Aye and Tiye, who shared a second, less grandiose chariot. Behind them, without the benefit of a chariot of any kind, came the senior members of court.

In Nefertiti's arms, clinging on tightly and looking overawed at the crowds, was Meritaten, the royal couple's first child. She shared her birthday with the first foundation stones of the city and seemed to have sprouted up just as quickly. She was not comfortable with her place as the object of so much adoration and was periodically unable to prevent herself from subsiding into fearful sobs, although her mother did her best to soothe and reassure her. Even Amenophis himself was seen to reach across with a comforting hand from time to time.

In Aye and Tiye's chariot, held in Tiye's arms, rode the divine couple's second daughter. Despite everyone's hopes for an heir and Amenophis' long talks with the Aten on the subject, Pentu the physician had been proved correct and the child had been born a girl. She was named Meketaten, and was elevated to a pedestal of love at least as high as that of her sister, despite her gender.

"It is of no concern," Nefertiti had told her husband, although he had shown no signs of needing reassurance on the matter. "We can try again."

"Of course we can," he had replied, kissing her on the tip of her nose. "There is plenty of time. For now, all I need are my little girls."

Nefertiti had smiled and silently prayed to the Aten that her husband was as unperturbed as he appeared.

The procession along the King's Way to celebrate the nominal completion of Akhetaten was well received, in the main. The crowd cheered and waved and threw flowers at the feet of the horses who pulled the royal chariot, although, as the royal chariot fastidiously stayed in the exact centre of the avenue throughout the procession, few flowers made it to their target. Some of the members of the crowd were less enthusiastic than others. Here after all was a king who had taken them from their homes and dragged them across Egypt, although even the most ambivalent had to admit that once he had got them here he provided for them like no pharaoh before him. Their homes were pristine and their food plentiful. Anyway, those members of the crowd seen not to be cheering as loudly as they might, or waving less than enthusiastically, soon found themselves in the vicinity of large, fearsome men who carried official looking clubs in such a way that they had been concealed, but not concealed well enough to be hidden from the sight of anyone that had cause to glance at their owners. Those who did have cause to glance soon found themselves cheering and waving as whole-heartedly as anyone in the crowd. The fearsome looking men would move on, never having spoken a word. In the procession Mahu would occasionally catch the eye of one of the men, and they would share a discrete nod of acknowledgement.

The king and his retinue passed northwards, through the southern suburbs and into the centre of the city. Everywhere was greenery such as had never been seen within city walls before. Some of the more enthused onlookers had climbed trees to gain a better vantage point. Others found their view obscured by the bushes and plants that lined every road and surrounded every building.

Once in the city centre the procession passed the smaller of Akhetaten's two Aten temples and then the king's house on the right and the royal palace on the left. The palace was the king's official residence. It had its back to the road, and instead faced out over the Nile, separated from the river by three tiered gardens of carefully landscaped exotic flowers. Straddling the road between the palace and the king's house was a covered bridge linking the two, too high to be reached by the hand of any man standing in the street. This drew as many stares as did the royal family itself. Few had seen its like before, and fewer still were prepared to risk standing beneath it. There was a brief hush as the king passed into its shadow, and redoubled cheering as he returned to sunlight.

The procession continued northwards until it came across the Great Temple to the Aten. Amenophis had designed the building with the intention of stealing the breath from the visitor's throat, and he had succeeded. Even the men who had built it and seen it grow day after day were staggered by its majesty. As its foundations had been laid some had compared it to the temple of Amun at Thebes, but such comparisons were soon abandoned as inadequate. Its scale was unique in Egypt and beyond. This single building was as long as the city was wide, and as wide as the entire northern suburb.

Amenophis and Nefertiti dismounted from their chariot and, having handed Meritaten to Tiye, made their way on foot through the first of the colossal gateways that dwarfed every other building in the city. On either side of the gateways, as if on guard, stood equally tall poles from which trailed dozens of multicoloured streamers reaching almost to the ground, hanging limply in the still air.

The gates were opened by unseen hands and the royal couple stepped forwards into a vast open space. Arranged before them in neat rows either side of the central pathway were three hundred and sixty five altars. Two priests, struggling under the weight of the food piled upon the trays they carried, took tentative steps forward. Nefertiti pointed towards the nearest of the altars and the priests gratefully laid the food upon it.

Nefertiti guided Amenophis back to the main pathway that led further into the temple. A small stage had been constructed at the far end, before a second gateway that led into the inner sanctum. Amenophis and Nefertiti climbed the steps on to the stage, followed by Aye and Tiye, and turned to face the crowd that had silently filed into the temple behind them. Perhaps a hundred and fifty people prostrated themselves before their king. Here was every noble and his wife and every member of court, however lowly. Amenophis wanted his message to reach everyone of any consequence. He wanted there to be no possibility of error, no opportunity for misunderstandings, either genuine or contrived for convenience.

Amenophis had allowed himself the conceit of recognising the founding of Akhetaten as a moment of inspired genius. Granted, the Aten had appeared to him and prompted him with a heavenly sign, but the fact remained that he and he alone had built the city. And yet, even now, with his glory reflecting off the walls and dazzling those who knelt before him, he was tormented by doubt. The long scar that lay across his back had faded with time, but the memory of the pain was as fresh as it had been as he had lain in his chariot and his blood that day in Thebes.

He knew he was not safe. He knew that Amun was not the sort of god to allow a rivalry to go unpunished, and that even here in the remote desert his tendrils may stretch yet. No number of policemen could protect him from a determined god, and so he had come to his decision. It was, he thought, rather inspired.

The trick was in denying Amun influence, for how could Amun turn men against him if he had no means of communicating with them?

He had spent days rehearsing his speech, a scribe writing and rewriting the drafts he dictated until neither of them could remember what had been discarded and what retained. The scribe had read it back to him until Amenophis had its every word at his command. This was not a time to rely on improvisation.

On the stage Amenophis and Nefertiti lowered themselves into their thrones.

"May you live!" Amenophis shouted to the crowd. The half nearest to the stage began to climb to their feet, the rest following a moment later.

"You will need to speak up," Nefertiti whispered to Amenophis, through the corner of her mouth.

Amenophis began to stand in order to be able to project his voice further, and then realised that it may appear undignified for a king to have to stand and shout at his audience. Halfway out of his seat he hesitated and began to sit down again before realising that he could have all the dignity in Egypt, but it would serve him little if nobody could hear what he had to say. Sighing, and thinking about the indignity of indecision, he pushed himself to his feet and to one or two faltering steps towards the front of the stage, aware of the greater indignity of walking too far and falling into the arms of the people standing below.

He took a deep breath and began the proclamation that would save him from Amun, that would cocoon him in Akhetaten as securely as if the city were his tomb.

"Nobles of Akhetaten! Today you witness history, for today marks the founding of Egypt's greatest city, built in honour of its greatest god!"

Somehow, the words did not seem as powerful as when he had rehearsed them. The open air seemed to suck at their vitality, leaving them hollow and transparent by the time they reached the ears of those who strained to hear them.

"May the Aten behold it and take delight in it!" he continued. "For it is the Aten who advised me concerning this place. No official advised me concerning it, and neither did any person in the entire land advise me. It was the Aten alone.

"I did not find this place provided with shrines, or plastered with tombs, or covered with any hint of civilisation. I found this place abandoned, not belonging to a god or a goddess, or a king or any other people. When this land was still barren the Aten appeared to me and proclaimed to me: 'Build a city on this site to belong to my majesty for all eternity!'

"And build it I have!"

This last sentence was designed as a rallying cry, a bearer of emotion that would swell the hearts of those in attendance. Amenophis had already paused for applause, but he heard nothing.

Behind him, Nefertiti felt a stab of anxiety. Amenophis had rehearsed parts of his speech to her, and she knew the significance of the line and the effect he had planned it to have on the crowd. It was not, she realised, that they were being purposefully unreceptive, but that Amenophis' rhetoric and delivery left them somewhat confused as to when they were expected to react.

And then, somewhere, someone started clapping. Nefertiti craned her neck to see who it could be. There. Perhaps two thirds of the way towards the back of the crowd. Nefertiti could not quite make out who it was, other than that he was a short but wide man. He was making a point with his applause, his hands held above his head. And then somebody else joined in, on the periphery of the crowd. Nefertiti recognised him as one of Amenophis' guards. One of Mahu's men. Another began to applaud, on the other side of the crowd. Another guard. Soon, the audience began to take notice and sporadic pockets of applause broke out. It was only a matter of moments between the first person applauding and the entire audience following suit. Nefertiti felt herself able to relax as Amenophis continued.

"The Aten has bestowed upon us all a great gift. The gift of his city, with myself and my Great Royal Wife Nefertiti as his representatives herein. The Aten is our great god, who shines over every land, and despite the distance that separates us, his rays shine upon the earth for the people of every nation to see.

"Behold this god, and think on his greatness! For when he is absent the land is a dark and dangerous place, where lions roam abroad. But when he is here he pushes back the darkness and the world awakes, because the Aten has given it life.

"But the Aten who gives us life also gives us this city, and he has brought us here to be with him in the place where he is most exalted. By coming here, we have all entered into a covenant with him, a covenant that I for one am not prepared to break."

The decisive moment had arrived. He was too far away from the people who shared his stage to be able to discern their expressions, but he quickly glanced in their direction anyway. He believed he saw Nefertiti nod her encouragement, but if his mother and uncle moved they did so too subtly for him to detect.

What he was about to say would come as much as a shock to them, he knew, as to anyone in the audience before them. Amenophis had consulted only the Aten, and then relayed the conversations to Nefertiti in order to successfully interpret the signs and portents.

Amenophis took a deep breath, but did not allow himself any further time for reflection before plunging ahead.

"I hereby declare that I shall not leave this city again as long as it pleases the Aten to allow me to remain among you. I have placed marker stones around the city. These *stela* are my city's boundaries. I shall not cross them."

A hum started up like the distant drone of a large insect. Nefertiti edged forwards in her seat and desperately tried to discern its meaning. It seemed not to be a sound tinted by malice; rather it appeared to be the sound of the crowd's consternation, and as such not nearly so threatening as she had feared it would be.

But then Nefertiti knew what Amenophis was about to say next.

"My tomb shall be in the eastern cliffs over which the Aten rises every day to give us the bounty and blessing of his light," Amenophis was saying. He paused. Nefertiti, without realising it, held her breath.

"As shall be yours," Amenophis said. "For you shall all enter into the covenant of the Aten. I hereby decree, under the gaze of the Aten himself, that this city shall be a very temple itself, and its inhabitants shall be its eternal congregation. Once entered, none shall leave."

There was a moment of stunned silence. Nefertiti looked out over the crowd. Heads were turning as though neighbours were having to silently confirm with each other the evidence of their ears. And then, in the same place as before, the applause began, although this time is was not nearly so infectious. The guards on the periphery of the audience cheered and clapped with easy enthusiasm, but they were joined by a negligible number of the rest of the audience, and Nefertiti could see none that were ready to add to the noise. The guards were almost rapturous, but arresting though such a noise was, it appeared feeble when viewed in the context of the heavy silence that surrounded it.

Indeed, the volume of the ovation did nothing to drown out a lone cry of dissent that dared voice itself from the crowd's anonymity.

"Shame!" the voice cried. "Shame!"

Nefertiti strained to see where the shout had originated, craning her neck and bobbing her head from side to side in the manner of a cat stalking its prey. It was impossible to tell, but she saw the reaction of the guards nearest the dissenter and that was enough. With no visible sign of hesitation, two of the guards ploughed into the crowd, their clubs already held high over their heads. The audience scattered before them, barging and climbing over each other in their panic until a rough, empty circle was defined, the central point of which consisted of the two guards leaning over a prone body, swinging their clubs high over their heads and bringing them down, again and again, on the man that lay quivering between them. The rest of the guards had remained at their stations around the periphery of the crowd, but to Nefertiti they looked to be conspicuously restless, their clubs held by the handle in one hand with the beating edge resting upon or tapping against the other. The crowd saw this as clearly as she and nobody dared move to the aid of the man on the floor.

Nefertiti pushed herself to her feet and strode across the stage to her husband, barging past Aye and Tiye, who were both out of their seats, too aghast at the spectacle before them to notice Nefertiti's hands and elbows upon them. Nefertiti grabbed Amenophis' arm and hissed into his ear.

"They are killing him! You must stop them!"

"Who?" Amenophis asked, half turning to face her.

"The guards. The man who shouted."

"They will not kill him," Amenophis said. "They will arrest him, nothing more."

"But I can see them," Nefertiti said. "They..."

But as she turned from Amenophis back to the scene playing out in front of the stage she saw that the beating had in fact ceased and that the guards were contenting themselves with dragging the insensible man from the temple. The crowd shifted out of the way as they went and closed up behind them. Nefertiti heard Meritaten and Meketaten crying heartily, caught up in the turmoil if not understanding it.

"What will happen to him?" she asked Amenophis, indicating the man being dragged from the temple.

"He will be taken to the police barracks. We have cells there."

"And then?"

"Nefertiti," Amenophis said, with gentle firmness. "I must finish my speech. They are waiting. Please."

She turned and resumed her seat. Aye and Tiye watched her progress as though she herself was responsible for the actions of the guards. She met their gaze as best she could as she passed them.

Amenophis too watched her go. He turned away when the attention of his mother and uncle turned from her to him. His perception of their expressions had more to do with intuition than vision, but to him their faces were questioning and angry.

Amenophis turned back to the crowd. He knew it was going to be difficult to reign their attention back in, but the problem was almost a welcome distraction from his mother's glare.

"If..." he said, addressing the audience.

Hardly a face was turned towards him and everybody was in a huddled conference with everyone else.

"If I could..." he said.

The guards had taken to patrolling the circumference of the crowd as though prowling for their next victim.

"*You stand before your king!*" Amenophis suddenly shouted, flecks of spittle spraying from his mouth. He stood for a moment in silence as though even he had been surprised by the vehemence of his outburst. Once again he felt all eyes on him.

"The Aten," he said, "is my father. I am one with him, as he is with me. We are two bodies of the same spirit, and so when you speak out against me, you speak out against the Aten. I cannot and I will not allow this to happen, for it is blasphemy and I will not tolerate blasphemy against the name of the god who brought me into being and led me to this place.

"It is through me, and through the Great Royal Wife Nefertiti, that the Aten commands you. It is through us alone that he bestows his blessings upon the face of the earth. Without your pharaoh to act on your behalf there would be no light, only darkness like death. There would be no seasons, no inundation, no crops. The forces of chaos would be abroad in the land, and everything would be marked with their swords. And yet you stand there and cry *shame* when I attempt to proffer to him your thanks?

"No, there is no shame. Only blasphemy and betrayal. Are there others among you ready to betray your king and your god?"

Amenophis surveyed the crowd as though he could see its members, as though it was more than one large amorphous mass. At least Nefertiti could see that nobody was prepared to meet his eye. Amenophis returned to the set text of his speech in a manner that informed the crowd that the matter of his rebuke was completed.

"The Aten is to be twice honoured this day, and there are those among you who have been informed of a further duty I have commanded to be undertaken. It takes place in the Small Aten Temple, to which we will now make our way. This is no concern of the majority of you. You may disperse as you wish, or you may wish to remain here to pay your respects to your god."

He had been fighting to resist the compulsion to turn and see what his mother and uncle were doing. He had not heard them return to their seats and he feared that they were standing behind him with expressions of fury displayed for all to see.

Recognising her cue, Nefertiti once more pushed herself from her chair and traversed the stage to her husband. Taking him by the hand, she began to lead him to the steps that would take them down to the floor of the temple. To reach these she had to take him past Aye and Tiye

"What is the meaning of this?" Tiye said.

Amenophis had no reply.

"*Now* he has nothing to say!" Tiye said to Aye. And then, once again addressing Amenophis: "Do you even understand the words you have just spoken? Am I to understand that you have just forbidden me from ever seeing your father again? Or Aye his wife? Or Maya his mother?"

Amenophis was genuinely taken aback.

"Forbidden?" he said. "No, of course..."

"Then I am going insane," Tiye said, "because that was the meaning I took from your little speech. 'Once entered, none shall leave.' They were your exact words."

Amenophis took a deep breath.

"Mother," he said, with exaggerated composure. "I am sure that the Aten will make a dispensation for such honoured members of the royal family as yourself and my uncle. I shall consult with him and personally see to it that he does so."

Amenophis squeezed Nefertiti's arm and she resumed her guiding of him towards the steps that led from the stage. Tiye watched their slow progress, her mouth agape.

From the vantage point of the stage Nefertiti had noticed a general reluctance on the part of the majority to leave the temple. Only once she was on their level and a path between them had materialised before her did she see the reason why. The guards had dispersed from their positions around the circumference of the audience and taken up stations instead around the gates that led back out into the city. Only those with further business at the Small Aten Temple were being allowed passage back out onto the street. Any others attempting to leave were being persuaded of the advantages of minding Amenophis' suggestion that they remain behind for some extra worship.

Once the royal party and the selected few that were to follow them had left for the smaller of the two temples the remainder were herded unceremoniously through the second set of gates into the inner temple. They were surprised to see that this, too, was without a roof to allow the life giving rays of the Aten to bathe the congregation without restraint and undoubtedly, it was noted by more than a few, to allow the Aten the advantage of seeing exactly who had made the effort to come and worship him.

If the worshippers had expected to be led into a room full of statues of their new god, perhaps in the traditional guise of a man with the head of an animal or bird, they were to be surprised further. There were statues, and plenty of them, but there were none of the Aten. From everywhere around the courtyard there glared down the visage of Amenophis, and wherever he was not there was Nefertiti, stern and just as godlike. The Aten himself appeared only in the wall paintings, and even here not as a man, but as an abstract, as the sun itself, shining down with long rays that terminated in hands, each holding an ankh, the symbol of life.

It was not lost on the congregation that the Aten shone for only two people; Amenophis and Nefertiti. The wall decorations did not show his rays continuing past the royal couple to the general population, and the population did not bow to the Aten, but to the king and queen that were always depicted between the god and the people.

It was quite clear to all in the courtyard to whom this temple had been built, and it was evidently not the Aten.

The Maya Papyrus, Fragments 85-89

Footsore, we trailed behind the royal chariot back along the route we had followed that morning, towards the Small Aten Temple. It had already been a long and tiring day and I would have been bemused to have seen a countenance not besmirched by boredom and misery. The king's news had thrown us all into profound confusion. Many, myself included, did not truly believe what we had heard. Of course it could not be the case that we had just been banned from leaving the city, for that would have made us prisoners, and even the most totalitarian of kings would not imprison an entire city on an insane whim. Even Amenhotep's grandfather, who had beaten men to death with his bare hands and then hung their bodies on the prow of his ship as a trophy had not stooped to such tyranny. But even those among us who had doubted the veracity of what we had heard were taught to believe our ears by what we witnessed in the Small Aten Temple.

I remember the heat being particularly fierce that day, even for that forsaken patch of desert, as though the sun had leant closer in order to better see the farce that transpired in his name. The crowds had thinned significantly by the time we paraded back along that morning's route, but we must have been a curious sight to those who remained at the side of the road, no doubt appearing like a beaten and bedraggled army returning from the field. The applause as we passed was sporadic. It swelled only as the king passed, although that may have been as much to do with the menacing looking guards that surrounded him as his royal presence.

Only one man seemed prepared to buck the displeasure of the guards. He appeared in a cloud of dust on the King's Way, heading towards us from the south. He did not check the pace of his horses as he drew near, but swept straight past us, rightly assuming that he need take no evasive measures, as we would be more than eager to leap out of the way of his hooves and wheels. The guards' formation tightened around Amenophis and swords were drawn, but there seemed to be no need of them. The man did not even glance their way, but continued whipping his horses into a foam mouthed frenzy. Almost as soon as we had noticed him he was by us, leaving us to reform our untidy formation to continue our walk. One or two guards peeled away and followed him and we watched until they had disappeared towards the Great Aten Temple. The king regained his composure and our column moved off.

Once back under the brief shade of the remarkable windowed archway that linked the king's private residence with the royal palace, we turned left and trooped through another pillared gateway into the Small Aten Temple. Even here there was precious little relief from the sun for us honoured guests, and even less relief for our aching feet other than when we knelt before Amenophis as he mounted yet another stage.

Somehow I had expected this gathering to be less punctilious than the first – and I think we were all praying for brevity to match – but I was to be disappointed. If anything, it was even more strictly observed. Amenophis stood upon his stage as though he had been carved from limestone by an honest but bad tempered sculptor.

"May you live," he said, and we reluctantly rose to our feet.

Before us was a tableau whose uses and meanings were not immediately obvious. The stage had been constructed hard up against the wall of the inner temple, which itself was heavily decorated with scenes that were unfamiliar to me, but that all seemed to feature Amenophis and Nefertiti in some intimate pose – holding hands, or embracing or even, in one case, kissing each other – whilst being drenched in the rays of a sun that shone only for them. The stage had been placed in such a way that the largest representation of the sun, or as I now had to begin to think of it, the Aten, appeared directly between the thrones of Amenophis and Nefertiti.

Between these thrones, though, sat a third, directly below the depiction of the Aten. It was neither as large nor as richly decorated as the king's, but it was still laden with enough gold and electrum and lapis lazuli to have made a very rich man weep with gratitude should he have ever come into possession of it. This throne remained empty, and Amenophis and Nefertiti sat either side of it.

Amenophis remained seated as he spoke, his hands grasping the two staffs of his office crossed at the base of his neck. His voice was quieter than it had been at the Great Aten Temple, and although he was here addressing fewer people, the impression was one of gravity rather than intimacy. And anyway, his first sentence made any need of volume redundant.

"I am not your king," he said.

Chapter Fourteen

Mahu's Men

TIYE WAS so paralysed by a transport of rage that she was unable, within the relatively limited confines of language, and with the added restraint of the child in her arms, to express herself to her own satisfaction, although she tried a number of times before settling for the expression of her contempt via a silent scowl.

"Well," she said, watching Amenophis' back as he tentatively descended the steps from the stage in the Great Aten Temple. "In all my…"

She turned to Aye. "I have never…" she said.

Aye placed a reassuring hand upon her shoulder. "I know," he said. "I know."

"But what is to be done?" she asked him.

"Perhaps this was all a mistake," Aye said. "Perhaps we should never have allowed the building of this godforsaken city in the first place."

"But we discussed it," Tiye said. "We decided that it was for the best. That it would have been unwise to stifle him. That our mother taught us the value of having an ally on the throne. These are your words that I use, Aye. Do you now dispute them?"

"Not at all, not at all," Aye said, concentrating more on his thoughts than his words. He too was watching the royal couple as they headed through the temple gateway and back onto the city thoroughfare. As the backs of their guard disappeared from view around the gateposts he was able to gather himself and attend with more alacrity to the subject at hand.

"Not at all," he said again. "I merely qualify them. Sometimes, being the friend of a bad king is more dangerous than being the enemy of a good one. We must tread more carefully than ever, but so too must we be more determined than ever in the effective application of our influence."

"Is it our place to influence a pharaoh in the ruling of his kingdom?" Tiye asked.

"You are a Great Royal Wife," Aye said. "If not you, then who? Egypt demands it of us."

"Egypt? Or the memory of our mother?"

Aye looked at her. "Both," he said, matter of factly.

"And the family? She used to call it her dynasty."

"And so it shall be," Aye said. "So it shall be."

"I always shared our father's view on talk of dynasties and control," Tiye said. "It unnerved me."

"And now?" Aye said.

"And now I am not so sure. I am beginning to think that hers was the only safe path. Look what happens when we loosen the reigns. The king goes mad, declares himself a god and imprisons his people. Imagine if we had not been here. Perhaps he would have done something stupid."

Aye managed a sardonic smile. "Perhaps," he said.

He was about to speak further when the wind carried the tidings of a commotion to him from the main gate. The crowd was thinning now, as the majority of its number filed into the inner temple. Of those that remained only an insignificant number were not guards or policemen, left behind to note who neglected to continue the king's worship within. It was too far away for Aye and Tiye to determine the details, although it seemed that the guards manning the gate had closed around someone like a tightening fist. Even without the details, the scene carried with it the unmistakable signs of violence.

"What now?" Tiye said, as Aye started for the steps that led from the stage. He broke into a run, the pace of which increased as he neared the gate and the scene being played out there unfolded before him. Four or five guards had surrounded a man. From within their circle Aye could see, as he approached, the occasional flash of a hand raised in a fruitless defence, the glimpse of a face bloodied and torn. Aye did not check his pace as he reached the guards. Rather, he threw himself forwards into their midst, knowing the deafness suffered by men in such situations and that pleas for mercy would be as pointless as those of the man to whom the attention of the guards was turned. They were too dedicated to their task to see Aye coming and he was able to pull two or three of them away before they gathered themselves enough to resist his remonstrations. One man pushed him away and two others stepped into the space he was forced to vacate, their clubs poised over their heads. Aye instinctively took a further step or two backwards and the men followed, their intent burning in their eyes before the recognition of their assailant brought them to a standstill.

"I am the Great Royal Wife Tiye's brother, and her husband's closest friend," Aye said, anger more than exertion quavering in his voice. "I am father to Nefertiti and uncle to Amenophis. I could crush even your master Mahu without a single thought or regret. Think what I could do to you. Now, will you beat me as you beat others who do not follow your master's lead?"

Aye looked from one man to another in turn. Each of those he surveyed looked to another as though unsure of the limits of their authority.

"No?" Aye said. The guards did not move.

"Then step aside," Aye said, "and question the wisdom of remaining in my sight."

The guards shuffled away, crestfallen, and revealed a man that lay on the floor behind them. His face was already swollen to such an extent that one eye was almost completely closed, but beyond that Aye guessed that most of his injuries were more painful than serious. Aye had not allowed the guards the time they had obviously needed to complete their work.

"What happened?" the man said, struggling to prop himself up on one elbow. Aye saw that one of his front teeth had been broken in half. "Is this how you treat visitors in this new city of yours?"

Aye bent to help the man into a sitting position. "It is no city of mine," he said.

"I am a messenger from His Majesty King Amenhotep," the man said. "I am on urgent business, bid to complete my commission with all speed by the king himself. I do not expect to be treated in such a way upon Egyptian soil. Perhaps in Mitanni or Hatti they may be savage enough to treat an Egyptian envoy in such a way, but here? Am I in a foreign land?"

"I fear," Aye said, "that you may be indeed. Now, you speak of a commission from Amenhotep. What of it?"

"I am instructed to speak to the Great Royal Wife," the man said. "I am permitted to say that it is a matter of the gravest possible importance and that any man who stands in my way can be thought of as treasonous."

He shot a glance at the guards, who were standing in a protective group a handful of paces away.

"Beyond that," the man said, "I am permitted to say nothing, save before the Great Royal Wife herself."

"And that is exactly where you find yourself, messenger," Tiye said. She had approached from behind Aye's back as the two men had been talking, a grandchild in each arm. Her voice was weak and faltering, as though the messenger had already delivered his news. She reached out for Aye's hand and, her eyes never leaving those of the messenger, said: "What is it that you have to say to me?"

The Maya Papyrus, Fragments 90-93

"I am not your king," Amenophis had said.

If only that were truly the case, I thought, undoubtedly as did all those who shared the temple floor with me. Of course, none of these thoughts were voiced. Not after the scene we had all witnessed in the Great Aten Temple.

I had known Amenophis since the earliest of our school days, and I think that I probably knew him as well as any in the temple that day, with the exception of Nefertiti. I could tell from the tone of his voice and the look on his face exactly the response he was hoping for from his audience. I am not your king, he had said, and waited, I knew, for a hushed but audible awe to fall over the crowd.

Nothing of the sort happened. There is a limit to how much a man can be overwhelmed in one day and we had all reached that limit at some point during the preceding hours. There was nothing left in us to shock, and so his nonsensical announcement fell upon us as it would upon a man asleep or dead. I took some malicious pleasure in noting the momentary consternation on his face before he continued with his speech.

"Neither is Amenhotep, my earthly father, your king," he said. "Egypt has only one king, and you are at his coronation."

Amenophis and Nefertiti both stood, turned to face each other, and took a step forwards. They both moved slowly enough and with enough surreptitious glances at the audience and reassuring glances at each other to reveal that is was a choreographed move which they had practised frequently but which they both believed to be under rehearsed. The movements were so simple and yet so full of nervousness that I can only begin to imagine the gravity they both believed to be bestowed in them. Nefertiti leant forwards and, with her arms rigidly outstretched, removed the blue crown from atop Amenophis' head. Amenophis took it from her, and both took a backwards step away from each other.

Amenophis turned to the empty throne that was placed between those of his and his wife. Slowly, painstakingly, Amenophis lowered himself to his knees, his crown held out before him all the while. He began to lower the crown towards the seat of the throne. Suddenly, his spell was broken, the majesty fled. Amenophis' eyesight was not good enough to judge the distance to the throne. He was about to crown the stage as Egypt's new king.

Nefertiti had to spring forward and stay his arm with a gentle touch.

She whispered something into his ear and stepped back out of the drama. I was close enough to Amenophis to make out the swell of every ill-defined muscle and trace the tracks of the beads of sweat that raced each other down his back and fled beneath the waistband of his kilt. I could see the tremors that exposed the weakness of his arms under the weight of the crown and the deep breath of frustration that he allowed himself before shuffling forwards on his knees to bring himself within reach of the throne.

He placed the crown on the throne and bowed his head.

"My father, the Aten," he said. "Living in Truth, who rejoices in the name of the light which is in the sun-disk, I name you king of your city and your country, to rule through me, Amenophis, your chosen son."

And then, remarkably, Amenophis began to sing. My first instinct was one of stifled amusement. To hear a pharaoh sing was such a startling concept that it was difficult not to laugh, as much through surprise as mockery. But very quickly I realised that there was nothing to mock. Amenophis could sing. His voice was light and reedy, but at the same time it was lilting, and carried on the breeze with no effort imparted by either the singer or the weather.

The melody and words that he sang were unfamiliar to me, and far from unpleasant. I only discovered later that the song was a composition of Amenophis himself. It was a hymn to our new king.

> *Beautiful you appear from the horizon of heaven* [he sang]
> *filling every land with your beauty*
> *for you are fair, great and dazzling.*
> *Your rays enclose the lands to the limit of all you have made*
> *for although you are far away, your rays are always upon us.*

Here Amenophis' voice fell almost to the level of a whisper, and the melody changed also, becoming melancholic and wistful.

> *When you set in the western horizon*
> *the land is in darkness in the manner of death.*
> *People lie in their bedchambers, heads covered up in the dark.*
> *Every lion is out of its den, all creeping things bite.*
> *Darkness gathers, the land is silent.*
> *The one who made it all has set.*

And then the key changed again, to become celebratory and joyful, but without warning so that for the first words of the next line it seemed to jar against the ears until they realised what they were hearing and how it worked, and suddenly the beauty of the hymn revealed itself in a rush, like the first taste of juice sucked from a fruit.

But the land grows bright when you rise,
pushing back the darkness as you give forth your rays.
The people of the Two Lands are in a festival of light,
awake and upright, for you have lifted them up
and their arms are lifted in adoration of you.
You made heaven just to rise in it, to see all you created
and you created the faces of men
so that you would not be alone in your creation

The hymn continued for some time, here praising the Aten as the greatest of gods, there doing the same for Amenophis and Nefertiti, but never straying from its sublime melody. When the song drew to a close it was greeted with silence, but at last it was the silence of awe, not disapproval.

Amenophis turned back to his audience.

"The Aten is crowned king," he said. "He shall be co-regent with me. His words will be law, as are mine. I shall consult with him and he with me. He will be my guide in the rule of the Two Lands, and I his. We are one and the same, the Aten and I, indivisible and true. We are the gods of Egypt.

"I am Amenophis no longer, for Amenophis means 'Amun is Satisfied', and he most assuredly is not and shall not be satisfied by my reign, and by that of the Aten's, which will eclipse Amun as if he were no more than a god of the hearth. Amenophis is dead, and from this moment I am Akhenaten, 'One who is Beneficial to the Aten'. I shall not satisfy Amun by using his name. I do not expect this fact to be forgotten."

At this the guards that surrounded us turned to give each of us meaningful looks, undoubtedly intending to convey the consequences of any lapse of memory on our part concerning the king's latest decree.

We in the audience swapped nervous glances with each of our neighbours in turn, as though as part of some obscure ritual. We did not have to communicate with each other with any more intimacy to divine each other's thoughts. None of us knew what to make of this. The change of names was an inconsequential aside: there was little chance that anybody in that congregation would ever be close enough to the king to refer to him any more informally than 'Your Majesty', so there was little chance of us confusing his old name for his new. More worrying was this new co-regency between man and god. I doubted that it had been represented in its truest light. Amenophis described it as though it was an abnegation of power in favour of something better suited to the job. Rather, it seemed to be a renunciation of responsibility, a declaration that whatever may yet befall us in this new city, we had someone other than Amenophis to blame.

A refusal to accept responsibility could never be a healthy disposition in one so powerful. Of course, had I known as I trudged out of the temple that day how accurate my musings would prove to be I would have walked with a nimbler step, and I would not have stopped until the city was far behind me.

At the very first hint, Amenhotep had known the worst. The dismay of it all was so acute as to be an almost physical sensation. It was a small but sharp pain on the right hand side of his jaw, just below the cavity that marked the place previously occupied by one of his extracted teeth. He sent for his physicians and they helplessly ordered medicines and spells that had already proved their inefficiency. They resumed their post in the antechamber outside the king's bedchamber, ready to be summoned in the night to fail to stem his pain with as much expediency as possible.

There were those who counselled the king to wait before sending for Tiye, those who told him that there was no need to ask her to traverse half the length of the Nile when he would undoubtedly be feeling hale and healthy again before she was halfway home. Amenhotep ignored them and the messenger was sent with all haste, although the king knew it would be upwards of a month before he would see the fruit of the messenger's labours.

Amenhotep, meanwhile, awaited the onslaught of his pain. It was not long in coming, and its ferocity was such that even Amenhotep had never known. With it came illness that the physicians and priests were unable to curb which ran rampant around his body as though the complicated potions designed to defeat it were water and the gods and goddesses invoked to combat it were nothing more than speculative thought and fond wishes. The king's descent was swift and merciless. Fever smothered him. His state of mind changed with each passing hour of the day, by turns irritable and unresponsive, anxious and lethargic. He complained constantly of being cold, and no fire could warm him. Large, purple lesions began to appear on the flesh of his chest and arms, appearing all the more angry in contrast to the pallor of his skin, and the doctors could do nothing to blanch them. He began, a number of days into the sickness, to slip in and out of consciousness, and it was only during the times when his senses left him that he looked as though he would ever again be capable of peacefulness.

By the time his messenger to Tiye had arrived in Akhetaten and fallen under the clubs of Mahu's men, Amenhotep was rendered incapable of all but the most trivial of activities.

The entire palace, and such court as had remained there after the exodus to Akhetaten, awaited Tiye's return as though she herself held the secret of the king's well-being, as though she carried around his good health in a vial. Once the Great Royal Wife returned, Amenhotep would be nursed back to health. She had the love in her touch to be able to pull him back from the precipice he was currently tottering towards. Nobody would allow themselves to believe any differently, although in reality they knew that for everything Tiye was, she was no physician, and the physicians had already failed.

When Tiye and Aye arrived at the palace there was a flurry of optimistic activity. Tiye and Aye's apartments were cleaned by armies of maids, as would be expected, but also Amenhotep's rooms were cleaned - his dressing room, the throne room, the audience chamber - as though to be ready when he miraculously sprang from the bed at the feel of his wife's touch.

Aye and Tiye had been travelling for the better part of two weeks, restlessly pacing the deck of the ship as though they could hurry the slow Nile current that bore them. Back in Akhetaten they had paused long enough only to collect enough clothing for the journey and to leave word with servants to give Amenophis the news and an invitation to follow should he so desire.

Once at the palace they had little time for pleasantries, almost racing each other through the corridors, always a step short of the indignity of breaking into a run. When they finally found themselves outside the king's quarters they had the air about them of two people who have arrived at the same location from entirely different directions. They took a moment or two to ensure they appeared as one should when about to be ushered into a sick chamber.

Passing through the doorway they were immediately struck by the stench of illness. They both stopped short and tried to become accustomed to the smell before continuing. Neither of them wanted to greet the king with grimaces.

Within, the bedchamber was dimly lit, the windows having been stopped up with sheets. Tiye thought the place to have about it the air of a tomb. Servants and lesser wives bowed out of her way as she approached her husband's bed. His face was indistinct, disguised by the mask of the room's darkness, but even from a number of paces away Tiye could discern the swelling around his jaw. He looked like his mouth was full of food. Tiye thought of Amenhotep's banquets and the stories he would tell around huge bites of chicken or bread. The memory sharpened the melancholy at the realisation that she had seen such a thing for the last time.

"Husband," she said, quietly.

Amenhotep opened his eyes.

"Wife," he said, although the constrictions of movement around his mouth meant that it came out as *Ise*. His eyes smiled and he reached out his hand for her to take.

"Majesty," Aye said, from over Tiye's shoulder. Amenhotep saw him for the first time.

"My friend," he said. *I syend.*

"Hush," Tiye said. "Do not try to speak."

Amenhotep nodded at her. "It hurts," he said.

During the following days, Aye and Tiye barely left Amenhotep's side for a moment, and never both at the same time. Amenhotep said little, but listened with fascination to their stories of Akhetaten. They were careful to omit the actions of Mahu's guards and the proclamations of Amenophis, but instead concentrated on the wonders of the buildings and any inconsequential news they could be sure would not upset him. Throughout the time they spent at his side Amenhotep's pain did not alleviate and his fever did not break. The proportion of time he spent conscious lessened, and the time he spent unconscious was a blessed relief for those around him, who felt themselves relaxing as the pain gradually faded from his brow.

The physicians and priests left their posts even less often than did Aye and Tiye, and their chants and invocations were a constant background murmur until it faded into the general hushed noise of the room and disappeared. Statues of gods were paraded across the room, and amulets were placed in strategic positions around the king's face and body. Unguents and balms were applied, and evil smelling concoctions dripped into his open mouth. None of these things had the slightest discernible effect and Amenhotep's grip on the world became increasingly precarious with every passing hour.

On the fifth day after Tiye's arrival Amenhotep was awake only briefly. He squeezed Tiye's hand.

"Have I been a good king?" he said. The question was so unexpected that Tiye felt her eyes briefly burning with unexpected tears. Her first instinct was to say *What sort of talk is this? You will be a good king for many more years yet*, but the look in her husband's eye was an entreaty for honesty and she could no more lie to him than leave his side.

"You have been a better king than generations of men risen from their grave could recall," she said. "The Two Lands have never known such peace and happiness. No man, even the poorest peasant, is hungry. We have more food than gold, and we have more gold than we have ever had. And when was the last time Egypt lost a son in war? Whole ranks of men have served their entire careers in the army and have never seen a spear thrown in anger. Egypt is a land as great as she was in ancient times, before she was stripped of so much by the invasion of the Hyksos. And why? Because you have been her bow and her stern, her shield and her tongue. It is through you that the gods are appeased, through you that the inundation comes every year. It is your diplomacy that made friends of our enemies. Egypt is feared and respected throughout the world, and her greatness is your greatness."

Amenhotep smiled as best he could.

"I could not have done it without you," he said.

"Thank you," Tiye said, "but you are too modest. You would have been a great king, whoever you married."

"Amenophis will be officiating at my funeral." It was more a question than a statement.

"Yes, of course he will," Tiye said. "He is your son who is to reign after you. Who else could it be?"

"I know," Amenhotep said. "Although I wish it could be almost anybody else. You will oversee everything, won't you? I cannot bear the thought of him making a hash of it. There is too much at stake."

"Everything will be fine. I shall see to it myself."

"If he does something wrong and I am denied life in the underworld because of it, I shall..." His voice, already weak, trailed off as he realised that there was no threat he could make that could possibly make sense. "Just watch him," he said.

"Of course," Tiye said. "But now you must rest."

"I do not wish to rest," he said. "There are many things that I wish to behold for the last time. Things that have never mattered to me before. Trees. The sun. The river. Do you think the gods will allow me to see them all one last time before they take me from them forever?"

The time for honesty having passed, Tiye nodded. "Of course they will," she said. "Of course they will."

It was dawn on the tenth day since Aye and Tiye had returned to the palace. Tiye, as always, was sitting on the edge of the king's bed. Aye was asleep on a mat usually reserved for physicians in the antechamber. The physicians still slept there on occasion but they had long realised that their ministrations were achieving nothing other than baiting the king's annoyance at their lack of success. They had gratefully ceded their roles to the priests, who had fared no better.

Tiye was holding Amenhotep's hand and watching his face as it was slowly revealed by the rising sun. His eyes were moving beneath their lids.

"What do you dream?" Tiye whispered, smiling.

Amenhotep was in his father's chariot, so close to his father's back that he could smell the sweat. The sun was high and the walls of the wadi rose menacingly on either side. Behind them ranged the king's army, and standing on either side of Amenhotep were Tjenuna and Maiherperi, although part of Amenhotep's mind tried to remind him that chariots were not wide enough to admit three people standing side by side.

"I have missed you," he said to them both.

"We have not missed you," Tjenuna said. "We have seen you every day."

The chariot was travelling at a fearful pace, and even the lea of Thutmose's back did not protect Amenhotep from the buffeting of the wind. On either side of him, Tjenuna and Maiherperi were holding his hands, but he found he did not need to grip the sides of the chariot, for he was neither unbalanced nor afraid. For although the walls of the wadi to his right and his left hid a host of Nubians, their bow strings taut and their spears held high in readiness, he had nothing to fear. He was in the safest place in the world, protected by his friends and his gods.

Amenhotep opened his eyes and Tiye slowly came into focus above him.

"I am Crown Prince Amenhotep," he said to her, "and I ride in the chariot of the pharaoh."

The focus slipped away from him, and the pain stopped.

"Dead?" Amenophis said.

Tiye said nothing. She did not want to repeat the word.

"But this is terrible!" Amenophis said.

"It makes you sole regent of the Two Lands," Tiye said.

"No, no, no," Amenophis said, distractedly, waving away her words. "I am co-regent with the Aten. Where is he to be buried?"

"The Aten?" Tiye said, unable to resist the temptation.

"My father," Amenophis said, testily. "Where is my father to be buried?"

"In the Valley of the Kings. Where else?"

"Impossible," Amenophis said.

"But that is where his tomb is. Do you perhaps have another one, more suitable, that we do not know about? Have you been building it in secret?" She made a show of tapping the floor with her foot as though searching for a hollow space. "Is it here perhaps?"

"No," Amenophis muttered.

"Then let me hear no more ridiculous talk. He will be buried in the Valley of the Kings in Thebes and you will officiate at his funeral. That is the way it has always been, and the way it will always be. You are pharaoh now. It is your duty."

"Not in Thebes, mother. I cannot."

"Why?"

"It is not safe for me. You saw what happened last time I was in Thebes."

"Last time you were not surrounded by a forest of bodyguards."

"Mother, I have enemies more powerful than you appreciate. I could have every soldier in the kingdom surrounding me and it would not deflect him from his aim by one jot."

"Him? Who?"

Amenophis began to pace nervously around the simple and unpresumptuous throne that Tiye occupied in the middle of the audience chamber. After committing her husband's body to the embalmers for the seventy days they would need to prepare it for the tomb, she and Aye had returned to Akhetaten, bearing their news with them. Tiye had decided that Amenophis should hear it from nobody but her.

"Who?" she asked again as Amenophis passed behind her and reappeared at her other hand. "Amenophis, who..."

"Akhenaten," he said.

"Akhenaten, then. Of whom are you so afraid?"

"I am not afraid," Amenophis said, stopping before her as though in sudden collision with a solid object. "I am cautious. I am wily."

"Of course," Tiye said. "You are so wily you have gone pale."

"I am not afraid of him!" Amenophis shouted.

Tiye was taken aback by the vehemence of his outburst.

"I am afraid of nothing," Amenophis continued, with more composure.

"Then there is nothing to prevent you officiating at your father's funeral in Thebes."

"No," Amenophis said, with reluctance greatly emphasised.

Tiye sighed melodramatically. "Thank you, Amenophis," she said.

"My name," Amenophis said, "is Akhenaten."

The Maya Papyrus, Fragments 98-101

Exactly seventy days after his death, Amenhotep's sarcophagus appeared before us in the streets of Thebes, carried at the head of a shuffling, subdued procession. More people than could ever be counted lined the route, the women kneeling in the gutter, wailing and throwing dust over their heads in the traditional ritual of mourning. Egypt had never before witnessed such an expression of grief, and I doubt it will ever do so again. Many people in the Two Lands could not remember a time when Amenhotep had not been on the throne and his absence left them lost. Their very lives were lived in his debt. Only his just rule and his intervention with the gods on their behalf had kept war and hunger from Egypt's borders for such an unprecedented length of time.

The death of any pharaoh is a time of turbulence, for it is a time when the gods of evil and chaos may rise and usurp the power that has been vacated.

Except, of course, that there was no vacuum left by the passing of this king. For here marched Amenophis, his son and heir, who was already king and in whose delicate frame so much was already invested. Had the people known of Amenophis what I and the other members of his court knew, the men of Thebes would have joined their wives and mothers on their knees in the dirt, weeping for what was lost.

As a member of court and a nephew of the Great Royal Wife I had been afforded a privileged position in the procession alongside Nakhtmin and Horemheb but behind my father and also, intriguingly, behind Mahu. Nefertiti was pregnant with her third child and by all accounts was having a difficult time of it. Nausea had prevented her leaving the comfort of the palace. I overheard one or two muttered witticisms prompted by her absence to the effect that Amenophis must have divorced his wife and married Mahu instead, so resolutely did the pair refuse to be parted from each other throughout the entirety of the proceedings.

I was close enough behind Amenophis to see him take a step closer to Mahu when we finally reached Amenhotep's tomb and he saw who awaited him there.

It was a figure who looked older than any man I have ever seen. He was standing with the help of two sticks and a man was standing either side of him, presumably to leap to his aid should he begin to totter. As if my thoughts were moulding the situation to which they were turned, the man took an involuntary step forward and his helpers sprang into life. They did not lay a hand on him, though, before he had steadied himself with the aid of his sticks. Although he had obviously not walked all the way to the tomb himself - his palanquin rested a few paces away - it was obvious that the day was taking its toll.

But for all that, for all the weakness and frailty, he was a man with gravity and authority enough to stop the procession in its tracks without uttering a word of command.

He smiled a greeting only after we had come to an undignified and prolonged halt, and it was not a smile I would be happy to see repeated. It was a cold smile, and it seemed to infect only the lower half of his face.

"Amenophis," he said, by way of acknowledgement.

Members of the procession shared one or two concerned glances. This was not a man for whom a respectful prostration would have been easy without a fair amount of advanced warning and the assistance of his attendants, but he had not put himself to the trouble even of bowing his head. He had not greeted his king with the deferential Your Majesty, *or even deigned to refer to him by his new chosen name. Every aspect of the salutation was an insult and had obviously been designed as such.*

I saw Amenophis swallow heavily before replying.

"Ptahmose," he said, as though he was not a god-king, an incarnation of the greatest of deities, a demigod able to crush all that stood before him with nothing more than a wave of his hand. Rather, he appeared to me to be a man, and a frightened man at that.

Ptahmose, on the other hand, was the very epitome of unperturbed calm. The swagger that his body was no longer able to provide was more than compensated for by the tone of his voice. If he no longer had the strength to stand unaided it was perhaps because that fortitude had been diverted elsewhere. He was no less the man than he had ever been, and his mind was as sharp as his body was fragile. I could see in his face that he immediately grasped that he had the advantage over his king, and he had never been a man to leave an advantage unexploited.

He stepped forwards like some ponderous four-legged animal, first his left stick, then his right leg, then his right stick, then his left leg, and then the cycle repeated, with each individual movement accompanied by a quiet gasp or grunt of effort. It gave his movements a threatening air and one or two of the observers around me could not help but take a step backwards. The king, perhaps drawing strength from Mahu, who drew even closer to his side, remained firm.

"What brings you here?" Amenophis asked, in a voice faintly tremulous.

Ptahmose laughed. "What brings me here?" he asked, emphasising the incredulity in his tone. "I was under the impression that we were here to bury a king."

"What business is that of yours?" Amenophis said.

"Do I hear you right?" Ptahmose said, making a play of tilting his head as though to hear better. Had he had a hand free I do not doubt that he would have held it to his ear. "What business? I am Amun's representative on earth. My absence at the burial of a king would be, shall we say, unusual, would it not?"

"You are not needed here, priest," Amenophis said.

"Then neither, I presume, is my god?"

Amenophis looked as though he was about to speak in anger. He went as far as inhaling in preparation for a torrent of words before Ptahmose spoke again.

"Think carefully before you answer, Amenophis. You are heard by more than the people who surround you."

Amenophis' mouth remained open but made no further movement. He looked as though his words had lost their nerve and retreated down his throat. His face turned such unexpected hues that he appeared as though he was about to choke on them.

Absolute silence reigned. Not a bird sang. This far from the city not a chariot wheel rumbled, not a dog barked, not a hawker shouted his wares. Every face was turned towards the king, and he was acutely aware of it. He turned to look at some of the faces before him; his mother, Aye, Mahu, even myself. He looked so hapless that even I was almost moved to pity for him.

"Well?" Ptahmose said.

Amenophis knew as well as we did, despite his pleading glances, that nobody could help him even in the unlikely event that anyone bar Mahu felt the urge to do so.
We, like Ptahmose, awaited his reply.

Amenophis wished Nefertiti was with him, if only to hold his hand until the termination of this trial.

Everything hinged on his answer. He knew that whatever it was it would be repeated throughout Thebes and, more importantly, Akhetaten. To deny the importance of Amun to the ceremony, especially before such an esteemed audience, would have been nothing short of an explicit declaration of war against Ptahmose's network of temples. Amenophis desperately tried to calculate his own readiness for such a conflict, and found himself wanting the courage.

But what was the alternative? To allow Ptahmose a role in the funeral would be an act of surrender before any war had even begun.

Amenophis felt a rage brewing within him as he watched this aged priest standing before him, smiling innocently. This had all been planned, Amenophis realised.

"Ptahmose," Amenophis said. He licked his lips. He was still unsure exactly what he was going to say. "My father's reign is now a thing of the past. Of course you may represent your god at his funeral. And I would thank you to remember that my name is now Akhenaten."

It was, Amenophis could not help thinking, a particularly clever answer.

"*Excellent*," Ptahmose said. "Very wise, Amenophis, very wise indeed."

He began the intricate procedure of taking his place at the head of the procession, directly between the sarcophagus and the entrance to the tomb.

No, Amenophis wanted to say. *You misunderstand me. I was toying with you. I was* insulting *you.* But it was too late. Ptahmose was already chanting his invocations, the members of the procession instinctively bowing their heads in reverence. Amenophis looked around incredulously. It was as though he was no longer there.

By the time Amenophis returned to his palace in Akhetaten his humiliation at the hands of Ptahmose had been fermenting within him until it had begun to bubble up and seep through his very pores. He swept in through the doors and along the corridors like a desert wind, ignoring those who prostrated themselves before him and pushing aside those who were not nimble enough to avoid his path. He flung open the doors to Nefertiti's bedchamber as though they had personally affronted him. He found her in bed.

"Treachery!" he shouted. "Foul perfidy! Shameful wickedness!"

"Amenophis?" Nefertiti said.

"*Akhenaten!*" Amenophis screamed, his face contorted in fury, the veins in his neck pulsing. "*My name. Is AKHENATEN!*"

Nefertiti edged backwards in the bed, her hand held to her lips.

"Husband, I am sorry if..." She began, but Amenophis waved away her apologies.

"You are the same as all the others," he said. "The world is full of buffoons who cannot remember a name, and dullards who refuse to. Which are you, Nefertiti?"

"Akhenaten, my husband," Nefertiti said, struggling to keep a quiver from her voice, trying to calm him with her tone. "I have never seen you like this. You have never spoken to me in such a way. Has something happened to bring about this transformation in you? Please remember that I am your wife and your friend. I am your ally, Akhenaten."

Amenophis' fury was barely sated by her words. His expression softened only momentarily, as though her speech had touched him until he remembered a promise to himself to remain angry. "An ally would remember my name," he said.

"When all forsake you, I am your only ally," she said.

"Nobody will forsake me," he said, sitting on the edge of Nefertiti's bed. "I shall forsake them. Nefertiti, I have been much in thought since my father's funeral. That priest will rue the day he became my enemy."

"What do you propose to do?" Nefertiti said.

"I am going to commune with the Aten," he replied, and stood up. "Rest. I have the feeling I will need your strength before long."

He commanded his chariot be prepared and rode to the Great Aten Temple. What was in his heart was so frightening that he hardly dared admit it even to himself for fear of which gods were listening to his thoughts.

He spent hours in the inner sanctum, prostrate at the temple's innermost altar. There was no roof, even here. Had there been anybody there to see him Amenophis would have seemed a forlorn figure, alone before the altar, feeling the sun on his back like the touch of a protective hand.

"What am I to do?" he said into the floor, after meditating on the matter for longer than he could remember meditating on anything. He received no answer. He lifted his head and pushed himself upright so he was kneeling before his god.

"What am I to do?" he said, again. "Am I really to carry out what is in my heart? I can think of no other way."

His own voice echoing off the walls of the temple served as his only reply. He knew he was utterly alone but he could not resist the temptation to turn his head to confirm the fact before he spoke again.

"I am afraid," he whispered. "It will be difficult. It will be dangerous. Egypt will resist me. Every priest will become an assassin. Amun himself will not tire in his pursuit of me."

Amenophis paused as though digesting the meaning of his own words.

"Is there really no other way?" he said, and paused again.

"Then so be it," he said, "although it saddens me to come to this decision. There will be much bloodshed and much misery. But if it is the will of my father the Aten, I cannot betray your wishes."

Once outside the temple his guards immediately moved to surround him.

He nodded at one. "Fetch me Mahu," he told him.

"Ptahmose needs to be taught a lesson," Amenophis told Mahu. "As does his master, Amun. They believe themselves to be a rival to my power, and that cannot be allowed. I have already come too far. Any threat to me now is a potentially fatal one, and I must guard against it with no check to my actions, for there can be no compromise. It is either kill or be killed."

"You want me to kill Ptahmose?" Mahu asked.

"No," Amenophis said, "not Ptahmose."

Even Mahu was aghast at what Amenophis told him. Mahu the torturer. Mahu the unshakeable. His hand trembled as he wiped it across his mouth in thought.

"Are you *sure*?" he asked.

Akhenaten shrugged. "It is the will of the Aten," he said.

Chapter Fifteen

Amun's Revenge

The Maya Papyrus, Fragments 107-110

I CAN only attribute the coincidence of the two events of this time to divine intervention. It is the only explanation that carries any credence, and it is an explanation accepted by my contemporaries as readily as it is by me. It is, I think, unrealistic to insult and injure the gods - especially those as powerful as Amun - without expecting ill consequences for your actions. Of course, Amenophis (or Akhenaten as I had now acquired the habit of calling him) was as unrealistic a man as ever I had met.

The first man I saw afflicted with Amun's Revenge was not Egyptian but Syrian who had arrived on a trade ship carrying building wood and copper, bronze and silver. He was an ambassador from Abdi-Ashirta, the king of Amurru in Syria, here to congratulate Akhenaten on his ascent to the throne as sole regent. By all accounts, the man was not well when he left the ship. In fact, those men in hale health and good spirits were very much in the minority on that vessel.

When they arrived at the palace gates they were already barely able to stand. The colour was gone from their faces, sweat stood proud upon their brows and they coughed with such long and painful exhalations that they were unable to catch their breath and would stagger this way and that as all their energy was diverted into the almost impossible act of breathing. It was obvious to all that they were close to death.

I can vouch for what follows because I was there. It was I who announced the guests to Akhenaten. I found him in his audience chamber, leaning head to head with Mahu over a map of Lower Egypt.

"Your Majesty," I said, prostrating myself at the threshold of the room, disinclined to enter further and risk being drawn into a discussion about whichever subject was currently occupying them.

Had I known what they were discussing I... Well, I have no idea what I would have done. Probably prostrated myself in the doorway and made my escape as soon as possible; which, in fact, is what I did anyway.

Akhenaten and Mahu looked up from their deliberations, but neither spoke.

"Your Majesty," I said again, once it became evident that he was waiting for me to continue. "Abdi-Ashirta, king of Amurru, sends his greetings."

Akhenaten looked as though he was not sure what to do with the news.

"Oh?" he said. "Really?"

"His ambassador awaits without," I said. "He has brought gifts to celebrate your accession to the throne."

"Oh," Akhenaten said. "What form do these presents take?"

"I am not sure, Your Majesty. I have not seen them. Items forged from gold, I believe."

"Gold?" Akhenaten said. "Gold I have. Bid them wait."

"As Your Majesty wishes," I said. "I shall escort them to the antechamber."

Mahu whispered something in his master's ear. There followed a brief discussion, none of which was audible to me. At its termination Akhenaten looked to me once again.

"How many of them are there?" he said.

"Three, Your Majesty."

"And you are sure they are from Amurru?"

"I have no reason to doubt their word, Your Majesty," I said, becoming slightly bemused with the line of questioning.

"Then," Akhenaten said, "you cannot tell me for sure that they have not travelled here from Thebes. That they are not, for instance, priests in disguise?"

"Your Majesty?" I said

"You forget that I have been attacked by Amun before, by those who were not what they appeared. I am surprised at you, Maya. I thought you were a man of intelligence."

"Well..." I said.

"And yet you seem to be happy to risk your king's well-being on the word of some stranger. I expected more from you, Maya."

I offered my most humble and abject apologies, aware that in the minds of men such as Akhenaten there was a very small step indeed from stupidity to treason.

"Bid the so called ambassadors to wait outside," Akhenaten said. "We shall leave them out in the gaze of the Aten. He shall judge them according to his wisdom."

I bowed from the room, Akhenaten and Mahu forgetting me and returning to their map before the doors had closed between us.

I returned to the palace gates and informed the visitors that they must wait outside in the sun before the king would deign to see them. I left them leaning against the palace wall, breathing tortuously and coughing, coughing, coughing. I ordered a servant to supply them with all the water they could drink and asked one of the palace physicians to treat them as best he could.

Beyond these basic acts of kindness I was powerless. Had I invited them inside the king would have seen it as treachery. Had I invited them to await the king's pleasure at my own home, Akhenaten would have seen me as a co-conspirator. And so outside they waited, growing weaker by the hour as the Aten examined their purity. Those that passed them by on that busy thoroughfare were already familiar enough with the strange happenings of this king's reign to have the wisdom to not slow their pace or voice their curiosity. One never knew who was watching and listening.

The physician informed me that he had administered honey, carob and mashed dates to the men at the gate, but that he could do no more. I paced the floors of the palace, unable to decide what to do for the best.

The king was busy and may well have forgotten the presence of the guests, but it was not for me to interrupt him once again and repeat news that he had already heard, for it was just as likely that he had forgotten nothing and would be less than pleased at my reappearance at his door. But then it was obvious, even without the grim prognosis of the physician, that the men would die should they be left where they were.

The correct thing, I knew, was to take my chances with the king. He may have forgotten, I told myself. He may even express his gratitude for the reminder. Although I knew that Akhenaten would be unlikely to admit such a lapse even if one had indeed taken place.

Every moment that my cowardice confined me to the corridors of the palace, the men outside grew closer to death. I forced myself outside to see them and found them, to my horror, no longer able to stand. They were sitting with their backs to the palace wall, their legs outstretched, insensible to the host of people who had to step over them to make their way past. The faithful servant I had entrusted to them moved from one to the next with an amphora of water, anointing in turn their foreheads and lips with it.

My resolve hardened at the sight. I rushed back into the palace and had myself announced once more at the king's audience room before I could change my mind.

Licking my lips, smoothing the creases in my kilt, my heart racing, I was admitted.

"I believe I have already given my instructions regarding this matter," Akhenaten said once I had reminded him of the ambassador's presence.

"Just so, Your Majesty, only..."

"In fact, I believe I have already explained to you my suspicion that these men may be something other than they appear."

"Again, Your Majesty, I..."

"And yet here you are, Maya. Would there perhaps be an ulterior motive in your attempt to persuade me to admit these men to my palace?"

"Your Majesty, these men are going to die if you leave them out in the sun."

"They are being judged, Maya. By a wisdom, believe it or not, even greater than your own. Do you question that wisdom?"

"Indeed not, Your Majesty."

"Then let the Aten decide. If the men are as innocent as you seem to believe, they are in no danger. The Aten is not a malicious god. He does not kill without good reason. If, however, they pose me some danger, they will undoubtedly die. Then, perhaps, your loyalty to them will be re-examined."

I had no answer to this, and I remained silent.

"That will be all, Maya."

I left the room, furious with myself. I had had the courage neither to speak my mind nor to remain silent, and I had achieved only the feeding of a paranoid man's suspicions.

They may have survived, the ambassador and his companions, had they been allowed shelter and the comfort of a good bed. As it was, out in the daytime heat they had nowhere to go but the underworld.

I watched them die, as though witnessing the tragedy, standing to one side and looking concerned, would somehow absolve me of guilt.

My guilt was not misplaced; neither was my grief. Both, at the time, consumed me, devoured the sinews of my being as though they were predators as manifest as anything found in the desert. Looking back, they were the nipping of ants, the stinging of insects. For real though they were, they are now diluted to nothing in the anger and sadness that followed them. The ambassador was the first death of many waged upon us by the twin curses of Amun and Akhenaten, and by the end of it all I barely remembered that the ambassador from Amurru had even existed.

Two years had passed since Amenhotep's funeral. It was a time spent planning and discussing, endlessly reiterating and reviewing. The jokes about Akhenaten and Mahu spread and were repeated so often they became standards. The only time the king was to be seen out of Mahu's company was on the friezes and carvings of the royal family that could be found around the city and encircling its public buildings.

Nefertiti had borne two more children, Ankhesenpaaten and Nefernefruaten-ta-sherit, who were already to be seen on their father's knee in the frescoes of the Great Aten Temple. Both were daughters, and Nefertiti was already pregnant with a fifth child, as though the fear of not providing Akhenaten with an heir had driven her straight from the parturition bed into the conjugal one.

She had begun to wear a nervous look around her husband, as though afraid not of him but of what he might think of her and her failure to bear him a son. He insisted on many occasions that he was not concerned about his lack of an heir, that he loved Nefertiti and her daughters more than ever, and that a son would surely come in time. The last assertion made something of a lie of the first two, but she clung to what she wanted to hear as though it was a cliff face.

Nefertiti tried to reassure herself that the Aten would not be so cruel as to give her another daughter. Akhenaten was the Aten's son after all, and he would want the king to have an heir as much as did Aye, who made no secret of his concern at the steady stream of daughters Nefertiti was producing. She made herself believe this, as she made herself believe her husband and tried to ignore the amount of time he was spending with Mahu. She was the only one at court who did not discuss it, although whether her reticence was caused by fear of upsetting herself or her husband was unclear.

It is doubtful whether Akhenaten would have paid heed even if she had pinned him to the wall and screamed her objections in his face. He was doing the Aten's work and nothing was allowed to interfere, even here, even now, as the ambassador from Amurru waited with diminishing strength outside in the sun for a summons from the king that would never come. Akhenaten was enthralled and engrossed by the slow fruition of his plans. It was obvious to Mahu and Akhenaten both, as they pored over the map of Egypt in the palace, that their actions needed to start in Akhetaten before spreading to the rest of the Two Lands. Once Akhetaten was subjugated, Thebes could follow. The pair spent the day alone together, as they had so many others, with few interruptions. Finally, as the daylight was beginning to fade, Mahu asked: "When do we start?"

Akhenaten thought for a moment. "When *can* we start?" he said.

"Almost immediately," Mahu said. "At least with Akhetaten. It takes only an order from myself."

"And we can trust your police to follow that order?"

"Yes," Mahu said.

"Without question?"

"Without question."

"Then," Akhenaten said, "give the order tomorrow. For now, order them to spread the word. I will speak tomorrow at the Window of Appearances and announce the decree. I expect every man of note to attend."

"Of course, Your Majesty."

Mahu left the room to set about making the necessary arrangements, leaving Akhenaten alone in the spreading gloom. He had no lamps lit that evening and the course of his thoughts followed the growing darkness.

Of course, there was no turning back now. The word was already out that he was to address the populace tomorrow. The Window of Appearances was an area in the bridge that spanned the King's Way between the palace and the king's private quarters. From here Akhenaten would on occasion throw trinkets to the crowd that gathered below, or bestow awards on those of his realm that he thought most deserving. It was an ideal stage; aloof from the crowd and out of their reach whilst remaining close enough to them to be seen clearly, and the width of the road below enabled a large crowd to gather in relative comfort, making them less irritable at the reception of bad news.

Akhenaten turned his thoughts to exactly how he was going to break the worst news that any of them had ever heard.

The crowd, as was usual on these occasions, gathered well in advance of the hour appointed for the beginning of the king's address. It was never clear whether or not he and Nefertiti would be distributing gifts from the window and everyone was eager to engineer themselves a place within throwing distance of the royal couple.

The crowd was extensive by the time Akhenaten and Nefertiti arrived at the bridge. Aye and Tiye were already there, still unaware of the nature of the king's announcement, although they both noted Akhenaten's nervousness and Nefertiti's ill-temper and both guessed the seriousness of the situation when the servants arrived, staggering as never before under the weight of the gifts which Akhenaten was to distribute.

"Why are we here?" Tiye asked, with little preamble and less good humour. Akhenaten paced to and fro before her, his lips moving in rehearsal.

"You will know soon enough," he said, and would be drawn no further.

Finally, the hour drew nigh. Akhenaten and Nefertiti stepped into view. Mahu's guards ensured the crowd's enthusiastic greeting. The royal couple waved, Akhenaten smiling while the flitting of his eyes betrayed the racing of his thoughts. Servants on either side of the window handed gift after gift to Akhenaten and Nefertiti, who distributed them through the crowd. Never before had such generosity been seen from the Window of Appearances, but few in the crowd had the presence of mind to wonder what it meant, so eagerly were they grasping at the gold and turquoise trinkets that showered down on them.

Finally, too soon for Akhenaten, the supply was exhausted. He held up his hands to calm the clamour and the audience quickly fell into expectant silence.

"People of Akhetaten," Akhenaten shouted. "I bring you glorious tidings! Today is a day that will live forever in history!"

A suspicious murmur skimmed through the crowd. These were words they had heard before, and what followed them was rarely welcome news.

"I have consulted the Aten and he has revealed his true nature to me. We have decreed that it is now time to share that nature with you, my people. You are honoured to be standing on the King's Way this day, for, in your dotage, when you are asked by the generations that follow you where you were when the true nature of divinity was revealed to the world, you can say 'I was there!'"

Scattered applause greeted the oratory, but for once Akhenaten was too nervous to register that it was less enthusiastic than he had hoped. He could not see well enough to note the guards who waded into the crowd to encourage a more ardent response in those it was felt were lacking.

"The Aten," Akhenaten continued, "is not the king of the gods. He is not the creator god, nor is he the god of the river nor the sky nor the earth. Neither is he the god of man, nor the god of beasts. And yet he is all these things."

The crowd made no sound to give any clue to their mood, but it was a silence deep enough for Akhenaten to recognize its nervous expectation.

"For," he said, "the Aten is simply God. There is no god but the Aten. Amun and Ptah and Osiris, all of these so called gods are nothing but manifestations of the One God, the Aten. They have no further need of your worship, for they are false gods!"

Now there was sound enough from the crowd for Akhenaten to judge their mood. There were shouts, and not only from the crowd before him, but from the bridge itself, from his right, and it sounded like Tiye.

He turned instinctively towards the sound, but then span around to his left when he felt Nefertiti tightly grip his arm.

"Husband!" she was saying. "Oh *no*, Akhenaten, stop them!"

"Stop who?" he began to say, but already his mother's voice was in his other ear and he did not hear Nefertiti's answer. At the same time, he was aware of the noise of the crowd, shouts and screams and other sounds, sounds of people running and falling.

"What is the meaning of this?" Tiye was shouting. "Akhenaten, I *demand* to know what is happening!"

"Akhenaten, *stop them!*" Nefertiti was shouting and vigorously pulling on his arm, and then the sounds of Aye stepping in and trying to placate Tiye, all three of them shouting at once, and the noise of anger and panic in the crowd below, all these things swirled together like the confused currents at the confluence of two rivers, panic swelling inside Akhenaten like the tide.

He took a deep breath, momentarily worried that if he began shouting along with the rest of them he would be unable to stop.

"*Enough!*" he shouted, trying to shrug himself free from Nefertiti's grip.

Aye was holding Tiye steady, his hands tightly gripping her shoulders. At Akhenaten's word of command Tiye ceased struggling and, while Nefertiti's hand remained where it was, holding her husband's arm, her grip loosened and her tugging trailed away like an unfinished sentence. Even the volume of the crowd's unrest seemed to dip, although few of its members could have heard Akhenaten's shout over their own tumult. It was more likely that the effect was occasioned not by the vehemence of the king but of the guards, who were beginning to gain the upper hand in their control of the crowd, with its more vociferous voices of protest either fled or clubbed into submission.

The scene became quiet enough for Akhenaten to hear the sobs of his wife and her whispered entreaties to *stop them, stop them* as she continued to watch the carnage below.

Akhenaten held up his hands again, and this time it took considerably longer for the gesture to calm the crowd. The sounds of distress hardly lessened at all, even when the beatings had been brought under control.

"This is a joyous day!" Akhenaten shouted. "Do not weep, but rejoice! I have delivered you! You are no longer slaves to the whims of myriad gods. Their tantrums are no longer your privations. Their fits of pique can no longer hold the river in its banks and the grain beneath the soil! For they do not exist! Do you not see what this means? Do you not understand? You are free!"

The more astute and fearful amongst the crowd's number began to applaud at these words, and the guards who prowled between them, stepping over those they had left prone, looked disappointed at the lost excuse to raise their clubs once again.

"Now you can see your god," Akhenaten continued, pointing over his shoulder at the sun resting behind him like the angry stare of a malevolent father.

"And we can see you!" Akhenaten said.

The soldiers embarked onto the ships before dawn's first glimmer. Silently, hardly yet awake, they tramped on board and felt the gangplanks bow and bounce beneath their cumulative weight. Once on deck they shuffled and shimmied, trying to find a position that was marginally comfortable on the planks beneath them. The morning was still cold, and they were grateful for the warmth of the men next to them. Before long they would curse that warmth, shaded from the direct sun though they were by large coloured canopies that were fixed over the decks.

A flotilla of ships waited in and around the docks, and as soon as one was loaded it would slip away from its moorings and its place would be taken by an empty companion, and the trudge of men would begin anew. It was a number of hours before the last of the ships was packed with soldiers and Mahu, who had embarked last of all, was able to signal for the convoy to pull out into the current.

Akhenaten had been reluctant for him to accompany the men on this expedition at all, but Mahu had gently and persuasively insisted. It was too important, he had said, to entrust to a less experienced commander. There were too many things that could go wrong, too many unforeseen circumstances and reactions which would need a quick heart if disaster was to be averted.

"But I need you here," Akhenaten had said. "I see my enemies everywhere. I am not safe without you to watch over me."

But Mahu had convinced him that the threats resulting from the failure of this mission were greater than any threat in Akhetaten. Besides, the king's extensive bodyguard would remain. Reluctantly, Akhenaten had agreed and sent Mahu on his way with entreaties for a speedy return bouncing around his head.

Some months had passed since Akhenaten's declaration from the Window of Appearances, and only now was he feeling the return of sufficient resolve to take the next step of his grand scheme. There had been discontent at first, even after news of the treatment of the dissenters in the crowd had spread around the city. There had been those who had made plain to friend and stranger alike their opposition to Akhenaten's religious views. They were so brazen they may as well have taken to shouting their opposition as they shouted the price and quality of their wares in the market.

Akhenaten mentioned it to Mahu, and Mahu spoke to his commanders. This was not to be allowed to continue.

Visitors to the city began to comment upon a change in the atmosphere, a subliminal tensing of the air as though the entire city was holding its breath, as though everybody was waiting for a great calamity to befall them. Police began to make house calls in the hushed hours of the night, when the quiet would aid their surreptitious arrival but only serve to advertise their departure, as the families of those arrested would wail and scream as their loved ones disappeared towards the barracks. Neighbours quickly learned that attempted interventions were unwise, and that to even raise a head from the pillow was not without risk. Rumours began to circulate that not every ear was as friendly as it would have its neighbours believe. Friends were treated with circumspection, acquaintances with outright distrust. It was judged safer not to inquire after those the police had taken away, and so nobody was ever sure what became of them. Relatives, visiting from Thebes or Memphis or any other town along the Nile that had given up its sons and daughters for Akhetaten, would find houses empty or occupied by tight-lipped strangers, and everywhere they turned would be the sound of people talking about *something else*.

Still, Akhenaten was eager for some reassurances as to his security. It was with an abundance of nervous energy that he paced around the perimeter of his audience chamber while he awaited the arrival of Mahu's police commanders. Mahu was by now surely aboard his ship, and Akhenaten was feeling his absence already.

The commanders were shown into his presence and promptly prostrated themselves at his feet. They were men who had seen at first hand what happened to those who engendered the king's displeasure and they were keen to ensure that there was no possibility of his anger being directed towards them. They rushed to assure him that there were far fewer naysayers on the streets and in the homes of Akhetaten than there had previously been under his less stringent rule and they furthermore begged to report to His Majesty that their officers remained ever vigilant in their zeal to apprehend any who would oppose His Most Excellent Majesty and that his rule was indeed, now that it had been pointed out to them, righteous beyond the wisdom of Man and ultimately could not fail to realise its aims, whatsoever they may be. They left their king's presence much relieved at having given a good account of themselves. For his part, the king was similarly calmed. His person was becoming more secure with every passing day and every successful arrest.

Mahu's thoughts, meanwhile, were turned only towards his men. They were not the elite of his police force, who were now employed exclusively in the personal service of the king. Some of the men on the fleet were experienced in matters of subjugation, but most were relatively new recruits and Mahu was vaguely worried about how they would perform. It was one of the reasons he had insisted he personally command the expedition. There had been an unprecedented recruitment drive in Akhetaten, and the poorer sections of the community had been eager to take advantage of the offer of regular food and reliable lodgings and so Mahu knew few of them personally, but he could tell the seasoned from the untested at a glance. One looked resigned to their uncomfortable journey, the other nervous about what awaited them at its conclusion.

It is a long way to Thebes, one appeared to be thinking. *But we will be there soon enough*, the other seemed to reply.

The priests who first saw the ships approaching from the north assumed that they carried the king and his retinue, and so while they hurried to the temple to alert Ptahmose to the unannounced royal visit there was no alarm in the shouts that preceded their ingress into the temple grounds. A guard was hastily deployed, but that was merely a matter of protocol, and the men that formed it were neither highly trained nor heavily armed. Their true purpose was nothing more than to remind the king of the existence of the temple armoury.

Mahu knew that there was little he could do to maximise his advantage of surprise. His ships were visible to the temple for a long time before they reached the docks, and it took even longer for them to manoeuvre into such a position so they could begin to disgorge their cargo of men. Throughout the docking procedure the colossal statues of Amenhotep peered at Mahu through the heat haze from the opposite bank of the river. Mahu found himself unable to meet their gaze, and ensured that he remained busy enough to justify avoiding it without making an overtly conscious effort to do so.

By the time the priests of the temple realised that this was more than a royal visit, most of Mahu's ships were already arranged around the sides of the harbour and were either being tied up or had already lowered their gangplanks to unload their men. Mahu's men were a great deal more numerous than the royal bodyguard that the welcoming priests had expected. The men in the honour guard lining the edge of the harbour began to exchange nervous glances as it became increasingly obvious that the lines of men striding down the gangplanks were going to take some time before they were exhausted.

The unloading continued. Not a word was spoken by the soldiers or those who watched them. The only sound was the tramp of the soldiers' sandals on wood and stone.

Finally, as though he had been counting the men from the ships and had been waiting for a predetermined number to be reached, the commander of the temple's honour guard barked an order and one of his men broke ranks to run pell-mell back into the temple grounds. This time the shouts were laced with fear.

The last to leave the ships, as he had been the last to board, was Mahu. He walked calmly and slowly. He shielded his eyes and turned to glance at the sun, perhaps to gauge how much its heat would dissipate the strength of his men during their labours, perhaps to gauge the beneficence of the Aten. He was aware that the commander of the guards was standing before him, patiently awaiting his attention. He paused long enough to illustrate his command of the situation, but not long enough for the high priest to appear from the temple gates, borne aloft on a wave of reinforcements.

Mahu turned to his opponent.

"And you are?" he said.

The commander was so flabbergasted by the question that he could not answer for a moment or two, and instead undermined his authority by blustering and stuttering before being able to bring his mouth under control.

"Who am *I*?" he said. "Who are you, who arrives on this sacred ground with what appears to be half of the king's army?"

"My name is Mahu. I am the chief of the king's police," Mahu said. He looked over his shoulder, a peremptory review of his troops. "And you may rest assured that this is a very small fraction indeed of the king's army."

"And what business brings you here?" the commander of the guards said.

"Business between the king and your false god," Mahu said. "Now stand aside or you will take a lesson from my troops."

"I shall do no such thing while there is breath in my body."

Mahu sighed. "So be it," he said. "Men!"

He pointed to the commander and his guards arranged behind him. Mahu's men drew their *kepesh* swords and advanced. The temple guards were for the main part brave but they were also outnumbered and badly trained and their ceremonial duties were no preparation for the savagery of opponents in battle. They were quickly subdued. Those few who survived jumped into the water to escape or ran for their lives back to the temple itself. Mahu's men lost more sweat than blood.

They wiped clean their swords and with Mahu at their head, they marched on the temple gates.

The gates alone were the size of a house and probably weighed only a little less. Those retreating guards with sufficient remaining presence of mind were struggling to close the gates before Mahu could breach them. Once they saw that Mahu was approaching and that they had neither the time nor strength to complete their endeavour they took to their heels and followed the rest of the temple's inhabitants into the building itself.

Mahu's men did not break step. Mahu ordered them onwards into the temple grounds, aware of the consequences of allowing them time to ponder on what they were doing.

Two priests remained at the doors leading into the first of the temple buildings, holding their chins high, trying but failing to look tall and confident.

"You may not pass," one of them said, as Mahu approached.

"Where is Ptahmose?" Mahu asked, looking from one to the other.

"*You may not pass!*" the second priest shouted.

Mahu's arm shot out suddenly, giving the second priest no time to dodge the fist that ploughed into his face. He fell backwards and slid inelegantly down the temple wall, clutching his bloodied nose and whimpering.

"Where is Ptahmose?" Mahu asked again, this time holding the terrified gaze of the priest who remained upright.

"I am not at liber..."

"Where is Ptahmose?" Mahu said again.

"I am not at liberty to say," the priest said, in a voice quavering with fear and determination.

Without removing his eyes from the priest, Mahu held out his hand towards the troops that waited behind him.

"A sword," he said. He felt the weight of a *kepesh* being placed in the waiting hand. Still staring intently at the priest, Mahu raised the sword above his head. The priest tightly closed his eyes and, holding his hands up to protect himself, tried to shrink back into the unyielding stone behind him. He heard the sword slice through the air, and then a slapping, crunching sound followed by a choking, gargling whimper, but there was no pain. The priest opened his eyes.

The *kepesh* was buried between the neck and the shoulder of the priest whom Mahu had punched. The blade had bitten into bone and Mahu struggled to pull it free until he put his foot on the priest's chest. He looked back to the second priest and raised the sword a second time.

"Where is Ptahmose?" he said.

"The inner sanctum," the priest said.

"Thank you." Mahu strode away into the gloom of the temple's corridors, his troops following. As his back disappeared into the shade, he gestured vaguely behind him to where the priest was standing. "Deal with him," he said.

Two soldiers remained behind, but stayed only briefly.

Mahu strode through the temple's labyrinthine corridors with a firmness of step that belied his ignorance of the inner sanctum's location. His troops walked behind him, each as eager as the next to avoid becoming separated from the group and falling prey to priests not discouraged by the rout on the dockside.

Here and there unperturbed pockets of defence lay in wait, ready to pounce out of doorways and crannies at the sound of a Memphis accent. One or two of Mahu's men were lost in the brief clashes but in the main it was the bodies of priests and guards who lined the corridors. Eager to reach his goal as quickly as possible, Mahu ensured that one of the priests was kept alive and marched at the point of a sword at the head of the column. He acted as not only as a guide, but as a buffer against further attack.

At each junction Mahu would stop and quiz the prisoner as to the best way to proceed, with force increasing in proportion to the prisoner's reluctance to talk.

Finally, and with his sword pressed closely enough to the prisoner's throat to draw a dark bead of blood, they reached the final junction. Before Mahu stood the small, unprepossessing door that led to the inner sanctum, to the home of Amun himself. Even Mahu's zeal was dampened somewhat by the enormity of what he was about to do. He stared at the door as though willing it to open of its own volition.

"You cannot," the priest whispered at his side.

"I can do anything I like," Mahu said, his gaze remaining fixed on the door. "I act on the command of the One God."

"The what?" the priest said, surprise momentarily conquering his fear.

"The Aten," Mahu said. "The One God. The Creator."

"But Amun is the king of the gods," the priest said.

"There is no king of the gods. There are no gods to rule. Only the Aten."

"You are mad," the priest said.

Mahu stepped away from the door and, with no change to his expression, pushed his sword forwards. It met brief resistance against the throat of the priest and then plunged inwards with ease. For a fraction of a moment the *kepesh* was taking the priest's entire weight and Mahu was able to picture himself holding up his victim by his sword alone. He smiled at the image, but the priest was too heavy and he sank to the floor. Mahu regarded him for a moment and then turned back to the door.

He hammered on it with his sword handle. As he did so flecks of blood darted from the blade and landed on his hand and arm. Mahu tutted and rubbed them off.

There was no answer to his knocking. Sighing at the inconvenience, Mahu stood to one side and signalled to two of his troops.

"Open it," he said.

The two men did not move except to glance at each other.

"Open it," Mahu said again.

They both knew there was no escape, and both were more scared of Mahu than they were of Amun. They stepped forwards. One of them grabbed the handle and, half expecting to be enveloped in flame, or ice, or perforated by flying spears, or any number of other deaths, he pushed.

The door swung open into shadow. Nothing more deadly emerged than the smells of incense and stale air. Mahu found the courage to step forwards and the presence of mind to do so without betraying his nervousness. The men behind him were palpably scared. Mahu knew that anything but calm determination from their commander could very quickly lead to panic.

Before him was a surprisingly small room. At the far end, only a handful of paces away, stood Amun, his expression sparkling in the light of the braziers that hung from the wall at his shoulder. He looked surprisingly serene.

Before him, on the floor, lay a hunched figure, prostrate before the god, his back rising and falling quickly and deeply with the breath of fear. He was so old that Mahu doubted whether he would have the strength to stand under his own volition.

"Ptahmose," Mahu said.

The figure did not respond other than to tense the muscles beneath his parchment skin

"Ptahmose," Mahu said again. He reached out with his foot and kicked the priest, without too much force, on the backside. Still Ptahmose did not acknowledge him. His breath quickened, and Mahu began to make out a murmured prayer, the words mumbled, quick and indistinct.

"You are wasting your time," Mahu said. "There is nobody there to hear you."

The mumbling continued.

Sighing, Mahu stepped around the high priest's frame and stopped in front of the altar. Reaching out, he placed the palms of his hands firmly on the centre of the statue, and pushed. After a moment's resistance Amun began to topple backwards. Only now did Ptahmose raise his head from the floor and he did so in time to see Amun land, head first, on the floor of the inner sanctum. The statue was heavy enough for its impact to send a brief tremor through the floor.

Crying out, Ptahmose tried to rise to his feet. Mahu effortlessly pushed him back down with a foot on his shoulder.

"If you are so intent to stay there, then stay there you shall," Mahu said.

"Is this how your king would have you treat an old man?" Ptahmose said. There was a quiver in his voice, but Mahu was unable to discern whether it was the product of anger or fear.

"My king has commanded me to root out the evil of Amun," Mahu answered. "You are its foundation and its core. I very much doubt that His Majesty will concern himself unduly with the details."

"He shall be hearing about this," Ptahmose said.

"Yes," Mahu said, signalling to one of the guards hovering on the threshold of the room. "Yes, I do hope so."

The Maya Papyrus, Fragments 114-115

Like smoke, a rumour began to permeate the city streets. People, it was said, had started to die in the same way as the ambassador from Amurru. It would be some time until the illness began to be known as a plague. Not long after that it became known in trusted circles as Amun's Revenge, so obvious was its provenance. Those who survived its victims began to privately curse the name of their king. The highest mortality rate was among the physicians and those who tended the sick and dying, as though there was a maliciousness within the sickness that bade it afflict those who least deserved it. Certainly the man who most deserved it remained hale within his palace.

I must have walked every street of Akhetaten at this time, trying to quash the irrational feeling that I was somehow responsible for all this, that somehow my actions had encouraged Akhenaten, or at least not sufficiently dissuaded him from his insanity. This was long before the days of deserted streets and silent markets, before the stink of unburied bodies began to infuse the very air of Akhetaten, but not before an atmosphere of dread had settled over the place. It was as though we, the city's unfortunate inhabitants, knew what was coming, and I bore the discomfort of this precognisance harder than any.

Had I been too ready to agree to Akhenaten's outlandish claims, too reticent to say what the whole world was thinking? To have acted any differently would have been to invite death, but what was my life weighed against the lives of those who had fallen to disease?

It was on one of my walks that I stumbled across a sight that brought me to an abrupt standstill. I must have looked a curious spectacle that morning, for I had stopped in the middle of the King's Way, forcing the chariots and pedestrians on the road to swerve around me and voice their concerns about my sanity and fitness to be using the road.

I am not sure to this day whether anybody else saw the girl in the alleyway, or whether they simply chose to ignore her, for she lay only half in shadow and other pedestrians passed her much closer than had I, their gazes suspiciously fixed on the ground before them. The girl's resting place was an alleyway that led off I know not where from the King's Way itself, and she lay a little way back from the road.

I held my hand to my mouth and took a few faltering steps forward.

She was, I could now see, a child of no more than eight. I could tell from her clothing and slight stature that she did not come from a family of means, and I could tell from her pallor that she was dead. I approached her gingerly, as though she was asleep and I was afraid of waking her. She was so thin that at first I thought she may have died from malnutrition, but then I saw the blood caked around her mouth and realised the real reason for her demise, and I cursed once again the vanity of my king which had brought this divine vengeance down around our ears. The same blood had dripped from the mouth of the ambassador from Amurru before he had breathed his last.

Perhaps, in his wisdom, Amun would have found himself able to blame me, in part, for what had happened. Indeed, the whole court could have been held to account for failing to prevent our king's idiosyncrasies. Had I become ill with the plague I would have been mortified and terrified, but in my heart I would have seen that, however circuitous the logic, I may have deserved it.

But what of the girl? What possible reason, other than innocent proximity, could the gods have had to lay her low in such a heartless fashion?

There could only be one reason, and it came to me as I hurried from the scene, shame colouring my face and fear fuelling my steps. Everybody would be afflicted by Amun's Revenge purely because his rage knew no bounds. There were no innocent victims, because everyone was guilty of life and of humanity, and in the eyes of Amun, we must all, by that association, have been nothing more than vermin to be exterminated.

The king hated to feel afraid, and it was clear to see that this emotion was not a difficult one to conjure in his breast. When the king was afraid, people suffered. When he was angry they suffered. When he was tired, or sad, or unwell, or irritable, or unhappy with the dimensions of the latest statue to be made in his image, people suffered.

And yet it fell to someone to speak to him about the sickness. Nobody nominated me, other than myself, and nobody hinted to me about the seriousness of the situation in the hope that I would take the onus from them and speak to the king myself. My only promptings were the sights that my own eyes beheld.

Of course, my moment of civil charity passed with the same rapidity with which it had arrived. I was no more a position to change the situation than was the poor girl in the alleyway. Only the frustration remained, but it was fuel enough to fire me into marching into the palace, my resolve and my anger matched only by my fear, which rose with every step that brought me closer to my goal.

I found the king in his audience chamber, alone save for Aye and what seemed like half a hundred torches. I prostrated myself at his feet, and told myself that I suffered to bow to him only because I was a diplomat and a politician, and not a coward.

He left me there for some time before he bid me rise.

"Good morning, father," I said to Aye after I had risen. He grunted a reply that was as divorced from the situation as was Akhenaten's wish that I may live.

"Your Majesty," I continued, undeterred. "I feel I must..."

"Read it again," Akhenaten said to Aye, as though I was not in the room. I stopped, mid-flow. However undeterred one was, one did not continue speaking when the king interrupted.

Aye unrolled a papyrus scroll he had been holding beneath his arm.

"'To His Majesty Amenophis...'"

Akhenaten looked at me for the first time since my arrival. "He has not yet heard," he said, explaining the correspondent's use of his old name. "I am prepared to forgive him his ignorance on this occasion. Continue, Aye."

"'To His Majesty Amenophis,'" Aye read. "'Lord of the Two Lands, etcetera etcetera, from your loyal servant, Ribaddi, Prince of Byblos, footstool for your feet, etcetera etcetera. Your Majesty has not replied to any of my earlier letters, and I am afraid that they have not been reaching you. I have sent copies of this one by several different routes.'"

Aye held up a handful of scrolls by way of illustration, and Akhenaten shook his head and snorted.

"'Your Majesty,'" Aye continued, "'the situation is becoming desperate. May the king, my lord, know that the war of Abdi-Ashirta against me is severe, and he has taken all my cities. I most humbly beg upon my knees for Your Majesty's urgent assistance.'"

Aye rolled up the scroll.

Akhenaten turned to face me. "Well?" he said.

"Well, Your Majesty?" I stammered.

"Yes, Maya. Well," he said, with a note of irritation in his voice. "Are you not an advisor to your king?"

I had never considered myself as such, at least not in matters of import, but I felt it perhaps unwise to deny it.

"Erm," I said.

"Maya," Aye said. "The king has received an alarming letter from one of his vassals. He is asking for your recommendation for his actions regarding it. A number of other people have given their opinions, and now it is your turn. Should His Majesty intervene against Abdi-Ashirta? Should he make peace with him? What?"

"Ah," I said. "Yes."

"Yes, Maya?" Akhenaten said.

"Your Majesty," I said. "You have taken me somewhat off guard. Ribaddi mentions having written to you before...?"

"On many an occasion," Akhenaten said. "In fact, on too many occasions. He is always complaining, Maya. These people are making war on me, those people are making war on me. This city has been lost, that city has been sacked, please send help. It is always the same with Ribaddi lately. Does he not realise that I have my own problems? Does he not know that the whole of Egypt stands against me and assassins stalk me at my every turn? Does he think he is the only one to have difficulties in life? He knows his letters have reached me because I have already replied to the last one."

"And in that reply, what did Your Majesty communicate to Ribaddi?" I asked.

"That he writes too many letters," Akhenaten said. "I told him to stop it. And yet here we are."

"Perhaps, then," I said, "Your Majesty would consider sending help."

"You sound like a priest," Akhenaten said, his eyes narrowing with suspicion.

"Your Majesty?" I said. I looked to my father for help, but he was engrossed in rolling up the papyrus scroll with no creases.

Akhenaten stood up and stepped down from the dais upon which his throne was situated.

"If there is one thing my father taught me, it was never to trust a priest," he said.

"But..." I began, and Akhenaten stepped in so close to me that I could smell his breath when he spoke.

"Do not interrupt me, Maya," he said. I nodded, but said nothing for fear it would be seen as another interruption. Akhenaten seemed to accept this, and continued.

"My father always said that the priesthood of Amun would try to persuade me to go to war in order to meet their own ends. And now I wonder whether you are taking their place, since the priesthood of Amun no longer exists."

"What?" I blurted out, before I could stop myself.

Akhenaten spun around and shouted into my face.

"I said do not interrupt me!"

I took an involuntary step backwards and looked to my father once more. He looked back, but offered no support.

"My most humble apologies, Your Majesty," I said. "It is just that the news took me rather by surprise."

"Surprise, Maya?" Akhenaten said. "Surprise? Why? Have I not decreed that Amun is a false god?"

"Yes, of course, Your Majesty."

"Then what on earth did you expect to happen to his clergy? Do you think for a moment that I would allow them to continue in their acts of blasphemy against the one true god?"

If I am honest, it was not a question that I had asked myself. To rid the world of Amun's priests was such a ridiculous proposition that I did not even consider it. The priesthood of Amun had existed since the dawn of time itself. They out-dated the pyramids. They were as inviolable and eternal as the sun and the moon and, well, as the god they served. To hear Akhenaten say they were no more was like hearing that someone had taken away the Nile, or the desert. It did not seem possible that the world could have continued functioning in their absence.

"What have you done with them?" I asked.

"I have shown them the error of their ways."

I looked at my father for the third time.

"Mahu?" I said. Aye nodded.

"You are trying to change the subject, Maya," Akhenaten said. "Why are you so keen for me to fight? Do you have motives of which I am not aware? How do you gain from my going to war?"

There is very little that can be said in conversation with the paranoid that will not foster their suspicion. There is no logic, only excuses; no denials, only subterfuge. And so once Akhenaten had decided that I was manipulating him for my own design, I feared that there was little I could do to dissuade him.

"I am concerned only for Egypt, Your Majesty," I said.

"For Egypt, or for your king? Sometimes the two are mutually exclusive," Aye said. I stared at him, momentarily staggered.

"Ah, very true," Akhenaten said. "A good point. Thank you, Aye." He turned back to me. "Well?" he said.

My mind was almost too full of my father's betrayal of me to be able to turn my thoughts effectively to the problem that I faced. For him to say such a thing so obviously placed me in danger that I could not believe it had been an accident. He at least had the good grace to look embarrassed by his words, but that was of scant consolation.

But some instinct made itself available to me. Perhaps words were put in my mouth by one of the gods; perhaps Amun himself, although certainly not the Aten, unless I had very much misjudged him. But whatever it was, I just opened my mouth and allowed to spill out the first words that came to my mind. I recognised my lack of eloquence at the time but decided that the longer I spoke, perhaps, the less obvious it would seem. I knew that I had the king's vanity on my side, and that he would be loathe to ask for an explanation of my nonsensical rant.

"But the king and the Two Lands are one and the same thing," I said. "If a man is lame in his leg, he does not blame his heart, although they are part of the same body and the heart still suffers because of the leg's shortcomings. In the same way, if Egypt's king is beset by enemies, I cannot turn my back on his kingdom and ignore its faults, although it harbours the very enemies that the king finds rallied against him. For if the king and his country are the same thing, to neglect one would be to neglect the other. It would be like cutting out the heart to cure the leg."

Akhenaten stared at me in silence for a moment.

"Well, yes," he said, finally. "Of course. Well done, Maya."

I allowed myself to begin breathing again.

"But nevertheless," Akhenaten continued, "I shall not be going to war on behalf of Ribaddi. He shall have to look after himself."

"A wise choice, Your Majesty," Aye said.

"Your Majesty," I began.

"Do not question me, Maya. My father always taught me to avoid war. That is what I am doing. My father was a master diplomat and politician. I would be a fool not to follow such wisdom. And anyway, I cannot spare the men. I have so many enemies at home that..."

His voice trailed into silence.

"In fact," he said, "it occurs to me that my enemies at home would be much emboldened by my involvement in a foreign conflict. With the army away, who would protect the king?"

"Your Majesty," I said, my imagination serving up the image of poor Ribaddi, loyal servant, attacked and executed by hordes of barbarians. "It would only require a token force. Once Ribaddi's enemies see he has your support they will not dare continue their attacks."

"No," Akhenaten said. "I have made my decision. I shall remain loyal to my father's memory. There will be no war. Aye, write to Ribaddi. Tell him he has my utmost confidence in dealing with the situation himself. And tell him that I expect only to receive good news in his letters from now on."

"I shall make it perfectly plain, Your Majesty," Aye said, bowing.

I knew from his tone that further discussion would be treated as suspicious. Had the king not already voiced the thought that the situation had been engineered by his enemies? It would have been foolhardy in the extreme to continue. Ribaddi was left to his fate.

And yet I knew I must now broach another subject, just as dangerous. My damnable conscience was reminding me of the girl in the gutter and however I tried to distract it, the image insisted on returning.

"There is one more matter, Your Majesty," I said.

The king sighed and returned to his throne. "Yes?" he said.

"It is the plague, Your Majesty."

"Plague? It is hardly a plague, Maya."

He was right, of course. I had heard nobody refer to it as such – not yet – but there seemed little point in not imbuing the situation with as much gravity as I could muster.

"Your Majesty, people are lying dead in alleyways."

"Nonsense, nonsense. You are exaggerating."

"Your Majesty, I have seen it with my own eyes. On the way here this morning; a child, dead in the street."

"But not without reason, Maya."

"Not without reason?" I said, failing to keep the incredulity from my voice.

"You have to remember, Maya, that the Aten has his hands in everything. We are all the Aten's children, and the Aten does not take his own children to his bosom without good reason."

"The Aten willed that girl to die?" I said.

"She was most likely a non-believer," Akhenaten said.

"Or a blasphemer," Aye added.

"Very true," Akhenaten said. "Very true."

"There is nothing you will do?" I asked, ignoring my father's contribution.

"What can I do?" Akhenaten said.

I knew the answer, but it was not one I was prepared to voice, for although I was outraged by the king's actions I was not courageous enough to endanger my own life in order to save others. Part of me saw this as cowardice, and I roundly condemned myself for it, but another part, equally strong, saw it as nothing more than sensible and pragmatic. And of course, I told myself, it is not as though my speaking my mind would have any effect. He would condemn me as a traitor, but he would not act upon my words other than to use them against me.

The answer was for him to turn his back on the new god he had created and embrace the old: Ptah, Amun, Ra and the rest. The gods that had watched over this kingdom since it was created from the formless sea of chaos. The gods that had been worshipped since the first Egyptians had walked the earth. The gods who were named in the oldest documents and carved into the oldest tomb walls. They were the reason for the dead girl in the alleyway, not the Aten. It was they who wished to punish us, and they were not without just cause.

No, I told myself, the best I could do was to remain silent and await the right moment to speak, for speaking now would help nobody, least of all myself.

In this was the logic that enabled me to sleep at night, safe from the taunting of my cowardice, and even when the plague finally became known as such and made its way into the palace and struck at those within, I did nothing but thank the gods that it was not me.

Upon his return, Mahu was afforded a hero's welcome, although few lined the route of his parade who were not soldiers. The general feeling in the populace was sympathy for Ptahmose rather than hatred for him, and if enforced enthusiasm was not enough to deter the idly curious, fear of Amun was. The market place behind the backs of the soldiers was all but deserted, and just a few streets away from the procession not a soul was abroad.

The soldiers' cheers were equalled in volume only by their jeers and whistles, for Mahu had brought with him a trophy of his victorious campaign.

Pulled behind Mahu's chariot, his arms tied at the elbow and wrist behind his back, was Ptahmose. He had been stripped naked.

It was obvious to everyone in the crowd that Ptahmose was no more than a few steps from death, and his doom was not only etched in his bruised and aged body but in the shame and dismay of which his eyes spoke. With every step he surveyed the crowd for a friendly face, but did so in vain.

By the time the procession reached the Window of Appearances Ptahmose was being more dragged than walked. His skin was almost invisible beneath a layer of dust and sand thrown up by the horses' hooves and chariot's wheels before him. Deep lacerations lined his feet, and also his legs and arms where he had fallen and been unable to clamber back to his feet before being dragged along the street.

When Mahu's chariot stopped, Ptahmose simply lay in the dirt and did not move. Akhenaten, from his vantage point in the Window of Appearances, said nothing but regarded Ptahmose like a man regarding a snake, too fascinated to turn away but ready to leap to safety at the snake's first sign of movement.

At a sign from Mahu a soldier made his way to the back of the chariot and lifted Ptahmose from the ground. It was not an onerous task: Ptahmose looked as though the soldier could have carried him all the way back to Thebes without noticing any burden at all. As the soldier brought him forwards Mahu held out a hand to momentarily detain him.

"Does he live?" Mahu asked.

The soldier leant his head close to that of Ptahmose and waited for Ptahmose's breath to brush his face.

"Yes, my lord," he said after a moment. "But barely."

"Barely is all we need," Mahu said. "Continue."

Up at the Window of Appearances, Akhenaten was beginning to appear agitated. His eyes could not rest, but switched every other heartbeat from regarding Mahu to Ptahmose, Ptahmose to Mahu. His hands went to the pendants that adorned his neck, his fingers working the beads that hung there as though trying to solve a puzzle. Mahu noticed his unease and made a fist of his hand, holding it to his chest in a sign of strength and solidarity.

Akhenaten's agitation was not tempered by the thought of the speech he was about to make. With Mahu in the security of the palace, safe in the knowledge that Ptahmose was a fortnight's sail away the speech had seemed erudite and effortless. Now, the prospect of delivering it to

Ptahmose's face terrified him, although he could see that the priest was in no state to even hear him, much less listen.

Akhenaten inhaled and exhaled deeply and slowly before speaking.

"Ptahmose," he said. The priest was incapable of making any sign that he heard or recognised his name.

"Here is a false priest of a false god," Akhenaten continued, choosing to ignore the fact that he was being ignored, and choosing to address the crowd, who at least could respond to him. "And his defeat is incontrovertible proof of my words. He claims to be the tool of the king of the gods, but look at him. What are we to think of such a pathetic sight? Are we to fear it?"

Akhenaten laughed and held up his arms to the audience of soldiers and police. To his delight they laughed along with him. They pointed at Ptahmose and jeered and mocked him. Ptahmose still sagged on the arm of the soldier that held him and made no attempt at reply.

"I think not," Akhenaten continued, buoyed up by the support of the soldiers. "There is nothing here to fear. And what god would allow this end for his chief emissary?"

The jeering increased.

"A weak god?"

A cry of *Yes* from the crowd.

"A defeated god?"

Yes!

"A *false* god?"

Yes!

"He is nothing now. There is nothing to protect him, nothing for him to worship, and without his god there is no reason for him to exist. Mahu, take him away. Deal with him in a way fitting with a man of no consequence."

The crowd erupted, and Akhenaten was unable to resist painting a broad smile across his face. He was elated. He had never addressed any gathering before with such eloquence, such understanding of the situation and the audience, such aplomb and such skill. Never had he received such a rapturous reception. He wanted to talk forever, and yet recognised that he should stop before he out-spoke his welcome.

Mahu signalled to the soldier who was supporting Ptahmose. He took a step back towards the chariot, and then stopped. Ptahmose had raised his head. All eyes had been turned to him to watch his ignoble exit and so everyone saw his face turn up to look at the Window of Appearances. Everything seemed to stop momentarily. The crowd fell silent as though at a command, and waited to see if Ptahmose would speak.

His mouth opened. The crowd assumed the air of someone leaning forwards to eavesdrop all the better.

"Amenophis," Ptahmose whispered, with such frailty that the words barely managed to clamber past his lips.

Akhenaten's smile froze. He had not heard what Ptahmose said, but then he had not needed to. The very fact that Ptahmose had spoken was enough to chill him. He had not expected to have to enter into some form of dialogue.

"Amenophis," Ptahmose said again, this time with enough strength to be heard by those closest to him in the crowd.

Akhenaten felt the euphoria of his oration leaking from him. Here was a situation that Mahu had promised would never happen. He had sworn that Ptahmose would be a broken man by the time he was presented before the Window of Appearances, that he would be beyond any form of resistance, that his spirit would lie at Akhenaten's feet to be kicked and mauled without impediment as the king saw fit.

Akhenaten now had to choose between two courses of action and neither appeared to him to be the way he wanted the audience to conclude. He could order Ptahmose removed from the scene before he could speak further, thereby preventing the possibility of humiliation at the priest's reply, or he could magnanimously invite the priest to speak, illustrating that Ptahmose could say nothing that held any fear for him. Of course, Ptahmose was a born orator and Akhenaten was unsure how he would fare in a debate with the man, but if he did not allow him to speak it would look like Ptahmose had defeated him merely by saying his name.

Akhenaten was at a loss. *What would my father do?* he thought. *Why did he never teach me this?* He looked to Mahu, whose expression said only that he was awaiting his king's decision.

Eventually, Akhenaten's indecision was a decision made for him. In the silence after Ptahmose had spoken his name the priest had gathered his strength and his breath. He began to speak, his words punctuated by long, painful breaths.

"Amenophis," he said again. "You have excelled yourself. You have employed thugs to take an old man from his home and beat him. This supposed god of yours must be powerful indeed to engage in battle with a man such as I, who has hardly the strength left to hold a sword in his defence."

Ptahmose stopped to draw in his breath, which seemed to have run away without him. It was a moment that Akhenaten recognised as his opportunity for rejoinder, but the words refused to form in his mind. He needed time to prepare, to rehearse, to ask Mahu's opinion. What if his words were foolish? What if he spoke and Ptahmose answered only with laughter? What if the crowd echoed him?

"I have seen your support, false god," Ptahmose said. "I have seen the crowds that bay and cheer for you, and I have seen the scabbards that hang at their sides. Is this your army, Amenophis? Are these the men who worship at your feet? Do you have nobody here to pledge themselves to you without being paid to do so?"

"Silence, priest!" Akhenaten shouted, finally finding the words within himself. Ptahmose sagged against the soldier who was still holding most of his weight, seemingly grateful of the interruption. The crowd turned to the Window of Appearances. Akhenaten could feel the expectation in the air and for once was grateful that he was unable to see the faces that beheld him. There were no more words. He had commanded Ptahmose to silence only because he wanted him to stop talking, nothing more. There were no more thoughts to follow the command. Ptahmose was at first unable to continue, but even when he had reined in his tortuous breathing, he waited. He could see the crowd doing the same, willing the king to speak further and being answered only with emptiness and vacillation. Ptahmose smiled to himself and drew strength from the king's weakness. He waited just long enough for the crowd to begin murmuring amongst itself before continuing.

"Do you see where your heresy has brought you and your damned city? Everywhere I hear talk of ruin. A man can hear much when he is held captive in such a confined and crowded space as a river ship, and rumour has a way of seeping on board with the provisions at each port of call. Do you know, Amenophis, that your soldiers were scared to return here after they butchered the priests of the god who has protected this land since it was formed from the void? Did you know that your city's guards are having to prevent people slipping away into the desert, people who know they will surely die in the sand, but who prefer to do so than stay here with you and your false church?"

Despite his infirmity, Ptahmose still carried with him the gravitas that had been his companion and boon throughout his long life. He had saved himself from more than one perilous situation merely by the strength of his character, but he knew that this was not a situation from which it would be so easy to claim victory. But the tone of his voice, the authority of his bearing, and the inner strength that seemed to project from his body all the more since his physical strength had deserted him, all conspired together to compel his audience to listen with an air approaching that of reverence. Even Akhenaten, whose jaw opened and closed silently in a reply that was still unformed, was spellbound.

"My god Amun has wreaked his mighty ruin against you and your city, Amenophis," Ptahmose continued, "and in this way he shows himself more clearly even than your god who hangs over us all now and watches these events in silence. I find such detachment inexplicable in one you profess to be so mighty, but no matter. You will take me away now and have me killed by your henchmen, but as you watch me depart and you tally my death against all those of the heretics in your city, ask yourself this: who has really won this war? Is the might of Amun truly extinguished, or does his wrath walk amongst you every day, even here in your stronghold? Your people will turn against you rather than suffer the consequences of your blasphemy before too long, Amenophis. As I am taken away now I walk into the bosom of my god, to sit at his right hand in the underworld for a million years. At whose hand will you sit, Amenophis, when you are taken away?"

The strength in Ptahmose's legs left him completely now, and he remained upright only because the soldier that carried him remained firm and took his weight. The thrall in which his words had held the crowd was broken, and an excited murmur skittered through it, loud enough only to reach the ears of the king without revealing any of the messages it contained.

"Take him away!" Akhenaten commanded. "Cease this madman's ravings! His god is too weak to save him now, although he would dearly wish to!"

He looked as though he was about to speak further but had thought better of it. He watched while Ptahmose was bundled onto the back of a chariot. Akhenaten took a step back towards the palace and then stopped. He held his arms out to the crowd.

"May you live!" he said, and then realised that it could have appeared to many that he was addressing Ptahmose rather than the audience that surrounded him. "Not..." he began, and then stopped again. There was nothing he could possibly say to salvage the day, he realised. He turned and stalked sullenly away from the Window of Appearances and back towards the palace.

And as he walked, so his rage and his fear grew. Ptahmose had made him look a fool, and the priest's imminent death was small consolation when weighed against the damage his words may have done in those who heard them.

But more than that; what if he had been correct? What if Amun was as strong as ever, even without his priests? What if he was as strong in Akhetaten as he always had been in Thebes? What if this rout of his temple was not enough?

As he walked, Akhenaten was unable to prevent himself from glancing from time to time over his shoulder, as though he expected to find there a man with a cobra's head.

The Maya Papyrus, Fragment 116

> *I saw little of Akhenaten during the days that immediately followed his confrontation with Ptahmose at the Window of Appearances. He spent almost all his time locked away with Mahu and to a lesser extent with Aye, who seemed ever more willing to answer the call of his king. What I did see of him, though, was of a man in distress. He was nervous in almost all company, even that of his wife and children, and he spoke quickly in short, malformed sentences as though he did not expect to be given the chance to finish a long speech.*
>
> *I am ashamed to say that I had been so engrossed with my own fate and the fear of disease that I had quite neglected my duties to my family, specifically, my sister. Surrounded as she was by all the pomp and majesty of Akhenaten's court it was becoming increasingly difficult to see her as I once did, as the pretty philanthropist who had taken the victim of school bullies under her wing. She was growing distant from me. I was, after all, only mortal.*
>
> *Determined to deal with at least one aspect of the guilt that dogged me, I had myself announced in her apartments. I am delighted to say that she appeared to be genuinely pleased to see me. I had been not a little concerned at the reception I would be given after such a prolonged absence.*
>
> *"It is good to see you again, brother," she said, giving me a polite kiss on the cheek.*
>
> *"Yes," I said. "I am sorry it has been so long, only I have been..." my excuse trailed away to silence.*
>
> *"It is all right," she said. "I understand. Please, take a seat."*
>
> *I could feel the love that emanated from her, and I believe it was genuine, but there seemed to be a formality about her that was unfamiliar to me. It was as though she was speaking to me as a brother, but also as a subject.*
>
> *"How is Akhenaten?" I said, conscious of protocol and the fact that there were few other things that we had in common any more.*

"He is... troubled."

"Ah," I said, in a knowing way. *There seemed little else I could do. "And you?"*

She sighed. "I am troubled also," she said.

It would have been an insult to ask her what was causing her distress. I opted to remain silent and allow her to tell me unprompted, as I knew she would.

"My husband Akhenaten is the Aten incarnate," she said. She spoke slowly as though she was explaining it not only to me but to herself also. "He is his son, but he is also the Aten himself. It sounds complicated, but we have spoken about it at great length, both between ourselves and with some of the wisest men in the kingdom. It is perfectly straightforward. I am Akhenaten's wife, chosen to be so before I was born. I am, therefore, not only the god's wife, but the god's daughter. I am Nefertiti the goddess."

She smiled quickly, as though the title was still something of an embarrassment to her, but she did not recant it.

"As such, I am as responsible and as much at risk as my husband," she said.

"Almost," she added, giving me that smile again.

"At risk?" I said.

"From Amun."

"But I thought that Amun was a false god," I said. I was less wary of questioning Nefertiti than I was of her husband. "How can he threaten you if he does not exist?"

"He is a threat not because he exists, but because people believe him to do so. With that faith he continues to be as powerful as if he was standing outside the palace door with an army at his back."

It was logic that I could understand, but I was still confused by Nefertiti's attitude.

"You seem happier about the situation now than you were when Akhenaten announced it at the Window of Appearances," I said.

"I was shocked," she said. "I have now had time to think on the subject. I have spoken to my husband, and I have consulted our father. Both have persuaded me of the legitimacy of their beliefs. Father was particularly forthright. He explained everything to me."

"Father?" I said, surprised that he would be included in the conversation.

"He has some very strong opinions on the subject."

"It did not seem like that so very long ago."

"He, like I, has had an epiphany."

"Has he indeed?"

"Do not be so cynical, Maya," Nefertiti said. "Everything makes perfect sense as long as you accept Akhenaten's divinity and the existence of the Aten, as I always have. It then follows that his wife must also have a similar claim to divinity. We are the holy triad. The Aten, Akhenaten and myself."

"Then," I said, "how does it follow that if the Aten exists, the pantheon of gods that should share his heavens ceases to exist?"

Nefertiti shrugged, as though it was the most obvious answer in the world. "Because the Aten says so," she said.

"Some would view that as a circular argument," I said.

"Some would view your doubt as blasphemy," she replied. "Is it so difficult to believe that your pharaoh is divine? Does Amenhotep's funerary temple not display images of his mother being impregnated by Amun?"

"Well, yes," I said, reluctantly.

"And Hatshepsut? Does her temple not show the same scene?"

"Yes," I said, seeing where the argument was going.

"And is it such a step from that to this?"

"We Egyptians have never worshipped living gods," I said.

"Well perhaps it is time that we Egyptians embraced the new and discarded the old."

I was not convinced, but then I had not had the benefit of my father's teachings on the subject. Moreover, I could see that there was little point in trying to dissuade Nefertiti of her beliefs. It appeared to me that Nefertiti needed her faith. She was not as blind as Akhenaten, and neither was she as hard-hearted as Mahu. Her faith was her only armour against what was being carried out in her family's name. However much Akhenaten's policies filled me with dread, and however much I blamed him for the current predicament I and the rest of the city found ourselves in, I had neither the ability nor the inclination to argue with Nefertiti. I did not want to chance removing her only defence against what was happening around her.

And so, when I was once again summoned to the king's audience chamber by Aye, I was overjoyed to discover that Nefertiti would be there also. It gave me the opportunity of meeting with the king for once without the guilt of holding my tongue against everything I wanted to address. With Nefertiti *there I could tell myself that I stayed silent for her, and not for myself.*

In the throne room the two royal thrones were occupied by the king and Nefertiti. I was the last to arrive, Mahu and my father already occupying the ground before the dais.

I prostrated myself.

"We have come to a decision," Akhenaten said, with no preamble. I raised my head from the floor and wondered whether his words constituted an order to get to my feet. I hesitated and then stood, waiting for a reprimand that did not come. Akhenaten seemed too preoccupied to even know whether or not I was present.

"We have deliberated hard and long, but there is no other way."

I speculated as to the identity of 'we'. He looked to nobody in particular when he used the word, and so it could have been any of us there present, except myself, although had I been asked my opinion I would have wagered that Mahu's name was not far from the king's lips.

"It is now obvious that my... reforms in the temple of Amun at Thebes were not wide ranging enough in their application. It is the only explanation for Amun's continued support, and such support is the only explanation for the Aten's continued wrath."

"His wrath?" I said, before I could stop myself.

Akhenaten threw me a disapproving look before replying.

"Can you think of another explanation for the sickness abroad in our city?"

"No, Majesty," I lied, wondering at the king's latest change of heart.

"The Aten demands obedience," Akhenaten continued. "He demands faith, and he demands respect. Currently, this heathen population is giving him nothing. They must be taught."

I can hear his voice now, all these years later. They must be taught. *I can hear the determination therein. I can see Mahu's humourless smile, and Aye's resolution, and Nefertiti's discomfiture.*

They must be taught.

They were the words that presaged a time that scarred all who lived through it, and all who survived it would refer to it for ever more, with a shudder, as The Terror.

Chapter Sixteen

The Terror

MAHU'S TROOPS swooped with callous efficiency. Their orders were clear, and beaten into them with such enthusiasm that they would sooner have turned on themselves than disobeyed any letter of them.

Their first group of targets were within Akhetaten itself. A decree was sent out around the city, warning the citizens within that their household gods were no longer permitted. Like everywhere in Egypt there was hardly a house, even amongst the poorest, which did not have a host of small gods to protect it. There were gods of the hearth and kitchen, gods of the bed chamber and garden, gods of the young and old. Each would live in the house as a small statuette, portable enough to be taken to a new dwelling place when the need arose, but large enough to be effective against the forces of chaos. Each house celebrated the larger gods with equal enthusiasm. Statues of Amun, Ptah, Osiris or any of the others, usually depending on the householder's birthplace, adorned the homes of everyone from highest nobles downwards.

All of these, all of them, without exception, were declared to be prohibited. A short amnesty was declared. Police chariots patrolled every street of Akhetaten, collecting the idols which were deposited outside the homes of those who feared the king more than the gods they were evicting.

After two days the idols were collected in the courtyard of the palace. They made a sorry pile.

"How many?" Akhenaten asked Mahu, who shrugged.

"Hard to say," he said. "Three or four hundred at most."

"How dare they?" Akhenaten asked. "Do they not realise with whom they are dealing? Three or four *hundred*? There should be ten, twenty times that number. Where are all the others?"

Mahu shrugged again. "They have not been volunteered," he said.

"Then we shall have to volunteer them ourselves," Akhenaten said. "Send in the police."

There was a systematic search, starting in the slums lining the sewers to the north of the city. The inhabitants of the district, the poorest of the people of Akhenaten, were lucky and unlucky in equal measure. They were lucky in that the stench of the sewers and the abundance of flies encouraged the police to perform what was nothing more than a cursory search in their eagerness to progress on to the more desirable neighbourhoods. They were unlucky in that their poverty left them with nothing but the love of their gods, and once these gods were confiscated many found themselves with homes entirely empty.

Those with the least to lose also had the most, and it was not unusual for the most disadvantaged citizens to fight and claw in defence of the gods which were ripped from their grasp. Those who did so, being the poor, were clubbed into submission or death without a second thought. The police split into two groups. One would enter the houses and throw out any contraband they found within. Others positioned themselves in the road to smash the statues that landed at their feet. Stories circulated the city about mothers throwing themselves under raised clubs to protect the gods who protected their children, and managing to defend them only until their bodies were pushed out of the way.

It was later said, perhaps apocryphally, that the wailing and crying of the poor could be heard as far away as the palace and that the king ordered his musicians to strike up to drown out the noise.

The police left a trail of ruin in their wake. On every street, in every alleyway throughout the entire district, mounds of smashed statues were left under the gaze of the Aten.

Many citizens sank into the dust of the street or the filth of their homes and watched the backs of the departing policemen and wondered what they could possibly do now to protect themselves and their families against the illness that was beginning to make its mark.

The police, meanwhile, were more than happy to leave the slums behind them and progress to the more affluent areas of the city. Here, though, their pickings were less bountiful. News spread quicker than the police's horses could gallop and many people, afraid to be caught in possession of an illegal statue, did the police's work for them. The police arrived in many a street to find that the piles of smashed statues had arrived before them, and that there was precious little left to smash for themselves.

Those found in possession of idols were treated similarly throughout the city, regardless of status. Beatings were common, vandalism mandatory. Houses were all but demolished in the search for hiding places and many a well-heeled citizen found themselves with as few possessions as the poorest by the time the police had completed their grim task.

Nobody was excepted barring the king himself, although those at court knew enough in advance to clear as many rooms as possible and dispose of anything that may have been taken for an idol long before the police arrived, thereby minimising the disruption to their homes and lives.

It was a number of days before Mahu was able to deliver the news to Akhenaten that the city was clear. Akhenaten was able to declare a beginning to the second, more complicated phase of the operation.

"You see," Akhenaten said to the two generals he had summoned to his audience chamber, "there can be no freedom from the heresy of Amun while any aspect of him remains in the kingdom."

The two generals there assembled were Nakhtmin, who had been rapidly elevated through the ranks owing to the happy chance of his father Aye's proximity to the throne, and Horemheb, whose similar string of promotions could be traced back to his part in the protection of Akhenaten when the young prince had been attacked by agents of Amun in Thebes.

The two men stared impassively to the front, both resisting the temptation to follow the king with their eyes as he marched to and fro before them.

"And so," Akhenaten continued, "it gives me great pleasure to be able to confer on you the holy duty that I am about to describe."

He stopped and took a moment to stare directly into the eyes of the soldiers standing before him. Even at this short distance their faces tended to smudge into a indistinguishable brown and he was forced to lean in close in order to be sure of their features. Each officer in turn felt the king's breath on his face.

"For you should make no mistake," Akhenaten said. "This is a holy duty indeed. Perhaps the most important commission of your entire careers. Do you understand perfectly?"

"Yes, Your Majesty," the generals chorused.

"Good," Akhenaten said, taking a moment to settle himself back into his throne. "Then I shall allow Mahu to furnish you with the details."

Mahu stepped forwards and acknowledged the throne with a bow of his head before turning to the generals.

"Throughout the entire kingdom, wherever our people look, they see Amun staring back at them. On temple walls, in palaces, on cornices, pylons and obelisks, the people of Egypt see paintings of Amun, they see statues of him, they see words carved into the very stone of these Two Lands, praising him and glorifying him.

"Well, gentlemen, it is high time that we put a stop to it. You have each at your command one division of five thousand men. You will split the country between you and you will visit every shrine, tomb, temple and palace and there you will expunge any mention of Amun. You will chisel his name and his likeness from Egypt's stone until nothing of this false god remains to tempt Akhenaten's people into evil. Questions?"

There was a short pause while each of the generals weighed the risk of speaking out against the dangers of making an incorrect decision once the mission had begun. Eventually, Horemheb spoke.

"Your Majesty," he said. "If we are to erase the hieroglyph for Amun wherever we find it, will we not also be removing it where it forms part of your father's name?"

"Quite so," Akhenaten said. And then again, as if to reinforce the point: "Quite so."

"Please forgive a poor mortal's ignorance, Your Majesty," Horemheb said, "but will we not then be destroying your father's immortal soul? Is it not said that a man's soul may only continue to exist in the underworld while his name is remembered by those who live?"

Horemheb was later unsure as to whether he saw the very faintest suggestion of a shrug from Akhenaten, but the king made no further effort at reply. The men looked to Mahu.

"It is as you say," he said. "But we have very little choice in the matter. The successful future of Egypt is at stake, and we cannot afford to allow sentimentality to cloud our judgement. This is a war, gentlemen. In war there are always casualties. Now, I believe your men await you."

Both generals knew the worth of silence and they bowed from the room without another word. It was not until they were safely away from the palace and the risk of eavesdroppers that they allowed themselves to voice their opinions. They were old enough friends to implicitly acknowledge that their words, however disloyal, would go no further but even then the habit of discretion was a difficult one to break. They continued walking as they spoke.

"Well?" Horemheb said, asking half a dozen questions without the risk of actually forming them.

Nakhtmin shrugged. "We are soldiers," he said. "We have our orders."

"Would you consider them wise?" Horemheb asked.

"I would not consider them at all, Horemheb," Nakhtmin said. "They are instructions, not conversation pieces."

Horemheb lowered his voice into an urgent hiss. "Yes, but is it a soldier's duty to obey an order that is so patently wrong?" he said. "An order that sins against the gods? An order that erases a pharaoh's soul? Surely…"

"Yes?" Nakhtmin said. "Surely? Surely what?"

Horemheb sighed heavily and kicked at a pebble.

"Exactly," Nakhtmin said. "What would happen if your officers began questioning your orders? *I'm sorry, general, but we have a moral objection to attacking the enemy's left flank.*"

"That is different, Nakhtmin, and you know it."

"Different for us, not for Akhenaten. Not for the man issuing the instructions."

"The instructions came from Mahu. Since when did he outrank us?"

"Since he saved the king's life," Nakhtmin said.

Horemheb snorted. "He is not the only one," he said.

"Ah, yes, of course, my friend," Nakhtmin said. "But you saved the king's life only the once. Mahu saves it every day."

The pair had passed under the Window of Appearances, thankful for the momentary shade, and on towards the Aten temple. They had been able to talk openly since passing through the palace gates.

"And so we sin against the gods, just because we have been told to," Horemheb whispered.

"Not at all. We cannot sin against those who do not exist."

"But do we believe that, Nakhtmin?"

"Of course we do, Horemheb," Nakhtmin said, with a mischievous smile. "We have been ordered to."

When Nefertiti gave birth for the fifth time and, despite all the favourable readings of her water by the court physician, she gave birth to yet another daughter, Akhenaten made no obvious sign of disappointment or frustration. The physician professed profound amazement at the outcome. His predictions, backed though they were by tried and tested methods, had been initially made with not a little nervousness. His trepidation had been increasing with each successive birth and each successive incorrect forecast of the baby's gender, but he had managed to persuade himself that now, after four daughters, the Great Royal Wife could do nothing but deliver to her husband the son that he craved.

To everybody's surprise and the doctor's dismay, the baby was another girl. Akhenaten named her Nefernefrure and vowed to himself and his wife that he would love her as dearly as he would have loved a son who sprang vibrant from the womb praising his name and singing a hymn to the Aten. Nefertiti was at first unsure whether or not to believe him but relented gratefully when his actions proved the veracity of his words. He doted on Nefernefrure as much as he had doted on any of the others; to such an extent, in fact, that Nefertiti began to wonder if he was not doting on her as much to make his point as he was to enhance the idyll of her childhood.

Before long, though, Nefertiti began to notice a certain distance in the king. He visited the harem more often than was his usual habit. He met with Nefertiti less often in her bedchamber, and when he did so, seemed to be there only because it was expected of him.

"That is how his father started," Tiye said one day, after Nefertiti had quizzed her about Akhenaten's behaviour. "It is probably how they all start."

"But what does it mean?" Nefertiti asked.

"That he is about to bring home another wife, my dear," Tiye said.

"Never," Nefertiti said. "He would not."

He did.

Her name was Kiya. She was a wife far down the ranking of the harem who had been brought over from her home in Mitanni as one of a series of diplomatic marriages arranged by Akhenaten's courtiers. Akhenaten himself had always paid her scant attention, as he had with all his other minor wives. He was disinterested in what amounted to good or bad diplomacy in the area of his wives.

"They are here, are they not?" he would say, and that would signal the end of any discussion of the matter.

Akhenaten made it abundantly clear to all at court, and all who saw the pictures of him frolicking and playing with his family, that he had only one priority when it came to women. Or, rather, he had six priorities, and those six were Nefertiti and her daughters. He had no room in his private life for anybody but them, and this was a fact in which he invested not a little pride. After Nefernefrure's birth, though, Akhenaten had no choice but to review his policy on rivals for his Great Royal Wife. There was the matter of his succession to consider.

"I am not surprised," Nefertiti told Tiye after Akhenaten had taken her by the hand into their private chambers to break the news to her and insist that it meant nothing. "You warned me that this was about to happen."

She was speaking the truth, but she was lying when she insisted that she was neither upset nor jealous about this new wife and the rooms she had taken over in the palace.

"Is she younger than you?" Tiye asked, and Nefertiti nodded and started counting the floor tiles in her head in an attempt to stem the flow of tears.

"Well, that is no matter," Tiye said, seeing her distress. "At least she cannot be more beautiful. Let him keep his ugly women."

Nefertiti made a noise that was half laugh and half sob. "Thank you," she said.

"What is she like?" Tiye asked, for although she realised that it may be a painful for Nefertiti to discuss, her curiosity could not be held at bay.

"Light skinned," Nefertiti said. "She wears short Nubian wigs and large earrings."

"Humph," Tiye said, as though she had never heard a more disgraceful description. "I am sure she is no threat to you."

"And what if she bears him a son?" Nefertiti asked.

"Well," Tiye said. "Someone has to."

Nefertiti broke down into unrestrained tears, and, cursing her own candour, Tiye held her and whispered soothing noises.

"I am sorry, my dear," she said. "I meant no offence, but the king needs an heir. To die without one would be a betrayal of our dynasty. I am sure that you would not like to see all your grandmother Thuya's hard work go to waste."

Nefertiti's weeping subsided into convulsive sniffles.

"I have always stood by him," she said.

"And I am sure you will continue to do so."

"But *this*," Nefertiti said. "I have *always* stood by him, from when he was bullied at school to when he was overwhelmed at his accession to the throne, to his deification, to his blindness. Everything. I have always been by his side, no matter what I thought or what he said. And this is how he repays me?"

"My dear, you must see this from Egypt's point of view. From your family's point of view. It is his duty to provide an heir."

"You mean it is mine," Nefertiti said. "How does he know I will fail to produce one for him?"

"I do not wish to be cruel, but you are hardly in your prime any more. You are still the most beautiful woman in the kingdom, but you must begin to accept that you cannot continue producing children as though you were conjuring them from nowhere. You have already confounded probability by surviving five pregnancies. Do you wish to tempt the gods to take you to their bosom more than you already have?"

"My next child could be the son of which we dream."

"Yes, it could," Tiye said, with a sigh, with just the mildest hint of impatience. "But then it could not. Perhaps it would be another daughter. Perhaps it would be the child that killed you. Is Akhenaten not showing his love for you by removing the risk?"

"No," Nefertiti said. "I think, rather, that he is showing his disdain and his ingratitude."

"Well, if that is what you choose to believe, there is little I can do or say to dissuade you. But you will see. You will see that Akhenaten loves you still."

It was little consolation for Nefertiti. Secretly, she did not believe Tiye's assertion that Akhenaten's actions were carried out with the best interests of the dynasty in mind. For what was the dynasty if outside blood had to be imported into it? This Kiya woman was not a member of the family and she had no place within it. Akhenaten and Nefertiti were both Thuya's grandchildren; it was their responsibility to continue the dynasty, not some Mitannite temptress.

But there was ultimately little she could do to change the situation other than pointedly snub Kiya in the corridors of the palace. Akhenaten would not be drawn on the subject, other than to repeat his mother's words so closely that Nefertiti began to suspect that he had been primed by her.

It was only a matter of days after Kiya's installation in the palace that Aye came to seek Nefertiti out in the privacy of her bedchamber.

"Did you know about this?" he asked her, before the door had closed behind him.

Nefertiti was being prepared for bed by her attendants, all of whom shrieked in surprise and leapt into positions calculated the most likely to protect their mistress's dignity.

"Father!" Nefertiti said, clutching her nightclothes tightly to her neck.

"Did – you – know?" Aye said, emphasising each word as though it was its own sentence.

"Of course not," Nefertiti said. "I... I had my suspicions."

"And you never came to me?"

"How could...?" she began, and then looked at the attendants, who still crowded her as though protecting her from physical harm. "You may go," she said. One or two looked at her doubtfully. "You may *go*," she said.

Aye tactfully turned his back to watch them leave the room, giving Nefertiti the opportunity to arrange her clothing.

"How could I come to you?" she asked, after Aye was once again facing her. "These last months you have been closer to the king than have I. You have surprised people with your about face."

"I have done nothing but show loyalty to whom it is owed. An example that you would do well to follow."

"Really?" Nefertiti said. "And to whom is my loyalty owed? To my family or my king?"

"They are one and the same," Aye said.

"You know what I mean."

"Yes," Aye said. "I do. But what is to become of your family if the king and this woman produce between them a son? What then for Nefertiti, the proud mother of five pointless daughters? What then for

Thuya's mighty dynasty that was destined to rule Egypt for a thousand years? Thrown away. Cast aside. Handed to this Mitannite and her bastard offspring."

Aye leaned forwards and, placing his hands firmly on his daughter's shoulders, he looked her in the eye.

"You cannot allow that to happen," he said.

"I cannot prevent it," Nefertiti replied. "What would you have me do? I am no longer in my prime. To have another child would be dangerous, especially if I became pregnant so soon after giving birth to Nefernefrure. Perhaps the Aten has decreed that I shall not produce a son. Father, we must accept the situation and make the best of it."

Aye flung himself away from her with such a flourish of impetuous annoyance that she was forced to take a step backwards.

"Never!" he cried, and took a moment to rein in his anger before continuing. When he spoke again it was quietly, and with slow deliberation.

"I have seen all this before, with Amenhotep. That was a terrible thing, and it cannot happen again."

"What happened?" Nefertiti asked.

"He took a Mitannite wife. She became pregnant."

"And what became of her?"

"She... she died. As did her child."

It had been guilt about the past as much as anxiety for the future that had sent Aye darting through the palace corridors into Nefertiti's apartments with such alacrity. As soon as he heard the news he had been able to picture the king's new wife as easily as if she had been standing before him, and she had looked like Giludkhepa's twin. In Aye's mind she was already pregnant with Akhenaten's child just as Giludkhepa had been pregnant with Amenhotep's, and Aye knew too well where that must lead.

He had not thought about Giludkhepa and her child with such clarity for a long time. Their deaths had never constituted an episode of regret for Aye, for without their deaths there may never have been a dynasty, but that did not mean his memories sat comfortably with him. He had hoped that the dreams in which he saw the figure of Amun standing motionlessly in the shadows of Giludkhepa's bedchamber while Aye found himself unable to flee were behind him forever, but he now suspected their imminent return. He was filled with dread at the prospect of Akhenaten taking another wife not because he did not want to have to take matters into his own hands as he had done with Giludkhepa, but because he knew that he would do so without hesitation should the need arise.

"You must become pregnant again," he told Nefertiti.

"At the risk of my life?"

"At the risk of everything," he told her.

Horemheb walked slowly along the dockside. He was contemplative, his hands behind his back, looking up at the façade towering over him. It was almost deserted now, quiet enough for him to make out the creaking of ropes on the ships tied to the landing stages behind him. Amun's temple did not only look deserted. It looked as though it had never been inhabited. Horemheb, at the prow of his ship, had noticed on the approach to the harbour that not only the temple but the whole of Thebes seemed to have been scared into hiding by Mahu's attack. Of the few people that Horemheb could see on the streets, none remained in evidence by the time his ships had docked, and now only the cries of birds accompanied him as he approached the mighty gates of the temple, still ajar as they had been left by Mahu's men.

It was only on passing through the gateway and into the temple courtyard that Horemheb appreciated really for the first time the power of the enemy that Akhenaten had joined in battle. Not a stone had been kicked from its place, not a statue touched, not a frieze scratched. Here was the love that the populace of Thebes felt for their god. The gates had been open and the temple unguarded for months, and yet Horemheb could see from the tableau before him that when he passed through into the temple proper he would find it just as pristine. Not a gold chalice removed, not a medallion stolen. Each room of this temple probably held enough gold to free any Theban from toil for the rest of his life, and yet the respect and fear for the god to whom it was dedicated had guarded it more effectively than an entire army could have done.

Horemheb sighed and signalled for his men to disembark. He could only hope that they were not so enamoured of the old gods as were the people who had not taken the opportunity to loot this temple.

The men assembled in ranks along the dock and were marched into the courtyard. Only half of them were armed. The rest carried hammers and chisels, or ladders and scaffolding requisitioned from the artisans and sculptors of Akhetaten.

"You know your work!" Horemheb shouted to them. "You will be allocated a space by your officers. Work it diligently, for I shall be personally inspecting every handspan of this temple, and personally meting out punishment to any man found lacking in concentration or application. Is that clear?"

"Yes sir!" the troops shouted back.

"Then to your duties," Horemheb commanded. The men were split into sections. Some busied themselves around the walls while others were led through the doors into the temple by their officers. Horemheb made a mental note to have them searched before they returned to the ships.

He patrolled the inner perimeter of the temple walls, behind the backs of the men who worked on them with chisel and hammer. He looked for all the world like an unhurried browser in the marketplace, but only because he was making a conscious effort to do so. In reality he felt every hammer blow as though it was made against his heart. Stone splinters flew around his head and fell at his feet like the tears of Amenhotep's statues.

Everywhere the name of Amun was to be found, everywhere likenesses of his face glared out from the wall, the chisels were applied. Everywhere the word Amun was to be found – even when it was within the names of Amenhotep III, or his grandfather, Amenhotep II – it was erased from existence. Huge scars were left in its place, for Akhenaten was not concerned with aesthetics, but only with results. All along the walls, offerings were now made to empty spaces and jagged holes. Sentences in praise of Amun and Amenhotep trailed off into nothing. It looked to Horemheb like a battle scene, and each expurgation was a casualty. It looked far more bloody than images painted onto stone had any right to do.

Horemheb wandered inside, but more of the same awaited him here. If anything the vandalism was more pronounced here, if only because of the increased frequency that the objects of worship appeared on the walls. Statues of Amun were being removed and thrown into baskets for removal so that they could, depending on their medium, be melted down or smashed up. It was less a battle here than a massacre of innocents. Horemheb's men worked in silence, each alone with their deliberations on irreverence and blasphemy.

Horemheb retreated to his ship with orders for his officers to come and find him once the task was complete. He sat for some time alone in the semidarkness of his cabin, his head in his hands. He never did inspect his men's work.

The Maya Papyrus, Fragment 118

> *I took no pleasure in this. Truly, I did not. For one thing, I was afraid. For another, I have never been one in taking pleasure in the misfortune of others, even when that misfortune serves me as loyally as did this. Do you see what you have done? I wanted to shout at him. But it would have done no good.*
>
> *"Your Majesty, I have news of Ribaddi of Byblos," I told him.*

"Ah, Ribaddi," he said, with a smile that exuded smugness like a lamp exudes light.. "Did I not tell you that he was fussing over nothing? I have heard nothing since I told him to keep his counsel. And, as I remember, you wanted me to go to war, did you not, Maya?"

"Your Majesty," I said. "Ribaddi is dead."

His smile evaporated. "Dead?" he said.

"Dead. Soldiers of Amurru invaded Byblos and took the city. They found Ribaddi in his palace. They marched him outside and they cut the throats of his wife and his children, and then his parents, and then him."

"How came you by this news?" Akhenaten said.

"Two of his household guards escaped by ship. They are being cared for by the court physician."

"They are here?" Akhenaten said. "In the palace?"

"Yes, Your Majesty," I said.

"And what, may I ask, makes you so sure that they are really members of Ribaddi's guard? What makes you think they are not emissaries of Abdi-Aširta, sent here to put me to death? Have you checked? Or did you simply wave them into my palace and bid them make themselves comfortable?"

"Your Majesty," I spluttered, momentarily forgetting myself. "Byblos has fallen! You did not help a loyal vassal against a common enemy and now he is dead!"

"That does not change the fact, Maya, that you have put the life of your king in jeopardy!"

Akhenaten shouted for the guards on permanent duty outside the doors to the audience chamber. There was the smallest hint of panic in his voice. For a brief moment I assumed that the guards were for me. I have never felt fear like it. In the space of a heartbeat my entire body flushed with cold and my legs lost all but the strength needed to keep me on my feet.

"Your Majesty," I began, fully prepared to beg for my life.

"Guards!" Akhenaten shouted again, and the doors burst open with the application of pressure from half a dozen men, all of whom spilled into the room at the same time.

"Your Majesty," I said. "Please..."

Akhenaten could not hear me. The guards immediately surrounded him as though to guard him from attack, weapons drawn, eyes wild.

I took a step backwards, my hands held up in some form of denial or calming gesture, I know not what. "Your Majesty," I said once again, and with each reiteration the words were imbued with less confidence and more fear. It was now more a question than a plea for his attention.

He spoke to his guards, but I did not hear what he said. I was calculating the distance between myself and the door and the probability of being able to reach it before the swords of the men arrayed before me. I had already concluded that success was unlikely without any element of surprise and I had begun to tense myself to dart towards freedom with no warning of my actions when the guards rushed at me.

I screamed and, covering my head, sank to my knees, praying only that Akhenaten would allow me to live long enough for me to be able to plead for my life. "Please, Your Majesty, please," I said, repeating myself as though to persuade him not with reasoned argument but with the sheer depth of my capitulation.

And then the guards were gone and the unexpected sound of the door slamming made me jump and whimper. I raised my face from the protective shelter I had formed from my forearms and looked up at the throne.

Akhenaten looked down, a confused but still smug smile on his lips.

"Maya?" he said.

I looked around me. The guards were gone.

"I thought..." I said. "I thought..."

"You thought what, Maya?"

I pushed myself to my feet.

"Nothing," I said.

"You clearly thought something, Maya," Akhenaten said. "A man thinking of nothing does not suddenly fall to the ground and shriek like a woman."

His words hurt me, but then I think they were calculated to.

"I thought you had summoned the guards to come and kill me."

"Do you think that would have been justified?"

I had no idea what he wanted me to say, so I told the truth.

"No," I said.

"And do you think me in the habit of making unjustified decisions?"

"No," I said again.

"Really, Maya," he said, sighing in the manner of a parent whose patience is exhausted with a wayward child. "Then if I am not in the habit of making unjustified decisions, why were you afraid that I had made one this time? Do you in fact expect me to make such bad decisions?"

"Not at all, Your Majesty," I said.

"Then logic dictates that if you thought I was summoning the guards to kill you, you must think I would have been justified in doing so."

I allowed him to humiliate me. Standing before the throne, I bowed my head and stared at my feet. I justified my attitude to myself. Sometimes, in my more self-obsessed moments, I believed myself to be the only sane man at the palace and as such the safeguard, however ineffectual, against the king's more preposterous follies. It was barely true, but it was enough to allow me to tell myself that it was better for everyone if I accepted my humiliation now, for then I could continue in my defence of the realm. I took my cowardice, held it close to my heart, and called it courage.

"Well?" he said.

"Yes, Majesty. I thought it would have been justified for you to order your guards to kill me."

"Because?"

"Because my mortal heart cannot comprehend your divine thought process and so I did not understand the reasoning behind your decision not to save Ribaddi's life. This led to unforgivable impertinence on my part and I throw myself on Your Majesty's mercy."

He seemed a little assuaged by this, even if I was not.

"Hmm," he said. "Perhaps there is no harm done. I have despatched my guards to deal with those whom you have invited into my palace."

"What will become of them?" I asked.

"They will be judged as are all strangers who come before me, by the Aten."

"Your Majesty," I said, weighing the wisdom of each syllable before daring to utter it. "They are men who have seen much horror and much hardship. I would beg you to bestow your divine mercy upon them."

"I already am, Maya. I am not killing them. I am merely allowing the Aten to judge the loyalty of their hearts. Now, you said that there were a number of matters that you wished to discuss with me. I hope those to come are more reverential than the first."

It was a clear sign that the subject was closed. I have done what I can, I told myself. There is no sense in angering him, I told myself. I can help nobody if I am dead, I told myself. Cowardice as courage.

"Your Majesty," I said, "it grieves me to the very depth of my soul to have to impart further bad news, but..." I indicated with the amount of scrolls I held exactly how much bad news there was.

Akhenaten sighed. "Is it really bad news?" he said. "Or is it just another half dozen Ribaddis, complaining over nothing?"

I took a deep breath and told myself I was holding my temper, while another part of me laughed at the thought that I would ever dare let it free in this company.

"The Hittites are on the move," I said. "We have had news of incidents all along our north eastern borders."

"Incidents?"

"Nothing more than skirmishes at this stage."

"Nothing to worry about then. Next."

"Your Majesty," I said. "They are only skirmishes because Hatti is unaware of the lack of troop coverage we have in the area. If they knew how vulnerable we are they would attack without a second's hesitation."

"Nonsense. Our army is the mightiest in the world. They would not dare."

"Just so," I said. "Our army is indeed, as Your Majesty says, the greatest in the world. But it is scattered around the country chiselling out the name of Amun from temples and palaces. It is in no state to defend itself or Egypt."

"Maya," Akhenaten said, with the measured approach of one who wishes the meaning to be wrung from every word. "After the wilfulness you have already displayed this morning, I dearly hope you are not calling into question the importance of my army's current assignment?"

The very idea.

"Nothing could be further from my mind," I said. "The army are protecting you from insurgency and false gods, and there can be no greater role than that, but even that is useless if while they are doing it the Hittites pour across the border and arrive at the doors of your palace."

For a brief moment, such that I would have missed it if I had chosen that moment to glance down at the scrolls in my hand, Akhenaten looked genuinely scared.

"Impossible," he said

"Your..." I began, but he held up his hand, which silenced me.

"Impossible," he said again, firmly.

I held the scrolls out, knowing they were useless to him. "The reports from the borders," I said. "I only ask that you consider Egypt's defence, and the defence of her loyal vassals abroad."

"I have considered it," Akhenaten said, "and I cannot in all good conscience countenance the distraction of my troops from their primary task, and their primary task is the protection of their gods."

"Yes, Your Majesty," I said.

"Anyway," Akhenaten said. "I have other concerns. I am to have an heir. The kingdom must be prepared. We have celebrations to arrange."

He was smiling again, proud, all thoughts of borders and aggressors forgotten.

"An heir?" I said. "A boy?"

"So the physicians assure me."

"The physicians have told you as much before," I said. "With Nefertiti's history it may not be prudent to rely too much on them."

"I am aware," Akhenaten said, "of what is and is not prudent without your petty little reminders. And anyway, Nefertiti is not the only one who is pregnant."

"Your Majesty?" I said.

"Kiya is also bearing my child. It is a glorious sign from the Aten. At least one of them will be a boy. It will be interesting to see which one it is, will it not?"

I bowed from the room, Akhenaten's mischievous giggle clinging to me like a parasite, my scrolls still tightly clutched in my hands, forever unread by anyone with the power to act upon their contents. They were almost entirely written in haste and untidy in execution, the ink blotted and smudged, the words misspelled and sentences convoluted and difficult to unravel. They were written by the officers of border garrisons and rulers of foreign principalities from within inner rooms and safe houses, in darkness and panic with Hittite soldiers hammering at the doors and climbing through the windows. They were the purest expressions of faith; faith in kingship, faith in responsibility, faith in loyalty and duty. And yet Akhenaten, the god aspirant, had reacted as though the need and nourishment of faith was *unworthy of him. I have always held that a god needs faith as we mortals need air, and Akhenaten was perilously close to suffocation, for faith unreciprocated is nothing more than wishing, and wishing rarely begets a satisfactory outcome.*

Nakhtmin was not enjoying himself. Not strictly speaking. Foremost in his mind, as always, as everywhere, was Duty. Everything else fell behind it and was judged only in comparison to it, coloured by the echo of orders, the burden of expectation. So it is not that Nakhtmin was not enjoying himself, or not happy. These emotions were not absent, they were just not relevant.

Nakhtmin did, however, allow himself to help out with a hammer and a chisel on the more exclusive sites to which his troops had been assigned. It was good for morale for the commanding officer to occasionally dirty his hands alongside his men. They respected him for it and if it was handled correctly it did not breed familiarity. Subordinates were much more likely to lay down their lives in battle for a commander they respected and slightly feared than for one whose orders were followed merely because of the lack of an alternative.

At the end of the day he remained in the temple a short while after his men had filed out towards the local barracks. Around him darkness closed in as the sun lowered itself below the parapet of the courtyard wall, and the sounds of Abu Simbel beyond the walls became muted as though the twilight was a blanket. Around him, on all four walls, was the evidence of his labours and those of the men under his command, and although the marks were being slowly consumed by the night they shouted out to him, unmistakable even in this light.

He wandered over to the wall that was facing him and ran his hands over the scars. It felt uncomfortable and yet strangely compelling, like brushing fingers over an open wound and being surprised at its depth. Some good work had been achieved here today, he decided. The questions of morality and religion did not surface in his mind. There was no morality. There was no religion. Only the king and the kingdom, and Duty.

The scrolls continued to arrive at the palace, and Akhenaten continued to dismiss them. As with all state correspondence they were engraved into stone tablets for permanent storage and then destroyed. The tablets were transferred to the House of the Correspondence of the Pharaoh and then forgotten. They were snapshots of trauma, as though a lamp had been lit in a darkened room to briefly illuminate two men about to embark on combat.

The kings of the neighbours of Egypt were like lions, circling their prey, so aflame with the prospect of blood that they snap and claw even at each other. The Hittites and Mitannites fought each other without mercy, knowing that only the annihilation of the enemy would secure their homelands from invasion. The land of Amurru, meanwhile, recognised that both were at their weakest when pitted against each other, and that an Atenist Egypt had no stomach for a fight, and so took the rare opportunity to help herself to any scraps that remained when the combatants had slunk away to regroup and replan.

Egypt's properties abroad were stripped one by one. The Hittites moved into positions that were only a few days' march away from the Egyptian border. Mitanni appealed for help and was ignored, King Tušratta's letters piled up alongside all the other cries for help in the House of the Correspondence of the Pharaoh. The alliance with Mitanni, uneasy even when at its strongest, crumbled away like old limestone.

Akhenaten would listen with growing impatience to his advisors and ministers. They were repeating themselves, he told them repeatedly. They had been scaremongering for weeks or months, and they were still here, bereft of sword wounds, their houses and families intact and safe. For how much longer would they continue to spread their malicious cowardice before they came to realise that Akhenaten was right, had always been right, would always be right as long as he had the guidance of the Aten to lead him by the hand through the darkness of politics and war?

Even Aye, who had been so ingratiating of late, began to harp on about the Hittites this and the Mitannites that. *Enough!* Akhenaten wanted to shout (and did, on occasion). *Do you have nothing better to tell me? Nothing more to ask? When I have my two wives by my side, their bellies racing to fecundity?*

Sometimes the two wives, Nefertiti and Kiya, would sit either side of Akhenaten's throne, Nefertiti looking sullen and embarrassed at being paraded for men to coo insincerely over, Kiya looking proud and noble for the same reason. They appeared to be growing at the same rate, as if their expanding waistlines were a changing fashion that they were both endeavouring to follow.

"They will almost be twins, these children of mine," Akhenaten liked to joke, as he stroked each woman's belly. His attendants and ministers would smile as though they had never heard him say it before and shuffle uncomfortably at the fact that they had to broach the subject for the Hittites and the Mitannites and the Amurruvians once more.

The court physicians examined the women and confidently predicted the gender of their unborn children. In actual fact, the result of the tests on the women's urine indicated the exact opposite of the results that were given to the king, but the physicians knew well enough by then that it was better to be popular than correct, that the previous predictions had been proved wrong five times on the run, and that surely Nefertiti would be able to manage to produce a boy at the sixth time of asking. The doctors had looked at the emmer and the barley upon which the two women's urine had been sprinkled. Kiya's barley grew, but the emmer did not, indicating that her child would be a son. Nefertiti's emmer grew, but the barley did not, indicating that she would bear yet another daughter. The doctors, after a brief discussion on the likelihood of this, simply swapped the labels on the flora and took Nefertiti the good news.

The Maya Papyrus, Fragment 119

> And still the defeats came. Abdi-Ashirta's son, Aziru, harried our lands and killed our subjects and allies in Asia. With Ribaddi dead, there was no intimidating the Amurruvian troops into leaving his soil. Half of Asia was lost to us. In Syria we heard only of defeats and retreats, which I announced to His Majesty on an almost daily basis, only for him to wave his hands at me in a weary manner and ask if I had anything joyous to tell him for once.
>
> I did not.
>
> In Palestine a local hoodlum rose from the ranks, calling himself Labaya of Shechem. He mounted an ambitious campaign against our interests in his homeland, and was defeated not by Egyptian troops as he deserved to be, but by Palestinian loyalists to Akhenaten's crown. But killing Labaya was like ridding a house of a bee's nest by smashing the nest. Labaya's sons rose and stung everything within reach. Palestine, it seemed, was to be lost to us as well.
>
> Only protracted begging on the part of his ministers pricked Akhenaten into taking action, and while the resulting defensive engagements were meagre, they were our lot and we had to be happy with them. The problem was not a lack of enthusiasm in the Egyptian forces, but a lack of discipline and training. Akhenaten's troops were not soldiers of the army, for the army was still scattered around the kingdom, chiselling walls and holding each other's ladders. No, the men sent out to defend

everything that Egypt held in foreign lands were themselves foreigners. They were mercenaries, and mercenaries fight for only one thing. They were Nubian archers; they were Semitic spearmen; they were Libyan slingers; they were unprincipled, loutish, dirty men with no allegiance other than to their purses, and every time I unrolled a scroll bringing news from the borders I held my breath until I saw that it was not telling me that the mercenaries had turned against their benefactors.

I almost fainted when I read of their exploits in Jerusalem, whence they were sent to protect Jerusalem's prince and Egypt's friend, Abdi-Kheba. Realising there was more money in fighting against him rather than with him, they broke into his palace and helped themselves to whatever was small enough to fit through the doors and windows. When an outraged Abdi-Kheba appeared in his nightgown to lodge his complaints against their officers he was hacked to the floor and left for dead.

Life at home was hardly much better.

The plague was still with us, and its virulence was becoming such that more people than me were beginning to give it that name, and Mahu's police were still making night calls, although unlike the plague they appeared to be running out of victims. It became customary, when asking after an acquaintance who had not been seen for a while, to simply ask "Plague?" If the answer was no, it usually meant that the police had got him.

All this, together with the stories leaking into the city via the river of defeats abroad and merciless enemies at the gates of Egypt, leant the city a claustrophobic quality as though the people within were struggling to breathe from the pressure they were under. Every conversation had a distressing premise; that an invasion, with its attendant rape and murder, was imminent; that the plague was on the verge of a devastating escalation; that Akhenaten was to have every other man, woman and child in the city executed as a lesson to his detractors. That none of these things happened did not seem to lessen the expectation that they were only days away. And still the stories came from the traders, still the plague claimed its victims, still there were families where the husband was not there one morning and the pale wife was never asked where he had gone.

It seemed that life would continue this way forever.

And then Akhenaten summoned us – myself, Aye and Tiye – to the palace. Audiences at the palace were becoming a daily trudge to hear one insane soliloquy after another. Sometimes it would be myself alone, sometimes, presumably, my father or Tiye alone. The more significant Akhenaten thought his announcement to be, the more of us who were summoned to hear it. When all three of us made our way into the audience chamber it was enough to set the heart at a gallop. Perhaps the fact that, on this occasion, Nefertiti was absent and the king's eldest daughter, Meritaten, was at his side in her mother's place should have given me pause, but my thoughts were too preoccupied with what may transpire to be alerted to it.

We prostrated ourselves before the throne, with varying degrees of effort and noise. Tiye was ageing quickly by now, as though racing to be back at her husband's side. Aye was more supple, but hardly likely to spring to his feet with anything approaching a flourish. I helped Tiye back up after we had accepted our royal blessing.

"I am to marry again," Akhenaten said. The three of us looked to Meritaten and thought we knew what was to come. In hindsight, it was hardly surprising. A king could marry his daughter, if he so desired, but only a king. A commoner, or even the most senior member of court, could not. It would be unthinkable.

For a king took his daughter's hand in a marriage that was different to the marriage of a man and his wife. A king's daughter, once she was his wife, was there merely as a helper, a crutch, as a foil in the religious ceremonies that required a king's wife to be present when the king's wife was detained elsewhere. They would sleep not as husband and wife but as father and daughter, as master and servant, not only in different beds or rooms, but sometimes in entirely different palaces.

"My daughter Meritaten and I are to be married," Akhenaten said, and I was already preparing to begin reading out the scrolls that I carried under my arm announcing our latest military defeats, the most recent betrayals by our mercenaries.

"Meritaten is to bear me a child," Akhenaten said, and I dropped my scrolls.

Chapter Seventeen

ta-sherit

The Maya Papyrus, Fragment 121

AS THE *most senior member of court not directly involved in the royal wives' fretful pregnancies I was expected to greet the returning heroes, Nakhtmin and Horemheb. I was also, of course, Nakhtmin's brother, and as such I could be trusted by my superiors at court to be both ebullient in my praise and lavish in my gifts.*

I hardly needed telling that they were no ordinary men, these two conquering generals. They had saved Egypt from a great evil, and had single-handedly defeated ruthless temples and dastardly tombs, vicious statues and bloodcurdling engravings, armed only with the swords in their hands, their fleets of ships and an entire army at their backs.

Nakhtmin and Horemheb disembarked from their ships in Akhetaten's harbour, each accompanied by an honour guard from their troops. The crowd waved and whistled and cheered, watched as they were by the king's agents. I was standing a little way back, separated from the crowd by burly soldiers, flanked on either side by servants holding the gifts with which I was to shower the generals to commemorate their glorious return. The generals stopped at the bottom of the gangplanks that led down from the decks of their ships. They waved at the crowd and the crowd waved and shouted back. I could tell that neither man wanted to move before the other. Horemheb's ships had arrived outside the harbour days before Nakhtmin's had returned, but he had made a point of waiting so that he would not receive all the glory and Nakhtmin would not set foot back in the city already as old news.

After two or three minutes they were still waving, and the crowd was still cheering. I could see out of the corner of my eye the arms of my servants starting to tremble under the weight of the gold they carried. Another minute or two, and neither the waving nor the cheering looked to be in any immediate danger of coming to a standstill. I looked to the heavens for help, finally realising what was happening.

Nakhtmin was not going to move so much as a hair on his wig while he continued to be cheered with such abandon. Horemheb, an indulgent and almost private smile upon his lips, was going nowhere without Nakhtmin. The crowd, meanwhile, were aware that they were being watched, that all gatherings of this kind were dissected and analysed to glean every morsel of information from them. Nobody wanted to hear their front door splintering in the night and awake to find an unfriendly face leaning over their bed, wanting to know why they had been the first to stop cheering Akhenaten's heroes.

Eventually I had no choice but to step forwards and wave my hands in the air in a calming gesture, quietening the crowd as I walked. Nakhtmin looked faintly aggrieved, Horemheb faintly grateful, but at last they were able to step forwards and feel the solid ground of the harbour beneath their feet.

I spread my arms in welcome and gestured to the servants, who stepped forwards. One by one I dipped into the trays that they struggled to hold out to me. My hands found heavy pendants, rings, bracelets, all delicately crafted from gold and bejewelled with turquoise and lapis lazuli. By the time I had finished the two generals could hardly be seen beneath their adornments. Had the gifts stretched as far as crowns, neither would have been distinguishable from a king. Such was Akhenaten's gratitude.

Three chariots were standing at the entrance to the harbour. I led Nakhtmin and Horemheb towards them, ensuring that my smile remained broad and my step light. I could not help noticing Horemheb glancing at me as we walked, meeting my eye in a way that I could only interpret as meaningful without being able to actually discern the meaning behind it. Nakhtmin, on the other hand, was unable to tear his gaze away from the crowd that lined the route. He would occasionally lean forwards over the linked arms of the soldiers who prevented the crowd from surging forward, and touch those who reached out for him in return. Horemheb obviously found this both ridiculous and risible, for he insisted on nodding in Nakhtmin's direction whenever he caught my gaze and smiling in a rather cabalistic manner. I smiled back, confused rather than conspiratorial.

As we reached the chariots, Horemheb touched my elbow and leant in close to me.

"He enjoys this, does he not?" he said, once more nodding towards Nakhtmin.

"I believe he does," I said, and Horemheb stepped onto his chariot, seemingly satisfied with my answer. I watched him for a moment. I somehow had the impression that there were more to his nods and questions than met the eye and ear. He seemed to be asking more than his words professed, and in these times of Mahu's men and the suspicion that they engendered, his actions prodded awake a distrust in me that never deeply slept.

The three of us headed off through the city along the King's Way, accompanied always by the crowds. We dismounted when we arrived at the palace gates, which had been opened for us in advance. I could see Horemheb engineering to walk beside me as we passed from the street into the courtyard. Here, for the first time, Horemheb and I found ourselves out of earshot of any of our entourage. Nakhtmin was still at the gates, once again playing the crowd with jokes and the grasping of outstretched arms. I could have screamed my disapproval at his back from an arm's length and he would not have noticed.

Horemheb touched my elbow again. It was a habit that was beginning to irritate me already.

"Your smile is much more transparent than I think you believe," he said.

"I have no idea what you mean," I told him.

He laughed gently and gave me a knowing nod.

"What?" I said, although I knew exactly to what he was alluding. I had tried to look welcoming and enthusiastic on the dockside but I was presumably no more an actor than I was a warrior. And yet, however obvious were my lies, it was not something that I was ready to admit to someone who I barely knew. It was not, for that matter, something I was ready to admit to a lifelong friend or my closest relatives.

"I can tell a lot from a man's smile," he said, and despite myself I almost began to enjoy the situation. He knew what he was saying, as did I, and we both knew that the other knew, but both of us were too wary to admit it. And yet I got the impression that Horemheb was willing to drop his guard further and quicker than was I. I felt as though he trusted me, and it was flattering to be seen as steadfast by one in whom so much power was vested. Of course, in hindsight I can see what a skilful diplomat he had already become. I was not feeling anything that he had not *decided I would feel, and he was no more ready to drop his guard than he was to take me by the hand and dance with me.*

"I can tell, for instance, whether or not it is genuine," he said. "Especially in one so unused to subterfuge."

"Ah," I nearly said. "But you are wrong. My entire life is artifice so close to this king."

But of course I could not, and he knew I could not, and his eyes glistened with mischievous pleasure as he watched me force myself to agree with him.

"And would you care to tell me what you were failing to hide?" he asked. "Your disapproval, perhaps?"

"Of what could I possibly disapprove?" I asked, trying to marshal my features into something resembling innocent enquiry.

"You disapprove of me, and of Nakhtmin" he said, still with a warm smile. "You disapprove of the task which we were given. It will profit you little to deny it. Every gesture, every forced smile tells me of it."

It was said with such warmth, such camaraderie, that it was difficult to deny. Even if it had not been true I think I would not have denied it, such was the persuasiveness of Horemheb's voice, the calmness of his tone. I felt like a confidante, and the fact was that I wanted to be the confidante of a man like Horemheb. And I reciprocated the trust he led me to believe he had in me. And anyway, if he was telling me the truth, he already knew.

I shrugged.

"If the gods are dead I do not see the point in defacing their temples. If they are alive I do not see the wisdom in it."

There was a moment when the two of us simply looked at each other. Knowing Horemheb as I do now, I believe that he paused purposefully, just long enough to let him have his private little joke, just to let me know who was in charge.

And then, quietly, he said: "I agree."

He turned away from me and headed into the temple courtyard. The conversation was over.

"What will be the child's name?" Tiye asked.

"What does it matter?" Aye replied.

"Did he not say?"

Aye looked at her. "Are you not listening to me?" he said. "The child is a girl."

"Yes," Tiye said. "I was wondering what he was going to call her."

"Setepenre," Aye said, with a gesture designed to convey the fact that he thought Tiye exasperating and her conversation trivial.

"It is a pretty name," Tiye said.

"A pretty name?" Aye said. "Our dynasty is ripped from our grasp, the throne is lost, and your considered judgement of the entire debacle is that Setepenre is a pretty name? Have you any conception of what has just happened?"

"Do not patronise me," Tiye said. "I am as aware as you."

"No," Aye said. "I do not believe you are."

There was a venom in Aye's voice but Tiye had never been afraid of him. He was a formidable man but she was, after all, Amenhotep's widow and a Great Royal Wife, and Aye at his angriest knew that there were limits even he must observe.

"What harm is there if Kiya has a son?" she asked him. "It will still be Akhenaten's child. The dynasty will continue."

"The child will be a foreigner, like his mother. A foreigner on the throne of Egypt. You can see what state the Two Lands are in under Akhenaten. Can you imagine the depths to which they will sink under a king raised by Akhenaten and a wife over whom we have no control? It will be the end of Egypt."

"You are exaggerating," Tiye said.

"Exaggerating? Tiye, it is almost the end of Egypt already. Enemies mass on our borders and the king does nothing. Plague walks the streets, and the king does nothing. Will he teach these values to Kiya's son? At least if Nefertiti were to have a son we would have some control over him via his mother."

"There is something else that has put you in this mood."

Aye looked at her. "There is nothing else. There need be nothing else to put me in a temper such as this. We are in the midst of a disaster."

"You are your father's son," Tiye said. "It is like having a conversation with him. Everything is a disaster. Every setback is an irretrievable loss. We will find a way around this. The gods will come to our aid."

"The gods?" Aye said, incredulously. "The gods? They have not been very conspicuous in their aid so far. Is that all that you expect us to rely upon?"

"They have helped us before. They will help us again."

"When?" Aye said. "When have they helped us? Did I miss it? Was I otherwise engaged when these gods swept down from the heavens and guided our family through its storms?"

"The messenger from Šuppiluliumas," Tiye said.

"Which messenger?"

"The one who never arrived," she said. "Are you telling me that was nothing to do with the gods?"

Aye remembered the messenger he had imprisoned in the palace in Memphis. It seemed inconceivable that the man could still be alive. Aye had locked him in his cell a lifetime ago, and there he would surely have withered within a few years, or possibly even months. He would already have been weakened by his long journey and the darkness and the food of prison would have done nothing to aid his constitution into recovery.

"I think it more likely that bandits played a role in that," Aye said.

"Perhaps, but who put the bandits there, where they would cross his path? It was the work of the gods."

It was something of which Aye had never been proud. He had never spoken of it to anyone bar his mother. It was not something for which he wanted to claim any credit, for he reasoned that there was no credit to be made from condemning an innocent man to a lonely death in a foreign prison, but then it was not something for which he wanted the gods to claim credit either. After all, he had helped preserve Amenhotep's tenure on the throne, which made it an act of heroism in its own way.

"It was me," he said, without enthusiasm.

"What was you?"

And so he told her.

"And what about Giludkhepa?" Tiye said when he had finished. Aye prayed that she did not see him wince at the mention of the name. "Are you going to tell me that the gods did not have a hand in that?"

"None of this matters," Aye said. "Talking of the past does not help us deal with the present."

"Giludkhepa and her child did not just die," Tiye said. "They were killed."

"Enough!" Aye shouted.

Tiye looked taken aback. "Aye, whatever is...?"

"Will you stop talking of the past? It cannot help us."

"But it can," Tiye said. "That is exactly my point. The gods will come to our aid as they have done before."

"The gods have never come to our aid."

"But Giludkhepa..."

"I killed Giludkhepa!" Aye shouted, and then, in a sudden vision of a host of servants within earshot on the other side of the door, he said again, but softly, as though to whisper would quieten his earlier utterance: "I killed Giludkhepa."

"You...?" Tiye said, breathless with astonishment.

There was a moment of uncomfortable silence. Aye did not want to speak, and Tiye seemed incapable of it.

Finally, she said: "And the child? Giludkhepa's baby?"

Aye nodded.

Both lapsed back into the silence of their own thoughts.

"I had no choice," Aye said, eventually. "The child was a threat to the dynasty."

Tiye grunted noncommittally, still lost in introspection.

"But do you see why we cannot rely on the gods to help us? In the past we have only helped ourselves."

"You have," Tiye said, in the tones of an accusation.

"We all have," Aye said. "Did you not persuade your husband to take courses of action dictated to you by our mother? Are you really better than me?"

"I did not kill a baby," Tiye said, quietly.

"You would have done differently?"

Tiye did not answer him. Instead, she said: "And what now? What of Kiya? What if she produces a son? Is she to die as well?"

Aye remembered the darkness of Giludkhepa's bedchamber and the sound of her breathing and her baby's quiet sighs. He remembered the weight of the cushion in his hands and the feel of her beneath him. He remembered the strength ebbing from her arms and the blows they dealt against his shoulders. He remembered his retreat, and he remembered turning and seeing the silhouette of Amun in the corner of the room, arms folded, a forked tongue darting from his cobra's head. It was only later that Aye remembered that Amun's presence had only been in the guilty dreams that had haunted Aye's sleep. It was a realisation of little comfort, for Aye knew that those dreams were not meaningless.

"Is she?" Tiye asked.

"If there is no alternative," Aye said. "If her life, and the life of her child, stand in the way of this throne and its rightful heirs, then those lives shall be forfeit. Would you have it any different?"

Tiye looked away.

Setepenre, the sixth of Nefertiti's daughters, was less than three weeks old when Kiya felt the first pangs of her own confinement. This birth was not as easy as had been Setepenre's. It was Kiya's first, and while she had all the attention and attendants that Nefertiti had grown used to, she did not have Nefertiti's experience, nor her build. The extremity of pain was something that Kiya had never felt before, nor hoped to again. But at the end of it, as she held the child in her arms, she professed to all that would listen that every moment of it was a debt repaid by the knowledge that this baby, this son, was born safe and well and heir to Akhenaten's throne.

"Ah!" Akhenaten said to Aye, when told the news. "I have a son! Are these not the most excellent tidings?"

No, Aye thought. They are not.

"Yes," he said, instead. "Indeed they are. Most excellent."

"Spread the news to my court and my kingdom," Akhenaten told the runner. "Let my people know that I have an heir, and that he is strong and healthy."

Aye left the king's company at the earliest available opportunity. He found Kiya in her bedchamber, where the priests and nurses had carefully carried and placed her, as though she was the baby. A nurse had followed, the prince sleeping in her arms, and had placed him in a crib at the side of his mother's bed.

By the time Aye arrived, both were sleeping, Kiya occasionally wincing and quietly crying out as she moved in her sleep and pain flared in her abdomen. Aye was never alone with her and the prince for more than a few moments at a time because of the constant stream of nurses to soothe her brow with water, doctors to hum and haw over the bed and the crib, and priests to offer their prayers. Throughout, Aye remained in the corner of the room, barely noticed, barely moving. He simply watched, at times intent on his subjects as though willing them to wake under the pressure of his gaze, at others distracted and seemingly unaware of his surroundings.

He was heard on occasion to be muttering to himself, although none who heard him could make out the words, strain as they might as they meticulously straightened bedclothes that were as flat as they were ever likely to be.

He was picturing how it would be to kill the princess and her baby. He could imagine it perfectly. The baby would not struggle. Although it may already have been old enough to possess a desire for life, it was not yet developed enough to do anything more than randomly flap its limbs. It would take seconds. Kiya was still weak from the birth, as Giludkhepa had been in her last moments, and would be unable to offer any significant resistance. The actions were replayed in his mind, again and again. He memorised the position of every piece of furniture, every ornament and gift. His eyes followed the route he would need to take after he gained access to the room in darkness. He sought a weapon that could be disposed of as easily as be acquired.

He remembered the terror of discovery and the summons to Amenhotep's audience chamber the morning after Giludkhepa's death and pushed it to the back of his mind, where it plotted with the dream of Amun to unhinge him. With a weaker man, he told himself, it may have a chance of success, but I know my place. I am the servant of this dynasty, not its master. If Thuya were here she would offer nothing but encouragement, and what I do I do for her and for Egypt.

He did not notice the expressions of relief on the nurses' faces as he made to leave the room, and he did not notice Kiya's eyes opening as he stepped past her bed.

"Aye?" she said, as he was about to cross the threshold.

He stopped, but he did not turn.

"Aye?" she said again, and this time he had no choice but to turn and face her. He had instinctively stopped at the sound of his name, and he could now hardly claim not to have heard her.

"Kiya," he said, by way of greeting.

"Does His Majesty know of the birth?"

"He does, Your Highness," Aye said, the title almost sticking in his throat.

"He knows it is a boy?"

"He does."

"Is he pleased?"

"Ecstatic, Your Highness."

"And does my son yet have a name?"

"Indeed he does, Your Highness. He has called the boy Tutankhaten. It means 'living image of the Aten'."

"Does it?" Kiya said. "Tut-ankh-aten."

She was asleep again before Aye had left the room.

When he dreamt, he always seemed to dream of Amun. He would wake feeling drained, as though he had never closed his eyes, as though Amun was still standing in the corner of the room, watching, his cobra's eyes never wavering, never blinking, his tongue flicking the air like a whip. He repeatedly relived moments that were yet to happen, feeling the guilt before the crime, the guilt of intention, the guilt that Tiye forced upon him with nothing more than a look and an intake of breath.

Eventually, Tiye began to notice the rings around his eyes that were pronounced enough to be seen clearly through the face paint that he had taken to smearing across his features with increasing vigour.

"So you have decided on a course of action I see," she said to him one morning over breakfast.

"I have not said as much," he said.

"You do not have to," she told him. "I have all the information I need."

She indicated his eyes with a piece of half eaten pomegranate. "Your decision does not allow you much rest."

"You know nothing of my decision."

Tiye shrugged. "You must do whatever you feel is right," she said, although her tone gave him more meaning than her words, and it was a meaning at odds with what she had actually said.

"Exactly," Aye said, but without enthusiasm. He picked at one or two pieces of fruit on the table. Part of him had regretted his confession to Tiye as soon as it had been out of his mouth, and she had done nothing since to make him feel that such regret was misplaced. Her every word was reproach, as though he had not saved her family from obscurity. Conversely, the confession was not something that could have been avoided for much longer. It had accompanied him for so many years it was almost like a limp or a scar. It had become part of him, although it was a part of which only he was aware. It was as though he had eaten fish and swallowed a bone. The bone was long gone, but the scratch in his throat reminded him of it every time he swallowed. And now he was an old man, or was at least approaching old age at a furious pace. It was no longer a limp he felt strong enough to bear on his own. Not when his judgement at the hands of Osiris was so imminent.

He was beginning also to regret his rush to a decision, although he considered it possible that this was coloured by his disturbed sleep. But the eyes of Amun would not leave him alone, and the memory of the weight of Giludkhepa's pillow was enough to drag him down in the lake of misery in which he floundered.

"I *have* come to a decision," he told Tiye, "and it is not the decision which you suppose. Tutankhaten shall live."

Tiye was startled enough to be caught frozen, her food halfway to her mouth. "How very magnanimous of you," she said, hiding her surprise.

"Do not mock me," he said.

"And what has brought about this turn of events?"

"Thought," he said. "Just thought. The boy is no threat. He may yet turn into an ally. We will have to see if he can be groomed for the throne. For our throne."

"But he will not be a continuation of the dynasty."

Aye shrugged. "At the moment there is nobody he is displacing. Should another son be born I may have to reconsider."

But when he awoke the following morning Aye could not remember his dreams for the first time since Tutankhaten's birth. He began to wish, despite his every instinct, that the king would have no more sons to upset the balance Aye had forged for himself.

The Maya Papyrus, Fragment 128-131

I believe I have never seen a man so transformed as was Akhenaten after the birth of his son. For him there were no worries about dynasty or family or tradition. All there was was an heir, a boy who could lead Egypt forever onwards in its glorification of the Aten after Akhenaten had himself gone to join his heavenly father in the sky.

The changes I saw were, of course, entirely superficial, but they were still enough to bring a smile to my face after too long an absence. The boy remained with him at every waking moment. After a month or two I suspect Kiya may have had trouble picking the baby out in a crowded room, such was Akhenaten's devotion to him. Tutankhaten would be bounced upon his knee, or chucked under the chin, or tickled or hugged, even when Akhenaten was in the midst of an official audience or ceremony. Only when the child cried or needed feeding or changing was he hastily handed over to his wet-nurse, a woman who excelled under the name of Maya.

Many a happy joke was to be had when Tutankhaten threatened to cry and Akhenaten would hold him out at arm's length, call for Maya to provide a breast at which he could suckle and then make to hand the boy to me. How we laughed every time this happened, until I thought we would still be laughing at it long after Tutankhaten had grown too old to cry or need suckling and would easier lift Akhenaten than the other way around. Even one's humour is subordinate to that of a king, no matter how low that may be.

But despite the falseness of the levity and the hands held against sides which steadfastly refused to ache, Akhenaten seemed happy, and happiness is stronger even than paranoia. With every laugh it seemed as though Mahu took a step back into the shadows that populated the corners of the rooms.

I too, I have to admit, was besotted with the boy. He was delightful company, more disposed, in those days of infant innocence, to laughter than to tears. A lack of care was wrought upon his features and it was easier to stare at him and smile than it was to be depressed or frightened by the daily roll-call of disaster that our audiences with Akhenaten had become.

There were many occasions when I reached out to take the child from Akhenaten as he held him out to me, only to realise after I had taken a step forwards that it was once again the joke about the wet nurse that shared my name. Akhenaten is nothing if not persistent.

Occasionally there to laugh along with us, and just as falsely, was Meritaten, Akhenaten's eldest daughter. The deceit of her laughter was different to mine. In mine there was simply the absence of humour; in hers was the antithesis of it. She seemed to me to be the opposite pole to Tutankhaten. In the baby there was innocence and naivety. In Meritaten there was nothing but Akhenaten's child. Her belly was by now swollen enough to trouble her when she sat down or stood up, and it was a sight that disturbed me greatly, as it did all who saw it and knew what was inside her. In unguarded moments, when she believed herself to be unobserved, I could also see that it troubled her no less than it did everyone else. Her smile would fade, and her colour with it, and she would adopt the expression of someone who had swallowed something unpalatable. I felt sorry for Meritaten, and those looks of despair that occasionally betrayed her nigh on broke my heart asunder. She was as loved by Akhenaten as much as ever – more so, in fact, since she carried his child – and Nefertiti loved her and pitied her in equal measure, but this could never be enough to offset the fact that she was pregnant with her father's baby.

Still, she bore her burden with all the grace that her station in life depended. In one thing at least, from the vantage of her future, I can call her lucky. Meritaten's life had stranger surprises yet in store for her that nobody, even one as twisted as Akhenaten, could ever have envisaged.

When the time of Meritaten's confinement came she accepted it with the stoicism that had characterised her pregnancy. I chanced to be in the king's audience chamber early one evening when the word came that her pains had started and I caught a glimpse of her being helped past the door along the corridor. She walked gingerly, with her hands resting on the shoulders of the nurses who flanked her, but her face portrayed only physical pain, and for that dignity I lauded her.

I was grateful that Nefertiti, Aye and Tiye soon arrived to hear news of the birth first hand. It was impossible for me to have left, and the prospect of spending the following hours with only Akhenaten and Mahu for company was an excruciating one.

It seemed, to the gratitude of everyone concerned, that Meritaten was not yet finished displaying her strength. At fourteen years of age she could hardly be described as a child, but this was her first baby and she was yet of slight build and so those *of us in the audience chamber ordered food and drink from the servants and settled down for a long night. To our amazement we were hardly comfortable when the doors from the main corridor opened and the guards bowed into the room, announcing the king's physician. The man looked slightly dishevelled, as though he had been taken by surprise before he had finished dressing.*

"It is over," he said, in the peremptory manner that doctors are wont to adopt, even with royalty.

Nefertiti gasped audibly. "Over?" she said. "So soon? Is she...? I mean..."

The doctor saw that his announcement was open to misinterpretation.

"I mean that the child is born, Your Majesty," the doctor said, at last observing protocol and bowing low to the king.

"I am a grandfather?" Akhenaten said.

"Er," the doctor said, looking from one of us to the other, unclear as to Akhenaten's exact relationship to the new baby. "Yes?" he hazarded.

"And the child?" Aye said. "Does His Majesty have another heir?"

"The baby is a girl," the doctor said.

Aye scowled but Akhenaten seemed disinterested in the news. "It is of no matter," he said, dismissively. "I have an heir already."

"Yes," Aye said, "but you have only one, and..."

Akhenaten held up his hand. Aye fell into an abrupt and unhappy silence.

"I am to name my new child," Akhenaten said. We gave him our undivided attention.

"She shall be called Meritaten," he said. We stared at him, and then at each other.

"Meritaten?" I said, speaking for us all.

"Meritaten ta-sherit," Akhenaten said. "Meritaten the Younger."

"Will that not be somewhat confusing, Majesty?" Aye said.

"I have spoken," Akhenaten said.

Aye bowed. "Majesty," he said.

"And should Meketaten have a girl, she shall be called Meketaten ta-sherit."

Nefertiti turned to him. "Meketaten?" she said.

Akhenaten smiled.

Tutankhaten charmed the palace. Courtiers and visitors – to whom he was always introduced - would congratulate the king on siring such a well behaved, happy little boy. Only to themselves would they acknowledge their amazement that such a man could father his exact opposite. The priests in the Aten temples, knowing wherein the safety of their future lay, would fuss and coo over him whenever he was taken there for worship with such enthusiasm that ceremonies, already seen as interminable by almost everyone but Akhenaten himself, could sometimes double in length.

Tutankhaten's earliest and happiest memories were of the Great Aten temple. The length of the ceremonies was not something that overly concerned him. They seemed primarily to be opportunities for the priests to express their love and loyalty to him and his parents, and for him to bow at the feet of carvings depicting the sun, which always seemed to be shining its rays solely for his family. The other parts of the ceremonies, the speeches and offerings and sacrifices, he was content to sleep through.

Kiya, too, was honoured. She was the woman who had provided the throne with an heir, and had, in that one act, been elevated to being the mother of a god. A temple was built for her in an area of the city known as Maru-Aten, wherein were built altars and shrines to the Aten, for her use alone. There were gardens and a lake to aid her relaxation, and even the pavements were painted with marsh scenes and flying birds to take her mind off the sand that blew in from the surrounding desert. She was often to be found here, away from the palace where an unexpected meeting with Nefertiti could never be ruled out. Whenever she was summoned to the king's side she knew that Nefertiti could be there, waiting with Akhenaten, refusing resolutely to give her so much as a smile.

Kiya had pitied Nefertiti at first. She could understand her chagrin, to spend so many years producing nothing but daughters and then to be upstaged so effortlessly, and by a foreigner at that, and one with only a fraction of her beauty. Kiya was under no illusions in comparisons of herself with that other royal wife. Kiya could not compare, neither in physical appearance nor stature nor temperament, and so she did not attempt to. After all, she did not need to. She was the mother of the king's son, and that counted for more than anything Nefertiti had ever possessed. But she was equally aware that her power made her vulnerable and that those who had been weakened by Tutankhaten's birth were also made all the more dangerous by of it.

Still, she estimated that neither she nor Tutankhaten were in any immediate danger. Although Aye privately did not believe her capable of it, she had analysed the situation with some prescience. On the occasions when the king was too busy or preoccupied to have his son sitting upon his knee to witness the affairs of state, Kiya was allowed to have him accompany her on her constitutionals around Maru-Aten. She would walk the decorated pavements with him in her arms or, later, with him at her side, his hand clasped tightly within hers. The boy was the only confidante in whom she invested any real trust, and even that was eroded with every passing month and the increasing possibility of his understanding her and accidentally repeating her comments to those at whom they were directed.

But on her early walks with him he was too young to either understand or repeat her and she was able to talk more freely than almost anyone in the city.

"My prince," she would sigh, glancing around even here to ensure they were as alone as she believed them to be. "What a blessing that you have no inkling of the weight upon your shoulders."

She tickled him under the chin and Tutankhaten laughed up at her as though to emphasise the lack of his cares in this world. She held out a finger to him and he grasped it tightly.

"What a blessing that you have no idea that this little hand holds not only the future of the Two Lands, but the life of your mother within its feeble grasp. We both walk a narrow path, my prince, with crocodiles on one side and snakes on the other. If we lose hold of one another even for an instant then we are doomed. Your father is mad, your mother is jealous and your grandparents are ruthless. What a world for a little prince to have to grow up in."

They came to the lake and Kiya sat down under an awning that had been erected at one end to provide some protection from the sun. Birds and insects glided over the surface of the water.

They would sit there often, mother and son, in the years that followed, until Maru-Aten was taken from them and Kiya's name was chiselled out of every inscription by Akhenaten's troops, before the entire construction was re-dedicated to the name of Meritaten and Kiya disappeared, leaving no legacy behind her save her son and Aye's insidious smile. Before all this befell her she was almost able to mark her son's childhood with their visits to Maru-Aten, for they were so infrequent that Tutankhaten seemed to have changed and grown visibly between each one. The rest of the time Kiya would spend here alone while Tutankhaten sat on his father's knee and, later, stood quietly by the side of his throne, observed by all with warm smiles.

As time passed and Kiya found herself able to talk less and less to her son about anything other than the banal, the pair would eventually sit mainly in silence, simply watching the wildlife and enjoying the opportunity of being in each other's company. She would not see

Tutankhaten grow out of the innocence that made her honesty with him so dangerous, and she would never have the chance to warn him of the fate that lay in wait for him.

The Maya Papyrus, Fragment 136-139

> *Here was the reason that I loved Tutankhaten: he remained perfectly still, a smile playing upon his face as though placed there by a mischievous breeze. He showed no signs of boredom or restlessness. He neither fidgeted nor fussed, he made no noise, he displayed none of the loathsome habits of other children of his age. Many of Akhenaten's progeny were well-behaved, for the gravity of their station in life was pressed into them at an early age and without respite, but even so Tutankhaten was the most good-natured of them all. He listened attentively by the side of his father's throne although it was doubtful that he understood anything but the most rudimentary episodes of what passed by his ears and eyes in the audience chamber.*
>
> *It was perhaps a miracle of temperament, or perhaps merely an indication of how little that Tutankhaten understood of the conversations and dramas that were played out before him (however remarkable I believe the boy to have been, I favour the latter), but his smile never faded, regardless of the worsening news that was brought in from the world outside Akhetaten's walls.*
>
> *Horemheb and Nakhtmin both begged to be permitted to act to prevent the slide down which both Egypt's internal politics and external diplomacy had begun to slip, but despite Horemheb's eloquence and Nakhtmin's obstinacy, both were prevented. It was not important enough for Akhenaten to wish to act. When the roads between each city and the next fell into such lawlessness that survival at a journey's end was celebrated with as much surprise as thankfulness, Akhenaten answered that the Aten would watch over the pious traveller and that all creatures, even the bands of robbers, were his handiwork and his tools. When the last of our cities beyond our borders fell to marauding robber bands and opportunistic foreign potentates, Akhenaten lauded it as a blessing that the heathen were once again amongst their own kind where they belonged. When Hittite troops crossed our borders and sacked the towns that were unlucky enough to lay in*

their path, slaying the women and children with as little compunction they did the men, Akhenaten expressly forbade Horemheb and Nakhtmin from taking their troops to extract their revenge. Egypt was strong, he told us. The Aten would not allow any fate to befall her that she was not capable of absorbing without so much as a bruise. And anyway, the troops commanded by Horemheb and Nakhtmin were needed for other, more important duties. For what was the security of our country and the well-being of its citizens when measured against the calamity of Amun's name remaining unexpurgated from a temple wall in Elephantine? What possible consequence could be the erosion of our borders when there were families in Akhetaten who insisted on risking the destruction of Egypt from within by hiding statues of their household gods in covered alcoves in the darkest corners of their homes?

And there were even more problems to divert the mind of our king, and thereby to test our wits and patience to their very limits. All of my days were spent fawning before the throne, for there was no longer any other way of dealing with Akhenaten whilst trying to persuade him to see the reality of any one of the horrendous scenarios that were being played out in and around Egypt.

Egypt, it transpired, beyond anything else that may have been happening to it, had been reduced to a state of poverty. This was almost beyond my comprehension, beyond what could ever seem possible not only to me but to any man at court; to any man, for that matter, throughout the entire kingdom. Egypt had been the most prosperous nation under the gaze of the gods since the gods themselves were young. When Amun spat out the pantheon that had gestated in his mouth, grown from his own seed, he spat them into a firmament that domed a land for which he and they would provide throughout the whole of history like no other god could provide for any other land. This would continue for a million years, so we had learned, Akhenaten and myself and our classmates, although it now seemed that their reign was to be somewhat shorter than our teachers and priests had led us to believe. Amun and Mut and Ptah and all the others had turned their backs on us, and who could blame them? We had, after all, turned our backs on them.

It seemed impossible but this guardianship had now been withdrawn, and with it had gone Egypt's wealth. Impossible for more reasons than one. During the reign of Amenhotep, and indeed during the reigns of all of this eighteenth dynasty as far back as Hatshepsut, the priesthood of Amun had been as rich almost as the throne itself. It owned almost as much land. It was no small contribution to the threat that Amun posed. And yet here we were, the temples of Amun dissolved and the priests scattered to the corners of Egypt or the underworld that lay beneath it, their riches stolen by the king's emissaries and brought within reach of the king's grasping arms. And within the reach, therefore, of his city's gulping mouth.

For although Akhenaten's riches were, for a time, almost unbounded in their staggering depth, they disappeared as easily and with as little trace as a cup of water poured onto desert sand. Akhetaten was a project so complex, its temples and palaces so opulently fashioned and filled, that almost nothing was left of the vast wealth of the temple of Amun.

So impoverished was the king that his troops were for a time diverted from their mission of desecration to another task, equally onerous, and were sent around the towns and villages dotted along the Nile to collect the king's taxes, and to do so with a fervour never previously seen in these lands. It was not enough. Had every inhabitant enjoyed the wealth of one such as I it may have made a difference, but peasants, farmers and servants have so little that to tax them at all seems unjust, and even a millionfold of their contributions could be nothing more than a kitten against a Sphinx of debt.

His diplomacies, never better than naïve, fell to immeasurable depths. Ambassadors of our neighbours began to appear at Akhenaten's palace gates, returning his gifts to their kings which, despite Akhenaten's assurances, it appeared were statues fashioned from wood and then covered with gold paint. Amenhotep had promised his contemporaries solid gold, and this was not a misrepresentation of the items that he sent out with his emissaries. Akhenaten also spoke of gold, but he meant wood. He spoke of lapis lazuli and turquoise, but he meant paint. He spoke of wealth, but he preached trickery. The kings of our neighbours saw this not as frugality but as a snub and an insult. When their representatives returned with the gifts Akhenaten granted them audiences and then informed them that he had only ever promised them wood and paint in the first place and that he was surprised to see again what he had sent from his country in good faith.

Of course, one could never have concluded with reference only to the appearance of the royal family that Egypt was becoming impoverished. No poverty was allowed to roam the corridors of these palaces. Akhenaten himself, and those within the shadow of his smile, continued to live as though the coffers were bulging at the hinges. Those who fell from favour, and those towards whom Akhenaten was ambivalent, soon began to feel the withdrawal of costly favours. Unfortunately, this included the king's contemporaries abroad. The avenues for diplomacy that Amenhotep had so lovingly tended began, one by one, to be closed off.

The emissaries were sent away with their gifts intact, too afraid and closely escorted to press their points home with too much force, but still bewildered as to how Akhenaten could ever hope to be believed.

Perhaps if Egypt's troubles during the second half of Akhenaten's reign had been limited to those of an economic nature events may still not have unravelled as they did.

Throughout Amenhotep's reign the granaries of these Two Lands had been in danger of bursting under the pressure of the food stored therein. Hardly a year passed when the Nile did not enter into her inundation with gleeful abandon, ensuring that our crops grew with equal enthusiasm. Now, though, we found that we could no longer so optimistically rely upon such a bountiful nature. The Nile was no longer so predictable in its rise and fall. It rarely now grew to the heights and depths and widths that it had seen under Amenhotep. It had, on one or two occasions, failed to rise at all. There is little so distressing or overpowering as an Egypt that has not seen an inundation of the Nile for two years. Egyptian soil is as dead as the stones that litter it. Without its annual bathing in the divine waters it cannot sustain a crop, and so when the waters do not rise the gods do not imbibe the soil with life, and when that happens the farmers would probably enjoy as much success if they cast their seeds on the pavements of Akhetaten as on their own fields. The first year that the Nile failed to flood there were one or two raised eyebrows around court, but of course, nobody deemed it safe to pass comment. In any case, there was nothing particularly to worry about. Amenhotep had bequeathed us such riches in food that the Two Lands could easily withstand one or two lean years.

The following year the Nile flooded again, and those (including myself) who had seen the previous year's crop failure as yet another facet of Amun's retribution began to relax and privately smile and shake their heads at their own scaremongering. We were so grateful to see the flooded fields that we did not pause to consider the quality of the harvest. It was enough to feed us, but only that. There was no grain left over to begin restocking the granaries. The next year was the same, and then the flood failed completely once again.

It was a cycle that was repeated, with varying degrees of severity, throughout Akhenaten's reign. It seemed as though every year we took a step towards famine, and whether that step was a giant stride or a half-hearted shuffle, it was always towards the darkness and the barren desert and never away from it.

The signs could not have been more blatant if Amun had descended on Ra's chariot, wagging his finger and shaking his head. His anger was matched only by his mercy. He was punishing us; of that no sensible man could have any doubt, unless his reason had been dazzled by Akhenaten's absurd teachings. But, while punishing us, he was offering us clemency. He was offering us the chance to halt our march towards disaster. All we had to do was forsake Akhenaten's false gods and turn our eyes back towards the light of Amun and the pantheon that ranked alongside him. There was no sense in him destroying us with one wave of his arm, although to do so was undoubtedly within his power. For what would he be then left with? An empty Egypt was as much use to him as it was to us. And so, every year, we were offered a warning. Every year we were escorted closer to our doom. And every year, under Akhenaten's unfaltering leadership, we relinquished the possibility of saving ourselves.

And now I brought to Akhenaten the worst news of all. Tutankhaten was, as always, by the king's side. His father had become increasingly severe and unforgiving as the years had passed and as his woes had mounted up against him. It was usually impossible to guess which of his many moods would be temporarily paramount from one audience to the next, and so now, more than ever, did one risk the consequences of careless speech. I would sometimes dare not even raise myself up from the prone position before the king's throne as I begged him to attend to the latest calamity.

"Your Majesty, I beg to report that the failure of this year's inundation has put further pressure on the granaries."

"Of course it has, you fool," Akhenaten said. "Did you come here to tell me that?"

"Not entirely, Your Majesty," I said. "Unfortunately, the drain on the granaries has been such that I have to report that they are now empty."

"Empty?"

"I have it on the best authority. I have checked and rechecked the numbers. It seems that we no longer have any safeguard against famine. If next year's inundation…"

He waved me quiet again. *"Do not patronise me,"* he said. We stood in contemplative silence for a few moments, both of us picturing the scene. Famine had not visited the Two Lands in the memory of even the oldest of its citizens, but tales had been related down to us from generations past; generations who had been so overwhelmed with corpses that piles as high as a man's head had been left to rot in every street in the land. Our thoughts may well have extended into the afternoon had they not been interrupted from an unlikely source. It was Tutankhaten who spoke, and this was uncharacteristic enough for the sound of his voice to startle me, even before the meaning of his words had time to chill me to the core.

"Good," he said, simply. The smile returned to his face.

Akhenaten and I stared at him for a moment. He looked from one to the other of us.

"Good?" I said. *"Good, Your Highness? Forgive me, but I am not sure you fully understand the situation."*

He looked uncertain for a moment, as though my gentle rebuttal had been enough to unseat him from his confidence.

"There is no more grain in reserve?" he asked.

"Yes, Your Highness."

"So, if the Nile does not flood next year, we will all starve?"

"Yes, Your Highness," I said again.

"Then I understand fully," he said. *"And I say again: good."*

Was this a monster, I wondered? Had he been growing before me every day and hiding his nature from me? Surely not. Surely there would have been some sign that would have betrayed him. I was floundering for an answer.

"Explain yourself," Akhenaten said to him.

"Father," Tutankhaten said. *"The Aten knows all, does he not?"*

"Of course," Akhenaten said.

"Then he must know that the granaries are empty."

"Yes."

"Then surely we are guaranteed a bountiful harvest next year?" Tutankhaten said. *"For the Aten would never bring down upon us a famine. Not while we worshipped him as the one true god."*

Akhenaten laughed. I simply gaped. It could have been Akhenaten talking, although Tutankhaten's words were couched not in malice but in genuine enquiry.

"But of course!" Akhenaten declared, delight etched into his features. "Maya, do you not see? Your constant doomsaying is entirely misplaced! The boy is correct. My father the Aten will never allow famine to stalk these lands. Not while he is revered as I revere him. This is a cause for celebration, not misery and fear. Fetch my chariot. We will give thanks this very day for this happy turn of events!"

"There is nothing I can tell him that will make him recognise the truth," I told Horemheb later that afternoon. I had just endured an interminably long service wherein Akhenaten made endless offerings at the altar of the Aten to give thanks for what was essentially the inevitability of famine.

In the time since he and Nakhtmin had returned from their sojourn defacing Egypt's temples I had grown increasingly close to Horemheb. His dry wit entertained me and his power and patronage flattered me. I was eager to reciprocate the trust he obviously held for me. Everybody I knew was, to a greater or lesser extent, associated with the king, and even those I trusted were not above a slip of the tongue. I had kept many a dangerous secret in those years, and they had long since ceased to be a burden that I felt privileged to carry.

Horemheb, though, I had grown to hold in a regard stronger than that of simple trust. I felt his integrity to be unquestionable and his self-discipline and restraint were such that there was negligible danger of him accidentally endangering me with the king. My only concern was his relationship with my brother Nakhtmin, for I had learned of old that Nakhtmin's discretion was such that he could be trusted with neither kind word nor cruel. I expected that Horemheb, as his closest friend, would be happy to share my words with him. My fears were quickly proved to be unfounded.

"You know, do you not, of your brother's reputation?" Horemheb asked me once, shortly after our discussion that day of his return from defacing the temples of Amun.

"Reputation?" I said, innocently. This was before I knew Horemheb well enough to trust him.

"He has never been malicious," Horemheb said, "but let us say he is not known for his quick wits. Your words to him may be repeated before ears for which they were never intended."

Since that day I had been happy to speak candidly with Horemheb. I had the added insurance that almost all of our conversations implicated him as much as they did me.

And so, when I told Horemheb of my fears that Akhenaten could not be forced to recognise the truth, I did so secure in the knowledge that this was a private conversation.

I told him of the morning's events in the audience chamber.

"It is a shame about the prince," he said.

"Just so," I said. "But he can hardly be blamed. Which of us would not have believed our father's every word at that age?"

"Very true," Horemheb said, distantly. "Very true."

"What are you thinking?" I asked. I knew Horemheb well enough by now to know when his mind was elsewhere.

"Nothing," he said, suddenly, as though returning from a daydream. "Nothing at all."

And now this.

After everything, the final blow. Akhenaten was alone, brooding in the semidarkness of his badly illumined audience chamber. Nobody expected him to be here, so there were no attendants. His servants assumed him to be asleep in his bed chamber, and so he was confident that they were not outside the door, awaiting his command. He had lit some of the lamps himself, stumbling and cursing at first under the veil of his night blindness, but became bored before the job was half finished. Only the lamps behind the throne were lit, and some of these had not caught properly and were guttering unpredictably, making his long shadow on the floor and wall in front of him twitch and shudder like an enraptured dancer. The gloom did not disturb him. It matched his mood, somehow comforting his black thoughts. He watched the shadows for a few moments, his elbows on his knees and his chin resting in his hands. His servants had not been here to provide a cushion for his throne and he shifted in the seat, trying to find a comfortable position on the bare wood. He had no idea where the cushions might be kept, and had no intention of risking being caught searching the ante-rooms and cupboards. Whatever else might be happening around him, he still had his dignity. He briefly considered summoning a servant, but quickly decided that he would rather be uncomfortable and alone. Anyway, he doubted if he would find any of them in their quarters. They would all be with his wife, with Nefertiti, crowded out into the corridor outside Meketaten's room, pushing and standing on tiptoes to see the tragedy all the better. Akhenaten wanted no part of it. It was a death, not a festival, and he had more intention of searching for cushions than he did of adding to the indignity of the situation and sanctioning it simply by joining it. Nefertiti would be sitting on the bed looking forlorn and tearful, with priests and physicians so desperate to help they would be getting in each other's way as they raced aimlessly from one part of the room to another. Behind them would be a press of lesser attendants and nurses and beyond them, pushing for a better view, would be everyone else. And in the middle, the quiet, calm majesty of Meketaten, already on her journey through the underworld, her daughter, Meketaten-ta-sherit, held in a nursemaid's arms. Akhenaten had no stomach for such a scene. It seemed to him that he had stomach for little of late.

Outside the audience chamber's door he heard bare feet slapping against the tiles as someone ran along the corridor. He looked up and watched the door, willing it to remain closed. It did so, and the footsteps receded. Akhenaten's head dropped and he once more began watching his shadow.

"She was your granddaughter," he whispered into the darkness. "How could you do this to your own granddaughter? Why would you take her away from me?"

But he knew why. He knew full well why.

"I am only one man," he said. "I am doing everything I can for you. Why must you punish me for that?"

When the voice in his head answered him it sounded like his own, but he knew it was not.

Tombs, the voice said. *Sepulchres. Pyramids, even. How many of those are host to Amun's cursed name? How many can you find? You have not even begun your father's work, and yet you expect him to revere you.*

"But what about the borders?" he said. "What about the Hittites?"

What did Amenhotep teach you about wars? the voice replied. *Who can better repulse your enemies? Will you trust it to men with all their failings, or your father the god who bestrides the heavens in glory every day?*

"Who will collect the taxes for your temples if my soldiers are scouring every handspan of the Two Lands for hieroglyphs?"

Who? said the voice.

"You," Akhenaten said. "I trust you."

But it was a lonely vigil.

Horemheb had been furious over the army's inactivity. From time to time Akhenaten regretted not dealing with him more harshly. He had allowed himself, on rare occasions, to utter words that no man should be allowed to speak to his king, however essential were his skills in the service of the crown. Had Horemheb been Nakhtmin, Akhenaten would not have hesitated in ordering his execution for treason and blasphemy, but although Nakhtmin was a superb general he was nothing compared to Horemheb. Still, he had taken his first steps along a dangerous road. He had been warned.

"Remember whom you address!" Akhenaten had shouted at him, on the morning of that very day, when the imminence of a Hittite invasion was still his main concern, before the news was brought to him that Meketaten was being dragged into the underworld.

"I address Egypt!" Horemheb had shouted back, to the general consternation of those who shared the audience chamber with him. "For you are she, and I cannot separate you. But I would rather risk impiety in addressing your most holy majesty than I would risk your land and your person. For both are at risk from the Hittites, and you should make no mistake about Šuppiluliumas. He is a savage and a heathen, but do not mistake him for a dullard. He has the intelligence to know that Egypt is militarily weak but he is prudent enough to limit his forces to meaningless skirmishes. He is probing us, Your Majesty. He is like a physician, feeling for the places of weakness, the places where the pain is most acute. In this assertion I tempt your anger, but I would rather be executed for a patriot than live as a sycophant."

Of course, Akhenaten had known he had no words to match this eloquence, but he had the might of the throne, the power over the just and the foolish alike granted to him by the crown on his head.

"My soldiers," he told Horemheb, emphasizing the phrase to make certain that all within earshot understood exactly whose soldiers they were, "My soldiers will not fight. My soldiers will continue the work of the Aten, for only through this can I guarantee the Aten's benevolence. And with his benevolence, we have already won any battle we would ever have to fight."

Even Horemheb, for all his bluster and bravado, knew where the limits of Akhenaten's patience lay, and for all the risks he professed to run for the sake of Egypt and her king there were some that were taboo even for him. He stopped short of his next outburst concerning his own personal lack of faith that the Aten was capable of influencing the outcome of so much as a game of Twenty Squares. That, he knew, would be an unforgivable outburst even for Tutankhaten or one of the princesses, and it would almost certainly mean Horemheb's head. Instead, with all eyes upon him, he looked at the floor, tried to remain calm, and kept his counsel.

"Good," Akhenaten had said, turning to his other courtiers to demonstrate that the subject was closed. "Then we will move on."

But now, sitting alone in the audience chamber and watching his shadow frolic across the opposite wall, he wondered whether it was possible for him to move on at all. If the Aten had allowed Meketaten to slip into death, then surely there was nobody at court who was safe.

He did not know the prophecy of his words; nor the imminence of the doom that he had unwittingly foretold.

Chapter Eighteen

Smenkharē

The Maya Papyrus, Fragments 142-150

WHEN *I received the summons I was in my bed. The hammering on my door was urgent and loud and I awoke in fear, for I had heard that knocking described too many times by the relatives of those who had become targets for Mahu's police. For a few moments I remained motionless, as though by doing so I could remain undetected. I listened to the sounds of a servant rousing himself and padding towards the door. He was no more eager to greet my visitors than was I, for Mahu's men were just as likely to call for servants as for their masters. I heard the door open and the sound of voices muffled by the walls that separated us. I hardly dared breathe in my eagerness to decipher the words, for the sound of my breath was enough to drown them out completely. I listened to every nuance, every change in timbre, and analysed each one in an attempt to allay my fears. Surely there would be more shouting, I told myself, had they come to drag me away to the cells. But that? Does that not qualify as shouting? How eager is that voice? What does it tell me of the temper of its owner? Surely there would be no conversation at all if they had come for me? They would simply barge their way into the house and shackle me before I had chance to make good any escape through another entrance. Surely.*

My thoughts continued in these circuitous dead ends and traps, and continued even as I heard the servant's footsteps retreat from the door and grow in volume as they approached the door of my bedchamber. Surely they would have more urgency if I was being arrested? Surely the police would come to fetch me in person?

The servant knocked upon my door and, although I could not explain my logic now, I did not answer. The thought that the servant would retreat and report that he could not rouse me, and that this would be enough to deter my visitors was ridiculous, but a fervent wish all the same.

The servant knocked again, a little louder this time. He coughed.

"My lord?" he said.

I did not respond.

"My lord Maya?"

I sighed. It was no longer likely, or even possible, that his knocking or shouting could not have awakened me. Now I was feeling not only desperately afraid but faintly ridiculous. There was no way I could not answer. There was also little point, for it must have been a matter of moments before the servant tried my door and found it unlocked.

"Yes?" I said, trying to lace my voice with what I hoped was a convincing tone of somnolence.

"My lord, you have visitors."

I cursed him then for his ambiguity. Visitors? Would he describe the police as visitors? Surely not. And yet they had perhaps instructed him to keep me at my ease.

"Visitors?" I said. "At this time? Tell them to return at a more civilised hour."

"My lord, they are quite insistent. They tell me it is a matter of great import. They are here at the behest of the king." The servant paused, and when he spoke again he tried to load his words with significance. "It is the police, my lord."

"What do they want?" I spoke in a whisper, as though to encourage my servant into collusion.

"You are needed at the palace," he said.

At once a sizeable proportion of my anxiety was soothed. Prisoners were never taken to the palace. It was deemed a risk for them to be allowed so close to the king.

Outside, the night was still and cold. Above my head glittered countless bright stars. The city was silent save for the occasional sounds of the night. The cry of a baby as it woke for a feed, the splash of the night's waste as it was thrown into the sewer, the mew of cats waiting for their owners to wake to let them in. There was no possibility that I could be in danger, I reasoned, for how could the city continue as normal if I was about to die? How could a baby cry and a mother soothe it? How could the just continue to sleep? Surely there would be an air about the place, a portent of catastrophe. It was an unforgivable detour into egotism, but it served to allow me to take one step after another. Of course, in my *eagerness to hear sounds of encouragement, I heard others. I heard the coughs of those who slept, unaware that they were coughing and yet to awake to the discovery of their infection with the plague. I heard the tramp of expeditions entirely similar to my own, with those whom they were escorting as desperate as myself for thoughts of comfort. I heard the sounds of Akhenaten's city, amplified by fear and night.*

We walked into the palace and through corridors I did not recognise, with turns and junctions enough to rob me of my sense of direction and location within moments. Eventually, we stopped outside a door. Mahu was there to greet us.

"You have seen the plague," he said, with the intonation of both a question and a statement.

"I would like to meet a man who has not," I replied, confused.

"The royal family are forbidden to enter lest the demons are able to contaminate them."

He did not explain himself further, but instead pointed to the door behind him. My guard parted to allow me access and I pushed it open, expecting it to lead me into a sparse cell. I was surprised to find the room beyond both much larger and much more tastefully decorated than anything I had been expecting. It was large enough to require pillars to hold the ceiling in place, and warmly lit by numerous lamps placed at generous intervals around the walls.

I pushed the door open, and gasped.

When Nefertiti arrived she found Aye on his feet, with a smile so wide it seemed almost predatory.

"Father?" she said.

"Please," Aye said, indicating the sumptuous seating arranged around the far side of the room.

Nefertiti regarded him quizzically, unused to the formality in his tone, but she followed his gesture and walked over to the chairs. They were arranged around large double doors which Aye had propped open before her arrival. Beyond the doors the palace grounds fell away sharply in a series of gardened terraces until they were dissected by the Nile, which flowed through the landscape like a dark cut through a lavishly embroidered gown. Ships and boats of various nationalities and application dotted the river and the harbour, each moving with an easy independence of the others to create a relaxed but chaotic scene. Sails caught the sun as much as the wind, making the hulls beneath them seem dark and dull by comparison.

Nefertiti settled into her seat. Aye sat opposite her.

"The breeze from the river here can be very refreshing," he said. Nefertiti nodded but said nothing. She was unsure yet exactly what to make of the situation.

"It is a beautiful apartment, do you not think?" Aye said. He looked around him as though he needed reminding of its appearance. He smiled ingratiatingly.

"It is," Nefertiti said. "You are very lucky."

"Yes, well, lucky is one thing," Aye said. "But do not forget that I am one of the most senior men in the kingdom. These apartments fit my station. And, of course, I am not here much of the time. Only when I am needed at the palace. But you know His Majesty better than anyone. I do not have to tell you how busy he keeps us all, and so how much use I am able to get from these rooms!"

Aye spoke with polite humour, and a smile to inform Nefertiti that he really had no objection to the long hours the king expected of him.

"Why am I here?" Nefertiti asked, suddenly.

"Can a father not seek the company of his daughter?" Aye replied.

"Surely," Nefertiti said. "But you must admit that it is not entirely within character? I cannot remember when you came to see me purely for the sake of seeing me. There is usually a motive."

"A motive!" Aye said, remaining jovial. "You make it sound like I am a criminal, or a plotter."

"Not at all," Nefertiti said. "Only that you are perhaps more consumed by your duties than by your family."

"Well, exactly," Aye said. "My duties are my life, as is my king and my country. I am sure that you are the same as I."

"Perhaps," Nefertiti said.

"But," Aye said, "it just so happens that on this occasion you are correct. I do indeed have a motive for asking you here today, but it is not nearly as sinister as you may believe."

There was a short pause, during which Aye seemed reluctant to continue.

"Well?" Nefertiti said, finally.

"Nefertiti," Aye said, taking a deep breath. "You are a sensible girl. You always have been. You have made me very proud. Your achievements are rivalled only by those of Tiye herself. You have cemented the right of this family and its descendants to wear the crown of Egypt and sit upon her throne for a million years. You are a woman whose name and beauty will be famed throughout history. It is my joy to be your father."

Despite her suspicions, Nefertiti could not help smiling.

"Is that what you brought me here to tell me?" she asked.

"Yes, it is. Although not that alone."

The sounds of a commotion drifted up from the harbour, carried on the breeze from the river. Nefertiti looked down and, by craning her neck for a moment, could see the crews of two ships gesticulating angrily with each other. By the time Nefertiti saw it the incident was over and the two ships drifted slowly away from each other as though the ships themselves had exchanged words.

"Then what else?" Nefertiti said.

"I need to speak with you concerning His Majesty. And concerning Egypt. And the family."

"Is that all?" Nefertiti said, smiling.

"I am concerned for His Majesty's well-being," Aye said. He leant forwards to offer a bowl of fruit to her. She raised her hand slightly from her leg and showed him her palm as a signal to refuse it.

"I am sure that the rest of the court and the city share your unease," Nefertiti said.

"Very true. But I am not so sure that I share with the court and the city the capacity to act upon that unease."

At the harbour the two ships had docked and the row had spilled over onto the dockside itself. Nefertiti could see a man she presumed to be the harbourmaster rushing to intervene, police closing in behind and to either side of him. She could see now that the crew of one of the ships had skin coloured much darker than was common in Egypt.

"To act?" she said. She knew her father well enough to be guarded in her responses. While she understood that her father's principle loyalty was to his family, she also knew that he saw the family as an entity in and of itself, and its members were merely dispensable constituent parts. In the same way that a man's life may be saved by amputating a limb or a tree encouraged to grow by lopping off its branches, Nefertiti knew that her father believed none of the family's individual members to be essential for its continued success.

"Yes," Aye said. "To act. I for one cannot allow myself to remain inactive when everything I see around me is in turmoil. The Hittites, the plague, the famine that breathes over our shoulders, a king who is all but bankrupt. You do see, do you not, the troubles that Egypt faces?"

"I would be a fool not to."

"Exactly!" Aye said, slapping his knee to reinforce the exclamation. "Exactly. And you are not a fool, Nefertiti. You are the most able woman of your generation. Never a fool."

Nefertiti could not help wondering where all this flattery could be leaving. "Thank you," she said, simply. She did not allow herself to comment further.

"I am concerned," Aye said, sighing, "that His Majesty may be in need of some assistance."

"His Majesty has all the assistance he could ever need. He is the Aten's son. No pharaoh has ever taken advice from one so wise. The Aten, remember, is omnipotent. Do you presume to offer counsel that could countermand anything that the Aten has contributed?"

Aye looked momentarily taken aback and Nefertiti could not help feeling something approximating satisfaction at the sight. He was her father, and as such she knew that she owed him nothing but respect and obedience, but she was the Great Royal Wife, and that made him her servant. It could only benefit him to be occasionally reminded of the fact.

A few moments of silence passed. Nefertiti looked back out through the doors, down towards the harbour. The police had cleared the area of troublemakers and only a handful remained. They were all dark skinned. All the local sailors, she presumed, had the good sense to disappear at the first sighting of Mahu's men on the scene. The foreigners did not understand how the situation had changed once the police arrived. They continued to argue, pointing back towards their ship. She could see now that a long scar ran down the starboard side, put there presumably by the bow of the ship with whom they had the quarrel. As Nefertiti watched she saw the first of the policemen raising his club. She wanted to shout out a warning, but it was impossible. It would have been an act of gross indignity for a Great Royal Wife to be seen shouting from a doorway. And besides, the harbour was too far away for her shouts to be decipherable. She turned back to Aye, who had once or twice in the silence between them opened his mouth to speak and then thought better of it.

"Nefertiti," he said, and then stopped. Nefertiti looked at him and said nothing.

"Nefertiti," he said again. When she could stand his discomfort no longer she opened her mouth to speak, but he waved her quiet. "No," he said. "Please, let me..."

Aye gathered a deep breath and exhaled slowly.

"Nefertiti," he said. "Have you ever considered that you may yet have an even greater role in the governance of the Two Lands of Egypt?"

Nefertiti's eyes widened. "I do not follow," she said.

"It just seems to me that a woman of such wisdom is wasted somewhat as the king's wife."

"Wasted?" Nefertiti said, incredulously. "As the king's wife? The Great Royal Wife? Father, have you lost your senses? What higher role could I possibly have in life? Perhaps you plan to have me lifted to the heavens, or married to the Aten? Or would you have me as king?"

Aye raised his eyebrows. Nefertiti regarded him with surprise.

"Father!" she said.

Aye shrugged. "It would not be the first time," he said.

"A woman as pharaoh," Nefertiti said. "It is ludicrous. It is unthinkable. A woman, indeed!"

"Do you know the story of Hatshepsut?" Aye asked her.

"Yes, of course I do," Nefertiti replied. "Akhenaten's father used to tell it to him as a child, and he has told it to me. But that was an entirely different situation. Hatshepsut was not a pharaoh. She was a regent, safeguarding the throne until her son was old enough to inherit it from her."

"Yes, that is what she used to say. But what do you think happened when her son reached maturity? Do you think she handed the crown to him? She did nothing of the sort. She would have been mad to do so. No, my daughter, she kept that crown in her powerful little fist until the day she died. She was a pharaoh. She responded to her country's call and was not found lacking at the day of her judgement. You would do well to follow her lead."

"This is insanity," Nefertiti said, beginning to rise from the chair. Aye stood up quickly and took a step towards her to prevent her from getting completely to her feet.

"Wait," he said. There was a momentary look of fear in his eyes, fear that Nefertiti would betray him, fear that Akhenaten would ask Mahu to discover the truth of this conversation. Aye was too much of a politician for the expression to remain in his features for more than a fleeting instant, but it was enough for Nefertiti to notice it. Now she recognised tension in Aye's every movement and word. His flattery was borne not of manipulation but of submission. His desire to keep her in her seat was more panic than threat. It calmed her somewhat. It intrigued her moreso. She sat.

It seemed to pacify him. He took a deep breath which he fought to keep steady. He too sat.

"You know, do you not," he said, "how much I risk in speaking of this to you?"

"You think I would betray you?"

"I think that treachery is beyond nobody if the alternative is sacrifice. All I ask is that you listen to me. When I am done you may deal with me as you see fit."

Nefertiti nodded.

"I am not asking you to depose your husband. For that I would gladly betray myself, for it is a thought unworthy of me. I ask only that you help him. You take some of the burden from his shoulders. Surely to do so would be less of a betrayal, less of a blasphemy, than leaving him to face these tribulations alone? You can be the staff upon which he can lean his weight when he is weary. You can be the advisor he can accept without embarrassment. Do you not see how you could serve your country?"

"Then you are not suggesting that I should be king?"

"I am suggesting that you be co-regent. Just as Akhenaten was with his father. I fear that the pressure of his position is not boding well for His Majesty. I am asking you as his wife, and as a patriot, simply to stand between him and that which would hurt him."

The arguments that Nefertiti had been forming to rebut him utterly evaporated. Had she not seen the fear in her father's eyes she would have believed herself to have been manipulated, but she was no longer so sure.

"You make a very persuasive argument," she said.

"I do nothing of the sort," Aye said, shifting in his seat. "All I do is speak the truth as I see it. There is no persuasion here, no argument. Only love and patriotism."

"I shall have to consider your words."

"I would expect nothing less," Aye said.

"And if I were to follow your advice, do you think it will simply be a case of my donning the crown? Do you really think my husband would allow such a thing?"

"I shall speak to him personally," Aye said, and could not help adding to himself: by the time I have finished with him he will practically be begging for a co-regent.

He walked Nefertiti to the door, his hand held lightly at the small of her back. As she retreated along the corridor Aye remained in the doorway, watching her until she disappeared around the nearest corner. He went to sit back at the open doors and watched the Nile silently for a long while.

Akhenaten paced the floor. Lamps had been lit in such numbers that their glow reflected off the white walls and caused a pain behind Nefertiti's eyes.

"Husband, why do you not sit?" she said.

"What is happening?" he replied, in answer to a question that he had not asked.

"I do not know," she said. "Why do you not sit down? We can discuss it. Your pacing is making me uncomfortable."

Akhenaten ignored her, and paced. Nefertiti rubbed her temples.

"Can we at least extinguish some of the lamps? Why have so many been lit?"

Akhenaten turned on her.

"*Because I must see!*" he shouted. He almost immediately regretted his outburst, and continued more calmly. "I need the light to see anything at all nowadays."

He held up his hand in front of his face and moved it back and forth, trying to force his eyes into focus upon it. He failed at any distance.

"My eyesight is deteriorating to such a degree that I can see nothing unless the Aten shines directly over my head. If I do not light the room in his image I am reduced to fumbling my way around as though my eyes are closed."

Nefertiti remained silent. She reached out her hand in such a manner that he would come across it as he walked past her. He stopped when he felt the touch of it against his leg and reached down to grasp it.

"Nefertiti," he said. "Help me. I can feel everything slipping away. All my decisions are wrong, and yet all my decisions are those of the Aten. Does he deliberately lead me into traps? Is he as unaware as I am of the correct route to take?"

Akhenaten sat down wearily next to his wife. "May he forgive me for thinking so," he said, and lay his head on Nefertiti's shoulder.

"Perhaps," she said, wondering even as the words left her whether or not she was making the correct decision. "Perhaps you should speak to Aye. He may be able to help."

The couple sat in silence for a moment.

So quietly is was almost a whisper, Nefertiti added: "He is a wise man."

The Maya Papyrus, Fragments 150-154

> *I remained in the doorway as though I had been paralysed, as though I was posing for a sculpture of confusion and fear. The room was as sumptuous as any I had seen. Each pillar – and there were more than I had time to count – was decorated with colours and images that could only have been placed there by the nation's leading artists. The ceiling must have taken those same artists many months lying on platforms beneath it. It was decorated with the images of wildlife frolicking over reed beds, executed in colours so vibrant the observer could be forgiven for thinking that they were illuminating the room all on their own, without the help*

of the lamps that hung from golden fittings around the tops of the walls. The floor was similarly designed, and with such aplomb that it seemed a shame to walk upon it.

But this was not what kept me from stepping forwards. In fact, I noticed none of these details until much later, when the entire field of my perception was not being commandeered by one image and one thought.

The thought was: It cannot be.

A nurse was sitting by a bed, mopping the brow of its occupant.

I held my hand to my mouth.

The occupant was Tiye.

Finally released from my paralysis I stepped towards the bed. Tiye opened her eyes for the first time since my arrival and attempted a smile.

"Ah," she said in recognition, and then descended into a fit of coughing so violent I thought she would expire from the effort alone, there before my eyes. Once she had managed to calm herself, she spoke again.

"A visitor," she said. "Such a rare thing. And I see you have brought a friend with you."

I followed her gaze over my shoulder and saw Mahu lurking in the doorway. He quickly turned tail and made his escape. I closed the door gratefully, using the action as a breathing space in which I might martial my thoughts. I found it inconceivable that Tiye could be dying. I had never known her in anything less than the pinnacle of fitness. That she might be its victim reinforced for me the hold with which this plague held the city within its grasp.

I turned back to the bed, entirely unaware of anything I could say or do to help the situation, or even make it less awkward. I could hardly ask after her health.

"Aunt," I said.

"Maya."

We stared at each other. In a moment of inspiration, I walked around the side of the bed to where the nurse sat. I took the cloth from her and indicated that she may leave for a few minutes. Gratefully, she fled the room.

I sat down and dipped the cloth in the bowl of water that had been placed by the side of the chair. I wrung it out and dabbed it on Tiye's forehead.

"How long have you been like this?" I asked.

She shrugged.

"Has anyone been to visit you?"

"One or two priests. They informed me that they had advised all members of the royal family to avoid me. I am unclean, apparently."

"It is not you, it is the demons within you," I said, as though this could possibly be of any comfort to her. She did not reply.

"Does it hurt?" I asked.

She looked at me blankly for a moment. "Yes," she said.

She dissolved into coughing once more and I devoted myself to wiping the sweat from her forehead as though it would make any difference to her condition, as if she was in any state where she could even notice me doing it. As she coughed, a fine red spray flew from her mouth and fell on her chest and chin. I wiped these with the same devotion, although I was beginning to regret offering to take the nurse's place.

"You have always been a good boy," Tiye said. "Always attentive, always polite. Even now you ignore the priests in order to attend to me. I shall not forget this." She realised what she had said and smiled ironically. "Although of course I may not have enough time left in which to forget it. Still, it does not change my gratitude to you."

I did not like to explain that the true reason for my visit was abduction rather than duty. Instead, swallowing my guilt like a mouthful of stale beer, I said: "I could not leave you alone at a time like this. Of course I came to see you. You are my aunt. You hold no fears for me."

I had never seen someone as ill as this and survive. Her skin was so pale and stretched as to be almost translucent, so wasted as to reveal the contours of her skull beneath. When she spoke it was more an exhalation of breath than a formation of words, and I had to lean close in order to understand her. I concluded that I was right to lie to her. It was a lie of love. Who would not want to know on their death bed that someone cared enough for them to accompany them into the darkness?

"I have always been fond of you, Maya," she said, which surprised me. I never really believed that Tiye had even noticed me.

"In all the politics and manoeuvrings and scandals and battles, you have kept yourself removed. There is a wisdom and a dignity in that which I can respect."

She turned her head and fixed me with a gaze. "If only you knew," she said. "If only you knew."

"If only I knew what?" I said.

She did not remove her gaze, and I felt it impossible to turn away. Even in the extremity of sickness, Tiye's eyes were captivating. She made so little movement that I began to doubt that she had heard my question and I felt the need to ask her again.

"If only I..." I began.

"If only you knew," she said, suddenly, "exactly what had been perpetrated in the name of this family."

She exhaled heavily, as though she had unburdened herself of a heavy weight. And now that she had made the decision to talk it seemed as though she wished to speak of everything at once and do so before the opportunity was taken from her.

"I am not an evil person," she said.

"Of course not," I said. "Who has said...?"

"I will not die with my conscience so beset," she continued. I doubted again whether she had even heard me. "When my time comes to be judged by Osiris, he will not find me with a heavy heart. I shall live forever. My husband awaits me."

This time I said nothing. Sure enough, she had stopped only to gather her breath.

"Crimes have been committed. My silence makes me a conspirator, if only after the event. It has weighed upon me for some time and I shall remain silent no longer."

As she spoke I continued mopping her brow and, on occasion, muttering words of encouragement that she neither heard nor needed. She told me everything, and her address lasted so long that I had as little idea then as I do now exactly how long it lasted. She told me about Thuya's obsession with the family and its dynasty, and how Aye became her tool for the fruition of her plans. She told me of Thuya's manipulations to ensure that her wishes became the king's commands. She told me how Aye imprisoned the ambassador from Hatti, and how he had never spoken about the ambassador to anybody. How he left the ambassador to die, alone and exiled, in a palace cell in Memphis.

She told me about Giludkhepa. She told me how my father had smothered her and her newborn baby and then disappeared into the night, in order to secure Akhenaten's accession to the throne, which, in turn, was to ensure the survival of the dynasty that Thuya believed she had created.

By the time Tiye fell into a broken, wheezing silence I was stunned beyond words. There was nothing I could say in response and the pair of us lapsed into a long silence. I believe that I even forgot what I was doing with my hands. The cloth I was holding remained firmly within my grasp, resting on Tiye's forehead. It remained there until she was able to find the strength to lift her arm and push my hand away.

My father. My own father. It did not seem possible. That he should be capable of murder, and worse, treason. For surely it was treason to influence the succession of kings? To kill a prince to ensure that a more favoured son comes to the throne? No wonder Tiye had felt the need to confess this. It was not her crime, but it was a crime so fundamental, so dire, that even a proximity to it must cast a pall over the soul.

Egypt was teetering over the precipice of disaster and it was my father who had brought her here. Without him there would have been no Akhenaten, for he would have remained Amenophis, the prince. There would have been no Atenism, for a prince's insane ramblings would have been seen as just that without the authority of the crown to give them credence. There would have been no Mahu, no police with clubs, no terror. Amun would have continued his long and prosperous reign over the gods, who would each have remained firmly in the firmament where they belonged. There would have been no bankruptcy of the nation, no friends becoming enemies through lack of thought and care and gifts. There would perhaps still have been a nation of Hittites camped upon our borders, but there would have been an army capable of meeting them on the field of battle.

Had I not been numb with disbelief and shock I would have been angry enough to take that palace apart stone by stone until I found my father, whereupon I would have wreaked my revenge on him with a cruelty that shames me even now.

I remained sitting there for a long time, even after the lamps around the walls had begun to sputter and fizzle into darkness. We neither of us spoke, nor moved.

Eventually, the door opened. Framed in the light from the corridor was the nurse I had relieved earlier. She entered the room nervously and coughed politely. It was perhaps not the most judicious method for attracting my attention in the circumstances, but it sufficed in its purpose. My thoughts had so encompassed my senses since Tiye had revealed the truth to me that I felt as though I was waking from a vivid dream. Although my eyes had been open I had not been using them, and when I

looked at the nurse they struggled for a moment to focus upon
her.

"How fares Her Majesty?" the nurse asked in a whisper.

I looked down to Tiye on the bed and regarded her for a
moment or two before looking back at the nurse.

"Her Majesty is dead," I said.

The nation mourned as though a beloved king had died, and they mourned not only for the royal family, but for themselves. This was especially true of the members of court. They knew that there were very few checks on Akhenaten's behaviour and decisions, but one of the more effective ones had been the word of Tiye. She had only a minimal influence over the king, but even in decisions in which she was not directly consulted, the influence was sometimes evident. Even the most wilful of kings will sometimes heed the opinion of him held by his mother. The extent of Akhenaten's grief at the news of his mother's death only served to emphasise the effect of her loss would have on him.

And this loss, this grief, was compounded by the death of Setepenre, Akhenaten and Nefertiti's sixth daughter. She had fallen victim to the plague only a matter of days after Tiye herself succumbed.

Both Tiye and Setepenre were buried, days apart, in the royal wadi in the cliffs of Akhetaten. Even Akhenaten's favourites – Mahu, Nefertiti, his remaining daughters – found it impossible to communicate with him for weeks afterwards.

Nefertiti was less conspicuous in her grief. She, after all, had only lost a daughter and an aunt rather than a daughter and a mother, and she thought it unseemly to try to compete with her husband in the sadness that consumed them. Even so, to lose a second daughter was as much as she could bear, and only after the immediate shock had receded to manageable levels did she find herself capable of functioning in anything approximating a normal manner.

"Now is the time," Aye told her one afternoon as they took a constitutional around the palace grounds. As if in response to Nefertiti's loss, the plants and trees were beginning to lose their flowers and leaves. Such was her fragile state that the sight was enough to tease the tears to her eyes. She sniffed heavily and Aye laid a supportive hand between her shoulder blades.

"I know," he said. "I know."

"You do not seem to be affected by all this," Nefertiti said.

"Believe me, daughter, I am affected. I have not slept undisturbed by nightmares since Tiye passed to the underworld. But I am a busy man and my duties do not allow me the luxury of tears during the day. To forsake those duties now and surrender to grief would not be a dignified way of remembering my sister. She spent her life in the service of the crown, and to neglect it now on her account would, I assure you, be something about which she would have one or two things to say."

He smiled, as though at a happy memory.

"Now is the time for what?" Nefertiti asked, between sniffles.

"For us to act. He is at his most vulnerable."

"You make it sound like betrayal," Nefertiti said.

"Not at all, my dear, not at all. But you must admit that His Majesty is not the sort of man who always accepts what is best for him. Perhaps now would be a time when he would be at his least resistant to our help."

"I think you may be mistaken," Nefertiti said. "But I will not oppose myself to you should you wish to try."

"Your Majesty," Aye said to Akhenaten the next morning. "I have urgent and crucial matters of state that I have to bring to your attention."

Akhenaten ignored him and Aye counted this as a blessing. They were alone in the throne room, Aye having remained behind after the end of the king's daily audience. The audience itself had proceeded as Aye had expected, with various courtiers and ministers giving their reports and being received with either silence or shouting.

"I am betrayed!" Akhenaten had screamed at one unlucky minister who had the temerity to ask how he was. "That is how I am! Betrayed!"

He turned to Mahu, who was by now a permanent fixture at the king's side.

"I am holding you personally responsible for this!" he shouted.

Mahu paled. "Me, Your Majesty? But for what?"

"I have a number of questions, but there is only one answer. How were the plague demons permitted to enter the palace where they could infect my mother and daughter? Why were they given the strength to defeat our every attempt at subjugation? Why were the priests so ineffectual against them? Why? Why, I ask you? There is only one answer, one irrefutable, unassailable fact. Can you tell me what it is?"

Mahu simply stared at Akhenaten, his eyes wide. He had no idea what the fact may be and could not decide whether or not silence was preferable to an incorrect guess.

"*Gah!*" Akhenaten shouted in frustration, and turned to the man standing immediately to Mahu's left. "You! Tell me why!"

Silence.

"*Imbeciles!*" Akhenaten shouted. Every courtier and minister in the room stared at their shoes, at the walls, at the ceiling, rather than accidentally catch the king's eye and be asked the question to which none of them had an answer.

"The reason why these things have happened," Akhenaten said, slowly, as though explaining a simple concept to an inattentive child, "is because of Amun. The Aten can see everything. He is everywhere at all times. He knows what is happening in his city and the nation surrounding it. He is angry, and he is vengeful, and there can be only one cause for this."

Akhenaten turned to Mahu. "Mahu, you have not been carrying out the tasks to which I have commended you."

Mahu began to protest, but a stern look from Akhenaten was enough to stop him before he had advanced any further than opening his mouth.

"Time and time again I have had to take matters into my own hands," Akhenaten continued, suddenly calm, but all the more threatening because of it. "Time and again I have had to instruct you to step up your activities and find any worship of Amun that may remain. You have one more chance to root out this evil. Should you fail this time it will mean your life. Do you fully understand me?"

"Your Majesty," Mahu said. "I can assure you that I have always..."

"Do you," Akhenaten said, "understand me?"

"Yes, Your Majesty," Mahu said.

"Good. But please also understand this: should the Aten continue to be angry with me because of your slovenly approach, I shall be as merciless as he."

Akhenaten turned from Mahu, back to the rest of the courtiers there present. "Now, if there is..."

He stopped and looked back to Mahu. "You may begin," he said. Mahu backed from the room hurriedly, almost tripping over his own feet in his haste and eagerness to bow as low as possible.

"Now," Akhenaten said. "If there is nothing else..."

The courtiers and ministers left gratefully. Aye remained where he was, alone with Akhenaten and the ever present Tutankhaten.

"Your Majesty," Aye said, once the room had emptied. "I have urgent and crucial matters of state that I have to bring to your attention."

Akhenaten had, it seemed, expended his energies by directing them at Mahu. He did not shout and bluster in reply to Aye. Instead, he acted as though Aye had left the room with the rest of the ministers.

"Your Majesty," Aye tried again. "I am concerned for your health."

Akhenaten's eyes flickered, and his gaze slowly came around to meet that of Aye.

"You?" Akhenaten. "*You* are concerned over *my* health? Do you presume? How dare you?"

Aye took a deep breath. "Your Majesty, the strain you are under would have killed a mere mortal many times over. I can only thank the Aten that he has the wisdom to have elevated you to the godhead. Please allow those who love you to care for you."

"I need no care!" Akhenaten shouted. "I have the Aten, and his care puts the breath in my body and the pulse in my wrists. Do you really believe that your puny contribution could ever have the slightest effect? You are very arrogant, for a mortal, Aye. It does not bode well for you."

"Your Majesty, your word is sufficient. I merely wished to ensure that you were well. Forgive me. I meant no offence by my question."

"Yes, well," Akhenaten said. "See that you take care not to overstep your station in future."

Aye bowed low. "Of course, Majesty. Only..."

"Aye," Akhenaten said, drawing the word out as though it was a sword he was slowly removing from its scabbard. "You are beginning to test my patience."

"Forgive me, Your Majesty, but I have a question of a theological nature. I cannot imagine anybody better to answer it than the son of the Aten, who reflects his father's light in a manner that is dazzling to the mortal eye. I do not wish to hear the garbled message from one of your priests. Rather, I would ask you, my god."

Akhenaten smiled, but there was little humour in it. "You were always one for flattery, Aye."

Aye shook his head. "Merely observation, Your Majesty."

"Very well," Akhenaten said, with a sigh. "Ask me your question so that I may answer you and send you on your way."

"Your Majesty, my question is simply this: what is the nature of the divine triad?"

"Ah," Akhenaten said. "I thought you were going to test me."

Aye smiled. "Remember, Majesty, that I have only a mortal heart. That which is obvious to you, in your divine state, may be imperceptible to my comprehension."

"Very true," Akhenaten said. "Very true. Well, it is very simple, really. The Aten is three gods, and he is one. His two children, myself and Nefertiti, are separate from him, but part of him also. I am his son, but I am him."

"And Nefertiti is his daughter, but she is also part of him?"

"Of course," Akhenaten said.

"Ah, I see," Aye said. "And you are, of course, as powerful as the Aten, if you are part of him?"

"Well," Akhenaten said, unsure whether this was flattery or blasphemy. He was also slightly unsure of the correct answer. "I am not as powerful, no. Not as such. The Aten is the great creator, remember. The father of the world. I am only his son."

"And yet you are given power by him to rule the Two Lands?"

"Of course," Akhenaten said. "Really, Aye, this is very basic knowledge. I am surprised that you need to ask."

"Your Majesty," Aye said, taking a deep breath. His questions thus far had indeed been very elementary features of the faith. Now, though, there was no escaping the dangerous line he had to follow.

"Your Majesty," he said again. "Why is it that the Aten weakens you so?"

Akhenaten had begun to enjoy the conversation. It was always a pleasure to talk about the Aten, because it followed that Akhenaten would inevitably have to talk about himself in relation to divinity, and to do so was something that he rarely found tiresome. The conversation had proved to be a diversion from his woes and so it was doubly annoying to have the enjoyment brought to such an abrupt conclusion.

"I beg your pardon?" Akhenaten said incredulously. He leant across and placed his hands over Tutankhaten's ears.

"Forgive me, Majesty," Aye said, "but it seems to me that there are three parts to a triad and that if only two of those three parts are utilised the entire structure is compromised."

"Are you questioning the Aten? The very fabric of the holy trinity?"

"Your Majesty, a man who would do such a thing would deserve the slow death of a heretic. It is not my intention to do so."

"Then what exactly *is* your intention, Aye?"

"Only Your Majesty's continued well-being and happiness, but to have both of those attributes you must be strong, and to be strong you must be part of a trinity, not a duality."

Akhenaten was about to berate Aye further when he stopped himself. Of course, he thought, the man is being impertinent, but perhaps he has a point. Perhaps I *am* weak. Perhaps we are weak, myself and the Aten. Perhaps this old man has chanced upon the solution which has eluded me thus far.

Abruptly, he dismissed Aye to give himself time to ruminate on the conversation. The more he considered it, and he considered it endlessly over the coming days and weeks, the more attractive the idea became until it was nothing less than the inescapable elucidation of the answer to all his problems. He discussed it with nobody, least of all Aye. For his part Aye did not have the temerity to broach the subject again. He knew better than to risk snapping the luck he had already stretched to transparency. He could only hope to have planted a seed.

As Akhenaten cogitated and considered, at least one thing became clear. As a mortal, these were thoughts that Aye could never have formulated himself. Akhenaten had to consider the possibility of the Aten's involvement.

But what was he to do?

There were two answers, both as preposterous as the other, and Akhenaten quickly discounted them both. They both restored the trinity by making commensurate two of its members. The Aten would remain at the top, of course, but his two children would be equal beneath him. The first was for Akhenaten to renounce the throne, which was impossible to contemplate and would be a laughable notion were it not so horrific. The second was to promote Nefertiti to be her husband's equal, which shared the outlandishness if not the horror of the first.

Akhenaten prayed until the imprints of the temple floor tiles seemed to be in indelible relief on the flesh of his knees, but the Aten remained inexplicably silent, and the only thoughts to trouble Akhenaten's brow were his own.

You cannot do it. There has not been a female king of Egypt for generation upon generation. Hatshepsut acceded to the throne but she was your grandfather's grandfather's mother. She is so remote as to be irrelevant.

But of course you can do it. Hatshepsut was a better king than half the men who preceded her. And are you not Akhenaten, the god and the king? Who is to tell you what you can and cannot do? Would you rather abdicate?

Finally, he was decided. Or rather the situation was resolved. A decision where there is only one possible outcome is hardly a decision at all.

He made the announcement before a select audience. Only Aye, Nefertiti and Tutankhaten were in the king's audience chamber. Even Mahu was absent. Tutankhaten was standing, as always, at Akhenaten's right hand. He occasionally hopped from foot to foot as though containing either great excitement or a full bladder.

"I have been in consultation with the Aten," Akhenaten said, "and we between us have reached a decision. It seems to us that we have not maximised the strengths of our trinity. Nefertiti, you are a child of the Aten, as am I, and it is not fitting for a woman with such a divine antecedent to be a mere wife of the king. The Aten and I hereby decree that you will rule the Two Lands alongside me, as my equal and my co-regent."

Nefertiti glanced quickly at her father. Imperceptibly to everyone but her, he nodded. Nefertiti turned back to the throne.

"I accept," she said, breathlessly.

There was a fleeting look of impatience on Akhenaten's face. "It is a decree," he said. "You do not have any choice but to accept."

He signalled for her to take her seat on the throne beside his.

"Now that you are a king you shall have a kingly name. This I have considered also. Nefertiti is your birth name. From now, you are to be known as King Smenkharē."

Nefertiti tried it once or twice under her breath. Smenkharē. It was an ugly name and she hated it immediately. She had no idea what it meant and she was loathe to ask in case its meaning was as unattractive as its pronunciation. Smenkharē. No, it would never do.

Her annoyance was fleeting. It was surely a small price to pay for the throne of Egypt. She was amazed and delighted and edging closer to euphoria by the second. It seemed impossible, and therefore it was impossible and at any moment she expected the others in the room to break into laughter and congratulate themselves on a joke well perpetrated. But as each moment passed the likelihood of this diminished until she realised that the room had been enveloped in silence for some time as her companions awaited her first utterance as co-regent. Of course, she was so bewildered to be entirely bereft of fitting words and so her first pronouncement as pharaoh was, simply: "I do not know what to say."

There was polite laughter, for those before her understood the difficulty in which she must have found herself and were to forgive this momentary loss.

The Maya Papyrus, Fragment 158

I like to think of myself watching him like a cobra watches its prey. Tall, regal, intense, invulnerable to distraction. Of course, I was none of these things. I was a bumbling fool, and the results of my clandestine investigations and surveillance show only that.

When my sister was pronounced co-regent I felt not a flicker of pleasure. No sincere smiles tarried upon my lips. My audience with Tiye was so strong in my memory that the proclamation of Nefertiti's accession struck me as no coincidence. I knew that someone was in danger. I do not now and I did not then profess to have Aye's mental stature. I could not guess what his next move would be. I knew only that there would be one and that it was my duty to foil it. It seemed to be ridiculous to be placing myself in the position of Akhenaten's protector, for one does not protect monsters from their just fates, but there was only one man in the kingdom who wielded power with more dread threat than he. Only the thought of Aye on the throne, or so close to it that it made no difference, was more terrifying to me now than the long health and happiness of the tyrant under which Egypt currently choked. Even Mahu seemed preferable, for Mahu was just a thug. He was Akhenaten's tail, and with Akhenaten removed he would thrash ineffectually for a while before subsiding into obscurity. Aye would only grow stronger and more dangerous.

Throughout this document I have never tried to excuse my actions. I present this as a history, not an apology, although there are some I do not doubt who believe such an apology to be overdue. And yet I will not be condemned where condemnation is inappropriate. There was simply too much to do, too much ground to cover, too many conversations to be overheard for one man to enjoy any real degree of success. There was nobody, not even Horemheb, to whom I could turn. I could hardly accuse Aye without knowing what it was that I was to accuse him of, and I could hardly expect any accusation not to reach his ears before long. If I was correct and the pharaoh himself was under threat from Aye, then I would be a target against which he would not hesitate to act. And so I do not apologise. How could I not fail?

I watched with no idea of what I was watching. I listened to inane and irrelevant conversations and weighed them with a significance that they did not deserve. But I could not be present at meetings between Aye and Akhenaten that I later discovered to be pivotal. I could not be present within Aye's heart.

Finally, by the time he acted, I was in no position from which I could prevent him. By the time his plans were complete I was in no position to denounce him, for by then his power was all but absolute.

Here was the problem: for all Akhenaten's professions of egalitarianism, Nefertiti would never be his equal. It was always going to be the problem and Aye had always known as such, however much he might have denied it to himself. He would undoubtedly have Nefertiti's ear and he could use her for the promotion of his own plans and policies but she would always be the weaker of the two regents. Akhenaten would never submit to much he did not already agree with in the first place. It would never be enough.

Akhenaten, Aye now acknowledged to himself, was still an obstacle. Aye knew that he was capable of much with an ally on the throne, someone who could be moulded, free from Akhenaten's restraints of paranoia and fear.

This was his goal. That Akhenaten was about to preside over Egypt's destruction either by disease or starvation or unopposed invasion, Aye did not doubt. That Aye was wise and judicious enough to rescue the kingdom from Akhenaten's indignities he was equally certain.

For a long time Aye had not even acknowledged to himself that there was a second half to the plan that had culminated in Nefertiti's accession to the throne.

But now of course, there was. There undeniably, unequivocally was.

He knew that he had to be careful. It was not even enough for Akhenaten's death to look like an accident, for accidents could be engineered and any accident that befell a man as unpopular as Akhenaten would be as suspect as a knife between the shoulder blades. Akhenaten's death needed to be seen as untimely but entirely natural, and Aye knew of only one method which could accomplish this. It was not easy and not entirely without risk, but it was the only solution which readily presented itself. There had for some centuries been known a method of extracting a substance from the kernels of peaches that, when ingested in even the most minute quantities, caused an illness that would more likely be explained away as the work of demons rather than men. It was almost invariably fatal.

Aye had gold. And he knew where to look.

The Maya Papyrus, Fragment 159

> *By my keen intellect and deductive genius I discovered that Aye was missing a mere day and a half after the news had already spread around the palace. There was no real mystery in it, at least for those who currently did not see a mystery if Aye was so much as three heartbeats late for a royal audience. He had mentioned to one or two people that he was to be unavailable for a brief time as he inspected the garrisons based around the city's border stones, beyond which it was forbidden to travel. It was an arduous task and one which Akhenaten saw only as confirmation of Aye's loyalty to him.*

For my part I was angered by the news. I did not like the idea of Aye being out of my sight. He had a day's ride on me: it would be impossible to follow him. I had no idea where he could have gone and less idea why he might have gone there. I did not know when he would be back, by which route, or what he planned upon his return.

Had anyone been able to ask me about the progress of my investigations I could only have told them the truth: that they were preceding exactly as well as I had expected they would.

Chapter Nineteen

The God of Death

SINCE NEFERTITI'S elevation to the crown of Egypt the atmosphere at court seemed refreshed. Indeed, it was an air that was echoed around the city as a whole. Nefertiti recognised it and she recognised its causes, and she was flattered but demure, as – everyone quietly decided – perfectly befitted her.

The news of her accession to the throne had been publicly announced two days previously and the celebrations were only now beginning to subside into hangovers and half-remembered embarrassments. The announcement had been made from the Window of Appearances, below which the optimists of the city had gathered to hear good news and receive expensive presents. When the word spread that the news was, against all rational expectation, not only good but celebratory, street parties had spontaneously erupted around the city. The people seemed intent on welcoming Nefertiti not only as their king but also as their saviour. Perhaps, it was thought (but never openly expressed), she may be a stay on her husband's hand. Perhaps she will be the harbinger of good sense and wise rule. The more cynical city inhabitants turned up their noses and sneered, commenting how Nefertiti and Akhenaten were merely each other's reflection, and how nothing would change, but most did not register their disapproval in such strong terms as refusing to drink and before the first evening was paling into dawn all objections had been quietly forgotten, at least until the morning's watery light had once again hardened celebrants into sceptics.

Nefertiti was unable to completely submit to the festive atmosphere of the city. Before his departure Aye had met with her and issued her with instructions as to what she should do in his absence. She was unhappy about it, yet at the same time recognised the logic and importance of what he had told her. She had never felt any love for Tutankhaten's mother, and the woman had hardly made a hearty effort to ingratiate herself with the palace and the members of court since the boy had been born, but nevertheless Nefertiti bore her no real malice.

And so the fact that Aye had decided that Kiya was an obstacle that needed to be removed was, at best, regrettable. But Nefertiti knew that he was right. Kiya was a pull on the king. The problem with her was not what she had done, for she had done nothing other than that one arbitrary act, but what she might do. Her potential for influence, not merely on the king, but also, and to a much greater effect, on the prince, was staggering and frightening.

For his part, Aye was almost relieved to be having the conversation about Kiya with his daughter. He had reached a stage where any of his plans were rendered useless by Kiya's continued presence at court. While Tutankhaten had remained young and while he had remained so resolutely by his father's side, Kiya had been a marginal threat. But now that Aye had decided upon the removal of the boy's father, Kiya would automatically become a much stronger force. Any thoughts she took upon herself to sow in the boy's mind would remain undiluted by Akhenaten's philosophy, and while Aye planned the disposal of the vast majority of that philosophy as soon as Akhenaten was removed, he needed Tutankhaten to learn that his true family was Aye and Nefertiti. He needed to embrace the importance of Thuya's dynasty, and that was very unlikely when someone entirely external to that dynasty had his ear.

Aye's plans involved danger and sacrifice, and more than enough of both, and he did not intend them to be sabotaged by a foreigner to whom he held no allegiance whatsoever. And so he left his commands with Nefertiti, couched as requests and entreaties, and the instruction that Kiya should be gone by the time of his return.

Nefertiti spoke to Akhenaten one evening after the pair of them had overseen the last prayers of the day at the Great Aten Temple. They had boarded their chariot within the temple walls and ridden it to the palace, although the distance was small and Nefertiti would have enjoyed the brief walk. It had been decreed by Akhenaten, in the light of the strengthening of the divine triad, that it could only hurt for royal feet to touch the ground in the city where it had been made impure by the touch of mortals. Teams of priests had been drafted into the palace to continuously bless its floors and the ground of the courtyards where mortals may dare to tread. The floor of the temple, it was decided, was pure by its very nature and was spared the rigours of constant prayers on its behalf.

Aye knew that Nefertiti would be aided by her husband's paranoia. It is easy to persuade the paranoid of anything as long as it is information to their detriment. He knew that she would need no corroborating facts, no team of witnesses. All she needed was her word, Akhenaten's trust and naivety, and some little preparation.

Kiya's Maru-Aten temple was not secured against access by whomever at court would avail themselves of its tranquillity. As Akhenaten himself was not tempted by its attractions, security was deemed unnecessary to prevent those who would intrude upon it. In reality, very few did so, concerned as most people were that, should there be a schism in the royal family, attendance at the Maru-Aten may indicate a predilection to fall on the side of Kiya rather than Akhenaten. It was not difficult, therefore, for Nefertiti to gain entry to the area unobserved. She knew that there was little danger of encountering Kiya, for Tutankhaten was with his father and Kiya rarely visited the place without him. Still, her heart raced. She knew that the package she carried under her arm, wrapped tightly in a linen sheet, would mean the death of anyone else apprehended with it in their possession. She was uncertain as to the nature of her fate in a similar situation but assumed with some confidence that it would not be pleasant.

She wandered the pathways and lanes of the Maru-Aten, unsure of exactly what she was looking for, clutching her package tightly to her as though worried that it might spring suddenly from her arms and make a getaway. She walked quickly and furtively, her eyes searching each intersection and darkened alcove for a suitable place.

For a long while nothing presented itself and she was beginning to consider retracing her steps back towards the entrance. And then she passed a crossroads, glancing to her left and her right. She stopped and backed up. It was the place she needed. She found it difficult, in fact, to imagine a place more suited to her purpose.

Before her stood a bench which looked out over a manmade lake. Above the bench was a banner designed to keep the worst of the sun off the head of whoever sat there.

Now, at the very moment of the execution of her task, Nefertiti hesitated. Her fingers played with the wrapping of her package, rearranging rather than uncovering it. She looked around her for a long moment, as if waiting to be discovered.

Finally, unable to delay any longer, she stepped forwards towards the bench. She crouched before it, unwrapped the package, and then reached beneath.

Once she had finished she hastened from the Maru-Aten as quickly as dignity would allow. She did not want to remain there for a second longer than absolutely necessary, but then neither did she wish to be witnessed running and have to answer all the questions that such a sighting would beget.

By the time she crossed the threshold back into the palace she was struggling to keep a grip on her breathing. She did not believe that she had been seen. She retired at a more relaxed pace to her quarters, where she sat and stared into the middle distance for some time.

The Maya Papyrus, Fragments 162-164

Suffice it to say, I knew nothing of this. I was so intent in watching Aye and attempting to fathom the reasons for and consequences of his disappearance I did not think that I needed to watch Nefertiti as well. I regret the events that unfolded subsequent to her visit to the Maru-Aten, but unlike Nefertiti I cannot find it in myself to accept any of the blame for them. Indeed, they could have been so much worse was it not for my intervention, belated though it was. Now I am unable to separate those looks of Nefertiti that were due to repentance and those that were due to fear of discovery.

I received a summons to attend the kings' audience chamber. It came at a more civilised hour than the one that summoned me to attend Tiye, but nonetheless I was left in no doubt of its urgency. After all, with Aye away, someone needed to be present to provide advice for Akhenaten to ignore. It was a very important job.

When I arrived I found that all the other players in this drama were there ahead of me. Akhenaten and Nefertiti were upon their thrones, both looking angry and afraid. Mahu was standing to one side of them, his countenance set equally dourly, but with perhaps a hint of pleasure in there also. I knew then that something dreadful had happened. To Akhenaten's right, as always, was standing Tutankhaten. I had never before seen him appear so concerned. His face was pale and his hands fidgeted with each other endlessly where normally they would be content to hang by his side or lean against his father's throne.

Before both thrones, her back to me as I entered the room, was standing Kiya. Her shoulders were slumped forwards as though she had recently been relieved of some heavy burden. Her head was bowed and as I watched, her back jerked as she sobbed. I walked around to the thrones, my eyes never leaving her. Her hands, I now saw, were covering her face, and while they hid her admirably, they were useless to muffle the sound of her crying.

"What has happened?" I asked, once I had risen from the prone position. I directed the question towards Akhenaten.

Although I was at liberty to address such questions to Nefertiti since her accession and although Nefertiti would undoubtedly furnish me with a more comprehensible answer, it did not do to needlessly bruise Akhenaten's fragile ego.

"Something unforgivable," Mahu replied, in Akhenaten's place.

"Heresy," Akhenaten said. "Damned heresy and treachery. I can barely believe it of her, but it is incontestable."

I looked in astonishment at Kiya. The majority of her face remained obscured by her fingers, but her eyes had risen above them like the sun rising over mountains. Fittingly, her eyes were as red as dawn.

"It is – not – true," she said, between sobs.

"Then perhaps you would care to explain this," Akhenaten said. He reached behind his throne and then thought better of it.

"Maya," he said. "Pick this up and show it to her."

I followed his pointing finger. There, in the shadows of his throne, lay a statuette. I stooped to retrieve it and saw immediately that it was a depiction of a man with a cobra's head, standing tall and proud, his feet together, his arms folded across his chest in the attitude of a king. It took a moment or two for me to fully grasp its significance, it having been so long since I had seen anything similar. And then I realised. It was Amun. I held it up in the light. Akhenaten frowned and turned away. Kiya's sobbing renewed its ferocity.

"I have never seen it before!" she said.

"Then how did it get there?" Mahu said. "Did it perhaps make its own way there?"

"Enough!" Akhenaten said to him. "Do not talk like that."

Mahu bowed his head in momentary embarrassment.

I gradually managed to deduce the events leading up to this audience. It was no easy matter, for each of my interlocutors was bereft of sense, brimming as they were with one emotion or another to the detriment of all else. However, it transpired that the idol of Amun had been discovered in the Maru-Aten, in the vicinity of where Kiya was wont to take Tutankhaten when his presence at the palace was not required. To be found in possession of such a statue was of course prohibited in the strongest possible terms. There could be no reason for owning one other than the celebration and worship of this most proscribed of gods. In a member of the general population of Akhetaten, such ownership was seen as heresy and treachery. In someone as close to

Akhenaten as was Kiya it was seen as all this, but as a personal affront as well. It was seen not only as treachery, but as treachery in its basest and most dangerous form; treachery by the mother of the heir to the throne, who by her very influence could turn her son against everything protected and lauded by the king and his court. There was no exaggerating the seriousness of the crime of which Kiya had been accused.

"It is not mine," Kiya insisted, and continued to insist throughout what now transpired to be a hearing.

"Of course," Akhenaten said, labouring the sarcasm in his tone. "Your protestations do you no good service. They only anger me further. Do not add to the insult you have thrown in my face. We are not here to decide your guilt. That... thing," – here he waved his hand dismissively towards the object I still held in my own – "has made that decision for us. All we can do now is decide your punishment. You would be wise to soothe my anger in any way that is still open to you."

"There is only one punishment for treason," Mahu said, leaning close to Akhenaten's ear.

Akhenaten nodded in confirmation.

"Your Majesty," I ventured at this point. "You have of course considered the fact that, as entry to the Maru-Aten is possible for anyone, this despicable item may have been placed within by someone other than Kiya. I am only mortal and do not have your wisdom and talent for deduction. Perhaps you could explain to your poor servant how you know this monstrosity to belong to Kiya?"

Akhenaten cast me a withering look to which, luckily, I did not pay too much heed. I was too busy at that moment silently apologising to Amun for referring to his statuette as a despicable item and a monstrosity. I am sure that he understood that I did so only through necessity.

"I have of course considered all the possible scenarios," Akhenaten said. "But who else would have put it there?"

I shrugged. "Anyone may have put it there," I said.

"Anyone may, but only one person did," Mahu said. "For what reason would they do so? You are introducing needless complications."

"How did you know to find it there?" I asked.

"An informant."

"Who?"

"They remain anonymous. A note was left at the palace gates. We do not know who left it there."

"May I see it?"

"No," Mahu said. "I did not keep it. It did not seem important."

"Not important?" It was more an exclamation than a question.

"Maya," Mahu said. "May I ask why you are defending a known heretic?"

I had no answer for Mahu's tortuous logic. If Kiya was accused of a crime then it was only because the king knew her to be guilty. If she was guilty, no man had business trying to excuse her actions. To be suspected was to be condemned, but to question the suspicion was to question Akhenaten's infallibility, which in turn would lead him to suspect and, therefore, condemn.

Akhenaten had decided Kiya's fate before I, or anyone else – excepting, perhaps, Mahu – had been consulted on the matter.

"It grieves me to say it, but I have no choice," Akhenaten said. "Kiya's execution takes place at dawn."

I knew what this meant, and from the cry that escaped his lips, so did Tutankhaten. There was only one punishment for a heretic under Akhenaten's rule. It was a punishment I had witnessed once, and only once. It had happened many times since, of course, but I had always succeeded in being elsewhere when it happened. That one sight was enough for me, when I saw the priest accused of Akhenaten's attempted assassination slowly impaled on a wooden stake at the palace of Malkarta. His pitiful cries and unheeded pleas for mercy had remained with me as clearly as if they were being forever whispered in my ear, and the vision of his feeble struggling against hands that held him firmly in the last touch he would ever feel from another human being remained as vivid as if they were being eternally played out before me by a troop of actors.

Tutankhaten and Kiya had reacted with equal abhorrence to the news of her end. Both were understandably inconsolable. It was the furthest I had ever seen the prince divert from his usual implacable calm. It was my dearest wish to console him, but Akhenaten was already addressing him and it would have been unwise to appear as though I was protecting him from his father.

"Now is the time for you to become a man," Akhenaten was saying to him, to my further distress. The king had leant over to put his arm around his son's shoulder, as though this could be any *consolation. "I realise that this must be difficult for you. Indeed, it is..."*

Akhenaten stopped to lean back momentarily and cough.

"Indeed," he said again, "it is equally difficult for me. But we both have to realise that there are more important issues here than the life of one person, or our grief, which will surely pass with the knowledge of the great good that has been done in defence of the Aten."

Tutankhaten was struggling to staunch his tears, and it was a sight far more moving than the tears themselves.

So intent was I on the young prince that, may her spirit forgive me, I had entirely forgotten about the condemned woman standing at my elbow. There was the sound of flesh on floor. I turned, and saw that Kiya had collapsed into an ungainly heap at my feet.

Nefertiti remained implacable. She had known that her actions would only ever have traumatic consequences. She remembered the words of her father. *It is for the greater good*, he had said. *Always remember Egypt, and the priority of needs. What benefits Egypt outweighs our own desires, and would do so if our desires burned for a million years. Be strong, my Nefertiti.*

Her strength would remain unbowed for she knew the importance and the significance of what she did. She knew its causes and consequences. She knew the future it shaped would benefit tenfold from this one sacrifice.

She reminded herself who this woman was, of the shame that she had laid over Nefertiti, of her accentuation of Nefertiti's failure to provide Akhenaten with a male heir. She forced herself to dwell on Kiya's reluctance to ingratiate herself with the rest of court, how she undoubtedly thought herself to be above such things.

These thoughts fed Nefertiti's bile with sufficient vigour for her to remain outwardly calm when Akhenaten announced Kiya's sentence of death. *Always remember Egypt!* her heart shouted to her.

She did so, and her voice did not speak in protest.

The Maya Papyrus, Fragments 165-166

There was no further opportunity to petition Akhenaten's mercy that day. Kiya, who quickly regained her senses, although not her composure, was marched firmly away to spend the night in a cold and comfortless cell. Akhenaten quickly declared the audience to be at an end and, followed by Nefertiti, strode from the room with as much purpose as the guards who surrounded Kiya. Akhenaten grasped Tutankhaten by the hand and gave him no choice but to follow him, although the boy's eyes never left the door through which his mother had been taken.

I remained in the audience room for scant moments, alone with Mahu. We looked at each other, he undoubtedly finding me as distasteful as I found him, and then I turned and left. I knew there was no point in my trying to defend Kiya further. It would be asking him to forfeit his measure of blood, and that had been a lost cause for many years.

Instead I persuaded the guards to allow me to visit Kiya. It seemed that I was destined of late to spend time at the bedside of those about to leave my company forever, like a god of death ensuring that his consignments are dispatched on time.

She was, as was to be expected, entirely inconsolable, for she was not only facing untimely death, which few of us can meet with the dignity that we like to foresee, but cruel death. Long, drawn out death of pain unimagined. She was barely coherent in answering my questions.

She quickly dismissed the idea that the statue had belonged to her and remained firm in her assertion that she had never seen it before it was presented to her that day. I earnestly expressed to her my desire to help her and that she would only be hindering me if she was not wholly truthful with me, but she would not be moved: the statue was not hers. I believed her, for I could not think that she had any reason to continue lying.

I wanted to know who she considered enemies, who would have cause to act against her so piteously. She could think of nobody, although to be fair she could barely think enough to acknowledge my presence. I tried to focus her thoughts with hopes of release. It felt cruel to do so but I believed that it was not an impossibility as long as I was able to encourage her cooperation.

At last she could only name one person who she thought capable of hatred towards her so malignant that it could lead to this, and while her logic was sound I could not bring myself to believe that her conclusions were correct. I had perhaps pushed her too hard in trying to reach a suspect, and in doing so I had forced her to name someone, however unlikely.

There was, of course, no question that Nefertiti could have been responsible for this. There was enough malice in this act for a thousand Nefertitis, and even Akhenaten could not have persuaded her to act in such a way.

I left the palace after I could no longer force myself to remain with a woman so destroyed as was Kiya. I left her with nothing other than whispered platitudes and the promise that I would not rest until I had explored every avenue for the pleading of mercy with Akhenaten. I did not share with her my estimation of the likelihood of success. She begged me, as I was leaving, with her hand suddenly outstretched and gripping my forearm, to arrange for her to see her son one last time. I promised to do what I could but secretly doubted that I would have any more success in this than in any of my other undertakings. Akhenaten would see it only as a plea for her to have one more opportunity at corruption.

Neither Akhenaten nor Nefertiti would receive me that afternoon. Both blamed urgent matters of state to which they had to attend but I did not believe a word of it. Akhenaten was trying to avoid having to answer my questions, although more through a weariness of them than a fear that I might change his mind, and Nefertiti was undoubtedly following her husband's instructions.

I retired to my home and awaited the coming of the morning. Images of Kiya's sleeplessness were enough to ensure my own.

The next morning found me at the palace before sunrise, pacing the bounds of the inner courtyard where I knew the execution was to take place. It was a small space made claustrophobic by the tall walls that enclosed it. It was a place that rarely saw the face of the sun, for the Aten knew of the events here without having to witness them for himself. In the exact centre of the square stood an apparatus that I recognised from Malkarta. A tall stake had been planted in the ground, beside which had been placed a small run of wooden steps. The stake and the ground around it were stained black, as though evil itself was seeping from it. It may be the imagination of my memory, but it does not seem as though any birds sang in that square.

Come the appointed hour I was still there, still pacing, unable in my fear to martial my thoughts into any coherent argument. The nearer the time of the execution party's arrival, the more my thoughts skittered from my grasp, so that when they finally arrived I felt as though I would flow forth such a meaningless torrent that they would deposit me on a stake as a gesture of mercy.

Akhenaten was there, of course, his face suitably grim. Mahu was with him. I was pleased to see that Nefertiti was not, but this was more than offset by my horror at the sight of Tutankhaten. Kiya was to have her wish to see him one more time after all, although I am sure she would have forgone the desire had she known in which circumstances their last meeting would take place. The prince was white and weak, his knees trembling with every step, his hands shaking as they repeatedly went to his face, his wig, his kilt, his chest, in a never ending cycle of fear. He looked for all the world as though the imposing presence of his father was all that kept the prince on his feet.

Last of all came Kiya, flanked by two guards who dwarfed her and barely acknowledged her struggles. She fought them with the strength of unrestrained panic but their hands gripped her arms with such implacability that she was unable to loosen them even for a second. Her legs were tied at the ankle and she was unable to pull her feet forward. They dragged behind her like the feet of a cripple, or a corpse.

And she screamed. She screamed with such ferocity that it seemed as though she was shredding her throat, and her cries emerged torn into unrecognisable syllables.

Akhenaten laid a hand on Tutankhaten's shoulder and the boy looked as though it was a physical effort not to shy away from it.

I stepped forwards, directly into Akhenaten's path.

"Your Majesty, on Kiya's behalf I beg mercy," I said. "On behalf of your wife whom you loved enough to bestow upon her the seed that became your son, the wife who loved you enough to bring your heir into the world, the woman, Your Majesty, who is and will always remain the woman your loving son looks upon as his mother, I beg that you reconsider this course of action."

I spoke hurriedly, not giving Akhenaten the chance to interrupt, although this was more through fear than design.

"That you have determined her guilt, holy king, cannot be questioned by a mortal such as I. Your wisdom is as fathomless as the ocean. But so, Majesty, is your clemency and your forbearance, and I beg most humbly that you allow these to be given voice."

"His Majesty has made his decision," Mahu said. Neither he nor the king had broken their step and I was forced to back away before them as I spoke. "It is not for you to question."

"Your Heavenly Majesty," I said. "Allow me the great honour of addressing you directly, and not through your minions."

I caught the look that Mahu gave me at this remark, and I noted that I had just made a very powerful enemy.

Akhenaten and Mahu stopped. It was not through anything I had said: they had merely reached the place where they wished to be.

"Your Majesty," I said again. "You are a god. You are not bound by the words of your servants." Again I looked at Mahu. Again he returned my gaze with the look I imagine he would have adopted had I slapped him in the face and insulted his mother. "You have within you the power of forgiveness. Yes, Kiya must be punished for her actions, but you may define the manner of her punishment. You are no more restrained by laws and traditions than you are by the words of those around you. I would beg you to consider the effect of this on your son. Are you not punishing him by these actions? Are you not condemning him along with his mother? Can you bring yourself to commune with the Aten in his temple and tell him that you have executed the mother of his grandson?"

This last ploy was the most desperate, and I had known as soon as it occurred to me as I had paced and waited for the sun to rise that it was an argument so riddled with dangers that had balked at its use until the very moment when it flew from my mouth. To call into question Akhenaten's authority, his relationship with the Aten, was bordering so closely on heresy that a different wording could have toppled it over the edge.

At least Akhenaten deigned to look in my direction. He was taller than me by a head and shoulders (as he was most men), but I suddenly felt much smaller before him.

By this time, Kiya's screams had cost her most of her remaining energy, and she was able to do nothing more than weep, in great wracking sobs that contorted her body. Tutankhaten was weeping also, staring up at his father with eyes yearning for relief from his pain. He had heard my words as well as had everyone else in the square.

"Father," he said. Akhenaten ignored him, intent as he was on me, and Tutankhaten tugged on his arm. "Father."

Akhenaten looked down at him.

"Please, father," the prince said. *"Spare her. Please."*

The tears had coursed a route through his face paint, which had smudged along the channel's edges. His face looked like the view of a flooded river from a cliff top. His nose was running, and the paroxysm of his grief had diverted him so much that he had not noticed a trail of saliva escaping from a corner of his mouth. He looked the very picture of pity and despair.

"Do not anger the Aten," Tutankhaten said. *"Listen to Maya. She is my mother. Perhaps the Aten will not take kindly to her death. Have you prayed over the matter?"*

Akhenaten shook his head. He was unused to Tutankhaten making such demands on him, and he looked as though he was unsure exactly how to deal with it. *"I do not need to pray over it,"* he said.

"Then you do not know the Aten's wishes," Tutankhaten said. His voice was rising as he began to sense the dawning of hope. *"What if..."* he said, and then cast around for something to follow it with.

"What if," he said, and then inspiration struck and I found that I could breathe again. *"What if this is a trap?"*

"I do not understand," Akhenaten said. Mahu began to speak but a waved hand from the king was enough for him to finish before he even began. *"A trap? By whom?"*

"You have many enemies, father. You have always told me so. Perhaps those who wish you harm had a hand in this, knowing it would lead to my mother's execution, and knowing equally well that such an event would bring you into disfavour with the Aten."

Suddenly, Akhenaten's face was a mask of confusion.

"Your Majesty," Mahu said. *"We are wasting time."*

Akhenaten ignored him, and Mahu knew his master well enough to know not to repeat himself.

"But she must be punished," Akhenaten said to Tutankhaten. *"She is a heretic. Do not question this, for it is not open to discussion. If she has been manipulated by my enemies it only makes the crime more serious. She was tempted into heresy in order to harm me even further. Are you suggesting that those who hurt your king and your god should be allowed free reign to act howsoever they wish?"*

The boy had no answer, and looked to me for help.

"She must be punished, Majesty," I said, solemnly. *"Of that there can be no doubt."*

Tutankhaten looked stricken once again, but I could do nothing to signal my benign intentions to his mother without alerting Akhenaten and Mahu to the same fact. I continued.

Or I would have done had Akhenaten not chosen that moment to explode into a fit of coughing. I watched him, wide-eyed and spellbound; so much so, in fact, that I did not continue speaking, even after his coughing had ceased.

He looked at me quizzically. "Well?" he said, as though nothing had happened.

"Er," I said, still astonished that only I seemed to have noticed what had happened. "I was saying, Majesty, that she must be punished. She is, after all, a heretic. But she should be punished in a manner that does not play into the hands of your enemies."

"Then what are you suggesting? Imprisonment?"

"An excellent idea, of course, Majesty," I said. "But I was thinking of something else. If she is imprisoned, you run the risk of her heresy still reaching out from wherever she is being held and infecting those around her. I have another suggestion, should it please Your Majesty to hear it."

"How very gracious of you to finally ask His Majesty's permission before airing your poisonous views," Mahu said.

This time we all ignored him. The courtyard had become silent. Kiya, who had been following the conversation so closely that her sobbing had abated to a level where I did not have to raise my voice to be heard above it, stopped struggling entirely and held her breath. Tutankhaten watched me with the intensity of prey. Even the guards seemed to have taken an interest.

"Exile," I said, and the courtyard seemed to exhale. Both Kiya and Tutankhaten resumed their weeping and Kiya, who's strength seemed to have been restored by her brief rest, redoubled her pointless efforts towards escape.

"Exile," Akhenaten repeated, as though he had heard the word for the first time.

Tutankhaten returned to tugging on his father's arm. All pretence at reasoned argument had fled. "You cannot!" he was shouting. "You cannot send her away! She is my mother!"

"I see," Akhenaten said to me. "Clever. Very clever. This way I punish all my enemies at once."

"Just so, Your Majesty," I said, with a deep inner sigh.

Tutankhaten would never see his mother again after that morning. She was put into a chariot before nightfall and whisked *away, her driver having been given special dispensation to cross the city boundaries. I believe she was taken north, and then eastwards until she reached the borders of her homeland, Mitanni, where she was deposited without ceremony at the first town over the border. What became of her after that nobody will ever know.*

All trace of her was removed from Akhetaten. The Maru-Aten was rededicated to Meritaten, Akhenaten's eldest daughter. Throughout the city, Kiya's name was excised from monuments and inscriptions. Her likenesses were chiselled out of walls, leaving nothing but ugly scars in her place. Her name was barely ever mentioned again around court, except by Tutankhaten, and then only in private conversations with me. She was destroyed as surely as if she had been hoisted onto that stake on the morning of her supposed execution.

It took a long time for Tutankhaten to forgive me for my actions that day, because he saw only that his mother was no longer with him, not that she was at least alive, albeit alive somewhere else. It took a long time for him to accept that the outcomes of my words with Akhenaten were the best that could ever have been hoped for, and to see me not as the man who robbed him of his mother but as the man who saved his mother's life. Once he had done this I flatter myself in the belief that I became his closest friend and keenest confidante.

I do not believe that he ever forgave his father.

Aye was away in total for perhaps a week. He returned to find the palace in a state of uproar.

He had a pouch of poison securely tied to the belt of his kilt and a report in his head fabricating the exact nature and readiness of the guard posts around the city based on the few that he had actually visited. It seemed he would need neither.

He quickly discovered that nobody could have cared less about the readiness of the guards on the city's borders. He could afford to hide the peach poison in a secure location in his home, wrapped in many protective layers of cloth and leather, because it seemed that the gods had read his mind and put into effect his plan without his intervention.

Servants and courtiers rushed this way and that as though heedless of their destination or what they were expected to do on their arrival. Women wept at the turmoil of it all. Priests walking the corridors would without warning drop to their knees and begin monotonic intonations and entreaties to the Aten, in the hope of encouraging his mercy. Physicians were to be found in almost every corner, huddled into groups where they would whisper and plot and, occasionally, disagree with each other loudly and volubly.

Nobody had enough time even to notice Aye as he passed, and he did not stop to ask questions. Whatever had happened was of such magnitude that he did not want to hear it from a servant's mouth. He sought the king.

There seemed little difference between the audience chamber and the rest of the palace. Even here were to be found the airs of panic and confusion. The room was crowded as he had never seen it before; so crowded, in fact, that he could not see the thrones from where he was standing, momentarily baffled on the threshold of the room. He began to push his way through, and only now was he recognised. His name preceded him in reverential tones. When he was halfway across the room he saw Nefertiti. She had heard his name and stood from her throne. He could see her on the dais, raised head and shoulders above those around her.

"Father!" she shouted, and waved to him unnecessarily.

When he finally reached the thrones, he saw that one of them was empty, and he did not let himself believe the first thought that sprang into his mind, because it was a conclusion too fortuitous to be the truth.

"Where is he?" he asked Nefertiti.

She sat down again.

"He is on his sick bed," she said.

"His sick bed or his death bed?"

"Father, really, do you have to be..."

"Tell me!" Aye hissed, clamping his hand over hers on the arm of the throne. "Which is it?"

Nefertiti did not answer immediately and when she did it was in a conspiratorial whisper. "It is the plague," she said.

Aye could barely contain his excitement and relief. The king was going to die. He had to fight to retain his composure and a suitably dire expression.

"I must see him," he said.

"He is in his apartments," Nefertiti said, "but there are very few people he will see. The priests have ordered that nobody should see him at all, but he has overruled their decision. He says he does not wish to be alone. I left him when sleep overtook him."

"Have you discussed with him the succession?"

"He will not discuss it. He says that he is not ill, that the Aten would protect him even if he was, and so there is no need to discuss anything of that nature."

"But he has all the symptoms?" Aye asked.

Nefertiti caught the eagerness and excitement in his voice that he had been trying so carefully to avoid. "You have no need to worry," she said, coldly. "He will most assuredly die."

"Then I say again: I must see him. We cannot allow him to die until he has confirmed you as his successor."

"I am already co-regent," she said.

"Yes, but you are a woman. It needs to be confirmed or it will be challenged."

"By whom?"

"Would you like to wait to find out?"

She did not answer.

"I shall wake him," Aye said, and pushed his way back through the crowd.

He found priests barring the way into the king's bedchamber. He made to walk past them without acknowledging their presence but they moved to block his access to the door.

"You cannot pass," one said.

"I am Aye, the god's father," he said.

"We are aware who you are," the priest said. "You cannot pass."

Aye took a deep breath. Although the king was still alive, there was no telling how long he would remain in that joyous state and Aye did not want to waste time with these buffoons that he could be using to confirm his daughter as the next pharaoh. He glared at each of them in turn.

"My daughter is pharaoh. I have her ear. Unless you let me in to see His Majesty with all alacrity you will be dead by morning. Or, at least, you will be a good way towards it. Perhaps dead by the afternoon."

He spoke so calmly, so prosaically, that his words carried with them a cold dread. Neither of the priests replied. They looked briefly at one another and then wordlessly stepped to one side. Aye did not acknowledge them further. He stepped forwards and pushed open the double doors that led into the king's bedchamber.

Within he found a team of physicians huddled, as elsewhere in the palace, in the corner of the room, discussing earnest matters in hushed tones. They raised their heads to regard him when he entered, looking for all the world like a troop of feeding hyenas having just noticed the proximity of a lion. They recognised him and returned to their discussion.

Aye stepped over to the bed. It was raised from the floor and Aye needed to climb four or five steps to reach it. Within lay Akhenaten. He looked weak and although he was asleep he breathed in shallow gasps. His eyelids fluttered spasmodically. Aye sat on the edge of the bed and looked down at him. He leant close to the king's ear.

"Pig," he whispered, and sat upright again.

Akhenaten made no sign that he had been disturbed. Aye leant close again.

"Idiot," he said, and smiled. "Heretic."

Akhenaten's head turned from side to side and he made some nonsensical noises.

"Halfwit," Aye said. He regarded Akhenaten's misshapen head, and the long spidery fingers that lay on the bedclothes. "Monster," he said.

Akhenaten opened his eyes, and Aye could see that it took a moment or two for him to find purchase on the world around him.

"Your Majesty," Aye said, and sat back as Akhenaten launched himself into a fit of coughing that shook the bed. The physicians rushed over from their side of the room to offer help. Aye stood and moved himself to one side to allow them access. He looked uninterested as they fussed and fretted over the king. Eventually, Akhenaten stopped coughing and managed to recover what little breath he had left, and his physicians calmed themselves and retreated to the safety of their huddle on the opposite side of the room. Aye sat back down on the bed.

"I understand Your Majesty is ill," he said.

Akhenaten looked up at him. "Nonsense," he said. "Nothing that I do not have under control."

"Your Majesty," Aye said. "You are plainly and gravely ill, and you need to recognise the fact."

"I will not have..." Akhenaten said, and coughed again for some time, although without the ferocity of his previous attack. "I will not have this blasphemy in my bedchamber," he said, finally.

"Blasphemy, Majesty?"

"I am the Aten's son, and the Aten will not allow harm to come to me. He has told me as much himself. Now, Aye, if you believe me to be ill, you either believe that I am lying, that the Aten is lying, or that he does not have the strength to save me. It matters not which. All are blasphemy."

"Even gods die, Majesty. Now is your time. The Aten is calling you to his bosom."

"Guar..." Akhenaten began, but there was little strength in his voice, and Aye had to expend almost no effort with his hand over Akhenaten's mouth in order to prevent him completing the word. Even the physicians did not hear. Aye nodded at them.

"Tell them to leave the room," he said.

Akhenaten's eyes bulged as he looked up at him.

"Tell them," Aye said, and Akhenaten nodded slowly. Aye removed his hand.

"We have matters to discuss," Akhenaten said to the physicians. "Leave us."

They did so, and not without looks of gratitude. They could not, after all, be expected to save his life if he had banished them from his presence.

When they had gone Aye calmly placed his hand back on Akhenaten's face, although this time he covered both his nose and his mouth. Akhenaten tried to struggle, but he hardly had the strength to move his bedclothes. After some moments Akhenaten's colour began to fade, and his thrashing became more laboured and ineffectual. At this point, Aye removed his hand.

Akhenaten's breath whooped in his throat as he fought to gather as much air within him as he could in as little time as possible. He only managed one or two deep breaths before the effort brought on another coughing fit. For a moment, Aye thought he may have gone too far and the effort would kill Akhenaten before Aye was ready, but slowly, painfully, Akhenaten was able to get his breathing more under control. He looked up at Aye with terror declaimed in his eyes as effectively as if he had the strength to scream it to the priests outside the door.

"Perhaps you are correct," Aye said to him. "Perhaps you are not dying. Perhaps this is a passing sickness from which you are destined to recover. Now, I happen to firmly believe that you are dying. If you disagree then so be it. In fact, it helps my cause if you do so. If that is the case, then you have all the more reason to listen to me. I want to make something absolutely clear to you."

Once again, Aye's hand went to Akhenaten's face. Akhenaten tried to move his head out of the way, but he was weak enough for Aye to hold it in place with one hand. Aye did not wait as long this time before removing his hand and letting Akhenaten breath again. He waited for him to recover fully before continuing.

"And that thing is this," he said. "I have at the moment absolute power over your life. Whether you are destined to recover from this illness or not is immaterial. I decide, and I alone, not your precious Aten, whether you live to see the sunset or whether you die in your bed now. You see, because I believe you are dying, I have no time to discuss matters with you, or cajole and persuade. I have no time for politics or tricks or intrigue. You will simply do as I say, because if you do not, I will kill you. Do you understand?"

"I understand the words, but not where they have come from." Akhenaten said.

"That is of no matter," Aye said. He lifted his hand again in an exaggerated movement.

"What would you have me do?" Akhenaten said quickly, his eyes staring at Aye's hand as though trying to push it away with nothing more than an exertion of will.

"Name Nefertiti as your successor."

"Her name is Smenkharē," Akhenaten said, and Aye laughed.

"You are a stubborn old fool," he said. "But very well. It is of little consequence. Name her as your successor to the throne."

"She already is," Akhenaten said.

"Then name her so. In front of witnesses. It will save a lot of distress when you are gone. There are some who would be reluctant to serve a female king."

"And what if I am not dying?" Akhenaten said. "You do know, do you not, what I will have done to you before you beg to be executed? Mahu is a very resourceful man."

"My future is nothing against that of my country," Aye said. "Now, am I to summon your courtiers? And the prince? Or shall we end it instead?"

Akhenaten looked at him, and at the hand poised above his face, for a long moment.

"Summon them," he said.

The Maya Papyrus, Fragment 171

> *We were a very select bunch, we who gathered outside the king's bedchamber. It was only a matter of minutes since the call had gone out that we had been summoned, for we had each spent all that day and the previous night at the palace awaiting news of the king's condition. Few of us could have truthfully said that we were in reality concerned for Akhenaten's health. I would never wish for any man to suffer – with the possible exception of Mahu, who I think is a special case – but I cannot say I was unduly distressed at the thought of Akhenaten's passing. Rather I (as well, I suspected, as most of the people around me) was interested in events and their relation to and consequences for the royal family and the kingdom as a whole.*
>
> *If I may be less circumspect: the day that Akhenaten died would be one of cacophonous celebration in the hearts of almost every one of his subjects. Of course, traditions needed to be maintained, and a certain dignity is called for in the death of the most savage tyrants, but while the country mourned and women threw dirt over their heads along the entire route of the funeral*

cortege, there would not be one of them who was not thinking: It is over! I am free!

. We had no idea why we had been gathered. We could assume that the king yet lived, for news of his passing could not have been kept a secret for this long. We each looked at each other quizzically, but nobody spoke.

As well as myself, Nefertiti was there, as was Tutankhaten. Horemheb and Nakhtmin arrived together, minutes behind us. Mahu was conspicuous by his absence. I could only think that he had not been told of the audience. I could not see him missing it otherwise.

We were ushered into the bedchamber and found that Aye had preceded us. He was sitting with surprising familiarity on the edge of the king's bed, smiling easily. Akhenaten himself looked as though he was clinging onto life with the very last of his strength. He did not turn his head when the door opened and we were ushered in by the priests. It seemed as though so much of his concentration was being taken up merely by staying alive that there was none left for us. We gathered at the foot of the bed, such as we could. Standing where we were we could see nothing more than the lumps in bed caused by his feet. There were no steps there for us to climb to bring us on a level where we could see his face.

Once we were in position, Aye spoke.

"His Majesty wishes to make an announcement," he said.

Akhenaten did not speak. He did not, in fact, acknowledge that he had heard Aye at all, or that he even knew that Aye or any of the rest of us were there.

"Your Majesty," Aye prompted.

And then we heard a voice from the top of the bed.

"I hereby decree and command," the voice said, and then descended into coughing before continuing: "and... command that, come the eventual time of my death, may the Aten postpone it for a thousand years, that my co-regent, King Smenkharē, shall rule this land without me."

"That is all," Aye said, standing up and signalling for us to leave. We did not react immediately, for it was a development that we were not expecting.

"Thank you for your time," Aye said. He stepped down from the dais upon which the king's bed was placed and ushered us towards the door. Akhenaten began to cough again. As we were herded in that direction, having time only to look at each other in *puzzlement, I thought I heard Akhenaten try to speak once more and I saw Horemheb turn his head in the king's direction. Later, Horemheb was to tell me that he thought he heard Akhenaten speak his name. At the time, the king's voice was so quiet and so distorted by coughing, and Aye was speaking over it so incessantly, that we both separately assumed that we had imagined it.*

We exited the room, leaving Aye alone with Akhenaten once more.

"Horemheb," Akhenaten said, as the audience was leaving. None had been given the opportunity to speak, nor to question what they had heard and seen. Akhenaten knew he only had one chance to alert them to the heinous crime that had been perpetrated here. Surely Horemheb, the general of the king's army, the man who had already saved Akhenaten's life from the hands of a priest of Amun, would leap to his aid once he was aware of Aye's treachery. But he did not have the strength and the word caught in his throat.

And now the room was empty once again, save for himself and Aye. Aye closed the door and returned to his place on the edge of Akhenaten's bed.

"You are going to die," Aye said. "You must reconcile yourself to this."

"I may yet recover, Aye."

"Recover and order my arrest and execution?"

"You have committed no crime," Akhenaten said. "Not yet. I have no reason to have you arrested."

Aye wrinkled his nose. He thought the lies pathetic in their transparency.

"Do you know," Aye said, "you were right about one thing all along." He raised his hand once again.

"No," Akhenaten said. "There is no need... you have my word... Aye, please..."

Aye's hand came down over his mouth, and his final words were muffled into incomprehensibility.

"You were right," Aye said. "This disease will not kill you after all."

He waited, his hand held tightly over Akhenaten's nose and mouth, until all resistance had ceased.

End of Part Three

Part Four

The Borders of Night

Chapter Twenty

The Architect

THERE HAD been no dreams of Amun. Or at the very least, there had been no dreams of a vengeful Amun. Occasionally, Aye would wake with the vague impression of a dream which contained the god with a cobra's head, but the flicking of the tongue no longer seemed malicious to him. It was closer to a smile than a snarl.

It made perfect sense. For how could Amun continue to be angry with him after the service he had done him? Aye had rid the world and the heavens of a monster and a heretic and surely the pantheon must be feting his name with loud huzzahs for the work he had carried out. He had no fear, for anything in the world with any strength, any real strength, any power to make a functional difference, was his friend and ally.

Fleetingly, he had been concerned about Akhenaten's shade, for a pharaoh, however malign, must surely leave a trace in the Underworld. But it was a concern that caused him no more than a handful of sleepless nights. After all, was it not true that all the dead, from paupers to kings, were judged by Osiris on their entry into the Underworld? Akhenaten must have had a heart so heavy that it would have toppled Osiris' scales to the ground. There was little chance that his soul lived on.

Of course there was the matter of Akhenaten's earthly allies, but Aye did not doubt that he had the wherewithal to deal with them easily when the time came.

He knew the value of patience. He had learned it by watching Ptahmose's posturing and manipulation during the years of the peak of his powers. He knew that his fellow Egyptians did not embrace change even when the change was patently for the better. Sudden change was unendurable by even the most radical of his countrymen and so he knew he must steer carefully and bring the ship around so slowly that even the current did not notice. But steer he did, and the course was already changing.

Nefertiti, it transpired almost to his surprise, was an able king. She had been a Great Royal Wife, and later a co-regent so entangled with the flora of the throne that its roots entwined her even when its flower was removed. Aye had allowed her the time to steady herself, for however prepared she was, however naturally she fell into the role it was one that demanded not a little acclimatisation. Anyway, for now she was not declaring radical decrees or throwing the country into a turmoil of revolution. She was only making the decisions that Aye had already decided she should make, and she was managing to do so with an almost complete lack of prompting from him.

The army was gradually being diverted back into a force for the defence of the kingdom rather than a force for the destruction of Egypt's temples. It was impossible, as yet, to remove all the soldiers from their duties as tax collectors but Nefertiti had at least signalled her intention to right the situation at the first opportunity. It was as much as Aye had hoped, and the threat from the Hittites had already diminished to curses thrown from capital to capital as increasing numbers of troops made their way to the threatened border regions. Horemheb and Nakhtmin were already there, organising their forces into some semblance of order and cursing the years of sloth that had allowed their men to become so flabby and ineffectual.

The country was content for the first time since Amenhotep's death, and Aye felt not a little measure of pride that he was the architect of its contentment. It was he who had despatched Akhenaten, although he recognised that he was perhaps only a day or so ahead of the plague that would have killed him anyway. That did not matter to him. It had been his hand that had snapped the shackles that bound the Two Lands, and for that he knew he would live forever.

So, no, there were no nightmares, for there were no possible evil consequences of his actions. No innocents had died, no babies. It felt instead as though a birth had taken place. Aye felt like a father all over again.

Mahu scared her. He was the only one, but he made up for a kingdom full of courage. At first, after the plague had dragged Akhenaten into the arms of the Aten, Nefertiti had been so afraid of him that even she, the king of Egypt, had been loath to anger him by banishment or some other punishment for his years of cruelty. Later, there was more than just fear. It was a secret feeling, one that she dared not name even to Aye – especially to Aye – but one which she harboured in her heart like shame. And her mortification was this: he was useful.

He had remained at the throne's side throughout the month's up to and following Akhenaten's funeral. He asked for nothing and he was granted barely a smile or a greeting, but he never left her side. He offered advice which at first she had ignored as a matter of principle. He had treated her with quiet respect. He had ensured her safety with guards that watched over her night and day.

At first she had dispensed with them. She saw them as an embodiment of Akhenaten's paranoia and she wanted nothing remaining that would remind her of the fact that once she had been persuaded that she felt a need for them.

And then at the funeral she had been carried by chariot at the head of the cortege and she had felt bare. The crowds had lined the route as she had known they would, as Mahu had warned her they would, and she found herself trying to watch every direction at once, waiting for the man who would be her killer to step forward from the women who lined the route and wailed the lies of their grief. Of course, no such man had done so and she doubted if such a man even existed, but it was only afterwards that her fears had seemed ridiculous. Throughout the funeral she had been distracted and anxious. The ceremony in the tomb, up in the cliffs overlooking the city, was a barely surviving memory, shredded as it was by the fear of facing the crowds once again. On the procession down from the cliffs back into the city Mahu seemed to sense the discomfort that went unnoticed by everybody else and engineered himself into position directly behind her. She was grateful for that, although at this stage she was still unwilling to show any favourable outlook towards him and she pretended that she had not noticed.

At her next audience she informed him that the tradition of the royal armed guard was to be resumed forthwith. She had been surprised by the lack of smugness in his face when he bowed his compliance, and even more surprised by the lack of objection from Aye. She had assumed that he would have a great deal to say on the subject and had prepared herself for having to flex her authority with her father, but nothing of the kind had happened.

He was, in fact, engrossed in another problem of Nefertiti's reign, but in any case would not have objected had he been giving the conversation the attention it merited. If Nefertiti felt the need for an armed guard it was not for him to question her. Or, more precisely, there was no need for him to question her. It made no difference to him if she surrounded herself with guards or not. Given time, she would see that she was not viewed by the general populace as was her late husband. With Aye's help, she would be loved, and she would soon see that her guards, and for that matter Mahu, were entirely superfluous.

It was not something that concerned him. What concerned him was the matter of the daily worship. More accurately, he had two concerns with the daily worship. The first was that Atenism shared with the religion that preceded it one crucial aspect, the aspect that Aye had used to engineer Nefertiti's place on the throne. It was the trinity, and it could hardly be discarded now after Aye had used it to such good effect. Except, of course, with Akhenaten gone there was no longer any trinity, and Aye had quickly come to the conclusion that one needed to be manufactured. The king needed a wife with which to worship that Aten, but similarly a king needed a wife to worship Amun, and once the transition was made back to the true religion the need for a wife would not be diminished.

It was a train of thought that he could not avoid, but it was one that he resented, for it unceasingly brought him to the second of his concerns, which was the nature of religion itself. That Atenism had to be discarded was without question in his mind, but how, and when? The Atenist priesthood had been so favoured by Akhenaten that their stature and power within the city was a model of the power enjoyed by the priests of Amun throughout the kingdom during the reign of Amenhotep. They would not be a foe easily vanquished. And for that matter, neither would Mahu.

It was a question of loyalties. Mahu was making a play of his loyalty to the throne, but Aye recognised that for what it was and knew him to be doing nothing more than manoeuvring for position. Mahu had his men, whose loyalty was beyond question. They had followed him into too many situations, enjoyed too many benefits and favours under his command, wielded too much sheer power for them to be anything other than fiercely devoted to him. They would be a problem, for Aye's success depended upon the removal of Mahu from court, and preferably from this mortal realm altogether. His men would not sit idly by and allow such a thing to happen.

At a time like this, Aye needed all the allies he could muster, and making enemies of an estate as powerful as the priesthood was not a sensible or desirable step in that direction.

And so for now Aye had decided to leave the priests be, but this did not help him with the question of a wife for the king. The priests would not be pleased if Nefertiti was unable to appease the Aten and his fanatical cohorts.

Luckily, he knew exactly who to appoint.

The Maya Papyrus, Fragments 181-192

> *The problem was that a king needs a wife, even if the king herself is a woman. No man could be a wife, and so the only real solution was to have our female king marry another woman. Still,*

although we recognised that there was nothing here other than the ceremonial, one or two of us at court continued to feel uncomfortable with the arrangements. I cannot say why with any level of certainty. Perhaps the idea of two women being married was so unnatural that it offended our sensibilities regardless of the circumstances. Perhaps we were not offended by that, but rather by the fact that Meritaten was Nefertiti's daughter, and we were reminded of Akhenaten's marriages to his daughters, and the offspring thereof.

I was sure that I was not alone in my hesitancy to celebrate the marriage, and one evening I mentioned my concerns to Horemheb. By now I believe I was as firm a friend to him as I was to Tutankhaten, or as he was to Nakhtmin. I felt that there was an implicit trust between us that was beyond compromise. We were at the palace, but we were alone, waiting for Nakhtmin to make an appearance before the three of us attended an audience with Nefertiti. Both Horemheb and Nakhtmin had recently returned from their regiments on the north eastern border and had been summoned to report their progress to the king. I was there because I was Nefertiti's most trusted advisor, perhaps with the exception of Aye. I had no doubt that once the audience chamber doors opened we would find that both Aye and Mahu had gained entrance to the room via some other route and would be waiting for us at the king's side, trying not to look as though they had just finished a conversation to which we would never be privy.

"I take it you have heard about the marriage," I said to Horemheb.

"I have," he said. "Once again we have been granted a time of great rejoicing."

I looked at him, and he looked back, expressionless.

"I am not so sure," I said.

"Nonsense," he replied. "It is a time to rival even the great joys brought to us by Akhenaten and the Aten."

There was another beat of silence.

"Are you mad?" I said, when I saw that he was not going to add anything. "Did I perhaps sleep through these great joys of which you speak? Did they all perhaps happen at once while I was otherwise engaged?"

Horemheb took me by the elbow and led me out from the antechamber in which we were awaiting Nakhtmin into the corridor that ran for some length along the side of the palace, bordered by windows looking out over delicately manicured *gardens and pools. I could hear the calls of hoopoe birds as they sought mates among the shrubs and bushes.*

"Maya," Horemheb whispered to me, his grip still firm on my elbow. "I would have you take more care over your words. We both know our true feelings over Akhenaten and the joys he brought us, but it simply would not do to allow those feelings to become public knowledge."

"Really," I said, "can you not sense the change in the air? Akhenaten is gone. My sister Nefertiti occupies the throne. I think that neither of us have much to fear from her."

Horemheb shrugged.

"You may be right," he said. "It may be that our monarch is as enlightened as Akhenaten was intolerant, but I would prefer someone else to take the risk before I will openly criticise her reign, or that of her predecessor. I would urge you to follow my example."

"I think you are overreacting," I said.

"I would rather overreact than offend a vengeful king. We still worship the Aten, do we not?"

"For now," I said.

"Then for now I shall not criticise him, or his offspring."

"Even when you are alone with people you trust?"

"You can never be sure of being alone. I have spies working for me against the Hittites, and I know how spies operate. I prefer to speak in a room full of people. As least then I know who is listening, and I can modify my words accordingly."

"Very well," I said. "I shall heed your advice, for you are a man whose advice is rarely without merit. But I still say it is an unnecessary caution."

"Ah, my dear Maya," he said, smiling. "There is no such thing."

When Nakhtmin arrived the conversation between myself and Horemheb came to an abrupt end. Horemheb and Nakhtmin were inseparable in almost all situations, but Horemheb knew both Nakhtmin and I well enough to know that I would be uncomfortable discussing matters of a private or delicate nature in Nakhtmin's company, and that Nakhtmin would be just as uncomfortable keeping any private information private. Nakhtmin's lack of discretion preceded him wherever he went. He was forgiven by those around him only because of the lack of malice with which he shared their intimacies, and because of his talents elsewhere. He may not have been the most intelligent member of our family, nor the most shrewd, for Aye was privileged enough to hold both of those positions. Neither was Nakhtmin the most pleasing to the eye or the most flattering to the spirit, for that was Nefertiti. Nakhtmin's overriding quality, though, was his skill on the battlefield. It was so well developed that it rivalled that of Horemheb himself, and it was a quality that Egypt relied on infinitely more than Aye's mind or Nefertiti's body.

The three of us were summoned into the audience chamber, where Horemheb and Nakhtmin reported on their progress at the border.

"There are skirmishes," Horemheb told Nefertiti. Aye and Mahu, as I had predicted, were installed on Nefertiti's either side. Tutankhaten waited by Aye's right hand. All listened with a grim intensity.

"Are they preparing for an all out attack?" Nefertiti asked.

"They are testing our strength," Horemheb replied. "They are searching for weak spots. They are a very meticulous people, the Hittites."

"And will they find weak spots?"

"Yes," Horemheb said, simply. "We have had very little time to prepare. I am a little surprised that they have not found them already."

Nefertiti looked momentarily outraged.

"You seem a little nonchalant about the fact, General."

"Nonchalant, Your Majesty? I can assure you that neither I nor General Nakhtmin are doing anything less than our absolute utmost in the protection of your kingdom. But I must remind you that the army is in a little less than the pinnacle of condition. The men of your army are only mortal, Majesty. They require time to adjust from the duties to which they have been assigned during your husband's reign, may the Aten keep his soul for a million years. While they do so they are being attacked by the Hittite advanced guard. They are continuing heroically under difficult circumstances."

I knew Horemheb better than anybody else in the room, and I could see the anger that he successfully disguised from the others. He remained entirely calm during his speech, which even went as far as placating Nefertiti. Mahu did not look so happy as his king, and Aye looked as inscrutable as ever.

"Then I would bid you continue your good work," Nefertiti said, in such a manner as to make it impossible to estimate the *ratio of sarcasm in her voice. It was clear, however, that the two generals were being dismissed.*

"Your Majesty," Nakhtmin said, stepping forwards. "We have travelled for over a week, mostly under the harsh desert sun, in order to present you with our report. Am I really to believe that our work here is done? Do you dismiss us so quickly to return to our men?"

Before Nefertiti answered, Mahu leant to her ear and briefly whispered something to her.

"Is there somewhere else where you can be of more use?" Nefertiti said, once Mahu had stood upright again.

"We are never more useful than when we are at the head of a division of soldiers," Nakhtmin said. "But by the time we return to them you have taken us away for three weeks. We are not messengers, Nefertiti. If you require reports of one sentence I suggest you employ a man of that trade instead. We have some to spare, should the need arise."

"I would remind you whom you address," Mahu said, from his position at Nefertiti's right shoulder.

"I do not address you, for one," Nakhtmin said. "I address my sister. I would have you remember the same thing."

"You address your king," Nefertiti said. "I am no longer simply your sister."

Nakhtmin looked briefly as though he was about to speak again. Horemheb firmly placed his hand on Nakhtmin's shoulder in order to interrupt the flow of his thoughts.

"I am sure, Your Majesty," Horemheb said, "that you will forgive Nakhtmin his quick tongue. He is merely concerned that he might serve you forever to the best of his great ability. Your Majesty knows him well enough to know that he means no slight."

Horemheb bowed deeply, and I could see from the way the skin on Nakhtmin's shoulder welled up around his fingers that he was putting not a little pressure on his friend to do the same. Nakhtmin took the hint.

"General Horemheb speaks the truth," he said, barely able to keep the reluctance from his voice. "I most humbly apologise, Your Majesty."

"You are forgiven," Nefertiti said, differentiating herself from her husband in three words. Horemheb and Nakhtmin bowed from the room. I thought I saw Horemheb glance in my direction before the doors closed behind him. It was a look that put the full

stop on the conversation we conducted while we waited to be admitted to the audience chamber.

I took it as the warning that it undoubtedly was, and from that day decided to show some restraint in my criticism of this regime, or the one that preceded it. Mahu's whispering to Nefertiti had gone unnoticed by nobody.

Aye thought himself a fool. He had been so busy with his preparations for the future that he had paid scant attention to the present and he had failed to appreciate that which was coming to pass under his very nose. While he had been meticulously plotting Nefertiti's decisions for tomorrow and the day after, he had failed to see that Mahu was plotting Nefertiti's decisions for today. There had, of course, been few visible examples of the machinations that Mahu had been quietly constructing. They had been as fragile as walls made from mud, but Aye knew that given time, mud dries into brick strong enough to construct palaces.

When Mahu whispered something into Nefertiti's ear at her audience with Horemheb and Nakhtmin, Aye had been flabbergasted, but not at the action itself, although this was shocking enough for a man with designs of his own on the ear of the king. What had surprised and appalled him in such generous measure was the ease with which Mahu had offered his advice and the nonchalance with which Nefertiti had accepted it. It was almost as though she had been expecting it and had delayed her judgement until she had weighed the merit of his words. Aye knew then that he had lost a significant battle, and that Mahu had successfully insinuated himself where Aye had failed. It was of no consolation (in fact it made it all the more galling) that Aye had failed simply because he had not applied himself to the attempt.

He could not gauge exactly how much ground he had lost, but any at all was more than enough. It was a situation that Aye did not enjoy, because he was being forced to act before he had fully deliberated on his options and their likely consequences. He knew, though, that to hesitate now was to lose much more than that which Mahu had succeeded in denying him.

He also recognised that a direct challenge to Mahu was as much a folly as would be a failure to take any action at all. A dislodged Mahu might be even more of a threat.

He decided on a different tack, although in all honesty he could not tell whether it was a good choice or no, whether it was the wisdom of a quick mind or the folly of a desperate one.

Two days after the audience with the generals, Aye was once again before the throne in the audience chamber. To his chagrin, Mahu was once again by Nefertiti's side, as, of course, was Tutankhaten.

"I have a proposition for Your Majesty," he said. He was careful to phrase his words formally, for he had the suspicion that Nefertiti revelled in it.

"You know I am always happy to hear your ideas, Aye," Nefertiti said, and Aye noted that she no longer called him 'father'.

"I believe that it is time for Tutankhaten to take a tutor."

"He has a tutor," Nefertiti said. "In fact, he has several. The priests of Aten teach him every day."

"Really," Aye said, looking at the boy. "He seems to have little spare time for them. He is always here before me and after I am gone."

Nefertiti smiled easily, choosing to ignore the slight in Aye's tone. She turned to the prince and ruffled his wig. "He is very keen to learn the ways of the king, are you not, Tutankhaten?"

"Yes, Your Majesty," Tutankhaten said, joining her in her smile. Nefertiti was now a long way past the first flush of youthful beauty, so much so that some would consider her to look stern, but still her splendour commanded enough awe to make her smile irresistible to those lucky enough to enjoy its glow.

"I cannot help thinking," Aye said, "that there may perhaps be more for him to learn than he can find in an audience chamber. Even this one."

"Do you indeed?" Nefertiti said. She was still smiling. "And I would be willing to wager that you just happen to have a name in mind of someone who would be the perfect tutor, do you not?"

"Perhaps, Majesty," Aye said. "I may."

"And what would you propose to teach him?"

"There is little doubt that one day he will be king," Aye said. "I am lucky enough to have spent my entire life at court, the companion and servant of three of Egypt's greatest monarchs: yourself, of course, and Akhenaten and Amenhotep. I think there is little the boy could learn from me that would not be of at least some use to him in his life ahead."

"You make a convincing case," Nefertiti said. She turned to Tutankhaten. "And what about you?" she said. "Would you like to be your grandfather's pupil?"

Tutankhaten looked at Aye, who smiled in return.

"Of course," Tutankhaten said, but his smile had faded somewhat, and what little of it remained did so against its better nature.

Nefertiti sat back in her throne, and although Aye could not discern its nature, some sort of cue evidently passed between her and Mahu, for he chose this moment to lean forwards and whisper in her ear, just as he had done during the audience with Horemheb and Nakhtmin. This time, though, he spoke at greater length and only straightened up after Aye had begun to wonder if he would ever stop.

Once he had spoken his fill, Nefertiti spent a moment in thought.

"No," she said, eventually, and Aye's consternation lasted only long enough for him to realise that she was addressing herself to Mahu and not to him. "No," she said. "I do not believe that it can do any harm. I think he may learn a great deal. Aye has always been a friend of the throne."

Mahu had the good grace to look embarrassed at such a public, if indirect, interpretation of his counsel.

"An excellent choice, Your Majesty," Aye said, bowing. He did not gloat to Mahu over the decision, but he looked him in the eye long enough for Mahu to know that he could have done had he so wished.

It was as much as he could have asked for. The granting of his boon, and the humiliation of Mahu into the bargain. Aye retired to begin planning his next move.

It had been almost as great a surprise to Nefertiti as it had to her father to discover exactly how much she had begun to rely on Mahu, and how this reliance increased from one day to the next. She found him surprisingly trustworthy and selfless. The advice he gave her was always honest and while she did not always agree with it she was sure that it was given in good faith and with laudable motives.

At first, despite the protection she felt he afforded her on the return to Akhetaten after her husband's funeral, she had been reluctant to allow him even into the palace and would hardly have imagined his place at her elbow within a matter of months. But there he was, and once there he was impossible to dislodge. He was not stubborn or wilful, but kept his place at her side simply by telling her the truth.

"Your husband, may the Aten keep his soul, was not a popular man, Your Majesty," he once told her. They were alone in the audience chamber, she having allowed him to remain behind for the first time after the departure of her other advisors. Mahu had offered her little preamble to the statement, and it caught her somewhat unawares.

"You think not?" she asked him, surprised not by the statement but by Mahu's confidence in its assertion.

Mahu smiled. "I think not," he said. "In fact, he was a hated man."

Recovering herself, Nefertiti glowered at him. "I will thank you to keep your opinions on your kings and gods to yourself, lest your words be overheard by those you discuss, who are less forgiving than I."

"My fate at the hands of the gods is nothing compared to my shame should I misrepresent the truth to you, Your Majesty," he said. "It is my duty, just as it was my duty to your husband, and it is one I will execute in this world and the next, regardless of the consequences."

"That is very loyal of you, Mahu," Nefertiti said, somewhat placated.

"It grieves me to say so, Majesty, but I fear that I speak the truth. Please do not mistake my belief in the opinion of men with my concordance with it, for I loved your husband as much as any servant has loved a master. He was to me a man of vision, of truth and beauty. He was, and is, the one true god. However, it does not change the fact that he was hated. He was hated by his servants, by his generals and his army. He was hated by his people and his courtiers and ministers. Perhaps, to some extent, it is not entirely surprising that this should have been the case. For men of small intellects fill their idle minds with hatred when faced with that which they fear."

Mahu was staring at Nefertiti now. Standing as he was, upright and proud, at the foot of the dais upon which she was sitting, their eyes were almost on a level and his gaze held hers like the arms of lovers destined to part.

"They did not understand him and so they feared him, and so they hated him. And yet, Majesty, despite the ire of everyone who had occasion to bow at his feet and the distrust of everyone else, he remained alive and healthy up until his last week on this earth.

"And for that, Majesty, he had me to thank. I watched him when he did not know he needed watching. I guarded him when he though himself alone and safe in his solitude. I guided him when he thought he had already made the correct decision, and cheered him when he thought he had not. He was safe always, Majesty, and if it is at all within my power and the power of my men, which is considerable, I would have you kept in the same safety.

"Gracious Majesty, is this an honour you can find it within yourself to grant me?"

Nefertiti was impressed. He had displayed an eloquence of which she thought him entirely devoid. Moreover, she knew that he was speaking the truth. She knew how her husband was regarded and she had not needed telling by a man such as Mahu. She had only to remember the procession of Akhenaten's funeral and the feeling of exposure to nameless danger she had felt when at its head. She had long feared that Akhenaten had not been the only royal to be so regarded by those around him and that the general populace would see her, especially since her accession to co-regent, as nothing more than his accomplice.

Viewed in these terms, it was perhaps surprising that Akhenaten had lived a life as long as he had, and that when he finally succumbed to death it was not at the hands of a vengeful subject, but at the word of the supernatural. Mahu had not needed to remind her of Akhenaten's fate before that loyal servant had taken up his role as chief of police, and the death they feared had overtaken him at the hands of a priest during Amenhotep's *sed* festival. It had been the only attempt on Akhenaten's life and to her knowledge there had never been an attempt on hers, and she was willing to believe that this was due in no small part to Mahu's watchfulness.

"Do you believe me to be in danger, then?" she said.

"We are all in danger, Your Majesty," he said, as she had known he would. "Even the most popular of public figures is in danger, and the more popular the figure the more acute the danger they live through every day. For it takes only one man, should his senses be addled enough, to threaten the lives of those around him. When a king is well loved, he is loved no more by the madmen of his realm than if he were a monster, because the mad do not have the faculties to tell the difference. If a king is loathed, an attack is expected. It is watched for. The palace and courtiers, the police and ministers, all are vigilant, all watch endlessly the parade of the public before them, ready to pounce in defence of their sovereign. If a king is loved, the attack, if there is one, must surely come from a man bereft of logic, and they are impossible to predict, their actions never evident until they have already been committed.

"It would perhaps make my job easier, Your Majesty," Mahu continued, "if you were as unpopular as your husband."

"And do you think that likely?" Nefertiti said.

"Not a bit of it," Mahu said. "And it troubles me greatly."

"If you are to serve me, you will do so in a way different entirely from the service you offered my husband," she said.

"Different, Majesty?"

"Entirely," she reiterated. "I do not like your methods, Mahu. I never have. I find them vulgar and callous. I like to think that I am neither of these things, and since you will act in my name, you will act in a way that does not bring shame to it. Do you understand me?"

"Majesty, sometimes there is a need of methods that are countenanced by nobody, myself included. But I have always acted in defence of the crown, and the protection of such a treasured institution does not allow limits for the sake of politeness or compassion. If people are hurt it is only because there is a reason for it."

"Nevertheless," Nefertiti said, and there the discussion had ended. She did not labour the point, partly because she expected her commands to be obeyed without the need for justification and partly because she was happy for Mahu to protect her using whichever methods he saw fit, so long as they were effective and her conscious was salved by the knowledge that she had forbidden him from using them.

But she kept him by her side from that moment forth as closely as Akhenaten had done.

Tutankhaten's lessons began almost immediately, for Aye recognised that where the allegiance of every player was already decided the only solution to tip the game in one's own favour was to bring another player to the table.

Tutankhaten listened with rapt attention whenever Aye spoke. He was more than a little afraid of the old man. It was not as though Aye had ever directly hurt him, or even raised his voice to him, but Tutankhaten had been present at enough royal audiences to know that Aye was not a man who would happily brook the questioning of his opinion. Whatever the cause, the fact remained that Tutankhaten was nervous enough in Aye's company to answer any questions eagerly, if not always correctly, and to listen gravely to every word that Aye directed towards him.

But however much he tried he could not begin to understand the concepts that Aye described as though they were merely the products of common sense. That there could be more than one god was as alien to him as if Aye had told him the Nile flowed with wine. That one god, Amun, could be king of the gods Tutankhaten had to grudgingly accept as logical, for presumably even gods would need somebody to rule them. To be subjugated to rule of one form or another was nature's way, he supposed. But that individual cities may worship their own gods he found preposterous. Was Amun not a god in Heliopolis? Did his immense and divine power suddenly dissipate once outside the city walls of Thebes? Did Ptah only rule in Memphis? What if the gods should meet? What if one man were to travel from one city to the next? Would not his previous patronage under a rival not anger the god of whichever city he found himself? How could the Nile have its own god? Was it not a part of creation? Was it not ruled by the god who created it? How could the sun be three different gods at once? How could the king be the manifestation of the godhead without being a god himself? How could he be *different* gods, depending on what he was doing?

All of this was ridiculous to Tutankhaten but he listened all the same, never giving any indication that he harboured doubts as to the veracity of Aye's claims.

Indeed, he wanted to believe. More than anything, he wanted the approval of this old man who seemed so slow to humour and so ready to scold. He wished his mother was here to tell him what to do for the best. He wished his father was here, for then none of this would have arisen in the first place and the Aten would still be in his throne in the vault of the heavens.

But now Aye was telling him that not only did he have to contend with a whole host of gods, the existence of which he had never even guessed, but that the one god in whom he did have faith was in fact a falsehood. He had never existed, this Aten. It seemed unlikely to Tutankhaten that a man as great as his father could have been so fundamentally mistaken about so many matters, and yet Aye seemed so determined in the facts that he reeled off.

Tutankhaten decided that it would be prudent to keep an open mind, and that any doubts he entertained would remain silent doubts in the keep of his heart.

For his part, Aye quickly concluded that Tutankhaten would be an able pupil, given some time and stability in which to develop his mental faculties. Aye had expected a greater reluctance to embrace the old gods, but the young prince absorbed the facts as readily as if he had been a young man embarking on a career in the priesthood of Amun. He did not question anything that he was told, for which Aye was at once grateful and suspicious.

But as the months passed Tutankhaten's attention wavered not one jot. He was always punctual and polite, always quiet and attentive, never once so much as frowning when Aye instructed that lessons that day would last somewhat longer in order to cover some important points.

By his tenth birthday he was as learned in the ways of the old gods as if Atenism had never been conjured into existence.

"We can spare no more men, Majesty," Mahu whispered to Nefertiti. He straightened up and stood with his hands clasped behind his back. Aye thought he could detect the vaguest glimmer of a smug smile, so slight as to be almost behind his lips rather than upon them. Aye turned his gaze back to Nefertiti, a quizzical look upon his face.

Nefertiti did not answer immediately. She was still running Mahu's previous sentence through her mind. *We* can spare no more men, he had said. Not *Egypt* or *Your Majesty*, but *we* can spare no more men. It was sound advice, she was sure, but she needed to speak to Mahu about his station and the ideas he seemed to be adopting which indicated that he was elevating it somewhat in his own mind. She would speak to him later. Now was not the time.

"We can spare no more men," she said to Aye.

"Your Majesty, I must beseech you," Aye said. "The borders are buckling under the pressure being applied to them by the Hittite forces.

Messengers from the front indicate that neither Horemheb nor Nakhtmin can guarantee with any certainty how long they can hold out."

Mahu bent to Nefertiti's ear once again.

"There is a limited supply of soldiers," Nefertiti said, once Mahu had straightened once again. "I cannot conjure them from thin air. I would not be surprised if neither Horemheb nor Nakhtmin are being entirely truthful when it comes to the straits in which they report themselves. They have been empire building since they have been in a position to do so. This could well be nothing more than a plea for power."

"And yet it may not," Aye said. "It may be that they are being entirely truthful. Are you willing to take that gamble?"

Mahu leant down to Nefertiti's ear once again, and Aye could contain himself no longer.

"Must you be forever begging for thoughts?" he exclaimed. "For once, daughter, speak to me from your heart and not the heart of this... this..." Aye blustered and waved at Mahu, unable to think of a suitable epithet.

Nefertiti sprang to her feet.

"You stand before your king!" she shouted. "I would expect you to remember it!"

Aye did not flinch. He met her gaze with neither fear nor defiance, but with calm dispassion. When he spoke he did so quietly, as if to emphasise the fact that he did not need to raise his voice.

"That is something your husband would have said," he said.

Nefertiti's rage dissipated in a moment and was replaced with confusion of equal potency.

"Akhenaten?" she said, as quietly as Aye. "Never."

"I remember him using those exact words."

"My husband was a great king," Nefertiti said, although there was no confidence in her voice and it carried with it a hint of the denial of an indictment as yet unspoken.

"He was at least a king who could speak his own mind," Aye said.

"Get you from my sight," Nefertiti told him coldly, and in doing so attempted to appear as though his continued presence before her was a grave risk to his well-being, although it had more to do with a lack of forceful answers than a surfeit of forceful wrath.

Aye bowed deeply, in such a way to indicate that he was happy to do so, and not wounded enough by Nefertiti's ire to resent having to do so.

"Majesty," he said, and backed towards the door.

However outwardly he forced a smile, however convincing he believed himself to be in his ability to appear happy to receive his daughter's anger, Aye could not persuade himself that he had come away from the confrontation the victor. It was not the first such altercation between them, and not the first to be decided by whispered words from Mahu.

Aye had lost arguments about the royal guard. He had lost arguments about the continued ham-fisted activities of the police contingent in the city. Nothing was determined until Mahu had leant, his hand raised to guard his words and bridge the gap between his lips and Nefertiti's ear, and offered his sibilant opinions.

When Nefertiti had first acceded the throne Aye had allowed her freedom. He gave her the opportunity to edge herself gently into the role. He did so no longer, and yet he had no more grip on the throne than he had over two years previously. It was not the way his plan had run. What was worse, what was infinitely worse, was that he could not rid himself of the image of Mahu laughing himself to sleep at nights at Aye's expense. He radiated smugness the way other men exuded sweat and took joy not in having the king's ear but in having Aye know he had her ear.

Aye had tried everything in his armour to try to wrest some power from undeserving hands. He had stormed, he had cajoled, he had begged. He had spoken to Nefertiti when Mahu was absent and she had merely delayed her decision until Mahu had been consulted. He had spoken to Mahu when Nefertiti had been absent and Mahu had merely ignored him and then informed the king. Nothing would work, and what was more, Aye had come to another, more distressing conclusion: he knew that Nefertiti was enjoying her power. If she listened to Mahu, she did so only because she chose to do so. If she listened to Aye it would be because he had forced himself upon her. It was not an act of free will. It was not an act worthy of a king, or of a goddess.

Aye had been able to dissuade her of the reality of her divinity with no more success than he had been able to persuade her of anything else. Mahu had her ear over this just as he had everything else, and it was to Mahu's advantage to have her a goddess rather than simply a pharaoh. It was a link to Akhenaten, and anything that reminded her of that time was profitable for him.

Aye had lost. He only had his tutelage of Tutankhaten to cling to, and as the boy listened to Nefertiti's words in the audience chamber with just as much intensity as he did Aye's in the schoolroom, Aye hardly knew whether he still had that.

Aye lamented the irony that Thuya's dynasty was at last secure – for her granddaughter was sitting upon the throne, and her great-grandson was next in line – but that such security had come at the price of Egypt.

He no longer attended royal audiences, for he could no longer stand the automatic gainsaying of his words, the instinctive ignorance of his pleas. He could no longer stand Nefertiti's frown, or Mahu's smile, or the way that the one led to the other.

He came to the decision at home. It was mid-morning, a time not suited to brooding or callous decisions, and Aye almost wished it was evening when the gloaming could spread like his malice and gradually swallow him up. But it was not. It was a bright day at a time when he knew that, had he not shunned the practice, he would perforce have been before the king's throne. Instead, he was sitting in the living room of his home at the table at which he would normally have taken his meals. The house now was empty, save himself. The previous night had not brought him sleep and he had been pacing the floor long before sunrise. He had heard the sounds of his neighbours and their servants rising and leaving their homes to meet the responsibilities of the day. His own servants had risen, as they always did, with the sun, in order to prepare the household for the coming day. Aye barely acknowledged their presence. He was unused to seeing them at this time of day, because he was either asleep in his bedchamber, outside of which his servants had long known the importance of careful steps and whispered words, or he was already at the palace. They worked silently around him as he paced the floors, rubbing his temples in thought.

Before long, with no instructions other than the expression on his face and the speed of his pacing, the servants divined his wish to be undisturbed and they fled each room as he entered it. He did not settle in any of the rooms for more than a few minutes and quickly tired of the sight of their backs disappearing via the nearest door. He ordered that they should vacate the house entirely and not return before nightfall.

He had then found himself at the table in the living quarters, after briefly returning to his bed chamber to retrieve a small package from a hidden cache located under his bed. He turned the package over in his hands, and thought of what he would do with it.

The day passed relatively uneventfully. There had been a representation from Syria which Nefertiti had charmed and entertained so effectively that they had largely forgotten the complaints of their government by the time they retired to their beds. Mahu had been as helpful as she had come to expect, remaining silent for long periods before leaning in with a piquant or insightful remark which, once repeated aloud by Nefertiti, would leave the ambassadors' arguments sounding petty and nonsensical. Their complaints that Egypt had not heeded their requests for help against the Hittites were dismantled point by point, so comprehensibly that even Nefertiti had been impressed, if slightly concerned that many of her arguments were lost to her by the time the discussions had concluded.

Well, she thought, as the Syrians left for the guest quarters, *it is important only that the argument was successful. The steps which brought about such success are immaterial.*

She was not entirely sure whether she herself was convinced, but she resolved to make herself so. It was not a king's lot to have to deal with doubts and insecurities.

Shortly after the ambassadors left it was the turn of her advisors, and she nodded her goodbyes to them as they bowed their way to the door. She wondered, not for the first time, where Aye had been all day. It was unlike him to miss such an important audience knowing that Mahu would have her undivided attention without him. Nefertiti smiled to think of the animosity between the two men. It was not her doing and there was nothing she could do to control or change it, and so instead she resolved to find it faintly amusing.

Soon, the audience chamber was empty except for herself and Mahu. It was so late in the evening by now that it was impractical for Mahu to travel all the way home only to have to return in the morning for further discussions with the Syrians. Nefertiti suggested he stay in his apartments in the palace and he bowed and thanked her for her consideration. She watched him leave before pushing herself out of her throne. She found herself exhaling with the effort and decided that she was getting old. She wondered how long it would be before her exhalations were replaced with groans and grimaces as her joints succumbed to the passing of the years and began to complain at the exertions she demanded of them.

She walked from the chamber and made her way back to her apartments, thinking about times not so very long ago when she would make this walk as Akhenaten's companion, and about how they discussed what it would be like to make the walk alone. Now she knew, and it was not as unpleasant as she had expected it to be. She had not expected to have the concerns of a kingdom on her shoulders as she made her way through these corridors, and work and worry provided a strange relief from grief.

She reached her apartments and let herself into her dressing room, where servants waited to prepare her for her bed. They were different rooms from the ones she had shared with Akhenaten, for she had quickly found that his absence had redefined them for her. They were no longer rooms, or even rooms that she was once shared with her husband. They were now simply rooms where her husband would never be again.

Her servants fussed about her, gently and quietly removing her clothes and her make-up, taking off her wig and placing it on its stand. They washed and perfumed her and then she submitted to having her head shaved, for it had been some time since it had last been done and the stubble was beginning to itch.

After every inch of her had been cleansed and purified the soft linen of her night robe was allowed to fall over her shoulders and body, its hem held by three servants to ensure that its placement was as regal and dignified as possible.

All but one of the servants then prostrated themselves while the one remaining on her feet opened the door to the pharaoh's bedchamber. Nefertiti smiled at her and thanked the rest for their care and consideration as she always did, and walked into the bedroom. Candles had been lit in alcoves around the wall and the room was full of warm light. She heard the door close behind her. Here more servants awaited her, already prostrate in a line across the floor.

"May you live," she said, and they rose and set themselves about their duties. Two of them turned back the covers on the bed ready to receive the king's person. Two more servants extinguished all but one of the candles, while two more escorted Nefertiti across the floor and up the steps. She climbed into bed and the servants bowed from the room, taking the last lit candle with them. Darkness engulfed her, and she thought about Mahu.

He had left the audience chamber before her and made his way with little ceremony back to his austere rooms. In the days of Akhenaten he had spent more time here than he had anywhere else. The practicalities of travel had, in those days, not been an issue, for Akhenaten had not felt comfortable whenever Mahu was more than a few moment's away from him. Although Mahu had been successful in impressing upon Nefertiti the danger that she constantly faced he was as yet unable to lead her into as deep a labyrinth of paranoia as he had her husband. He thought that it would probably only be a matter of time, and that each step she took was a step to his advantage. A fragile king was one in need of security and there was nobody in the kingdom with a greater gift for the provision of security than Mahu. His position at court had suffered somewhat with the passing of Akhenaten, but Mahu was nothing if not resolute, and a man in the habit of achieving his goals. He knew that what he had been before he could be again, and that there was very little, other than the unpredictable whims of a woman in power, that could prevent him.

Mahu began to prepare himself to go to bed. He did not have the servants at his disposal who attended Nefertiti, but he was able to remove his make-up and clothes with two hands quicker than she was with half a dozen. He carried his own lamp across the bedroom, watching the shadows play before him as he walked. Once in the bed he extinguished the lamp and lay back with little preamble. He fell asleep quickly, his thoughts muddling into nonsense before his waking mind could latch onto any one of them.

Aye was in the palace. It was quiet and he was alone. The palace had rarely been so deserted under Akhenaten, regardless of the lateness of the hour, for there had forever been the patrols of guards to meet, even in the remotest and least travelled corners. Since Akhenaten's death there had been a relaxation and the patrols were much easier to avoid. Nefertiti still felt the need for them but was happy knowing that they at least existed. Aye was confident that he would not be intercepted, although he recognised still the necessity for caution. A man who marched through the corridors with no secrets, no malevolent intent to lighten his step and sharpen his eye would be apprehended within minutes. Although the patrols were fewer, they were still there, and they were still a keen danger. He carried with him a small vial that any man of education or suspicion would recognise. There would be little chance of persuading any of Mahu's men that he was not here for an ill purpose.

He ducked from one corridor to the next, secure in the darkness and knowing the plan of the place well enough to recognise both exactly how to get to where he was going and that he was taking the longest but safest route. It was a course that took him past the room where Tiye had breathed her last and he could not help stopping at the door and gently pushing it open before glancing into the room, as though recognising the presence of his sister's spirit and seeking absolution from it.

Before too long, and having heard only the rumour of a patrol via the shuffle of its members' distant footsteps, he was at his goal. Here there were guards, as Aye had known there would be. They were tired and listless, for there had never been anything on this shift worth relating to their companions the following morning, nothing to disturb their monotony, nothing, until this night, that would make them value their posts as something worthwhile.

Aye had to get past them, and he had to do so in a way that would never lead them to suspect that he had been here. He could march up to them, of course, and demand entrance, or laugh and joke with them and tell them how he had a message to deliver, but subterfuge was the key, not brazenness. Subterfuge and malice.

The door to the room was placed at a junction in two corridors. One corridor formed the wall in which the door was to be found, the other faced the door directly, so that if the door was open Aye could have marched down the corridor and into the room without checking his pace. In a small alcove to one side of the door was a lamp which cast a pale glow around the area where the two guards were standing. Its strength was insufficient to illuminate the corridors for more than a few paces around them. In front of them, facing the door, safe in the darkness, was Aye. He waited, forcing himself to inhale and exhale in measured, calm beats. To his left was another door, slightly ajar. The room beyond it was dark, and therefore empty, and therefore ideal for Aye's purpose.

He continued to wait and watch for his opportunity. He remained absolutely motionless. It seemed as though the guards had recently finished eating. The room to Aye's left contained their supplies for the night, and Aye knew he had enjoyed at least a modicum of luck. Had he arrived minutes earlier he would surely have met one of the guards appearing from the room, laden with food. The guards were drinking beer from a large jug and talking. Aye listened to every word, from lack of choice rather than interest.

"He wants to move in with us, the buffoon," one of them was saying.

"I take it you are not exactly happy with the situation?" the other replied.

"Of course not. Would you be? You have met him, so you know what he is like. The man is a drunk. He will sell my furniture for wine."

"So refuse."

"Refuse? How can I refuse my wife's father? He has nowhere to go. If I refuse him I will be as destitute as he is."

"And therefore probably as drunk."

"Don't take his side," the first guard said.

"I'm not taking anybody's side. I am just saying..."

"Well, try to restrain yourself. If you like him so much, have him move in with you."

"You know I would my friend, but I am a single man so my furniture is not as tasteful as yours. If he took it to the market he would barely raise enough to get you drunk, and you have a woman's tolerance for wine."

The first guard laughed quietly. "True," he said, "but how can I be any other way? I cannot afford to support her father's taste for beer and pay for one of my own."

The two men drank their beer for a few moments, passing the jug between them, each staring into nothing.

"Well," the first guard said, eventually. "We should make a patrol."

"You stay here. I will go. If I meet your wife's father I shall be sure to stand him a flagon of ale. I may save you a chair."

The first guard feigned anger, although the two were obviously close enough friends to be able to ridicule each other without offence.

"Go," he said, "and take your mouth with you, before I fill it with more than beer." He clenched his fist and made a play of waving it beneath the other man's nose.

The second guard wandered away. He left his sword where it was, leaning with its companion against the wall. Aye waited until he had disappeared around the nearest corner before stepping forward.

"Guard," he whispered.

The guard looked up, straining to see in the gloom. He could just make out a face in the dark, the light catching the nose and the brow ridges.

"Guard," Aye said again. "It is Aye. You must help me."

"Aye?" the guard said. "My lord?"

"You must help me," Aye said again. "The palace is in grave danger."

"But..." the guard said. Aye could see him looking around in the hope that his companion would return. Aye knew the patrol would take much longer, but he did not want to give the guard any time to think.

"Now!" he hissed. "I am the king's father!"

"But my post..."

"Forget your post, man!" Aye said. "You must come to the aid of the palace!"

The guard came to a decision and began to run forwards before suddenly stopping after only a couple of paces. He looked around for his sword. He felt a fool. He had guarded the same door for almost his entire career and had never once needed to brandish his sword. Now he needed it and it lay forgotten where it could threaten nobody.

Aye saw his hesitation, and scarcely able to believe his good fortune, said: "Leave it! There is not time."

After a moment's more indecision the guard ran on without it. As he advanced, Aye backed away into the deeper dark. The guard did not see him raise his hand. He did not see what the hand held. As he passed by where Aye stood he neither heard nor saw Aye's movements, but only felt a hand clamp across his mouth and a sharp, slicing pain across his throat. The strength immediately left his legs, but there was no sound to fade and the passageway was too dark for his sight to dim. He hardly knew that he was dying at all.

Aye dragged his body into the store room and went to stand back in the corridor, careful to avoid the blood. He had yet to make his escape from this place and being covered in blood would not help his chances at all.

He did not have too long to wait until the second guard returned. He was already joking before he arrived.

"I saw him," he was saying. "He said to thank you for the table. At least I think that was what he said. His voice was a little... Sobekhtep?"

Aye saw him approach the doorway and stop in almost exactly the same position that the first guard had occupied before Aye had called to him.

"Sobekhtep?" he said again. "Are you there?"

Aye stepped back towards the store room.

"In here," he said, loud enough to be heard, but too quiet for the guard to recognise that it was not his friend's voice.

"Sobekhtep?" the guard said, blindly looking at where Aye was standing in the impenetrable dark.

"In here. Look."

The guard advanced.

"Sobekhtep," he said. "If old Mahu finds that you left your post unguarded..."

The sentence would remain forever unfinished, and Aye never found out what would have happened if Mahu had discovered that Sobekhtep had left his post. The second guard joined the first on the floor of the store room and Aye stepped back out into the corridor and made his way to the door that had been so poorly guarded. He slipped his knife back into the belt of his kilt.

He paused only momentarily at the door. There was little point in delaying what he had decided must happen, and every moment out in the corridor was a moment in which he could be apprehended.

He pushed the door open gently and stepped into a darkness rendered deeper by the absence of light from the lamp in the corridor. He knew that in the daylight it was a different room from that in the palace in Memphis in which Giludkhepa had lain on the night he killed her, but in the darkness the room and the victim could have been exactly the same. He was sweating and it felt like ice on his skin.

He knew the layout of the room and he stepped across it confidently. He reached down to his belt and removed the pouch that was tied there. He reached the bed and sat down on the side of it. The contents of the mattress creaked as he allowed it to take his weight. The bed's occupant moaned quietly and shifted position. Aye toyed with the pouch for a moment before pulling the string that was tied around its neck. It opened.

He shifted his weight on the bed and leant forwards. He could vaguely distinguish the shape of a head on the pillow below him. He did not want a struggle this time. He wanted it to be painless, quick enough for him to be confident of his escape, and certain enough to have no doubt of his success. He could not use the knife, for his victim was facing towards him and he would not be able to avoid the blood.

But as he watched the face and listened to the breathing, he knew that he could not do this in cold blood. He could not do this like he had done Giludkhepa. He could not face Amun's stares again. This time his victim had to see him, had to know him, had to know that what he did he did not for himself or for hatred or spite, but for Egypt and the future. He took the vial from within the folds of his kilt and shook it gently. It contained a solution of the poison he had not needed to kill Akhenaten. He removed the top.

"Nefertiti," he said, and the word almost caught in his throat.

She awoke with a start.

"Father?" she asked, and he clamped his hand over her mouth just as he had the mouths of the two guards, but he tried to do so with more tenderness, if such a thing was possible.

He knew that he did not have the strength to smother her. That was a death fit only for the sick and feeble. Instead, he removed his hand from her mouth just long enough for her to take a whoop of air in preparation for a scream and to empty the contents of the vial into her throat.

There. It was done. All he had to do now was keep her quiet. She flailed with the energy of one unconcerned with preserving any strength for later, her fingers like whips in the air. A nail caught him on the side of his jaw, tearing a ragged hole in the flesh. He flinched but tried not to show his anger. He could not blame her.

"Shh," he said to her. "This will only take a moment. You are to sit at the right hand of Amun. You are to secure your family's dynasty for a million years. Ssh."

And as he talked the poison constricted her throat and her breaths became nothing more than painful rasps and wheezes until Aye thought it hardly worth the effort to breathe. He thought that would be the end of her, but her struggling did not subside until a huge spasm enveloped her with enough force to dislodge his grip. She doubled over on the bed and Aye did not attempt to restrain her further. She was beyond screams. He stroked her hair as she trembled and spluttered.

He left her only when she was done. As he walked from the room he checked his cheek for blood.

Chapter Twenty-One

Tutankhamun

The Maya Papyrus, Fragments 202-203

WHAT CAN I say? How can I describe in words the sense of loss? I cannot, and so I shall not try. Even now, after the healing of years, my eyes blur and my hands tremble under the weight of my grief, at the thought that I will never see my Nefertiti again. She was the last remnant of my childhood, the last person in whose company I could say to myself: I am home. I found myself suddenly without a tether, without roots.

Nefertiti died shortly after the third anniversary of her accession to the throne. I had commissioned Bek, the sculptor, to fashion a bust of her in honour of her anniversary. Its delivery had been delayed by technical difficulties and I felt it a cruel blow that I was not given this last opportunity to show her my love for her. It was meant to be a surprise, so she never even knew of its existence. Once she was dead I did not want it, for in the passing of one moment it had changed from a thing of love to a thing of loss, and would serve forever only to remind me of what was no longer there and of the fact that she never saw it. I never saw the finished product and although Bek was too modest to make the claims himself, those few who had seen it in the various stages of its manufacture declared it to be a masterpiece surpassing anything they had ever encountered, and that its beauty was so great, so ingrained in its very fabric that it rivalled the face of the great Nefertiti herself. The news only drove me further from it. I did not even permit Bek to finish it, and it will remain forever missing one eye, lest its completion truly does allow its beauty to rival her upon which it was modelled. As far as I am aware it remained on a shelf in Bek's workshop, and would remain there still had the entire city of Akhetaten not been destroyed and looted and driven into the ground with the same fanaticism with which it had been raised. Hardly two bricks remain upon one another now, and I trust the bust of Nefertiti lies safe in the desert sand.

There was no choice after Nefertiti's death but to declare Tutankhaten king. Not that any other choice would have been made even if there had been a dozen princes from whom to choose, for, despite his father, or perhaps because of him, perhaps because any prince would appear flawless in the reflection of Akhenaten, Tutankhaten was as loved as any man in the kingdom, as adored as any king that had preceded him. He was now nine years of age although those who did not know him as well as I assumed him to be older. He had perhaps seen so much in those nine years that time needed to pile upon him in order to separate the events of his life from one another. He was tall, as his father had been, and as serene and stoic as his mother.

Even at this young age, as remarkable as it seems, I regarded him as a friend. His integrity was unsurpassed, and I found myself comfortable discussing with him matters that I would baulk at mentioning even to Horemheb.

He officiated, as was required, at Nefertiti's funeral. She was laid in a tomb cut into the cliffs surrounding Akhetaten, although she would lie undisturbed only as long as the city remained unmolested. How could I have known that she would remain interred for less than two years and that I would have to defend her mummy with my own body? I loved my sister as much as I ever loved anyone, and I witnessed scenes in my defence of her that I would not wish upon Akhenaten himself. Of course, I did not protect his tomb when the crowds came howling around the door. I will risk my life for love, but I will not do so for duty.

Tutankhaten, for all the years that his body did not betray, was too young to steer the Two Lands alone. He needed the help of those around him, those he could trust, who had no interests other than those of Tutankhaten and Egypt herself. His principle ministers were chosen from his court by his tutor and guardian, Aye, my father. He undoubtedly saw in me some courage and talent that I did not see in myself (although his decision was undoubtedly swayed by his young charge's enthusiasm) for I was chosen as his treasurer. It was a position the importance of which I did not underestimate. My duties were many and varied, and could hardly have been more important. I was responsible for the treasury, of course, but that made me responsible for everything that fed it, and it was a voracious beast. The taxing of Egypt became my domain. The payment of her soldiers and officials. The investment in her granaries, and therefore, by implication, the feeding and survival of the entire nation. The second minister chosen for Tutankhaten was a choice that surprised me even more than my own, although it was one infinitely more welcome. Horemheb was ordered to return from the front, which would be left in the capable hands of Nakhtmin, in order to advise His Majesty on military matters. Aye made himself vizier, which was the only unsurprising aspect of the entire affair. It quickly became evident that Horemheb was there simply because it was a place where he could be watched, monitored and controlled. I soon began to wonder on the motives behind Aye's choice of treasurer and it was only Tutankhaten's assertions that I had been as much his choice as Aye's that soothed my nerves.

How naïve I was.

His plans had been too long in their formulation to permit error of any kind. Everything was meticulous. Everything was beauteous in its simplicity.

The triumvirate of rule was set up behind the throne before anyone could catch their breath. Mahu had been his principle problem but he had acted with such aplomb, such confidence and guile, that Mahu was left outside before he even saw the door closing upon him. Before he even realised there was a door to be closed. Had Aye not acted with instinctive speed his opportunity would have been lost. On the morning of the discovery of Nefertiti's body and the murdered guards outside her room Aye had forced himself to remain in his apartments to ensure that he could be found there when one of his servants entered, breathless with fear and shock, in order to be as surprised by the news as anyone else. He had waited at the mirror, a razor in his hand, for a knock at the door. When it came he brought the blade up to his face. He shaved while he heard the news, and as the fateful words were spoken he sliced the blade across the cut that Nefertiti's fingernail had scored across his face. He had rushed directly to Nefertiti's room, for he knew what was expected of him, but he left strict instructions with his servant to summon Tutankhaten to meet him there and to ensure that he stopped for nothing and no-one on his way to the rendezvous. He had appeared suitably distraught over his daughter's body. It was not entirely an act for when he saw her, pale and stricken in her bed, her beauty distorted by death, he felt something akin to guilt stirring within him, although it was muted enough for him to notice it with curiosity. He grieved at the bedside, not raising his head until he heard the door open and close behind him. He sensed a presence behind him and knew who it was.

"Your time is over," he said, without turning around.

"I fear that you may be mistaken," Mahu said. "It has been my time since the first bricks of this city were laid. Nothing has changed."

"Oh, but it has," Aye said. "I am in charge now. You may find that more things have changed than you thought possible."

"*You* are in charge?" Mahu asked. "Who has granted you this honour?" He looked down at Nefertiti's body. "Her?" he asked, with a sneer.

"I have granted it," Aye said, "and I have all the power I require in order to do so. For there is a new king of Egypt and he is making his way here as we speak. He does so at my bidding."

For the first time in as long as Aye could remember there was a look of insecurity in Mahu's expression.

"When the king answers your call you have little to fear from his servants," Aye said, keen to press home his advantage. "I am Tutankhaten's tutor and guardian. He will allow himself to be guided by my word. Even at his young age he recognises the way of wisdom."

Before Mahu had the opportunity of rejoinder the door to the corridor opened. Two servants stepped over the threshold, looking slightly overawed. One of them was the man whom Aye had commanded to fetch the prince. Following them, and looking equally nervous, was Tutankhaten. He came into the room and the servants arranged themselves on either side of them.

Without comment, Aye prostrated himself before him, and Tutankhaten looked down at him, his agitation hardly eased by the gesture.

"What are you doing?" he said.

"My beloved Nefertiti is dead," Aye said. He could feel the eyes of the room upon him, and he was beginning to feel self-conscious, like a man who begins to applaud only to discover that the rest of the crowd are not following his lead.

Tutankhaten looked towards the bed as if noticing its occupant for the first time.

"What does this mean?" he said, his eyes fluttering between Aye and Nefertiti, not allowing himself to believe his suspicions.

"You are Akhenaten's only son," Aye said. "There are no other princes to challenge you. Your Majesty, the throne is yours."

One by one, realising the import of the situation, the servants around the room lowered themselves to their knees. Tutankhaten simply stared, his head turning from one to the next and then back to Nefertiti, as though in an appeal for help. Mahu was the last to follow Aye's example, and when he finally did so he wore a scowl upon his face that belied the subservience implicit in the gesture.

Moments passed.

"May you live," Tutankhaten said at last, in a quiet voice.

The occupants of the room climbed to their feet.

"What has happened here?" Tutankhaten asked.

"It is not entirely clear," Aye said, "Although the evidence would point to foul play."

Tutankhaten looked at him blankly.

"She was murdered," Aye explained.

Tutankhaten gasped and put his hands to his mouth. "Murdered?" he said. "But who would do such a thing?"

Aye shrugged his shoulders. "That is something that we may never know, although I shall appoint a team of men to endeavour to discover it," he said. "And there is perhaps another question that needs to be asked. A question equally important. Luckily for us, there is a man here who can answer it."

Aye looked at Mahu. "How was this allowed to happen?" he asked him.

Mahu was not so much surprised by the question, for he knew it would come, as by the bluntness with which it was asked. He was accustomed to more reverence than this, to the people addressing him being fearful rather than angry.

"I will need to do some investigations of my own," Mahu said, and then added, as though as an afterthought: "How came you by that cut on your face? Have you been in a struggle?"

Aye touched his fingers to his face as though he had forgotten that the cut was there. "It is a shaving cut," he said. "Hardly a battle scar."

Mahu stepped forward and made a show of examining the incision. "You must shave very vigorously," he said, "or with your eyes closed."

"Sir," Aye's servant said, from Tutankhaten's side. "I can vouch for what Aye says. I saw it happen."

Aye could barely prevent himself from a victorious smile. *So easy*, he thought to himself.

"How convenient," Mahu said, although his voice had lost some of the bombast with which he had been speaking.

"You talk as though you were accusing me of something," Aye said. "I do so hope that is not the case."

They were civil words but Mahu did not have to dig deeply to find the threat within them. He was on untried ground, and knew that attacking from an insubstantial foundation was as unsafe as building on one. He had no option but to bide his time.

"I am accusing nobody," he said.

"Good," Aye said. "Then I believe you mentioned something about conducting an investigation into your failure to protect the king from her enemies."

"If there was such a failure..." Mahu began.

"*If?*" Aye interrupted.

"If there was such a failure," Mahu said again, "it was made by men in no position to repeat it."

"Nevertheless," Aye said, "I am sure His Majesty would appreciate you giving the matter your urgent attention. Is that not correct, Majesty?"

Tutankhaten looked momentarily surprised to be included in the conversation. "Yes, please," he said.

Mahu had little choice, and Aye managed to gesture towards the door just as Mahu took his first step towards it, as though Mahu was following his command.

As soon as the door had closed upon Mahu's back, Aye turned to Tutankhaten.

"Your Majesty," he said. "There is much to be done, and little time in which to do it. May I suggest that you summon your ministers to your audience chamber?"

"What for?" Tutankhaten said.

"Well, first of all, you will need to conduct a review of your security arrangements," Aye said. "It is obvious that Mahu is no longer up to the job."

"You mean I should remove him?" Tutankhaten asked.

"It may be for the best, Majesty."

"I am not sure I would like to do that," Tutankhaten said. "Mahu is a scary man."

"I am your servant, Majesty. It will be my pleasure to carry out your wishes on your behalf."

"All right then," Tutankhaten said.

"One more thing, Majesty, if I may."

"Yes?"

"There is no longer any need for you to use the word 'please', as you did just now with Mahu. You are the king. You should issue commands, not make requests. It is just a small thing, but you may find it useful in dealing with your subjects. It is what they will expect from you."

"But what will I command them to do?" Tutankhaten said, as Aye ushered him gently towards the door.

"Ah, Majesty," Aye said. "I believe there I may be of some assistance."

The Maya Papyrus, Fragments 208-211

"I pride myself on being a man who can learn from the mistakes of others," Aye said to us. He addressed himself as much towards Tutankhaten as he did towards myself and Horemheb. "The reigns of Nefertiti and Akhenaten were inglorious and flawed. They were hated by the general populace, and not without good reason."

Horemheb was taking the opportunity to glance meaningfully at me every time Aye's head was averted for the briefest of moments. I saw him (in fact, I saw him the first time he did it, and every time afterwards, throughout the entire audience) and each look was more meaningful than the last, more loaded with significance, couched as it was in exaggerated head movements and looks of increasing intensity. I had seen him, and I saw him each time, and each time I did not have the courage to return his look, to return it as if to say I have seen it. I have seen it and I know. I had heeded Horemheb's warning to me on the day he told me that Akhenaten's death had not negated the need for circumspection in the sharing of thoughts about the condition of the royal family. Now, it seemed, Aye had divined that such circumspection was no longer needed.

At least for him.

"It was not an assassin that killed Nefertiti," he continued, and I readied myself for some staggering insight. I was to be disappointed. "It was not disease, nor gods, nor old age. It was unpopularity. It was the hatred of her people. That is what killed her."

I thought it was a disrespectful comment and it angered me. Another look from Horemheb told me he felt the same way. Nefertiti was never hated. Perhaps she was viewed with suspicion because of her association with Mahu, but she was never hated. Not my sister.

"But for now there are more important questions to be addressed," Aye said, and I was astounded at his flippancy.

"More important than apprehending the king's killer?" I said.

"They are questions of the survival of Egypt," Aye said. "They outweigh all the murders you care to think of. From now on Egypt comes first, and last, and everywhere in between. Our waking thoughts will be of Egypt and her wellbeing. Our dreams will be of the health of the Two Lands. Neither gods nor man will divert us from our devotions. Too much has already been lost, and I will not permit these losses to count for nothing."

"And what of His Majesty's protection?" Horemheb said. "He is Egypt now. Our thoughts need to be of him. If Nefertiti's killer remains at large how can we guarantee His Majesty's safety?"

"In two ways," Aye said. "Nefertiti was ill-served by the man charged with protecting her. You may have noticed his absence from this audience."

"Mahu?" I said. "What has become of him?"

"He has been given a less strenuous assignment," Aye said.

I was not to discover it until much later, but as we spoke Mahu was boarding a ship to travel southwards along the Nile. He was guarded closely by trustworthy men of Horemheb's regiment and his ship would not dock until it reached its destination. It was a place that both Akhenaten and Nefertiti would have recognised, for it had been the first stop on the tour that had concluded with Akhenaten's discovery of the future site of the city where we were now standing. It was the quarry at Gebel el-Silsila, and Mahu would spend the rest of his career commanding the garrison there, breaking up fights and burying the victims of accidents. Aye had deemed it remote enough to preclude the possibilities of Mahu's return.

"And the second way?" Horemheb said.

"The appointment of a man who will not be as careless in His Majesty's protection."

"That man being...?" Horemheb said.

"You, Horemheb," Aye said. "From this moment forth you are the king's protector. I will hold you fully accountable for any failure on your behalf."

"You will hold me accountable?" Horemheb said.

"If you fail in your task, who else will there be?" Aye said.

Horemheb had no answer.

"Good," Aye said. "I believe you are a man to be trusted. The king is in safe hands. Now, we must continue. The king must be found a wife. I have a suggestion with which I doubt you will take issue."

He looked from Horemheb to myself and back again, as though defying us to challenge him. We did not yet know who his candidate was. He did not once look to the king.

"Ankhesenpaaten," he said, after a pause measured for maximum drama, and then added, as though someone had questioned his decision and he was being forced to defend it: "She is Tutankhaten's half-sister. He was not born of Nefertiti, and we *must guard against challenges, although I am sure there will be none."*

He looked us in the eye again, perhaps wondering whether either of us were about to spring into life in defence of some obscure princess of whom he was not aware. Neither of us did so. Only Aye seemed to have the wherewithal to consider questions such as this so soon after the tragedy that had befallen us all. At the time I could not decide whether he was clear of head or cold of heart. Of course, now I know.

"She is the daughter not only of Akhenaten, but of Nefertiti. If Tutankhaten is married to the daughter of two kings nobody could mount a challenge and expect to be taken seriously. If I was married to the daughter of two kings I doubt anyone could challenge me."

As he spoke the last sentence he laughed to accentuate the fact that he meant it as a witticism. Horemheb and I smiled politely. We did not know then that it was more prophecy than humour, and it is a moment that makes me shake with anger even now. It makes me wonder exactly how much Aye had the future planned in his mind.

Neither myself nor Horemheb had any objection to marrying Tutankhaten to Ankhesenpaaten, and so the decision was made. Throughout the entire audience, Aye did not ask for or defer to Tutankhaten's opinion even once.

The troops struck in the darkest hour of the night, for it was an hour that seemed apt to those who organised the attack. It was the hour furthest from the sun's zenith, when the Aten was at his weakest, when he could do nothing but lumber through the underworld as though dragged by lame oxen, hearing the sounds of his world being torn from his grasp and shattered with glee at his feet.

They were scenes that Horemheb remembered well from the plundering of the temples of Amun. The only difference was the glee with which the men set about their task. They ran through the hundreds of altars, their swords chipping and sparking against them as they ran, one or two stopping long enough to topple them or grab handfuls of food from them as they passed.

Another difference that Horemheb noted from his vantage point at the front of the temple was the lack of fight in the priests as they were dragged from their places of sleep, half dressed and half awake, into the light of the moon. Akhenaten had never made the effort to provide them with the means to defend themselves. Mahu's men were ample for that task and Akhenaten never truly believed that the Aten would allow something of this magnitude to occur. But now the Aten was toppled from his throne and the only men still loyal to Mahu and within the distance to make a difference were locked securely in their barracks, surrounded by jeering soldiers and throwing themselves at the door. By the morning their god and their fighting spirit would have been entirely excised.

The priests were marched in silence through the city to the docks, where they were counted onto ships that queued out into the river.

Some ships headed north, some south. Each would anchor at different settlements and towns along the river, from the delta in the north to the border with Nubia in the south. Most places had heard of the Aten, and had been visited by the iconoclasts with their clubs to smash the idols of family gods and the heads of those who persisted in worshipping them.

Few priests were given the succour they craved, and many would end their lives in the street, condemning exile as nothing more than an extended execution.

Aye was in his villa, a glass of wine in his hand. He was staring at nothing in particular. In other rooms he could hear the sounds of his servants bustling to and fro, cleaning, tidying, preparing. They knew better than to intrude into the room in which he was sitting. They noticed that there was a cut on his face which would not heal up. Although the more conscientious among them quietly swapped recipes for balms that would mend it in no time, nobody felt able to approach him about it.

Aye looked down at the goblet in his hand and swirled the contents. He had not sipped from it for some time, and did so now only to avoid wasting it. It was Syrian, and the vintage was of the fourteenth year of Akhenaten's reign, which was a particularly good one, but a mere taste, exquisite though it was, would not be enough to lift his embattled spirits.

He drained the goblet and put it to one side. Across the room from him was a bronze mirror. He stood from his seat and walked across to it. He looked into it impassively for some time and if any servants had been courageous enough to silently enter the room behind him they would have thought him in a trance. Finally, slowly, he moved, bringing his hand up to his face where his fingers traced the route of the cut Nefertiti had given him as she struggled against her death. The scab was raised in relief from his face, so many times had it been picked away and allowed to reform. A line of reddened skin had formed around it, and it was sore to the touch.

Wincing, Aye pinched the top of the scab between his fingernail and thumbnail. He inhaled sharply as he pulled his fingers away. The scab came with them, bringing tears to his eyes, but they were tears well-earned and just. He wiped an eye and sniffed. There was no blood, but the cut seemed deeper than it had first been. It looked like a valley cut into desert sandstone. It was all that was left of her. It was a thing of her making and to allow it to fade out of existence was somehow as big a crime as any of those that had preceded it.

It seemed, at this early juncture, as though Nefertiti's death was going to be entirely justified. He tried to think of it from Thuya's point of view, or from history's. Nefertiti had been thirty years old when she died; she had easily lived more than half of her life. In a hundred years, or in a thousand, or five thousand, how much difference would those extra twenty years have made? In the eyes of history, the distinction between a thirty year life and one of fifty was negligible. And yet consider the difference her death had made. Egypt was saved, her foundations shored up. Nefertiti's death had guaranteed Egypt's survival, and that was something that was big enough for history to see, for in a hundred years or five thousand, the ramifications of it would still be felt.

Aye had this conversation with himself every day, and every day it failed to lift his mood. Every day he picked away the scab that Nefertiti had left him, and every day the cut behind it grew deeper. He turned his thoughts to the future, to this glorious Egypt which he had created, or at least nurtured in her sickness and raised from her sick bed. Every aspect of the years of Atenism needed to be erased. The people had to become once again accustomed to a king who would not torment them or baffle them with superstition and suspicion. Aye believed he had achieved a great deal when he had resisted the temptation to cut the throats of every priest in the city. He had shown the world that Tutankhaten was not a barbarian, that his mercy was as boundless as the desert. Mahu's men had been disbanded, although some had been fanatical enough to put up a fight and a small number of deaths had been unavoidable. There were few enough of them left to be sent to different units at the front line, where the fighting with Hittite forces was at its heaviest. They would find themselves volunteered for the riskiest of missions. Soon there would be none left, but Egypt would think them forgiven by a compassionate king, and given the chance to redeem themselves of their crimes, and they would gradually be forgotten.

And yet there was so much more to be done that the thought of it was daunting even to a man who had considered and reconsidered it a thousand times before the opportunity had come along to put it into action. Akhetaten was not the capital of Egypt, not in the eyes of the people and the gods. Only Akhenaten and Nefertiti had ever considered it to be so. It was time, Aye had decided, to leave this forsaken canker on the face of the desert. Memphis had been Egypt's capital before Akhenaten's madness had robbed it of the title, but Memphis was not the answer. All this had started because the capital had been too far removed from the heart of the nation. Akhetaten would be abandoned, yes, because such a thing was unavoidable, but the court would not decamp to Memphis. Aye had decided that Thebes would be the new capital, and he had decided that now was the time to allow the king to know. He would call an audience in the morning. Preparations would be made, and at last the desert would be allowed to reclaim the land that had been stolen from it.

Aye returned to his seat, the left hand side of his face throbbing. He poured some more wine, but he did not drink it for a long time.

The Maya Papyrus, Fragments 214-217

> *Tutankhaten and Ankhesenpaaten were married with little ceremony. Aye saw it as neither necessary nor dignified to parade the arrangement even before us at court, and certainly not before the commoners in the city. Some paintings were commissioned, and one or two statues, but they were for the benefit of posterity and mainly showed events of rejoicing which had never taken place. We were invited to an austere affair, surrounded though it was by the riches of the nation. Aye officiated, there being no high priest yet to do his bidding. The ceremony itself lasted mere minutes. The royal couple were seated upon their thrones before we arrived and still there when we left. Between these two events, Aye intoned the simple facts; that Tutankhaten and Ankhesenpaaten were thenceforth to be married, and that Ankhesenpaaten, daughter of Akhenaten and Nefertiti, was to be considered the Great Royal Wife. We then trooped out, leaving the newlyweds looking confused and overawed on their thrones.*
>
> *They were, after all, nothing more than children, and the marriage meant nothing more to them than the opportunity to sit together during royal audiences, and hold hands when Aye's disapproving gaze was not upon them. He did not hold with such public displays of affection from a king and members of his entourage. He seemed to reason that Akhenaten and Nefertiti had shown enough of that during their time together, allowing themselves to be shown in friezes, paintings and sculptures holding hands and playing with their children, who were permitted to cavort upon their knees. Akhenaten was hardly a fine*

example of upstanding morality – for who could be more
bankrupt than a killer of gods? – and so Tutankhaten's reign was
to be a reaction against it. In public Aye scowled should they allow
themselves more comfort than a shared glance, and reverted to
his role of tutor once he had them in private, scolding them with
all the anger in his armoury.

The move went so smoothly that it was as though it was an annual event, as though moving the court from one city to another, removed from it by an arduous journey of some days, was something that had been achieved so many times before that it had become second nature. During the entire time Aye did not spend more than a handful of moments at a time away from the palace. He did not return to his villa throughout.

Aye consulted Tutankhaten and Ankhesenpaaten at every opportunity, although it seemed to them that sometimes he only paused briefly on his way somewhere else, and even then did so only for the sake of appearances. For the most part they merely agreed with him, although both were too young and inexperienced in the way of kingship to notice that the only questions he asked were the ones to which he already had the answers, and the opinions he sought were asked in such a way as to allow them only one response.

"Would His Majesty care to offer some guidance on the matter of his name?" he asked one day.

Tutankhaten did not answer immediately, but looked to his wife for counsel. She looked back but offered him nothing but an expression as quizzical as his own.

"Perhaps His Majesty considers that his name, including as it does the name of the false god Aten, may be something of an anachronism?" Aye said.

"Yes," Tutankhaten said, thankful for the prompt. "Perhaps."

He was torn between looking pensive over the matter and revealing that he did not understand the word *anachronism*.

"What are your thoughts on the matter, Aye?"

"My thoughts, Majesty, are entirely inconsequential. You are pharaoh. My thoughts bow to yours."

"Yes," Tutankhaten said. "Of course."

"It merely struck me, Majesty, that you may have decided to change your name. I am sure that it would be a marvellous boost to the morale of the people. The gods, too, would surely smile on the gesture."

Aye allowed Tutankhaten to think about this for a moment before continuing.

"Of course," he said, "if you feel that I am putting words into the king's mouth..."

"Not at all," Tutankhaten said. "I was about to suggest the same thing."

"How very wise, Majesty," Aye said, bowing. "Have you considered which name you would like to take?"

Tutankhaten looked blank.

"Well," Aye said, "what does Tutankhaten mean?"

"The Living Image of the Aten," Tutankhaten recited.

"Ah, then you are considering replacing one god's name with another?"

"Er," said Tutankhaten.

"With Amun, perhaps?"

"Amun?"

"Yes, Majesty. You could simply replace the Aten in your name with Amun. Tutankhamun. The Living Image of Amun. That *is* what you were about to say?"

"Yes, Aye, of course. It is the obvious solution." He tried the name once or twice.

"An excellent idea, Majesty. And presumably you were going to do the same for your wife?"

"For Ankhesen..." Tutankhaten said, and then stopped. He smiled mischievously. "You mean for Ankhesen*amun*?" he said.

Aye laughed. "Precisely, Majesty! Such wit in one so young! I shall make all the necessary arrangements for your decree."

"My decree?"

"The wise decree that your name is to be changed, Majesty. The country will need to know. I shall tell them that it is to become effective immediately."

Aye bowed from the room, leaving the king and his wife to recite each other's names and laugh at the unfamiliar sounds.

As he walked, Aye permitted himself a thin smile. He was remembering his mother and her manipulations of Amenhotep, and how she not only managed to have her name mentioned in all his messages but also persuaded him that it had been his idea. Looking back, Aye thought her vanity somewhat crude, and he was glad that he was not afflicted by it. His actions were for Egypt, not for himself. He judged some of his actions in service of the crown to be nothing short of heroic, and yet they would forever remain a secret. He imagined himself in ten years, twenty, a wizened old man lying back in soft cushions, servants feeding him fruit and meat, laughing at the irony of saving the world and being able to tell nobody. These were not the actions of a man desperate for the kiss of history as his mother had been; they were the actions of a man with too many things to hide. His hand went to his face and the scab that by now ran almost its entire length. It had grown and deepened and reddened since Nefertiti had first gouged it, but in the months since her death its nature had changed in more than its extent. It was something that he no longer saw as having been forced on him. Rather, it had been bequeathed. He tended it like a gardener would tend a flower, or a child a sick pet. When the pain became unbearable he would let it alone until its complaining eased and then he would pick at it again, and by doing so, remember her. He would soothe it with balms when it wept and absentmindedly stroke it when he was thinking of something else. He wished often that there could have been some other way and his only hope more fervent was that no alternative would ever occur to him, for he could not bear to think that he could have achieved his aims without taking his daughter's life.

He played through endless scenarios in which Nefertiti was allowed to live, and without exception they failed. Aye's hand would lift again to the scab on his face, and he would thank her.

Chapter Twenty-Two

The Man King

The Maya Papyrus, Fragments 232-235

IT IS *perhaps nothing more than nostalgia for a time of peace, or perhaps it is that I see it now set in relief against the misery of the times that came immediately before and after it, but those first years at Thebes were, I think, the happiest of my life. They seemed to roll by so effortlessly that I sometimes find myself struggling to remember their details, so gloriously insipid were they. Nobody died unexpectedly. There were no revolutions, religious or otherwise. The wars on the borders against Hatti, while never dying away completely, were held effectively in check by Nakhtmin and his troops. There were no plagues.*

There was only peace, and rebuilding, and the return of all the old gods, and happiness, and Tutankhamun. Only Horemheb seemed unhappy during our time in Thebes under the rule of Tutankhamun. He could of course see what I refused to allow myself to notice. Aye was, as far as I was concerned, the king's regent and carrying out a regent's duties as was good and proper. It was his lot in life to advise and nurture the king as a father would. The king would still be a prince if his father was still alive, and have the opportunity of learning at his father's knee. Tutankhamun no longer had such a luxury – if that is the correct word for lessons learned at the knee of someone such as Akhenaten – and so Aye, who was almost Tutankhamun's grandfather, took the mantle upon himself.

Of course, if you had asked Horemheb at this time for his thoughts on the situation, he would have a slightly different interpretation.

"Who is the king?" he would ask me, after an audience wherein Aye had been particularly loquacious. "To whom do we bend our knee?"

I would cluck and chuckle and pat him on the back and tell him that he was overreacting and being paranoid, and he would scowl at me and look as though he was going to explode with rage. The colour in his face would sharpen and then subside and he would stalk away, muttering oaths and imprecations to the gods for patience.

He was right. I was wrong. I forget how many times I have apologised to him for this, but it never quite seems to be enough. I am no longer even sure to whom I am apologising. I think I would give the world itself to apologise to Tutankhamun and Ankhesenamun, but of course I cannot.

Still, if I manage to put away from my mind the misery around which this time was enveloped, I can smile about it with very little prompting.

Tutankhamun and his wife were growing up. Like most royal couples, they had wed at a preposterously early age without the luxury of knowing each other particularly well. And like many royal couples they grew to love each other in the years following their wedding. It is a curious phenomenon, this relationship of a king with his Great Royal Wife. There are very few who do not grow from almost complete strangers to devout lovers over the course of their marriage, although I do not think this any happy reflection on the skills of royal matchmakers. Rather, I think Hathor, the goddess of love, is compelled to smile upon those who share the isolation of power.

Here were two children in awe of the world. Where else could they turn but to but each other?

Even I, who tried so hard to be more than just Tutankhamun's treasurer; I, who had always taken pains to be more to him than just another faceless servant at court, could never be anything other than an outsider, although he had always embraced my friendship. We met socially, or at least as socially as is possible within the restraints of etiquette. By this I mean simply that we saw each other outside the audience chamber. The only other person to do this on anything approaching a regular basis was Aye, but I suspected, prompted by Tutankhamun's hints, that even these meetings had their parameters strictly defined. They were opportunities to continue Tutankhamun's schooling, a matter over which Aye was as zealous as he was over any other, or they were continuations of the day's business which could wait no longer. On more than one occasion Horemheb, who was aware of my cordial relationship with Tutankhamun and

Ankhesenamun, tried to prime me to press the king for a description of exactly what happened in these meetings, to which myself and Horemheb were never invited. I risked his wrath on just as many occasions by refusing. A king was not a man from whom answers could be gleaned if he was not readily forthcoming with them.

In my social appointments with the royal couple they both afforded me some leeway in my propriety and allowed me to father them, albeit in a way to which they were wholly unfamiliar. Both remembered Akhenaten well enough to know that he was never an easy man with whom to conduct any form of familial relationship. Tutankhamun had the advantage of having spent much more time with Akhenaten than had Ankhesenamun, although that was hardly any advantage at all. Since their father's death Ankhesenamun had been given no replacement, and Tutankhamun had been given only Aye.

I was old enough to be their father, but I acted more like an elder brother and this, I think, they appreciated as a break from the strictures of court. In return I tried to care for them as best I could. From the earliest days at Thebes we would meet in their private quarters and I would bring with me an amphora of wine, half a cup of which both the king and his wife were permitted. It was a time of great pride and happiness for me. Happiness that I was able to walk the palace corridors with jars of wine under my arms fashioned into the shapes of the gods Hathor or Bes, simply for the joy of knowing that they had been welcomed back from their banishment by Akhenaten. It was a matter of pride to see the royal couple's faces when I was announced, and to be able to educate them into the ways of the oenophile, one sip at a time.

"This is an acquired taste," I would say. "It is a sweet date wine from the Delta." And they would sip it and grimace, and I would laugh and tell them they would grow into its enjoyment.

Or, "This is a dry wine, and it is a very special vintage, from the nineteenth year of King Amenhotep's reign, may he live forever. Be careful with it. Savour it, for it is very rare and highly valued." And I would watch with paternal sternness to ensure that they savoured every touch of it on their tongues. They both favoured a dry wine. On occasion I would mischievously tell them a dry wine was sweet, or vice versa, and watch to see if they noticed my trickery. It was not long before they were catching me out every time.

My greatest pride, though, was to be found in none of these moments. My greatest pride was to be found after the wine tasting, when both the king and queen protested (with little conviction) as I retrieved their cups.

"You have had enough," I would say. "You are yet children. What would Aye say if he discovered I had allowed you to get drunk?"

They would make a pretence at sulking, and I would make a pretence of firmness, and someone would suggest a game of Twenty Squares or Senet, and our words would be forgotten. Here lay the pride that nearly burst through my chest every time I thought of it, for here I was close enough to the king and his Great Royal Wife to be allowed to forbid them their wishes. The only other man in the kingdom with this honour was Aye, and this was due more to fear of him than any affection. Technically, Tutankhamun could have had me imprisoned for daring to speak to him in such a way. Instead, we were firm enough friends for him to not only allow it, but to submit to it also.

I miss those times of simple happiness more than I can say.

As the royal couple grew I allowed them a little more wine, although I always guaranteed their sobriety and they still yielded to my commands to stop.

I did not notice until later, when it was all too late, that a subtle change had been taking place over these years. Fear is never as enduring as love, and where trepidation may fade over the years, friendship grows only ever stronger.

Ankhesenamun was sixteen years old when she fell pregnant for the first time. Tutankhamun was three years her junior. The news was announced to the people of Thebes via means of a stela and word of mouth and spontaneous parties erupted throughout the city. The court physicians carried out all the tests at their disposal and declared with confidence that the child would be a boy. Aye greeted the news with such relief that a brief rumour circulated the palace that he had come to some arrangement with Amun to remove the lines of a number of years from his face.

"See how you have been blessed?" he told the royal couple. "You are hardly a man, Majesty, and already Amun has done for you what the Aten could never do for your father and Nefertiti."

"Are the physicians always right?" Tutankhamun asked him, in honest innocence.

"Nothing is always," Aye said, "but they are right often enough to trust their word."

"Then my child will be a boy?"

"So our best minds tell us, Majesty."

"Then I shall have an heir."

"Indeed, Majesty," Aye said, smiling.

Tutankhamun looked shocked for a moment. Ankhesenamun reached across and squeezed his hand.

"Are you not pleased, husband?" she said.

"I am..." Tutankhamun said, struggling for the words. Slowly, he brought his gaze up to meet hers. "I am going to have an heir," he said, and laughed.

"Congratulations once again, Majesty," Aye said. "Now, on the same subject, if we could turn to..."

"My son will have no tutors," Tutankhamun said, and Aye stumbled to a halt, surprised at the interruption.

"No tutors, Majesty?" he said, still smiling.

"No," Tutankhamun said. "He will learn at my side. He will have no need of tutors."

"You will be very busy with matters of state, Majesty. I am sure your son will understand that you will not always be available for him."

"No, Aye," Tutankhamun said. Aye raised his eyebrows. "I have decided. I was deprived of my father. My son will not be."

Aye bowed, but with an expression on his face that would lead an observer to conclude that his back was troubling him. "As you say, Majesty. Perhaps it would be prudent to discuss the matter at greater length nearer the time?"

"Yes," Tutankhamun said. "Of course. We will discuss it then."

He looked unsure as to whether he had been the victor in the argument. Aye turned back to the papyrus scroll and unrolled it slightly to reveal its next item.

"Your Majesty will be aware," he said, "of the importance of the morale of the general population. Your father was despised by the populace, and we know how we wish to avoid that. What are unhappy people?"

"Dangerous," Tutankhamun said, by rote.

"Good," Aye said. "And so Your Majesty may wish to celebrate your good news in such a way that includes the people of the city."

"Yes," Tutankhamun said. "I shall. I shall command a grand feast."

"Excellent idea, Majesty," Aye said. "And what else?"

"There should be more?"

"I am not a man to command his king, Majesty. I wish only what you wish."

"Then I think there should be more," Tutankhamun said.

"Very wise, Majesty. And what form should these extra celebrations take? Games, perhaps?"

"I was just about to suggest the same thing," Tutankhamun said.

"Of course, Majesty," Aye said, bowing. "Then if I may take your leave in order to begin the preparations?"

"Please do so."

Aye bowed, and noted with slight distaste that Tutankhamun and his wife could not wait to be alone before they turned to each other, Tutankhamun reaching out to gingerly place his hand over her stomach, and for them both to start giggling like children at the thought of what was within. Sighing, he took his leave. He had services to perform.

He contacted the priesthood and issued them with instructions about which they were not pleased but were unable to complain. He summoned the army's greatest fighters and charioteers, its most skilful swordsmen and strongest spearmen, organised the herding of as many lions and bulls as were available at short notice and supervised the crews who were allotted the task of preparing an area of land outside the city walls large enough to accommodate everything he had planned. Awnings were erected, under which rows of seats were placed, and around which large banners of red and blue fluttered, proclaiming the names of the royal couple interspersed with earnest declarations on the divinity of Amun. Opposite this was constructed a stage upon which were placed two thrones and a smaller, less conspicuous seat which was placed to the rear and one side. Before the stage and the rows of seats were situated rows of tables. Teams of labourers walked in lines along the thoroughfare created between the stage and the seating area, meticulously removing stones and dumping them further out into the desert.

Come the day of the celebrations, Tutankhamun and Ankhesenamun rose with the sun, feeling childish excitement for the coming day. By the time Aye arrived to escort them to the area he had prepared outside the northern walls, Tutankhamun was hopping from foot to foot with anticipation and Aye had to rest his hands on his shoulders and look him squarely in the eye and remind him of his position. It was unthinkable that the king should be allowed out of his private apartments in such a state. Aye enlisted the help of Ankhesenamun and made her promise to hold her husband's excitement in check.

Tutankhamun breathed deeply and gradually brought himself under control.

"Are you ready?" Aye asked him.

Tutankhamun nodded.

"Are you sure?" Aye asked. "You may not leave until you are ready."

"I said I am ready," Tutankhamun said, with a hint of irritation in his voice which Aye silently noted.

"Good," Aye said. "Then follow me."

He led the couple from the apartments and through the palace corridors into the courtyard that abutted the main doors, where three chariots awaited them, the horses skittish in anticipation.

"If I were a horse I would be like them," Tutankhamun said.

"I dare say so, Majesty," Aye said, signalling for him to mount the leading and most ornate chariot.

They rode in convoy through the city streets to the northern gate. Crowds on either side were held back by troops. Flowers and kisses were thrown in the king's direction. He waved to the crowds and felt Aye's gaze on his back. He knew what Aye would be thinking and could imagine his words next time they were alone for long enough for Aye to set off on one of his signature tirades on the subject of royal dignity. Well, Aye had no control of him while they were in separate chariots, and there was little he could say or do in front of this crowd, and anyway, Tutankhamun was king and he could choose to do as he wished, so he beamed at the crowd and waved with the enthusiasm of a man summoning help. He would just have to be reprimanded and have done with it. It was becoming frustrating because Aye was so old fashioned and Tutankhamun failed to see why being king had to be such a solemn affair. Nowhere was it written that the king had to be miserable. His confidence buoyed by the crowd's reaction, he decided to confront Aye at the first available opportunity. It was time he stamped his authority on the situation. After all, when all was said and done, the man was little more than a servant and he had no choice but to bow to the king's will.

The chariots trundled through the northern gate and presently reached the area set aside for the celebrations. The whole of court and the principal representatives of the temple of the Amun were here already, occupying the rows of seats opposite the king's stage. On either side of the seats, held back by makeshift barriers and more troops, stretching off into the distance, were rows of people from the city, all as enthusiastic as the crowds that had lined the city streets.

By this time the reaction of the crowds and his excitement for the coming day had conspired within Tutankhamun to create levels of exhilaration approaching euphoria. He jumped down from the chariot and walked the length of the crowd, holding out his hands for the people to grasp, laying his hands on the foreheads of babies held out for him to bless.

Aye rushed over to him, forgetting for a moment his reliance on the walking stick he had occasionally taken to leaning upon. Standing behind him, he leant in to speak into Tutankhamun's ear.

"Majesty," he said. "I hardly think that this..."

"What?" Tutankhamun shouted.

"I said, Majesty, that this is not the..."

"What?" Tutankhamun said again, laughing. "I cannot hear you for the noise of the crowd!"

"Majesty, you must stop this indignity and make your way to the stage!"

"I must make my way to the edge, you say?" Tutankhamun said, pointing along the length of the crowd. "But that is what I am doing!"

"To the stage, Majesty, to the stage!"

"Yes," Tutankhamun said. "To the edge. I *am* doing!"

Aye lost the little restraint to which he had been clinging.

"Your Majesty, you will stop playing games with me this instant! You are acting like a common market stallholder touting for business. You are making a fool of yourself and your wife. I demand that you cease this carnival at once and make your way to the stage."

Tutankhamun's bravado was somewhat punctured by the severity of Aye's anger. He turned to where they had left Ankhesenamun. He could tell even from this distance that she was not embarrassed by his actions. She was struggling to smother a smile. He could not help smiling back, but he sensed that he had pushed the situation exactly as far as he would be permitted. With an overdramatic sigh which was entirely for Aye's benefit, he turned and made his way to the stage. On the way he met up with Ankhesenamun and purposefully held out his hand for her to take. She did so and leant close enough to him to whisper.

"Did you see the colour of his face?" she said. "I thought he was going to melt into the sand."

By the time they reached their thrones they were almost helpless with laughter. Aye took his position in the seat behind Tutankhamun's throne, from where he could be heard muttering to himself.

At last, the festivities were allowed to begin.

They started with games: wrestling matches, archery and spear throwing competitions for distance and accuracy, foot races and chariot races, between each of which a short rendition of music was performed by a troop of Anatolian minstrels. Eating and drinking continued throughout. Beef, mutton, pork and goat, wild hare, duck, goose, gazelle, quail and pigeon, Syrian chicken, eggs, butter and cheese, jugs of wine, milk and dark barley beer, plates piled high with dates, bowls brimming with honey, all were paraded before the king and his wife, all sampled and nibbled and sipped until neither Tutankhamun nor Ankhesenamun thought themselves capable of leaving their chairs.

The final event was a prestigious chariot race in which the king himself would take part. His chariot was brought to the foot of the stage. This one was not so ornate as his state chariot, for all the weight of the gold in that would make it difficult for him to win a race against a man on foot. The race chariot was somewhat more fragile, but every superfluous element of it had been excised, so much so that it looked unfinished. Tutankhamun enjoyed its functional look. He could imagine that he was a charioteer in the army, riding into glorious battle. He climbed aboard. The two horses that would pull the chariot were from his own private stable and were confidently reckoned to be the fastest in the kingdom. He cantered them past cheering crowds to the start line. His opponents were among the best, at whose feats he had been marvelling throughout the day. They were daunting men to be racing against, but Tutankhamun had the confidence of a boy, and a king, He greeted them happily, and they prostrated themselves on the floor by the side of their chariots. He bid them rise.

"For the duration of this race I am not your king," he said. "I am but a simple charioteer in a plain chariot."

The men bowed and muttered their affirmations.

"I don't want you to let me win," he said, in case the point had been lost on them.

"As you wish, Your Majesty," they chorused.

The race was a close one, which somewhat allayed Tutankhamun's fears that he had been allowed to win; in fact he had thought the race was lost until he managed to coax an extra burst of speed from his horses as the finish line came into sight. After the race he checked with his opponents, and they all swore on the name of the gods themselves that no favouritism had been given, and he allowed himself to believe them. He returned to the stage with the adoration of the crowd in his ears and could not help but smiling and waving at those who so exalted him. He was only barely able to prevent himself jumping up and down on the spot with the accumulation of excitement throughout the day. Aye scowled, as Tutankhamun had known he would, but Tutankhamun pretended he had not noticed.

There remained only for the king to make his address to the courtiers and public arranged before him. Many would later profess to him that it had been their favourite part of the whole day, and he would thank them graciously while privately suspecting that they were not being entirely honest with him.

His words had been prepared by Aye, as were the words to all his speeches. As he stepped forward a silence fell that Tutankhamun felt was slightly eerie in the presence of so many people. There was a moment's pause before every member of the crowd went down to their knees and prostrated themselves before him. Tutankhamun patiently waited for them to sort themselves out, and then waited for five heartbeats before speaking.

"May you all live!" he shouted. There followed another short interval while the crowd rose back to its feet.

"People of these Two Lands!" he shouted. "Your joy is my joy!" This was greeted with enthusiastic cheers and frantic applause, as was almost everything he said for the duration of the speech.

"I have gathered you here to share my happiness, for I am to be a father. A future pharaoh is to be born, direct in line from the great kings of our past, such as my grandfather Amenhotep and his father, Thutmose. Amun has blessed these lands! His is the glory of my kingdom, his the power of creation. It is he who has placed this child in the belly of my wife!"

Sustained applause followed this statement, and continued for so long that even Tutankhamun began to tire of it. He held up his hands for silence before continuing.

"I ask that you give thanks to him and the gods of your hearth and family as you and your countrymen have done for generations immemorial. But for now, I must bid you farewell."

Groans and lamentations, which Tutankhamun quieted again with his raised hands. "Now, now," he said, light-heartedly. "I must go, for I have an appointment. I believe the god Bes is awaiting me."

This was greeted with laughter and a huge cheer, for Bes was the god of drunkenness and merry-making.

Aye watched the young king's performance with a critical eye, but he had to admit to himself that the boy had the power of oratory. There had been no mention of Bes in the prepared text. He wondered where such skills had come from – certainly not from the boy's father, who could have bored even the most fanatical of royalists. Perhaps I deserve some credit, he thought. Aye smiled and rose to congratulate the king on a job well done.

They rode their chariots back to the palace and the crowd slowly dispersed, if anything more in love with their king now than they ever had been.

The Maya Papyrus, Fragments 241-248

Nakhtmin had returned from the border. Tutankhamun was not old enough to remember him from the last time he had been at court and so the king had ordered that a meal would be held in his honour, with a select gathering of those closest to the throne. I attended, as did Aye and Horemheb and, of course, Ankhesenamun. The child within her had granted her a certain radiance in her composure and complexion. It was something I had seen in other women in her condition, but rarely had I seen it so gracefully displayed.

Tutankhamun was hardly less glowing, although he tried to hide it behind a screen of maturity and masculinity. It was a screen full of holes, and on occasion I would catch him acting like the boy he was – trying to catch an insect, perhaps, or experimenting to see how far he could walk with his eyes closed before bumping into something – and I would slip from the room, smiling, for fear that I would embarrass him, or that my interruption might steal away the precious little that was left of his youth.

Earlier in the day of Nakhtmin's feast Tutankhamun had led me by the hand to a suite of rooms close to his private quarters. These were to be the child's rooms and they had been decorated with childish motifs along each wall. Here miniature furniture was already arranged, little chairs surrounding little tables, despite the fact that they could not be sensibly used for at least another three or four years. Here lay a cot, and next to it a bed, as though the child would grow from one to the other in the space of a night.

"Look," Tutankhamun said, leading me into a separate room. "I have been collecting these for months."

In the room were arrayed a substantial collection of toys. I wandered into the room, smiling and remembering the toys of my own childhood, which had been remarkably similar, and realising how little the world changed from one generation to the next.

"Watch," Tutankhamun said, and picked up a figurine carved from ivory with strings tied through holes that had been drilled in its arms and legs. Tutankhamun jerked on the strings and the figurine came to life, as though dancing to frenetic music.

"Is it not fantastic?" he asked me, and I had to agree as though I had never owned one myself as a child. He put it down and searched for something else, too excited to remain on one

choice long enough to actually pick it up. Watching him reminded me that it had not been so long since he had not needed the excuse of fatherhood to find enjoyment in trinkets such as these. Finally he picked up a wooden lion and held it up to my face.

"Rar!" he said, and pulled a string that had been fed through the lion's head and attached to its jaw in such a way that it opened and closed its mouth at Tutankhamun's bidding. He laughed, and I laughed with him, although I felt a small thrust of sadness. I was not entirely sure why, but I found something vaguely tragic in the sight of this boy playing with toys for which he was too old, but that had been denied him by the duty of kingship at the age when they would have given him the joy for which they were fashioned.

"My son will adore this," he said.

"I would not doubt it for a second," I said, in a voice slightly strained by emotion.

He turned back to find more toys.

"Tutankhamun," I said. "I am sorry to say it, but we must have a care not to be late for the feast."

He acknowledged me, but I doubt he would have been able to repeat my words had I challenged him.

"Tutankhamun," I said again.

"Yes," he said, his arms buried up to the elbows in an unruly pile of toys. "I know. Just a few more minutes."

"We must not keep Aye waiting," I said, slightly shameful of my use of the name as a wedge. Tutankhamun straightened up, sighing.

"Of course," he said. "How remiss of me."

He looked disappointed to be leaving the room for something so boring as a meal, but brightened up almost immediately, in the way of which most children are capable, as his thoughts turned to happier subjects.

"I shall teach my son to use a bow like no man before him," he told me, as we walked. "And I shall ensure that he has the fastest horses in the kingdom – faster even than my own – and the sharpest sword, and the... Maya, is it too soon to find his horses? I do not want them to be too old before he is old enough to drive them. But then I do not want to leave it too late, so that he is left wanting them when he is my age and they are not grown. How old should a child be before he lifts his first sword? I was old, but that was because my father did not like tools of war. Perhaps my son should be younger. Certainly with a bow. With a bow you must start very young, so that your muscles become accustomed to the strain. My tutor tells me I am doing very well, considering how late I started."

Tutankhamun stopped and turned his back to me.

"Can you see the muscles in my shoulders? They are the important ones for bow work."

He was too young for muscles of any real definition, but I assured him that I would have to be blind to miss them. He continued walking.

"My son will have a smaller bow than mine, but only for a while. Children have to have smaller bows. It is nothing to be ashamed of. I will take him hunting in the desert. Lions can be dangerous, but when you are as quick and accurate as I am you have nothing really to worry about. It is all in the action."

He stopped again, long enough to demonstrate how quickly he could retrieve an imaginary bow from an imaginary quiver and bring down an imaginary lion with it. I felt rather sorry for the lion, it took so many accurate shots before submitting. Each arrow was accompanied by a 'shtoof' sound from Tutankhamun and each shot was separated by one or two fleet steps, as though he was dodging the lion's attacks.

"I can see you are something of an expert," I said.

"Well," Tutankhamun said. "I have had more experience than you. I shall teach my son everything. He will be famous throughout history for the glory of his hunts and the number of lions and bulls he kills. Even more than my grandfather Amenhotep, and he was the greatest hunter ever. Do you know how many bulls he killed?"

I shook my head. Tutankhamun looked at me.

"Lots," he said.

We were at the door leading to the banqueting room. I smoothed down Tutankhamun's kilt.

"Are you ready?" I said.

He nodded.

"For Aye?" I said.

He nodded again and took a deep breath. "Ready," he said.

I entered first, and then he waited for Ankhesenamun to join him before the pair were announced. We prostrated ourselves and Tutankhamun bid us rise. I caught a glimpse of Ankhesenamun's face as I did so, and she did not look happy. Her mouth was set into a grimace and her gaze fell upon the table, although it did not fix there, and I would warrant that she saw nothing that was upon it. I watched her as she sat down, hoping to catch her eye to *ask her with a raise of the eyebrows what it was that was bothering her, but she did not look in my direction.*

Along with the royal couple, myself, Horemheb, Aye and Nakhtmin were present. As is often with scenes that are impressed indelibly upon the memory, I remember seemingly trivial details with as much clarity as those which changed all our lives. I remember how much Nakhtmin and Tutankhamun enjoyed each other's company. They seemed to share a sense of humour and a taste for tittle-tattle, and although Tutankhamun kept a hold of his tongue I could not help noticing his eyes sparkling with delight as Nakhtmin recounted tales of debauchery and infidelity in those at court who were not lucky enough to be present. Horemheb scowled throughout, but I could tell that he could no more remain angry at Nakhtmin than he could at me, and that there was a tolerant humour behind his frown. Even Aye was talkative that evening.

Only Ankhesenamun seemed quieter than I would have expected and she picked at her food, so that the contents of her plates went back to the kitchens more rearranged than diminished. She was five months into her pregnancy.

Poor, brave Ankhesenamun had said nothing to any of us, including Tutankhamun. She had spoken briefly to her physician, who had examined her and told her that the spots of blood she had discovered between her legs were nothing to be afraid of. When I later confronted him about his prognosis he stood by it; he told me that if there had been a problem with the pregnancy there was very little he could do about it because it was in the hands of the gods, and the greatest of doctors cannot stay the hand of the divine. He told me that he had to accept his helplessness and to scare Ankhesenamun with morbid possibilities would not serve her cause in the least. He told me that the symptoms very often really are nothing to worry about. I stopped listening long before he stopped talking and I tried to let the drone of his voice in my head take my mind from what had happened.

At the time I assumed that Ankhesenamun's reticence was because she disapproved of the subject matter, not being a woman too enamoured with the comings and goings of those below her at court. Even I was enjoying Nakhtmin's stories for once, so animated was he in their telling. I paid little attention to Ankhesenamun, for I did not want to repay what I saw as a rare petulance with the reward of attention. It is undoubtedly this that prevented me from seeing her illness creeping upon her. I am comforted, albeit negligibly, by the knowledge that even had I nursed her through the entire meal it would have made not the slightest difference.

It was during the fourth course that she pushed her plate away from her across the table with enough force to spill its contents over the side. The conversation stopped abruptly and all eyes turned to her. She was pale. Every inhalation was a gasp.

My first thought was that she had been poisoned and I cried out in alarm. She later told me that she wished she had indeed been poisoned, but I upbraided her for making such remarks, and I knew the king would have done so too, had he lived to hear them.

Such painful details. I remember the scrape of Tutankhamun's chair across the floor tiles as he pushed it away to stand up. I remember him taking a step towards her, holding out his hand to cup her cheek. I remember the expression on his face, and on hers.

"Ankhesenamun?" he said.

Suddenly enough to make me jump in my seat, she screamed and folded up, her head almost hitting the table, her arms hugging her stomach and abdomen.

"Fetch a doctor!" I shouted to Nakhtmin. He regarded me for the briefest of moments (so brief as to make me think in my more charitable moments that I imagined it) as though about to ask who I thought I was to order him around in such a peremptory manner. Then he was running from the room, leaving his chair upturned behind him.

Between us, Aye and myself lowered Ankhesenamun gently to the floor. Aye gathered together cushions and laid them under her head. Tutankhamun knelt and held her in his arms, whispering her name over and over as though it was a prayer. Her screams only increased in pitch and volume and desperation as she lay and hugged her knees to her chest. Tutankhamun looked from her to me, the threat of panic in his eyes, and there was nothing I could say.

The doctors arrived with Nakhtmin at their heels and quickly bundled her up and carried her through the apartments to her bedchamber. Tutankhamun walked with them, his hand clinging to hers. We guests followed nervously behind at a respectful distance, swapping glances and wringing our hands. We only stopped when the door to the bedchamber slammed in our faces as though we were spurned lovers.

We remained there, for we knew not what else to do, and we paced and bit our nails and prayed that each of Ankhesenamun's screams would be the last, looking for the subtlest clue that our prayer had been answered. We timed the interval between them in our heads, taking comfort when it was longer than the interval before, and wincing in despair and disappointment when it was not. A groan was seen as a positive sign, merely because it was quieter than a scream.

Perhaps an hour into our vigil the noise finally stopped, but it was replaced by something, in its way, much worse. It was replaced with the sound of sobbing. I knew both Tutankhamun and Ankhesenamun well enough to discern that it was the king's weeping that I could hear.

Tutankhamun remained alone for as long as he could bear it. He had expressly forbidden even those closest to him – in fact, he had placed special emphasis on those closest to him – from disturbing him. He was motionless in the toy room, sitting cross-legged on the floor. He held in his hands the toy lion, turning it around and around, as though perpetually expecting to find answers engraved on whichever side faced away from him. Occasionally he would pull the string that opened and closed its jaws and somehow this would always prompt the tears, but the tears were good. The tears made him feel cleansed. He felt he could cry when he was not observed by those who believed he needed to be stronger.

The doctor had explained it to him in words so simple that Tutankhamun had felt slighted at the implication that he would not understand anything more complicated. Aye's hand had been on his shoulder, one man giving comfort to another, and Aye had evidently sensed his tension at the doctor's condescension for he had squeezed his shoulder tighter momentarily, as though to hold him in place. Tutankhamun breathed deeply and tried to listen, for he knew that it was important.

"It is to do with the spirit," the doctor was saying, and Tutankhamun found himself nodding as the physician spoke, urging him to reach the point. "The human soul is split into two facets: the *ka* and the *ba*."

"I know that," Tutankhamun said.

"Of course, Your Majesty," the doctor said. "The *ka* is easy to define and understand. It is what makes us who we are. It is the eternal spirit that dwells within the shells of our bodies."

"I *know*," Tutankhamun said.

"Of course, Your Majesty," the doctor said. "But what of the *ba*? What can we say of the *ba*?"

He waited for Tutankhamun to answer, because he was beginning to sound patronising even to himself. Tutankhamun did not know the answer and remained silent.

"Well," the doctor said. "The *ba* is the spark of life. There is a *ba* for every person, from peasants to kings, but there are a limited number, so when one is no longer needed, it is reused. When a man dies, his *ba* goes into the unborn baby. It brings the baby to life, but it is not the baby's soul. It is the difference between a statue and a man. It is the difference from a healthy baby and... well..." The doctor's voice trailed away for a moment before he remembered where he was. "Sometimes, sadly, there are not enough *ba* to go around. They are all used. Everybody is alive who can be alive. Unfortunately, it is not an uncommon occurrence. This is what happened to your baby. It was nobody's fault."

"Is that supposed to make me feel better?" Tutankhamun asked him.

The doctor looked flustered for a moment. "Well, no, Your Majesty, I meant only..."

"Leave me," Tutankhamun said to him.

Gratefully, the doctor bowed from the room.

"Majesty," Aye said, from over Tutankhamun's shoulder.

"You too," Tutankhamun said.

"Really, Majesty, there is no..."

"I command that you leave me, Aye," Tutankhamun said, the firmness of his tone surprising even himself. He was not aware that he had the strength to address Aye in such a way. "And I am not to be disturbed under any circumstances." He felt the weight of Aye's hand leave his shoulder. He did not turn around as Aye left the room, partly so that Aye could not see his tears, but also because he did not want to feel the sudden urge to apologise.

From there he went to the toy room and sat amongst the presents he could not give. They would not allow him to see Ankhesenamun because they told him that she was too ill, and he did not know whether or not he believed them. He could not command them to allow him to see her in case they were telling the truth and his presence excited her to such a degree that it endangered her further. But he had the terrible suspicion that she was dead and not a man among them had the courage to tell him. Perhaps they were waiting for a better moment, when the weight of his daughter's death – they had told him that she would have been a daughter, in a manner that suggested this could be another consolation – was not so crushing. He wanted to tell them that he would never feel any less desolate than he did now, and that no news they could give him could make him feel worse, but even he did not believe that.

He turned the toy lion over and over in his hand, but there were no answers to be found anywhere upon it.

The Maya Papyrus, Fragments 249-256

It sometimes seems to me that the gods play us all for sport, that they place wagers upon us and laugh and joke at the calamities that they cause to befall us. It sometimes seems to me that they test us and our resolve and our strength not for the betterment of our souls or the focusing of our knowledge and minds but simply for their own entertainment and idle curiosity. For what other reason could they have piled misery upon fear for me in the manner that they did after that night at the palace? What other explanation could there be for the news that greeted me only three days later?

I rushed to the palace with such haste that the shanks of my horses were flecked with foam by the time I arrived and my legs ached from the buffeting they had received at my unwise disregard for the stones and potholes of the roads. I left the messenger, who is after all paid for his speed, coughing in my dust.

The palace was sombre, and the usual smiles I received upon my arrival were muted into nods and grimaces. I did not care. I hardly noticed. I ran the corridors with such abandon that I found myself unable to stop at corners and was forced to use the opposite wall as an uncomfortable yet effective brake on my progress. By the time I reached the audience chamber I was out of breath almost to the point of suffocation, and I rather undid all my frantic haste in getting there and quite failed to grasp the scene that greeted me.

The industry of the room was abruptly interrupted by my dramatic arrival and although all eyes were turned towards me, the people frozen in the attitudes in which I had found them, I could not find the breath to speak for some time.

"Akh..." I said, unable to force anything more sensible from my mouth. "Akhet..."

But now it was not only breathlessness that was preventing me from speaking. The tableau that presented itself to me was far more breathtaking than my headlong flight to the palace. Aye was there, as were a number of courtiers and lesser ministers. Horemheb was absent, as, of course, was Tutankhamun, who was still in mourning for his child. He had ordered that the baby be mummified, and declared that he would mourn until the child was entombed.

Aye looked at me from where he sat upon Tutankhamun's throne.

I had been standing with my hands upon my knees until my breathing and heartbeat reined themselves in to what appeared to be safer levels. I straightened up and regarded Aye with suspicion.

"The kingdom needs ruling," he said to me. It was the first time I had ever heard the subtlest hint of uncertainty in his voice. "Would you have us without a king?"

"We have a king," I said.

"He is hardly at the reins at the moment," Aye said. "He is currently sitting alone in a room full of toys. I believe he has favourites among them."

"And you think that excuses this?" I said. I walked forwards and the courtiers parted before me. Aye stood up, looking guilty.

"I presume you are here for a reason," he said, and I suddenly remembered why, and all thoughts of the man's irreverence were discarded as though I could only contemplate one outrage at a time.

"Akhetaten," I said. "They are ransacking it."

"Who are?"

It was a question that had not occurred to me and I did not know the answer. All that mattered to me was that it was being destroyed. The vandals could have been locals or Hittites or Nubian revolutionaries or demons for all I cared. I knew only that they needed to be stopped, because I recognised that people are never satiated, and that there are always more to come and envy the pickings of those who came before them, and that as soon as the city was emptied of treasure there was only one other place for them to go.

"I do not know," I said. "Brigands. Criminals. It is unimportant. Only the crime is important."

Aye shrugged. "It is a city that did not deserve to be made," he said. "Perhaps this is for the best. Let them unmake it. Let them consign it to the desert, where it belongs."

"But you must protect it!" I said.

"What is there to protect? If any gold remains there, let them have it. We are no longer the slaves of Akhenaten. Gold is plentiful again. You are the king's treasurer. You know how full are the coffers. What do we care for a handful of carvings and statues?"

"The tombs!" I said, turning from him and making my way towards the door. "Who will protect the tomb of my sister? Your daughter?"

I opened the door to leave but gave him the opportunity of reply before I crossed its boundary. However angry I was with him, however this was the most I could ever have hoped to rail against him, I could not leave without allowing him the end of the argument. He was still my father, and I was still afraid of him. To leave too abruptly seemed more disrespectful than I was prepared to allow myself.

"They will not touch the tombs," he said, but the fearful expression on his face told me whom he was trying to persuade. "If tombs are robbed they are done so at night, in stealth, by shameful men. Not in broad daylight by marauding gangs. It does not happen. And anyway, we have left a garrison of soldiers there to protect them."

"How many?" I said.

"They are highly trained men, faced with delinquents and thugs."

"How many?" I said.

"A dozen. Maybe two."

We stared at each other, and with each beat of my heart I felt my rage rising, my hands beginning to tremble, the almost uncontrollable urge to scream and throw myself at him. Of course, I did nothing of the kind, but I shouted at him in frustration and felt almost as brave.

"I will do it!" I shouted, and I stormed from the room, unable for the sake of appearances to return and retract my hasty words. But all the while, as I stamped along the corridor, I was thinking only one word: How?

Aye could not deny to himself the fact that he was enjoying his new position. People could not help but give him that extra touch of reverence. He believed he deserved it, for all the hardship he had suffered and toil he had contributed towards the kingdom, but such a belief was almost a secret even from himself. They were thoughts that he was not comfortable to entertain for very long. It seemed vaguely sacrilegious to wish the love of the people upon himself.

When he first sat himself on the king's throne he did so with the most harmless of motives. He had been dealing with the king's business since before the sun had risen and now, as the sun slid down the western side of the heavens' vault he was still there, working as hard and as ceaselessly as he had been for the entire day. He had been tired. He was neither a man as young as the king, to endure a day of labour such as this one had been, nor one with the advantage of an Aye looking over his shoulder with endless advice and the answers to all the most taxing questions. There had been, perhaps, a time when he would have taken it all without a moment's weary contemplation, without ever having to stretch his back with a grimace and a groan, without ever having to shake the feeling back into his extremities. But no longer.

Aye had sighed heavily and ordered the nearest servant to bring him a bowl of fruit and had leaned against one arm of the throne. It had looked so soft, so comforting, that he could almost feel it drawing the ache from the small of his back, almost feel the tingling in his legs as his weight was taken from them and the back of his thighs were caressed by the red cushions of the seat.

He had tried to make the move look nonchalant, as though it was the most natural thing in the world, as though it meant nothing, as though this was just a chair like any other. His thoughts drifted away from the voice of the minister addressing him, who was talking about the distribution of grain in the settlements near the southern border. He stepped across the front of the throne and slowly sat down, unable to prevent a satisfied little sigh escaping his lips as he did so. He could sense one or two glances being shared across the room by the courtiers therein, but the absence of pain was too soothing for him to care. He decided that there was nothing to do but continue as though nothing out of the ordinary had happened. The minister talking about grain distribution had drifted to an untidy halt, his mouth open but forgotten.

"Well?" Aye said.

The minister gradually recovered the thread of his speech and Aye made a show of his rapt attention.

From that moment he had noticed a change in those around him. It was as though the throne was the thing to be revered and those who bowed to him were in reality bowing to that.

Perhaps bow was too strong a word. They certainly did not prostrate themselves, and Aye would have been horrified had they done so, but there was an unmistakable deference when they addressed him, a glance at their feet, a nervousness with the hands.

He enjoyed it. He tried to tell himself that it was not the enjoyment of being treated almost like a king but merely the satisfaction of knowing that he was making a difference to Egypt, safeguarding her when she was at her most vulnerable. But another voice would answer that he could protect the kingdom without sitting in the throne, without the ministers of court having difficulty meeting his eye, without inclinations of the head that were almost bows.

The king was to remain in mourning for the duration of the mummification of his daughter's body which, like all royal embalmings, was seventy days. As the days slipped past and ministers and servants asked after the king's welfare, Aye found himself answering with less and less enthusiasm. Each day that passed made it easier to slip onto the throne, and each day that passed brought an added reluctance to have to surrender what he had found.

The Maya Papyrus, Fragments 258-270

> *Even the quickest route to Akhetaten took days. I paced the deck of the ship continuously during the journey, paranoid that we would be too late. I had paused long enough to gather together as many soldiers as I could fit onto one ship and set sail without further delay. The waters were smooth and the wind strong enough to push us against the current at a healthy pace but it could never be fast enough for me and I found myself time and again at the prow of the ship, trying to pull the horizon towards us with the power of my impatience.*
>
> *When Akhetaten's harbour finally came into view I almost laughed with relief. The ship drifted towards the dock as though drawn there by its own motives and as we approached I was gripped with a sense of apprehension. The docks were deserted and it was disquieting to see such a place so lifeless and barren. I felt almost as though I had never been here before. During our time in Akhetaten every need of the city had come through this place, every visitor, every commodity, every piece of food that could not be grown or raised in the hostility of Akhetaten's environs, it all came through this port, and to see it empty, to hear the silence in which it was cocooned, was like looking into the eyes of a corpse.*
>
> *We disembarked in silence, the captain of the troops marshalling his men into columns along the dockside. The sailors*

were ordered to remain with the ship and to guard it at all costs. It was our only way back out of the city, for the desert between here and anywhere else was impenetrable to all but the hardiest of bandits.

We marched out of the docks and through the city to the King's Way. The streets echoed with the tread of the soldiers' sandals and the clink of swords within their scabbards. We would occasionally hear the sounds of activity coming to us through alleyways and across junctions, but we saw nobody. In a city where silence reigned so effectively, sounds became treacherous and it was impossible to determine from how far away they came and what the nature of their activity might be. It was a disconcerting feeling and I was glad to walk at the head of a troop of such heavily armed men.

Everywhere was in the grip of decay. Without the artisans and craftsmen to maintain it, the city was crumbling into the desert from whence it sprang. The white paint on the walls had faded from its brilliance and here and there had fallen away from the walls entirely, bringing great slabs of the plaster with it. Debris littered the roads, and it was not debris that had simply fallen from the walls or through the windows that lined the streets. No mere decay could account for the furniture that the troops were forced to skirt, lying as it did in the middle of the road. The encroaching desert sand, which had started to drift into streets and doorways, was not the agent that had smashed doors to splinters or chiselled out the eyes and mouths of the royalty represented on the frescoes on the palace and temple walls.

At the royal palace and the Small and Great Aten Temples we encountered nothing but destruction. Although we searched as thoroughly as only a group of men who do not care about the wellbeing of the furnishings can, we found no living thing. I was hardly surprised. Whoever had preceded us here could have walked from these rooms with the wealth of a lifetime in their arms. They would not have hesitated before racing to the nearest market or smithy.

We marched on.

Past the last of the houses the desert began. Before us were the imposing eastern cliffs in which the royal tombs were situated. The sand sapped the energy from my legs so quickly that within a few steps my thighs and calves were burning with the effort of picking one foot up after the other. Sweat poured from me and stung my eyes, taunting me for the dryness of my mouth.

Still we marched. The desert sand gave way to the rock of the cliffs. I marched at the head of the column, thinking only where the first arrow would fall if we were attacked, and brought the men finally into the Wadi Abu Hasa el-Bahri.

I guided us to the entrance of Akhenaten's tomb. The steps leading down to its door had been revealed and the sand that had covered them dug away. The seal on the door at the base of the steps had been broken and the door itself lay open.

I knew the layout of the tomb just as well as I knew its location and I continued to lead the men into the darkness. It was as empty as the city over which it gazed, which was a matter of immense relief to me, but we had been preceded. The lid of Akhenaten's sarcophagus had been prised open and lay to one side where even its riches of gold had taken second place to unwrapping the linen from his head, removing his eyes and smashing in his mouth, rendering him blind and mute in the underworld for all eternity.

I remained staring at the desecration for a moment, shaking my head.

"Where will it all end?" I said to nobody in particular. "There used to be respect. The modern world is a place made bankrupt."

The soldiers remained silent behind me but when I turned to face them I could see that they did not seem too distressed at Akhenaten's fate, for they had no more love of him than had the bandits.

I marched them back out into the sunlight. I was terrified at what awaited us at Nefertiti's tomb. I had not forgotten the distant activity we had heard in the city and I knew that whoever we had heard had heard us. If there was anybody still here, there was only one place they could be. I was just as terrified of finding them as I was of not doing so, for if I did not it meant they were already gone and the damage done.

We clambered through the rocks. The route was tortuous and we could not see our goal until we were almost upon it.

Only I knew the path and so I was leading the way when we rounded the final corner. There was a shout. I stopped suddenly enough for the man behind me to stumble into my back. An arrow fizzed past me and clattered on stone.

I quickly found a vantage point behind the nearest sizeable rock. I could see nothing overhead but arrows and I could trace the accuracy of our archer's aim by the screams of their targets.

By the second volley the sword and spearmen were already racing forwards, shredding their throats with screams.

The commander of the troops almost passed me by, so instinctively had I found cover, but saw me at the last moment and clawed at my arm.

"Come!" he shouted at me.

I did not move. He threw a sword at me and I had to scuttle out of the way to avoid injury.

"Now!" he shouted. He grabbed my forearm and dragged me to my feet. "Pick up the sword. Pick up the sword!"

I did so simply because the thought of disobeying him did not occur to me. Somehow I found myself running alongside him. He was shouting as we ran.

"We do not know if we killed them all. Some may have escaped into the tomb. We have to be after them before their friends have too much warning of our approach."

We were by now at the entrance to the tomb. I could not help but notice that none of the soldiers had ventured within. I genuinely had no idea what was happening.

"I have no time for if-you-pleases and thank yous," the commander told me. "A confined space is not difficult to defend. We must arrive with as much speed as possible. You know the layout of the tomb. You must lead us."

I actually took a step backwards.

"But..." I said.

"My lord, you will be able to count the moments you argue by our dead."

"But..."

"Go!" he shouted.

And, Amun help me and protect me, I did.

The time before Tutankhamun was informed that it would be once again safe for him to visit his wife was interminable.

Since the baby's death Tutankhamun had been becoming increasingly paranoid about Ankhesenamun's wellbeing. Aye took every opportunity to assure him that her health was improving day by day. He brought endless updates of her progress and messages of love that Tutankhamun secretly doubted were authentic. Still, he was unable to prevent himself from pleading with Aye to return to Ankhesenamun's bed chamber to gather more. Aye would dutifully oblige and return with declarations of undiminished devotion that Tutankhamun would once again be unable to trust.

Finally, after one day and two nights the physicians came to him to tell him that Ankhesenamun was well enough to receive him. He rushed to her bedside with all the speed he could muster from legs weak with excitement and nervousness, leaving Aye with his walking stick gasping in his wake, his urgings to dignity ignored.

He skidded to a halt in the antechamber to the room in which Ankhesenamun was recovering. Two physicians awaited him, both with grim expressions set on their faces. Tutankhamun felt an immediate lurching in his chest.

"What?" he said.

"She is still very weak, Majesty," one of the doctors told him.

"I know," Tutankhamun said.

"Try not to excite her."

"I *know*," Tutankhamun said.

The doctors shared a brief glance. "You must try to be calm, Your Majesty," the second doctor said.

"I *am* calm," Tutankhamun said, his agitation belying his assurances. "Let me in!"

The doctors looked at each other again, the expression of each telling the other that there was nothing left to be done. They opened the door. Tutankhamun stepped forwards, the reverent silence of the room beyond the doorway doing more than the doctors ever could to calm him.

The bed upon which Ankhesenamun lay faced across the room. Pillows had been arranged behind and around her to prop her up into a position somewhere between the horizontal and the vertical. It enabled her to turn her head as Tutankhamun approached and smile at him through silent tears.

Tutankhamun signalled to the nurses and physicians who were arranged around the room endeavouring to appear as though they had no interest in his arrival.

"You may leave us," he said. They all filed to the doorway and Tutankhamun and Ankhesenamun were alone.

"I have been so afraid," Tutankhamun whispered.

He was standing two or three paces from the bed, his fingers playing nervously with the belt of his kilt.

"My husband," Ankhesenamun said, her voice trembling under the strain of trying to keep her tears in check. "I am sorry."

"It is not for you to apologise," Tutankhamun said.

"I have let you down," Ankhesenamun said. "I have not cared for our baby, and I beg your forgiveness. I have disappointed you, and for that I am truly sorry."

"I am not disappointed," Tutankhamun said. He stepped forwards and gingerly lowered himself onto the bed near the little mounds that signified the whereabouts of Ankhesenamun's feet. "My grief is deeper than the Nile and my anger flows with the rage of an inundation but it is not directed towards you, for you are no more at fault here than am I. My anger is directed towards the gods, who did not provide a *ba* for this child. It is Amun who has let us down, and only him do I hold responsible."

"Thank you," Ankhesenamun said, with deep feeling. "You may come closer, you know."

"Are you sure? I do not want to hurt you."

Ankhesenamun smiled again. "Hold me. It will not hurt."

"I can hold you?"

"Please," Ankhesenamun said.

Tutankhamun carefully edged up the bed. Ankhesenamun's smiled remained, although when she blinked it caused tears to overflow and run down her cheeks. Tutankhamun brushed them away with his thumb.

Wincing, Ankhesenamun leant forwards and reached out for him. He enveloped her in his arms and held her so tightly that she groaned with the relief and security of it.

"Does it hurt?" he asked.

"I am a little tender in… certain places," she said, "but it is manageable. I am weak, though. I lost a lot of blood, and it has taken my strength with it. For a while I could hardly raise my head. The doctors tell me it was serious, but not unknown. They tell me I am going to recover."

"What about another child?" Tutankhamun said.

Ankhesenamun made a noise that Tutankhamun did not immediately recognise as a laugh, hidden as it was within a sob and a sniffle. "I am expecting the nurses to bring me some food. Perhaps we could wait until after I have eaten?"

Tutankhamun pulled away from her, his brow furrowed. "No," he said, "I did not mean…" but then he saw that she was teasing him and he returned her smile. "You know what I meant," he said.

"As soon as I am well we can try again," she said. "Because a *ba* was unavailable for our little girl this time does not mean that there will not be one available if I become pregnant again."

It was the words *our little girl* that were too much for Tutankhamun. He had so wanted to be a man when he saw Ankhesenamun again. He had harboured such romantic visions of a quiet strength with which to reassure her, of a regal composure to compensate for the runaway emotions of her femininity. But after she referred so tenderly to *our little girl* he was no longer able to retain control of himself, and for a long while afterwards they remained in each other's arms, his forehead resting upon her shoulder, his shoulders shrugging with the effort of weeping. She stroked the top of his head as he wept, noticing that its stubble was beginning to grow.

"You have not shaved," she said, simply in order to say something.

He lifted his head from her shoulder and sniffed voluminously, wiping the back of his hand across his nose and mouth.

"I know," he said. "I have not eaten either. Yesterday I did not dress."

Ankhesenamun tutted. "I shall have to speak to your servants once I am recovered," she said. "They have been neglecting you."

"I ordered them to leave me alone," Tutankhamun said. "It is not their fault."

The couple lapsed into silence, holding each other, gently swaying from side to side as though in time to music.

"We will have many more children," Tutankhamun said, and then corrected himself: "Many children. We will have a great family, and not a corner of the palace will be free of their laughter and play. We will have armies of girls and boys, and the boys will be great warriors and hunters, and will take wives from all the kingdoms of the world, and will lead Egypt from strength to greatness."

"I know we will, husband," Ankhesenamun whispered. "I know we will."

"You will undoubtedly be the father of a great dynasty, Majesty," a voice said, from across the room.

Both Tutankhamun and Ankhesenamun had been so immersed in their grief and sating themselves on the unique comfort that only they could bring to each other that neither had heard the door opening and Aye letting himself into the room. He had in fact been there for some time but having decided upon a discrete entrance he then found himself at a loss with how to announce himself. He had listened to their conversation self-consciously, his fingers running over the knots in the wood of his walking stick, but had been unable to find an opportune moment to interrupt. He had listened to Tutankhamun's words and smiled at them, but there had not been the surge of pride that he had found to be usually associated with such talk of strong kings and heirs and dynasties. It would normally bid images to his mind of his mother and what she had achieved, how her machinations had furnished the Two Lands with not one but three kings, all of whom were her own progeny. How the wife of a soldier had plotted and planned and finally succeeded in becoming a God's Mother and the matriarch of an entire kingdom. It brought tears to his eyes to match

Tutankhamun's when he thought of it and he recognised just how much Thuya would have rejoiced at the young king's words.

And yet, despite all this, for the first time he had felt something lacking from Tutankhamun's words, or if not from the words themselves perhaps from his reaction to them. It was not something to which he could put a definition, although it was not unlike loss. Neither was it unlike disappointment. It felt as though something was being taken from him, and it was not without some degree of alarm that he realised what it was. It was the throne.

When he spoke he did so not only to announce his presence, but because he needed to distract himself from his realisation. They were not healthy thoughts.

"How long have you been there?" Tutankhamun asked him.

"Not long," he said. "I was awaiting you without." He indicated the doorway, and presumably the anteroom beyond it, with a movement of his head.

"And what brings you within?" Tutankhamun asked.

"The doctors wished me to relay the message to you that Ankhesenamun must be allowed to rest. We all realise how difficult it must be for you, Majesty, but you must force yourself to leave her side. You may visit her again tomorrow, and the next day, and each day you may remain for a little longer, but for now she must sleep in order to regain her strength."

"I will remain," Tutankhamun said. "Ankhesenamun may sleep with me at her side."

"I applaud your loyalty, Majesty, but I am aware of the love that you both share and I doubt she could ever be truly rested in your company. She will not be able to help conversing with you."

Tutankhamun looked unsure for a moment, torn between devotion to his wife and the desire not to hinder her recovery.

"Please," Ankhesenamun said. "I am being cared for admirably here. You do not have to spend every moment with me. Just be sure to visit me whenever the opportunity presents itself. Anyway, I am sure I will be back on my feet in a day or two. If you busy yourself with matters of state you will hardly notice that I am gone."

"There are no matters of state," Tutankhamun said. "Aye is attending to it all. I shall not be king while I am in mourning for my child."

"Husband, I think it will help you. It is not a betrayal of her to try to surmount your mourning. It is only a betrayal if her death destroys your life. Your kingdom needs a king, and privilege is no respecter of calamity."

Tutankhamun looked at the floor between his feet.

"Your Highness," Aye said. "If His Majesty feels the need for time to adjust to his loss, I am more than happy..."

"Of course you are, Aye," Ankhesenamun said. "But you have already done enough. We are both grateful. But with all due respect, you are not the king."

Aye bowed, but said nothing.

"My wife is correct," Tutankhamun said, unable to filter the reluctance from his voice. He turned to Ankhesenamun and took one of her hands in both of his, one above and one below, the palms gently pressing together. He looked at her with all the gravity he could muster, and said: "Though I leave your side, my thoughts do not."

It was a pleasant sentiment, but it was delivered with such solemnity that Ankhesenamun could barely restrain herself from laughing.

"Thank you," she said, simply, in the hope that Tutankhamun would leave the room before she lost the battle.

Aye and Tutankhamun left the room and Ankhesenamun found the battle all too easily won. Her husband's company had, for all too brief a time, kept her grief at bay. As soon as the door closed behind him it all came crashing back with an almost physical force. It served only to remind her what an accomplished father Tutankhamun would have been. She lay back in the bed, covered her eyes with the heels of her hands and began, very quietly, lest her husband hear her through the door, to weep.

In the corridor, Aye and Tutankhamun were making their way to the king's quarters.

"I should call an audience," Tutankhamun said.

"Really, Majesty, there is little need. Despite Ankhesenamun's wishes, if you would prefer me to continue acting as your regent until you are ready to resume your duties, I will regard it as an inestimable honour and a singular privilege."

"Thank you, Aye, but Ankhesenamun is right."

"She need never know, Majesty."

"Know what?" Tutankhamun said. He stopped and regarded Aye, who walked on for one or two paces before also drawing to a halt.

"If you would prefer me to continue acting in your stead there is no need for us to tell Ankhesenamun, if you would rather she did not know."

"As I said, Aye, I think she is right. I shall resume my duties."

"As you wish, Majesty. If you are sure."

"I am," Tutankhamun said.

There was a firmness in his tone that Aye was noticing with an increasing frequency. It was coming with adolescence and the growth of self-belief. Aye very much doubted there was anything that he could do about it, for he had coached the boy in kingship as well as any king before him had been trained, but it worried him exceedingly.

But despite the resolve in Tutankhamun's voice Aye could not resist the temptation of one more remark.

"As long as you are certain that the weight of your responsibilities will not be detrimental to your wellbeing at this trying time."

"*Aye!*" Tutankhamun said. "I have spoken. Listen when your king speaks!"

Aye raised his eyebrows to himself (once they had resumed their walk and he was sure that Tutankhamun would not see). It had been an interesting reaction, and one that was neither expected nor welcome. But, Aye reasoned, it was the logical progression of Tutankhamun's attitude towards him. The child's fear had been transformed into the adolescent's truculence and was now evidently becoming the impatience of the young man. Aye would perhaps have to shift his approach once again. He was beginning to see the advantages of cajolery over commands.

Either way, it was an ominous development. Aye was already feeling the loss of the privilege he had felt when in the king's audience room. Although it had tired him to the brink of exhaustion his weary bones had been steeped in satisfaction. When he fell into his slumber each night, knowing he would have to be awake again within a few hours in order to resume his duties, he wore his fatigue like a medal. He had already known what was expected of him because he had spent most of his life at the side of one king or another and he had seen what had been expected of them. He had been Tutankhamun's tutor and Nefertiti's father, he had been vizier and advisor and confidante and friend, and all this had given him an aptitude for the job that he doubted had been in the possession of many of his predecessors. It was almost as though it was a role that he was fated to fill by the gods. It was almost as though Amun had trained him for it in the same way that he had trained Tutankhamun.

It was almost as though it was his right to occupy the throne.

He looked askance at Tutankhamun as they walked, and wondered on the calibre of his reign if he had not had Aye there to advise his every move. He wondered how much of a king this boy really was, in comparison with him.

The Maya Papyrus, Fragments 271-285

> *The men lit lamps and torches and we stepped into the tomb's*
> *retreating darkness. From the entrance a long straight corridor*

sloped into the ground, interrupted twice by flights of stairs. The corridor was so small that I had to bow in order for it to accommodate me, which was undoubtedly the intention. I could not see the end of the corridor. In fact, I could see no further than a handful of paces before the light quickly gradated to impenetrable blackness, within which, I realised, an army could await me with no hint to their existence. The men had become very quiet, awed partly by the reverent surroundings in which they found themselves, but also, I think, at least in part because they were as scared as was I.

We reached our goal after two or three turns. The descent to the burial chamber itself was not entirely level and it was only when we were within fifty paces of it that we saw the glow of light emanating from within. The men extinguished their lamps and suddenly the light from below seemed all the brighter. Now that we had stopped we could hear their voices and the noise they made as they looted whatever they could lay their hands on, so intent on their wicked task, and so determined to grab whatever they could before their neighbour reached it first that they had set no guard and cast hardly an eye in our direction. Evidently, the commander needed more faith in his archers. Nobody had preceded us.

I had no option but to move forwards. The confines of the passageway prevented any possibility of rearranging the order of our attack into a more satisfactory formation. I cursed myself for lacking the courage to refuse the commander's orders. I could have shouted directions from the back. Perhaps even from the entrance.

I edged forwards towards the doorway. Around the sarcophagus, which was situated against one wall, and in which the reflections of the bandits' torches and lamps flickered, gold upon gold, were standing a group of men, much fewer than I had been expecting but enough to run me through as effectively as if there had been a hundred or a thousand of them. In truth, there was very little room for them, such were the riches arrayed around them.

Luxurious beds, chariots (both ceremonial and war), statues, canopic jars, shabtis, a painted wooden chest containing uncountable jars and bottles of perfumes and cosmetics, bottles upon bottles of wine, linen, furniture, amulets, gods, model boats, vases, pottery, thrones: all of this and more had been amassed in the chamber. All of it was essential to Nefertiti in the afterlife, so where it had been found that there was not enough room for a particular item to be delicately and aesthetically placed it had been piled on top of something else with little ceremony. Much of the clutter had been accentuated by the haste and recklessness of the bandits who had thrown anything that could be lifted and could not be sold into one corner where it tottered in a rather threatening manner. In another corner were the items of value that they were presumably intending to take with them.

I could see from my vantage point that their interest even in these items had waned and been superseded by the riches promised by Nefertiti's outer sarcophagus. It was a mask fashioned almost entirely from gold and turquoise, and was a thing of hypnotic beauty. I found my eyes drawn to it even here, when they had so many more things of import to observe. It hardly resembled her, for the goldsmith's art was not such that he could encapsulate a beauty as intense as Nefertiti's, but then there was no need for it to. Gold has its own intrinsic beauty, and it needs not be fashioned into anything in order to capture the attention of all those in its presence.

It was only when I saw the sword wielded by one of the bandits that I was forced into action. He lifted it and it was obviously his intention to use it to lever off the gold of Nefertiti's mask.

The process of thought abandoned my heart. I was instantly and uncontrollably consumed by the vision of my sister's face removed by this plunderer. I screamed. I howled with the injustice of it all, with the rage of the helpless assailed by the remorseless, with the revenge of every king robbed of an afterlife by those intent only upon their own enrichment. They heard me, of course, these devourers of souls, but the chamber was sufficiently small for the man nearest to me to not even have time to raise his arms in defence. I lunged with my sword, the weight of my entire body thrown forwards into the thrust. It penetrated his belly at the exact point of his navel. He did not scream. I jerked it out of him and he fell forwards, forcing me to step to one side to allow him an unimpeded journey to the ground. By this time my comrades had gained my side and they were hacking and chopping with the energy of my own anger, which had been slaked not one jot by the blood of the man at my feet. I stepped forwards again, and again I lunged forward and withdrew, lunged and withdrew, stabbing at anyone within my reach.

Save for my initial scream, we fought mostly in silence. The surroundings were too cramped to do anything, once engaged, other than fight for survival which, I discovered, is the most fierce and cruel of conflicts. At least one man was cut down by the panicked flailings of his own comrades. Each man came at least within a breath of death. Not one of us at the end of the fight, when at last it came, were unmarked, although many of us would feel no pain until our racing hearts had calmed somewhat. I had somehow suffered a cut which ran the length of my left arm, from which ran blood that formed itself into a delta around the outcrops of my knuckles. I have no idea to this day how I came by it, although I am reminded of its existence every day by a scar which I do not think will fade any further.

I estimate that the conflict lasted no more than a matter of minutes but by its conclusion the bandits were vanquished and adrift in their own blood. We had lost six men and one who would succumb to his wounds before we once again reached the ship awaiting us at the docks.

A strange elation overcame me, although my heart and muscles were almost too weak with the exertion and fear to carry it. I had fought, and I had prevailed. I had defended my sister's memory and protected her immortal soul. I had around me men that I could stand proudly alongside and call my comrades, and they, I think, these rough men who could kill without compunction and feeling, had somewhat more respect for this timid scribe than they had at the outset of our adventure. They had seen my fury and, in their own way, admired it. I was proud and euphoric and decided there and then that I would forever cherish the comradeship of these men and fight alongside them, share this joy of victory with them, whenever the opportunity arose to do so. Of course, this was a fanciful resolution that faded with the rapture of survival, but it was real enough while it lasted.

We dragged the bodies of our fallen and theirs and laid them out under the desert sun. Our dead would be transported back to the ship for burial in Thebes; the bandits would be left where they lay to be picked at by the vultures, ensuring that their souls endured the same fate as that which they intended for my sister.

I came to a decision while I was carrying the feet end of one of the bandits up the steep slope towards the open air. This could never be allowed to happen again, and short of a permanent military force stationed in Akhetaten, which Aye would never allow, there was only one way to ensure the safety of Nefertiti's mummy.

I decided that I would return to Akhetaten once I had the chance in Thebes to recover from my exertions and injuries – the cut along my arm was already beginning to sting – and bring with me servants and soldiers in sufficient numbers to empty the royal tombs of Akhetaten and transport their contents to the Valley of the Kings in Thebes where they could be safeguarded with the devotion that they deserved.

I promised Nefertiti that I would not forget her. I promised her that I would return to rescue her from her husband's fate.

Of course, by the time I had returned to Thebes affairs had overtaken me to such a degree that any promises I had made were subsumed by the events around me and it was some time before I could honour them.

It was seven years before I returned to Akhetaten.

Chapter Twenty-Three

The Fall of Carchemish

A PLAN had developed. It had gestated almost independently of him and presented itself fully formed. The king was becoming troublesome; of that there could be no doubt. Aye had perhaps been too accomplished in the schooling he gave him. It had always been his intention to give Tutankhamun the education and ability to make his own decisions. It had never occurred to Aye that these decisions would ever be contrary to Aye's own wishes.

It was ingratitude. Ingratitude and arrogance. The king had taken Aye's teachings and suddenly believed himself capable of colouring them with the brush of his own meagre experience. He thought his own opinions somehow worthy, or at least he thought them more worthy than Aye's, which had after all only had the benefit of a lifetime of cultivation.

Perhaps, Aye thought, it was time for the king to come to know his own shortcomings. Perhaps then, when he had been allowed to fail without Aye to prop him up he would see the worth in Aye's counsel.

It could not be a simpler strategy. Simply do nothing and wait for the king to come to him.

He could hardly have picked a better time for his defiance, but then neither could he have picked one worse. It was a time of pressure unprecedented in this reign and it was all coming from one place.

The people were happy, and vocally so. Whenever the king emerged from the palace, which he did on his daily trip to visit the shrine of Amun within the great Theban temple, he was greeted with nothing less than ecstatic enthusiasm. There were few empty bellies in the kingdom. The roads between the major settlements were safe to travel, at least with a small escort. The gold routes were secure and although the levels of plenty in the granaries and temples had not reached the abundant heights of Amenhotep's reign, nobody really expected them to. Amenhotep's reign had been one of such boundless wealth that it was almost seen as an aberration, a golden time of legend that could never return. Tutankhamun's reign, by contrast, was compared more often with that of his father than that of his grandfather, and in so doing the populace could hardly find the son wanting. Tutankhamun could have grown up to be a dribbling simpleton, Aye often thought, and the people would have hailed him as a divine hero in comparison to his father.

But, as was often the way, the gods were not content with the happiness of their creations. There was a blemish on Tutankhamun's reign and, if it was the only one, its significance was perhaps enhanced by its uniqueness. Nevertheless, all at court recognised it for what it was; a dangerous and frightening development.

The Hittites were on the move once again. There were few years in which the Hittites did not make some attempt at the extension of their borders, but these were a series of military adventures different in tone from the many that had preceded them. They seemed both more determined and more purposeful. They were aiming towards a goal rather than aiming merely to destabilise their neighbours and pick up the morsels which were left unguarded after the fighting stopped. Now, for the first time since Amenhotep's reign the Hittites seemed set on all out war. Egypt's military forces, after the deprivations of Akhenaten's day, and despite Aye's best efforts at their rehabilitation, were far short of the manpower necessary to be confident of victory in any major campaign, especially one against so determined and powerful an enemy.

The Hittites had moved south and east from their capital at Hattusa and laid waste the land of the Amurru, and from there marched without pause into the Beqa Valley area of Lebanon, thereby wrenching it from Egypt's control. Short of marching into Egypt herself, the Hittites could hardly have challenged Tutankhamun more directly.

Of course, Aye knew that his own victory would be worth nothing if he enjoyed it at the cost of Egypt's defeat at the hands of Hatti. But he thought he knew Tutankhamun well enough to know that Tutankhamun loved his kingdom more than his pride. He was confident that the king would come crawling to him for his help before the situation with Hatti became intolerable. And anyway, he had played with kingdoms as stakes before and he had never lost.

Aye could not blame the king for poor decisions. He was fourteen years old and Aye could not imagine himself in Tutankhamun's position at Tutankhamun's age. Only Amenhotep had been man enough at that age to grasp power and Aye did not expect that the world would ever again see a pharaoh of Amenhotep's calibre. Still, he had little sympathy for Tutankhamun. He had brought it all on himself, and the point needed to be made.

Despite the reports coming from the lands that were falling before the Hittite advance, it quickly became apparent that Tutankhamun was almost as reluctant to act as had been his father. His one submission to the situation had been to send Nakhtmin out to the lands bordering the Beqa Valley to reinforce the Egyptian troops and local militia stationed there.

Aye detected no religious reckoning in Tutankhamun's decisions: there were no declarations of the Aten's protection or of the intention to seek his guidance. Aye would have been horrified and perplexed had there been any. No, the reasons behind his decisions were purely political and military. Aye was as proud that he had raised a king with the ability for such sound reasoning as he was frustrated that the king's reasoning was leading him to the wrong conclusions.

Each messenger would arrive breathless and filthy at court with the same news: that Hittite soldiers had been reported at some-town-or-another and had been engaged by local forces, with these losses on the side of the Egyptians and their allies and those losses on the side of the enemy, and the local garrison commanders would most humbly request the king's gracious command. They would depart with the same instructions each time.

"We must continue our current policy of seeking out the enemy wherever we may find him," Tutankhamun would say. "Where possible, the enemy must be destroyed without mercy."

After one such audience, Tutankhamun turned to Aye. "He thinks I do not know what he wants," he said, "but I do. I just will not grant it."

"Who?" Aye said, raising his eyebrows. "Grant what?"

"You know full well. Nakhtmin. He wants permission to attack."

Ah, Aye thought. A breakthrough.

"Does he?" he said.

"Really, Aye," Tutankhamun said. "I thought you would have picked that up."

Aye bridled, but said nothing. He was determined not to fall prey to Tutankhamun's barbs. He would let the king think what he would.

"But we cannot attack," Tutankhamun continued. "To do so would be the utmost folly. It would leave our borders unguarded against a foe of whose numbers we have no real measure. We have no idea where their bases are. We have no hope of finding them before they know we are vulnerable to attack. It would be suicidal."

Tutankhamun stopped talking and stared at Aye. Aye stared back. Neither spoke.

"Do you not have an opinion?" Tutankhamun said, eventually.

"Your great-grandfather, Thutmose, used to have a friend and an advisor called Tjenuna, of whom I have heard tell," Aye said. "He was a wise man to whom not only Thutmose but your grandfather, Amenhotep, used to turn for counsel. He died saving Amenhotep's life in battle. He used to tell Thutmose and Amenhotep that whatever they decided must be the correct decision, because it was one made by a king, and therefore guided by a higher power. As I said, he was a wise man."

"So you will not help me?"

"What help could I possibly be?" Aye asked. "You are His Majesty Tutankhamun Nebkheperurē. You do not need the help of a man such as I. You are already guided by Amun and the pantheon of the gods. You are infallible, Your Majesty." Infallible, he thought, but wrong all the same. To continue in the present manner is to invite defeat. It will not be a quick defeat, but it will come all the same. If they can probe our weaknesses forever, and at their leisure, then they have, for all intents and purposes, limitless resources. If they make a mistake they lose nothing but men. If Nakhtmin makes a mistake we lose something much more difficult to replace: land. The only way to safeguard Egypt is by forcing the Hittites to defend what they have already won outside our borders, and the only way to do that is to attack.

I am a stubborn man, he thought to himself, as he watched the king cogitate over the matter at hand. Aye still had the capacity to surprise himself on occasion. Both the extent of his obstinacy and the faith he held in his ability to discern how far to take the situation before it became counter-productive were traits that consistently seemed to vie to outdo each other. Still, he trusted his judgement more than he was surprised by it, and it never occurred to him to back down. *The king must learn* was an adage that he found himself silently repeating to himself over and over again. *He must learn wherein lies the real wisdom of the throne, and thereby its power.*

"We cannot leave the borders undefended while we send troops on adventures abroad," Tutankhamun said, but seemed more to be thinking aloud than addressing Aye. Aye, in any case, made no answer.

"No," Tutankhamun said, with a suddenly resolute tone to his voice. "My mind remains unchanged. We cannot afford to attack. We have not the resources, and I have not the inclination."

"Very good, Your Majesty," Aye said, bowing. "I am sure the gods are guiding you along a path of wisdom."

He left the room, thinking: *fool.*

The Maya Papyrus, Fragments 292-296

> *When the ships docked in Thebes harbour and the men sang enthusiastic and colourful songs declaring exactly what they*

intended to do upon returning home to their wives and sweethearts, I joined in with just as much gusto, and with a tear in my eye.

My farewell to my newfound comrades was an emotional one on the dockside of Thebes, at least for me. They seemed a little nonplussed at my gushing rhetoric and declarations of undying camaraderie that I felt lay between us, but they had the good grace to appear saddened by my departure.

I had one consolation for our separation, and that was the imminence of my reunion with Tutankhamun and Ankhesenamun. I was overjoyed not only at the prospect of seeing them once again, but at the opportunity of regaling them with the tales of my heroism in the defence of Ankhesenamun's mother. I had been away many weeks.

I found the king pacing the floor, and his wife following him as though in an attempt to catch him. I was announced, and both rushed towards me, their arms outstretched.

"Whatever is the matter?" I exclaimed in alarm, immediately trying to imagine the worst of all possible scenarios.

"Disaster!" Ankhesenamun said, before Tutankhamun had the opportunity to open his mouth. Perhaps realising she had been pushed into speaking out of turn by the passion in which she found herself, she did not continue.

"Well?" I said, when neither of them spoke.

"Hittites," Tutankhamun said at last. "They have attacked again. Nakhtmin was too far away to react in time. They have taken the city of Carchemish, although I am told it withstood them for eight days before they breached its walls. Their brutality is matched only by their intelligence. Carchemish sits upon the Euphrates. They have effectively severed half of our trade routes. It will be almost impossible to dislodge them. Šuppiluliumas has installed one of his sons, Piyassilis, as the city's king."

"Your Majesty," I said, instinctively. "I am sure it is not as bad as all that. The Hittites have been attacking us and our allies for years."

"Not on this scale," he said. "Not with this degree of success. Horemheb is on his way now with the men of his command, but I doubt it will be enough. The turrets of Carchemish are impassable when manned by soldiers with the skill of the Hittites."

"Does it matter?" I asked, quickly rephrasing my question in response to the angry look favoured me by the king. "I mean to say, will it affect Egypt?"

"Apart from cutting off our imports from the north east, they are at the gateway to the Lebanon. They will undoubtedly advance, and when the Lebanon falls it takes with it the source of our imports of cedar wood. Without it we can build neither ships nor chariots. Hatti will impoverish us and then leave us defenceless and then conquer us. And I can but watch as the world falls."

"How did this happen?" I said, perhaps unwisely, for if I had considered my question I would have realised that there was only one way for these events to have transpired, and that was the misjudgement of the king.

Tutankhamun scowled. "I was misadvised," he said. "It is a question to which I shall address myself when the time is more propitious."

At that moment, as though summoned by Tutankhamun's words, Aye arrived. He looked stern.

"Your Majesty," he said. "Maya."

I inclined my head. "Father," I said. Such was the gravity of the moment that nobody yet had professed their pleasure at seeing me returned safe and relatively unharmed from my adventures in Akhetaten. It was not a subject I felt able to broach without prompting.

Aye looked as though he was host to an angry inner dialogue. He would look to the king and go as far as opening his lips to speak before thinking better of the idea and turning away or staring at the floor. The rest of us remained silent. The king resumed his pacing and Ankhesenamun resumed anxiously following his footsteps. Only I remained watching my father and the curious struggle with which he appeared gripped. Such was his agitation that he did not notice my staring at him.

Finally, after some moments, he seemed resolved to actually speak.

"Majesty," he said. Tutankhamun stopped his pacing and met his gaze. Ankhesenamun stopped a pace or two behind him, wringing her hands.

"Aye?" Tutankhamun prompted.

"Majesty," Aye said again, inhaled and exhaled slowly and deeply, and then spoke in a rush, as though wanting to expel the words before fear clogged them in his throat. "Majesty, I feel that it is imperative that we launch an attack against the Hittites at the first available opportunity. It will force them into defence, and thereby prevent them from launching any more attacks of their

own. It will safeguard our... your kingdom, and to do otherwise is dangerous folly, which I can no longer allow."

Tutankhamun stared for a moment. "Which you can no longer allow?" he said, at last, speaking slowly.

"You are placing the Two Lands in an unprecedented danger," Aye said.

"Which you can no longer allow?" Tutankhamun said again, incredulously.

"There was a time, Majesty, when, king though you are, you would have given some respect and credence to the words of your tutor and advisor."

"There was a time, Aye," Tutankhamun replied, "when my tutor and advisor would not pick and choose his moments to provide advice and would never presume to allow or disallow anything."

I had never seen Tutankhamun so determined in the face of Aye's authority. His hands were balled into fists.

"Your Majesty," Aye said. "You must recognise the wealth of my experience in these matters. I was your grandfather's closest companion and I learned at his side."

"My grandfather was no fighter," Tutankhamun said.

"He was a diplomat."

"Are you suggesting that diplomacy can extricate us from this situation?" Tutankhamun said. "My grandfather was a great man, but I fear that even he would baulk at this particular challenge."

Aye sighed. "Your Majesty..." he said.

"What is it exactly that you are asking me to do?" Tutankhamun asked him.

"Majesty, give me command of the situation. Listen to me. Issue the orders that I provide for you. You are yet a child. It is time that you stopped playing at kingship and allowed me to act as your regent. It is our only hope."

"You are seriously asking me to revoke my throne?"

"I am merely asking you to recognise the wisdom and authority of your elders. Nobody need know. You can trust those of us in this room as you can trust no others. The country, the court, the generals: all would believe that you had as firm a grasp on your throne as ever you have. Let me save us from this threat."

"I cannot believe what I am hearing," Tutankhamun said. He looked to Ankhesenamun and myself as though for confirmation that he was not imagining the entire scene.

"Then," Aye said, "I suggest that you persuade yourself of the reality of the situation immediately. I shall assume control. Your next command will be that when Horemheb's troops arrive they are to reinforce the troops under Nakhtmin and move to surround the city. They will then attempt to..."

"I am your king!" Tutankhamun shouted. It was a reaction chillingly reminiscent of his father and it was the only time in his life that I saw him allow the temperament of his forebears to flood to the surface. Even Aye was taken aback and, in a moment as rare as the temper that prompted it, was unable to reply.

"I rescind no power to you!" Tutankhamun said. "I categorically deny you the right to issue orders in my name. I will hear no more of this, Aye. You are dismissed from my sight."

"Majesty!" Aye said, but he was blustering under the ferocity of Tutankhamun's words.

"Get you gone!" Tutankhamun shouted, and Aye actually took a step backwards. He then looked to each of us in turn and, finding there neither succour nor support, turned and left the room.

Once Horemheb arrived he moved quickly to consolidate his forces with those of Nakhtmin. Nakhtmin made a show of greeting him like a brother while secretly resenting him for the implication that he could not cope on his own. The troops of both generals were eager for the fight, despite the foreboding look of the towers built into the walls of the city, where they could sense the Hittite archers who were undoubtedly stationed within.

But there was nothing to be done. Nakhtmin had despatched messenger after messenger to court with reports foretelling doom and woe. The replies came back so quickly that the king's messengers were passing those of Nakhtmin on the road, and the answer was always the same. Wait. Watch. Do not waste the lives of Egyptian soldiers on a battle for a well defended town. Your king commands patience.

Both Nakhtmin and Horemheb could wait, if waiting was ordered, but neither could grant the king their patience. They drilled their men endlessly, as much to exorcise their own frustration as to maximise their troops' fitness to fight, but they could do no more. The tone of Nakhtmin's messages soon changed from emphasising the difficulty of the situation to downplaying it. If he was to be exiled indefinitely in this uncivilised land he could at least salvage some respect by being the sole general in charge. If he was lucky enough to become embroiled in some kind of fight he was reluctant to have to share the glory with Horemheb, friend though he was. Nakhtmin preferred to live without the worry that he was being overshadowed.

Nakhtmin's messages eventually had the desired effect and Horemheb, along with his army, was recalled. He left without comment, enjoying the feeling that he did not suffer from Nakhtmin's insecurities.

Back at court a frigid atmosphere held sway over the throne and those closest to it, which seemed to Aye to be not unlike the atmosphere in a home after a domestic disagreement, where both parties were cold but civil towards each other in an attempt to prove themselves more refined, and therefore more mistreated, than the other. No mention was made of the words thrown in anger in the king's quarters, but the manner of both Tutankhamun and Aye would have left even a stranger in no doubt that relations between them were, to say the least, strained. Even at their most relaxed, dealings between the pair had been formal affairs. Now when they addressed each other they sounded like bad actors reciting lines.

The situation had not improved by the time that Horemheb completed his long march south and his arrival with every man of his command unscathed in fact only served to remind Tutankhamun that he had been right not to order an attack on Carchemish, and Aye that Tutankhamun had become obstreperous and stubborn. Tutankhamun was by now wily enough to ensure that Aye was present to hear Horemheb's reports of the success of the policy of deterrence. Aye's congratulations were as unenthusiastic as his smiles.

Aye, however, was not present when Tutankhamun hosted a delegation from the temple of Amun, who, without the formalities and preamble that Aye had impressed upon the king to be compulsory when addressing Amun's high priesthood, were bluntly asked to explain the Hittites' current success.

Two priests were present, one of whom being the High Priest and the other the man expected to replace him, and neither had been expecting the question.

"Your Majesty?" the High Priest ventured.

"It is a simple question, Raneffer," Tutankhamun said. "I have given a great deal of time, effort and expense in the rehabilitation of Amun. I was given to understand that in return he would offer his protection."

"But he has, Your Majesty. Have the Hittites not been prevented from reaching the Two Lands?"

"Momentarily."

"I was led to believe that our armies had prevented their advance, Your Majesty."

Tutankhamun looked at them both. He had not yet given them permission to rise from their knees and their heads were bowed to the floor, their arms outstretched before them, their voices muffled by the proximity of the tiles. It looked like a painful position to have to hold for any significant amount of time. Their voices were thin and hesitant with fear. He noticed for the first time that they were trembling. Neither were young men and their age only added to the indignity of their position. He had never spoken to them in such terse tones before.

He suddenly felt a wave of pity for them. They had not, after all, offended or attacked him or attempted to browbeat him into relinquishing the power of his throne. They were men he had met many times in the past. He held no dislike of them and he believed that this was reciprocated. He was, perhaps, being a little harsh.

"Please," he said. "Stand. May you live."

The priests gratefully clambered to their feet, looking abashed. They regarded him like wayward children and his pity surged afresh.

"Do not be offended by my actions," he said, quietly, feeling suddenly ashamed. "I mean you no harm."

"Of course, Your Majesty," Raneffer said, while making it perfectly clear that Tutankhamun's words of reassurance had done nothing to comfort him.

"I only mean to know what I am doing wrong," Tutankhamun said. He was now doubly glad that Aye was not here to witness the conversation. He felt like a supplicant at the priests' feet, and while Aye would have given him the strength to stand his ground with them, he knew that he would not feel the better for it afterwards.

"What could you possibly have done wrong, Majesty?"

"Raneffer, even during my father's days the borders of this country were never so unprotected by our gods. When Amun could have been no more insulted we did not find Hittites knocking at our door. Why is it that we do now? I am the link between the world of men and the world of gods and through my actions do the deities see us and judge us. I cannot have these catastrophes upon my head. There must be something I can do in order to gain Amun's affections once more." His voice trailed off. "There is so much that depends upon it," he added, his voice cracking on the verge of betraying the tears that were lodged in his throat.

Everything seemed to rush at him at once and it all suddenly seemed so unfair. He had tried to be as good a king as it was within his power to be. He had respected the gods and he had listened to his advisors until such time as they made it impossible for him to listen any further. He had been attentive and well-mannered to those who deserved it. And yet everything seemed to be collapsing. The people had greeted him as their saviour and instead he had led them to the brink of disaster.

"Majesty," Raneffer said. "You are as good a devotee of Amun as he could ever wish you to be. If your duties were somehow lacking it would be our obligation to bring it to your attention. The order of the world would depend upon it and a calamity even greater than invasion would befall us and everything under the heavens."

Tutankhamun looked down at his priests and had the sudden and horrible conviction that there was nothing they could do to help him. He suddenly felt terribly alone. He wished more than anything that he could see his mother and shelter within her arms from everything that beset him. He remembered his walks with her along the shaded paths of the Maru-Aten in Akhetaten. He remembered her voice, and how it could soothe him to sleep when she sang him gentle songs.

He even wished he had a father to whom he could turn, although he had lost count of the lessons he had endured where Akhenaten's wickedness had been explained and illustrated over and again. There had been a time when he had hated the memory of his father. He was no longer so sure of his emotions. Time had dulled them as surely as it had dulled all the passions of his childhood, and he now at least had a perspective that had been denied him then: that of Akhenaten the king facing a unique panorama of the worlds of men and gods, with nobody in the kingdom or beyond who could truly empathise with him. He recognised now how difficult was the life of a king and he found himself more able to forgive his father's shortcomings and unwise choices.

He prayed for just one fraction of his father's self-assurance and confidence. His father had been deformed and as good as blind. How had a man so burdened been able to lead with such zeal?

Tutankhamun looked down at the priests before him and he knew. He knew that they could not help him but now he knew that they did not have to. He knew what he had to do, and he knew, with a need for revenge born of a simmering bitterness, exactly how to do it.

He dismissed the priests and sent word to summon the finest court craftsmen to the audience chamber. He realised he was being impish and he even wondered momentarily whether he was risking too much, whether there was a safe limit to how far Aye could safely be pushed. He tried to reassure himself with words taught to him by Aye himself, that a king should fear only gods, not men, and that no man, whomsoever he may be, was able to look him in the face and call him equal. But still, Aye was as formidable in old age as he had been at any time in Tutankhamun's life, and Aye vexed was never a comfortable sight.

But, no, the decision was made and he left the craftsmen in the audience chamber, exchanging glances and scratching their heads, vowing not to return until he knew their task to be complete. And in any case, he had a great deal to prepare.

The Maya Papyrus, Fragment 300

I suppose I was as surprised as any by the news, although the king did me the honour of preparing me for it in as gentle a way as possible. We were in his quarters when he told me.

I had arrived for an evening's wine tasting, struggling to prevent the amphorae from slipping from where I had clasped them between my arms and my chest, Tutankhamun and Ankhesenamun laughing as they rushed to relieve me of my burden. It was not unusual for the king to have dismissed his servants for the night and so my suspicions were not aroused by their absence. I should perhaps have noted the change in the king's demeanour. I had not seen him this carefree for a considerable time.

It was obvious from the start that this was not an ordinary evening. Neither the king nor his wife were able to concentrate on the tasting.

Of course, neither would tell me anything but that they had something to tell me and it was most infuriating to have to endure their knowing looks and conspiratorial winks, and it quickly drove me to the point where I gathered together the various amphorae, both open and sealed, and snatched the cups from their protesting mouths.

"Now," I said, guarding my hoard, and despite myself starting to laugh at their attempts to grab at it from behind my back. They were now old enough to drink much more than I had previously allowed them and I am sure the wine was influencing their behaviour towards the playful. I had been drinking alongside them, and while my age afforded me a somewhat sturdier tolerance, I was still feeling the effects. "Now," I tried again, "there will be no more wine until you tell me what it is you are sniggering at behind your hands. It is like we have lost five years and you are both children again."

There followed a two pronged attack which would be indiscreet of me to describe in any detail. Suffice to say it resulted in Tutankhamun dancing away, holding a half-consumed eight year old Cypriot medium white over his head in triumph, and I, almost crippled with laughter, following him around furniture, demanding its return.

I apprehended him eventually, but not before he had taken some more hearty swigs and passed it to Ankhesenamun, who, smiling, refused to be caught up in the mischievousness and handed it back to me. Tutankhamun pretended to scold her for her treachery and gradually we came back to rest in our original seats, with many a shake of the head and a chuckle to punctuate our progress.

And then, quite suddenly, he grew grave and said: "Well, my old friend, our games cannot postpone this coming moment forever."

He told me his news. The sound of laughter stopped, and there was no more humour that evening.

When Aye was next summoned to the audience chamber he was three quarters of the way across the floor when Tutankhamun stood from his throne and took a step to the side, where he remained, leaning awkwardly against the shoulders of the throne as though unsure exactly what to do with himself. Aye faltered at the unusual move, but then continued and was about to commence the lengthy old man's procedure of prostrating himself when he noticed what had changed, and the world tilted so forcefully that he was almost cast to his knees and had to lean against the nearest pillar, speechless and gasping until the strength returned to his limbs.

Tutankhamun was beginning to have concerns for his health and began to step forwards to offer help when Aye at last spoke.

"Are you...?" was all he managed, but it was enough to stop Tutankhamun advancing any further.

"I mean...?" Aye continued. Tutankhamun was unsure how to respond until he had something direct to answer. To ask Aye what he thought seemed superfluous.

"Is this some sort of an appalling joke?" Aye said, after catching his breath. "Am I supposed to be laughing at this point? If that is the case, my boy, you have sadly misjudged my humour."

"It is no joke," Tutankhamun said.

"I know," Aye said, straightening up.

He was regarding the throne in the way that a condemned man might regard the stake towards which he was being carried. It had changed since he had last seen it. There was a relief on the chair's back which depicted Tutankhamun and Ankhesenamun in this very room. There was little colour in it other than gold, polished by the rub of Tutankhamun's back, apart from the occasional blue of turquoise decoration and the brown of the subjects' skin. Tutankhamun was pictured sitting on a throne, his feet resting upon a footstool, one arm over the back of the chair in relaxation. Before him was pictured Ankhesenamun, standing and holding a crucible in one hand while the other anointed his shoulder with oils. It was a scene of domestic devotion that Aye had seen so many times it had lost any meaning it might have had for him.

But now it was different. It had been doctored. The roof over the royal couple's heads was no longer solid. There was a break in the middle of it, and within the break, which effectively opened the room in the picture to the heavens, there was a golden disk. From the disk, which was obviously intended to represent the sun, there emanated perhaps a dozen rays, each of which ended in a hand, each in turn holding an ankh, the symbol of life, for the royal couple. It was unmistakably the Aten, and the royal couple were now basking in its glow.

"I have come to a decision," Tutankhamun said.

"That I can see," Aye said. "Did you at least consider asking my opinion first?"

"I have to confess that I did not," Tutankhamun said, "For I was fully aware of your opinion without having to take the trouble to do so."

"It would perhaps have been considerate to ask, all the same," Aye said.

"I am pharaoh," Tutankhamun said, shrugging, and did not have to elaborate further.

"Forgive me, Majesty, but I am an old man, and this has come as something of a shock," Aye said. "I wonder if I could perhaps impose on you for the use of a chair."

Tutankhamun smiled and opened his hand.

"Not that one," Aye said.

Tutankhamun summoned a servant who brought in a chair. It was placed before the dais and Aye sat in it and leant his elbows on his knees. He stared at the floor below his feet for some time before speaking.

"What does this mean?" he said, at last.

"Probably not as much as you fear," Tutankhamun said, and Aye snorted. Tutankhamun ignored him.

"Egypt was never so threatened by foreign aggressors under my father's reign," Tutankhamun said. "Even the Hittites were neither so adventurous nor so successful as they are now."

"No," Aye said. "Very true. No foreigner ever raised his sword against the men and women of Egypt. Only your father's men did that: his soldiers and police, who fell upon the innocent in the night in the name of the abomination you have carved into your throne."

"None of that was in the name of the Aten. It was only ever in the name of my father."

"The Aten does not exist!" Aye said. It was the first time he had raised his voice above a murmur during the conversation and he had surprised himself as well as Tutankhamun with his composure until now. "It was a figment of your father's fevered imagination!"

"Something was protecting the kingdom. Something that has since been removed. How else do you explain the precarious position in which we find ourselves?"

"We are recovering from a bad king," Aye said. "Your father led the entire kingdom into turmoil. Do you expect us to thrive immediately after such unmitigated catastrophe?"

"You blame much on my father, Aye," Tutankhamun said. "I think perhaps you are too ready to do so. I think perhaps your decisions and opinions are shaped still by your enmity towards him."

"And now you are a man and beyond the help of wisdom you believe him to be much maligned, I presume?"

"Let us say that I can appreciate his position. He was an honest man driven to desperate means. There should be no condemnation for that."

"No condemnation!" Aye shouted, and laughed, a solitary *ha!* that was far from humour. "No condemnation, you say? Have you any idea what he did? Have you any idea what this... this..." – he pushed himself to his feet and pointed at the throne with his walking stick – "this *thing* was responsible for? It threatened everything I had worked for! It took the dreams of your family, of your ancestors, and it trampled upon them! And what of the dynasty? What of the dynasty built from nothing by your great-grandmother and her children? It meant *nothing* to the man! It meant... it meant *this!*" He snapped his fingers with a flourish. "And you want to take us back to that? Are you *insane*? Your name could live forever. Think on that. Your name, and the names of your children and grandchildren. The names of Tutankhamun and Aye and Nefertiti and Tiye and Thuya – all these could be honoured throughout history! Do you not want that?"

Tutankhamun remained resolutely calm. "What dynasty?" he said, quietly.

Aye ignored him. "And what is the next step?" he said instead. "Will you be closing the temples of Amun? Will you be executing the priesthood? Exactly how far do you intend to follow your father's road?"

"What dynasty?" Tutankhamun said again.

Aye had never been comfortable discussing it with anyone other than Thuya and, with significant reservations, Tiye. He preferred to be able to manipulate the players in his drama without their knowledge, for those ignorant of motive are least likely to fight against it. Recently, though, perhaps prompted by Tutankhamun's rebellious behaviour, he had begun to recognise the necessity of bequeathing his knowledge and plans to those who came after him, for he knew that everything he had achieved could be lost if they were to die with him. Thuya had always intended the dynasty to last forever, not just until its architects were taken from this world, and so, however much the idea galled, Aye had no choice but to pass on its secrets.

Now, of course, was hardly the apposite time for the confession of confidences. Perhaps there was no such time, Aye thought. Or perhaps this was the best time there had ever been, for the news could always inspire the king into realising the dreams of his forefathers and giving up on this insanity.

"You never knew my parents," he said at last. "My mother's name was Thuya, and she was an incredible woman. She would have liked you, and I daresay that you would have liked her, although you would have been a little frightened of her. Everybody was a little frightened of Thuya, even Yuya, my father." Aye smiled at the memory of her. "My parents were not part of your grandfather Amenhotep's court, but they had the ambition to be. Yuya was a charioteer in the army, and my mother was a singer at the temple of Min. But my mother had eyes that could see over the horizon, and she craved for more than she had ever had. She set about achieving it, and she succeeded, although not without cost, and the fruits of her toil, and the toil of those who continued after her, are before you today. Without her, you would never have become king."

"And what about my father?" Tutankhamun asked. "Was his throne down to her as well?"

Aye nodded. "As was Nefertiti's," he said. Tutankhamun listened intently as Aye related the tale of his family. Or, at least, the tale as he was prepared to tell it.

"Then this would explain your eagerness to take the throne from my hand," Tutankhamun said. Aye gave him a sharp look.

"No," he said. "I will not accept that. I work only for the good of the kingdom."

"You work only for the good of your family," Tutankhamun said, "and if the kingdom also prospers that is a happy coincidence."

The conversation was slipping from Aye's grasp and he spoke quickly in an attempt to tighten his grip upon it. He knew he had to change the subject but his pride would not allow him to avoid answering the king's last rebuke.

"There is no separating the king and the kingdom," he said, "and so everything I did for the dynasty was done for the king, and so the Two Lands have only ever benefited from my intervention. But," he continued, eager to continue with a separate point before the king could answer, "we are straying from the matter at hand, which is this." He gestured dismissively towards the throne and the depiction it proudly wore.

"I fail to see why it causes you so much pain," Tutankhamun said. He sat down on the throne, and Aye was grateful for the picture being obscured.

"How so?" Aye said. "How is it possible you do not see the legacy that the Aten brings with him? The legacy of pain and betrayal and deceit. The religious police, the paranoia, the plague. Your father used to leave foreign emissaries out in the sun until they died because he believed them to be assassins. I am still yet to reattach the bonds of allegiance that your father's actions severed with our allies. How do you think they will feel when news reaches them that this madness has been resurrected?"

"It has not been resurrected," Tutankhamun said. "It is just no longer being dismissed."

"It is madness," Aye repeated, putting his head in his hands. He could think of no more pertinent a word, and no more constructive a gesture.

"My childhood, it seems to me, consisted only of two other things," Tutankhamun said. "One was listening to my father's decrees at his side in the throne room and the other was accompanying him to the altar of the Great Aten Temple, where he and I together would be worshipped as gods incarnate. My father desired to leave me with nothing more than the love of his god. He was my father. Am I to deny him still?"

"After everything I have taught you..." Aye began.

"You taught a child, Aye," Tutankhamun said. "You now address a man and the inevitable change has taken place. That is perhaps the defining difference between a child and a man. A child's mind can be nothing more than a pale reflection of the minds that raised it, whereas a man owes his thoughts to nobody but himself."

"You are undoing so many years' work."

"I am enhancing it."

"You are betraying Amun. He will withdraw his protection from Egypt."

"I am no longer betraying the Aten, and he alone seems to be the successful protector of these Two Lands."

"There is no dissuading you?" Aye asked.

"None," Tutankhamun said, as Aye had known he would.

"Then can you at least assure me that you will not be revisiting the more gratuitous excesses of your father's years?"

"There will be no banning of gods," Tutankhamun said. "I am proud of my kingdom's religious freedoms, and prouder still to protect them. There will be no paranoia, no killing of diplomats, no religious police. There will be no Mahu. There will be no founding of new cities. I will be merely resurrecting a neglected god, dusting him down, and asking for his protection."

Aye grunted. He was not convinced. "That is how your father started," he said.

"My father was always zealous," Tutankhamun said. "I am more restrained. You should know me by now."

Aye could too easily recognise that the argument was irretrievably lost and that further debate was not only useless but most probably counterproductive. He decided that the best he could do was wait and pray, and keep his counsel to himself. There was nobody with whom he could discuss these developments for there was nobody who was cognisant of all the relevant facts. And besides, there was nobody whose opinion he would trust as much as his own. It was only afterwards, in the seclusion of his palace apartments, that Aye's anger really began to take hold. He found himself pacing from one wall to the next, muttering to himself and biting at his nails as though it was they who had offended him.

It is blasphemy, he told himself. Worse. It is betrayal. It is unthinkable. It is... it is... he could think of no expression worthy of the ignominy heaped upon the kingdom by this rashest of acts. It is worthy only of Akhenaten, he thought at last, and could think of nothing more fitting. He could not read Tutankhamun the way he had been able to read Akhenaten, or even Nefertiti. There was an impenetrability about him that made him unpredictable, and, Aye thought, there is nothing more dangerous than capricious power.

Aye continued to pace and pray for the remainder of the night. There was nothing more productive that occurred to him.

The Maya Papyrus, Fragments 308-311

Of course, it was only much later that I discovered my father's true feelings about Tutankhamun's decision. And by that I do not refer to his displeasure or scorn, although these were obvious enough, and had the inclination taken me I could have consoled him with the observation that there was hardly a soul in court who did not agree with him. No, I mean his true feelings. The opinions he hid even from himself for a time. The feelings that grew from his scorn and displeasure like weeds from filth that he was not to confess until I looked down on him in rage as he lay in the bed where he would die. Had I known them at the time – and in the intervening years I have felt myself both cursed and blessed that I did not – events would perhaps have transpired differently.

As it was, there were plenty of other distractions with which I could not help but try to contend. News spread as only news of great import and significance can. I think that in the whole of Egypt, in everyone who heard the news with varying degrees of horror, perhaps only two people were not quick to condemn the king. One was his wife Ankhesenamun. The other was me.

It may appear hypocritical. It may appear fawning. I care as little now as I did then. The fact was that I knew Tutankhamun as well, if not better, than I had known his father, with whom I had grown from my earliest memories. I knew his character. I knew his moods and thoughts and feelings. I knew that he was as likely to resurrect Akhenaten's terror as he was to grow into his father's grotesque shape. Perhaps Ankhesenamun and I were the only ones to see this, but then perhaps nobody knew him better than did we.

Even Horemheb, with uncharacteristic candour in matters of court, confided his fears to me.

"It is not healthy," he hissed at me one evening. He had waited until we were alone in my villa, even having the temerity to dismiss my servants for me, which I thought rather rude, although I said nothing.

"Healthy?" I said.

"Least of all for us."

"Us?" I said.

"Of course us," he said. "It puts the entire court at risk."

"I hardly think I am in any danger from Tutankhamun," I said, immediately realising how pompous it must have sounded. Horemheb seemed not to notice.

"Make no mistake," he said. "There is nobody safe."

"You are exaggerating," I said.

"That is not the first time you have accused me of that," he said. "Do you remember the last time?"

I considered it for a moment. "No," I said, honestly.

Horemheb smiled for the first time that evening. "When you remember, let me know whether you were correct or not."

He stood to leave.

"What are you going to do?" I said.

"I am going to return to my home and go to sleep," he said.

"I mean in general."

"Do, my good Maya?" he said. "Why do you assume that I will do anything? Do you think I would act against my king, even in my country's interest? Do you think I would admit as much to you even if I did?"

I returned his smile, for I genuinely did not think him capable of such actions. He took his leave and I went in search of my servants.

I remembered his words, though, and the next morning, even as the sun rose, unseen behind the city's roofs, I was making my way towards the palace. I found the king in his audience chamber and waited without until his audience ended and ambassadors I did not recognise, although their language seemed to have the cadence of Hurrian about it, emerged. I was announced, and found His Majesty in an vociferously ebullient mood.

"Ah, Maya!" he exclaimed, and came down from his dais, his arms held wide to enfold me in his embrace. I was more than a little taken aback and I am afraid we must have made a comical picture, the king enthusiastically embracing his subject who merely leaned against him, his arms at his side, sporting an expression of wonder and confusion.

"Maya," Tutankhamun said. "It is good to see you again."

"Your Majesty," I replied, hardly less bemused after his outburst. "You saw me yesterday."

"Yes, but it is still good to see you again. You can never see too much of friends, I always say."

"Do you?" I said, smiling. "When?"

"Well," he said. "Sometimes. When you are not there. Come. Sit with me."

"Your Majesty," I said, choosing to sit on the floor at the edge of the dais. Tutankhamun resumed his place on his throne. I paused before speaking further, for it was a difficult subject to broach. "I am concerned about your decision to move back towards Atenism."

Tutankhamun sighed melodramatically. "I see," he said. "You as well."

"I have been in discussion with... someone, and I am concerned that your actions are causing undue fear around court."

"There is no need to protect your confidante," Tutankhamun said, smiling ironically. "I know exactly who it is."

I was surprised. "I am sure that you understand that this person only has your welfare in his heart and speaks only through love, but that his words are such that they may be open to misinterpretation and for me to reveal his identity would perhaps unfairly taint your outlook towards him."

"Very well put, Maya," Tutankhamun said. "I applaud your loyalty, but you and I both know we are referring to your father, and furthermore we both know that his comments are not motivated entirely by love."

This put me in something of a quandary. There were a limited number of people with whom I could have discussed the matter and to discount any of them would only serve to increase the suspicion on the others. I decided that discretion was the best policy.

"I can neither confirm nor deny..." I began, but Tutankhamun waved me quiet.

"It is of no matter. I do not have the time for guessing games. Speak to me of that which you feel you must speak, but I would appreciate you doing so quickly, for I also have some news to impart and the effort of not telling you so far has almost killed me. I am bursting with the excitement of it."

"Really?" I said, forgetting for the moment why I had come to the audience chamber. "But what...?"

Tutankhamun held up an admonishing finger, but not without humour.

"Speak to me first," he said.

I ensured that I was brief. I told him of Horemheb's concerns, concerns I am sure the whole of Thebes felt in their hearts. Tutankhamun listened, although I could see the impatience in his eyes.

"They fear me becoming my father," he said after I had finished. It was a statement rather than a question but I nodded anyway.

"I can understand their concern," he continued, "but there really is no need for it."

"Your Majesty, you do not have to tell…"

He held up his hand once again and I dutifully fell into silence.

"No," he said. "You do not understand. There is no need for their concern, and I can prove it."

"Prove it, Majesty?"

"I can do more even than that. I can prove that I will not turn into my father. I can prove that my rediscovered faith in the Aten is well-founded. I can prove that the wellbeing of the kingdom can only be enhanced should the rest of the population follow my example."

"I would keep statements such as that last one between ourselves," I said, daring to interrupt only because I could foresee the tumult should Tutankhamun begin publicly claiming that the kingdom could be protected by the general populace bowing their heads once again to the Aten. From there it would be a short step indeed back to the horror of monotheism.

"I can prove it," Tutankhamun said, again. "My Ankhesenamun is pregnant again."

I was reduced momentarily to nonsensical monosyllabic mutterings before I recovered from the shock of the news, whereupon, my eloquence restored to its usual glory, I said: "What?"

"This is what I have been waiting so patiently to tell you," he said. Now that the news was out he was unable to restrain the indignity of exhilaration and he jumped from his seat and ran into the centre of the room before spinning around to face me once more, laughing all the while.

"Pregnant!" he shouted.

"Please, Majesty," I said. "Try to contain yourself. What if someone should see?"

"You sound like your father," he said. "And what if someone did see? I hardly care for anything at the moment. Nothing matters, only that my wife is to bear my child."

As if to illustrate his point he broke into an impromptu dance, laughing all the more at my worried glances towards the door. He rushed to me and, kneeling before me where I sat and holding my two hands within his, he spoke again with great excitement, seeming always on the verge of leaping to his feet and continuing his dance.

"But do you not see what this means?" he asked me. My blank look gave him my answer. "When has this happened? Only after I have made certain prayers and certain offerings to a certain god."

Tutankhamun must have seen some light of recognition ignite behind my eyes.

"There!" he said. "You understand!"

"Do you mean to say that Ankhesenamun has fallen pregnant because it has been so willed by the Aten?"

Tutankhamun spread his arms and raised his eyebrows, as if to ask whether there could be any other explanation more obvious.

"It is not impossible, I grant you," I said. Taking into account everything I had been telling him about the Aten's reception in the rest of the city, I was somewhat reluctant to fuel Tutankhamun's enthusiasm any more than it already was.

"Are you seriously telling me you think it is merely coincidental? That I begin praying to the Aten, and then, after all this time, Ankhesenamun becomes pregnant again?"

"I remember that she has been pregnant once already without the Aten's help," I said.

"And do you also remember what became of that pregnancy?"

"Yes," I said, quietly.

"Well, then," Tutankhamun said. "Do you still think me a fool for my belief that this time Ankhesenamun will be protected? And if you do, do you blame me for my foolishness?"

"No," I said. "Neither."

"Well, then," Tutankhamun said again, but said no more.

Aye found himself unable to join with the rest of court in their celebrations over the news of Ankhesenamun's pregnancy. His mood had not lifted since his discovery of Tutankhamun's return to Atenism, and no matter what he tried to tell himself – that this was always going to be a pale diluted form of Akhenaten's religion, that Tutankhamun's mind was as unreliable as his character was proving to be and this would be nothing more than a passing fad – he could never quite bring himself to believe his own reassurances and he found himself slipping into a despair so profound that it was almost an indulgence. He found himself purposefully waiting for people to ask after his health, which was surprisingly easy to engineer given a long enough conversational gap, merely so that he could snarl at them and profess his despair at the royal family in particular and the world in general. Those to whom he addressed himself found themselves shocked not only at his honesty and audacity, but also in the power of a man who could say such things with no fear for the consequences.

In truth, Aye cared little for the consequences and so did not take the trouble to analyse what would be the most likely outcome of his harsh comments. He had never thought himself prone to pessimism, only cautious in the face of obstacles. Perhaps a little overcautious from time to time, but that he considered to be the cost and nature of success. Now, though, there was a different timbre to his temper. There was a sense of defeat he had never before encountered, for even at the darkest junctures of his life and career he had always been able to glimpse hope like a single star in the night sky. Now Tutankhamun seemed to have plucked that star from its heavenly source and the future offered nothing but misery and danger and failure.

And so, when the news of Ankhesenamun's pregnancy reached him, Aye's first thought was *Well, here comes another little Atenist*. He took some strange pleasure in allowing himself to be drawn into conversations about the news so that he could profess his indifference. He knew that his words would reach the king's ears before long. He found himself almost hoping to be tried for treason and sentenced to death merely so that he could profess his indifference to that as well.

The first months of Ankhesenamun's pregnancy had been something to endure rather than enjoy. The baby had made her ill on a daily basis but the doctors had assured her that such a thing was not uncommon, especially with babies who grew up to be men or women of power and influence.

"He is merely stamping his authority on the situation," they told her. "He wants you to rest and he is ensuring that you do so by making you feel dreadful."

She had done as the doctors and her husband and her baby had told her and she had rested from that day forward. The memory of her first pregnancy informed her every moment. Every day that she awoke peacefully in the morning light when she so expected to awake in the dark and in pain was blessing enough to bring tears to her eyes. She sometimes dreamt that she was losing the baby and would awake in the dark, clutching her belly, and would have to wait to discover whether or not she was dreaming of pain because the pain was real.

But she knew that every day that passed without incident was a day's more strength for the child she carried and was a day less in which disaster could strike. As her nervousness at the beginning of the pregnancy began to abate its place was taken by her nervousness at the thought of what would happen at its end. She expected to remember for the rest of her life the agony she had felt when her body had expelled her first baby, and she wondered whether the pain of a healthy childbirth would be in any way comparable. Tutankhamun tried to reassure her by telling her that it would be painful but that it was a pain that countless women before her had endured. That she would feel as much pain as someone else she found to be scant consolation but she would smile and pat his hand and thank him for his concern and then try to think of something else. She turned for comfort instead to the gods. She prayed to the Aten with as much faith as she did to Amun and Ptah and every other god who occurred to her during that anxious time. She had found it easy as had Tutankhamun to slip back into her childhood faith. As with Tutankhamun, Atenism had been her companion during the formative years of her childhood, and belief was more natural to her than scepticism. When her husband had announced the Aten's rehabilitation it had been like slipping back into comfortable old clothes that she had not worn for a long time. It felt like a secret shared only by her and Tutankhamun, a club to which only they could belong. It brought them closer, and the bonds of her relationship with Tutankhamun had only grown tighter and stronger since she had lost their first baby.

Ankhesenamun had been scared at first that Tutankhamun would blame her for the loss, and later that he blamed her but was hiding it. It took her some time to recognise her paranoia for what it was, because even she had to admit that a man could not feign the affection that Tutankhamun showered upon her. She went through a period of blaming herself and feeling unworthy of a man who could love her after she had failed him in such a way. But after it all, after the wounds were nothing but scars, Tutankhamun and Ankhesenamun were inseparable.

When Ankhesenamun first felt the pains that signalled that the child was ready to come into the world she felt a brief flutter of panic play around the edges of her mind, for although she had been briefed many times on what exactly to expect, and although her instincts told her differently, it acted as the most vivid of reminders of bereavement and mourning. She called out to her doctors, who ran to her side as though making their way to the death bed of a rich old relative. It was not proper for Tutankhamun to be present at the birth and so he was left to pace nervously the length of the corridor outside the room of confinement, counting his steps in a futile attempt to take his mind from what was happening within and succeeding only in losing count of the minutes and the hours. He had been in this position before, he remembered, and then he had only awaited bad news. This was somehow worse, for although the risk was smaller, the stakes were much higher, and because he was not expecting disaster he was not sure he would be able to cope should it arrive.

When it did, he felt a sudden rush of cold, and his legs buckled beneath him.

Chapter Twenty-Four

The Chapel

AYE HAD not waited with the king while the king waited for news of his wife and child, for Aye was unable to bring himself to care for the welfare of anybody involved. The king and his wife were nothing more than ingrates and turncoats and the baby would be raised in the ways of Tutankhamun's religion and would undoubtedly prove to be nothing but a curse upon the kingdom. He did not wish the child or the mother harm, but then neither did he wish them well. He prayed for neither a girl nor a boy, for neither would bring rest to his troubled spirit. He found himself profoundly unable to care about any subject that occurred to him. He had taken to spending long hours and days in the sanctity of his villa in Thebes, his servants dismissed, hardly moving from his seat except at nature's command. Sometimes he would not emerge from his bedchamber from daybreak to sunset, whereupon he would retire to bed never having taken the trouble to get dressed.

He was in his bedchamber, and had been there since the night before last, when a messenger arrived from the palace with news of the birth. The messenger was warned by servants that Aye was not to be disturbed but was not to be dissuaded from his mission, however much he hesitated with his knuckles raised to rap on the bedchamber door. One or two servants watched from around a corner in the corridor outside the room, half afraid and half curious. The messenger took a deep breath and knocked. There came no reply. The messenger waited for a moment and knocked again. Again there came no reply. The messenger turned to the faces that poked nervously around the corridor's corner.

"Is he definitely there?" he asked them, but before they could reply their heads disappeared from view and the messenger heard the door swing open behind him. He whirled around to find Aye's face a hand's breadth away from his own.

"What?" Aye hissed. He breath stank of stale wine, but the messenger had the forethought not to grimace as it washed over him.

"My Lord," he said. "I bring tidings from the palace."

"Oh?" Aye said. "Invent a reply from me and take it back. Tidings from the palace are no concern of mine."

The messenger was nonplussed and had no idea how to react. After a moment he decided the safest course of action was to continue with his script as though nothing out of the ordinary had happened.

"My Lord, His Majesty Tutankhamun bids me bring you news of his wife and child."

Aye sighed and decided it would be quicker to get rid of the messenger if he co-operated than if he was obstructive. "Very well," he said.

If the doctor had emerged from the parturition room with any more reluctance he would not have been moving at all. By this time Tutankhamun had been forced by weariness to abandon his policy of pacing the length of the corridor and back and, having ignored the entreaties of servants and courtiers for him to retire to somewhere more comfortable and more fitting, had taken to sitting on a chair which someone had scurried away to bring for him. When he saw the doctor he stood and rushed towards him, coming to a sudden stop only after covering half the distance. He had seen the doctor's expression. The two men regarded each other across the floor of the corridor, both afraid.

"I am sorry," the doctor said. "We did everything we could."

"What?" Tutankhamun shouted. "What has happened?"

"Your Majesty, the baby was stillborn."

Tutankhamun needed to put his hand out to the wall to steady himself. His gaze lost its focus.

"And the Great Royal Wife?" he said.

"There has been no physical ill effects of the labour," the doctor said. "Her Royal Highness is perfectly healthy."

Tutankhamun pushed past him without another word. He was still at that age where it was important to him that other men did not see him cry.

Tutankhamun and Ankhesenamun were inconsolable. Their baby, another girl, was mummified and laid next to her sister, ready for when they would both be able to join Tutankhamun in his tomb.

Later, looking back, Aye saw that this was the moment when everything changed. He took no pleasure in the baby's death, even later, when it became apparent that it was the one event that pushed the royal couple into the downward spiral that would lead, circuitously and tortuously but inevitably all the same, to both of their deaths. He was not a petty man. He did not revel in the calamities of those who opposed him but all the same he could never profess to being surprised that this particular calamity had come to pass. He did not regard it as healthy to entrust a nonexistent god with the safety and well-being of something so fragile as the life of an unborn baby. And so when the messenger delivered his news he was not surprised, but then he would have had some difficulty to explain exactly how he felt, had the messenger had the temerity to ask him. He certainly was not saddened, because a great evil may have been averted, but then neither was he gladdened, because at the time he had no inkling of where this would lead, and as far as he could see this was a small victory that would ultimately change nothing.

"Send them my condolences," he told the messenger, before turning to return to his wine. "Only, make it more convincing."

The door closed.

The Maya Papyrus, Fragments 323-331

> *The baby's death could have had any number of effects on Tutankhamun. He could have become morose and depressed. He could have blamed himself. He could have built a sepulchre with which she could be forever remembered. The problem was, I think, that he fell upon the worse combination of all the possibilities. He became angry, yes. Angrier than I had ever seen him. But that anger was not directed at himself, or even at Ankhesenamun, but at the gods that he felt had betrayed him. And perhaps even then, if his reaction had stayed on that keel, the situation could have been salvageable but Tutankhamun became reckless in his rage, and it seemed at times as though he had become possessed by the shade of his father.*
>
> *He seemed to waste no time with mourning.*
>
> *"I have mourned enough for the whole world," he once informed me. "I am not going to begin again, for I fear I would never stop."*
>
> *Of course, the eyes are terrible liars, and his eyes revealed the truth. I never again saw them hold the life they had held before all this came to pass.*
>
> *Before Ankhesenamun's confinement Tutankhamun had ordered a chapel built for the Aten within the walls of the palace. It was a simple affair by the standards of those built by his father, but it had been deemed adequate while plans were drawn up for the construction of a replacement in central Thebes. For the*

moment Tutankhamun had to be content with the simplicity of the chapel, although simplicity is, of course, a relative term.

We were there now. Tutankhamun had spent much time kneeling before the Aten's altar, under the glow of the golden sun disk mounted upon the wall. I had taken to accompanying him on his sojourns in the chapel ever since news reached me of his behaviour there. Time did not seem to be mellowing his reaction to the death of his second baby and he was as unpredictable in the chapel as he was anywhere. The attendants and priests could not judge his mood from one moment to the next. One or two of them were afraid to be in there alone with him. Mid-prayer he might change from placid to raging and have changed back before the prayer's end. I decided that I was as safe as anyone in Tutankhamun's company and began to accompany him with a view to protecting him from himself. At first my attendance seemed to have a somewhat calming effect, but this was transitory. Before long I began to see exactly what it was that was making the priests so nervous. I saw him in turns weeping and screaming and raging and even, at one point, sleeping, curled up on the floor like a cat. On more than one occasion I felt the need to physically restrain him. I was glad I was there. The priests would never have had the courage to do as I did, even to save the king from harm, and it was only my restraint that stopped him, on at least one occasion, dashing himself against the wall. It was only my hand that stopped his mouth from shouting obscenities and insults at the image of the Aten on the wall before him.

"You cannot hold the gods responsible," I told him. "They cannot lend their hand to every baby born."

He snarled at me when I said this. He actually snarled. "They can lend their hand to mine," he said. "I am pharaoh, and my babies are kings. These gods of ours, of yours, they bathe in my worship and they gorge themselves on my offerings, and then sit back and laugh at my misfortune."

"I am sure..." I began in a placatory tone.

"You are sure of nothing, Maya," he said. "You do not know the minds of the gods. I do. I am pharaoh."

I had never seen him this way before. He had never spoken to me with such vitriol. Even the character of his voice seemed to have changed, as though a tenderness had been excised. It seemed as though his fury not only ran through him like bones, but that it was the stuff from which he was made. Throughout our conversation he had been kneeling before the sun disk on the chapel's wall. Now he stood, although he did not turn to face me. Instead he remained motionless for a time, regarding the depiction of the Aten before him. He approached it, and somehow I knew what he was about to do and I stepped forwards to intercede. Even as I did so I saw him raise his arms and bring them crashing down towards the icon of the Aten on the wall before him.

I was too late, although by that I do not mean that I was unable to prevent him striking out at the god. I was only a step behind him and hardly had to move in order to grab his forearms before his fists were able to do any damage. He was a strong young man and his strength, combined with his rage and his impetus, was enough to almost lift me from my feet. At any rate, it was enough to overbalance me, and I completed my noble act of self-sacrifice by tottering forwards like an aged invalid and falling in a heap at the king's feet.

But I reiterate that I was too late. I have never been an overly suspicious man but there are certain things that are enough to chill me, even in the safety of intervening years. The memory of my friend the king raising his hands in anger against a god – even a god in which I held neither faith nor belief – is one. No good can come from such a thing. I have since become convinced that his actions were viewed and judged by those who were in a position to do such things, and pronouncements were made against him in the underworld.

As it was, I had more immediate worries. Tutankhamun was staring down at me with an expression that was some distance from the fond looks to which I had become accustomed.

"You dare lay your hands on me?" he said, although this was not the first time I had done so.

"Your Majesty," I began. "Think on what you were about to do. You were about to attack your god."

"Does that excuse your actions?" he said.

"Yes," I said, firmly. I clambered to my feet. "Your Majesty, do you remember the evening you informed me of your desire to resurrect the Aten?"

It was not a question he had expected, and just for a moment I saw an unguarded expression.

"Yes," he said.

"And do you remember the laughter?" I said, forcing myself to smile. "Do you remember how you stole the wine from me and refused to return it?"

"Yes," he said, quietly.

"Remember that I am your friend," I said. "Your loss is one which has injured you and you are fighting those who love you most. That is understandable and I cannot find it in my heart to berate you for it. All I ask is that, when the pain has eased, you remember your friends."

I turned to leave, for if the truth be known I thought my words to be the most eloquent and persuasive I would manage under the circumstances and I wished to be alone before I added something disastrous to them in the thought that I was improving my argument.

"Where is your father?" Tutankhamun asked me. His face, which had softened at my words, had found a new target for anger and desired the excuse to express it.

I had no idea, and had not done so for some time. I told him as much.

"Not good enough," he said, but there was no longer any enthusiasm behind his harsh words and they had lost their vehemence. It was as though he spoke thus against his own wish. "I expect answers to my questions. He has been conspicuously absent for a while. It is not behaviour I expect from a vizier. Find him. Tell him I demand his attendance and if he is not willing to obey me I shall demand a great deal more."

I bowed and backed towards the door, bowing all the while, reasoning that now was as good a time as any to begin treating His Majesty in a more formal and respectful manner. My head remained bowed as I crossed the threshold, but before the doors could close between us Tutankhamun spoke.

"Maya," he said. I looked up, and saw that for one brief moment the anger and torment had left his eyes. He looked for all the world like the little boy who had been led out into a courtyard to see his mother's execution.

"I am sorry," he said. I nodded and turned away.

Aye did not answer the king's summons. He saw little point in doing so and part of him did not want the king to see him in his current condition. He was, he had to admit, beginning to look slightly dishevelled. His appearance was suffering without the attendance of his servants, none of whom he had encountered in a number of days. His kilts were no longer washed and were beginning to smell. There were three in the bedchamber and he dressed himself in whichever one lay closest to him on the floor when he forced himself from his bed. At night he would slip it over his legs and leave it wherever it fell. He was accustomed to being shaved by his servants, and without them a dark stubble had grown around his jaw and over the top of his head. His growing hair soon began to itch his scalp when he wore his wigs over it and so he soon dispensed with them and left them to keep his kilts company on the tiles. He knew that neglecting to shave his head was inviting infestation by lice, but he cared as little for this as he did for anything else.

He would venture forth from his bed chamber only when absolutely necessary, and even then only at the unlikeliest of times. He had become used to navigating the corridors of the house without the benefit of light and had even ventured, under the oppression of necessity, into the areas of the house usually reserved for his servants in search of food and water. He only went there when secure in the knowledge that he would meet nobody at any point in his journey. His servants knew him to be alive only through the occasional inadvertent sound that seeped through the bedchamber door and the absence of any truly offensive stench.

Had he but realised it, Aye would have to have acknowledged the mirror that his life was holding up against that of Tutankhamun's. The paths of their grief, although starting at very different points, were wending their way over similar terrain and were presenting their respective travellers with vistas that, if not identical, could at least be recognised as being from the same country. Both had felt their initial grief be transformed into anger, and both turned their anger against that which was more powerful than either would care to admit. Tutankhamun knew that there was no way of avenging oneself on a god, just as Aye knew that he could not defeat an entrenched and determined king. This wisdom profited neither of them, for both continued to fight, in their own way.

But this was where their journeys began to diverge. The essential difference lay not within but around them. Aye surrounded himself with nothing but his bitterness and the accoutrements of loneliness. Tutankhamun had Ankhesenamun. She had mourned with as much intensity as had her husband, but she had neither the wherewithal nor the inclination to attack the gods for her loss and her grief did not transmute into anger. She was able, instead, to soothe and calm him where no other had met with the slightest success. Her hands were the agents of her accomplishment as much as her voice, for she would soothe and kneed the tense muscles of his shoulders and neck as she whispered reassurances she did not believe into his ear, feeling him slowly relax under her fingertips.

Gradually, over the days and weeks following the birth, Ankhesenamun was able, through diligent work, to guide Tutankhamun's sorrow into a place where it obscured his anger and, finally, smothered it.

"Perhaps," she said to him one evening as they watched the sun set over the far bank of the river from a vantage point in the palace gardens, "perhaps it is because we are neither one thing nor another."

She was sitting behind him, her fingers teasing the intractable muscles of his neck, and he half turned to look at her. She applied the gentle pressure of one finger to his cheek and he turned without complaint back to the falling sun.

"I do not understand," he said.

"Did father ever speak to you of the development of his religion?"

"Rarely," Tutankhamun said. "I was too young. I remember him mainly speaking of the threats that he believed faced him."

"Was there anything mentioned about Amun?"

"Once or twice," Tutankhamun said. "Father seemed to simultaneously believe Amun to be his nemesis, and yet nonexistent. I never really understood it, to tell you the truth."

"Something must have happened."

"Ankhesenamun, are you being deliberately mysterious?"

"Sorry, husband," Ankhesenamun said. "I am thinking at the same time as talking. Something must have happened for father to choose to turn his back on Amun so wilfully. The Aten must have shown him his power, or father would never have forsaken Amun so readily and so completely."

"It does not matter how powerful are the gods," Tutankhamun said. "Amun and Ra are both gods of immense power, but the followers of one do not denounce the other."

"Perhaps they would," Ankhesenamun said, "if it was demanded of them."

"But by whom?"

"By the gods," Ankhesenamun said. "For who else could make such a demand?"

This time Tutankhamun did turn around to regard her. She made no attempt to prevent him, for something in his demeanour told her that it would be pointless. He met her eyes with his, and held them.

"What are you telling me to do?" he asked. He watched for a moment as her gaze flicked from his left eye to his right, his right to his left.

"I would not presume to tell you anything," she said, honestly. "I am just like you in many ways, Tutankhamun. I am just looking for reasons."

The Maya Papyrus, Fragments 338-344

Perhaps it was just that I knew him so well, but the change in Tutankhamun seemed obvious and immediate to me.

It would be inaccurate and naïve to claim that he was much happier after his talk with Ankhesenamun, but all the same it seemed as though the veil of depression that had threatened to smother him was at least lightened by his transformation and he was once again able to walk without dragging his feet like a cripple, able to meet the eyes of those who bowed before him in the corridors. The priests quickly learned once again that he was not a man to be feared, only held in awe. His violent temper seemed to have dissipated into the night and he became merely the melancholic reflection of the man he had once been.

He called me into his presence not long afterwards.

"I wish to apologise for my behaviour," he told me. I thought the very idea to be preposterous and I told him so, although in a slightly more ingratiating way.

"Your Majesty," I said. "There really is no need. A king should not apologise to his subjects."

"So your father has often told me," he said.

"Perhaps he is correct," I said.

Tutankhamun shrugged. "On occasion," he said.

"Your Majesty," I began.

"Tutankhamun," Tutankhamun said.

"Tutankhamun," I said. "I have been afraid."

"For me or of me?" he asked.

"Both," I said, with a restrained smile.

"Well you need be afraid no longer," he told me. "The Tutankhamun you saw was an aberration, nothing more. I have seen the error of the ways in which I was led. Grief held me by the hand, and she is not a travelling companion I would recommend."

"And now?" I said.

"And now I lead grief by the hand," he said. "It is a subtle difference, but a welcome one. I have given the matter much thought and it was irresponsible of me to offer the Aten so much disrespect. You were right to restrain me and I know how much you risked in doing so. I owe you not only my apologies but my thanks."

"They are more than I deserve," I said, bowing.

"And I owe the same to more than you," he said, as though to refute my modesty. "Your father, for one."

"My father?" I said, genuinely surprised.

"The same. I feel as though I have mistreated him. I have not seen him at court since all this business began, and I cannot help but think that it was I who drove him away."

"Your Majesty," I said, "you have not seen my father at court since long before all this. I fear your behaviour may have driven him away, but it was not your behaviour since the tragedy. He has seen precious little of that."

"Nevertheless," Tutankhamun said. "My mind is made up. I feel as though I have committed injustices. It will harm nobody for me to make some amends to those closest to me."

"As you wish, Majesty," I said, "but I cannot help thinking you are watering the desert. However much you offer I doubt it will be enough."

"And perhaps I am not the only one to be portioning the injustices," he said, rising from his throne and clapping me on the back. I walked with him to the doors leading to his private chambers. "I hope you have not been so eager to judge your king." There was no malice in his voice. He was teasing me. Just for a moment it felt as though he was a prince again, and his troubles unborn.

"It is good to see you again, Tutankhamun," I said. "I have missed you."

Aye ignored the first two messengers who brought the king's summons. When the third hammered on the bedchamber door Aye flung it open and threw pots at the man until he was forced to retreat over their shards. The fourth arrived with reinforcements and orders from the king that a refusal from Aye was not an acceptable response. The men accompanying the messenger were visibly armed. It was nothing more than a method of persuasion, Tutankhamun had told himself.

When Aye answered the bedchamber door, he did so with the air of a man so resigned to the world that he felt it easier to allow it to take its shots at him unimpeded rather than try to avoid them.

"Yes," he said, without inflection or further comment to the tableau that presented itself to him.

"My lord," the messenger said. "You are commanded by the king to attend him with all due speed. He has instructed me to inform you that you are to restrain from acts of violence against my person and to this end he has provided me with the protection of an armed detachment." He gestured exaggeratedly over his shoulder. The king in reality had said nothing of the kind, but the messenger thought that it would do no harm to elaborate slightly on the script he had been given.

Aye looked over the messenger's shoulder with no visible display of interest at the men waiting there.

He sighed heavily. "Very well," he said. "I shall answer my king's call. What else could I possibly do? Tell him I shall attend him at the earliest available opportunity."

He turned to close the door, and then stopped. "Tell him I shall see him tomorrow," he said, and closed the door.

The messenger was somewhat nonplussed. This was not what he had been expecting, which had been either a flat refusal or the opportunity to gain the king's thanks by returning with Aye in tow. He exchanged a glance with the men behind him, but they offered no help.

"Er," he said. He thought about knocking on the door again, but it was not a thought that he entertained for long. He decided that this news could be dressed in such a way to resemble a success. He turned and led the soldiers back to the palace.

The following day Tutankhamun would not allow himself to await Aye. A king waits for no man, he told himself, although he was almost hoping that Aye would not arrive. The thought of seeing him again and becoming reacquainted with the man's vitriol was not one that sat easy in his stomach.

When the servants arrived to advise Tutankhamun that his midday meal awaited him, Aye still had not arrived. The king had been toying with the idea of sending men to Aye's villa with instructions to physically bring him back to the palace but had easily discarded it. Tomorrow, Tutankhamun decided. He would take no further action until tomorrow.

Despite the decision that he would allow Aye until the following day to keep his promise, by mid-afternoon Tutankhamun had come to the reluctant conclusion that Aye was not going to arrive. He was disappointed and angry and slightly relieved and scared at the thought of what he would have to do to ensure Aye's attendance. It was becoming a matter of pride. To have a courtier, even one of Aye's standing, so flagrantly disregarding the express wishes of the king was more than an insult. It was humiliating, and Tutankhamun could not allow it to continue.

But for now he had to resign himself to the fact that he no longer had any realistic reason to delay his trip to the Aten chapel. If anything, it was a meeting that frightened him even more than the audience with Aye. He decided to make the journey alone for he wished nobody to see the abjection that he would have to perform once inside. He felt humiliated enough for one day. He traipsed along the corridors to the chapel, leaving behind him instructions that he was not to be disturbed.

Once in the chapel itself he remained standing in the doorway for some time, silent and unmoving, watching the Aten's disk as though afraid that it would suddenly fly from the wall, propelled only by the god's wrath. Eventually, he closed the door and stepped across the floor before lowering himself to his knees and prostrating himself before the golden disk. When he began to pray, he did so quietly at first, almost inaudible even to himself. He was still unsure exactly how to express his shame at the way he had behaved towards the Aten, but decided on balance that honesty was perhaps the only sensible method of dealing with a god.

"My father, the Aten," he said, from a prostrate position that he intended to hold for the entire interview. He remembered too late that he should have brought cushions for his knees, but was not prepared to leave now in order to get them. Anyway, the discomfort was fitting. It could be part of his penance. He cleared his throat and began again.

"My father, the Aten," he said. "I am here to beg your forgiveness with no restraint, as a captive of war begs the victor for mercy, as a slave begs his master, as a peasant begs his king. For I am a king of men, but you are a king of kings and I may do nothing but await the execution of your justice, should you so deem it necessary."

For a moment, Tutankhamun found that he was bracing himself as though awaiting a blow. His forehead remained resting on the cold stone of the floor.

"Oh, very worthy," a voice said, and Tutankhamun was so tense that he cried out at the shock of the break in the otherwise perfect stillness of the room. He pushed himself to his feet with as much speed that dignity would allow. In the doorway, leaning on his walking stick with the air of a man who did not really need the support, was Aye. He was not smiling. He turned and closed the door, allowing the king a moment to gather himself.

"Aye," Tutankhamun said. "What are you doing here?"

"What am I *doing* here?" Aye said. "I was somewhat under the impression that you wanted to see me. I took the endless string of increasingly agitated messengers as a clue. I am sorry if I misinterpreted it."

"You know very well what I mean."

Aye shrugged. "Your audience chamber was empty. Your father could always be found at the end of the day in one of two places. If he was not in his audience chamber blabbering on about something or other, he was in his temple pouring his heart out to his god. I took a chance, and look, here you are. What a remarkable coincidence."

Tutankhamun was taken aback.

"You will show me some respect," he said, a tremor in his voice. "And you will show my father some respect."

"Will I?" Aye said. "We shall see."

"Aye," Tutankhamun said. He was struggling to keep himself from shouting. The sheer effrontery of the man had incensed him. "I summoned you to the palace with the intention of apologising to you. I can see now what a mistake that was. I should have left you to rot in your house."

"Yes," Aye said. "Yes, you should. But you could not. Every day you become more like your father. He could never resist the temptation to interfere where he was not wanted, and neither can you." He lifted his walking stick and used it to point towards the sun disk on the far wall. "You have perverted everything I have fought for with this, and you could not resist the temptation to bring me here to taunt me with it."

"You have always been the enemy of the Aten," Tutankhamun said. "It is now as it always was. You are blinded to him by your hatred of my father."

"Blinded to him?" Aye said, and it was the first time he had reacted with anger to Tutankhamun's words. "Blinded to whom? Your father concocted him! How can I be blind to that which does not exist?"

"My father was guided to him, just as the kings of old were guided to their gods."

Aye laughed, and he did so with such genuine, patronising amusement that it was all that Tutankhamun could do to refrain from throwing himself at him. It was a laugh only calculated to infuriate.

"You are a naïve child," Aye said.

"And you are an old fool!"

"Better an old fool than a heretic. An old fool will be rejuvenated on the day of his death. What will become of you, Tutankhamun? Do you think Osiris will allow you passage into the underworld? Do you think your deeds will be looked upon kindly by the gods?"

"I have injured no gods," Tutankhamun said.

"You have injured no gods?" Aye repeated, all pretence of calm now abandoned, his voice raised and cracking with emotion. "Look at you! Look at where you are! Look at this!"

He reached forwards and grabbed at the golden disk on the wall. Tutankhamun jumped forwards and grabbed Aye's hands and for a moment there was equilibrium between them, Aye not strong enough to pull the disk from the wall but Tutankhamun not strong enough to force him to release his grip. And then, suddenly enough for it to take them both by surprise, the disk came free. The shock was enough to loosen Aye's grip and the disk hit the floor with a thud and both Aye and Tutankhamun fell backwards.

Tutankhamun was the first to react. He scrambled to his feet and rushed over to where the disk had fallen and began frantically wiping the dust from its surface. He did not turn to look at Aye when he spoke.

"Idiot!" he hissed. "What do you think you are doing?" He began meticulously searching the disk for damage, running his fingers lightly over the surface and moving his head from side to side in order to find the most helpful light. Behind him he could hear Aye making the groans of an old man as he laboriously clambered up from where he had fallen, leaning heavily on the stick he had retrieved from the corner of the room.

"It is *nothing*," Aye said. "It is a piece of gold, nothing more. It would better serve its country if it were melted down and used for currency. Look at you, grovelling before it. You look like a washerwoman on her knees at the river. You look like a servant."

The argument had by now deteriorated in each man's mind to such a degree that point making was now a secondary consideration behind finding comments that would cause the maximum possible insult. Both men wanted to do nothing but outrage the other.

"I am his servant!" Tutankhamun said. "Just as you are, and I will see you bow your head to him before I am finished with you."

"I am the servant of the gods who have ruled these Two Lands since the creation, and no other. I would die before I bowed my head to that abomination."

Tutankhamun had once again assumed the posture of a penitent before the disk as it lay on the floor. His fingers had found dents along its underside, and, being somewhat at a loss as to what to do about it, he assumed that begging the god's forgiveness would be as good a strategy as any. His knees were drawn up under him and he was leaning forwards, his arms either side of the disk and his forehead almost touching the floor. In between hurling insults at Aye, his mind was full of entreaties.

"That can be arranged," he told Aye. "I could have you executed for your actions this day."

"Then do so!" Aye shouted. "For I would rather die a thousand times than live in a kingdom ruled by the figment of a child's imagination."

"You will worship him!" Tutankhamun shouted back. "You will get on your knees and bow to your god!"

"Never!"

Aye was leaning over Tutankhamun, spittle flecking from his mouth as he shouted, his knuckles white with the pressure of the grip he held on his walking stick.

"He is the one god," Tutankhamun said, and although he did not believe it himself he thought that it was the statement that could cause

Aye the most hurt. "There are no other gods but the Aten, and you will bow your head to him or I will have it removed!"

"*Never!*" Aye shouted again. Although Tutankhamun did not see it, he raised his walking stick in a threatening gesture over Tutankhamun's head.

"*I am your king!*" Tutankhamun shouted. "*I demand obedience!*"

"*Never!*"

Afterwards, Aye would not remember doing it. He would not remember the feeling of a lack of control, the sensation that his body was working entirely independently of his mind, that this was the outcome, that this had always been the outcome, and that there was nothing he could do about it. He would not remember thinking, even as he acted, that this was the wrong thing to do, that there was no forgiveness for this, that all of his previous crimes together were nothing but misdemeanours in comparison, but that even as he was thinking it he could feel the walking stick jar as it connected with the back of Tutankhamun's skull, just above the neck. He would not remember the sound that Tutankhamun made as, after the first blow, he tried to rise to protect himself.

"*Never!*" he shouted, and each time he brought the walking stick down on Tutankhamun's head in a quick succession of blows, he shouted it again. "*Never! Never! Never! Never!*"

He would not remember that Tutankhamun only reacted once, after the first blow, and that after the second and all those subsequent, he lay on the floor, face down, and made not the slightest movement.

All he would remember afterwards was the blood, and the silence. The blood bloomed under Tutankhamun's face in a steadily expanding pool. It was caked on the handle of the walking stick. It had splashed over Tutankhamun's back, over the golden disk that lay near his head, over Aye's legs and kilt. Aye could see droplets as far away as the wall. All he could hear was his own breathing, and after the noise of the argument the silence seemed almost like a judgement.

For a moment Aye was devoid of all thought and merely stared down at the king, listening to the silence. Then, awaking from his reverie as suddenly as if he had been slapped, he looked to the door and turned his attention to listen for the sounds of approaching footsteps. There were none, for now. He wiped the blood from the walking stick and his legs and kilt as best he could before opening the door just enough for him to be able to listen all the better. Still nothing. He risked a peek and saw that the corridor beyond was empty. With a brief last glance at Tutankhamun, he slipped through the doorway and closed it. Nobody had known he was here. Nobody would suspect him of this as long as he was able to leave the palace unseen. With the knowledge he had of the palace's endless corridors, half hidden alcoves and unused rooms, this would not be a serious challenge. Should his crime be attributed to him he had no doubt that he would be brutally tortured and executed in the most barbaric fashion, but there were no witnesses and Tutankhamun was certainly in no position to be able to point an accusatory finger. Once he was outside the palace walls, Aye considered himself safe.

Had he known that when he left the chapel that Tutankhamun was still alive, it is doubtful he would have considered himself quite so far beyond peril.

Chapter Twenty-Five

The Almost King

The Maya Papyrus, Fragments 345-351

I ARRIVED *only shortly after Ankhesenamun, whom I found in the anteroom to Tutankhamun's bedchamber, distraught to the point of incomprehensibility. When I asked her what had happened, she could do nothing but mutter words I could not catch and gesture towards the door that led to the inner room. I sat her down before she fell, gripped her firmly by the shoulders, and gave her a look that told her to be strong and that I would not be long. She looked through me as though in a waking sleep. I saw that there was no discernable effect to my presence one way or the other and satisfied at least that the taking of my leave would not leave her in even more desperate straits, I quietly let myself into the bedchamber. For all the silence and stillness inside I could have been walking into a tomb. The light within had been dimmed and priests and physicians crowded the bed.*

I crept closer, the urge to be quiet in a quiet room too much to ignore, although I wanted to shout questions at the physicians and priests, I wanted to shake them until they made my friend well again. Most of all I wanted to shake Tutankhamun and order him to snap out of it, to stop playing games. I thought that if I shook him enough, if I wanted him to recover with enough will, he would have no choice but to do so.

Of course, I did not. I merely sidled up to the bed and touched one of the physicians lightly on the elbow. He turned, somewhat startled out of his devotions, and looked ready to berate the man who had interrupted him until he recognised me. He nodded a solemn greeting and walked me to a less populous corner of the room.

"It does not look good," he whispered to me, before I had chance to ask.

"Is he going to die?" I asked.

"We cannot tell. He has not woken since the priests found him. We have only recently been able to staunch the flow of blood from his nose and ears. We are doing everything it is possible to do. The egg of an ostrich has been mixed with grease and applied to the wound. But we cannot contend with this, no matter how many spells we cast."

He nodded over to the bed, and I followed his gaze. I could hear the low tones of the physicians, speaking in chorus.

"Repelled is the enemy which is in the wound," they said, as the ancient scrolls prescribe. "Cast out is the evil that is in the blood, the adversary of Horus. The temple does not fall down; there is no enemy of the vessel therein. I am under the protection of Isis; my rescuer is the son of Osiris."

They paused, and then repeated the spell.

"What happened to him?" I asked the physician, becoming aware that I was keeping him from his duties but unable to prevent myself from asking.

The doctor shrugged. "We are not sure. Perhaps an accident, perhaps not."

"Perhaps not?" I said. "Perhaps not? Is that a diagnosis worthy of a doctor at court?"

He shrugged again.

"I am less concerned with the execution of the crime than the rehabilitation of the victim."

"Then it was a crime?"

He shrugged. It was an annoying habit. "The king was found on the chapel floor, having received a blow to the back of the head. The disk of the Aten lay nearby, splashed with blood. Perhaps it fell from the wall by accident."

"Are you saying that it fell of its own volition?"

"Gods have been known to perform greater miracles than moving," he said.

I stared at him and then turned and stared at the huddle of men around the bed. I turned back to the doctor.

"Are you telling me that the disk of the Aten flew from the wall of its own accord and battered His Majesty about the head?"

"No," the doctor said. "I am telling you how His Majesty was found. I am telling you that there are rumours of divine intervention. Everybody knows how he had been acting in the chapel in front of the god. It is of no surprise to some people that the Aten was angry with him. I have heard tell that you yourself felt the need to restrain him on at least one occasion."

We made our way back to the bed and I peered between shoulders to afford myself a view of him. He was lying on his back, his arms by his side, a bandage wrapped tightly around his head. His expression was one of serenity.

"Tell me this," I whispered. "If the Aten did this, do you think him incompetent enough to leave his victim alive?"

The doctor shrugged. I turned on my heel and left the room. I remembered even as Ankhesenamun looked up at me to smile encouragingly.

"There," I said, sitting down beside her and putting my arm around her shoulder. "I knew it would be something and nothing. He has had a bang on the head, that is all. The best doctors in the land – and therefore, I imagine, in the world – are looking after him. There is nothing to be upset about. He could not be in better hands."

Ankhesenamun looked at me, and I permitted myself the familiarity of wiping a tear from her cheek.

"But will he survive?" she said.

I forced a quiet laugh. "Survive?" I said. "What sort of talk is this? Of course he will survive! He is young and strong. He is a pharaoh. How can he not? No, in a day or so he will be walking out of that room rubbing his head, but when he does, I should steer clear of him."

"Why?"

"Why? Because his head will feel like he has spent a week drinking nothing but Syrian wine, that is why. You know what he is like with a hangover." I put on a passable imitation of him on the occasions I had seen him suffering from the indulgences of the night before. "Ooh, Ankhesenamun, my head, my poor head. I command you never to let me drink again! I declare a pox on the men who work the grape!"

I rose from the seat and staggered towards the door, holding my head and rubbing my throat. "Water!" I moaned. "Give me water! My insides are turning to dust!"

It was quite an accurate portrayal, if exaggerated somewhat for comic effect. Despite herself, Ankhesenamun laughed. It was the half-laugh, half-sob characteristic of women who are reassured but whose recovery is fated to be nothing more than transitory. Still, it was better than nothing, and for now it would have to suffice, for I needed once again to take my leave. There was somewhere I needed to go. I begged my lady's forgiveness and slipped from the room, leaving her in the hands of servants who I am sure meant well but whose own lamentations were hardly likely to buoy the Great Royal Wife into anything approaching everyday sensibility.

I, meanwhile, made my way with all speed to my father's house. I was unaware whether or not he had yet heard the news. I could scarcely believe that intelligence of this magnitude had failed to reach him.

When I arrived I found the place strangely silent. At this time of day the home of any gentleman was usually in something of a bustle of movement. Night approached, and now was the time when many of the errands that could be put off during the heat of the day were finally accomplished. Almost anything, in fact, that involved the servants venturing into the air of the city was completed during the very early morning or the very early evening, and the wealthier areas of the city were known to come alive at these times of the day. Not so, though, with Aye's house. As I approached I was greeted with silence and I could discern not even the warmth of a lamp from within. I began to wonder whether Aye was in the city at all, but I knocked on the door anyway. I had come too far too quickly to simply turn around and retrace my route. I was dishevelled and out of breath, and I welcomed the break in my exertions.

And then the strangest thing happened. I heard a noise from within. I wondered at first whether I had heard some bizarre echo of my own knock, but it had not sounded remotely similar. Perhaps, I told myself, it was the sound of the house settling down for the night after a hot day. In truth, it had sounded for all the world like someone banging into something in the dark. I knocked again, with a little more urgency.

"Hello?" I shouted. There came no reply.

I hammered on the door with the side of my fist.

"Hello!" I shouted. "It is I, Maya!"

There was a pause, but just as I had raised my hand to beat the door again, I heard a voice I recognised.

"Maya?"

"Father?"

The door opened, and I was ushered inside.

"What are you doing?" I asked him. "Have you not heard the news?"

"News?" he said. "What news?"

"The news that the entire city must be talking about. The news that Tutankhamun has met with... what may be some kind of accident."

"Then they know it was an accident?" he said.

"You have heard?"

"No, no," he said. "I know nothing about it. But it was an accident, you say?"

"We are not sure. Father, why are you sitting here in the dark?"

"I was alone," he said, as though that was explanation enough. "I dismissed my servants for the evening. I was trying to sleep. We never agreed on an heir. Who is going to assume the throne?"

"What?" I said. "Nobody. His Majesty is not dead."

If anything, my father looked more shocked at this than he did at the initial news of the accident.

"Not dead?" he said. "But you said..."

"I said only that he had met with an accident," I said. Aye sat down, and did so rather heavily, I thought. "Are you all right?"

"Yes," he said, absently. "Then has he not told you what happened?"

"He is unconscious," I said.

"But when he awakes..."

"If he awakes," I said. Aye looked up at me.

"Then he might not?"

I shrugged and thought of the doctor.

"Father," I said. "We must go to the palace."

"Yes," he said. "We must. Wait. I need to prepare myself. I am hardly dressed for the palace."

He stood and left the room for a moment. When he returned, he was carrying a lit lamp. For the first time I noticed that he was only half dressed. He lit one or two other lamps in the room from the flame of the one in his hand. The last of these was placed on the floor near to the chair in which he had been sitting. In his haste he did not trouble himself to pick it up and find a more practical resting place for it. Instead, he simply leaned down and lit it where it was. I watched him, and followed his movement down to the ground. He groaned as he leaned, as old men do, and I was about to tell him to leave it, or at least let me do it for him, when my gaze, naturally following the curve of his pose, was brought to the sandal upon his right foot and, inevitably, to the

*small splash of dark colour that he had overlooked on the side of
the sole.*

For the first time in as long as he could remember, Aye was unable to
think. He had banished his servants from the house as soon as he had
returned home and reached his bedchamber without being seen, washed
the blood from his clothes as best he could and then simply paced through
the rooms of his house in the gathering darkness.

He had not meant to act in the way he had. The deed was done before
he could even realise he was doing it. And while he did not feel happy
about the death and his responsibility for it, at the same time he was not
unduly saddened by it. What was done was done, and regret was the
refuge of fools who had no command over their future. The key now was
to ensure that the death was not without profit, for there was nothing so
irksome as a pointless death. A death in which a greater good was
embraced was almost a thing of beauty.

The nature of the greater good, however, was not something that
immediately sprang to mind. That Egypt should be strengthened by this
entire unfortunate episode was a hope shining so bright that it obscured
the details by which it might be brought about. That this should be the
death not only of Tutankhamun, but also of Atenism was undoubted, and
from that basis would strength and prosperity flow. But how?

Aye's mind skirted the issue in various directions before he was able
to confront it with anything approaching honesty. Tutankhamun has not
named an heir, he thought. The kingdom needs a strong king, a traditional
king, a king not likely to lose his head under the pressure of his
responsibility. A staunch conservative king was needed who had the
stamina to restore Egypt to her former greatness without resorting to fads
and fashions, without feinting from one religion to the next depending on
the vicissitudes of life.

Aye was trying to justify the obvious conclusion that presented itself,
and he knew the solution even before he admitted it to himself. With no
named heir there was the unsettling possibility that Ankhesenamun may
well attempt to follow her mother's rash example and claim the throne for
her own. Nefertiti had set a dangerous precedent indeed when she had
donned the crown, and Aye feared that Ankhesenamun on the throne
would be a disaster of unrealised proportions. She was too close to her
husband. Aye did not doubt for a moment that Atenism would be as much
of a threat under Ankhesenamun as it had been under Tutankhamun. With
Tutankhamun's death the gods had presented Aye with the opportunity of

righting many wrongs, and it was not an opportunity that he intended to squander.

There was no longer any doubt in Aye's mind, after pondering the matter for only the time it took to complete two circuits of the house, that his solution was the only one viable, practical or realistic. It was his destiny, he realised. Every moment of his life, from his first introduction to the child Amenhotep, had been leading to this moment. Even his mother would have lost her breath and clasped her hands to her bosom at the thought of it. She, who had dreamed such lofty dreams, even she would not have had the temerity to believe this possible. And yet it *was* possible.

The house was fully dark now and Aye stopped pacing for fear of crashing into something. He came to rest, by chance, in his living room. He remained in the centre of the room, unmoving.

He would make himself pharaoh.

As yet, he had no idea how he was to go about it, but that was almost irrelevant. That he had acknowledged the thought was enough, for now.

By the time he heard the knock at the door he was already imagining himself at the head of the procession at the festival of Opet.

For a moment he did not know what to do, for two thoughts simultaneously sprang into his mind and collided there, paralysing him.

It is the palace, he thought. *Of course, they have come to inform me of the death of the king.*

They are soldiers, he thought. *Somehow they have discovered the truth. What if I was seen? Are they here to arrest me?*

He decided to make his way to the doorway and listen for noise. Soldiers in groups of more than two were incapable of remaining quiet for any length of time. He crept forwards in the dark, cursing himself when he stumbled over something which clattered loudly across the tiled floor as though protesting at its mistreatment.

"Father?" a voice said, and Aye felt relief rush out of him like an exhaled breath. He was safe. His own son would not be sent here to arrest him.

But the reprieve lasted only as long as it took for his son to tell him that Tutankhamun was alive yet. It was inconceivable. He remembered the sight of the broken mess that lay at his feet on the chapel floor. Nothing so damaged could possibly survive.

He followed Maya to the palace. When the doors opened for him he was silently grateful that the emotion of the day seemed to have been too much for his son, who pleaded for some time to gather his thoughts. Aye gratefully acceded in order to be given the time to gather his own.

He left Maya alone and made his way to the king's bedchamber, where he spent some time by the bedside, making the sympathetic noises that were expected of him, occasionally putting his face in his hands, now and then simply tutting and shaking his head. He asked the questions that he felt he should ask, and the doctor shrugged his replies. But all the while Aye's mind was detached. Although his eyes saw the king in his bed and his ears heard the priests and doctors conducting their scripted laments, although his nose detected the pungent scents of eggs and grease slipping from beneath the king's bandages, none of these senses impinged on his heart, for that organ was engaged entirely with analysing the situation in which he now found himself.

During his time as the boy's tutor, Aye had always taught Tutankhamun that a wise man did not dwell on current problems. A wise man, he used to say, concentrated on future goals. And then it was merely a case of plotting a course from here to there. Aye considered himself a wise man. There was no profit in staring down at this king and wondering whether a great evil or a great good had been done. The only profit was in ensuring that the outcome was a favourable one.

Aye knew that the throne was not beyond his reach. Not with a little management and a little manipulation. Now that he had imagined himself before the adoring crowds it was an image he was loathe to surrender. Aye was still to grasp his chance and he did not see why a bad king selfishly clinging to life should have the capacity to take that chance from him.

Aye resolved that he would not give up his throne without even noticing that he had already begun to think of it as his to give up.

But the question remained: *how?*

After an indeterminate wait, Ankhesenamun was ushered into the room. There was nothing to be said beyond platitudes and the pair quickly lapsed into silence, both watching the king as though expecting him to spring to life at any moment.

At one point, thinking that she was about to speak, Aye turned to face the Great Royal Wife, only to find that she had been clearing her throat or swallowing an undignified sob. He did not turn back to face the king immediately. Instead, he regarded her momentarily from the side. There was no emotion in his eyes, neither sympathy nor malevolence. He looked at her jaw line, her cheekbones, her eye makeup which had spread under the washing of her tears into a black smudge, the ringlets of her wig falling across her forehead and over her ears. He watched her for a moment, saw her blink and swallow. And he knew how he was going to take the throne.

The Maya Papyrus, Fragments 354-360

We walked in silence, my father and I. When we reached the palace I pretended that the day's emotions and fears had bettered me and that I needed some time alone. Aye agreed and walked on without me. I watched his sandals as he receded along the corridor.

I was not being entirely untruthful when I told him that I needed time to think, for that is exactly what I needed, although I could not of course reveal to Aye the true nature of my consternation and bewilderment. I had seen the stain upon the sole of his sandal. It was a stain the like of which I had seen before, but once. It had been in the tombs at Akhetaten after I had proved myself in battle against the bandits who came to rob their contents. There is nothing so draining as a fight in which one's mortal fate is to be decided. In almost all human activities there is a reserve that we unconsciously stockpile. Contestants in a chariot race do not sprint their horses from the start, for they know that while the lead may be initially theirs, they will quickly become exhausted. Commanders do not march their men everywhere at the double for they know that while they may reach their destination all the quicker, they will be fit for nothing when they arrive. In a hand to hand fight to the death there is no such luxury. Nothing is held in reserve for fear that one will not live long enough to call upon those reserves. Everything is thrown into the fight and when that everything is exhausted, more is found from the depths of the human spirit and thrown in as well, until you think you will die simply from the effort of staying alive.

After the fight in the tombs I was not too proud to lie on the floor and whoop in great gulps of breath, ignorant of orders and the activity around me until I was sure that I would be able to walk again after the sapping of so much strength. After a time I was able to sit up and did so, my arms wrapped around my knees. I began to watch the activity around me. Soldiers passed to and fro each carrying something from the tomb. Some carried fallen weapons, others, in pairs, struggled under the weight of corpses, still others carried severed arms or legs, occasionally waving them around in triumph or jest. It was then that I saw the stains so reminiscent of that which I saw on Aye's sandal. They were everywhere. I will never forget the colour, for it was very apt. I was not a glorious scarlet, as storytellers would have us believe, but dull, dirty and brown. It was the mark of spilled blood and my sandals, and those of the men around me, were caked in it.

Of course, the most obvious conclusion, once I had seen the stain on Aye's sandal, was also the most ridiculous. That my father could have anything to do with the king's current condition was one that did not bear the slightest amount of intelligent scrutiny, although I had to admit that it was more likely than an act of revenge by the Aten.

I found Horemheb at home, as yet unaware of the developments at the palace. I quickly appraised him of the situation, for I knew he was a general and familiar with the need to assimilate a great number of shocking facts in quick succession. He duly did so, watching me intently, as though waiting for me to make a mistake, not speaking until my story had drawn to a close. I left out none of the salient facts and included everything up until I left Aye at the palace doors.

"You left him?" Horemheb said. It was the first time he had spoken since greeting me on my arrival.

"Yes," I said. "I needed time to think."

"You left the man you suspect of attacking the king to visit the king again, unaccompanied?"

I stared.

"Not unaccompanied," I said. "The king is surrounded by doctors and priests. And anyway, I do not suspect him. I am merely commenting on what I saw and asking for your opinion."

"Suspect him," Horemheb said, simply.

"You really think him capable of it?"

"I think any man capable of anything until it is proven otherwise. And I know that the king is surrounded by priests and doctors, but who of them is watching Aye? Watching how he reacts, what he says, how he looks? Does he look nervous? Does he look guilty? Is he a man beset by angst at what he has done or genuine concern for the king's welfare? We could have learned everything we need to know from his behaviour at the bedside."

I leapt to my feet. "Fetch me a chariot and your swiftest horses," I commanded, and then felt slightly ridiculous when Horemheb reached up and grabbed me by the forearm. He pulled me back into my seat.

"Too late," he said. "He has either left or has grown used to the sight before him. He would tell us nothing now. And you would do more harm than good bursting into the room and suddenly *trying to appear the vision of calm and concern. He would see you looking sideways at him and suspect your suspicions."*

"Your suspicions," I said.

"Our suspicions. Admit it."

I looked at the floor.

"Good. When we act, we need to do so as one man. We can achieve nothing unless we are both of the same mind. If either of us..." – here he looked pointedly at me – "if either of us was to waver from our task it would be disastrous for both. I do not relish the prospect of enmity with Aye, but if it is to come I want it to come on my terms and in my time. He is a powerful man, and a man of cunning, but let him try to oppose me on my terms and he will wish his mother had never dragged him from the backwater that spawned him."

I found myself staring at Horemheb again. It was not a speech I had been expecting, and I said so.

"This has been a long time coming, in one way or another," he said. He did not elaborate, but I gathered his meaning.

The moment passed and he told me exactly how we must proceed. I confess I rather felt like a man finding that the Nile's current had pulled his oars from his grasp and was taking his boat wherever its whims decided. It seemed that the current was far too fast for me to consider jumping.

I returned to the palace shortly afterwards, Horemheb's instructions reverberating around my mind like excitement, or fear. My heart raced to keep pace with my chariot's wheels. I was once again going into battle on behalf of those I loved, but this time I had neither a sword nor a detachment of the king's troops to protect me.

When I reached the palace I summoned the captain of the guard and instructed him to place both Tutankhamun and Ankhesenamun under his protection. Troops were to be stationed in the king's bedchamber and there was to be no less than two men in there at any one time. The Great Royal Wife was to be afforded the same guard and they were to follow her wherever she went. I warned the captain that I acted under the name of General Horemheb, and that even the slightest deviation from these orders would result in the captain finding himself at the bottom of a Nubian gold mine within the month. Suitably impressed, the captain fled to carry out his duties. I had no doubt that he would be meticulous.

I then went to see Ankhesenamun. I felt as though my visit was half imposition and half support at a difficult time. She was still to be found in the anteroom outside Tutankhamun's bedchamber, from whence her servants had failed to remove her. She looked drawn, and the smile with which she greeted me was meaningless.

"Any news?" I said, fearing that she would say yes. She shook her head. I sat down next to her and leant forward to match her pose, my elbows upon my knees.

"I have taken the liberty of taking some precautions," I said. Throughout the conversation, we barely looked at each other, our gazes instead focused on the area of the floor between our feet.

"What sort of precautions?" she asked me.

I sighed. I had not been looking forward to this. "Your Highness," I began, and she looked at me briefly, her eyebrows arched, before returning to look at the floor. I rubbed my forehead with the tip of my index finger and started again. "Ankhesenamun," I said. "There is a chance that this was a malicious act on behalf of someone at court who had access to the king." I held up my hands to silence her objection before it could be voiced. "I know, I know," I said. "He is as beloved as any king before him, but the fact remains that this assault was perpetrated by man or god, and I am willing to wager everything I own that it was not an act of any god with whom I am familiar, and that leaves only one other solution."

"What sort of precautions?" she said again.

At that moment, as though they were actors awaiting a cue, two soldiers walked into the room. They looked nervous and apologetic and, without a word, took up position by the door, facing away from us. Two more followed them but, instead of stopping, made their way through to the bedchamber proper.

"This," I said. "This sort of precaution."

"Are my husband and I to become like our father?" Ankhesenamun asked me. "Never venturing anywhere without a phalanx of guards to protect us against suspected assassins?"

I would be delighted, I thought, if I considered it possible for Tutankhamun to venture anywhere again, escorted or otherwise, but of course I said nothing.

"Believe me," I said. "If I did not think it necessary I would never have considered it."

She was too weary to put up anything of a fight. I remained sitting with her in silence. Eventually I heard her breathing soften and deepen, and I put my arm around her and gently guided her head to my shoulder.

Aye had his speech constructed almost verbatim in his head. It was not a long speech, for it needed to be forceful and engaging, and long speeches were usually neither. It was not complicated or convoluted because it needed to be persuasive. It needed to be worded in such a way that the thought of opposition would not be given room inside the listener's heart. It was the most important speech of Aye's life. It was intended for the ears of Ankhesenamun alone, and its goal was to secure him the throne of Egypt. He was by turns confident and terrified. He knew his powers as an orator, he knew that he cut an imposing figure, and that to impress his will on the mind of a young woman should not, under normal circumstances, pose too much of a problem. On the other hand, she *was* a woman, and what was more, she was the offspring of Akhenaten, and so anything was feasible.

Timing, he knew, was as important as the words he had prepared. He would not be the only person intent on the Great Royal Wife's ear and he knew that he would have no support from any other quarter. He needed to act quickly, before her mind could become swayed in favour of another of her entourage.

Aye was of the opinion that he had the advantage of everyone at court. Even Horemheb. He knew what they did not. He knew better than the doctors and the priests, the soothsayers and the seers. Everybody else worked under the assumption that the gods would protect their own, and that a young man with the strength to survive thus far would have the strength to recover. They could not bring themselves to face what Aye knew to be Tutankhamun's inevitable death. He knew this because, at home, in a cache in a corner that would never be discovered, Aye had hidden what was left of the poison he had used to rid the cares of the world from Nefertiti.

He did not want to use it against Tutankhamun, and began fervently hoping that the boy would die of his own accord to prevent Aye having twice the guilt, but if he did not, if he began to show signs of improvement, the option was available. Aye did not have any choice, even if he had not been influenced by dreams of power. Should Tutankhamun regain consciousness there was nothing to stop him revealing the identity of his attacker and Aye's sense of self-preservation was far too well developed to allow such an eventuality.

Nobody else would be keen to interrupt their lamentations long enough to plan for a successor while the king still lived. If he had any rivals for the throne, Aye could have them outmanoeuvred already.

He arrived at Ankhesenamun's quarters only two nights after he had kept his brief vigil beside her at Tutankhamun's bedside. He had learned that she had only recently vacated her seat in the anteroom to Tutankhamun's bedchamber and he considered that this was something that could only be to his advantage. If she was tired and confused, all the better.

Once shown into her presence he bowed formally, but he did not prostrate himself. He noted the guards in the corner of the room and wondered who had ordered them there. He doubted it was Ankhesenamun. He doubted her capable of anything so calculated in the current turmoil of her life. He wondered if they were a permanent fixture and whether their presence had closed off one of his avenues of attack. He rather thought it did, but then it was not so great a loss. He had never been a man to rely upon a single plan.

"May I once again offer my sincere condolences at this difficult time," he said to Ankhesenamun. "I am sure that you are entirely overwhelmed, and I wanted to come to tell you that you can always rely on me as a friend and confidante, should you so desire it."

"Thank you, grandfather," she said. "That is very kind. I shall do so."

She looked momentarily as though she was going to say something else, but her open mouth instead widened into a yawn which she failed to conceal with any degree of success.

"I fear that you may have to," Aye said.

"I am sorry grandfather, but I am exhausted. I am finding it difficult to concentrate. I do not take your meaning."

"I will not keep you from your bed a moment longer than I have to," Aye said. "I only mean that the death of a king is a trying time for a nation, but for a royal court most of all."

"Grandfather, please!" Ankhesenamun exclaimed, suddenly animated. "Tutankhamun is far from dead! You should not talk like that. The doctors have assured me that the greatest medical and religious minds of the kingdom are working to aid his recovery."

"Nevertheless," Aye said, "while I pray hourly that he may be restored to us, I am afraid that it would be irresponsible to neglect to plan for the unthinkable. Should the worst happen, this court will become a cauldron. You have no heirs, Ankhesenamun. Every man at court will believe he has a claim on the throne. We must act now to prevent a harmful struggle."

"Harmful struggle?"

Aye smiled a patronising smile. "The throne is a powerful thing," he said. "It has been known to push men to the extremities of action. Blood has been spilled over thrones many times."

"You are telling me that there will be bloodshed should my husband not survive?"

"I am saying that it is a possibility, but that if we act now we can prevent it entirely. We can secure a smooth succession, and nobody, least of all yourself, needs to come to any harm."

"How?"

"Well," he said. "It will not be easy. But before we discuss matters of such delicate privacy, it may be a good idea to ask your guards to step outside."

She agreed without questioning him. Aye smiled broadly as he watched them leave, and he did so for any number of reasons.

The Maya Papyrus, Fragments 373-378

> *The king's condition dragged on, with little change in either direction, for months. I sometimes felt as though the gods were teasing us, or him. They kept him alive and close enough to recuperation to allow him to occasionally wake, but did not allow him to recover. His waking moments were irregular and transitory and, after the first handful had been and gone with no general improvement, they soon failed to arouse in us any sense of increased hope. They did, however allow us a moment here and there to be able to give him water and some bland, mashed food.*
>
> *It pains me to say it, but the king's moments of wakefulness may have done more harm than good in the long term. They served only to prolong the king's discomfort and it upset Ankhesenamun that he was never aware enough of his surroundings to understand or react to her whispered words of love and devotion.*
>
> *After three months I began to notice that his periods of wakefulness were becoming shorter and further apart. It was plain to me that he was slipping away. Even had I been tactless enough to share my belief with Ankhesenamun, she would never have believed it. Up until the very end she believed that there was hope, and the increasing reluctance of the doctors and priests to countenance optimism went unnoticed, or at least ignored. She left his bedside only when absolutely necessary. She would*

sometimes sleep sitting in the chair at the side of his bed, leaning forwards with her head on the bed next to him. She told me that she wanted hers to be the first face that he saw when he awoke.

We were all there when Tutankhamun finally died. A messenger from the shrugging doctor had found me at home and begged my attendance, as other messengers were doing with other senior members of court. Tutankhamun's breathing had changed, we were told. He had not woken for days. When I arrived Aye and Ankhesenamun were already there, and Horemheb was almost catching my heels as I ran in.

Nothing was said, for no words were worthy of the situation. Ankhesenamun was at the side of the bed, looking strained and tired. We were standing behind her; the general, the vizier and the treasurer, the men who had watched over Tutankhamun from his earliest days, his friends and mentors. We had accompanied him on his journey almost from the moment he came into this world, and now we were here to witness his leaving of it. His breathing was laboured, as the doctor's messengers had warned us. It bubbled in his throat, and occasionally caught for moments at a time so that we thought the end had indeed come.

He did not wake at the end. He did not, in the manner of a heroic history, open his eyes one last time and point accusingly at Aye before whispering his love to his wife and passing from us with a dramatic sigh. Nothing is so easy, nothing so clear. Instead he breathed out and simply did not breath back in again. It was a moment before anybody reacted. He had been doing this since we arrived. Then I noticed one or two of the doctors sharing a glance between them, and the shrugging doctor stepping forwards, preparing to speak.

"I am afraid His Majesty has gone," he said. "His injuries were such that we were powerless to prevent it."

Even now, Ankhesenamun was reluctant to accept the reality of the situation. She looked up at the doctor and then, as if for support, at me.

"There must be something you can do?" she said. "Why are you not chanting over him? Why do you just accept this? Are there no potions, no poultices? With all your combined medical knowledge and the ear of the gods, you are telling me that there is nothing?"

I leant forwards and placed a comforting hand upon her shoulder.

"He is gone," I said, quietly.

Ankhesenamun stared at me, and then back at the doctor, and then, in turn, at each face in the room, all of which were looking down on her. From each she craved an answer, silently begging that one of us would step forwards and say Wait, have you not tried such-and-such, *thus finding the miracle cure. The room remained in a bubble of oppressive silence. Slowly, as she realised that no miracle was about to ensue, Ankhesenamun's expression collapsed into immeasurable grief, and she turned to press her forehead against the back of Tutankhamun's hand.*

Aye made the arrangements for Tutankhamun's funeral. It was unthinkable that Ankhesenamun should be left with the task, although traditionally it was the king's heir or widow that issued the commands. She was too sick with grief to be able to carry out such morbid duties.

The change in Aye since Tutankhamun's death was remarked upon by everyone that knew him. He threw himself back into the role of vizier with something approaching glee. While his servants would never hold him in renown for his politeness and civility, he was no longer someone they would dread passing in the corridor.

He remembered with fondness the time Ankhesenamun lost her first baby, when Tutankhamun had been too distraught to rule effectively and Aye had stepped into his place. It had been an exhausting but glorious time, and this was no different.

So far, everything was going according to plan. He had taken effective control of the kingdom and nobody had questioned him. There had, as yet, been no power struggle, although he could sense its approach, despite the mood of preoccupied apprehension that infused the palace. It was not possible for a new king to be crowned for seventy days; the time it took to embalm and entomb the body of the previous king. Without a king there was no interaction between this world and the world of the gods, and without the gods' protection, the world was at the mercy of the forces of chaos.

All of this helped Aye. A nervous populace was much more likely to accept any king that came along, as long as he offered them some form of stability. Furthermore, a nervous populace infected the palace, which became less likely to offer resistance to the seizing of the throne.

Speculation was rife around the palace concerning the matter of the succession. Obviously there were no heirs to lay a claim on it, and those at court began to look to each other to see who would possess the courage to make the first move. And all the while, Aye was continuing his meetings with Tutankhamun's widow.

She had begun to dread the times when she would hear Aye's name announced at the audience chamber door. In fact, she had grown to detest the audience chamber itself. Without Tutankhamun to sit next to it was a room that made her feel vulnerable. There was a flood of foreign dignitaries who wished to pay their respects to the Egyptian throne in the aftermath of the king's death, undoubtedly to ensure that Egypt's new king, whomsoever that may be, would be more inclined to return their friendship. It fell to Ankhesenamun to suffer translated lamentations and declarations of alliance and loyalty. There seemed to be no end to them. Syrians, Nubians, Hurrians, Mitannites, Babylonians, all came and bowed at her feet. Only the Hittites were missing, and were roundly criticised for it by all at court. Secretly, Ankhesenamun was grateful for their absence. It was one less audience to endure.

She would, though, have undergone a hundred audiences with ambassadors if she could have done so in place of one meeting with Aye.

He only ever had one topic of conversation and it was one which made her shudder. She had remained determined, at least at first, to stay noncommittal to his request. Despite the horror with which she regarded his proposition, she did not think it prudent to bind herself to a decision one way or the other until she absolutely had to, partly because she thought it wise to give herself the opportunity to examine the buck and weave of popular opinion and partly because she had no real idea which was the appropriate course of action.

And recently it seemed as though her indecision was pushing him towards anger. He was becoming frightening.

"Your Highness," he would say, spitting the words as though he held them in particular disdain. "I must press you for an answer. If you cannot answer me today you jeopardise the well-being of the entire kingdom. You place yourself in danger from those who would wrestle the throne from you. You encourage our neighbours to take advantage of our lack of a king by launching their forces against us. You anger the very gods themselves, Ankhesenamun. Is the constitution of your conscience sturdy enough to take such punishment? Your Highness, I *must* have an answer."

"I do not know!" she shouted at him, after his most recent, and most animated, plea for a decision. "Aye, I am confused. You are confusing me. I do not know what to do for the best."

Aye sighed melodramatically. "I have told you what to do for the best," he said, in a voice weary of the argument. "It is very simple. Surely even a woman can understand it."

"But you must understand, Aye, that it would be remiss of me to act without taking the proper advice."

"You have..." Aye shouted, and then forced himself to stop and breath slowly for a moment before starting again, in a much calmer voice. "You have all the advice you need, Your Highness. I must again stress to you the importance of keeping this matter between ourselves. There is nobody at court during these troubled times upon whom you can rely. The most trustworthy may simply be the most devious. The closest friends may be the schemers with the greatest cunning. And anyway, I have explained everything a number of times. The situation – your situation – is clear."

"Nevertheless, Aye," Ankhesenamun said, in a voice that she hoped carried more authority than she believed. "I am very tired. You must let me have my rest."

Aye bowed, as though every joint pained him as he did so. "As you wish," he said. "I shall return shortly to see if you have considered my offer further."

He walked stiffly to the doorway and Ankhesenamun allowed herself to sag. She did not doubt that he would return, but she doubted that what he was giving her was an offer. Neither was it intimidation. It was, though, somewhere in between, and it was edging further towards coercion with every audience. She could see the sense, though, in keeping Aye's cajolery to herself, much as it pained her to do so. However much he may have been exaggerating the situation to further his own cause, there was an atmosphere around court that she had difficulty describing. It was not threatening, but it was waiting for a threat to appear. It was not deceitful, but it was waiting to be deceived. Everybody, it seemed, was waiting for everybody else. If news got out that Aye was acting before all of them she did not know what would happen.

Aye was tired of waiting. He wanted it to be over, one way or the other, for he could no longer continue being the almost king. He wanted the throne or he wanted nothing. This limbo would no longer suffice. In any case, he doubted he had the energy to continue in this manner for much longer, even if his patience had proved boundless. The government of the country was enough of a strain in itself without having the stress of attempting to manage his own fate as well. But more than anything, he was tired of waiting.

The next day, he returned to Ankhesenamun's quarters as early as decency would allow.

"Your decision, Your Highness?" he said, still marching across the audience chamber floor, without making the effort to bow.

"Aye, it has been only a handful of hours since we last spoke. Do you really expect anything to have changed so quickly?"

"Not if I am honest, Highness, no," he said.

"Then why are you here?"

"Merely to remind you of something."

Ankhesenamun was tired. She did not feel the need to be reminded of anything.

"Which is?" she said, without enthusiasm.

"Which is that I am still vizier of this kingdom."

"Of course you are, grandfather," she said. "Did you think I needed reminding of that?"

"Not of that," he said, "but perhaps of the fact that the vizier, after the king, has complete control of the kingdom's armed forces."

Ankhesenamun was taken aback. Although she had recognised that Aye was becoming increasingly forceful, she had not expected this.

"Is that a threat, grandfather?" she said.

Aye had been expecting the question, and he had already decided how it should be answered. His intention was to shock Ankhesenamun into a decision. There was little point in denying the very subtext that he wished her to appreciate.

"Yes," he said, simply.

Chapter Twenty-Six

The Hittite Letters (1)

The Maya Papyrus, Fragments 380-388

BY THE time I arrived at Ankhesenamun's quarters, her sobbing had started to subside but I could tell by the look of her eyes that she had been crying for some time. My first thought was that the strain, with which she had been coping admirably since her husband's death, had finally begun to take its toll and that she had summoned me merely in my capacity as a friendly face in order to comfort her. I had no idea of the true purpose of the audience.

For some reason her first sight of me was enough to reduce Ankhesenamun to the tears from which she had so obviously only just recovered. I rushed to her side and took her in my arms.

"Hush now," I said, in my best approximation of soothing tones. "Tutankhamun is not so very far away. You will meet him again soon enough."

She did not reply until the sobbing had released its grip on her breath.

"It is not that," she said, and then corrected herself. "Yes, it is. Of course it is. How could it not be? But it is also something else, something that I have sworn never to reveal to anyone, or at least, not until it is too late."

I pulled away from her slightly in order to be able to look her in the face.

"What?" I said.

"I want you to prepare yourself," she told me.

"Just tell me," I said.

"Your father – my grandfather – wants to take me as his bride," she said.

I almost laughed. I thought it was the start of some tasteless joke, so ridiculous did the words sound. When I saw that she was

*as far from laughter as ever I had seen her I decided that I must
have misheard, and asked her to repeat herself.*

*"He wants the throne. His blood is not thick enough to be
able to claim it without some reinforcement to his claim. I am that
reinforcement. If he marries me, nobody will be able to stop him."*

*I was mortified. Until that moment, I had always secretly
believed it unlikely that Aye was responsible for Tutankhamun's
death, despite the evidence I had seen with my own eyes. He was,
after all, my father.*

*But this changed things considerably. Not only did I have the
evidence of the blood on his sandals, I now also knew of a motive.
He had always been an ambitious man. We are, after all, an
ambitious family, although this particular affliction seems to have
left me relatively unscarred. But was he so ambitious that he
would dream of taking the throne as his own?*

*I listened as Ankhesenamun told me of Aye's insistence that
the pair be married as soon as possible, and that his intention was
to be crowned king even before Tutankhamun had been laid to
rest. There seemed to be no taboo that the man was not prepared
to trample upon in order to secure his foothold on power. She told
me also of his latest threat, the one which had prompted her to
confide in me, that if she continued to refuse him he would use the
army to reach his objectives, in a much less tidy but just as
effective manner.*

*"Did he actually say that?" I asked, still torn in my beliefs by
familial ties.*

*She shook her head. "He did not need to," she said. "He made
it perfectly clear that this was his intention."*

"And what was your reply?" I asked.

"I said that I would not submit my kingdom to civil war."

"Then you will comply?"

*Ankhesenamun looked at the floor, and when she spoke she
did so very quietly. "What choice do I have?" she said.*

*I took a deep breath. I had not wanted to tell Ankhesenamun
of my fears and suspicions concerning Aye, for I knew that it
would only serve to deepen the wounds of Tutankhamun's death.
But what choice did I have now? Now that the victim's wife was
about to be forced into marriage with the victim's killer? There
was no longer simply the matter of Ankhesenamun's pain to be
considered. Neither was it simply the matter of a man ruthless
and murderous coming to the throne of Egypt. Now there was the
matter of my injured sense of justice, and sometimes this can*

provide better sustenance for revenge than even the noblest of causes. The thought that my father could act in such a way made bile rise in my throat and I determined to ensure that he would not be allowed to succeed.

"You cannot marry Aye," I said. "The very idea is preposterous. It is an abomination."

"Well," Ankhesenamun said, a resigned tone in her voice, "if it leads to a stable kingdom and the crowning of a strong ruler and the avoidance of bloodshed, then..."

"No," I said, firmly. "You do not fully appreciate the situation. I am sorry, Ankhesenamun, but there are certain cogent facts about which you are ignorant, for I have purposefully kept them from you. I assure you that I did so only for reasons to which your welfare was central. Now, though, I fear I have no choice."

I told her everything, although everything was really not all that much, and it did not take long. She did not interrupt me, and when I finished she did not immediately speak.

"He killed Tutankhamun," she said, at last.

I held up my hands. "Please," I said. "I have fought with myself since that day not to be hasty. We do not know that he killed him for sure. The best that can be said is that we have cause for concern."

"He killed him," she said again. "He killed him so that he could get his vile hands on the throne. All this is part of his plan. I am part of his plan."

"We do not know that."

"Yes," she said. "We do. How else would he have got blood on his sandals?"

I thought for a moment. "Perhaps he had been out walking," I said, "in the market."

"Oh, please," she said. "Since when does a man like Aye go to the market for himself? He would rather starve than buy his own food."

"But if he is guilty it is all the more reason to oppose him. There must be something we can do."

Ankhesenamun raised her eyebrows. It was an expression of resignation, of weariness. "Such as?" she said.

"Horemheb has as much control of the army as does Aye. He could meet Aye's challenge."

Ankhesenamun shook her head. "No," she said. "He could not stand against Aye and Nakhtmin together."

"Nakhtmin," I said, quietly. "I had forgotten about him."

"He would surely side with your father, and his men with him. And between them, they would present an unbeatable force."

I sank into my seat and stared at the opposite wall.

"Then we have no hope?" I said.

"We have no hope," she said.

"We have one hope," Horemheb said, when I relayed Ankhesenamun's news to him later that evening. "But you are not going to like it."

We were drinking a heavy wine in the gardens that backed onto his palatial quarters in the most affluent part of the city. Here you could smell only the flowers, and hear only the calls of evening birds and the buzz and flutter of insects and could easily believe you were in some obscure outpost of the Nile, far from the hubbub of Thebes. Far in front of us the sun was slipping quietly to his bed, and so close to it that he shone only on the upper part of the walls behind us while the bottom was in shadow. A chill was beginning to appear, like a skulking nocturnal animal, and we took gulps of wine to warm ourselves in advance. We looked not at each other, but at the sunset.

"Anything," I said. "It is of no relevance whether I like it or not. I cannot dislike it as much as I dislike the thought of Aye forcing her to marry him."

"You marry her," he said. I snorted wine down my nose and almost dropped my cup.

"Me!" I said. "My apologies. I thought you had a sensible proposal."

"Think about it," he said. "If you were to marry her you would have as strong a claim on the throne as Aye. Stronger, if anything. It would stop him in his tracks."

"It would stop him long enough for him to pick up his sword," I said.

"He would not kill his own son," Horemheb said. I turned to look at him.

"Do you really believe that?" I asked him.

"No," he replied, looking into his cup and swirling the contents around.

"Well then," I said. "It would be an act of suicide."

"But think of what is at stake," Horemheb said. "You would be pharaoh! Think of the afterlife. You would be elevated to the godhead! Did you ever imagine such a thing would be in your grasp?"

"No," I said. "And I still do not. I have no interest in being King Maya, thank you very much. Anyway, she is my niece. It would not be natural."

"Natural? When Akhenaten married his own daughters? And had children by them? When you are pharaoh, you decide what is natural."

"Well I am not pharaoh now, and I am fully capable of deciding that putting myself in Aye's way would be suicide, and suicide is unnatural enough for me to want to avoid it. Why not you? What is preventing you from marrying her? She would be delighted with the protection of a powerful man like you."

Horemheb sucked air through his teeth in thought. "No," he said, and I thought I detected genuine regret in his voice. "It would not work. It would simply face my armed faction against those of Aye and Nakhtmin. It would lead to war. They would be able to claim I had usurped power, and what is more, there is not a man in the kingdom who would not believe them. In short, it would be the same result as if I were to announce my opposition to Aye now. War."

"Then we have no hope," I said, for the second time that day. But Horemheb's suggestion had set me thinking, and it was a thought that dogged me as I struggled to keep my balance on the back of my chariot as it later sped me homewards. The amount of wine we had consumed was undoubtedly having as an unsteadying effect on my mind as it was on my legs, but I was not so drunk that I did not recognise an intriguing possibility.

It was desperate. It was, some may have said, tending towards the insane. Others may perhaps have called it treacherous, but I cared not for the judgement of imagined critics. It was a solution, and it involved little personal risk to either myself or Ankhesenamun, and, what was more, it completely negated Aye's threat of civil war. It mattered not if he had the armies of a dozen sons ranged behind him. It would be something over which he had no power. There was, though, one small drawback.

I would have to keep it entirely secret from Horemheb.

That the wedding would happen was something that Aye no longer questioned. He knew that the threat of civil war was something that Ankhesenamun would not countenance.

But the question of what would happen after the wedding was one which Aye had only answered up to a point. He would become pharaoh by dint of his marriage to the woman who was not only the most senior surviving royal, but also the widow of the late king. His claim would be incontestable. But what then? He had come to realise that his relationship to Ankhesenamun would most likely change the moment he donned the crown. She would immediately change from the woman who enabled him to climb to such a lofty position to the woman who could cast him down with one word. He could not guarantee her continuing silence. And just as she was proving to be his road to the throne, so could she be someone else's.

She would expose him to risk. Risk was unacceptable.

Once he was convinced that his plan was to succeed he returned, content, to his home, where he checked once again that the last of the poison that he had administered to Nefertiti remained safe in its cache. He weighed the package in his palm. It seemed so slight, so insubstantial, this little packet that effortlessly changed the course of kingdoms. It would perhaps be a suspicious death so soon after the wedding, but by then he would be pharaoh and beyond reproach.

It was not a scenario without regret for him, but then it was not a scenario where feelings of regret were terribly relevant. It was a necessity, not only for his own wellbeing, but also that of the nation as a whole. Ankhesenamun was his granddaughter, and he had entertained a certain fondness for her during her youth but she had become a hurdle and a threat, and as such she could not be allowed to prosper.

Aye placed the packet back into its hiding place and thought little more of it until, much later, he came to retrieve it once more.

The Maya Papyrus, Fragments 390-393

> *I did not rush directly to the palace with my idea half-formed in my mind. It was too momentous a thought to release into the world without at least some of the pains of birth. I returned home and cogitated over the matter with the help of some Cretian wine which had a bitter taste of which I was not particularly fond, and which I had been saving for a night such as this when that which had preceded it down my throat had done me the favour of numbing my sensitive palate. I quaffed it in unceremonial gulps as I paced the floor of my living quarters, cup in right hand and amphora in left.*

There were, I knew, any number of scenarios in which my idea, if implemented, could easily turn disastrous. There were others where cataclysmic may have been a more accurate description of the potential outcome. But then, for every ruinous circumstance my pessimism was able to conjure, there was but one answer: is that any worse than that which is sure to happen if we do nothing at all? The answer was always no. I could think of a hundred different conclusions, but even the worst of them was no worse than Aye acceding the throne. Of course, the irony of the situation was that the only outcome that did not occur to me was the one that actually came to pass.

There were many who would have disagreed with me, including those who would otherwise have sided with me against Aye. I think that even Horemheb, who would rather have plucked out his own eyes than see Aye on the throne of Egypt, would have baulked at my idea. He would have said that it was too unpredictable, that it placed Egypt in danger, that I had no right to imperil the kingdom so. I could hear the exact words he would have used, every subtle inflection in his voice. I would have disagreed with him. How can it imperil the kingdom? *I would have asked him.* There are so many ways that it could help, even beyond the obvious. Can you think of a more dependable way to prevent the inevitable Hittite invasion? *He would have argued with me, and he would probably have won, but that does not mean that he would have been right.*

Perhaps the wine I had been pouring into myself helped strengthen my resolve. It certainly heightened my sense of urgency. I decided that any further delay would be an unacceptable risk and immediately woke my servants. I ordered them to prepare my chariot for another sojourn into the night.

I rushed to the palace and left my chariot in the courtyard, the horse untethered and looking a little confused at the untidy abandonment in which he had been left. I marched towards the palace doors with what I hoped would be perceived as a dignified gait but was, in fact, one in which every step seemed to be slightly too long for my legs. The guards were familiar enough with me to not only open the doors but to pass smiles between them that they thought I was too drunk to notice. In fact I was not, but I was too drunk to care, which amounts to the same thing.

There is rarely a time in a royal palace when there are not some servants on duty, if you know where to look to find them. I did, and I found a handful of them in the anterooms off the kitchens. I diverted one from her task and sent her to wake Ankhesenamun's attendants in order that they could then, in their turn, awake the Great Royal Wife and prepare her to receive me.

I waited nervously for the process to play itself out so that I could be summoned to Her Highness' presence. When the summons came I rushed into the audience chamber.

"I was sleeping," Ankhesenamun told me, rather unnecessarily, I thought, as I stumbled to an undignified halt before her throne. "I hope this is of sufficient import to drag me from my bed. Have you been drinking?"

"Your Mighness," I said, meaning highness *but almost saying* majesty, *and thus confirming her suspicions and deepening her frown. "I have reached a conclusion that will solve all of our problems."*

I could tell that she did not greet my words with anything other than the deepest scepticism.

"Really," I said, hoping that this would sway her.

Reluctantly, she waved her hands in a dismissive gesture and her attendants and bodyguard bowed from the room, leaving the two of us alone.

"Come," she said, signalling the throne where Tutankhamun used to sit. "Sit down before you fall over." I was too deep in my cups to have any qualms about accepting her invitation.

"Well?" she said.

I told her, and when I had finished she gave me a cold look.

"You are drunk," she said. "Or insane. Or both. Go to bed and sleep it off, and come to see me tomorrow. I suggest you prepare a comprehensive apology for disturbing me."

When I awoke the following morning I was still sitting on the throne.

Ankhesenamun did not sleep for the rest of the night and was fully dressed and sitting on the edge of her bed by the time her servants arrived to wake her. They fussed about her, but she hardly acknowledged their presence. As she had been since her return to bed after scolding Maya, she was preoccupied with what he had said to her. She could not deny, now that her initial shock had somewhat subsided, that the idea did have its attractions, cocooned though they were in risks and misgivings. And she had to admit that it was a way guaranteed to prevent Aye from seizing the throne. She would have continued to think about Maya's words for some considerable time, perhaps to the exclusion of ever acting upon them, had her hand not been forced.

Aye had waited for some days without venturing into the palace and yet still no word came, of submission or otherwise. He could not discount the possibility that he was simply being ignored.

And yet he could not countenance another trip to the palace. It would seem, at least to him, to be too close to begging. He had given her her chance. He had been more than reasonable for such a long time that it was beginning to look like weakness, and if he had any chance of success whatsoever it was in persuading others of his strength. It was no longer the time to ask and wait for the Great Royal Wife's opinions and decisions. It was time to make the decisions for himself and act accordingly. He would no longer allow a woman's vacillation come between him and what was rightfully his. He did two things.

Firstly, he summoned the generals he knew he would be able to rely upon to be loyal to his cause. Secondly, he sent a messenger to the north western borders to find Nakhtmin. It was time to bring matters to a head.

News came to Ankhesenamun that the army had begun carrying out exercises on the desert plains to the west of Thebes. Ankhesenamun had ordered no such exercises, and upon investigation discovered that Horemheb had not done so either. Only one other man in Thebes had the power to do so.

A week later, Nakhtmin presented himself at court for the Great Royal Wife's blessing. Aye had ordered him to do so the very moment he returned to Thebes, to be absolutely sure that Ankhesenamun was aware of Nakhtmin's arrival. It was unavoidable that most of his troops remained on the border, for the threat of attack from the Hittites had not abated, but he brought with him enough for the point to be made.

Horemheb hastily arranged his troops on the opposite side of the city and put them to the same manoeuvres as were being carried out by their erstwhile colleagues, but it was little more than a gesture. It was obvious to all who saw both forces that Horemheb's men were heavily outnumbered and significantly more prone to desertion should hostilities break out.

There was little doubt at court that civil war was unavoidable. Day by day, people were seen to be passing through the city's gates and heading north or south towards other, less dangerous, cities. As the days wore on the exodus increased until the people were leaving the city at such a rate their passage began to interfere with the armies' exercises.

Ankhesenamun too had come to the conclusion that war was inevitable, and the impending tragedy of it all was more than enough to prompt her once again to consider Maya's idea. She ruminated on it for a day more before coming to her conclusion. It would have to be tried. She would not be able to live with so many deaths on her conscience if she did not know without doubt that she had tried everything she could to prevent them.

She summoned Maya to her side and ordered him to prepare the letter.

The Maya Papyrus, Fragments 397-409

> To His Majesty Šuppiluliumas, king of the Hittites, conqueror of Carchemish, may he live. Thus writes Her Royal Highness Ankhesenamun, Great Royal Wife and widow of His Majesty Tutankhamun, king of the Two Lands of Upper and Lower Egypt, son of Ra, perfect of diadems, beloved of Amun, may he live:
>
> Your Majesty, I bring you greetings and felicitations. May all go well with you. I offer you the hand of friendship between our kingdoms. My husband is dead and a son I have not. But of you, they say your sons are many and grown. If you would give me a son of yours he would become my husband. I am loathe to take a servant of mine and make him my husband, but I have no sons who may inherit my husband's throne. I am afraid! I offer you my friendship and the friendship of my country and in return I beg your assistance and kindness.

> I composed the letter and the one that followed it. Let not men jealous of momentous times level their accusations towards Ankhesenamun. It was me. Ankhesenamun may have inscribed her name at the bottom of the papyrus (and wept for the thing she was doing even as she did so), and the words may have been a faithful rendition of her thoughts and wishes, but it was my hand that recorded them, just as it is my hand that records the words before you now. I stand by it. I do not regret my words, for regret is not appropriate to actions carried out in good faith as this one was. Judge a man not by the fruits of his life, but by the intentions of it. Judge less still a woman, for she acts with the good intentions of the men who advise her.

The letter was signed and a messenger was given it with the king's seal and a passport around his neck to help afford him safe passage.

Having watched his ship sail from Thebes harbour I returned to the palace to wait, which was the only option left open to me. I rarely saw Horemheb alone now, for I was afraid to venture beyond the city walls lest I become mistaken for an enemy of either side, so I saw him only when he made his brief reports to Ankhesenamun regarding the state of the factions surrounding Thebes. Ankhesenamun and I took every opportunity to remind him that his primary duty was as a deterrent. Horemheb, however, was growing increasingly intolerant of the situation. I knew him well enough to know that his patience was not inexhaustible and I feared what would happen once its well ran dry. He had never been an impetuous man, but I did not doubt that he was capable of launching into a battle in which he was heavily outnumbered, simply because he saw no alternative.

I persuaded Ankhesenamun to resist the temptation to tell him the truth until we had an answer from Šuppiluliumas. It would not be too long, I believed, before a Hittite messenger arrived with the news that a prince was following behind, ready to take the throne.

I was correct in at least one aspect. A messenger did indeed arrive from Šuppiluliumas, and he did indeed arrive before the factions outside the city walls put each other to the sword. I gathered with Ankhesenamun in the audience chamber before the messenger was admitted. We smiled warmly at each other, the first time since Tutankhamun's death that I could remember genuinely forming such an expression. I actually rubbed my hands together as I walked towards her throne as though a sumptuous repast had just been placed before me. I believed that our troubles were over. I believed that Ankhesenamun would shortly be summoning Horemheb to escort the Hittite prince through the city gates. I believed that Aye was thwarted, that bloodshed was averted, that safe harbour was reached.

I believed wrong.

Chapter Twenty-Seven

The Hittite Letters (2)

The Maya Papyrus, Fragments 411-416

THE MESSENGER *prostrated himself before Ankhesenamun. I was standing by her right side to let him know that I was here as a trusted advisor and that Ankhesenamun was happy to have me hear anything he had to say. However, I was careful to stand a discrete distance from her. I did not want the messenger returning to his prince with news of a rival suitor.*

"May you live," Ankhesenamun said, and the messenger rose to his feet. Without further ceremony, he unrolled a papyrus scroll that he had been carrying under his arm. He cleared his throat and began to read.

"To Her Royal Highness Ankhesenamun, Great Royal Wife and widow of His Majesty Tutankhamun, king of the Two Lands of Upper and Lower Egypt, son of Ra, perfect of diadems, beloved of Amun, may he live. Thus writes His Majesty Šuppiluliumas, king of the Hittites, conqueror of Carchemish:

I send you greetings through this, my humble messenger, and pray that for you all is well. For me all is well. The lands of Hatti and Egypt have never married their sons and daughters to each other. Why do you write to me with words of untruth and deception? Do you think me so naïve to send you one of my sons so that you may imprison him and hold him as a hostage? In this way do you hope to return my conquests to your own dominion? If you wish to recapture Carchemish, send your men to claim it. Do not expect it as a gift for the return of one of my sons. Thus speaks Šuppiluliumas."

The messenger rolled the papyrus and placed it back under his arm. He regarded the throne with a mixture of fear and suspicion. Messengers have been known to be executed for delivering such harsh words. Ankhesenamun ordered no such thing. In fact, she ordered nothing at all. She simply sat, open mouthed, and stared at the messenger.

"But..." she managed to say, and the sound of her voice brought me back to myself, for I fear I had reacted in a way similar to her own.

"The prince does not follow you?" I asked the messenger. It was not the most intelligent question I have ever formulated, and the answer was so obvious that the messenger was slightly at a loss to it.

"Er," he said. "No, er..." He did not know how to address me, and I had neither the time nor the inclination to explain to him the intricacies of life at court, and so I ignored him until his stammerings trailed off.

"Then that will be all," I managed to say. The messenger looked to Ankhesenamun for confirmation. "That will be all!" I snapped, and he made a grateful rush for the door. After he had taken his leave of us we remained silent for a moment. The plan's failure only seemed to accentuate its qualities. It had been such a good plan, I thought. It had not been flawless, but I was yet to come across any political scheme that was. And now it was dashed and with it went our last hopes of success and survival. Neither of us was under any illusion as to the fate that now awaited us. Ankhesenamun would have no choice but to marry Aye, for that was the only way she could possibly avert civil war, and yet in doing so we knew full well that she protected the lives of her people at the expense of her own. There was little chance that Aye would allow her to live once her usefulness had been exhausted. And as for her most trusted advisor, the man who had sided against his own father? The prognosis of my own fate was as grim as that of the woman I served.

I sat down heavily on the steps that led up to Ankhesenamun's throne, and found nothing of value to say.

"Well," Ankhesenamun said, after a significant pause. "I shall just have to ask him again."

I looked up at her. "Again?" I said.

"He does not believe that the offer is a genuine one. He believes it to be a trap. I simply have to convince him that such a view is erroneous, and he will not be able to resist sending a son to me. How could any man resist the throne of Egypt, even at a risk?"

"But how?" I said. "His letter was hardly worded by someone open to persuasion."

"We will find a way," she said.

"We will not," I said.

"Then perhaps your solution is better."

"What solution?" I asked.
"Exactly," she said.

To His Majesty Šuppiluliumas, king of the Hittites, conqueror of Carchemish, may he live. Thus writes Her Royal Highness Ankhesenamun, Great Royal Wife and widow of His Majesty Tutankhamun, king of the Two Lands of Upper and Lower Egypt, son of Ra, perfect of diadems, beloved of Amun, may he live:
Why do you say "They may try to deceive me like that?" You do not believe me and say so even to my face. If I had a son would I write to a kingdom in a manner which is humiliating to me and my country? He who was my husband is dead and a son I have not. Shall I then perhaps take a servant of mine and make him my husband? I have written to no other country. I have written only to you. People say that you have many sons. Give me one of your sons. To me he will be my husband, but in Egypt he will be king. I send to you my most trusted minister. I pray that he may be able to convince you of the truth of my words. Thus says Ankhesenamun.

I was desperately unhappy about the situation and was in something of a stupor as my servants packed my belongings ready for the journey. How had this happened? How did I suddenly find myself about to journey through bandit infested country in the hope of reaching a place even more dangerous? How did I expect to survive an audience with a vicious king who believed my very presence to be a plot to kidnap one of his sons? How in the name of Amun and all the gods had I allowed Ankhesenamun to talk me into this? My first thought had been to enlist the aid of the men with whom I had travelled to Nefertiti's tomb, before I realised with dismay that I did not know on which side they had cast their allegiance and that, even if they had declared their loyalty to Horemheb, I would not be able to ask for his aid without revealing the nature of my mission. I was almost tempted to do so in the knowledge that Horemheb would do everything in his power to prevent me from leaving, but my devotion to Ankhesenamun prevented me from doing anything so underhanded.

In my own defence I was not simply afraid for my own life. I knew I would be away from Thebes for some time, even if I was to return safely, and I was distinctly uncomfortable at the thought of leaving Ankhesenamun so unguarded. Of course, Horemheb would remain, but he could not be expected to be everywhere, and even if he could he was a masterly general but a poor politician, and I worried that he would be on hand to give bad advice in good faith. I could not even advise him of his new duties as Ankhesenamun's lone protector, for he would have wanted to know where I was going and why, and I would be in the same position as if I had asked him for an escort. No, he would find out soon enough. At least I would be beyond his reach when he did so.

I felt terribly alone as Thebes slipped from view around the bends of the Nile. I wondered whether I would ever again see her temples shining in the sunlight, or smell the incense drift from their doorways and windows. I have never felt so dejected, or so afraid.

All too soon, the ship docked in some little town that was not much more than a harbour and a road into the north-western desert. Here was the route I must take. Less a road than a parting of the dunes, it would have been fearsome even if it had not contained the sort of men I had fought in Akhetaten in Nefertiti's tomb. I imagined them skulking behind every bend, of which there were a disconcerting number.

The chariots were loaded up with enough supplies to cross the desert and reach Hatti. There was not enough room to pack enough food and water for the return journey but then there was little point in doing so. Either we would be greeted as friends, in which case we would be supplied with enough to see us through the return journey, or we would be received as enemies, in which case there would be no return journey to make.

Perhaps six or seven chariots set out into the dunes, my own afforded the laughable protection of being in the middle of the train. Each of my retinue was armed, but they had even less experience wielding a sword than had I, and the thought that I was the most battle-hardened fighter amongst us was not one that filled me with confidence. Signs of civilisation quickly disappeared from view, and we rode onwards.

It was three days before we saw another town, although town is perhaps an ambitious word to describe what was essentially a collection of huts which seemed to have huddled together for protection. Still, it was a welcome sight. The previous two nights had been spent in the bitter cold of the remote desert, where the darkness was so complete that it was impossible to tell whether one's eyes were open or closed. If you have not experienced it you will not believe the noises that can be heard in the desert at night. Looking back they were undoubtedly harmless animals and birds, but in the blind night every single one sounded uncannily like a murderous bandit crawling not quite silently towards my throat. By the time we crossed the border and began once more to come across settlements and small towns, I was almost delirious with lack of sleep.

We all had the alarming impression that we were being pushed forwards by forces beyond our control. Each night, as evening fell, we would see campfires in the desert behind us, perhaps a day's march away. We had no idea who they were, but whoever it was, it was a large force. The campfires were numerous, although they were concentrated mainly around the road we had used. Throughout the desert crossing they remained at a constant distance behind us, as though we were being followed by a force more interested in our destination than in preventing us from reaching it.

Once or twice during our passage we saw the lights of campfires in the distance before us as well and we would be forced to alter our route to give them as wide a berth as possible without becoming hopelessly separated from the course we had plotted.

We crossed the border into Hatti and began to yearn for the nights we had spent crossing the Egyptian desert. Here we felt as though our foes were multiplied tenfold, for while the bandits remained, the rest of the populace was hardly likely to welcome us as returning brothers. One consolation was that we seemed to have shaken whoever had been following us since our departure from the Nile. The campfires to our rear did not return once the border had been crossed.

At our first major settlement I presented myself at the nearest barracks and, through sign language and the display of the king's seal, managed to rouse the commander, who escorted me to the nearest official with whom I would be able to communicate. Through my training as a scribe I was fluent, if slightly lacking in practice, in the language of Akkadian, the diplomatic language used between kingdoms.

The official was remarkably more helpful than what I had been led to believe was the Hittite custom and he arranged safe passage for my retinue and I through to Hattusa, the Hittite capital, where I was vigorously assured that I would be granted an audience with King Šuppiluliumas himself. Although this was the very reason for my mission I cannot say that the prospect filled me with joy. His reputation as a fierce and merciless man did not encourage optimistic thoughts for the future. The only thing that prevented me turning and running was the thought of Ankhesenamun and the danger in which I would be placing her if I did not complete my assignment with any degree of success.

We travelled onwards and tried to remain undaunted by the ugly, guttural language spoken around us by our guards. They seemed too alien to be here for our protection and I wondered exactly how far they would be willing to risk themselves in order to protect us should we encounter any hostility on the way to Hattusa.

Everything seemed unfamiliar. This was the first time I had ventured into foreign lands and I was amazed to discover that the architecture was different, that the roads and temples and chariot designs were all outlandish and slightly unnerving. In my naivety I had always assumed that there was only one way of building a house or a temple. Now I realised that there were probably as many different ways as there were kingdoms, and every glance served only to remind me that I was far from home and the comfort of a friendly face.

It was another day and a half on the road before we reached the walls of Hattusa, and a day further before I was summoned to an audience with the king. I expect he knew why I was here and that he was as eager as was I to see how the situation would play out, but it would have been undignified for him to have seen me without delay. He needed to give me the impression that he was a very busy man, and that I was distinctly unimportant compared to his other duties.

Šuppiluliumas' palace was a dark and terrifying place, the inside of which I hope never to see again as long as I draw breath. There were not enough torches along the walls to cast sufficient light, and the low roofed corridors seemed to be knitted from a string of shadows. Every face was a mask of hostility, for word had surely spread that here was the man from Egypt, the hated enemy, the vile kingdom, the place of treachery and deceit. Of course, these were all terms used in Egypt to describe Hatti, but I had no doubt that Šuppiluliumas was a master enough of propaganda to be able to twist history itself to transform the people of the Two Lands into the evildoers and warmongers. The atmosphere did *nothing to alleviate my sense of foreboding. There was no finesse here, no sense of decorum or good manners. Every word was barked, every touch ham-fisted, every request an order.*

By the time I was manhandled into place outside the audience chamber doors I was barely able to keep hold of my panic. When the doors opened I almost fainted. An unexpected hand fell on my shoulder and pushed me forwards, and I finally entered the king's presence with the indignity of a stumble and trip, which I tried to disguise as intentional and lowered myself quickly into a prostrate position.

"Rise," a voice said, and I did so.

Before me, upon his throne, was King Šuppiluliumas. He was a small man whose face was almost obscured by long hair and beard. In one hand he was holding an axe so large that the end of the handle was resting upon the ground by the side of his throne. I was amazed that he had the strength to hold it aloft, for while he was undoubtedly an imposing and frightening figure, he was without doubt the oldest living person I had ever seen. I did not know it was possible to look so ancient. I wondered briefly whether his courtiers had anticipated his death by embalming him early. All I remember besides this were his eyes, which were dark and intense, below eyebrows bushy enough to almost obscure them.

"Speak," he said, in Akkadian.

"Your Majesty," I said, my voice quivering. "I bring you warm greetings from Ankhesenamun, widow of King Tutankhamun, who called you his brother."

Šuppiluliumas snorted at this, but I continued.

"I bring with me a letter from Ankhesenamun, who greets you as your sister."

I read him the letter, throughout which he did not so much as blink. When I finished I rolled the papyrus up and placed it under my arm. Šuppiluliumas did not speak, thereby creating a silence I felt compelled to fill.

"Your Majesty," I said. "If I may be so bold I would like to speak on behalf of your friend, Ankhesenamun. She is a woman alone in the world. Her husband has died in the first bloom of his manhood, and her two children were taken from her in the womb. There is nobody in the kingdom she can trust to take the reins of power from her hands. She is a woman. She is too weak to hold them for herself."

This was nothing that Šuppiluliumas had not been told in the letters, and he was beginning to look bored.

"But," I added. "There is one man. One man alone feels able to challenge for the Egyptian throne. And what is more, he is a man with the strength and intelligence to take it. Although this man is cunning and courageous, he is also warlike."

Šuppiluliumas raised his formidable eyebrows at this, but again said nothing. I realised I was dealing with a man who regarded openness as a sign of weakness. I was more than happy to appear weak to him if it was needed to make my point.

"This is a man who regards the world entire as being his for the taking. He is afraid of neither man nor god, and perhaps with good reason. He is a general with an expertise that is unprecedented in either Egypt or her enemies."

"I too fear no man," Šuppiluliumas said.

"Just so," I said. "From the tales I have heard of your daring and heroism and your prowess on the battlefield I would be honoured indeed to meet a man worthy of your fear. Yet I have heard also of your intelligence and wisdom, and I know further that a man with such attributes would be able to assess a threat and act accordingly. Imagine if you would, Your Most Gracious Majesty, your son on the throne of Egypt, this man of which I speak devoid of power and influence, Egypt no longer a threat and an enemy, but a friend and ally. Think of the power and strength of a Hatti standing shoulder to shoulder with Egypt instead of sword to sword."

I could tell by this stage that I had managed to tease his interest. I was feeding him fantasies that few kings would be able to resist, and I had been brought up to believe that Šuppiluliumas was a king whose hunger for power was unrivalled even amongst kings, who are hardly known for their indifference towards pre-eminence.

"I have heard," I continued, eager to feed the fire, "that your sons are also brave and wise men."

"True," he said.

"And that each of them would regard the throne of Egypt as almost as great an honour as the throne of the great Hatti herself."

"True," Šuppiluliumas conceded.

"And that each of them, being sons of Šuppiluliumas, would laugh in the face of any danger they may encounter along the way."

"You know," Šuppiluliumas said, "that if this is a trap I shall march upon Egypt in numbers to smother a swarm of locusts. If harm were to befall any son of mine at the hands of Egypt I would not rest until your entire kingdom was reduced to being a hole in the sand. Your men I would kill without a second thought. Your women would be given to my soldiers for their own entertainments and your children would become my slaves. If any son of mine were to be taken as a hostage to persuade me towards mercy I would consider him dead and I would level your country with a sweep of my hand. Do not think that I am not aware of the state of your armed forces after the reign of Tutankhamun's father. Any attempt on my behalf to subjugate your kingdom would be costly for my own troops, but I would consider even the elimination of my army as a small price in the face of such an insult."

I sensed that this may have been the longest speech of Šuppiluliumas' life, and that furthermore I was honoured to have heard it. It impressed me with the gravity of his thoughts on the matter.

"I can assure Your Majesty," I said, "that your son will be treated as Egypt's king from the moment he steps into the kingdom. You have the word not only of myself, but of Her Royal Highness Ankhesenamun. There is nothing else I can offer you."

Šuppiluliumas lapsed into silence again, but it was the silence of thought and I did not dare interrupt. After a moment he spoke again.

"I have decided," he said. "It is a prize worth the risk."

I sagged with relief.

"You may rest in my palace tonight," he continued, "and I shall gather together an armed escort. You will accompany my son and the escort back to Egypt. I shall expect to hear within the month that he has arrived safely and has been ensconced upon the throne. Any other news will be met with my wrath."

I bowed. "Your Majesty's wisdom is unparalleled," I said, and gratefully took my leave.

We left Hattusa the following morning with an armed escort of roughly thirty men, all of whom I was told were from the king's own elite guards. The prince's retinue numbered anything up to seventy-five, and I was informed that these were only those who had been able to come at such short notice. Another hundred or so were packing up the prince's considerable belongings ready to bring over once he was installed in Thebes.

The prince himself was a slight man, hardly credible as the son of his father. Where the king was fierce and imposing, the prince was softly spoken and seemed rather overawed by the position into which he had been unexpectedly thrust. His name was Zannanzash. I rather gathered that this was not the king's most able son. If this indeed was a trap, he did not wish to risk those with genuine talent for rule.

It was three weeks since I had left Thebes. I prayed that the situation had not changed in my absence. A lot can happen in three weeks.

Aye was in the midst of his army. He felt secure and confident and, he had to admit, not a little smug. The morning had dawned like any other since the standoff between his army and that of Horemheb's had begun, with little to suggest that the day may develop into anything other than the usual dull slog towards nightfall. Up until this morning his spirits had begun to drop. He may have been a warrior and a man hardy enough to endure a campaign, but the inescapable fact remained that he was also now an old man. It was painful to remain seated for too long, and the cold of the night seemed to ignore his parchment skin and chill his old bones directly. Things only became clear to his eyes if they were held a precise distance from his head. It was a considerable effort to either push himself out of or lower himself into a chair. There was no longer any denying that living in the field among the troops, while initially exhilarating, was an occupation designed for much younger men. He missed the comfort of his quarters. He missed the warmth of his bedchamber and the lavishness of his furnishings. He missed decent food. He missed the refreshing coolness of tiles beneath his feet in the heat of the day.

Now, though, something had happened. Something that gave him the opportunity of action, if only by proxy. Something that told him exactly how the enemy were thinking. Something he thought he could thwart with a snap of his fingers.

Aye had men in the city. They were few and they were not in positions of power, for all of those men were loyal to Ankhesenamun. Still, he had men, and it was better than nothing.

One of Aye's men was Tjanni, an old soldier who eked out a living down at the city's docks, loading and unloading ships for donations of food. His military career had been brought to an ignominious halt after his arrest in Akhetaten by Mahu's men, who had been reliably informed by another prisoner that Tjanni had been overheard making drunken and disparaging remarks about Akhenaten and Nefertiti. Tjanni was duly paid a visit in his barracks in the third watch of the night, and dragged, confused and protesting, onto a chariot which transported him to the police station, whereupon his shins were beaten with clubs until he named the men with whom he had been in discussion when he insulted the royal couple.

He survived only because Mahu lost his influence with the inner circles of court before Tjanni's execution was scheduled, and he was freed to return to his old life. There were, however, few places available in the army for a man who had been beaten so viciously that he walked with a pronounced limp and needed to rest every few paces. He gradually gravitated towards the docks, where he joined the ranks of the crippled and unemployable, sleeping in warehouses and begging or earning bread from those embarking and disembarking from the ships.

Tjanni had no love of the royal family.

He had not recognised the first messenger who left with the letter for Šuppiluliumas. He could not be expected to; he was as far as it was possible to get from the palace corridors where he might have been expected to have seen the messenger before.

He did, however, recognise another man when he came down to the docks some time later, also to embark upon a ship, with chariots and a retinue to accompany him. Tjanni found this most interesting, and there was little doubt in his heart that it was something of which Aye would wish to be informed.

He made his way to Aye's camp, where he was ushered in immediately to see Aye, who took his report, asked one or two questions and then thanked him and sent him for a good meal.

Aye called his generals to him and discussed the matter briefly. The reasons for a senior member of court to travel northwards were few, the most likely being an attempt to gather reinforcements.

"Nakhtmin," Aye said. "You know your brother. Perhaps you would like to follow him? You will recognise him as well as any. Furthermore, you will, perhaps, have some insight into the workings of his mind. Follow him. Discover his intentions. Whatever they are, I expect you to thwart him using whatever means you see fit."

"Consider it done, father," Nakhtmin said.

"I shall, Nakhtmin. I shall."

Nakhtmin took his men northwards as soon as they had been gathered into their units. There were two hundred of them altogether, packed onto ships which they boarded north of the city. Maya was a day's travel ahead of them.

They stopped at each town they came across, asking pertinent questions of those expected to know the answers, but they were in the far north of Egypt before receiving the replies they were looking for. They disembarked and prepared for a journey across the desert.

Maya crossed the border before Nakhtmin was able to catch him and Nakhtmin knew better than to take Egyptian soldiers onto Hittite territory. He doubted they would be seen again. Still, the fact that Maya had not held such qualms himself was an intriguing one. Nakhtmin set up an encampment and waited. There were, he thought, two possibilities. Either Maya would return with an army of Hittites at his back, which Nakhtmin thought at best to be unlikely, or he would not return at all. Nakhtmin knew that Maya was far from being a warrior. Perhaps he had simply fled Egypt altogether.

When Nakhtmin's patrols reported that Maya had been seen once more, and that he was now accompanied by a handful of soldiers and a much increased retinue, Nakhtmin was confused about everything except his duty. *Whatever his mission is*, Aye had said, *you must thwart it.*

He drew his men into ranks in order to address them.

The Maya Papyrus, Fragments 420-424

> *I felt much safer on the return leg. Not only was I surrounded by men who were numerous and trustworthy enough to protect us (or, at least, to protect their prince, which amounted to the same thing), but I had my journey's end in sight. I could almost smell the Theban incense on the warm breezes that blew from the tops of the dunes.*
>
> *I spent much of the journey at Zannanzash's side. He knew a limited amount of Akkadian, enough at least to enable us to conduct rudimentary conversations. By the second day I had begun teaching him Egyptian in the hope that he would have enough in his vocabulary by the time we reached court to greet Ankhesenamun and make favourable comments about her beauty. He was a remarkably fast learner.*
>
> *In him I saw much of myself. Neither of us were fighters, and so we were both slightly disdained in cultures where the sword is the most honourable of men's tools, and we had both compensated for this by the exercise of our minds. Like me, he was*

a man who had been thrust into a life with which he was not comfortable, but to which he felt duty bound to be true. Like me, he was frightened. I warmed to him immediately.

We crossed back into Egypt on the third night, and I noted that the distant campfires had not returned, confirming that whoever had been following us on the outward journey had either lost our trail and disappeared or had been dissuaded from further action by the size of our force. I went to my bed content. Content that I was relatively safe, that I was returning home, that I had completed my mission. Content that I would soon see Ankhesenamun again, and be able to provide her with the protection of a husband.

For the first time since leaving Thebes, I slept soundly and was not troubled by anxious dreams.

When I was awoken by a scream, therefore, the shock was all the greater, and I shot from my bed as though fired from a bow. There was a brief moment when, the scream seeming to have no sequel, I began to believe that the noise had existed only in my dreams, before I heard the fearful whispers of my retinue around me in the dark and the shouting of orders in Hittite from the royal guards. Everything was chaos. The fire I had fallen asleep nearby had collapsed into embers and I saw only legs as they flitted by, glowing red with reflected light. I groped for my sword, feeling little of the protection that it afforded me, and shouted for Zannanzash. He appeared at my side, looking as frightened as I was feeling.

Suddenly the noise of battle erupted around me. Sword clanged against sword, men screamed and cried, bodies fell into the sand. As my eyes grew accustomed to the dark I began to be able to make out shadows and figures in the glow of our campfires. We were obviously surrounded. I could see hordes of men around the periphery of our camp, pushing inwards, slowed only fractionally by the defence of the Hittite guards, who were valiant but hopelessly outnumbered. I grabbed Zannanzash's wrist and searched desperately for an opening in the ranks of those who assaulted us. There were too many of them, and no such opening presented itself. I had no option but to drag Zannanzash towards the centre of the camp, which was as far from our attackers as it was possible to be.

There we waited, for want of any alternative. The guards before us were falling, rank after rank, before the relentless tide of men marching into them. Swords flashed red in the firelight as they rose and fell. The noise grew more chaotic. For the first time I saw that the men who attacked us were Egyptian soldiers. I prepared myself to embrace death and tried to hold at bay the grip of panic. I barely succeeded, and felt the pressure of a pointless scream for help rising in my throat, despite the fact that all available help was currently being given and it was having a negligible effect. At some point I lost my hold of Zannanzash. I found myself spinning as the soldiers closed in, still searching out some avenue of escape and still failing. Beside me, Zannanzash had started to scream, and this, together with the arrival of a sword wielding Egyptian soldier into our circle of light, was the trigger that unleashed my own terror. I began to scream in unison.

As the soldier stepped forwards my scream seemed to transform itself in my throat and became a cry not of fear but of anger. To have travelled so far, I thought, to have surmounted so many obstacles, to be murdered here by my own countrymen. I knew them immediately for what they were; Aye's men sent to destroy Ankhesenamun's last hope. How they had found us was not a question with which I currently troubled myself. The irony of the situation, the sheer injustice of it all, suddenly consumed me. I was transported back to the tombs of Akhetaten, to the glory of my conflict with those who would have denied Nefertiti her right to an afterlife, and I suddenly knew what I had to do.

I stepped forwards, shaking now more with righteous anger than with fear. My assailant was standing by the fire, illuminated only to the waistband of his kilt. He approached to meet me. Behind me, Zannanzash continued to cry and weep for his life.

"Have at you," I said, quietly, more to myself than my enemy, and leaped into action, a war cry in my throat.

The soldier raised his sword and batted me with the flat of the blade. My own sword flew from my grasp and I toppled sideways, landing with my face within searing distance of the embers of the campfire. The soldier stepped forwards again to stand over myself and Zannanzash, his sword raised above his head, the blade pointed perpendicular to the ground, ready to stick us both.

The blade came down and plunged into the sand, a hand's breadth from my face. I cried out.

"Who is this?" a voice said.

"He is Prince Zannanzash," I gasped. "His father is Šuppiluliumas, who demands safe passage for his son on pain of war."

I thought this may be some deterrent to murder.

"Really?" the voice said. "Interesting." The blade was removed from the sand and then brought down with considerable force on what I assume was Zannanzash's neck. At any rate, it was a blow forceful and accurate enough to silence his cries and splash his blood onto my leg. The sword was retrieved from its victim and raised again.

I drew up my knees and wrapped my arms around my head, as though this would have been any protection for me. And yet the blow did not come. I remained motionless for some time before risking a movement of my head to glance up at the man who would be my murderer. He was standing as though posing for a sculptor, his sword raised above his head, poised to strike at me. I cried out again and put my head back under the nominal protection of my arms.

Still, nothing. What torture was this? Was he playing with me? Did he enjoy the fear as much as the death?

I glanced up again, and the sword came down. But it came down slowly, and not towards me. Instead, the soldier leant forward, close enough for me to make out his features for the first time.

"I cannot do it," Nakhtmin said. "Run."

News concerning the death of Zannanzash spread quickly in two directions. Nakhtmin sent runners southwards to inform Aye of Ankhesenamun's latest gambit, and the failure thereof. They were received like sons and then sent back to Nakhtmin with the news that he had been declared his father's official heir to celebrate such a monumental achievement. Aye was under no illusions as to the importance of the victory over the Hittite incursion. It was such a desperate attempt by Ankhesenamun to disarm him that it could only be her last chance. If she had any other alternatives she would have tried them a long time before inviting a foreign prince – and a Hittite prince at that – into the country. Aye knew as soon as the glorious news reached him that Ankhesenamun was now a spent force. There had been little bloodshed, and none that truly mattered, and suddenly the conflict was over.

He sent messengers immediately into the city under flags of truce to take the news directly to the palace. He demanded Ankhesenamun's promise of her hand and Horemheb's immediate demobilisation.

Ankhesenamun received the men with a sense of foreboding. She doubted that they were here to announce Aye's surrender. As they relayed the news she felt the strength flow from her limbs and was glad that she had not received it whilst standing. After they had advised her of the situation they issued Aye's demands, but Ankhesenamun barely heard them.

"What news of Maya?" she asked them.

"We have none, Your Royal Highness," they replied.

Horemheb was at her side. He had received news of the mission to Hatti without comment. The thin line of his mouth was comment enough. She turned to him.

"General," she said. "Your advice?"

Horemheb cleared his throat and stared at the floor, his hands clasped tightly behind his back.

"None that you would wish to hear," he said, quietly. "We have lost. Should Your Highness wish it I will fight, and I shall do so gladly with Your Highness' name on my lips, but I will lose. We concede now or we concede later. It is Your Highness' command."

"Tell your master that we accede to his demands," she said to the messengers. "Our troops will return to the city. Aye has my word that he may return to the palace with safe passage."

"And your hand, Your Highness?"

"Betrothed to my grandfather," Ankhesenamun said, and shuddered.

News also travelled northwards. However thorough Nakhtmin's troops were, the night was simply too dark to prevent a handful of men escaping with their lives. None of the Hittite guards survived, but some of Zannanzash's retinue did, scattered though they were in every direction. Most were at least wounded, and almost all of these died over the ensuing days under the desert sun, lost and bewildered, wandering whichever way they happened to be facing. Others fell prey to bandits or lions. A small number, though, escaped unharmed, and a smaller handful still managed to make their way back northwards towards Hatti.

Within a week almost every available Hittite soldier, whipped into a frenzy of patriotic pride and nationalistic zeal, was marching purposefully towards the Egyptian border.

Chapter Twenty-Eight

A Wedding, Of Sorts

AYE ENSURED that there was little delay in the execution of his plans. His troops marched into Thebes the same day that Ankhesenamun signalled her acquiescence.

His chariot swept into the palace courtyard and came to a halt at the doors, which were opened without comment or expression by the guards, who knew enough about politics to avoid alienating those who appeared to be in the ascendancy.

Aye found Ankhesenamun in the audience chamber with Horemheb at her side. He made a point of making no bow before the throne.

"It appears that you have won," Ankhesenamun said.

Aye smiled. "It appears so," he said. "But please try not to look upon this as victory for one side or defeat for another. This is simply victory. For all of us. For Egypt. You need to understand that if our marriage is going to be a success."

Ankhesenamun winced.

"Is there any news of Maya?" she asked.

"I have not heard any," Aye said. "Horemheb, you are remaining remarkably quiet."

"I do not have a great deal to say," Horemheb said.

"Will you baulk at prostrating yourself before me, General?"

"I shall prostrate myself before my king," Horemheb said. "It is not a soldier's prerogative to judge the fitness of a king, only to serve to the best of his ability."

"I suppose I would be naïve to expect anything more," Aye said. "But you are an able general, Horemheb. Egypt needs your loyalty." He turned to Ankhesenamun. "Now, to the wedding. It must be a public affair. There must be not a man in the kingdom who is not aware of it, and who is not entirely confident that you enter into it without hesitation or reservation. That said, it must happen quickly. It is a shame that Maya is not with us. He has a flair for this sort of thing. Still, I am sure we will cope. The wedding will take place in three days' time. That should be enough time to organise some rudimentary public celebrations. My coronation will take place at the same time."

Ankhesenamun gasped.

"But my husband is not yet entombed," she said.

"I am aware of that," Aye said.

"Then how can you hope to take his crown? It is unprecedented for a king to assume the throne before his predecessor is in his tomb."

"Then, my dear, we must break with tradition," Aye said. "There is not a moment to lose. There is little point in me pretending that my case for the throne is any stronger than it is. I will officiate at Tutankhamun's funeral not as heir but as pharaoh. Who can modify tradition for his own ends if not the king?"

The celebrations were indeed rudimentary, but their lavishness or otherwise was no concern of Aye's. The fact that they were public and prominent was enough. Banners were raised around the entire city proclaiming the marriage. Rings were cast portraying the happy couple in profile and distributed to members of court. Wine and beer poured from the temples and the people soon forgot their misgivings, at least temporarily. A stage was constructed outside the palace gates from which Ankhesenamun and Aye waved to the crowds and watched regiments of soldiers march past.

Once the people were gathered in sufficient numbers, and the wine had flowed in sufficient quantity, the High Priest of Amun and some of his most respected acolytes took to the stage. The High Priest carried before him the blue crown of Upper and Lower Egypt and knelt with it held at arms' length before Aye's throne.

The crowd cheered as the crown was placed atop his head, and Aye surveyed the people who were arranged before him. He concentrated for a moment on the weight of the crown upon his head, for it was deceptively heavy, and revelled in the feel of it.

He wondered whether his mother was looking on from the underworld. Aye felt a tear threaten to spill from his eye and smudge his meticulously applied face paint. He turned to smile at his new wife but she pretended not to notice and continued staring impassively into the crowd.

The Maya Papyrus, Fragments 431-442

> *I ran. I was able to find my way between the combatants who were now somewhat scattered in the chase for victims, out into*

the darkness of the desert. Luckily, panicked though I was, I retained enough clarity of mind not to allow my legs to carry me too far. I cleared two or three dunes before I felt safe enough to stop, and there I waited. I discovered later that most of the other survivors ran until exhaustion stopped them, and then found themselves hopelessly lost. They did not have a hope of finding civilisation and almost to a man they were never seen again.

I, on the other hand, knew that the troops would not remain behind for long after their victims were rendered limbless and lifeless. I prayed that they would leave our chariots and horses unmolested.

By the break of day I was sure that all sound from the camp had ceased and I crawled back towards it, tense in preparation to turn and run should my ears be lulling me into misguided optimism. As I crested the last dune I could see corpses strewn in various degrees of mutilation over the entire camp. Not a man remained alive.

The soldiers had released the horses from where they had been tied for the night but had not been too enthusiastic about shooing them away. One or two remained within sight, looking slightly lost and bewildered. My own horse was nowhere to be seen and so I picked the healthiest and fastest looking of the specimens available and harnessed him to the nearest chariot. I was probably closer to Hatti than Egypt, but guessed that showing myself there would be more suicidal than remaining where I was and waiting to die. I urged my horse to a gallop and let him rest only when it appeared that he was about to collapse from exhaustion. Despite my cruelty he served me well and I was at some nameless border town by nightfall. I made for the nearest occupied building, hammered on the door and collapsed. I am told that the priests and physicians of the town were not able to revive me until late into the following morning.

I had no idea, at this stage, exactly what had happened, but I did know that the men who had attacked us were Egyptian soldiers and that my brother Nakhtmin commanded them, so I could not assume that we were a randomly chosen target. Still, this knowledge only served to accentuate my uneasiness, and I did not feel that I could in good conscience allow myself to rest while disaster and tragedy may be befalling my friends in Thebes. As soon as I had gathered the strength to rise from my sick bed I commandeered a chariot and made my way back to the Nile with all the speed that my desert ravaged constitution would allow, where I found the ship that had brought us from Thebes patiently awaiting our return at the water's edge. I was informed by the captain that nobody else had returned and I was reluctantly obliged to order him to set sail without waiting to see if any survivors followed behind me.

The ship arrived in Thebes within the week. I could see from the prow as we approached the harbour that a significant change had taken place in my absence. There were no distant regiments of soldiers stationed in the desert around the town and as I made my way through the city streets to the palace there was no atmosphere of claustrophobia among the people. The tension had been lifted.

I was barely through the palace gates when I was called in to an audience with my father. It was a bizarre experience, having to prostrate myself before him, and he left me on the floor just long enough to make an obscure point about power and surrender.

"May you live," he said, eventually, and I rose to my feet.

"I am glad that you are alive," he said.

"Despite ordering my death?" I asked him, with a certain amount of courage. His imposing nature was hardly weakened by the sight of him in a crown.

"I did no such thing," he said, and I almost found myself apologising for the accusation. "I merely ordered your brother to prevent the success of your treachery. Had I explicitly ordered your death I doubt you would be here to accuse me of it."

"Yes, father," I said.

"You may refer to me as Your Majesty," he replied.

"Yes, Your Majesty," I said, the words passing through my throat as easily as a handful of sand.

"You know that I have named your brother as heir?"

"I know nothing about anything, Your Majesty. I have come straight from the ship."

"Does it trouble you?"

"Nakhtmin? Not in the least, Your Majesty. I can assure you that I have no designs on the throne."

"Very good, Maya. It pleases me to hear it. You will forgive me if I do not believe you?"

"Just so, Your Majesty, but I can assure you that nothing would cause me greater grief than to wear the crown of Egypt."

I was telling him the truth. Despite the rewards it bequeathed its occupant, the throne seemed to be far too hazardous an employment for the likes of me. I was far happier where I was. Or, at least, I would have been with a different master.

"And do you feel comparable grief with the current situation?" he asked me.

Of course, the question was a trap. What was I to say? Could I deny it when he knew full well that I had travelled to Hatti to employ a foreign prince in the position he coveted?

"I am delighted that the prospect of civil war has been averted," I said.

Aye laughed. "You are as fine a politician as any man I have met," he said. "And I do not forget that you are my son. There is a place for you in this court should you feel able to take it. I cannot pretend that we will not view each other with a degree of suspicion at first, but I daresay you will not find me as fearsome a king as some of those under whom you have served."

"I am greatly honoured, Your Majesty," I said, bowing.

"Does that mean you accept, Maya?" he asked me.

"Just so, Your Majesty," I said.

"Excellent. Then you may take charge of the arrangements for Tutankhamun's funeral. But I would ask you, Maya, to bear in mind that this is something of an untraditional event. It might be preferable to keep it as low key as possible. There would be little point in drawing attention to its more unconventional aspects."

I bowed my way from the room.

The funeral was eventually attended by just eight people. There were no weeping crowds, no lines of women in mourning throwing dirt over their heads, no caravan of chariots and honour guards. Only myself, Ankhesenamun, Horemheb and Aye were there, together with the High Priest of Amun and three of his acolytes, who were to assist in some of the rituals. For the first time since Creation, a reigning pharaoh carried out the opening of the mouth ceremony on his predecessor while those of us in attendance waited nervously for the offended wrath of Amun to collapse the tomb around our ears.

After the necessary rituals had been carried out, Aye made no secret of his desire to return to the city. The priests followed him, leaving myself, Horemheb and Ankhesenamun to quietly offer respect to our friend, husband and king. I had prepared a simple meal and brought it with me from the city. After Aye and the priests had left, the three of us sat outside Tutankhamun's tomb while workmen sealed it forever, and shared this simple repast

together in silence. What we did not eat I buried, as a final
offering to my friend.

Reports began to arrive in Thebes of attacks along the length of the north
western border by Hittite forces. Every available soldier, and, moreover,
thousands of men who had never before lifted a sword, were sent
northwards by ship to intercept the incursions. Šuppiluliumas had been as
good as his word. Every settlement the Hittite soldiers came across was
burned to the ground, its men killed and its women and children marched
back to Hatti, where they would spend the rest of their days as slaves and
paupers, seeing neither their families nor their homeland again.

Aye appointed Horemheb and Nakhtmin as generals in command of
the armed forces in the field. He expressed his regret that he could not
accompany them, but the frailty of his advanced years, while no handicap
to strong rule, may have proved to be something of a burden on the
battlefield. He was somewhat uneasy about returning Horemheb to
command but then he did not feel that he had the luxury of a choice in the
matter. The Hittite attacks were so numerous and unrelenting that even
men with Horemheb's unreliable history, and especially men with
Horemheb's undeniable military talents, were indispensable in the face of
such a vast invasion force. He would simply have to trust that Horemheb's
loyalty to his country was enough to supplement his lack of loyalty to the
king.

Aye's trust was not misplaced. Horemheb was delighted to be posted
to the front. He was happy to fight for anyone, as long as his enemies were
Egypt's enemies.

There were a number of generals in the field but Horemheb and
Nakhtmin were by far the most powerful. Out of the two of them,
Nakhtmin naturally assumed overall command, as was fitting for the heir
to the throne. He knew better, though, than to refuse to seek Horemheb's
opinions on any number of military matters.

They were quartered near to each other in a small town near the
border. It had been a day of desperate fighting. They were both filthy with
the sand of the desert, and both caked in blood, some of which was their
own. They sat together in silence while their attendants cleaned the grime
of battle from them and applied rudimentary dressings to their wounds.
Only their hunger was keeping the two men awake.

Food was brought for them and they dissected the day's events while
they ate. Once the table had begun to look less like a meal and more like

the results of the day's fighting, both men sat back, their hands on their stomachs and contented smiles upon their faces.

"Of course," Nakhtmin said, "there is so much more at stake for me now."

"More than what?" Horemheb asked. "I fail to see how the stakes could be any higher than they already are."

"I think you must be forgetting," Nakhtmin said. "This is my land that we are fighting for."

"And mine also," Horemheb said, knowing full well what Nakhtmin was driving at but finding it much more enjoyable to play the ignoramus.

"No," Nakhtmin said. "You do not understand. It is my land not because I merely live in it, but because I am due to inherit it."

"Ah, yes, of course," Horemheb said. "You are quite correct. I had forgotten."

Nakhtmin snorted a laugh. "You had done nothing of the sort," he said. "A man does not forget when he is addressing the heir to the throne."

"Not at all," Horemheb said. "To me, you will always be the little boy who was once roundly scolded by the child Akhenaten."

Nakhtmin sat forwards. "You are doing this deliberately, are you not?"

"What?" Horemheb said, accentuating the innocence in his voice. What had started as a harmless game had suddenly become much more, and he had no real idea why.

"You know," Nakhtmin said. "Protocol demands that you refer to me as Your Royal Highness."

Horemheb raised his eyebrows. "Does it indeed?" he said.

"You know it does."

"Oh, Nakhtmin," Horemheb said, in the tone of voice that he might use to address a confused child. "Please try not to forget yourself. You are addressing Horemheb, with whom you have grown from boyhood. Anyway, you do realise, do you not, that you will never actually wear the crown?"

"Really?" Nakhtmin said, now as annoyed by Horemheb's air of condescension as Horemheb was annoyed by his air of superiority. "And what fantasy enables you to come to such a bizarre conclusion in the face of all the facts?"

"Only," Horemheb said, "that your father has a young and nubile bride."

"And what of it?"

"Nakhtmin," Horemheb said. "Just suppose for a moment that by some freak occurrence, you were to die in battle tomorrow. Who would be heir to the throne then?"

Nakhtmin thought about it for a moment. "Well," he said. "Maya, I presume."

"Exactly," Horemheb said. "And do you think that such a prospect affords your father secure and untroubled dreams?"

"Not especially," Nakhtmin said, pensively.

"And should Aye ensure the successful continuation of his line on the throne by producing sons with Ankhesenamun, do you not think that, having royal blood on both sides, they would take precedence over you?"

Nakhtmin sat back and stared at the floor in thought. Horemheb smiled to himself. It was never unpleasant to deflate an oversized ego.

"And so," Horemheb said, unable to prevent himself from pressing home his point, "I do not address you as Royal Highness, because I think it a little premature."

Nakhtmin's gaze rose from the floor to meet that of Horemheb. His look of perplexity had been replaced by one of barely suppressed anger, and Horemheb's smile faded.

All of a sudden, he realised what he had done.

The Maya Papyrus, Fragments 453-459

> *It became evident later that our victory over the Hittite invaders was due to equal parts of luck and courage. It is unquestioned that our generals outsmarted the enemy as much as our rank and file outfought them, but we also had considerable help from an unlikely source, without which it is doubtful whether Egypt would have survived.*
>
> *It seems that the plague which had blighted our cities and decimated our people was indeed sent from the gods. The general belief at the time of its first manifestation was that Amun had sent it as punishment for his dethroning at the hands of Akhenaten, and that belief was only reinforced when it became apparent that those who fell captive to the Hittites somehow took with them Amun's Revenge and handed it unknowingly to those who had taken them. Before very long the Hittite forces were lying dead not from the wounds of Egyptian swords but the wounds of Egyptian gods, who were not content to allow the taking of their lands and peoples by such barbarians. They had no choice but to withdraw.*
>
> *But Amun was still not content. His revenge followed the Hittite soldiers as they retreated to their own lands, so that it*

could find their strongholds and seats of power. It followed them all the way back to Hattusa itself, where they led it to the palace of the king. Some months after the last of the Hittites were chased from our lands, news reached the palace that Šuppiluliumas himself had succumbed, and was no more.

I was called in to see Aye after the worst of his hangover had passed. Despite his age he had celebrated our victory with as much gusto as any man in the city.

He had held a number of audiences by this stage, but I continued to view them with an unshakable sense of trepidation. He was still suspicious of me – as I suppose he was right to be, considering what happened later – but he allowed himself to trust my judgement on matters that were not related directly to the throne. He allowed me to continue in my role as overseer of the treasury, but he also let me know that he was periodically checking my work to ensure that I was not tipping the balance of my books away from him and towards the temples.

On this occasion, as with many before and since, I believe that he was not consulting me for advice. Rather, he just wished for his own opinion to be reinforced. It was my job merely to agree with him in a way that sounded as though I was doing so of my own free will. Subtle as Aye could be, it was rarely a difficult task to detect exactly which answers he wished to hear.

"Do you think perhaps that public opinion is swinging in my favour?" he asked me.

"Surely, Your Majesty," I said, "public opinion has never been anything but firmly in your favour."

"Do not patronise me, Maya."

"No, Your Majesty."

"Do you think it possible for me to capitalise on this newfound popularity?"

"Not only possible but wise, Your Majesty."

"But how best to accomplish it?"

I saw an opportunity to rid the court of his presence for a while, and I assumed that not only would I enjoy his absence, but that the rest of court would thank me for it.

"Perhaps Your Majesty would consider a short tour of the major cities. It would perhaps also be beneficial to your health to relax aboard the royal ship for a week or two. You could announce the victory in Memphis and Heliopolis and anywhere else it took your fancy to stay. It would be an opportunity to introduce yourself to the people with the best possible news."

"A capital idea, Maya," he said. "Organise it with all due haste."

I bowed.

"Oh, and Maya," he said. "While Nakhtmin is still at the border I shall need you to accompany me."

I tried not to sag.

By the time Nakhtmin and Horemheb returned to Thebes, Aye had already set out upon his tour. The two generals found nobody to whom they could make their official report other than Ankhesenamun. They were shown into the audience chamber to find her upon her throne.

"Your Royal Highness," Horemheb said, and bowed. Nakhtmin shot him an angry glance before doing the same.

"May you live, saviours of Egypt," Ankhesenamun said, smiling.

"Too kind," Horemheb said. Nakhtmin said nothing.

"I must apologise for the king's absence," Ankhesenamun said. "He has asked me to greet you in his name until his return."

"To be greeted by one so fair is consolation enough," Horemheb said. He gave her his report and his assurance that the Hittite force was spent.

Throughout, Nakhtmin remained silent. After Ankhesenamun had once again expressed her thanks for their steadfastness, the two men bowed from the room.

"I do not like her," Nakhtmin said.

"What is there not to like?" Horemheb asked him, already knowing the answer.

"Who does she think she is?" Nakhtmin asked. "She is nothing but an upstart."

"Need I remind you that she is your father's wife, and Egypt's Great Royal Wife?" Horemheb said.

"Hardly," Nakhtmin said. "She is a usurper."

"A usurper?" Horemheb exclaimed. "A usurper of what? The throne that she has been married to twice? Your throne, which you have not yet been robbed of?"

"When my father returns I shall have to speak to him," Nakhtmin said. "This business of the succession troubles me."

"That would be prudent," Horemheb said. "But in the meantime, please remember Ankhesenamun's position. It is not one you can rally against with any hope of success. She is, after all, your father's path to the throne."

That night Nakhtmin allowed himself to fall under the influence of copious amounts of wine. He was unable to shake the strange feeling that he had been cheated of something. He drank alone, his spite matching pace with his inebriation. By the time that he had begun to feel nauseous he had picked up his knife and begun to pass it from hand to hand, watching the light from the lamps along the walls of his bedchamber glinting along its edge.

Before long the dance of light began to make him feel dizzy and he put the knife down.

How dare she? he thought to himself, slightly confused about the actual chronology of events. *How dare she steal my throne from me?*

He picked the knife up again and unsteadily pushed himself from his chair. The room span for a moment and he had to put out his hand to steady himself. Once he had found his equilibrium he marched from the room, banging his shoulder against the door frame on the way, and made his way down the corridors. He passed one or two servants, each of whom had experienced or heard tell of Nakhtmin's drunkenness enough to avoid his gaze and his path, their eyes safely averted until he was out of sight around the nearest corner.

As he neared Ankhesenamun's quarters the servants began to be outnumbered by the guards, although the soldiers were, if anything, less likely to confront him. Outside the doors to Ankhesenamun's room were standing two more guards, who drew themselves up to their straightest posture as they recognised the man who approached them.

"Ankhesenamun is at home?" Nakhtmin said, stopping before them.

"Yes, sir, but she is..."

"Then I shall see her."

"Sir, Her Royal Highness has retired for the evening."

"I said I shall see her. Do you presume to decide whom she sees, and when?"

"No, sir," the guard said, somewhat at a loss as to the proper protocol in this situation. "I shall announce you."

He turned to open the door before feeling a hand grasp his shoulder and pull him to one side.

"I shall announce myself," Nakhtmin growled, and was through the door before either guard was able to protest.

He found Ankhesenamun in bed, but not asleep. Startled, she drew the bedclothes around her as though in the belief that they offered her some protection.

"Nakhtmin," she said. "What is wrong? Has something happened?"

"Perhaps you could tell me," he said. He made to move towards the bed but did not see the step leading into the bedchamber and he tripped on it and fell heavily, sprawling across the floor.

"You are drunk," Ankhesenamun said.

Nakhtmin took some time to climb back to his feet.

"Of course I am drunk," he said. He was now standing by the bed. He held his arms wide and swayed for a moment. "Look at me," he said. "Do you blame me for being drunk? For seeking consolation from every source?"

"I do not understand," Ankhesenamun said.

Nakhtmin leant forward.

"I know what you are doing," he whispered, and straightened up again.

"I am not doing anything," Ankhesenamun said.

Nakhtmin chuckled and waved his index finger in the air. "I *know*," he said. "Do you think me stupid? Perhaps you think me weak? Did you think that I would stand by and simply allow this to happen?"

"I do not follow you," Ankhesenamun said. "You are not making sense. I do not know what you mean."

"Pah," Nakhtmin said.

"Allow what to happen?" Ankhesenamun asked him.

"Are you to provide my father with an heir?"

"No!" she said. "Nothing could be further from my mind."

"Then why marry him?"

"Nakhtmin, is your memory so short? Did I have any choice but to marry him?"

"You are lying," he said. "This is all a scheme. I am not stupid. I am not weak. You intend to steal my throne from me and present it to your son."

"You are your father's heir," Ankhesenamun said.

"Yes!" Nakhtmin shouted. He stepped forwards and grabbed her shoulders, shaking her as he spoke. "I am my father's heir! Not you, not your offspring. You may have fooled my father, but you cannot fool me!"

Ankhesenamun had begun to cry. "I have fooled nobody!" she said. "You are drunk! You are imagining things!"

Without warning he withdrew his hand from her shoulder and slapped her across the face. She had no opportunity to recoil from the blow and the force of it was such that it killed the scream in her throat. She was simply able to gasp. She closed her eyes, awaiting another blow, but none came. Instead, when she opened her eyes she found that Nakhtmin had retrieved his knife from the waistband of his kilt and was holding it in front of her face.

"Are you carrying my father's child?" he asked her.

Her eyes never wavering from the blade, she shook her head.

"Do you intend to?" he asked her. Again, she shook her head.

"Liar!" he shouted. He pushed the blade towards her and she tried to back away, but there was nowhere to go.

"I swear, Nakhtmin," she said. "Had your father not forced me to marry him..."

"Quiet," Nakhtmin hissed.

"I never wanted..."

"I said keep quiet! I am sick of your lies, harlot. You think that I will sit back and allow you to wrest my birthright from me? Thief!"

"Please, Nakhtmin," Ankhesenamun said. "Think. Think about what you are saying. Think how ridiculous it all is. Go back to your quarters and wait until the morning. Everything will seem so much clearer in the morning."

"Believe me, thief, I have never seen things so clearly as I do now."

"You can have the throne," Ankhesenamun said.

"Oh, can I? How very gracious of you! I can have the throne?" The pitch of Nakhtmin's voice was rising, the volume swelling with indignance. "And you think it is yours to give? Who do you think you are? Whom do you think you address? I am Crown Prince Nakhtmin! I am heir to the throne! It is for me to take, not for you to bequeath! Harlot! Thief! Traitor!"

Suddenly, he jabbed the blade forward. It caught her throat but did not penetrate too deeply. Blood flowed from the cut but Nakhtmin had seen many throat wounds and he knew that this one was not fatal. Still, Ankhesenamun's eyes widened and her hands flew to her neck, her fingers quickly becoming drenched with her blood. The sight of it did nothing to assuage Nakhtmin's anger. He stabbed again, this time with more force, with the weight of his body behind the blow. Her hands were still in front of her neck, and the blade severed the third finger of her left hand before entering her throat, where it sank up to the hilt. Blood pumped from the wound and quickly soaked the bedclothes.

Nakhtmin withdrew his knife and wiped it on the bed. Ankhesenamun sagged to her right hand side. Her hands fell from her throat. Nakhtmin walked from the room with a steadier gait than that with which he had entered. Suddenly, he felt entirely sober.

He opened the door and the guards turned to face him.

"Do you have any idea what I will do to you both," he said, "should you ever admit to anyone that you have seen me this night?"

The guards simply stared, wide eyed.

"Exactly what you are imagining," he said. "Only much, much worse."

He turned and walked away.

Chapter Twenty-Nine

A Nubian Rebellion

WHEN AYE returned and heard the news he did not have to feign the sadness he felt, only the degree of it. He had not borne Ankhesenamun any ill will. She had merely been a necessary step along his path to power, just as a chariot was necessary for a journey, or a meal necessary to assuage a hunger. A man need feel nothing towards them in order to use them, but he would still feel a tinge of sadness if the chariot was smashed or the meal ruined. But then there were always more chariots and more meals, and each would serve their purpose as effectively as the last. His consolation was that he may have been saved an unpleasant task.

There was, at first, no inkling as to the identity of Ankhesenamun's killer. The guards on the door had seen nothing out of the ordinary, but neither was there any sign that any other method had been used to gain entry to the bedchamber. There were windows that were accessible from the courtyard outside the room but guards also patrolled this area and also reported having seen nothing, although it was not impossible that someone may have slipped by them in the darkness.

Aye ordered an investigation and made his feelings perfectly clear regarding his desire to see it successfully concluded. After all, without a perpetrator it was impossible to make any conclusions regarding motive and Aye could not feel entirely safe until the reasons for Ankhesenamun's death were known. In the meantime his guards were doubled and accompanied him everywhere, in the manner that he had so scorned in Akhenaten. Nakhtmin was given command of his personal guard.

The police investigation continued without success for a number of days. Its commander, the Theban chief of police, was nervous, for without witnesses there was almost nothing he could do. The guards at the door and those patrolling the courtyard had been questioned again and again but had been unable to offer anything that was not already known. He was reluctant to employ methods of torture in seeking information for he suspected that there was no further information to be had, but then he was just as reluctant to give the king the impression that he was anything less than enthusiastic towards his task.

Aye had returned a week after Ankhesenamun's death. The investigation thereafter continued for four days before anything of note came to light.

The two guards who had been stationed outside Ankhesenamun's bedchamber that night both knew that they had to remain steadfast, but they also knew that a slip by one would condemn them both. It was an unnerving and entirely unpleasant experience. They became suspicious of each other to the extent that they were rarely to be seen outside each other's company. They knew full well that Nakhtmin was more than capable of carrying out his threat should their information leak, and neither were keen to discover which imaginative way he would choose to have them dispatched. The repeated questioning by the chief of police did little to allay their fears.

On the fourth day, the first guard, whose name was Yey, made a suggestion to the second, Tiya.

"What if we were able to tell someone without Nakhtmin having the opportunity of revenge?" Yey asked him.

"Then I would tell everything in a second," Tiya said. "I cannot stand this any longer. Sooner or later they will find out that we have been lying, and then we are dead. They will kill us for protecting the man they seek, which will be infinitely better than what he will do to us for failing to protect him well enough."

"But what if we could name him with no risk to ourselves?"

"Then I would have done so already."

"We could speak directly to His Majesty," Yey said. Tiya stared at him.

"Are you insane? First of all, we would never get that far. Secondly, you may have forgotten that Nakhtmin is his son."

Yey shrugged. "It is not entirely without risk," he said. "But perhaps a grateful king will offer us protection."

The two discussed it for the rest of the day, and repeatedly returned to the same conclusion. It was a massive risk, but if they could manage to speak to the king before Nakhtmin discovered them they had a better chance of seeing the end of the nightmare than if they simply waited for the information to be beaten from them by impatient policemen.

The following day they presented themselves at the door to the king's audience chamber, praying that Nakhtmin was not within. After a brief discussion with the commander of the guards, who nervously went to consult Aye himself, they were shown into the room. They were both shaking with fear as they prostrated themselves.

"May you live," Aye said.

The Maya Papyrus, Fragments 462-467

> *The two men rose from the floor.*
>
> *"Do you have something to tell me?" Aye asked them.*
>
> *They looked so frightened that I was somewhat surprised when one of them was able to find his voice in reply to Aye's question.*
>
> *"Your most gracious Majesty," the first one said. "We humbly beg a moment of your time. We have news regarding the death of Ankhesenamun."*
>
> *"You are the door guards who were on duty outside Ankhesenamun's bedchamber on the night of her death, are you not?"*
>
> *"We are, Your Majesty."*
>
> *"And you have news regarding what you saw or heard on that night?"*
>
> *"We do, Your Majesty."*
>
> *"News that has been in your possession since that very night?"*
>
> *The men hesitated. "Yes, Your Majesty."*
>
> *"And yet you volunteer it only now? Have you been questioned by the police regarding the matter?"*
>
> *"Yes, Your Majesty."*
>
> *And so it continued. I wanted to scream. I wanted to shake Aye and shout into his face:* Just let them tell us! What does it matter, what does anything matter, if they can tell us who killed your granddaughter?
>
> *Since my return from touring the country with Aye, I had been the victim of a deep depression. It seemed to me that my friends and my relatives were being taken from me one at a time, and that whenever I was lucky enough to find anybody to replace those who had been taken from me, it was only a matter of time before they too became the target of the gods' anger, or the desperate acts of men. In my selfishness I almost felt as though I was the victim. I was as keen as Aye professed himself to be to find the man responsible for Ankhesenamun's death, and the depth of my grief was matched only by the searing heat of my anger and desire for revenge.*
>
> *"You can answer for your reticence on another occasion," Aye was saying by the time I focused myself once more on the matter at hand. "But for now you may be able to redeem yourselves to some degree. Tell me, what information have you?"*

The two men looked at each other. One of them nodded encouragement to the other, as though one had been nominated as the spokesman and was now regretting his acceptance of the position. The second man cleared his throat.

"We saw someone," he said, finally. "That night, we saw someone."

"Who?" I asked, unable to restrain myself any longer.

"He went into Her Highness' room and remained there for some time. The next morning, she was dead."

"Who?" I asked again.

"Nakhtmin," the man said.

I was stunned, although Aye did not seem to take a breath. He shouted the guards from the door and instructed them to summon Nakhtmin to the room. At the mention of his name the two informers seemed to shrivel up into themselves.

"Your Majesty," the spokesman said, much more eager to speak than he had formerly been. "Please, Your Majesty, allow us to take our leave before the general arrives."

"I think it only fair," Aye said, "that he should be able to answer the charges you have levelled against him. They could hardly be more serious."

"But..." the first man said, before being interrupted by the second.

"Your Majesty, General Nakhtmin has threatened us with death should we reveal his whereabouts that night. We take the threat seriously. It is the reason we have not spoken before now on the matter. Please do not force us to confront him."

"You are in the presence of your pharaoh, gentlemen," Aye said. "Do you believe that you are in any danger that I myself do not explicitly desire?"

This seemed to do little for the men's state of nervousness, but they were fully aware that questioning the king would hardly serve to lessen the danger in which they believed themselves to be.

For my part, I awaited Nakhtmin's arrival in silence. I did not trust any words to leave my mouth in any sensible arrangement, such was the fury in which I was enveloped. My own brother. A double blow. Such was my anger that I would have placed him upon a stake myself, and shed not a tear as I did so. I began to breathe heavily in an attempt to stifle a scream of rage that was building inside me. Aye regarded me curiously once or twice, but said nothing.

Eventually, Nakhtmin arrived, marching into the room with as much purpose as ever he had until he caught sight of the two informers, cowering as far from him as the dimensions of the room would allow, which was enough to cause him to stumble as effectively as an outstretched foot. His expression crumbled into one of confusion and outright fear and somehow this seemed to selfish to me, his obvious desire for self-preservation so perverse and without honest foundation that I was unable to prevent myself from rushing forwards and slapping him across the face with all my strength.

"How could you?" I was shouting. "How could you?"

He was too shocked by the presence of the informers to defend himself. Instead, he drew his sword before I could set upon him again.

"Do not forget to whom you owe your life," *he whispered. I had no choice but to step backwards, contenting myself with the red weal that had bloomed where my hand had struck his face.*

"Murderer of women," *I said.* "No man can fear one such as you."

"Then fear this," *he said, and held the point of his sword up to my face.*

"Accusations have been levelled against you," *Aye told him.* "Very serious allegations."

"They are liars," *Nakhtmin said, indicating the informers with his sword.* "See how they snivel, like disobedient children."

"And how do you know they are not here to defend you?" *Aye said.* "Considering Maya's reaction, an innocent man would be forgiven for concluding that he was responsible for the denunciation."

"It is self-evident," *Nakhtmin said, but he was fumbling for his words.* "Maya is not in a position to accuse anybody. He was away with you when the crime was committed."

"Which crime?" *Aye said.*

Nakhtmin did not reply.

"I see," *Aye said.* "My poor, uncomplicated son. You do realise, do you not, that you have just confessed?"

"I have confessed nothing," *Nakhtmin said.*

"Why did you do it?" *Aye said.*

"I have confessed nothing!"

Aye sighed and rubbed his temples with the tips of his fingers.

"The worst possible gambit for you now is to annoy me, Nakhtmin. You have murdered the king's wife and you have been caught. These men have explained the entire incident to me. Your denials only serve to drown the little dignity you have remaining. Now, tell me. What possible reason could you have had for this distasteful episode?"

"Distasteful?" I exploded. "That is hardly..."

I was stopped by Aye's raised hand and stern look. I returned to simmering. Aye turned back to Nakhtmin.

"Well?" he asked him.

"I was safeguarding my position as heir to the throne," Nakhtmin said. "I was doing nothing you would not have done in my position."

"I would never have taken such a risk unless the threat was real and undisputed," Aye said. "Nakhtmin, you have disappointed me. I am disappointed that you felt so threatened by Ankhesenamun, for I had named you as my heir and had no intention of changing my decision."

"But if Ankhesenamun..." Nakhtmin began.

"Then that would have been the time to act. Even if she had borne me a son to take precedent over you, who would have been regent until he was old enough to rule alone? Would there then not have been ample opportunity to remove him from your path?"

Perhaps realising that he had said too much on the subject of regents removing kings, Aye changed the subject.

"I am disappointed that your methods are so lacking in subtlety. I am saddened that you have placed me in this position."

"Father, please..." Nakhtmin said.

"And what of Maya?" Aye said, looking to me. "What would your judgement be?"

"That he is guilty," I said.

Aye sighed. "Of course he is guilty," he said. "What would you pronounce his punishment to be?"

Nakhtmin looked at me, his eyes brimming with self-pity, with pity that he could not grant to his victim, and I felt nothing for him other than disgust. I held his gaze without qualms.

"Death," I said. "As is traditional."

"But Maya," Nakhtmin said. "I am your brother."

"No," I said. "You are not."

Nakhtmin turned back to Aye.

"Father," he said. "I beg you..."

"Do not beg," Aye said. "It will only add to my disappointment."

Nakhtmin swayed slightly on his feet, as though he was about to pass out.

"Luckily for you," Aye said, "I do not have the high moral standing of your brother, or such a literal eye for the law. I shall not punish you as Maya sees fit. You are, after all, my son and heir to the throne, and the continuation of my line is something in which I take particular interest. My family and I did not fight our way to such an exalted position just to have it torn from our grasp upon my death, and unfortunately, I think that Nakhtmin is the only remaining member of the family with the aptitude for power." Aye glanced at me. "However," he continued, "letting you live presents me with a further problem, for it would not do to allow news to spread around court that I had been so lenient with a man responsible for such a heinous crime."

He looked towards the two informers, who up until now had been forgotten in the corner of the room.

"Take these men away," he said to Nakhtmin.

"Yes, Your Majesty," Nakhtmin said, once again drawing himself up to his full height.

"And I expect them to have confessed to the crime before they die," Aye said.

Nakhtmin could not help but break into a smile. "Certainly, Your Majesty," he said, and called in the guards.

The two informers begged for their lives as they were dragged struggling from the room, with Nakhtmin following closely behind.

"Your Majesty," I said, feeling ashen. "I must protest!"

"You cannot protest, Maya. I am your king."

"But you are sending innocent men to their deaths!"

"Better that than sending the guilty man to his death and punishing the entire kingdom for one man's crime. For who then would inherit my throne?"

"That is hardly relevant," I said, knowing the answer full well but not wishing to acknowledge it.

"It would be an outcome that neither of us would want."

"But you are murdering two loyal men!"

Aye shook his head. "Loyal only to the truth," he said. "And that is hardly any loyalty at all."

"And so poor Ankhesenamun's death goes unavenged," I said.

"Regrettably so."

I turned and made for the door. Aye called me back.

"Before you leave," he said. "I shall overlook your unseemly outburst, but I shall also give you fair warning. The events of this day are matters only for the audience room. I do not expect them to travel any further, for that would be another threat to the dynasty of this family, and you know that I cannot allow such a thing. It would be a terrible thing to have to choose between my two sons but you should know that I would do so, should the need arise. And you would not win."

I left the room without further comment.

"If there is a single word that could be used to summarise my reign," Aye enjoyed telling people, "it is *stability*."

It was true: life had settled into a constancy that had not been known since the reign of Amenhotep, or at least the early years of Tutankhamun. Each inundation was as good as the last, and the crops responded accordingly. One or two minor campaigns in Nubia restored the public's faith in the army. Court life was almost entirely bereft of scandal and gossip, other than the inevitable rumours about who had been seen sneaking out of which bedchamber in the middle of the night. Relationships with the neighbouring kingdoms of the region were mended after the disastrous diplomacy of Akhenaten's years and new alliances and treaties were not only signed but trusted.

There was only one slight cause for concern in Thebes and at court, which was that Aye was by now very well advanced in years, and while it was going to be pleasant to have a king live long enough to die of natural causes it would not be long before there would be the unavoidable stress of passing into a new reign.

No matter how Aye tried to hide it, there was no getting away from the tell-tale signs of his frailty. He now needed help to both sit and stand. When he did manage to walk without the help of his courtiers he leant so heavily on his walking stick and moved so timorously that it often seemed as though he was not moving at all.

Worse were the embarrassing slips that were beginning to creep into Aye's conversation. On occasion he had been known to refer to people by the wrong name or, more perplexingly, by a name that nobody had heard mentioned before. This was bad enough in the privacy of the court but when it involved diplomats and ambassadors it was almost shaming, although few could deny the amusement that it occasionally caused when the ambassador was too polite or too nervous to correct him and would then have to answer to the wrong name for the rest of the audience.

At first, Aye had recognised his mistakes and had become increasingly angry with himself with each passing slip. He would refuse to allow courtiers to leave the audience chamber until he had remembered their names. As time passed, though, he would notice less and less, and would even deny that he had made a mistake if someone had the temerity to correct him.

His deterioration was not a slow one.

"Bring me my... erm..." he would say, clicking his fingers and pointing across the room.

"Your walking stick, Your Majesty?"

"Yes, my walking stick," he would say. "That is what I said. Are you entirely stupid?"

He would forget who was alive and who was dead.

"Tell Ankhesenamun I wish to see her," he would say. Or Thuya, or Tutankhamun, or names that few at court recognised, like Maiherperi or Tjenuna.

"Fetch me Tutankhamun," Aye one day instructed one of his servants, who by now had become adept at dealing with the king's lapses of memory.

"Your Majesty," the servant said, bowing. "I have to humbly and regretfully inform you that Tutankhamun is no longer with us."

"No longer with us?" Aye said. "What do you mean, no longer with us?"

"Your Majesty," the servant said. "Tutankhamun is dead."

"Dead?" Aye said, startled. "Dead? What are you talking about? Tutankhamun is not dead."

"Your Majesty, I can assure you..."

"Assure me? Assure me what? That I have taken leave of my senses? Would you perhaps be kind enough to tell me when this sudden occurrence came about, bearing in mind that I spoke to him only this morning?"

"Your Majesty, Tutankhamun has been dead for two years."

"You dare question your king?" Aye shouted. "Guards! Take this man away. He is a blithering buffoon. And fetch me Tutankhamun!"

The guards made a show of escorting the servant from the room.

The Maya Papyrus, Fragments 477-490

I am not the sort of man to take pleasure in the misfortune of others, even when that misfortune is thoroughly deserved. It would be tempting to claim that Aye's deterioration was a judgement from Amun, but many men come to this end and few of them have committed the crimes that Aye had on his conscience.

When I was called to see Aye after he had demanded to see Tutankhamun, it was a strange interview. At first, he did not recognise me.

"Ah," he said. "Tutankhamun. They tried to tell me you were dead, but I did not believe them. Not for a second. We must begin our preparations for the Festival of Opet. It is the first time it has been celebrated since before your father's reign, and so it needs to be memorable. I shall inform the High Priest of Amun that it will begin at the first sign of inundation."

"Your Majesty," I said. "I am Maya."

Aye squinted at me and I stepped forwards in order to aid his failing vision.

"Maya," he said, as though trying to place the name.

"Your son," I said.

"Yes, Maya, of course," he said, realisation dawning at last. "I was just... er... we need to... the festival..." His voice trailed away.

"The festival is months away," I said.

He stared at me in confusion and I let myself out without another word. It would have perhaps been apposite for me to offer some sort of comfort to the man but my ability to do so had passed away with Tutankhamun and Ankhesenamun, and the men executed for her murder, and while I took no satisfaction in Aye's suffering, I no longer felt duty bound to alleviate it.

Nakhtmin was sitting by his father's bedside. The king had not been out of bed for two days. Periods of infirmity were not unknown, and sometimes these days would coincide with times of relative lucidity and Aye would be happy to receive visitors whom he recognised instantly and with whom he was able to hold sensible conversations.

Nakhtmin would sit by the bedside on those days when he had been informed that Aye would know who he was and he would feel none of the unease that plagued any of the other visitors. He rather enjoyed himself, in fact. It reminded him how soon it would be before he was able to claim the throne as his own. Besides, there was a hostility missing from his father's conversations that was a constant undercurrent in Nakhtmin's interactions with other members of court. Most people, Maya and Horemheb excluded, were cautious enough to try to hide it, although it was always detectable. He treated his servants no differently than did his father, but Nakhtmin's servants seemed to resent it, while his father's appeared happy to accept their station in life. His dealings with ministers and ambassadors, sometimes necessitated by his father's infirmity of body or mind, were carried out exactly as his father would have done, and yet those same ministers and ambassadors would accept his words begrudgingly and his father's without malice or rancour. It depressed him, from which condition he found succour in a reliable retreat.

"You drink too much," Aye said to him, before Nakhtmin had even sat down. Nakhtmin's eyes were rimmed with red, and the furrowing of his brow betrayed the throbbing pain within.

Nakhtmin did not try to deny it. He simply shrugged his shoulders and squinted past the bed towards where the sun fell through the windows.

"How are you feeling, father?" he said.

Aye thought about it for a moment. "Refreshed," he said, at last. "As though I have awoken from a long sleep."

"You have," Nakhtmin said.

"I was speaking metaphorically," Aye said. A bird sang at the window.

"What is this unhappiness that has you running for the wine?"

"There is an atmosphere. It pervades everything. We have discussed it before on more occasions than I would care to count."

"I am not a well man, Nakhtmin, and there is little point in you denying it." Nakhtmin had not thought of denying it. "But, well or not, I am still pharaoh, and as pharaoh I continue to take an interest in my court."

"Please," Nakhtmin said. "Listen to the birds. Concentrate on the sun on your skin."

"This atmosphere," Aye said, undaunted. "Describe it to me. Is it one of rebellion?"

"No, no," Nakhtmin said. "Not rebellion."

"Then what?"

Nakhtmin sighed. "Distaste," he said, at last.

Aye made a show of pushing himself more upright on his pillows, but gave up after a short struggle. He sank back down to his original position with a look of mild irritation.

"Nakhtmin," he said, in a tone that made Nakhtmin wince, the voice of a father explaining the self-evident to his child. "I know that you are not a weak man. I know that you are a man of leadership and of decision and of immutability. I recognise these attributes in you because they are in me also, and they are the facets of my personality that have brought me to this position in life. You do understand your destiny, do you not? You do understand the weight of history upon your shoulders, the responsibility left to you by the members of your family, who have built the pedestal upon which you are about to tread by risking their lives and their freedoms in pursuit of your goal?"

"Of course," Nakhtmin said.

"Good," Aye said. "Then I ask only this of you: that if we share so many attributes, do not let the difference between us be that I was prepared to use mine where you were not. When you decide that the time has come to act, do so resolutely, and without mercy."

"Yes, father," Nakhtmin said, and began the process of persuading himself that it was the advice he would have given himself anyway.

After he had left the room, Nakhtmin began to feel emboldened. His father was correct, of course. There was little profit to be had from refusing to face his detractors. Those were the actions of a coward. Of course, there was no clear indication as to exactly who his detractors were. He could only assume that some of the actions of his past had become common knowledge around court. And if that was indeed the case, then they could only have one source. Maya.

Only Maya had been present when the two guards had been brought before Aye to accuse Nakhtmin of Ankhesenamun's murder. But then Nakhtmin could not believe for a moment that there was any real possibility that Maya would be capable of standing against him. The man, after all, was little more than a scribe, and scribes did not defy the threats of generals.

Except, Nakhtmin thought to himself, if scribes have powerful allies. Horemheb had shown once already with whom he had made his allegiances, and Horemheb was less likely to switch his loyalties any more than he would switch his nationality.

When Nakhtmin reached his quarters it was approaching the time that he liked to enjoy a small meal of cold meats and poultry. His servants were well versed in his preferred daily routine, and when he reached his quarters the meal was already laid out. A servant, a young girl he had seen on one or two previous occasions, was at the table, carefully pouring a cup of red wine. When she caught sight of him she straightened up suddenly, as though she had been caught doing something of which he would disapprove. He stepped towards her and she backed away. She was not unattractive, and while there was not outright fear in her eyes, there was at least some degree of nervousness. He found the darting of her eyes not entirely without aesthetic merit. He noticed with some amusement that her head flicked once or twice to her side as she tried to estimate her position in relation to the door.

"Do not be in such a rush to leave," he said. "Please, take a seat."

She had no option. Her hand went out to grope for the back of a chair that she knew to be somewhere in the vicinity. She sat down without taking her eyes from him.

Smiling, he sat opposite her. There passed a moment when they simply stared at each other.

"Now," Nakhtmin said, clearing his throat. "I can see that you are more than a little uncomfortable to be alone in my presence."

She started to protest, but he held up his hands to silence her. "To deny it would be to accuse me of blindness," he said. "And you would not want to do that, would you?"

She shook her head with some enthusiasm.

"Good," he said. "Now, you are very wise to be afraid of me, for I am a man whose power is matched only by his capacity for malice. Having said that, I am loyal to my friends. Would you like to be my friend, little serving girl?"

She nodded vigorously.

"Very wise, very wise," Nakhtmin commented. "Then, as we are to be friends, it would perhaps only be fair for you to share with me some of the observations people are making about me behind my back."

"Your Highness," the girl stammered. "I can assure you that..."

"I have no use for your assurances," he said. "I want only the truth." He stood up and leant against the corner of the table, looking down on her. "Without the truth, I am afraid that we can no longer be friends." He thought his threats to be almost dashing, almost charming, almost beguiling and hypnotic, and he was astounded when she did not respond. Instead of gushing forth with innuendo and accusations as he had expected, she merely shrank further into herself and shook her head, staring at him with watery eyes.

He said nothing and stared back, well aware from his experience questioning prisoners and subordinates of the power of a silence begging to be filled.

"Your Highness," she said, when the silence could no longer be tolerated. "I have only ever been a loyal servant to you and I swear that I have never..."

"Enough!" Nakhtmin shouted and, leaning forward, grasped the young girl's face in a clamp like grip between his fingers and thumb. He was done with subtlety and beguilement. The girl squealed, but made no further sound.

"Now you listen to me," he hissed, holding his head close enough to hers for them each to feel the cloying warmth of the other's breath on their faces. "I could have you buried in the desert before nightfall, where you would never be found. If I was feeling generous I could have you killed first. Picture your mother, and see her weep for you, never knowing, never really knowing whatever became of you. Is that your desire, child?" He understood a slight change in the rhythm of her trembling to be an attempt at a shake of the head.

"Good," he said. "I want you to understand that the only way to keep the image from becoming reality is to keep it at the forefront of your mind. Think only of her tears, and the answer to my question. Who have you heard discussing me, and what have they said?"

For the briefest of moments the girl considered lying, but she knew that to protect the guilty she would need to betray the innocent, and that was a prospect infinitely worse. The idea of self-sacrifice in the pursuit of the salvation of others was not discarded, for it never so much as made an appearance in her mind; she was simply too afraid, and the image of her mother was too vivid. And so she told him of the first two names that came to mind which fitted Nakhtmin's desire. She remembered the day well. She had been removing the dirty plates and dishes from a table in the king's audience chamber. Outside the door a picked bone fell from the top plate and rolled under a nearby table in the corridor outside the room. As she had stooped to pick it up she heard the voices of men who obviously believed themselves to be alone after the exit of the king.

"I have heard Maya speaking of a crime," she said.

"What crime?" His grip tightened again, and this time the girl found the breath to cry out. Nakhtmin shook her until she stopped.

"He did not say," she said. "A murder, but I know not of whom. Please, Your Highness, I speak the truth. He could not say more because the man he addressed silenced him for fear of being overheard."

"To whom did he speak?" Nakhtmin asked, already knowing the answer.

"Horemheb, Your Highness," the girl said.

Nakhtmin felt angry, yet vindicated. He let the girl go, but not without a final flourish that pulled her from the chair and sent her to her knees on the floor.

"You have done well," he said to her, although she gave no indication that she was listening, such was her distress. Nakhtmin was paying as scant attention to his words as was she. His mind was elsewhere. "You will not regret your candour today," he said. "Some will, but not you."

The girl scampered from the room, as remorseful as she was scared. It was too great an ordeal not to immediately share its details in the protective arms of her mother.

The Maya Papyrus, Fragments 500-501

I recognised immediately that something extraordinary had happened. It was so unlike Horemheb to appear in person at my front door rather than send a servant to summon me that I was shocked enough to almost fail to notice his state of agitation. I could perhaps be forgiven this. Horemheb's agitation is so unlike the similar emotion in any other man that it would take a close friend indeed to recognise it in the most fortuitous of circumstance. He does not, as some may, fluster or panic, and neither, as others may, does he babble insensibly until his breath deserts him and his energy dissolves. He merely becomes sterner and more focused, until it seems as though his stare would be enough to cause scars. It is advisable, under these conditions, to keep one's questions, answers and general comments short, and to stick to the matter at hand with a resoluteness not often exercised in conversation.

"What is it?" I said, forgoing my usual pleasantries.

"Nakhtmin," he replied, pushing his way passed me into the entrance hall of my house and beyond.

"Is he dead?" I shouted after him. It was the first possibility that sprang to mind and I did not know whether or not it caused me any sadness. I was merely curious.

"Sit down," he told me, after I caught up with him in my day room.

He spoke rapidly and without emotion. There was no judgement, not a trace of blame or rebuke, despite the fact that Horemheb had warned me on several occasions that I spoke too loudly and too openly. Everything was merely a fact.

"News has reached me that Nakhtmin blames us for his image at court and believes us traitors. He will undoubtedly act to avenge and protect himself. Unless we do so first, we are dead."

I stared. My mouth may have been open. Horemheb was waiting for a decisive answer, a cogent analysis of the situation and our recommended responses to it.

"How?" I said, meaning 'How shall we act?'

"What?" I said, meaning 'What shall we do?'

I was bereft of ideas thereafter and reserved my cutting insights until I had given Horemheb chance to speak. He did so soon enough, although he prefixed his words with a weary sigh that I could not really begrudge him.

"I need to know that you are with me," he said.

"With you?" I asked. "With you for what?"

"That does not matter. Either you are with me, and we work together without reservation, or we are dead."

"Well then," I said. "I am with you. Obviously."

"Good," he said. "Remember you said that, and remember what is at stake. For you will not like what I am about to say."

And he was right.

News had reached Thebes of rebellion in a town less than a day's travel north of the border with Nubia. Its name was Nabod, and it was a town so insignificant as to be absent from any of the maps that Nakhtmin had consulted before his departure. He knew that it was a walled town, but that it was a town so poor that the wall was constructed from mud brick and could well keel over under the firm application of a soldier's foot. The walls, though, were ample protection for the contents of the town, for there was nothing there. It was hardly worthy to be called a town at all. And yet such a pointless little place somehow believed itself to be equal to the might of Egypt. Nakhtmin found it laughable. He could picture the little men he would soon annihilate, cowering under the volleys of arrows he would send into the town. He could not help but smile. They were not innocent victims. They had volunteered for their fate, and, knowing this, Nakhtmin saw their deaths as nothing more troublesome than a sport, an excuse for exercise, an opportunity to drill his men and assess their readiness for a real fight.

Nakhtmin was happier than he had been for a long time, and it was not just the prospect of a fight that made him so.

He was not a man to whom invidious plotting came easily, but it came easily enough for him to have made arrangements for the demise of Horemheb and Maya in his absence. There were men whose loyalty to him was unquestioned, men who had remained by his side in the standoff against Horemheb, Maya and Ankhesenamun, who regarded that trio with almost as much loathing as did he, and there was one in particular whose skills of stealth and subtlety were undeniable. The man was said to have been born with a knife in his hand and nobody claimed to remember how many men he had dispatched with it. He had gone so far as to thank Nakhtmin for the opportunity to serve in such an esteemed manner and Nakhtmin had been unable to prevent himself from smiling at his own cunning. He could hardly be suspected of a crime while he was not even in the same country.

The man felt no nervousness. He did not allow himself to. It was a matter of pride. The only people entitled to feel nervous were those who were not fully prepared and those who were victims, and Surer never intended being in either category. Certainly for this assignment, Surer felt himself to be entirely prepared. There was little, in any case, that he needed to arrange. His targets were public enough figures for there to be very little need for the sort of prying that was likely to provoke suspicion. There was no secret to the location of their homes, just as there was no secret to their daily routines, which differed so slightly from one day to the next that Surer's job could not have been any easier had he issued them with instructions.

He estimated that Maya was going to make far the easier target of the two. Neither Maya nor Horemheb felt the need to maintain a personal guard and neither of their homes appeared to pose any formidable puzzle with regards to easy and undetected access, at least for a man of Surer's undeniable talents. The only difference between the two was that Horemheb was patently more able to offer at least a modicum of resistance, even when surprised and unarmed. For this reason, Surer had decided that Maya would be his first target, for if Surer was to be involved in any form of struggle or was forced to flee the city, it was more likely to be because of events at Horemheb's house rather than Maya's, and Surer did not want the responsibility of another house call to hinder what may have to be a swift escape.

He dressed respectably, in a starched kilt with a modified waistband that hid his knife well enough for it to pass unnoticed in the dark of the city streets at night. It would not survive close scrutiny but then he did not intend to allow himself to be so carefully examined.

He knew that Maya customarily worked late at the palace and so it was long into the night before he ventured outside. The streets were deserted, the only sounds coming from the crunch of stones beneath his feet and the distant shouts of the market traders preparing their goods and stalls for the coming day. The moon was bright and high enough to cast shadows that dogged his steps or, on turning a corner, pounced in front of him like an ambush.

He waited close to Maya's home. It was in an area of the city wherein there were plenty of alleyways in which he could hide and await his quarry.

Maya appeared around the nearest corner only minutes after Surer began to expect him.

He watched his target pass through the doorway, briefly silhouetted against the warm glow of lamps left lit for him in the entrance hall. Once the door was closed, Surer sprinted to the perimeter wall and peered through the gateway to the house. He watched as a lamp's glow flowed from one room to the next, and he counted windows as it went. It stopped in the last room on the right, paused, and was extinguished. Surer remained crouched where he was until his legs ached to such a degree that he was forced to move. He stepped through the gateway and moved into the deeper shadows that dwelt in its lee. He settled down to wait, turning his mind from the chill and the dark. His mind was on more important matters and, in any case, he was a man used to shadows.

Horemheb was concerned about Maya. The general at least knew the value of a sharp knife within easy reach of the pillow. Maya with a similar weapon was more likely to be a danger to himself than any assailant. And there was an added concern. This had been Horemheb's plan, and it was a plan towards which Maya had expressed profound misgivings. It was a scheme conceived by a man of action, by a soldier, and Maya had the heart of a scribe, much happier to describe the daring deeds of others than to perpetrate them himself.

But there were always necessary risks. It would, for example, have been impossible to avoid alerting Aye and Nakhtmin to the fact that there was something out of the ordinary if Horemheb had sent a detachment of soldiers to watch over Maya's every step. Horemheb's success depended almost solely on undetected preparations and so Maya remained unguarded. It was a risk that they had discussed, with starkly different levels of enthusiasm. Horemheb knew that Maya was not a coward. He was simply a man whose sense of self-preservation was manifested in a different way to his own. And the man who acted in spite of his fear was ten times the man who felt no fear at all. Still, he had not offered what could be called broad support for Horemheb's suggestion. He was more sensible of their vulnerabilities, and Horemheb had to concede the fact that there was very little chance of their scheme succeeding if they were both dead.

Even so, Horemheb's opinion held sway, propelled as it was by his strength of character and, perhaps, a little bullying. He doubted if he was going to achieve much in the way of a restful night, and sat staring into the darkness until well into the third watch. Before very much longer, though, his eyes became dry and irritable, and his head began to sag towards his chest. He lay down with the intention of continuing his vigil and was asleep almost immediately.

The Maya Papyrus, Fragments 507-511

During the course of the days – or, rather, the nights – following the formulation of Horemheb's ghastly plan, I found it almost impossible to remain in one place for any length of time. There was not a seat in the land comfortable enough to tame me, not a bed that could still my fluttering heart. The slightest noise, the faintest footstep or click of a door latch was enough to fling me from the deepest sleep into wide-eyed wakefulness within a moment and would leave me gasping in the dark, my heart thumping so enthusiastically in my chest that I would be able to feel it in my throat.

There was not a single moment when I did not regret agreeing to this monstrous act of insanity and pray for a way to retract my acquiescence. But matters had already progressed far beyond any point of safe return, and to attempt to do so now would undoubtedly be more dangerous than continuing along this most dangerous of routes.

I berated myself endlessly over my malleable character, so easily overcome by those with a more forceful oratory. What I had agreed to do was folly, and not only because it placed both Horemheb and I in the gravest danger (although I must confess that I found this fact rather compelling) but because it was an act of moral bankruptcy. There was nothing we would be able to present to Osiris in our defence when the day of our judgement came, no mitigating circumstances we could quote to lighten the sentence that would be passed upon us. There are some things that are simply wrong, and no provocation can excuse them. Of course, I did not know then what I know now. This was before Aye had bared his ugly past to me, and I did not know without doubt of the crimes of which Aye was guilty. I find it hard now to say whether or not my attitude would have been the same had I been fully cognisant of the facts.

As it was, I cursed myself with each breath and waited for untimely death until I could wait no longer and would have almost welcomed an assassin's blade as a relief from the suspense. Horemheb had expressly forbidden me to take any precautions, beyond vigilance, to protect myself, in the fear that it would alert our enemies to our intentions. But what was I supposed to do? Would Horemheb have patiently waited for death? Would he have been prepared to sacrifice himself in the name of his cause?

Surer made his way to the nearest window. It was small, and placed high in the wall where it could provide access to a refreshing breeze without admitting the heat of the Egyptian sun, but it was neither high nor small enough to prevent Surer pulling himself up by his fingertips and squeezing through to the room beyond with the easy air of a man who had practiced such a manoeuvre many times. On the other side he dropped down, landing in silence. He remained perfectly still for a short time, his fingertips resting on the cold floor tiles, listening for any reaction to his ingress. There was none, and Surer began to slowly make his way across the room. The villas in this district of the city were undoubtedly plush and comfortable, but they were surprisingly uniform in their construction, and even in the dark Surer knew exactly where to find the room in which the lamp had been extinguished. As he walked he slipped the knife from its hiding place in the waistband of his kilt. He came to the door leading to Maya's bedroom and held the knife briefly between his teeth as he used both hands to quietly push the door open and step inside. The room beyond the doorway was as dark and silent as the rest of the house, but Surer could sense the spaciousness. He walked across to the darker shape that marked the position of the bed occupying the middle of the floor, and took the knife back in his hand.

He raised it above his head and brought it down once, in a fast, slicing arc.

Nakhtmin's soldiers were ranged outside the walls of Nabod in units, eager for the command to attack. Hardly a one of them was feeling unduly nervous. The walls appeared relatively feeble and easily scalable and the men beyond them were hardly worthy to share a battlefield with them. They could see no activity whatsoever on the walls, which was indicative of a lack of preparation and, more importantly, a lack of archers within the enemy's ranks.

Nakhtmin walked before the ranks of his men and poured scorn upon their enemy, ridiculing the weakness of its men and the ugliness of its women. He made his men laugh and cheer and lavished them with the praise he told them they deserved. They were the cream of Egyptian manhood, he told them, and did not doubt for a second that they would effortlessly sweep aside any army insane enough to oppose them. He thanked them for their loyalty and joked that the forthcoming battle was going to be so easy that he might detail some of them to forage food rather than fight so he could watch the day unfold in comfort from the rear.

"But would you expect such a thing of your General Nakhtmin?"

"No!" they chorused.

"Would you expect your general to place you in a danger to which he would not commit himself?"

"No!"

"Would you expect him to lavish himself with comforts that his men could not share?"

"No!"

Nakhtmin pretended to look momentarily confused.

"Then," he said, as though testing the idea out on them, "perhaps you would want your general in your front rank, standing shoulder to shoulder and sharing with you his shield?"

A great cry went up. "Yes!" they shouted.

"Then so be it! I shall ride with you, and I shall call you my friends as I do so! Now, let us take ourselves..." (here, Nakhtmin turned and pointed towards the town with his sword) "...*to the walls!*"

The men sprang forwards, and Nakhtmin ran with them. He knew there was little risk in a minor skirmish such as this one, and the respect he would gain by personally leading the charge far outweighed it. The fact that he was on foot with his men (there was little point in using chariots against city walls) only increased the feeling of camaraderie.

As the men came within reach of the walls, ladders sprang up from within their midst, and many had men clambering onto their bottom rungs before they had even settled upon the walls. A steady stream of men began to flow up the ladders, and yet still there came no sign of defence from within the city. No arrows flew, no warnings were shouted or orders given. Nothing happened, and Nakhtmin's men, with Nakhtmin himself among them, climbed into the city, looking from a distance like a river negotiating cataracts.

For all that, Nakhtmin's men were not so numerous that the flow could continue for any significant length of time, and the last of them were cresting the wall even as the advance guard were jumping from it into the streets below.

They were in a small square which looked as though it had been created by the simple levelling of the houses that once stood within it. There was nothing to indicate that this space was marked for anything

other than the absence of purpose. The houses on the periphery of the
square all faced into it but looked as though they had been carrying the
burden of neglect for some years.

Nakhtmin's experience of soldiering and battles stretched back into
his childhood, almost as far as he could remember, and during that time
his experiences had granted him something that every soldier needs if he
is to guarantee his longevity, and that is an instinct for the unexpected.
The moment after his feet hit the ground of the improvised courtyard
Nakhtmin knew that something dreadful was afoot. He had no time to
shout orders or otherwise make preparation. He had time only to swear
quietly to himself before the first of the archers stepped from the
doorways of the houses that surrounded his men on three sides.

Their arrows were already notched, and several of Nakhtmin's men
were dead before they even saw their adversaries. Once the arrows were
loosed the archers stepped back into the darkness of the doorways to
reload and were replaced by others, who in turn fired and stepped back.
By the time the third volley of arrows had been loosed the scene in the
square was one of unrestrained panic. Very few retained enough of their
senses to band together and make a dash for one of the alleyways that led
between the houses. Even fewer made it this far, and those who succeeded
found themselves facing bands of swordsmen who had been lying in wait
behind the buildings.

Nakhtmin's only hope lay in the men still standing upon the wall. The
archers were always the last into any charge. Consequently, the men on
the wall were the ones most able to deal with the situation. Even as
Nakhtmin turned to shout his orders, the first of the arrows flew down
into the doorways of the houses, felling their occupants. The men who
stepped into their place made the mistake of redirecting their fire
upwards, towards the archers on the wall, which gave Nakhtmin the
opportunity to gather a handful of his men around him and make for the
nearest alleyway. He had seen what had befallen the men who had
preceded him on this route but the situation was no longer so
disadvantageous towards him. His assailants no longer had the benefit of
surprise, and Nakhtmin's men now had their general among them. He had
no idea as to what he would do once he had fought his way clear of the
alleyway, but he decided to let that strategy present itself to him once his
immediate objective of survival had been resolved.

As he had expected, as he and his men neared the alleyway's exit, the
enemy stepped into view. It was the first proper look that Nakhtmin had
managed to get of them but he did not allow his surprise to blunt his
instincts. At the very moment of their first appearance around the corner
of the house he leapt into a sprint, screaming for his men to follow him.

The two groups met with such ferocity that the ambushers could do nothing but fall back under the onslaught and after only a few moments only three were left alive. They turned and ran.

Only now did Nakhtmin allow himself pause. He looked down at the bodies of the enemy in consternation. They were not Nubian. The military planning and skilful execution of the ambush told him that they were not simply a band of disaffected rebels, but obviously a unit of a standing army which had the advantages of training and experienced commanders. Their kilts and body adornments told him that they were Egyptian.

More of Nakhtmin's men were now fighting their way free of the square and Nakhtmin sent the men with whom he had escaped to reinforce them by attacking the ambushers from the rear. Meanwhile, Nakhtmin surveyed his surroundings. He was in a maze of crooked streets and passageways, all claustrophobically lined with small, connected houses. If a secondary ambush had been placed here, Nakhtmin knew, then there would be no way of surviving it. His men had, by necessity, moved into the town, away from the walls and the support of the archers upon them. His forces were few, and many of the survivors were wounded and quite beyond the exertion of even the briefest of skirmishes.

The fight at the mouths of the alleyways leading to the walls was far from over, but Nakhtmin could not afford to await its outcome. If his troops prevailed they would need to be immediately prepared to meet the next obstacle. If they did not then his fate was sealed anyway. Reluctantly, he turned his back on them. There was little he could provide for them in either leadership or swordsmanship that would make any difference in a close quarters fight like this one. He was a general. His job was to decide what came next.

In the first house he reconnoitred he found nothing but the stale, musty smell of neglect. A hole had been hacked out of one wall, leading directly into the corresponding room of the house to the left. Through the hole he saw, in the far wall, another hole. His instincts had been correct. These houses had been prepared for an ambush. With the walls half demolished it would be a simple matter for the occupying troops to run from one to the next to give support where it was needed. He could only surmise that the troops who had intended to occupy the houses were the ones currently fighting outside, whose option to retreat to safer ground had been denied them by the swiftness of Nakhtmin's soldiers' response. If he could somehow disengage from the fight and retreat here himself there may be some chance of salvaging the day.

All the while these thoughts were occupying his mind, another was trying to gain prominence. He was trying to ignore it because neither the question nor the answer were immediately relevant, but he could not prevent the words from forming. *Why was he the victim of an ambush perpetrated by Egyptian soldiers?* For the moment, he told himself, it did not matter. It was unimportant whether he was facing Egyptians or Nubians or Hittites or anyone else, for all that was important at the moment was survival. Once that had been achieved there would be ample time to peruse the nature of the enemy. Until then, nothing but saving his men and himself mattered. And then, just when he thought he had managed to smother the nagging of the question, its answer stepped into the room opposite him, and smiled.

Chapter Thirty

The Purest Motive

SURER STARED down at the bed. Its contents had not reacted to the feel of his blade. There had been no sound, no struggle, no movement of any kind. Suddenly the darkness seemed to be more oppressive than protective and the silence only served to accentuate the sound of the blood rushing in his ears. He threw back the blanket that covered the bed as though a man of Maya's dimensions could have been hiding within its folds. The bed was decidedly, irrefutably empty.

There was no exit other than the one through which Surer had entered. He turned two full circles slowly, waiting for his eyes to become more accustomed to the night. He edged slowly back across the room to where the lamp that Maya had carried rested upon a small table by the wall. Beside it, in case Maya needed to rise before the sun, was a tinderbox. Surer opened it and lit the lamp.

It was a dull glow which barely reached the walls, which disappeared into the gloom. Surer took one pace forwards. He was not nervous, he told himself. He was merely alert. The situation had not slipped from his grasp sufficiently to warrant fear. He was still in control. He was still an unexpected man with a knife in the darkness of his victim's house. He was still the hunter.

And then, with another forward step he saw in the corner of the room a feature which had escaped his notice in the darkness. There was a small alcove in the far corner, across which was drawn a heavy curtain which reached from the ceiling to the floor.

As he watched, the curtain moved. Surer smiled. Raising the knife once more, he advanced.

"Hello, Horemheb," Nakhtmin said. "I thought I might find you here."

"Really?" Horemheb said. "I think perhaps that you are a little more surprised than you care to admit."

"This is a coup," Nakhtmin said. It was not a question, for he already knew the answer.

"I am genuinely sorry," Horemheb said, "but there is no other way."

He drew his sword.

"There is always another way," Nakhtmin said.

"No, there is not," Horemheb said, shaking his head. "Words are for those without the strength for actions. We are both the same, you and I. We both know this."

Horemheb advanced across the room, hefting his sword in his hand as though estimating its weight. Without hesitation, and without warning, Nakhtmin turned on his heel and fled.

For a moment Horemheb was aghast. Surprise delayed his reaction, but when he gathered himself enough to follow he did so at a breakneck pace, his shoulders bouncing off walls and door frames in his haste.

Once outside he found that Nakhtmin had not made a great deal of progress. His immediate goal had been to make his way back to the positions occupied by his men, where he could at least try to form a successful defence or, in the attempt, die with allies at his shoulder. He saw as soon as his left the house that this would be impossible. The skirmish showed no signs of abating, his men gallantly refusing to yield one pace without taking its worth in blood. Between Nakhtmin and his men was the main body of Horemheb's force, through which Nakhtmin would have to wade should he wish to reach any semblance of safety. His archers were tortuously making their way along the top of the crumbling wall, but even if they had wings to carry them to the worst of the fighting there was little use they could be, so intertwined were their comrades and enemies.

The time it took for Nakhtmin to dwell upon all of this was roughly equivalent to the time it had taken for Horemheb to react to his unexpected flight from the room, but more importantly it was time enough for Horemheb to come flying through the door from which Nakhtmin himself had so recently emerged.

"So unlike you to turn tail," Horemheb shouted, above the noise of the fight, which was perhaps thirty paces distant.

"I have my men to think of," Nakhtmin shouted back. "They need their general by their side if they are to carry this day and enable me to deliver unto you the justice that befits a traitor."

"It is no besmirching of character to betray murder."

"Your king answers neither to you nor your laws," Nakhtmin shouted. "He answers only to his gods."

"And you, Nakhtmin?" Horemheb asked. "To whom do you answer?"

"To my king!" Nakhtmin screamed. Once again, he turned and ran. He was hoping that he had managed to engage Horemheb in conversation long enough to allow the archers along the top of the city walls to reach positions wherein he and Horemheb were in range of their bows. He was further hoping that they were sufficiently alert to loose a hail of arrows the very second that there was enough air between himself and Horemheb for them to be confident of hitting the one and not the other.

But Horemheb was too wily a soldier to be taken aback by the same surprise twice. He sprang forwards at almost exactly the same time as Nakhtmin turned, and he was after him before either had the chance to take three paces. He did not turn his gaze for the briefest flicker from Nakhtmin's back but all the same he knew that the archers had lifted their bows and pulled taut the strings. He raised his sword and brought it down without breaking step. It connected neatly in the centre of Nakhtmin's head and split the crown of it in two. Nakhtmin did not have time to cry out before he was dead and his body fell to the ground in a shambles of arms and legs. It was a wound of sufficient depth, with a sufficient outflow of blood and the pointless grey mush that packed the inside of the skull, for Horemheb to be certain that the blow had been a mortal one.

He did not break his stride but darted away, back towards the houses in which he had first encountered Nakhtmin. Even as he moved he tensed himself for the sting of arrows launched from the city walls, knowing as he did that Nakhtmin's death removed the only factor that had prevented the archers from firing. In fact, Nakhtmin's body had barely lifted the dust from the ground where it fell before the archers had fired their arrows, although not a man among them had taken Horemheb's unexpected change of direction into account. Their arrows fell exactly where he had been standing had he continued in the same direction. Without hesitation, more arrows were removed from quivers, notched into bowstrings and released in a high arch. Horemheb heard a whine, a whistle, a rush of air as the projectiles accelerated down towards him. He could see that the doorway he sought was too far away.

He saw the faces of his officers screaming at him in the windows of the houses, urging him onwards as though they could ensnare him with their shouts and pull him to safety, some watching him, others watching the arrows as they fell towards him, their gaze dropping and dropping until, Horemheb knew, their eyes would meet his, and he would see no more.

Had I been a younger man I would have made it, Horemheb thought to himself, and what a glorious tale I could have told. What a glorious, glorious tale.

The Maya Papyrus, Fragments 518-521

I threw myself into the air, bringing one foot up behind me and pushing against the back wall of the alcove to give myself extra velocity. I was wasting my time. The heavy curtain which had up until this time proved such a reliable friend now decided to conspire against me and endeavour to wrap itself around my every limb. I did not fly from the alcove but rather fell from it, fumbling towards the floor and taking the curtain with me.

I had seen him approaching the house. I presume he must have scaled the gate or the walls, for the gate creaked when it opened and I had heard nothing. I had been standing on a chair in the darkness for some time, staring out of the window. It was a habit I had acquired ever since Horemheb had convinced me to follow his plan. Every evening before retiring I would watch the grounds for movement, cursing the chirruping of insects as I strained to hear the tell-tale rasp of the gates being opened. I forced myself to laugh at my own paranoia in order to lighten my heart, but even so my stints at the window grew longer with each passing night as the continued absence of an attack merely made one seem increasingly likely.

I forced myself to remain calm as I walked into my bedroom, set the lamp on the table, extinguished it, and went to hide in the alcove behind the heavy curtain that would so soon ally itself against me. I waited, trembling and praying that he would find the room empty and by some miracle be persuaded to search elsewhere.

Of course, he did not, and all too soon the night brought to my ears the unmistakable absence of sound within which a man envelopes himself when advancing carefully towards that which he fears may be a trap. I could see him no more than he could see me and I was sure of his whereabouts no more than he was sure of mine, and so the judgement I employed in deciding when to lunge really was no judgement at all and entrusted everything to fortune.

I jumped, and the curtain folded itself around me. I felt my body collide with my assailant, and my head clash painfully with his before we both met the floor. The curtain now was upon him and was preventing him from taking any action more decisive than a blind, restricted, and ultimately harmless flailing beneath what had now become a carpet.

What I did next makes me shudder even now, but I had little choice other than the acceptance of death, and I was very far from that particular road.

I lifted my bare foot and brought the heel down with as much force as I could muster on the place where I assumed his face must be. I was accurate enough. I believe my first attempt made contact with his temple and was powerful enough to bounce his head off the floor, momentarily slowing his struggles to a degree which allowed me to take a much more considered aim. I did so, and my heel connected squarely with the bridge of his nose. It was much softer than his skull.

I repeatedly stamped on his face as he gradually subsided into unconsciousness. It took much longer than I was expecting and when he had remained still long enough for me to lift the curtain from his face, I saw that he was in the grip of a sleep from which nobody but the gods ever wake. His face was unrecognisable as such, and it was the source of many dark rivers which were making their sluggish way across my floor. I fell to my knees.

Horemheb jumped.

He felt the sting of arrows even as the path of his flight meant that he would reach the safety of the doorway regardless of whether he was alive or dead when he reached it. He tumbled into the room and was immediately surrounded by his officers. It was only after some time that the crowd deigned to part and, in doing so, revealed that two of the officers were holding Horemheb between them and helping him upright. Two other men quickly moved to the door and immediately announced with an air of some confidence that the battle outside was all but over, the death of the opposition's general robbing them of their will to continue as surely as any number of mortal blows. The archers had already departed the scene and their compatriots were beginning to rout, leaving holes in their lines that those who remained were finding increasingly difficult to defend.

"Take me to my chariot," Horemheb said, on hearing the news.

"Sir," the officer supporting him to his left said. "You can hardly expect to ride."

One of Horemheb's legs was held at an awkward angle. Two arrows protruded from it; one from the calf, the other from the back of the thigh.

"I am dead if I rest here," Horemheb said. "Now take me to my chariot. Find a physician. He may prepare dressings for my wounds. I shall wait for nothing else. Move!"

The men around him sprang forward at his command, despite their misgivings. Two went to prepare his chariot and two helped him in the direction in which it awaited, while the remainder raced off in search of a physician. Horemheb's progress was necessarily slow and by the time he reached his chariot he found not one but two doctors preparing bandage strips along the ground. He was requested to lie on his stomach, and he was unable to prevent a scream ripping from him as the arrows were removed, his face buried in his arms and his fingers clawing at the dust which lay beneath them. Dressings were wrapped tightly around the wounds and he was lifted once more to his feet, dust and sand having become encrusted in the sweat on his face. He was helped into his chariot. He looked around at the faces turned towards him and spoke.

"Await my word," he told them. "Should you hear nothing, assume that I am dead and prepare for the fate of traitors. Should my word come, return to your homes and expect your loyalty to be recompensed a hundredfold."

It was not a rousing speech and nor was it meant to be. It was a quiet promise, and it was received with smiles and nods, not cheers. Horemheb turned from them and whipped his horses into a gallop.

He knew that he did not have time for his wounds to be dressed properly or for the luxury of succumbing to his pain. The routed enemy had only one place in mind, the same place held so dear by all defeated soldiers: home. They would head first for the ships that had been left with a minimal guard, moored further up the river, where they would find a small but determined force between them and their goal. Horemheb did not have men enough at his disposal to lavish this ambush with troops. It was designed, rather, to be a delaying force, able to grant Horemheb the time to steal a march on Nakhtmin's officers.

He expected his delaying tactics at the ships to split the enemy forces. Some would stay and fight because they would not know what else to do. Elements of the enemy's forces, he knew from experience, would simply saunter home, wounded, hungry and disconsolate.

Others, though, would be much more reluctant to impede their own progress any more than was absolutely necessary. These men would be officers, and they would be much more interested in returning to their king with news than with booty and, what was more, they were as cognisant of the need for speed as was Horemheb himself. The men who had accompanied Nakhtmin into Nubia were only a fraction of the armed forces at Aye's command. If Nakhtmin's men could effect a return before

Horemheb, those remaining forces would be immediately mobilised against him and he would be consigned to the Underworld in time for Nakhtmin to greet him.

If, however, Horemheb could reach Thebes first, an entirely more satisfactory history was eminently possible.

He spurred his horses on, every pothole and hillock making his leg feel as though it had been shot all over again. Before long his other leg was causing him just as much pain, for he had no choice but to put all his weight onto it. He could feel the jarring of the chariot all the way up into his spine.

He had been riding long enough only to break the horses' sweat when he saw the first signs of enemy troops. This was the reason for his decision to travel alone. He had known that his path must cross with that of the enemy at some point, and probably before the ships were reached. He had also known that there was more chance of his being able to slip through undetected as long as he had no retinue with him. The enemy were likely to be disorganised and confused and Horemheb's chariot was nothing out of the ordinary.

There were perhaps thirty or forty of them. There did not appear to be any officers commanding, and Horemheb did not expect there to be. For the column to have reached this point so quickly they must have abandoned their positions remarkably early in the battle, and Egyptian soldiers did not do that while their officer was alive to command them.

Horemheb wheeled his horses to the right, a manoeuvre which provoked a stab of pain from his injured leg, and attempted to pass the column to its rear. The area he was traversing would have been described as a road in only the most optimistic of portrayals and the desert to either side of it was nothing short of treacherous for horses and chariots alike. His speed immediately dropped as the wheels sank into the loose sand and the horses struggled to find purchase. The entire frame of the chariot listed to this side and that, and swapped from one to the other with much violence and little warning. It was all Horemheb could do to remain upon it. It was not long before he could feel the warmth of blood soaking into his bandages and trickling down the back of his leg.

One or two of the men in the column watched him pass with disinterested expressions, but did no more. His only dilemma was in judging the amount of interaction with the column that would prompt the least suspicion. Should he issue them orders? Would their suspicions be aroused if he simply rode past without acknowledging them?

As he passed, he was unable to prevent himself staring steadfastly towards the front, feeling conspicuous for it but somehow compelled to continue. Each movement felt so contrived to appear nonchalant that it seemed to him to be the surest advertisement of his true identity. It was only when the column was out of sight that he allowed himself some degree of relief.

The afternoon sun was already high in the sky by the time he had set off and it was not long before it was sinking towards the horizon. He had been riding steadily northwards, unsure of the local geography but confident that he would have to come across a settlement of some description before too long. And now, slowly merging with the approaching dusk, he thought he espied the uniform silhouettes of buildings in the distance. He spurred his horses on as quickly as their exhaustion would allow them.

Their tiredness and discomfort was matched only by his own. The pain in his leg had grown steadily during his journey. Swollen flesh bulged out above and below his bandages as though his leg belonged to a much fatter man. On occasion during the journey he had felt the world tip away from him and the light of his vision fade, and it was an act only of sheer will that prevented him from succumbing to unconsciousness. It would have afforded him all the joy in the world to simply step down from his chariot and lie on the ground.

But here was respite. Here was a village or a town, perhaps large enough to have a dock and river craft large and swift enough to take him home in relative comfort. He was sure that he must be here ahead of Nakhtmin's men, for he had encountered no others on the road after the first column.

He allowed his horses to slow slightly on entering what would perhaps one day evolve into the streets of the ramshackle town in which he found himself. It was nothing more, really, than a conglomeration of poverty. Horemheb made his way towards what was less a harbour and more simply a flat piece of land adjoining the river. He knew before he saw it that he was wasting his time but he could not risk missing the chance.

He approached the river and found a group of fishermen there, mending their nets. They looked up as he approached and gave each other meaningful glances but did not seem unduly surprised at the apparition of neglect they saw before them.

Already knowing the answer, Horemheb asked them if there was in the vicinity a craft that could travel as far north as Thebes faster than a chariot could carry him. The reply, as he had correctly surmised, was in the negative.

"Is there then one that can at least take me as far as the next northward town?"

The men shook their heads.

"There is not," one of them said. "We have but one boat, it is powered by oars, not wind, and I can assure you as a regular passenger of that vessel that you would be lucky if it carried you to the far bank without wetting your knees."

There was a general good natured murmur of assent from all but one of the fishermen, the exception presumably being the boat's owner.

"It has served you well enough on many an occasion," this one man now interjected.

"Well enough when I was in need of a wash," the other replied.

"Gentlemen, please," Horemheb said, fearing a general discussion on the river worthiness of the boat in question. "Can you tell me of anywhere I may be able to procure myself of a ship?"

"A ship, he says!" another fishermen said, feigning the accent of a man of nobility. "His Majesty would like a ship! Does one have one, Meryra?"

"Do you know, one may have left it in one's palace," Meryra answered.

This display of wit was well appreciated by the gathering, who seemed for the moment to have forgotten that Horemheb was there.

"I do not have time for jokes!" he shouted, an act which resulted in the somewhat premature conclusion of the laughter and the turning of all heads towards him.

"I presume you are from the battle to the south?" the first fisherman asked.

"Yes, and..." Horemheb said, and then stopped. "How do you know about the battle to the south?"

"Listen, friend," the fisherman answered, standing up with some effort. "I know you need to get to Thebes, but I can only tell you what I told your comrades. There is nothing for you here. I would suggest you try further north."

Horemheb barely heard the conclusion to the man's statement. He was already turning his horses to resume his sprint for home.

The Maya Papyrus, Fragments 526-529

> *It was my cue, this intrusion, this body on the floor. It was all the information I needed concerning the knowledge and intentions of our adversaries. In fact, I now knew more of these matters than I did of the fate of those whom I would call allies, for no news had reached me from Nubia and I did not know whether Horemheb was alive or dead, or whether Nakhtmin was consigned to the*

sand or at that moment racing back to relieve my shoulders of the weight of my head.

Horemheb had prepared me for such an eventuality. In fact it was integral to his plan, for not only did he expect it but he relied upon it to force me into action when my ill-advised sense of self-preservation may have persuaded me of the merits of inactivity.

"If you are attacked," he had told me, "and if you are prepared but appear not to be, there is a fair chance that you will survive."

"I shall keep your words as a great comfort to me in the dark hours of the night," I said, drily. Horemheb ignored me.

"And if you survive," he continued, "then you must act immediately."

"And what if you have not shared my luck and lie dead in some Nubian backwater?"

"It changes nothing," he told me. "For if I am dead Nakhtmin will be coming for you, and you will need to manoeuvre yourself into some position of power before he returns. It will be your only chance."

"And if you have been victorious?"

"Then I need you to act in exactly the same way, for you will need to prepare the way for me. Without your decisive grasp of the situation in Thebes I shall have nothing to return to, and however great my victory in Nubia I shall meet nothing here but my executioner, who, I might add, will work on you just as enthusiastically."

"I think we are taking a terrible risk," I said, not for the first time.

"Men cannot achieve greatness without risk."

"But I think I may live just as happily without either."

There was a flash of anger in his face and I decided that, on balance, continuing might carry slightly less risk than defying him, and I silenced my objections.

"Are you clear on your actions should Nakhtmin's agents act before my return?"

"I am," I said. "Should I be lucky enough to be drawing breath I shall take myself directly to the palace, where I shall crave an audience with the king."

"And then?"

"And then I shall probably be executed. Horemheb, I know all this. We have been over it so many times I not only know my answers, but I know the questions you are about to ask. Please, try

to resist the temptation to remind me of the idiocy with which I am about to act."

"I merely wish to impress upon you the importance of the successful execution of your duties."

"Believe me," I said, "there are few men on this earth who are more aware."

And I remained so, even now, as I looked down upon the man who had come to kill me. I was dreading what I must do next, for it would take more than a little courage and even more nerve, and now there was no longer any consolation to be had in the notion that the necessity of it might never materialise, or that if it did, it was to be in some undetermined future that could be safely ignored.

Still, there was little I could do before the break of day, and so I occupied myself with the removal of the body.

I did not even attempt to sleep for the rest of the night, but remained in my living quarters, watching the rectangle of darkness framed by my window pale slowly into dawn. I set off for the palace.

I called in at the temple of Amun on the way and spoke briefly to the High Priest, who was not altogether surprised by my request and agreed to it readily enough.

At the palace I found Aye sitting up in bed, eating a breakfast of fruit. Between mouthfuls he would regard each piece as though he was not entirely sure what it was and was momentarily undecided as to what to do with it next. I took this as a favourable sign.

"How is he?" I asked his manservant, who was waiting by the door.

"Confused," he said.

I nodded, as though in sympathy.

"We have matters of court to discuss," I said. "You may leave us alone."

"I am not sure that he will be able..." the man started, but I silenced him with a gentle hand on his arm.

"I know," I said. "But they are matters of some import. I must try."

The servant bowed and left the room.

"Father," I said, approaching the bed. He regarded me in the way that a man might look at an old acquaintance whom he once knew but can no longer remember from where.

"Yes?" he said, in an uncertain tone that suggested that he was not convinced that it was he whom I was addressing.

"Do you know who I am?" I asked him.

"Of course I do," he said.

"Who am I?"

"You need to ask?"

"Yes," I said. "Who am I?"

"You are," he said, hesitantly, and undoubtedly remembering that I had just addressed him as father, "my son."

"Your memory serves you well today, then?"

"Of course," he said. "I am pharaoh. The gods would never rob me of my faculties. I am as fit as I have ever been."

"Of course you are," I said.

"Do you have matters of court which you would like to discuss with me?" he said, pressing home the point. "Would you like my advice on political matters? Should I dictate policies of diplomacy and war? In the whole of Egypt there is not a man with such a grasp on the minutiae of life."

I looked at him.

"Have you seen Akhenaten today?" I asked.

He was about to reply and then stopped. He exhaled and stared for a moment over my shoulder.

"No," he said, and for a moment I feared that he had regained his lucidity at exactly the time which would be the most injurious to my well being.

"No," he said again. "It is yet early. I expect he will be along shortly."

I all but fell to my knees and thanked Amun for the gift of my father's fragility of mind.

"We have matters of great import to discuss with him," I said.

"Yes," Aye said. "Yes, of course."

"Do you know," I said, leaning forwards conspiratorially, "I think we shall need to tread carefully with him at the moment. He is in a rather zealous mood."

"Zealous?" Aye asked.

"With regards to the Aten," I said.

"Ah," Aye said, nodding. "Yes. The Aten. I see."

"I think it better if we play along for now," I said. "There is no telling what he will do if he is questioned. He is most indignant." My voice now fell to a whisper. "Yesterday, he began executing heretics. Mahu has the army behind him. If we are to fight him we must bide our time."

"Yes," Aye said. "We shall."

I stared at him for a moment and watched his gaze flick around the room as though searching for something familiar. There was confusion and not a little fear in his eyes, as though he had woken up in a room he had never seen before. He looked lost and I could not help feeling a twinge of sympathy for him. He was still my father, and there is something inimitably sad about a man falling from such pinnacles of authority to such trenches of helplessness.

"Akhenaten is without," I said, at last.

"He is?" Aye said, the look of concern on his face growing more pronounced.

"He demands that you see him."

"About what?"

I shrugged. "I have no idea," I said. "But I think he may have somehow got wind of the fact that you oppose the Aten."

"What? But how could that have happened? Who could have told him?"

"I think you did, father."

"I? But..."

"Surely you remember?" I said, and he stammered to a halt.

"Well," he said. "Yes, yes, of course, but..."

"Mahu is waiting in the palace courtyard."

"For what?" Aye asked.

"I am afraid to hazard a guess," I said. "Although he has men with him, and they are erecting a stake."

Aye swallowed. "A stake?" he spluttered. "For what purpose?"

I did not reply. Instead, I retreated to the doorway.

"I shall bring him in," I said. "Do as your wisdom commands."

Aye nodded. I left the room and found, looking nervous in the corridor outside the anteroom, the High Priest of Amun.

"His Majesty will see you now," I told him, leading him through the antechamber into the king's bedroom. "Please try to remain calm. He has been unpredictable of late and he may not recognise you. He becomes agitated if his misconceptions are challenged, so simply agree with whatever he has to say."

By this time we were at the door to the bedchamber and I pushed it open and ushered the High Priest over the threshold before he had the opportunity to question me.

I stepped in behind him and saw that Aye was climbing out of bed. He looked slightly panicked, and the High Priest's arrival did nothing to calm his spirits. His feet had hardly touched the floor before he was sliding to his knees before the astonished priest, who could not help but halt his progress and take a step backwards where he met my hands, which put paid to his retreat.

"Your Majesty," Aye said, prostrating himself with some effort on the floor before the High Priest's feet.

"Er..." the priest said.

"May the Aten bless you and your family a thousand times and a thousand times again," Aye said.

"The Aten?" the priest said.

"Of course, Your Majesty," Aye said. "The Aten. The greatest of gods. The one true god, the giver of life, the creator who brings order from chaos."

"You believe the Aten to be the one true god?" the priest asked.

"Of course," Aye said. "Who could doubt such a thing? I have given the subject much thought, as you know, and I now feel able to speak with some conviction." Aye glanced at me with a knowing look before he continued, and it was a look that weighs heavily on my heart to this day. "I would suffer indeed to believe that you considered my sometimes sceptical nature to be a sign of heresy. I merely wish to ensure that my beliefs are founded in wisdom and meditation. It is only after putting the subject under such scrutiny as I have that I can confidently proclaim the Aten as the creator, and Pharaoh as his emissary on earth."

I stepped forwards at this point, for the interview had proceeded along lines that I would never have been so optimistic to expect. If I had written it myself it could not have been so perfect, for I would undoubtedly have scripted some semblance of dignity for my father. I touched the High Priest's arm and tore him from the fascination that was Aye. Gently, I guided him towards the door, neither of us speaking.

Only in the antechamber did I raise my eyes from the floor.

"You see my problem?" I said.

"How could I not?"

"The question is, what can we do about it?"

The High Priest was silent for a moment, as though suspicious of the route that the conversation was taking.

"No," he said. "The question is surely whether we have any right to do something about it."

I shrugged. "Just so," I said. "Perhaps it is not our place to question the mind of a king, for surely there lies the domain of gods."

"Indeed," the priest said, thoughtfully. "Indeed."

"Of course," I said, as though the thought had at that moment occurred to me, "if His Majesty is absolutely determined to bring back Atenism, who are we to prevent him?"

"What?" the priest said.

"I said…"

"I know what you said. What did you mean by it?"

I gave him an incredulous look. "Were you in the room with me just then? You heard the king's words as well as I did. Was there any ambiguity to be had in them?"

"But he was just confused," the priest said. "He did not mean…"

"He meant every word," I said. I was beginning to wonder whether the scheme had gone as smoothly as at first I had believed. "Do you think I would have asked you here to witness meaningless ravings? I have brought you here because we face a great danger, and we need to act lest it consumes us all."

"He really speaks of returning us to Atenism?"

"He speaks of little else."

"But he must know that it is impossible! The people would never hear of it!"

"The people?" I said. "Do you think the people will have any choice but to hear of it, and to troop to worship at the Aten's feet and to demolish, stone by stone, all the temples of Amun?"

"But he is mad!"

"And you think that diminishes his power? Did it diminish Akhenaten's power? Madness is a strength of kings, not a weakness."

There was a long silence, during which time the priest considered the situation.

"What can I do?" he asked me, quietly, at last.

Horemheb had never before felt such pain, or such frailty. He had been travelling for two days without rest. The wig he wore over his shaved head had shielded him from the malaise which overtook men who stayed unprotected too long under the heat of the desert sun, but that same sun had lashed him without mercy during his journey. His skin, especially across his shoulders and along his forearms, was blistered and weeping. He had found that his leg wounds would stop bleeding only as long as his leg remained immobile. Blood had caked around the wounds and into the bandages and started to form scabs, but these were ripped away whenever the leg bent or straightened. His vision was suffering, for nothing in it was fixed; rather, the sights he saw before him melted and blurred into each other as though he was seeing them through undulating waters. But there was another discomfort which eclipsed all others. The leg without the wounds had been carrying almost his entire weight without respite for the whole journey. It felt as though the muscles were nothing more than frayed ropes holding a hide loosely together. Every change in the chariot's attitude was a precipice of agony, over which he repeatedly fell without control or hope of salvation. It was a torture such that only the gods could conjure, and the intensity and relentlessness of it, the sheer monotony of its application, brought from him howls and screams and cries for mercy loud and persistent enough for all the gods to hear, and ignore.

All he had to preserve himself was the greatest of determinations. He had seen traitors dragged before baying crowds to be deposited on sharpened stakes and abandoned to be killed by their own weight. They were memories he forced himself to keep forefront in his mind, for they were a more effective fuel for his resolve than the release from any amount of pain.

Every settlement he came to gave him news of men who had preceded him, also heading north and seeking a ship to carry them onwards. Each settlement proved to be as poor as the last. In places his route led him alongside the river, where the land was lush and fecund and some shade was to be had. Here and there he would allow himself to stop long enough to drink from streams or pick fruit, and, for however short a time, there would be the slightest of respites from his agony. Other times he would be forced to take short cuts across the desert where the river looped out to the west in the hope of being able to keep his course true enough to meet it again when it meandered back to meet him.

On two occasions his vision cleared to the extent where he could see for some distance before him and he thought he saw a faint dust cloud on the northern horizon. He thought that he was closer to it on the second occasion. He forced his horses to gallop onwards and tried to imagine the pain of impalement.

The Maya Papyrus, Fragments 531-538

> *It happened the day after I gave the High Priest his unforgettable audience with the king.*

I was at the palace, for I had decided that the safest place to be when the lion is away is in the lion's den. I was making a show of carrying out duties, the nature of which I could not have told you then and I cannot tell you now. Although I walked and talked and ate and worked, everything seemed to pass through me. When I copied court documents the words went from my eyes to my hands without me having any knowledge of them or their meaning. I could hold conversations and turn away without knowing anything of their subject or outcome. I have had dreams on occasion where I have known that I am asleep but have been unable to wake up and prevent the dream from taking its course. This was not unlike that distracting state.

My fear consumed me. It tainted the very air I breathed so that I would sometimes find myself gasping in empty rooms, leaning against whatever surface was closest to hand, my chest heaving and my heart pumping as though exhausted from some physical exertion. This happened to me on four separate occasions and each time I feared that I was at the very extremity of my life, able neither to move nor to call for help, and all I could think about was the danger in which I had placed myself and the fate that may await me should I be lucky enough to see the setting of another sun. Each episode passed after a short while and I was left to catch my breath and wonder if the gods were punishing me for my actions and had decided to taunt me with my life rather than simply taking it.

As it was, events quickly unfolded in such a way as to put even these fears into perspective.

I remember exactly where I was. The time of the Festival of Opet was approaching and I was surrounded by scribes, desperately trying to concentrate on some simple work in its preparation. It was an employment usually entrusted as a first duty to newcomers for there was little that an intelligent man could get wrong. I was surrounded by torn and crumpled papyri, each piece discarded with increasing vigour as I noticed that I had omitted words or, on occasion, entire lines. It was so distant from the famous festival presided over by Tutankhamun that it was as though my memories were dreams.

I was suddenly startled by the door flying open with such violence that its hinges were hard put to take the strain and a young priest flew into the room, took a moment to locate a friend and then whispered to him in urgent tones before leaving with all the energy with which he had entered. For all the time it took for his whisper to multiply and travel the length and breadth of the room he may as well have shouted his news as he passed.

There was, it seemed, a chariot at the gate, and within it there was standing a man so haggard that it seemed he was remaining upright simply through force of habit. He had arrived, it was also duly reported, after an uninterrupted journey from a battle on the Nubian border. At this portion of news I climbed hastily to my feet, disturbing the small mountain of papyrus leaves that was forming around my crossed legs.

"This man," I said. "Is he a general?"

The faces in the room all turned to me and then to each other, each with an expression as blank as the last. The priest who had brought the news had taken with him unspoken any part of it which I may have found to be of use.

I let out a cry of frustration and waded through the scribes, pushing away those not sprightly enough to quit my path. Few of them had ever seen me so animated and gasps of astonishment followed me from the room.

I ran to the door which opened out onto the palace courtyard. I stepped outside, squinting at the sky and pitying any man, friend or foe, who had travelled so far under such heat. I raced forwards, one or two of the more curious palace inhabitants accompanying me, and bounded up the steps which led to the viewing platform from which the gate guards could look down upon those who approached.

I poked my head over the parapet, a cry of greeting garrotted in my throat. There was indeed a chariot at the gate, and it did indeed contain a man a step closer to death than he was to recovery, but I had not expected the chariot to be accompanied by two others, each with a cargo as frail as the first. I recognised none of them.

"We demand to see His Majesty the king!" one of them shouted.

"It is a matter of the gravest urgency!" another added, as if their appearance could hint at a social visit.

The guard commander appeared next to me on the parapet. He looked like a man who had been interrupted doing something prohibited and who now feared that the sudden flurry of activity might prove his undoing. Weeks, and sometimes months, can pass for a gate commander with nothing of even the remotest interest happening and it was not unknown for them to while away the time whoring and sleeping. By this man's tousled appearance, he *may have been doing either when the news of a commotion at the gates reached him.*

"Who are you?" he shouted down at the three chariots. "What business have you with His Majesty?"

"Be careful," I whispered to him, before they had chance of reply. He glanced at me as though noticing me for the first time.

"What?" he shouted down at the men when he realised he had not listened to their reply.

"We are officers in Nakhtmin's army!" one of them repeated, emphasising each word, as though shouting them to someone much further away. "You must admit us immediately! We have news of Nakhtmin for His Majesty!"

"What news?" I whispered to the gate commander.

"What news?" he shouted to the men below.

"News of treachery!"

"What treachery?" I whispered to the gate commander.

"What treachery?" he shouted to the men below.

"We have no time to waste!" came the reply. "We have news that is for the king's ears alone! We have no desire to discuss it with soldiers and courtiers. I ask you again: will you allow us passage to impart news of the greatest urgency to the ears of His Majesty the king himself? Do you intend to endanger his kingdom with further delay?"

The gate commander moved as though to order the opening of the gates, but I stayed him with a hand on his arm.

"Wait," I said. "What are you doing?"

"You heard them," he said. "I must admit them."

"On their word?"

"My lord?"

"Do you intend," I said, slowly, "to admit men to see His Majesty the king purely on their word alone? Do you really know who these men are?"

I was desperate and could only hope that the commander would take my desperation for genuine concern for the safety of the king. I knew that should these men pass through the gate the game was up. There would be no hope of rescue or reprieve, for once through the gate there would be nothing preventing them being granted an audience with the king and Horemheb's coup being laid bare for all to see. My mind flooded with opportunities to impede the men's progress: I could persuade the gate commander that they were not to be trusted and were to be delayed until their identities could be confirmed, I could insist on an armed escort for them and then wait for one to be assembled, I could announce that I would arrange the audience myself and then find a million reasons to defer it, but there was nothing, absolutely nothing that I could do to cancel the audience rather than simply postpone it.

Still, desperation is a stubborn master and I was willing to cling at anything that might delay the inevitable, however inevitable it may be.

"If there is treachery afoot," I said to the gate commander, "had you not better ensure that these men are not the traitors?"

"But..." the commander said.

"What would be the best method for traitors to breach the palace walls?" I asked him. "A frontal assault? It would cost them days, and far too many lives. Would they not be better sacrificing one or two skilfully disguised and persuasive assassins?"

"I will arrange an escort for them."

"Not good enough," I said. "Not to guarantee the king's safety."

"But what if they are not assassins, my lord?" the commander said. "What if they speak the truth?"

"Commander!" one of the men shouted from below. "Do you side with the traitors? Are you so keen to prevent us bringing them to justice?"

"You cannot admit them!" I said to the commander, grabbing his shoulders.

"Are you in league with Horemheb, commander?" another man shouted. "Is this why you would stop us?"

My desperation was naked, and for the first time the commander saw it for what it really was. He looked at me in amazement and then, slowly, brought up his hands to remove mine from his shoulders.

I was beginning to panic.

"Please," I begged.

He turned his head to one side, swivelling his eyes so that his gaze continued to meet mine.

"Guards," he said. "Arrest this man."

People heard him coming from streets away. A horse and chariot galloping through a city made a noise that was difficult to ignore, and he found that it gave sufficient warning for a clear path to open up before him. Clearing the centre of the streets of people had the effect of gathering them all at the sides and it appeared almost as though Horemheb was the principal rider in some bizarre procession. It appeared to the people of the city as though a dead man was in their midst.

Horemheb knew the route to the palace well enough to concentrate on other matters as he guided his horses to their destination. He had no idea what awaited him, but knew that the cloud of dust he had seen before him in the desert was not too far ahead of him, and that he had been gaining on it but that he had never overtaken it. If, as he feared, it was evidence for Nakhtmin's men, they must by now have reached the palace and were perhaps already within, persuading the king and his court of the necessity of Horemheb's immediate and prolonged death.

He rounded the last bend and saw that he had indeed been beaten to his objective. This much he had expected, but he had never expected the gates to be open. A mob had formed and there was evidently some confusion, as there is wont to be when several groups of people occupy the same space with no common goal. The mob had at least two centres of attention, which became manifest as Horemheb drew closer. As he approached, the clatter of his wheels and the resounding of the horses' hooves drew the attention of one or two of the participants in the gateway who, as it became increasingly obvious that he had no intention of stopping, forgot their immediate concerns and grabbed the attention of those too involved to hear the approaching commotion. Before he reached them, the more prescient members of the crowd began to move out of the way but others, as was sometimes to be expected with those who were confident with their own place in the world and unwilling to yield it, even to their own detriment, waited until he almost burst through them before sense prevailed and they threw themselves to either side in a sudden outbreak of activity.

Horemheb wheeled his horses around in the courtyard, coming to a halt by the great doors that led inside, and examined the chaos he had left in his wake. Men were clambering to their feet and drawing their swords. Others, whom Horemheb assumed to be the men he had been following all the way from Nubia, seemed too exhausted and stunned to make any discernible reaction to his appearance other than to feebly urge the guards to respond.

"Wait!" he was about to shout, before another voice pre-empted him.

The Maya Papyrus, Fragments 540-546

"Wait!" I shouted, and rushed forwards. I had been marched from the wall down into the courtyard, a guard holding each of my arms. Horemheb's arrival was surprise enough for me to wrench myself free from their grasp. I waved my arms frantically as I ran, fearful that my exclamation may not have been enough to fully capture the attention of those nervous men around me.

Everything stopped and I became the focus of everyone's interest. Only Nakhtmin's men looked as though they had something to add to the situation. They puffed up their chests as best they could and stepped forward to match my advance.

"You are a traitor, sir!" one of them proclaimed. "And you are in league with this man - " here he gestured dismissively towards Horemheb, " - who dares to masquerade under the guise of His Majesty's service."

"Do you know who this man is?" I asked the gathered masses, generals and guards together, walking towards Horemheb and holding my arms out to him as though tempted to fold him into my embrace. I knew enough of public address to recognise the importance of launching my own verbal offensive before the audience fell prey to the oratory of my opponents. "Have you any idea of the station of the man you dare to threaten with your swords?"

It was enough to waft the scent of doubt towards the guards, and was enough to persuade them to allow their swords to wilt somewhat.

"This," I declared, "is General Horemheb, commander of the king's armies, loyal servant to my father, His Majesty the king. How dare you challenge him?"

I looked to each of them. The guard commander even paid me the compliment of looking at the ground to avoid my piercing gaze. It was all the encouragement I needed to continue.

"And what of these?" I said, moving towards the men who had arrived before Horemheb. "Who are they? Are they princes? Are they courtiers? Or are they common officers, with much to gain from a swing of power?"

Nobody seemed to be very willing to volunteer an opinion. "They are nothing!" I said, careful not to meet the eyes of the men I so denigrated for fear that their glares would rob me of my so recently acquired confidence. "And yet they arrive here unannounced and have the temerity to accuse others of treachery!"

Horemheb was climbing down from his chariot and the sight of him trying to move shocked me. He looked like a man at the very extremity of old age, who takes every slow step as though unsure whether he will live to see his foot make it to the ground.

"Do you see how this most venerable of men has suffered in the service of his king? See the wounds he has endured? And yet men arrive from nowhere, unbidden and unexpected and you jump to their command! What are you thinking?"

I was addressing my words mainly towards the guard commander, for he seemed by far the most likely to be swayed by them. Horemheb obviously suspected the same thing. He had taken one or two steps towards the doors leading into the palace and was now in fact close enough to reach out and touch them. When he spoke, he did so as though the commander was the only man there to hear him.

"There is treachery indeed," he said, "but you must turn to these creatures to find its source. I have rushed from the heat of the battle in order to report their sedition directly to the king himself. The fact that their rebellion failed is no reason to treat them with leniency."

He reached around and opened the door, never for a moment allowing his gaze to move from the face of the guard commander. "And to think," he scoffed, "that you almost allowed them access to the king. Prince Maya, you may accompany me to the audience chamber."

And with that, he turned and walked into the palace, leaving me to scramble in behind him.

"Inspired," I whispered as the doors closed behind us and I reached out to steady him.

"Hardly," he said. "They will be on our heels before we reach the next corner."

I glanced nervously over my shoulder. "Do you really think so?" I said.

"Without a doubt. You know what you have to do."

We took a couple of steps in silence.

"I cannot," I said.

"Maya," Horemheb said, his breath bubbling and rasping in his throat at the frustration of it all. "They must capture me. It is our only hope. We both have our duties."

"It would seem that walking slow enough to be captured would be the easier of the two."

"Perhaps you would care to swap?" he asked me. "You would perhaps prefer to be captured by your enemies, with all the risk that it entails?"

"You know what I mean," I said. "I said I cannot, and I mean it."

"For once in your life demonstrate that you have the thinnest sliver of courage in your character."

It was a comment that I resented at the time, and Horemheb has since apologised for it. I think it was born of frustration and a desire to shame me into action. It did shame me, but it was far from enough to grant me the courage I lacked. We reached the junction of two corridors, one of which led to the left, the other stretching straight ahead before us.

"Maya," Horemheb said. "For the love of everyone you have lost, for the life that you cherish, for the life of the one friend that Aye and Nakhtmin have allowed you to retain, in the name of Amun and Tutankhamun and Ankhesenamun, act now. Grasp your world by the throat and shake it until all the injustice you have suffered and all the crimes against those you loved are punished. Be a man, Maya. Choose. Will you be the man who walks the streets with his footsteps cushioned by the knowledge that he has done the right thing in the name of good people, or the man dragged to his execution, grateful for death to take away the shame of cowardice and apathy? There is no key to the Underworld like a principle honoured."

I looked at him, desperate for some excuse for dishonour.

"If those doors open and you are seen, we are finished," he said.

I did not speak, but I turned towards the king's bedchamber and I walked away, already weeping for the crime I was about to commit. Even the most cynical of killers, even those possessed by the most reckless of demons, would balk at the murder of his own father.

Horemheb continued onwards at his own melancholy pace. He was not very much mistaken with his estimate of the success of his delaying tactics. He heard the door swing open behind him before he was very much further and the sound of footsteps advancing towards him in haste.

He tensed for the guards' assault, but none came. Whether it was because of his position or perceived frailty, or whether his words outside had been more effective than he had imagined he could not tell, but the guards did not attempt to manhandle him. They merely stopped beside him and held their swords before him in such a way that made it impossible for him to continue.

"The commander says you are to come with us, sir," one of them said.

"And if I refuse?" Horemheb asked them, with no intention of refusing.

"Then we are instructed to bring you by force. Sir."

"Most regrettable," Horemheb said. "It is little wonder that revolutionaries feel safe to ply their trade in this country, when the most powerful of Egypt's generals are held to account by clerks and knuckleheads."

"We are also instructed to return with Prince Maya, sir."

"Ah, well there I am afraid I cannot help you. You see, Maya has fled." Horemheb gestured vaguely in the opposite direction to that of the king's bedchamber.

The guards hesitated.

"Bring him back if you must," Horemheb said. "But I do not imagine that he will be very pleased with the idea of a gate guard feeling mighty enough to restrict his movements around his own palace. Still, I have known men more vengeful, so I am sure that you will be fine. Remember that he is a prince. Only the king ranks higher than him in the Two Lands."

"And Prince Nakhtmin," one of the guards said.

"And Prince Nakhtmin," Horemheb conceded, quietly.

The guards looked at each other before shrugging and leading Horemheb, whose injuries now seemed to be further sapping his strength and his speed with every step, back towards the door.

Once back in the courtyard, Horemheb quickly saw that Nakhtmin's men had been similarly placed under arrest and he could not help but smile to himself. It was perhaps the only sensible option open to the gate commander, and he had hit upon it at last. When in doubt, swiftness of action is often the wisest course and then you can arrest everyone left standing.

"Now," the commander said. "Perhaps we can get to the bottom of this."

The Maya Papyrus, Fragments 547-551

Oblivious to everything, Aye was asleep when I opened the door. I watched him for a moment and then, wiping my eyes and taking a deep, faltering breath, I stepped into the room and closed the door behind me, never once letting my gaze stray from him. He was lying on his back, his mouth open, snoring gently. I walked across the room, picking up a cushion on my way and then hugging it as though it was an instrument of comfort rather than murder.

I sat down on the edge of the bed, roughly enough to disturb him, for I was not about to kill a man in his sleep. I think also that I wanted to give him the opportunity to plead for his life; not for the pleasure of hearing it, but the opportunity of heeding it.

Aye snuffled and snorted and muttered something I did not catch, but he did not wake up. I turned the cushion over in my hands and cleared my throat enthusiastically and then fussily made myself more comfortable on the bed.

"Father," I said.

"Aye," I said.

Aye opened his eyes and looked at the ceiling for a moment before focussing on me.

"Maya," he said, and I raised my eyebrows.

"You recognise me?" I asked him.

"Of course I recognise you," he said, testily. "Do you think me incapable of recognising my own son?"

"On the contrary," I said. "I think you capable of anything."

He made a brief noise that may, in some circumstances, have been taken for a laugh.

"What do you want?" he said.

"To tell you that the end is come."

For the first time I saw a look of concern pass across his face, although it arrived and departed in the briefest of moments.

"I am not sure that I like your tone," he said. "What end?"

"The end," I said. "The end of everything. The end of the family, the end of the dynasty, the end of the dream."

"Then it must be the end of me as well, for that is the only route to these heinous goals that you parade before me."

I said nothing.

"Do you intend to kill me, Tutankhamun?" he said.

"I am Maya, father," I said.

"I know that," he said. "My question remains the same, whoever you are."

"I have no choice," I said. "Events seem to have gathered a pace of their own, like a stampede that starts with one bull."

"Very poetic," Aye said, with a sneer. "Hardly a likely attribute of a killer."

"I am not a killer," I said.

"No," Aye said. "But I am, and I have crushed men with more mettle and power than you will ever know. You are not going to kill me, Maya. You have only one hope, and that is to leave the room and never speak of this again. Should you do so I will not reveal the details of this visit to your brother and he will not feel the need to protect me from possibilities of its recurrence."

"Nakhtmin is dead," I said.

"What? When? Who is responsible for this?"

"Horemheb," I said.

"Then he is as good as dead. I shall see to it with my own hands."

"No," I said. "You will not."

Aye then did something I had never seen him do before, something I suspected he had never done, with or without witnesses. He began to cry. There was no sobbing or renting of garments or railing with fists at the sky; simply a reddening of the eyes and a tear or two on the cheek, a sniff and a wipe of the face, but all the same he was weeping, and I have never seen him looking so human.

"Then you are my only hope," he said to me, after a moment or two of silence had passed. "You are my heir. The dynasty's heir."

"There is no dynasty," I said. "You are its last member. After you, Horemheb will take the throne."

"Nonsense," he said, rallying briefly. "Listen. You are the heir. There is no need to submit to Horemheb's will. Together we will ensure that you inherit the throne from me. You can be pharaoh, Tutankhamun."

"I am Maya, father, and I do not want to be pharaoh."

"Nonsense," he said. "Of course you want to be pharaoh. What would your father say if he heard you speaking like that?"

"I am Maya," I said. "You are my father."

"But if you will not be pharaoh, who will?"

"Horemheb will," I said.

"No," he said. "This will simply not do. Fetch my mother. She will know what to do. She always knows what to do. She knows that I have only ever acted for her."

"Thuya is dead," I said. "She has been dead a long time."

"Did Amun tell you to come here?" he said, surprising me with the sudden change of subject.

"Amun?" I said. "No, of course not. Why?"

"I saw him once," he said. "I saw him in the shadows in the corner of the room after I had killed Giludkhepa and her baby."

"You killed a baby?" I asked, astonished that even Aye would be capable of such a thing.

"I had no choice," he said. "He was standing between your father and the throne."

"You are my father," I said.

"Amun was watching me that night. I sensed it at the time. He was in the corner of the room, a man with a cobra's head."

"Who else have you killed?" I said.

"Oh, he never came back," Aye said. "He knew better. He knew that I was his champion, and that my actions were only for his glory, and that the dynasty was his only protection from your father and his ridiculous religion."

"I am not Tutankhamun," I said. "You are my father."

"He never came back. Not when I was forced to send Nefertiti to him. Not when I was forced to kill..." He trailed off and regarded me with a curious expression, realising that I could not be who he had convinced himself that I was. "Not when I was forced to kill Tutankhamun," he finished, quietly.

By now it was I who was weeping, but with much less dignity and much more emotion than my father had done.

"You killed Nefertiti?" I said.

"I had no choice," he said. "I have never acted for myself. Only the family. Only ever the family."

"As do I now," I said, standing up and lifting the cushion before me. "You are a monster."

He lifted up his hands to ward me off, and whether by accident or design they fell upon mine where I was holding the edges of the cushion. I paused.

"Do you see," he said to me, "how the purest motives can lead to the foulest actions?"

Undeterred, too stricken by grief and rage to be deterred, I pushed the cushion down into his face, and I held it there while his struggles ebbed away. I would have difficulty describing my feelings upon entering the room. Fear, certainly, presided over any other emotion and tinged everything with its own bitter flavour, but there was mercy also within me and even, to some extent, respect, for respect for one's father is not something that can be *muted simply because he does not deserve it. But by the time I was standing over him, leaning onto the cushion and feeling the weight of myself in my shoulders, any sense of mercy or fear had left me, replaced only by fury. Were I a more superstitious man I would tell you that the spirit of my sister and nephew watched over my shoulder with quiet approval as the life of their tormentor stole from his body. I would tell you that Amun himself applauded my actions and that the gods rubbed their hands at the prospect of their new arrival. The truth is, though, that I cared nothing for the judgement of the gods. I did not even care about the judgement of Nefertiti or Tutankhamun. I cared, at that moment, only about my judgement, about the person I would have been had I permitted Aye's admissions to go unpunished. I cared only that refusing the opportunity to mete revenge would make me an accessory to the crimes he had committed.*

I was a good man. I am a good man. I could not give myself such an epithet had I acted any differently that day in my father's palace, for in acting any differently I would have been condoning his crimes, and a good man cannot do such a thing.

And so I leant, and I pushed, and I waited. Aye's struggling grew weaker with every flail of his arms until, finally, it stopped and his body lost its rigidity and relaxed, his arms lolling over the sides of the bed. I removed the cushion and placed it back where I had found it.

My family's dynasty had come to an end.

When the guards found me, they found me on the floor of the king's bedchamber, wailing like a penitent sinner before his god. The king, who at first seemed to be asleep, was discovered on closer examination to be dead and the guards comforted me as well as was possible and brought wine, which I held in shaking hands and gulped down in one draught.

There was little cause for suspicion. Aye had been old and frail and this moment had been expected for some time. I explained that I had retreated to the bedchamber in order to ask my father's advice about the standoff with Horemheb in the courtyard and had arrived to find my father already dead. There was no evidence of injuries to the old man and, while a murderer may fake grief, it was judged difficult for anyone to feign the level of distraction to which Aye's death had pushed me. Indeed, I was not that good an actor and I doubt that had my story been true that I would have displayed quite the same extremity of symptoms.

Besides, with the news of Nakhtmin's death in battle, everyone there assumed that I was now Egypt's uncrowned king and even if Aye had been found with a knife in his chest and had died pointing directly at me there was little that anybody could do. An Egyptian king cannot commit a crime and so I was treated with the awed respect that a king deserves, and no mention was ever made of the fact that I had been alone with the king at the time of his death. Horemheb, of course, could prove that he was not involved. He was in the hands of his enemies in the palace. I had ordered his immediate release and proclaimed him the saviour of the throne. There were few who would dissent and those who were in any position to do so were exiled forthwith, against Horemheb's urging. He had wanted them executed but had I ordered it I may as well have left my father on the throne. They were no longer any danger to us, which was security enough for me.

Privately, I assured Horemheb that I had no intention of taking the crown and that arrangements had already been made with the High Priest of Amun to ensure that it was never asked of me. It was enough to placate him.

I had had very little time to oversee the arrangements for the Opet Festival, and falling as it so soon after the death of the king, it was of necessity a muted affair.

We waited for Amun's procession in the avenue of the sphinxes, surrounded by the adoring citizens of the city. There were perhaps a dozen of us; ministers and priests and generals, and Horemheb and I waited at either end of the row which they formed. I, as the heir to the throne, engineered it so that I was at the far end of the line.

As Amun progressed along the avenue the crowd fell silent and, space permitting, fell to their knees in supplication. The priests staggered onwards towards us.

They came in time to Horemheb, who waited at the head of the row of courtiers to greet the god. The priests did not slow their pace, for to do so would have been to stop, but they did not quicken it either, and allowed each member of court the time to prostrate themselves on the ground until the god passed.

They progressed perhaps four or five paces past Horemheb before they halted, as if on command. They were before the man whom most at court expected to inherit the role of treasurer from me. He was prostrate on the ground and after a second he risked a glance upwards to see what was causing the delay. The priests before him seemed to be swaying, as though struggling with their load, as though (although the minister could barely believe such a thing) Amun was resisting their forward progress. And then, to the accompaniment of gasps from the watching crowd, the priests each took a step backwards, and then another, until they were passing once again the man tipped to be my southern vizier, who was too confused to do anything but stare until his neighbour nudged him and he remembered to prostrate himself all over again.

And so it continued, step by backwards step, until the priests were once more before Horemheb, whereupon the strange swaying increased in magnitude. The priest at the front and right suddenly cried out (a vocalisation echoed by many members of the crowd and even one or two of the courtiers) and he and the man following him both fell, their sacred load tumbling from the palanquin to land in the dust of the avenue. It came to rest directly at the feet of General Horemheb, who somehow retained the presence of mind to look regal and yet flattered at the same time.

The crowd erupted into tumult at such a palpable sign of the god's favouritism.

Had anybody been looking towards me at this time, they may have detected the faintest of smiles upon my face.

Epilogue

IT WAS an especially hot day. Hardly the sort of day to be hiking through a desert, and yet this was what he was doing. Despite the heat, his gait was eager and brisk. His goal made the journey seem nothing less than a delight. He was following a road through the hills. Behind him, across the river, Thebes was shining white in the sun but seemed unsubstantial in the haze that hovered above the ground.

Maya tramped on. Under his arm was a large bundle of papyrus sheaves, rolled up carefully and tied into place with twine. He seemed to be treating it with much more respect than a simple document may have been entitled to expect. He shielded it from the sun with his own body.

Before very much longer he began to hear the voices of those who had preceded him; coarse, workmen's voices, but welcome for all that, for they showed that he was not far from his destination.

Before very much longer he reached it. The path looped around the base of a large hillock, hiding the entrance from him until he was almost upon it. He stopped and stood in wonder at the view.

The doorway to the tomb itself was necessarily nondescript, for it was an hour away from being sealed and hidden for all eternity so there was little point in any extravagant decoration. Still, it was a wondrous sight, not only because he knew that this tomb contained the mummy of his sister but because he knew that somewhere in these surrounding hills lay the bodies of generations of kings, all forever hidden and incorruptible.

The last remaining workmen were idle now. They had been issued instructions to leave the tomb open until Maya had visited it. He approached and they fell silent and bowed their heads as he passed into the cool darkness beyond the doorway.

He walked down a long, steep passageway that seemed as though it would continue to the Underworld itself, one hand on the wall to steady himself and the other guarding the papyrus scrolls he carried. The passageway was lit with lamps which turned the air acrid and he coughed once or twice as he descended.

At the bottom of the passageway lay the Chamber of Royalty. Nefertiti's sarcophagus lay in an adjoining room to the right, and Maya walked past funerary beds and statues and chests and boxes containing food and wine in order to reach it. This doorway did not yet contain a door. Once Maya had made his way back to the surface the workmen would come down here and seal the doorway up in a way that intended it never to be opened again.

He stepped into the burial chamber. There was nothing to be seen of Nefertiti. She was lying within several layers of sarcophagi, across the outermost of which Maya now ran his free hand.

"I have brought you home," he whispered.

He walked slowly around the periphery of the sarcophagus, as though expecting it to appear different from some other angle.

"Horemheb is king," he said. "He was the only choice after the incident at the Opet Festival. Of course, I graciously stepped aside to allow Amun's choice to ascend to the throne, and he kept his side of the bargain and retained me as treasurer."

Maya stopped walking. He was at the back of the chamber. Standing before him was a jar, similar to the canopic jars which stored the entrails and organs of the deceased. He took the leaves of papyrus out from under his arm.

"I have brought this," he said. He held it up for Nefertiti to see before placing it carefully in the jar and pushing the lid down on top of it. He cleared his throat and walked solemnly back to the entrance to the burial chamber.

"That is my account of everything," he said. "I have avenged your death, but nobody may ever know of it. I hope that it may reach you in the Underworld, for I want you to spend forever with the comfort of knowing that I loved you and I love you still. I failed you, my dear Nefertiti, and for that I beg that you might one day forgive me. Where I failed you in life, I have honoured you in death."

He cleared his throat again and looked at his sandals for a moment before looking back at the sarcophagi.

"Goodbye, my sister," he said, and turned to leave.

Once outside he began the long slow walk back towards the city. Before long he heard the hammer falls of the workmen as they began sealing Nefertiti's tomb forever.

The End

This book is dedicated with all the love in the world to my grandfather and grandmother, William and Marjorie Ford.

Author's Note

This book is set during the latter half of the Eighteenth Dynasty in ancient Egypt, around the second millennium BCE.

The history of the period is relatively well preserved. Many of the events related within these pages actually happened and will be recognisable to those readers with a prior interest in the subject. All but the most minor of characters in this novel are based on real people whose names and deeds are recorded in history.

There are, however, an infuriating number of gaps in our knowledge and probably as many theories about certain events as there are Egyptologists. This, though, is a novel. Where there are conflicting theories on a particular topic I have made a subjective choice to include one of them, based on my own beliefs as to which is the most likely. And, of course, which makes the best story. I have filled in the historical gaps with my own imagination, although I have tried to base this imagination on the best information we currently have on the topic.

One problematic area is the spelling of names. A particular quandary was how to refer to Amenhotep the king, and his son, Amenhotep the prince. To ease confusion I have adopted the Greek spelling of the younger Amenhotep's name. Within these pages he will be referred to as Amenophis. Other characters have names which seem to be spelled differently in every resource. For example, in other books you may see Aye spelled as Ay, or Tutankhamun spelled as Tutankhamen.

The British Journal of Egyptology is a fictitious publication.

At the time of writing, Nefertiti's tomb remains undiscovered, although to this day teams of archaeologists continue the search.

For further information about *The Maya Papyrus*, please visit www.richardcoady.com.

Acknowledgements

Many people have been kind enough to read and comment on early drafts of this book. I would like to give my heartfelt thanks to Harry West, Gary Smith, Conrad Williams, Irene Coady, Bill Coady and Tom and Sylvia Leatherbarrow.

Special thanks go to Vicki Hardy and Carolyn Prosser for their enthusiasm, kind words and the time it took them to proofread the Kindle edition of The Maya Papyrus.

As always, my love and thanks go to my wife, Miriam, who gave me her unswerving support every day of the 12 years it took me to write this book, and to my son, Adam, who makes me proud every single day.

Finally, I would like to thank Robert Partridge, respected Egyptologist, author, lecturer and editor of the leading Egyptology magazine, *Ancient Egypt*. Robert, with typical generosity, donated his time to this project with no expectation of reward. His knowledge of the period, his insight and his factual and creative input were genuinely invaluable. It goes without saying that any mistakes herein are entirely of my own doing and are no reflection on Robert's expertise. Sadly, Robert died before this book could be completed, but his contribution to it remains incalculable. Thanks, Bob.

www.ingramcontent.com/pod-product-compliance
Lightning Source LLC
Chambersburg PA
CBHW032249020726
47495CB00001B/30